COLORADO

*Love Carves Out a Home
on the Mountainside*

ROSEY DOW

BARBOUR
PUBLISHING

Megan's Choice © 1996 by Rosey Dow
Em's Only Chance © 1998 by Rosey Dow
Lisa's Broken Arrow © 2000 by Rosey Dow
Banjo's New Song © 2003 by Rosey Dow

ISBN 978-1-59310-581-5

Cover art by Comstock

All scripture has been taken from the King James Version of the Bible.

Published by Barbour Publishing, Inc., P.O. Box 719, Uhrichsville, Ohio 44683, www.barbourbooks.com

Our mission is to publish and distribute inspirational products offering exceptional value and biblical encouragement to the masses.

ecpa Member of the
Evangelical Christian
Publishers Association

Printed in the United States of America.

Dear Reader,

I was raised in an Amish/Mennonite family. My parents divorced when I was thirteen. My mother soon remarried, and everything changed. Deeply wounded by that abusive family life, I was an introverted teenager who hated meeting new people and had a fierce dread of public speaking. Then, I was cut off from my parents in 1992. During the healing process, a marvelous transformation happened in my life. My true personality slowly unfolded. Suddenly filled with abounding joy, I loved talking to people, making new friends, and learning about others. Joy overflowed to my computer keyboard, and my books suddenly began to be published.

My first release, *Megan's Choice*, was a reader's favorite. That same year I was chosen as a favorite new author for **Heartsong Presents**. My third release, a novella in *Fireside Christmas*, was on the CBA's best-seller list. Then in July 2001, my historical mystery, *Reaping the Whirlwind*, won the coveted Christy Award.

I never dreamed that one day I'd love to address churches, women's groups, homeschooling organizations, writers clubs, and even appear on radio and television. My husband, David, and I served as missionaries on a tiny Caribbean island for fourteen years. We have seven children and have been homeschoolers for sixteen years.

Check out my website at www.roseydow.com.

Megan's Choice

Dedication

To Dave,
my husband and best friend.

Chapter 1

"**M**r. Steven Chamberlin, please," Megan Wescott told the lanky hotel clerk. She had a pleasant, poised voice. It didn't give away the secret that her stomach was full of flying butterflies.

The young clerk gave her a friendly smile as his eyes approved of her large, brown eyes and creamy complexion. "One moment, please," he replied and held up his hand to summon a bellboy. "You can wait inside if you like."

Glancing around, Megan entered the hotel lobby to wait. The grandeur of the hotel snatched away her breath for an instant. She hesitated inside the door, feeling out of place and alone. She wished she could slip her hand into the warm shelter of her father's coat pocket, her habit as a child whenever she was troubled or frightened. If only he were here to help her now.

But she was no longer a child. Daddy was gone, and she would have to look after herself. And Jeremy.

"A–hem."

She realized a woman in a stylish black hat was standing close by with an impatient grimace on her painted lips.

"Pardon me," Megan murmured and hastily stepped aside. The woman sailed past without another glance, the swish of silk skirts and the heady scent of French perfume lingering after her. Megan drew a quivering breath. She fought down the desire to turn around and escape to the anonymity of the street. Instead, she crossed the thick carpet to a chair.

Resolutely, she drew the newspaper ad from her handbag and read it for what must have been the hundredth time.

Industrious young woman needed to cook and clean on a ranch in the Colorado Territory. Between twenty and twenty-five years old. Orphan preferred. Top wages. Inquire for Mr. Steven Chamberlin at the Olympus Hotel.

The mended edge of her glove slipped from its hiding place beneath the sleeve of her jacket. Carefully, she tucked it back in.

Maybe Mr. Chamberlin has already found someone, she thought, mingling hope and fear. The ad had been published that morning, but she hadn't been able to get away from the shop until quite awhile after lunch. Mrs. Peabody had grudgingly given her the last part of the afternoon off.

She noticed a distinguished gentleman who was sitting on a gold sofa reading a newspaper. Discreetly observing his features, she wondered again what Steven Chamberlin was like. Her mind drew a picture of a short man with a middle-aged paunch who smoked smelly, black cigars and had a booming voice. His wife, no doubt, was the kind who would be constantly peering over her shoulder and making clucking noises. She cringed inwardly and again stifled the urge to run away.

It was unthinkable that she, the daughter of a Virginia plantation owner, should be applying for a housekeeper's position. Her family had suffered many forms of humiliation through the last ten years, but nonetheless she was thankful her mother could not see her now.

It's a waste of time worrying about family pride, she reminded herself again. Jeremy, her little brother, was desperately ill, and the sanitarium was far beyond her means. If Jeremy was to get well, she had to have more money than she could earn at the dressmaker's shop.

The years since the War Between the States had been a nightmare for Megan. The loss of her father and brother in the war, living in poverty in Baltimore, and her dear mother's death would have been enough to break the spirit of most girls.

How could they have survived without Em? Dear Em, who had been with the family for more than twenty years. Em, who had stayed when the other freed slaves were sent away to find livings elsewhere. Thankfully, Em could watch over Jeremy if Megan had to leave.

Blinking, Megan held back the worried tears that blurred her vision. She drew the scrap of newsprint between two fingers, and the words "top wages" caught her eye. She had to get this position.

A tall, dark-haired man slowly descending the wide staircase drew her attention. He scanned the lobby, pausing a moment at the foot of the stairs. Megan noticed his tailored black broadcloth suit, white silk shirt with tiny red pinstripes, and black string tie. He had broad shoulders and a square, purposeful chin.

Was that Steven Chamberlin? Her throat tightened when she realized he was striding in her direction.

"You were asking for Steven Chamberlin, ma'am?" he asked, bowing slightly. He spoke pleasantly enough, but his faint, polite smile didn't quite reach his eyes.

"Yes." Megan's tongue felt thick and uncooperative. "I came to apply for this position." She handed him the ad. Her hand was icy and shaking.

"I am Mr. Chamberlin." He sat in the chair facing her. "May I ask your qualifications?"

To her dismay she felt her cheeks growing hot. The speech she had rehearsed all morning flew beyond her reach. Frantically, she groped for it.

"I can cook and clean," she managed at last, then added with spirit, "and I can work as hard as anyone."

The young man took stock of her clothes, which were carefully made but showed signs of wear; the sweet, anxious mouth; the quiet courage in her eyes, and his manner softened slightly.

"What is your name?"

"Megan Wescott. I need employment badly. You see, my little brother is ill, and the sanitarium is expensive."

His wife would be about my own age, she thought, not sure if that was good or bad.

"Your parents?"

"Father was killed in the war, and Mother died five months ago." She met his gaze openly, candidly, and realized for the first time that his thick black eyebrows almost came together. "I've been working in a dressmaker's shop doing fine needlework, but with Jeremy sick I'll have to earn more."

"I'd like to talk to you about some details." He glanced around. The man she had observed shifted position and turned a page of his newspaper. Two men engrossed in conversation walked past. "Would you mind stepping into the hotel restaurant where we can talk more privately? There are some things I need to explain about the position."

"Will your wife join us?" Megan asked, confused.

"That's one of the things I'll need to explain," he said, standing.

Is his wife ill? A vague doubt sprouted in her mind.

An aloof waiter showed them to a small table in a back corner of the dining room. Megan allowed Mr. Chamberlin to seat her. She removed her gloves, clasped them tightly in her lap, and waited. Alive to his every expression, she tried to determine what lay behind the handsome, self-assured face across from her.

"It's quite a long story," he began after ordering coffee for two. "Two years ago, my father bought a four-hundred-acre ranch near Juniper Junction—that's about fifty miles north of Denver in the Colorado Territory—from a man who went back East. It's deeded land. I guess my father was planning to go there sometime, but he never did. He died a month ago, leaving a small fortune to my sister and me. My mother died several years ago, you see.

"My half of the inheritance comes with a condition—my father's idea of giving me a test of character." His right eyebrow lifted slightly, giving him a vaguely cynical expression. He paused while the waiter set their coffee before them. "In order to inherit, my wife and I must live on the ranch for a full year and make it profitable."

"And you want a housekeeper for her?" Megan prompted. *Won't he ever come to the point?*

9

He added a spoonful of sugar to his coffee and stirred it thoughtfully. Megan watched the slow movement of his large, well-groomed hands. She looked up to find his measuring gaze upon her.

"I don't have a wife."

"I don't understand." *Maybe I ought to leave. This doesn't sound right.*

"I mean," he spoke slowly, distinctly, closely observing her reaction, "I'm looking for a housekeeper and cook who would be willing to become my legal wife for that year." He leaned forward, speaking softly. "I'll be frank. I could find a mail order bride if I wanted to. There are plenty of folks who are doing it these days. But I'm not ready to be saddled down with that responsibility. I wouldn't even go this far if it wasn't for losing a fortune in the process.

"After the terms of the will have been met, I'll have the marriage discreetly dissolved. No one in the East need ever know of the arrangement. I'm willing to pay one hundred dollars per month."

"But as your wife. . . ," Megan faltered. She struggled between dismay at his scheme and the knowledge that she desperately needed the amount of money he had quoted.

"A legality only, I assure you," he said. "Call it a make-believe marriage if that eases your conscience. I turned down two women this morning, but I think you and I could be partners. Why not? You need a sizable income, and I need a wife for a year. We can work together to accomplish both."

"But why would your father put your wife in his will if you aren't married?" It didn't sound reasonable.

"He thought I was," Mr. Chamberlin said, ruefully. "The last time I saw him was before the war. I was engaged at the time. What a foolish boy I was." He shook his head. "She was a hostess on the *Mississippi Queen*. I thought she cared for me, but she was only after my winnings at the poker table. She dumped me when a brighter star came along." His lips tightened. "I won't be so foolish again." He shrugged, and his expression softened. "Anyway, I didn't have any contact with my father after that visit. I guess he naturally assumed I had married."

"Couldn't you go to the solicitor and tell him you're not married?" Megan persisted, still puzzled.

"It would break the will." Again that hard look. "And Georgiana, my older sister, would dearly love to chisel me out of my half of the money." He leaned back in his chair and shook his head. "No. There's no other way."

Megan's slim fingers toyed with her china coffee cup. She stared at the painted yellow rose on the inside rim, weighing the possibilities. One hundred dollars a month was almost twice as much as she had hoped for. And what a relief not to have to please the tastes of another woman.

"What kind of work do you do?" She looked keenly at the man across from her. He didn't look unscrupulous, but there must be some reason his father hadn't trusted him.

Chamberlin laughed mirthlessly, gesturing with his hand.

"That's a good question, ma'am," he said, sobering. "It's right prudent of you to ask. I left home at sixteen and found out I could be handy with the pasteboards. That's the cards, ma'am. I rode the Mississippi riverboats for a few years, fought for the Confed'racy under Bragg, and then wandered around New Orleans after the war, trying my hand at this and that, gambling enough to keep me from starving.

"To tell you the truth, I was at a loss until this will came up. I think I'd like to have a go at ranching. Put down some roots, maybe." He shrugged. "At least I'd like to have a chance to prove I can do it even if I decide to come back East later. I don't have a predilection for the idea of marriage, that's all. I've been a loner for too long."

The simple directness of his answer convinced Megan he was being honest with her. There was a lengthy silence while she thought it over.

What would a meaningless marriage matter? Wasn't marriage a commitment of the heart? All he asked was what the ad said: a housekeeper and cook. It would be pleasant on a ranch, too. A ranch and a plantation were practically the same, weren't they? She remembered the corrals, the riding stable, the spreading lawn, and columned plantation house she had known as a child. The ranch would be different, of course, but there were similarities.

What a relief it would be to go back to that life even if she was only a servant.

But I won't be a servant, she suddenly recalled. *I would be the mistress.* Some of the cloud lifted from her mind. *Yes*, she rolled the idea around on her tongue, *I would be the mistress.*

"When would we have to leave?" she asked, slowly.

"Three weeks." He peered at her with half-closed eyes. "Does that mean you accept?"

"I can't see that I have any choice," she said, steadily. "Yes, I accept."

"Good." His expression relaxed. He reached inside his coat. "Here's my card. I'd like you to go to the Hurlick's General Store on Market Street and purchase any household goods you feel will be necessary. I'm afraid I wouldn't know where to begin when it comes to housekeeping, and I think it would be better for you to make your own choices. Give Hurlick this card, and he'll put it on my account. Have everything packed and sent to my address."

"What should I get?" Megan asked, taking the card and glancing at it.

"Whatever you'll need to take care of the house and fix things up a mite. The house isn't large, I understand, but it has been empty for quite some time. Cooking utensils, curtains, and such like would be in order, I suppose."

Megan slid the card into her purse. Her hands were clammy, and she had the strange feeling she was somehow watching herself from far away.

"We can have the ceremony performed in a quiet corner of the city in about a week," he continued, "but I see no need to change our living quarters until we leave. If you need to contact me in the meantime, you can reach me here. How can I contact you?"

"I live at 148 High Street, Apartment 3B," she said. She pulled on her gloves and stood up. She wanted to have some time alone to adjust herself to the new circumstances.

"Thank you, Miss Wescott," he said, rising with her, the shadow of a smile on his lips.

"Megan," she said seriously. "It's foolish to continue formalities."

"Yes, Megan." He sobered. "I'm sure I don't need to tell you our arrangement shouldn't be known to anyone else. Will you meet me at the park near the big fountain with water spraying out a carp's mouth, say a week from today? At two o'clock?"

"I'll be there." She offered him her hand, and he clasped it briefly. His hand, though uncalloused, was surprisingly firm and strong. "Good day." With a nod, she left the hotel.

Conflicting emotions swept over her as she stepped, blinking, into the bright afternoon sunlight. A flash of exhilaration tingled through her as she mouthed the wage he had offered her. *A hundred dollars a month!* Her brightest hopes had never been audacious enough to rise up that high. The marriage contract was a little disturbing, but livable for a few months. However, now that she knew the problem of the sanitarium fee was solved, she had to face the dark side: leaving behind all she loved to brave the unknown. Many who ventured into the wild new territories were never heard from again.

A whole year. She was heartsick at the thought. *Can I do it? Can I say good-bye to Jeremy and Em?* She pushed back the walls that crowded in on her. She would not succumb to her fears and heartaches. If she caved in, Jeremy would sense it and be afraid, too. She must be strong for him.

She walked blindly along the cobblestone streets, unaware of the chilly May breeze that tickled her burning cheeks. Her feet beat a steady cadence on the sidewalk while she reminisced about the past and wondered about the future.

Chapter 2

The years since the war were a series of murky shadows in Megan's memory. When the Southern cause was lost, her family left Virginia and traveled north to Baltimore to stay with Mother's Aunt Alice. Daddy had fallen with a Yankee bullet in his chest. Silverleigh, their home, was a blackened heap of ash and rubble. Friends were scattered, never to be seen again. Gone forever was the world they had loved. They hoped to find rest and build a new life, but those hopes were shattered when Aunt Alice had a stroke and died. Debt swallowed her estate, and again the Wescotts were homeless.

Mother was left without friend or advisor. It was up to her to provide a roof to cover their despairing heads and food to ease their gnawing stomachs. She walked the streets of the poorest, dirtiest section of Baltimore until she found an apartment, a dark, wretched cubbyhole, for a dollar a week. Intended for one or at the most two people, it had two closet-sized bedrooms barely big enough for a cot and a chair, a kitchen that was about the size of their dining room table at Silverleigh, and a sitting room that could be crossed in four strides from either direction.

The landlady, Mrs. Niles, looked Mother up and down as though mentally pricing every piece of clothing Mother wore before she grudgingly admitted she had a vacancy. She was a thin-lipped woman who had been middle-aged all her life. Her gown was a cheap imitation of the morning dresses that had filled two of Mother's closets at Silverleigh. However, the cut of the cloth was as far as the resemblance went; because the collar and cuffs were smudged, and there was a small tear under the arm, something Mother would never have permitted even in a servant. Though disgusted, Mother pretended not to notice and handed over the first week's rent, her last dollar but one, and in her mind playfully nicknamed the landlady Nilly-Willy. She made a joke of it to the children later that evening.

What it must have cost Mother's aristocratic pride to knock on door after door asking women if she could do their washing and ironing. The family lived on bread and tea the first few weeks they lived at Mrs. Nile's tenement house. Finally, the news of Mother's and Em's excellent work with soapsuds, starch, and hot iron traveled across the grapevine of Baltimore's housewives, and the amount of work grew until they had money to buy enough food to satisfy a growing boy and, of course, pay their rent.

Mother insisted that Megan, scarcely more than a child, continue her schooling. She found a church with a mission that taught slum children and made Megan attend the classes. Mother filled the gaps in their meager program by teaching Megan by lamplight after a twelve-hour day of bending over a washboard or iron.

Megan watched her mother's soft, white hands become red and coarse from hours in hot, soapy water. She knew Mother would never allow a word of complaint to pass her lips, and she would not allow anyone else to grumble, either. She never let it be spoken, but she could not hide her suffering, worry-filled eyes.

How could they have made it without Em? Always near with a strong back and willing, loving hands, Em comforted them and offered her earthy wisdom to chase away discouragement.

Years of brutal work and the lack of fresh air broke down Mother's health. She grew weaker and weaker until she had a fainting spell over the washtub. Unable to hide their tears, Megan and Em lifted Mother to her tiny cot, brought her hot broth, and tried to make her comfortable. There was no money for a doctor.

Megan stopped going to school. Instead, she took Mother's place in the soapsuds until Mother, broken in spirit and body, called Megan to her side a few months before she died. Mother's smooth, clear face now had deep creases around the eyes and mouth. In two months' time her hair had turned the color of moonlight reflected on new-fallen snow.

"I want you to get a position in the city, Megan," she wheezed, stopping often to take a breath. Her translucent hand reached out to touch Megan's cheek. "You'll ruin yourself with this backbreaking work. It's not fittin' for a pretty young thing like you to spend her life with her hands in wash water."

How courageous Mother had been through all their struggle, never thinking of herself, always thinking of Megan and Jeremy.

Cold hard emptiness had filled the apartment when Mother was taken from them. The burning ache was still fresh in Megan's bosom.

Following Mother's advice, Megan took samples of her work and applied at a shop close to the center of town. She had learned to weave lace and sew fine embroidery from her governess, who had considered it a necessity for a young lady destined to join the higher ranks of society. Megan was an artist with her needle, and she loved her work. At her first stop, Mrs. Peabody, the owner of the dressmaker's shop, had hired her instantly when Megan had spread out her handiwork.

It had been enjoyable to sit in the back room of the shop and handle the beautiful threads. However, the sense of enjoyment lasted only a few months. Mother's death squeezed the last ounce of joy out of Megan's life, and when Jeremy contracted rheumatic fever a few months later, Megan felt desperation grip her. The responsibility weighed her down until she felt she would smother.

The light was beginning to fade when Megan at last set a course for home. She reached her neighborhood with her thoughts still far off. Habitually stepping around bits of broken glass and refuse, she walked on. She didn't notice the thin children huddled together in doorways and on the front steps of their homes or the starving mongrel dogs sniffing the gutters for a morsel of decaying food. When she reached High Street, she stepped off the crumbling sidewalk to pass a group of ragged boys playing marbles on the corner.

" 'Lo, Megan," one urchin called.

"Hello, Joe." She smiled absently in response and walked on. Suddenly, the chance to leave the city gave her a new awareness of her neighborhood. She awoke from her sleepwalking and looked around at the soot-covered buildings and trash-laden street. The acrid smell of unwashed bodies and rotting garbage pricked her nose. In the depths of the building nearby, a man and woman raised their voices in a heated argument, while a baby wailed relentlessly. High Street had never seemed so dismal as today, the tenement houses never so dirty and depressing.

How wonderful it would be to get away from the city. To breathe fresh air, to feel free-blowing breezes in her hair, the sun on her face. To see wide, unbounded country crowned with a clear, sapphire sky.

The soothing smell of Em's thick stew welcomed Megan when she opened the apartment door. She was pulling off her gloves, adjusting her eyes to the dimness, when a tall, lean black woman came to stand in the kitchen doorway. She wore a faded gingham dress with a white apron. Her gray hair was pulled back from her face, seamed by years of hard work and sorrow. She held a dish towel in her hands.

"How is Jeremy, Em?"

"Sleepin'. I gave him some supper 'bout an hour ago." Em peered at Megan, her narrow face creased with worry. "Did you find you a new job, Miss Megan?"

"Yes, I did." Megan removed her bonnet and laid it on the shelf near the door. Hanging her jacket on a peg, she followed Em into the tiny kitchen wondering how to tell her the rest of the news. Saying it aloud made their separation seem more real. "It pays almost twice as much as I had hoped for, Em," she said, slowly, "but there is something I didn't tell you about."

"What do you have to do?" Em asked anxiously.

"I'm keeping house and cooking like I told you. . . ." Megan paused, avoiding Em's eyes. "But I have to go out to the Colorado Territory."

"The Colorado Territory! Lord have mercy, child, whatever for?" She stared at Megan, her lips slightly parted. The dimple in her right cheek, the one Megan called her worry mark, deepened as Megan continued.

"The gentleman has a ranch out there, and he needs a housekeeper. I've agreed to go for a year," Megan said softly.

"A year!" Two tears slid slowly down Em's anguished face, and Megan felt her resolve bubbling away.

"Please don't cry, Em," she begged, putting arms around Em, her face on Em's shoulder. "I don't want to go. You know I don't." The tears she had been battling all afternoon finally won out. In a moment she drew back, wiping her eyes. "I have no choice. You see that, don't you?"

"Yes, child." Em's seamed, careworn face was wet also. "I know." She sank into a chair with a heavy sigh, her face a picture of misery. "It's the lonesome days ahead I'm a-thinkin' on."

"I'll make enough money so you won't have to work so hard."

Megan knelt by Em's side and clasped her bony, work-hardened hands between her own. "If we can find you a place in a rooming house near the sanitarium, you can visit Jeremy every day. And you can get away from this dark, crowded tenement house. It will be better for us all." She searched Em's face for a sign of comfort.

"When you leavin'?"

"In three weeks. We have so much to do before then. I'll have to keep my job with Mrs. Peabody for another week or so. We'll have to make arrangements with the sanitarium and find you a place to stay." She looked around the kitchen. "We'll have to pack all our things, too."

"Em!" A faint call came from the bedroom.

"I'll go to Jeremy," Megan said, rising. She gave Em's hand a squeeze and ran to wash away the traces of tears.

The coal oil lamp Megan carried into Jeremy's bedroom cast a golden light over the child's hollow cheeks. His skin was almost transparent, his lips tinged a faint blue. His large nightshirt made him seem smaller than his ten years. Tousled, straw-colored hair came down to his eyes, now sunken and dulled by weeks of illness. His languid expression faded a little when he realized who it was that carried the lamp.

"How is my little soldier?" Megan asked, smiling tenderly. She set the lamp on the small table beside a chipped enamel basin. The splash of lamplight touched both walls in the narrow room.

"Megan," Jeremy murmured, a drowsy smile on his lips. "I'm glad you're home. Can you stay with me for a little while?"

"I'll stay with you as long as you like." She plumped his pillow and straightened the counterpane. "I have some grown-up business to talk over with you tonight."

"What is it?" His tired eyes showed a spark of curiosity.

"Well, part of it is good, and part of it is kind of hard." She eased into the straight wooden chair by his bed. "You know what the doctor said about having to take special care of you to protect your heart?"

"Sure," he said impatiently. "That's why I have to stay in this old bed all day long."

"Today I found work that will make it possible for you to get the treatments you need to get better."

"You did?"

"Yes. I'm going next week to make the arrangements with the doctor." She hesitated, dreading the rest of her news.

"What's the hard part?" He tried to sit up by supporting himself on his elbows. "Don't worry, Meg. I can take it. I'm no baby. Did the doctor tell you something bad about me?"

"Oh, no, Jeremy," she assured him quickly. "Don't even think such a thing. He said with proper care he has good hopes you'll soon be well." She pressed her bottom lip between her teeth. "It's that the job I found is far away in Colorado. I'm going to be a housekeeper on a ranch."

"Is Em going, too?" His voice had a touch of anxiety.

"Of course not. Em will stay near you and come to visit you every day. We wouldn't leave you all alone."

"Long as Em's with me, I won't mind." He lay back against the pillow, his restless hands feeling the texture of the nubby counterpane. He lay still a moment, absorbing the news until a new idea struck him. "Out West?" He raised himself on one arm again and looked more boyish than before. "Will there be Injuns and rustlers and everything?"

"I don't think so," Megan said, smiling gently. "There will be horses, though, like we had in Virginia. But what I wanted to tell you," she went on, "is that I'll have to stay there a year."

"Do you think I could go, too, when I get better?" he pleaded.

"I don't know, dear. We'll have to see." Dismayed by his flushed face and his quick, shallow breathing, she warned, "Don't get too wrought up. You must stay quiet."

"Wow, cowboys and everything!" he whispered. Reluctantly, he relaxed against the pillow. His eyes closed for a moment, then flew open to seek Megan's face in the dim light. "I'll try hard to get better, Meg, so I can come out and be with you."

She turned the lamp lower and whispered the platitudes she hoped would calm him, thankful he couldn't see her tears through the shadows. When he was dozing, she padded softly back to Em in the kitchen.

"He took it like my soldier boy," she told Em who was dishing up two bowls of stew. "He wants to come out to see the Indians and the rustlers when he gets well." She filled a thick, white mug from the metal water pitcher on the table and sipped it.

"That boy's a reg'lar angel." Em shook her head, smiling sadly. "I'll take care o' him, Miss Megan. Don't you grieve yourself 'bout that."

The next week was emotionally exhausting for Megan. Like a saber-wielding duelist, she beat back her fears. Her head knew that going away with Steve Chamberlin was the only answer to her predicament, but her heart moaned in torment. Each evening as she sat with Jeremy, white-hot daggers pierced her through.

I can't do it, she'd despair. *You must,* she'd argue back. *You must. You must.*

She spent the nights tossing fitfully on her hard, narrow cot. The days found her working her usual ten hours at the dressmaker's shop, making lists of things to do and take, and sorting their few possessions. The night before the wedding she didn't close her eyes until the faint gray light of dawn crept wearily through her tiny window.

Chapter 3

The next morning was as tedious and long as the morning at Silverleigh when Megan broke Mother's favorite china figurine while her parents were away. She had spent four dreadful, restless hours waiting for them to return and discover her guilt. Like then, Megan couldn't concentrate on anything else except the dreaded event. This time it was her appointment with Steve Chamberlin that overshadowed all else.

She had asked Mrs. Peabody for the day off, but when the day arrived, she wished she had asked for only the afternoon, because her job would have filled the empty morning hours. Instead, she had to pass the time wandering from room to room, looking out windows, sitting down with a book only to put it aside five minutes later with barely a line read. She absently straightened pillows and ran errands for Jeremy. At ten thirty she lay on her cot, feeling tired after her sleepless night, and hopped up in two minutes to continue pacing. Her taut muscles must keep moving. She could not think of closing her eyes.

After forcing down three bites of lunch, she took her time changing into her best dress, a pale lavender cotton with a faint ivory swirl woven into it. She parted her waist-length hair slightly right of center and pulled it back into a wide, brown bun at the nape of the neck. Putting on her navy bonnet and coat, she left the house early to walk off some of her nervous energy.

There was a chill in the air when she reached the street. The sky over the city was dotted with small, puffy clouds, and a warm, fitful breeze toyed with the strings of her bonnet. Without any haste, she headed in the general direction of the park Steve had mentioned. She still had an hour to wait, and the walk would normally take only twenty minutes.

The park, carpeted with a freshly grown crop of young grass and trees tinged with waxy, yellow-green new leaves, was almost deserted when she arrived. Mothers had their tiny charges at home for naps while older children were still in school. Megan wandered aimlessly on the path near a duck pond until she found a perch on a bench near the fish fountain Steve had told her about. With a detached attitude, she watched three mallard ducks dive for breadcrumbs thrown by a grizzled old man in a tattered felt hat. Across the path a clump of daffodils swayed in the occasional breeze, bobbing their heads toward Megan.

Can I really go through with it? The question that had been battering her mind for the past week reverberated again in full force. She suddenly realized she was clenching her teeth, and she tried to force herself to relax.

Sunshine spilled over her back, slowly warming and loosening her tense muscles. Her lack of sleep from the night before took its toll, and little by little she began to feel drowsy. Her eyes were drooping when the old man with the breadcrumbs carefully folded his empty sack and put it into the pocket of his faded, blue overcoat. He lingered a few moments longer before stomping down the path out of the park. Megan's gaze idly followed him until she saw something that roused her from her lethargy.

With a gray derby pulled low over his forehead, Steve Chamberlin strode past the old man, looking left then right as he came. He was dressed all in gray from overcoat to leather shoes. His face cleared when he spotted Megan, and he closed the gap between them in seconds.

"You came!" He settled down beside her. "I had almost convinced myself you would change your mind." The indecision on Megan's face stopped him. He looked at her carefully. "You're still going to do it, aren't you?"

"I can't afford to change my mind," she answered hesitantly. Seeing him again had brought a rush of panic over her.

"How is your brother?" he asked politely.

"He's about the same, thank you." She studied the tiny stitches on the back of her gloved hand lying in her lap. Her own words echoed in her mind. Jeremy was the same, and he wouldn't get better unless she fulfilled her duty to him. When the full impact of that realization came to her, her pulse quieted. The confused, troubled thoughts fell into order.

"Did you find a sanitarium?"

"Yes. There's one on the western edge of town on Oak Street called Pinefield Nursing Home. They have an open bed and can take Jeremy as soon as I bring the first month's fee."

"We'll take care of that today. After the wedding, we'll visit my solicitor and make all the arrangements."

She rose, and they strolled to a closed carriage waiting nearby. Steve curtly called out an address to the driver, handed Megan up, and they set off at a brisk trot. Megan clasped her purse in her lap and kept her attention on the scene passing before the side window of the carriage. She felt too wrought up inside to take part in small talk. Evidently, Chamberlin either sensed or shared her mood, because he was silent for the entire journey.

The wedding was cold and mechanical. Without raising his head, a white-haired preacher read the solemn words from a small black book, his stout, red-cheeked wife looking on. Steve slid a plain gold band on her finger, and it was over. Megan's hands trembled, and she felt chilled clear through, yet she felt a bit lighter, a trifle less burdened. She breathed a deep, silent sigh. There was no turning back now. Her future was sealed.

The wedding was followed by an uncomfortable trip to Cyrus Tump's, the solicitor's office, where Steve introduced Megan and notified the ancient, spectacled gentleman of their plan to move to Colorado. Megan was afraid the steely, gray eyes of the lawyer would bore right through her, but she resolutely met his gaze and even managed a smile and nod in response to his greeting. Steve made arrangements for Jeremy's sanitarium fee and a monthly allowance for Em to be paid from Mr. Tump's office.

Back in the waiting carriage, Steve handed her a white envelope. "This is your first two months' pay."

"Thank you." She put the envelope in her handbag, then slid the gold band from her finger and placed it carefully into an inside pocket of the handbag for safekeeping.

"Is there any way I can help you?" he offered kindly when she pulled the drawstring tight.

"Em needs a small place to stay near the sanitarium so she can be near Jeremy. We haven't been able to find anything yet."

"I'll see to it," he said easily, and wrote it down in a small notebook he withdrew from his pocket.

"When exactly are we leaving?"

"That would be May twenty-fifth at six thirty in the morning. We travel to Chicago, then change trains and go on to Denver. It'll take about a week."

"Only a week to go so far?" She had expected him to say twice as long.

"I want to get there in time to plant some corn, so it's none too fast. We'd leave this week if I could have gotten tickets." He returned the pad to his pocket. "Can I see you home?"

"Well, I was going to make the arrangements at the sanitarium for Jeremy. . . ."

"I'll take you there, then." He gave the order to the driver. "I don't have anything pressing this afternoon," he said, settling back on the black leather seat.

Megan was buoyed up with relief when Steve left her on High Street later that afternoon. A place in the sanitarium had been secured and a carriage engaged for Jeremy's transfer there. It was beyond marvelous to know that skilled hands would be caring for him tomorrow.

The next two weeks were a blur of activity. Megan and Em packed their few belongings and scrubbed the apartment. They were leaving it far cleaner than they had found it. It was heartbreaking to go through Mother's things, a task Megan had shied away from thus far. Mourning was momentarily replaced by excitement when she found some forgotten treasures in an old trunk. There was the forest green riding habit that had been Father's last gift to Mother before the war period. She tried it on and found that with a few alterations she could wear it.

She hesitated when she found Father's old Bible, wrapped carefully in black velvet and brown paper. Never read, it had been kept by Mother as a memento. Reverently, Megan unwrapped it and ran her fingers gently over the black leather cover. Replacing the wrapping, she put it with the rest of her treasures. It would be comforting to have a few familiar things with her when she was far away.

Shopping was exhausting but also exciting. She bought blankets, feather ticking, coal oil lamps, vegetable seeds, a large cast-iron pot, needles, thread, several bolts of gaily colored fabric in checks and small prints, and many other things.

She tried to concentrate totally on the task of clearing out the apartment and getting ready to go, pushing thoughts of good-byes far into the back recesses of her mind. The twenty-fourth of May soon arrived, however, and she could ignore good-byes no longer. She visited Jeremy that afternoon as she did every afternoon. Only today it was with a sinking spirit.

At the door of the ward, she hesitated on the threshold to see what he was doing before she came closer. His eyes closed, Jeremy seemed to be asleep. Megan tiptoed toward him, studying his face, savoring the sight of him. In spite of the fact that she had not made a sound, his eyelids fluttered when she reached his side. Slowly, he focused on her.

"Hello, Meg."

"How are you feeling, Jeremy?" She pushed his hair back from his forehead, letting her hand rest near his temple.

" 'Bout the same." He paused, gazing listlessly at her face. "It's tomorrow, isn't it?"

"I'm afraid it is," Megan whispered, suddenly choked. A powerful hand gripped the core of her being. "I'm leaving in the morning."

"I'm going to miss you, Meg." A single, lonely tear slid slowly down his pale cheek. Megan gathered him in her arms and held him close. She shut her eyes hard, squeezing back the tears.

"Be my soldier, Jeremy," she said, forcing calmness into her words. "While I'm working in Colorado, you work hard on getting well. I'll try to send for you when you're better. I promise." She laid him back on the pillow and gently wiped away his tears with her handkerchief. "You keep remembering those horses and cowboys you want to see so bad, okay?" She attempted a bright smile through stiff lips.

"I will," he said bravely. His lip quivered, but he didn't cry anymore. His fingers clutched at her hand. "Will you write to me?"

"Of course. You don't think I'd forget about my best beau, do you?" she asked lightly. "I'll write so much you'll get tired of reading."

"I'll get better as hard as I can," he promised solemnly.

"One day this will all be past, and we'll be happy again," she said softly, "but until then we'll both have to be good soldiers." She held his hand to her lips. "Always remember I love you."

"I love you, too, Meg." His lip quivered again. "Don't worry. Em will look after me."

Gently, she kissed his cheek, hugged him, and whispered a good-bye in his ear. She left the room without looking back. She couldn't endure the sight of him small and ill and alone, looking after her. But not looking back wasn't the answer, for the image of Jeremy in the sickbed was branded into her mind.

Tears coursed down her cheeks. She pressed her handkerchief to her mouth to stifle wracking sobs. Outside the door of the ward she leaned a shoulder against the cool wall, trying to get composure. In vain she drew in huge gulps of air and squeezed her sodden handkerchief tightly to her burning eyes. Finally, with tears still flowing, she straightened her shoulders, lifted her chin, and walked on.

~

The next morning, Megan and Em rose while it was still dark to get ready for Megan's departure. The apartment had a strange, hollow quality that echoed and amplified their voices and the little noises of their moving about. Megan's trunk stood locked and ready near the front door. Em's was in the middle of the living room. Em would finish the transfer of her things later that morning and return the key to Mrs. Niles.

Megan couldn't swallow a bite of food. Though Em pressed her, she could force down only a few sips of hot coffee. After placing a few final things in her case, she walked through the apartment one last time to check for anything forgotten. Her shoes made a resonating *clump-clump* sound on the bare wood floors. The faint light of day glimmered through the curtainless windows, making vague patterns on the walls and floor.

Memories swept over her during her stroll from room to room. In this remote, dark place she had laughed and wept these past eight years. Her mother had died here. Here she had grown to womanhood.

She stared sightlessly down at the street, hazy in the new dawn, until she felt Em's hand on her arm.

"He's a-comin' soon, Miss Megan."

"I know." Megan looked up into Em's sad face. The worry mark was deep. "Oh, Em!" Her courage wavered for an instant.

"Just take it one day at a time, Miss Megan," Em said, putting a strong, loving arm around her. "That's the only way to git through the hard times. I seen a-plenty, but they always pass, child. They always pass."

The *clip-clop* of hooves and the squeal of iron rims on cobblestones sounded below.

"He's here." Dread put an edge on Megan's voice. She hugged Em hard and a few tears spilled over. "I'll send a telegram when we arrive."

"You in the hands o' the good Lord, Miss Megan. If prayin' ever helped anybody, you be all right, 'cause I'll sure enough be a-prayin'." Tears flowed down her dark, wrinkled cheeks.

A light tap sounded at the door. Trying futilely to dry her eyes, Megan opened it. It took but a moment for Steve's man to remove the trunk, and Steve took the case.

Moving mechanically, Megan put on her bonnet and coat against the chilly morning air. She took a step toward the door, then paused. With a sob, she threw herself into Em's arms, squeezing her hard. Then she tore herself away and ran down the stairs, her heels beating a staccato tempo in her haste.

When she thought back later, all she could remember of the trip to the train station was a blur of impressions: the *clop-clop* of the horses pulling the carriage, the soft, steady pressure of Steve's hand on her arm guiding her through the waiting crowd, the aroma of cigar smoke in the passenger car, her wet cheeks and puffy, burning eyes.

They were in their seats less than five minutes before the train lurched ahead with a *chug-chug-chug* that grew into a throbbing *clackety-clack* as it gathered speed. The sound pounded in Megan's tortured brain until it rang in her ears: *You're-not-coming-back. You're-not-coming-back.* She rested her head against the high back of the red plush seat and turned toward the window. The exhaustion of the past three weeks washed over her. The sound and sway of the train lulled her anguished mind until she fell asleep.

It was near noon when Megan next opened her eyes. She blinked against the glare of the sun streaming through the train window and dazedly looked around. For a long second she couldn't remember where she was. It was Steve, beside her, reading a newspaper that brought her to herself. Catching a glimpse of herself in the gleaming mirror between the windows, she reached up to straighten her bonnet. She felt scruffy and had a nagging ache in her shoulder.

"Good morning," Steve said, smiling pleasantly, "Though I believe it's closer to noon." He looked at her closer, realizing her discomfort. "There's a powder room near the back of the car if you'd like to refresh yourself."

"I believe I will," she said, picking up her handbag from where it had slid into the corner beside her. She avoided Steve's gaze as she passed by him and half-stumbled down the aisle of the pitching, swaying car.

Megan bathed her red, swollen eyes and smoothed her hair back into its thick, brown bun. The cool water revived her somewhat and cleared her muddled mind. Taking advantage of the privacy, she placed the gold wedding band on her finger, this time to stay. Light though it was, it weighed heavily on her hand. She could feel it even when she replaced her glove.

On the return trip she braced herself by holding the backs of the seats and noticed for the first time how crowded the car was. Two fat businessmen, one puffing a long, black cigar, were deep in conversation. Several coatless young men is silk pinstriped shirts with black sleeve garters were engaged in some sort of card game near the front of the car, shrilly encouraged by three gaudy young women with rouge-reddened cheeks. A fine lady in a black satin traveling suit sat alone near a window, waving a tiny square of black lace in front of her nose. Megan felt particular sympathy for the mothers. There were several of them with fussing, wriggling children. With the exception of the one next to the woman in black, every seat was occupied.

The sound of many voices, the mechanical noises of the train, and the smell of box lunches, tobacco smoke, and sickly sweet perfume filled the air.

"Care for some lunch?" Steve asked, reaching under the seat for the box he had brought.

"I couldn't." Her stomach was a leaden knot.

"You'll be sick if you don't eat." He watched her thoughtfully.

"You must think I'm a crybaby," she ventured impulsively.

"On the contrary. I believe I could be a little jealous."

Surprised, she glanced at him to see if he was mocking her, but his face was serious. He met her eyes.

"When I left, no one noticed in the least," he added soberly. "No one has noticed for a long time." He broke the mood by studying the contents of their lunch box. "There's cold chicken, rolls, a piece of cheese, and a bottle of water and two cups. Surely you can take something."

"I guess I could take a roll," she yielded, holding out her hand. She was surprised at how good it tasted after she got past the first bite.

Grassy, rolling meadows skimpily dotted with horses and cattle skimmed past the window. Megan drank in each scene. She had been in the city for so long she had almost forgotten how lovely the countryside could be.

"How long until we reach Chicago?"

"About three days. Give or take a day." He handed her a cup of water. "We'll stop for dinner in Philadelphia, then on to Ohio and Chicago. There's an overnight stay in Chicago before we can get a train for Denver."

Hour by endless hour the journey stretched on. It seemed to Megan she was in limbo. Nothing existed but the *clackety-clack* of the train, the continuous pain in her heart, and Steve.

Chapter 4

The stagecoach waiting for them in Denver was brilliant red with shiny gold trim. Over its double doors the name *Concord* glowed proudly. Megan was surprised to see that even the wheel rims were scarlet. The team of four sleek black horses jangled the harness impatiently.

So this is the great West, Megan thought, hungrily absorbing every detail. Men in cowboy garb were lounging at various storefronts, engaged in desultory conversation. Now and then one would break away and amble down the boardwalk, six-shooter swinging, chaps flapping with each long stride. The women were dressed much more simply than those in Baltimore. Calico and homespun were everywhere.

Some of her self-consciousness had faded during the eight-day trip to Denver. Steve was casual and kind. She found soothing support in his presence. In Chicago there had been an embarrassed silence when they had reached their hotel suite, but he had arranged his blankets in the outer room and had given Megan privacy. Only twice did she have to hide tears of homesickness, though her thoughts strayed often to Jeremy and Em.

She felt a thrill of anticipation when Steve handed her up into the stage. In a few hours she would see her new home and begin her new life. What would it be like?

As soon as the stage pulled away from the broad streets of Denver, the rough country road jarred Megan to the core. Her already-aching muscles begged for relief, but the hard leather seats were unrelenting. The four other passengers, three men and one woman, exchanged introductions with Steve.

"Coming for a visit?" asked the stout, talkative woman known as Mrs. Pleurd.

"We're going to settle on the Cunningham place," Steve said, steadying himself by holding the edge of the seat.

"The Circle C?" blurted Mrs. Pleurd. Her mouth dropped open for half an instant before she recovered herself.

All of a sudden every eye was fastened on Steve. There was an uneasy silence.

"Why, yes," Steve said lightly. "My father bought the land about two years ago, and I've come to take possession."

No one offered any more conversation, but Megan could sense the strain.

Something in these otherwise friendly people was amiss. Was it something Steve had said or done? Megan probed her mind for an answer, but none came.

The shallow, winding stream where the driver chose to stop for lunch was peaceful and cool. Megan moved apart from the rest of the party to sit in the shade of a wide cottonwood tree, her back resting against its broad, steady trunk. She closed her eyes, breathing deeply of the clear air and resting her mind in the quietness while Steve went to the stream for some water.

In a few moments, hushed voices jarred her to full attention. She sat still, her head tilted to one side, listening to Steve's voice.

"I'm much obliged for your concern, Kip," Steve was saying to the man who had introduced himself as the foreman of the Running M, "but we'll go ahead with our plans."

"I'm just thinking of the little lady," a deep voice said. "Them Harringtons are plumb mean, and you'll have yourself a whoppin' fight. I hope you know what you're doing."

"I know." Steve's voice had a deadly, still quality. "I've been down the river a ways myself. We'll go on."

The snap of a boot on a twig told Megan they had moved away. She relaxed against the rough bark once more, but the memory of those voices lingered on, and her peace of mind flew away on silent wings.

A hot, lazy June afternoon gave them a drowsy welcome when the stage rumbled into Juniper Junction. From under the brim of her gray traveling bonnet, Megan eagerly watched the town roll by. The street was deserted except for two weather-beaten wagons and three sleepy horses standing three-legged next to various hitching rails along the dusty street. At various places a tepid breeze blew the sand into a small, swirling cloud.

"Whoa!" the driver bellowed as the stage lumbered to a halt. The clamor of the jouncing, jolting stage still sang in Megan's ears, and her stiff muscles complained when Steve helped her down. She stepped up onto the boardwalk and looked with interest at the shops and houses. There were one, two, yes, three saloons, and two blacksmith shops, a hotel, a bank, and a general store, as well as the stage station where she stood. Someone was building a small shop between the livery stable and the jail. It was a lonely place even compared to Denver and wouldn't bear comparing to the crowded, pulsating streets of Baltimore.

Brushing aside a tinge of disappointment at the forsaken little place that would be their main supply point, Megan entered the stage station to send Em a telegram and ask if a letter had arrived.

"Sorry, ma'am." The boyish clerk with pock-scarred cheeks shook his head. "The mail comes through ever' Wednesday. Maybe there'll be somethin' tomorrow."

Twenty minutes later Megan sank gratefully into the wooden chair Steve held for her at the hotel restaurant. He looked anxiously at her weary face when he took his seat across from her at the small, square table.

"Do you think we should wait until morning to go on?" he asked.

"A little rest and some hot food is all I need," she replied, trying to smile. "I want to get to the ranch today. I don't think I could wake up and face another day of traveling." In her mind she pictured the wide fields and spreading trees on the ranch. She could already feel the long, refreshing bath and the bed waiting for her there.

Two thick steaks and a plateful of fried potatoes later they walked outside to see four horses hitched to a buckboard in front of the general store next door. In the wagon were their suitcases and baggage.

"Aren't they beauties?" Steve asked, a hint of pride in the words.

"Where did you find them?" Holding his arm, she stopped on the edge of the boardwalk, looking eagerly at each horse in turn. There were two blacks, a buckskin, and a strawberry roan mare.

"Man at the livery stable had the three geldings and the buckboard. I got the mare from Harper at Harper's Emporium."

Megan rubbed the neck of the strawberry mare. Memories of happy days in Virginia came back in a flood. Morning rides with Father, all but forgotten, were revived again. The mare nuzzled her hand.

"Looking for a treat?" Megan laughed happily and patted the star between the horse's eyes. "What's her name?"

"Candy. Harper tells me she loves sugar and carrots. His daughter had her until she went back East. Treated her like a baby. She married a man from Delaware a few months ago, so Harper has no need to keep the horse around anymore." He checked a strap on the harness. "The black with the star and three stockings is Star, the one with the blaze is Caesar, and the buckskin is Billy."

"Will it take four to pull the buckboard?"

"It's a steep climb to the ranch from what I hear. When the wagon is loaded down like it is now, we'll be glad to have four." Steve finished his inspection of the harness. "We'd better get our supplies and head out." He pulled his watch from his vest pocket and glanced at it. "Billy has a loose shoe that must be attended to before we set out, and we ought to get to the ranch before dark."

It was shadowy inside Harper's Emporium after the glare of the hot afternoon sun. Megan paused on the threshold while she waited for her eyes to adjust to the dimness. The inviting aroma of new leather, fresh ground coffee, and tobacco drew her inside. From that moment, the smell of a new saddle reminded her of Harper's.

In one corner on a table were two saddles with some bridles and spurs; a few leather belts hung on the wall above them. There were large, copper-banded barrels of pickles, crackers, and coffee beans near the end of the counter where the coffee grinder stood. The rows of shelves that lined the wall behind the counter were filled with bolts of fabric, shirts and pants folded in a neat stack, an assortment of guns and ammunition, and various staple food items. On the counter was a thick glass jar of peppermint candy with a small sign: PENNY CANDY.

"Hello." A slim young woman standing near the counter spoke to Megan. Her strawberry-blond hair was pulled back into a wavy, shoulder-length ponytail. "Mr. Harper went into the back room for a minute." She had clear blue eyes and an open, friendly smile. "I'm Susan Harrington."

"I'm Megan Wes. . .ummm, Megan Chamberlin," Megan faltered. "We came in on the stage."

"Are you going to be here long?" The woman's friendliness touched Megan's heart and made her want to reach out.

"We've come to settle on a ranch."

"Oh, good!" Susan's smile broadened. "Elaine Sanders and I are about the only young women near Juniper since Alice Harper left. Where are you going to be?"

"I believe it's called the Circle C."

Susan's pleasant expression froze on her face. She grew pale, and her eyes opened wide.

"The Circle C?" She paused, searching Megan's face.

"Yes. I hope you'll come and visit me if you can," Megan said, offering a tremulous smile. She hoped Susan would be a friend in this friendless, faraway place.

"I will." A spark shone in the local woman's eyes. She glanced toward the curtained doorway at the rear of the shop. The noise of boots scuffling on the wood floor came from the other side of the curtain. Susan moved closer to Megan. "I will come and visit you," she hurriedly whispered on her way out.

A slim, gray-haired man with stooped shoulders stepped through the curtain-covered door.

"Can I help you folks?"

"We need supplies." Steve spoke from the corner near the leather goods. "My wife can tell you what she wants."

Megan walked to the counter. "Twenty pounds of flour, two pounds of brown sugar. . ." She gave Mr. Harper the list of supplies, enough for a month.

"I want five hundred rounds of .45 shells and five hundred .44s," Steve added when she finished. "And I'll take those two Colts, a Winchester, and the Henry rifle." He nodded toward weapons on a shelf to the left.

Harper's bushy gray eyebrows raised a mite. He dropped the shells into the burlap sack he was filling.

"Expectin' trouble?" he asked, his eyes still on the sack.

"We've come to settle on the Circle C," Steve said conversationally, "and we aim to stay."

Harper looked up, startled, to meet Steve's gaze for a long moment. The storekeeper's eyes shifted, and he continued filling their order in silence.

"I'll be needing a hand."

"You'll not be finding one for the Circle C," Mr. Harper said. His face was expressionless.

"Mr. Harper, I'm not on the prod, but if a fight comes my way, I'll handle it. With or without a hand." Steve lifted a burlap sack in each hand and carried them outside. Megan followed him, her heart pounding.

"I saw a blacksmith at work near the end of the street," Steve said, picking up the reins. "He ought to be able to take care of Billy's loose shoe in short order."

The pounding of a hammer on an anvil reached Megan's ears long before she saw the giant of a man who wielded the iron. He stood inside the wide open door of his shop shaping a red-hot horseshoe. His bulging, hairy arms were streaked with soot and sweat. When their buckboard creaked to a stop, he straightened, lifted the horseshoe with a pair of tongs, and plunged it into a bucket of water, making it boil over.

He was the biggest man Megan had ever seen. At least six feet, four-inches tall, he must have weighed close to three hundred pounds. He wore a ragged shirt so faded and dirty that it was impossible to tell its original color. Wide suspenders made two furrows over his shoulders, and his front was covered by a blackened leather apron. "Gud afternoon!" Nodding and wiping his hands on his apron, he lumbered toward them. His broad grin revealed a missing front tooth.

Setting the brake and winding the reins around the whip stand, Steve jumped down. "I've got a horse with a loose shoe. Can you take care of it for me right away? We have some traveling to do before nightfall."

"Five minute," the blacksmith announced in thick German tones. He picked up Billy's foot and examined the shoe. "Two nail vill make it gud as new." He slid a hammer from a loop on his side and dug two nails from his apron pocket. Four taps and he slid the hammer back through its loop. "I never seen you before. You live here?" It was a friendly question.

"We're settling on the Circle C." Steve's voice had become defensive.

"Dat's gud. Dat's gud." The big man's round blond head bobbed up and down. "I'm Logan Hohner. I have de Horseshoe Ranch just north of dere. Dose be my two boys, Al and Henry." He indicated two young men in their early twenties slouching in wooden chairs in front of the gray, wind-scoured building. At the mention of their names, the one with buckteeth protruding through his lips raised his hat a fraction then slid it over his eyes and tilted back in his chair.

The other nodded sullenly. Both were of large build like their father, except the father was hard and muscular and they were soft and lethargic.

"Come by my place any time," Hohner invited.

Steve thanked him and climbed aboard. He released the brake, shook the reins, and they were off. The bouncing of the buckboard was as bone-jarring as the stage ride. Megan clenched her teeth and held on. She wondered about her strange conversation with Susan Harrington.

Susan had been frightened at the mention of the Circle C. Susan Harrington. Harrington. Hadn't that been the name she had overheard Steve and Kip use that afternoon when they were beside the stream?

"Steve?" Megan looked at his profile. "What is the problem about the Circle C?"

He looked straight ahead, studying a moment before answering.

"I guess you'd better know." Looking at her, he held the reins loosely and shifted slightly on the seat. "It seems we've bought some trouble by coming out here. The Harringtons are the big landholders, and they don't like squatters."

"But I thought you had deeded land."

"It is deeded. And that's exactly why I'm not backing down."

His jaw was set in a hard line. "Evidently Harrington has some pull around here, and he has some sort of claim on the Circle C. The problem is that the law is in Denver. A deed is only a piece of paper. Unfortunately, paper's not much protection against a loaded six-shooter."

"You think there will be shooting?"

"No doubt there will." He glanced at Megan again. "Don't fret, though. I didn't fight under Bragg for nothing. We'll get through." He glanced at the sinking sun and clucked to the horses to get along faster.

The buckboard continued across the prairie to the rolling hills at the foot of the mountains. The horses started pulling, and Steve slackened the reins to give them their head. Soon prairie grasses were replaced by wildflowers, sagebrush, and piñon pine. A clean breeze swept over them as they neared the high country.

Megan gazed at the orange and brown rocks upthrust to the sky, the scrubby, green hillsides, and the jagged cliffs. She savored the scent of sage and pine. It was rugged country, but she fell in love with it at first sight. Simply being there made her feel happier than she had in a long time.

"It's not far from here," Steve said when they passed over a rise. "I believe it's through this stretch of trees and across a stream."

"There it is!" Steve pulled the horses to a stop. A sprawling, thirty-acre meadow sloped gently up until it was cut off by a stone wall. On the eastern side of the wall were a stone cabin and a smaller gray building. The two buildings were joined by a high board fence. The setting sun shone full on them, bringing life to the rock wall and house. They glowed like bronze against the darkening sky.

It was more beautiful than Megan had imagined. A cooling gust of wind bathed her face. It felt refreshing after the long, hot days of traveling.

"Giddap!" Steve called to the team, and they rode slowly down the bank. The water came a few inches below the axle of the buckboard. Megan held her breath until they were climbing up the other side. Skirting the field, Steve held the horses to an even, moderate gate. Timothy grass brushed the bottom and sides of the buckboard.

By the time they reached the house, the wind had taken on a definite chill. It pulled at Megan's dress and reached down inside of her. She picked up the shawl she had draped over the back of the seat and wrapped it closely around her shoulders. Shadows filled the hollows and crannies of the dooryard, bringing with them a strange foreboding. Uneasy, Megan looked around the dooryard that was little more than an extension of the meadow, full of thigh-high grass and brush. She pushed through the grass toward the stone house while Steve rummaged for a lantern and the lamp oil.

The floor and roof of the porch sagged wearily. A few boards were missing from each. The door leaned on cracked, dry leather hinges. The smell of dampness and mold caught at her nostrils. Resting her weight cautiously on the broken porch floor, she reached a tentative hand toward the door.

"Oh!" she cried sharply, drawing back. Inches from her face an enormous spider web covered the top half of the partly open door. Cringing, she pulled her shawl tightly about her and returned to the edge of the porch. The nightly cricket chorus had begun, punctuated now and then by the ghostly "who—o—o—o" of an owl.

She shivered and dug her nails into the palms of her hands, holding in the discouraged, exhausted tears that sprang to her eyes. How could they sleep here tonight? And she yearned for a relaxing soak in a warm tub.

"Here's a lantern," Steve called from the buckboard fifteen minutes later. "I'd better see to a fire. It's getting cold." All she could see of him now was his middle, next to the swinging lantern held high above the tall grass as he walked toward her. Never giving the spider web a thought, he pushed the groaning door open and walked inside.

With many nervous glances, Megan squeezed herself into the smallest proportions possible and followed him into the gloomy house.

Chapter 5

There's a fire already laid," Steve said when he had set the lantern down. He knelt before the fireplace and struck a match on the edge of his boot sole. The dry wood sparked into a flickering flame.

Megan hovered nearby. She was afraid to move around or look too closely at the shadowy corners of the room. The fire gnawed with gathering appetite at the kindling, so Steve added a larger piece of wood. Megan felt a hint of warmth and moved even closer to the smoldering light.

"I'll bring in some things for the night." Steve stood up, brushing off his hands. "You sit down and rest yourself. You look all in."

"I'm sure a night's rest will set me right," she replied automatically as she moved to an upholstered settee near the fireplace and sank to the seat. Without another word, Steve took the lantern and stepped into the night.

In a few moments he was back carrying Megan's trunk with several blankets stacked on top. Working quickly and efficiently, he spread out a crude bed near the fire and told her to lie down. She felt her eyes drooping as soon as her head found a resting place.

The cabin was dusky from sunlight shining through the cloudy windows when Megan awoke. Gingerly, she sat up. She ached in every bone, and her head throbbed dully. Steve was nowhere around.

A pail of water with a metal dipper hooked on the edge stood on the dusty stone hearth. Megan drank greedily, then bathed her face. She unlocked her trunk and was searching for a fresh dress when the door hinges groaned.

"Mornin'." Steve dropped an armload of split logs into the woodbox near the fireplace and brushed off his bark-flecked arms. "I'll move your things into the bedroom yonder if you want." He nodded toward a door on the wall opposite the front door. "I laid claim to the loft last night." He added a log to the small fire. "There's a spring out back if you want to wash up."

"I'll cook breakfast first," Megan responded. "I'm starving." She grinned in spite of herself.

Steve answered with a relieved smile. "The supplies we bought at Harper's are there." He pointed to two burlap sacks beside the moth-eaten settee. "I brought them in last night. You'd better use the fireplace until we can clean up the cookstove and check for a bird's nest in the chimney.

A hot breakfast improved Megan's outlook. She armed herself with soap and towel and went in search of the spring. Opening the back door, she peered outside. A wide stream of water flowed from a crack in the rock wall behind the house to fill a stone-lined basin in the ground. Through the clear water she could see the basin had some loose stones and moss inside, but it was in good condition. She touched the stream pouring down only to jerk her hand back. The water was like liquid ice.

The bath, though not quite the long soak of her daydream, was invigorating. While she finished dressing, she noticed that when the water left the basin it continued through a stone-paved trench that led through a springhouse and drained down a bank. Megan walked to the edge and looked down. Gasping, she took a step back. It was forty feet to the bottom! The eastern side of the house was on the edge of a small cliff.

Megan looked out at a vast expanse of blue-green rolling hills that melted to meet the level prairie. The sun was a glowing yellow ball barely resting on the flat horizon. The radiant light made the prairie grass gleam like silver as it swayed in the continuous breeze. She stood spellbound, feeling like an ant on the edge of an endless wilderness. No trace of human handiwork marred the landscape. It was magnificent.

How long she stayed there, she didn't know, but finally she realized she ought to get back to the business at hand, and she turned away from the panorama with a promise to visit this spot many mornings in the future.

Back in the house, she wrapped a navy kerchief around her head, tied an old work apron over her blue calico dress, and made a careful, critical inspection of the house.

The front wall of the house was built of rock, and the floor was made of smooth, flat stones. Both walls and floor were fitted together as perfectly as a broken piece of pottery glued back together. The walls and open-beam ceiling were swaddled with dust-laden spider webs. The windows, cracked and pocked, were covered with a thick layer of fly-specked grime. There were two wooden chairs and a three-person settee positioned in a semicircle around the fireplace. The cushions were moldy and full of holes with small tufts of gray cotton showing through.

At the western end of the house was a dining area with the kitchen branching off toward the back, making an *L* shape. A thick oak table and four chairs were covered with the ever-present dust but seemed in good condition.

Megan looked about her with an appraising eye. The marks of a craftsman were all around her. The house had definite possibilities.

She moved into the kitchen to examine the rusty range, two counters, and many cabinets. The single window revealed a small stretch of grass and one side of the gray wooden building she had seen last night. She also saw the high board fence.

The fence intrigued her. Why was it there? What did it hide? She went through the back door to find out the answer. When she had come out earlier, she had been too taken up with the spring and the breathtaking view to think of looking in this direction.

The fence was six feet tall and parallel to the face of the rock wall, making a corridor about fifteen feet wide. Seeing nothing unusual behind the fence, Megan walked on until she came to the wooden building. Applying a little pressure, she lifted the reluctant door latch and was rewarded by a small shower of dirt when the door swung open.

She looked inside before she stepped over the doorsill. Six stalls stood before her with a single manger running the length of all six. The buckboard was beside the far wall, still loaded with the stacks of grain for the horses and the corn seed Steve had brought from Baltimore. On the wall near the open double doors hung a wooden bucket and a bit of chain. There was a door on the left side of the back wall, probably a ranch hand's modest quarters.

Steve stood in the second stall, a pitchfork in his hand.

"I was wondering where the fence led," she said when he looked up.

"This is a nice place, isn't it?" he asked without waiting for a reply. "I can say one thing for Cunningham, the man who built it." Steve rested his forearm on the pitchfork handle. "Besides being a craftsman, he knew how to prepare for a battle."

"A battle?"

"Sure. There's a rock wall behind the house, a cliff beside it, and no trees within shooting range. No one can approach the house unseen." He propped the pitchfork against the wall and picked up a shovel. "That fence was put there so he could get to his stock without going out in the open. And water back there, too."

"The house is well-made. I can see that."

"That's another thing. It has a stone front. The rest is made of squared logs. No bullet can get through them."

"You think he had a lot of trouble?"

Steve lifted a shovel full of hardened straw and manure from the floor and heaved it outside. "Judging from the town's reaction to us, I think it's pretty obvious," he answered, bending for another load.

"I guess I'd better get started in the house," she said in a moment and went back to the house the way she came.

It was noon when Megan walked out to the sagging front porch for a cold lunch and a little rest. She was tired, but it was a satisfied feeling. The morning had been spent in the kitchen, for she couldn't tolerate the thought of no clean place in which to cook. She had scoured and scrubbed until her shoulders ached.

Steve joined her for bacon and biscuit sandwiches, leftovers from breakfast, and cold spring water. They passed the lunch break in companionable silence. In spite of the hard work, Megan was enjoying herself immensely. Those few minutes of sitting on the rickety porch, absorbing the blueness of the cloud-strewn sky, and drinking in the hay-scented air, pumped life back into her tired limbs.

It was past dark before Megan permitted herself another rest. The windows in the house were as clean as she could make them, cracked as they were, and the four-poster bed in her room had been stripped of its rotting mattress and replaced with a fresh hay-filled one. Steve had cut the hay from the front yard.

The kindred atmosphere of Steve sitting near the fire cleaning his new guns, thick stew bubbling cheerily on the shiny black kitchen stove, gave Megan a tender, contented feeling she hadn't known for a long, long time. She ladled the soup into bowls and set them carefully on the table.

"Tomorrow I'll scout around and get acquainted with the country," Steve said, drawing a knotted string through the barrel of his Winchester. "I left word at the livery stable, the hotel, and the emporium that I need a hand. If we can't get one, I'll have to work double to get the corn crop in. It'll be late as it is. Not to mention a garden."

Megan had to force herself to wash up after supper. She moved with leaden feet and arms, but somehow she managed to finish. That night she lay alone in the darkness trying to sleep in spite of her sore shoulders and aching back. She pressed the heels of her hands against her eyes to ease her throbbing head. It had been nine days since she had seen Jeremy. Was he better? Worse? How much longer would it be until she got some news? Her mind flitted from question to question. In a few minutes a soft rain started a soothing, tapping lullaby on her windowpane. The tune hushed her restless brain, and she fell asleep.

The next morning Steve rode out before the sun shone its face full over the prairie. Megan stood in the doorway watching until horse and rider disappeared into the stand of oaks and pines. She was about to go inside when a movement in the tall grass caught her eye. She studied the edge of the yard, expecting to pick out a rabbit frozen in its tracks, when two pointed gray ears moved slightly at the edge of the grass.

She drew in a startled breath. *A wolf*, she thought. Even as the impression touched her consciousness, she rejected it. Wolves came at night and were shy of people.

The large gray head moved higher and came into her field of vision. The shaggy face ended in a pointed nose, further confirming her first impression, but there was a nagging doubt.

"Here, boy," she called softly. She spoke more to judge the animal's reaction than in hopes he would indeed come to her. The shaggy gray head bent down out of sight and raised up again. The mouth opened, and its red tongue rolled out in a wide yawn that ended in a low whine. The black button eyes were still fastened on her face.

It was a dog.

What is a dog doing so far from anyone? She wondered. She went inside for a leftover piece of biscuit from breakfast. She dredged the biscuit in partially hardened bacon dripping in the bottom of the frying pan. From the edge of the porch she threw the biscuit toward the dog as far as she could. It landed ten feet from him. Still watching her, he didn't move.

She waited a moment, decided she was wasting her time, and went back inside. She threw open all the windows in the house to let the clear, pine-scented air sweep through before clearing up the breakfast dishes.

That task finished, she glanced out at the spot where the biscuit had fallen. It was gone, and so was the dog. Whether the dog or some other wild animal had taken the food, she couldn't tell. It was an unusual happening, but not significant, and she forgot about it.

Late in the afternoon she was rubbing the wide, stone fireplace to a shine with pine oil when an odd sound stopped her midmotion.

It was a voice as rough and rasping as a frog with laryngitis singing, "Rock of ages, cleft for me, let me hide myself in Thee."

Half-curious and half-alarmed, Megan peered out a front window. Someone rode toward the house on a lop-eared, gray donkey.

"Let the water and the blood. . ."

It was an old man wearing faded, dust-covered clothes and a brown Stetson with a frayed crown. He rode up to the porch and pulled up on the donkey's reins.

"Anybody to home?" he shouted.

With shaking fingers, Megan lifted the latch and stepped outside. The man swung from the saddle and took off his hat.

"Howdy, ma'am." He wasn't as old as Megan had first imagined. She was relieved to see his mild blue eyes had a friendly twinkle. "I heard you folks are needin' a hand."

"Yes," Megan said, smiling in response to his polite manner. "My husband is looking over the country today. I'm expecting him around suppertime." She hesitated. "I've got some water on for coffee. Could I offer you a cup?"

"I'd be much obliged." He picked up the donkey's reins from where they trailed on the ground.

"You can put your donkey in the stable. There's a spring out back." Megan went back into the house to finish making the coffee.

"My name's Megan Chamberlin," she said as she handed him a steaming cup at the dining room table. "My husband is Steve."

"Thank you, ma'am. I'm Joe Calahan, but most folks call me Banjo on account of I'm always making music." He chuckled. "It seems like there's always a song on the inside o' me that's scramblin' to get out." He sipped his coffee and sighed appreciatively. "That's a mighty fine cup, Mrs. Chamberlin. A good cup o' coffee is a great comfort to a man." With a work-gnarled hand, he smoothed the spot on his graying black hair where his hat left a crease. "What type o' hand was your husband wantin'?"

"As far as I know, he's planning to put in a corn crop as soon as possible. He says it's almost too late already. He wants to get some cattle, too."

"I've turned my hand to just about ever'thin', so I reckon it don't much matter."

That evening when Megan introduced Banjo, Steve's relief was easy to see.

"After we mow the hay in the lower meadow, we can plant it in corn," Steve said after supper. They sat around the small flame in the fireplace. The June days were warm, but the nights still had a chill. The flickering firelight made the polished stones glow. "Know much about cattle?" he asked Banjo.

"I've punched a few cows," Banjo said. Thoughtfully, he rolled the toothpick he was chewing to the other side of his mouth. "Ever heard of the Harringtons?"

Megan started at the name.

"Kip Morgan told me a little about them."

"I know Kip. He's a good man. As for Victor Harrington, he was one of the first ranchers to open up this country. He fought off the Indians, built a ranch, and brought in about twenty thousand head o' cattle.

"He pushed out a few small ranchers in the process, but mostly folks stayed out o' his way. The bulk of the land he claims is government land, but the law is in Denver, so government land or no don't make no difference. What he can hold with a six-shooter is his."

"That's what I figured," Steve said.

"I suppose you could try to do things through the law, but that would only get Harrington to ride over to Denver and buy himself a lawyer, a judge, and a jury. You wouldn't have a Chinaman's chance.

"Well, sir." Banjo cleared his throat. "To get back to facts. Five or six years ago John Cunningham bought these four hundred acres. He came in quiet-like and had this house pretty nigh built before Harrington got wind of it. You see, Harrington only comes around this neck o' the woods once in a blue moon. But there's plenty of water coming down off that mountain behind you. If there was to come a drought, he'd need that water in the worst way."

"I found a lake just south of here, too," added Steve.

"That's on your property," Banjo said, nodding. "Cunningham dug in for a long fight and did a good job o' holding Harrington off, too. He had to go all the way to Denver for supplies there at the last, because Harrington put the strong arm on the shopkeepers in Juniper."

"Why did he quit?" Steve asked. "He'd done so much here."

"His wife died in childbirth. It took the heart out of him, I guess. I worked for him time and agin since he come here. A little over two years ago I was passin' through and stopped by to swap howdies. He was gone." Banjo looked at Steve. "I never heard tell what became of him."

"I don't know much myself, Banjo," Steve answered. "He sold the property to my father about two years ago. I never saw him. My father left the land to me in his will. That's all I know."

"We'll be gettin' an early start, so I'd best say good night to you," Banjo said, rising. "Thank you for the fine meal, ma'am," he said, settling his hat on his head. "I'll be gettin' to my room in the stable." After Steve's return that afternoon, they had swept out the back room of the stable and cut a new mattress full of hay for one of the two bunks. The quarters seemed bare to Megan, but to Banjo, who had lived in many places like it or worse, it was homey.

"You're welcome, Banjo." Megan smiled. She was glad he had come.

Chapter 6

The next morning when Megan glanced out the living room window, the same gray shaggy face she had seen the day before appeared at the edge of the meadow. The dog stayed still, ears high, watching the door of the house. Megan scooped a piece of bacon and the end of a loaf of bread from the table she had been clearing and darted for the porch. When she reached the door, she slowed down and was careful not to make any sudden moves. She stepped to the edge of the porch and threw the food toward him. The dog didn't flinch or make a move toward her.

"It's okay," she said quietly. "I want to be your friend." After a few moments she decided the creature was not going to come closer, and she went back inside. She made a mental note to tell the men when they came back that afternoon. The stray dog intrigued her. She wished she could learn more about where he came from.

The sun was slipping down behind the mountains the next day when a group of riders appeared at the edge of the meadow and galloped toward the house. Hearing the hoofbeats, Megan came to the open doorway to watch. Steve and Banjo were on their way to the house for supper when the group reached the dooryard.

"You Chamberlin?" A wafer-thin, freckled young man with a thick crop of fiery red hair stepped his pinto horse to the front.

"I'm Chamberlin," Steve acknowledged.

"You get out," the red-haired young man ordered in a strident voice. His hard, green eyes looked down coldly at Steve.

"This here's Rocking H range, and we don't cotton to squatters."

"I've got a deed for this land," replied Steve, his voice still even, "and I don't bluff." He looked around the group of five riders. "You fellows are welcome if you come peaceable. Otherwise, consider yourselves warned."

The leader edged his horse forward until it almost touched Steve. "You consider yourself warned." He dropped his hand toward his holster.

"Easy, Beau."

Beau hesitated and looked toward a tall, black-haired man with a narrow face and a deep scar running from his temple to his jaw. The man who spoke stepped his horse forward three steps. He was chewing thoughtfully on a twig.

"They'll git what's comin' to 'em if they don't go. No need to fly off the handle. Your pa don't want shootin' trouble. We can handle 'em another way."

"You heard my answer." Steve stood straight, right hand tense and ready beside his six-shooter. "Now get off my land."

Four of the riders turned their horses, but the one with the red hair hesitated. He looked scornfully at Banjo.

"You joinin' this outfit, Banjo?"

"That's right, Harrington." Banjo's twinkle was nowhere to be seen. "I'm with 'em. And you'll get a run for your money."

Beau considered this news then slowly turned his horse. "Get out!" he repeated and joined his friends.

Megan was shaky with relief and alarm when the group of men rode off. She went inside to set the table, but her ears were tuned to hear Banjo's comments on the incident.

"That Harrington's son?" Steve asked Banjo when he came in from washing up in the basin out back.

"In the flesh," Banjo said, pulling out a chair and sitting down at the table. "He's like a banty rooster. His pa's the big rooster, and he tries to carry the same weight." He glanced at Steve. "But don't underestimate him. He's mean as a snake. I was in town one time when a stranger call him 'Red.' He bumped into Beau and said, 'Sorry, Red,' just like that. Well, sir, the young feller hauled iron, and that hombre almost got hisself shot. If Clyde Turner, the feller with the scar, hadn't been there, who knows what would have happened. That boy's mighty tetchy about his hair."

"Who's Turner?" Steve asked, forking a piece of beef onto his plate.

"He's the foreman. Been with Harrington five, six years."

"He looks familiar, but I can't place him."

"He scares me," Megan said, shivering. "Both of them do."

"Don't alarm yourself, Miss Megan," Banjo said, setting down his coffee cup and smiling kindly. "There's not many men in these parts would harm a lady."

Banjo's words were small comfort when Megan thought of all that was at stake for her in this lonesome place. What if Steve were killed or they had to leave? What would happen to Jeremy? She brooded over those questions until she was worn-out with thinking. They had to make it.

Fear tightened Megan's lips and creased her brow as she watched Steve strap on his gun belt before leaving the house the next morning. He noticed her anxious expression and paused at the door.

"A gun is a tool out here, Megan. I'm not asking for trouble by wearing it, just preparing in case it comes."

"I know," she said, tearing her gaze from the gun to meet his eyes. "But it frightens me to think of what could happen. Please be careful." Through the window she watched him cross the distance to the stable. By sheer will she forced down the fear and went about her chores.

Three days after Harrington's visit, Steve pulled his shiny new plow from the stable and hitched up Star before dawn. They had a long day in store for them planting their garden, and Megan would work alongside the men. The black was restless, eager to get going. He bobbed his head and blew until Steve took the reins and they walked across the freshly cut meadow. Banjo followed him carrying a hoe over his shoulder and his old buffalo gun in the crook of his arm.

Megan finished the breakfast dishes and packed a lunch before she followed the men to the large, sunny plot near the stream at the western edge of the meadow. She carried a cloth-covered basket on her arm and many small sacks of seeds in her apron pocket. The air was sweet with the smell of newly cut timothy. A playful breeze made the wide brim of her sunbonnet flap up and down. It tugged at her full skirt, wrapping the cloth around her ankles so she almost tripped. She heard birds twittering in the woods. The beauty of the morning made her want to spread her arms wide and twirl around until she had to sit down for dizziness.

"There's power in the blood, power in the blood." Banjo's hearty voice drifted with the breeze.

What does he have to sing about? He seems so poor and alone. Like me. But he's used to it, she decided. *He's probably always lived like that.*

"Beautiful day, Miss Megan," Banjo called cheerfully. He knocked his hat to the back of his head and wiped his brow on his sleeve. "That sun'll be mighty hot come noon, though."

Onions, carrots, green beans, and limas—she set the sacks of seeds near a cottonwood tree. She'd already put tomato, cabbage, and sweet potato seeds to sprout in a tray in the kitchen. Peas, turnips. . .she could almost taste them already.

"What should I do first?" Megan asked Steve, waiting on the edge of the plowed plot.

"Banjo will hoe you a furrow. You follow along and drop the seeds in. He'll tell you how." Calling to the horse, Steve bent over the plow handles and moved slowly away, cutting a brown strip from the edge of the meadow.

"Banjo, I've been meaning to ask you something, but I keep forgetting about it." Megan was dropping green bean seeds into a furrow three steps behind Banjo. The sun was high in the cloudless sky.

"What's that?" He didn't look up. His hoe kept chopping and pulling back the dark earth.

"A strange dog comes to the edge of the meadow every morning. When the grass was tall, he'd stay hidden, but since the meadow has been cut he sort of crawls up to the edge of the yard on his belly and crouches there. At first I thought he was a wolf, but he's got some brown and black patches on his back, and he whines sometimes when he sees me. I was wondering if he may have belonged to Cunningham."

Banjo paused to mop his brow with a splotchy handkerchief. "Now that you mention it, I believe Cunningham did have a dog. I never paid much mind." He stuffed the handkerchief into his back pocket and bent over the hoe. "If I saw the critter, I could tell you if it's the same one."

"I've been throwing food out to him, but he hasn't come to get it while I'm outside. I've watched from the window. He never barks or growls, just whines."

"I'll have to get a look at him."

"Maybe Steve will be ready to break for lunch soon." She put her hands on the small of her back and leaned backward. "It will be noon shortly. I'll ask him the next time he comes close to this end of the garden."

An hour later the men sprawled on the ground under an oak tree, and Megan spread out a blue-checkered cloth to serve sandwiches. She tried not to notice her dirt-stained and rough nails. They were still ugly, though she had scrubbed vigorously in the stream.

"You in Mr. Lincoln's war?" Banjo asked Steve. The sun now was glaring down upon the garden plot, and the shade of the trees was a welcome relief.

"Fortieth Mississippi." Steve lounged against a tree, chewing a long piece of grass.

"I served under Sheridan the last few years of the war," Banjo continued. "I lived in Texas then, you know." He leaned back until he was resting on one elbow. After some talk and laughter, they rose and went back to work.

It was close to dusk when Megan plodded wearily back to the house. She turned to look back at Steve and Banjo finishing the last strip of rich, brown earth. Tired as she was, it was gratifying to know she belonged here. This was her own home and these were her men to care for, at least for now. If only Jeremy were here, and Em. She tried to push aside the anguish that lingered in the back of her mind ready to steal every morsel of happiness she might know here.

During the next several weeks, life on the ranch fell into a routine. Day by day Megan worked in the garden pulling out the weeds until her hands became tough and strong. Her face grew tan in spite of the sunbonnet she wore. It wasn't long before she grew to love the smell and feel of rich earth.

The morning Steve came to tell her his news, she was on hands and knees seeking out the latest interlopers among the two-inch-high sprouts. She stood and brushed the dirt from her hands when he came near.

"Banjo and I will be leaving for a few days," he said. "He tells me Jim Sanders, the owner of the Running M, may sell me some cattle. I want to get several hundred head to fatten up before winter."

"How long will you be gone?" Megan tried to hide her dismay. How would she feel being at home alone?

"It'll only be two or three days. I'd like to leave tomorrow if I can finish putting in the corn today."

Megan looked at the lower meadow, all plowed and planted except for a small patch. Steve had chosen the lower ten acres so the edge of the field would still be out of shooting range when the corn grew tall. She swallowed to ease the tightness in her throat.

"All right. I'll bake some biscuits for you to take along."

"You've done well for a city girl, Megan." He smiled down at her. Megan looked away, her cheeks burning.

His smile stayed with her when he and Banjo rode out the next morning. It warmed her inside where she couldn't reach. When the men disappeared from her sight, she lingered at the open door watching for a familiar face at the edge of the yard. As usual, a shaggy gray figure came to rest just beyond her throwing range.

"Here, boy," she called again. She held out a piece of bacon rind. "Come on. I won't hurt you."

The dog moved forward a pace and sat down. He tilted his head to one side and whined.

"What are you afraid of?" she kept talking in a soothing voice. With an underhanded throw, she tossed the meat. It landed near his feet. "I won't hurt you, you know. I would like to be friends." She continued cajoling and coaxing a few moments longer. The dishes were waiting, as always, and finally she decided to go back inside and attend to them.

Before she moved, the dog crouched down and crawled to the bit of bacon. Grasping it in his teeth, he backed to the edge of the grass to eat it, always watching Megan.

"Well, you're getting braver, are you?" She went inside for a piece of bread and threw it to him. "Friends. See?" She brushed a crumb from her hand. "You could use a friend. . .and so could I." With a last wistful smile, she went inside the house.

That day Megan cleaned the loft, taking advantage of Steve's absence, and made doughnuts for his return. The dog returned the next morning. Megan sat on the steps and talked to him for half an hour. He watched her closely and whined twice, but he wouldn't come near.

Early in the afternoon of the second day, she was spreading out some navy gingham to make a tablecloth when movement on the edge of the meadow caught her eye. She ran to the window for a closer look. The sight filled her with horror.

Several men on horses circled the garden. One had flaming red hair and rode a piebald pinto.

Beau Harrington.

With a motion inviting the others to follow, he stepped his horse into the garden and began tramping around.

At first Megan couldn't move. She stood, mouth open, staring as they started through the garden plot. Abruptly, she came to herself. Indignation grew into outrage, and she overcame her natural fear. She ran to the fireplace, tore Steve's extra rifle from its pegs above the mantel shelf, and raced outside, holding it clumsily in her arms.

"Stop! Stop!" she shouted. One time she almost stumbled on the rough ground, but she never stopped or even hesitated. She ran to the edge of the garden and awkwardly raised the rifle. "Stop, or I'll shoot!"

"Well, well," Beau Harrington was the first to speak, "what have we here? Chamberlin lettin' a woman do his fightin' for him now?"

"He's not here, or he'd take on the lot of you," Megan fumed. She raised the gun higher. "But it doesn't take a man's finger to pull a trigger. You get out of here before I do."

"She means it, boss." A long-legged, skinny man with a beak nose spoke up. He watched Megan warily.

"Slim's right," Clyde Turner added. His flinty eyes sized up Megan and the long gun in her arms.

"You tell your man he can expect more of the same if he doesn't move," Beau sneered. He hesitated after the others moved away, then slowly followed them.

The closer Megan came to the house, the weaker her knees became and the sicker her stomach felt. Her arms were too limp to lift the rifle back to its pegs, so she propped it against the wall and sank into a chair. She realized tears were streaming down her face. Covering her face with her hands, she gave way to frustrated sobs.

Their beautiful crop was ruined. Crying relieved some of her pent-up emotions, and she stared blindly at the cold fireplace. After the first waves of despair had passed, discouragement slowly transformed into smoldering anger.

How dare those scoundrels! She wouldn't let the likes of Beau Harrington stop her. Too much was at stake.

She washed her face in the spring. Weren't there some seeds left? Yes, the sacks were in the kitchen. Armed with a hoe and the Henry, she marched out to inspect the damage. She glanced at the sun, still high above the horizon. If she hurried, there may be time to make repairs before dark.

Kneeling over her injured seedlings, she discovered the damage wasn't as overwhelming as she first thought. She crept along on all fours, straightening a seedling here, planting new seeds there until the sun sank low and the seeds were spent. She stood and stretched her tired back as she looked over her work. The garden wasn't as large as it had once been, but they would still have fresh vegetables on their table.

Candy came to the fence and nickered when Megan walked past the corral. She propped the hoe and rifle against a post and rubbed the roan's nose. *I wonder if I can still ride,* she thought, resting her aching forehead against the mare's smooth cheek. *One of these days,* she promised herself, *I'll give it a try.*

It was noon the next day when Kelsey, Banjo's lop-eared donkey, stepped out of the trees. Billy wasn't far behind. Was that a third horse with them? Megan strained her eyes but couldn't tell. Quickly, she slid her freshly risen rolls into the oven, smoothed her hair, and ran out to meet them.

"There is a fountain filled with blood, drawn from Emmanuel's veins. . . ." It was Banjo's voice, as sweet and rough as ever. "And sinners plunged beneath its flood lose all their guilty stains. Hello, Miss Megan." Banjo smiled warmly and raised his hat.

"We brought you something." Steve stepped out of the saddle on the off side and came around his horse holding a rope. Slowly, a short black and white animal followed.

"A cow!" Megan clapped her hands in delight.

"Sanders had two, and this one just weaned a heifer calf, so he let me have her. For a price, you understand." He chuckled wryly. "She's a Holstein. They're supposed to be good milkers. Her name's Bess."

"She's beautiful!" Megan couldn't take her eyes off the creature. "Oh, Steve! A cow! We haven't had milk or butter or cheese for ages."

"We bought eight hundred head of longhorns from Sanders, too. We left them in a grassy canyon east of here. A nice looking lot, don't you think, Banjo?"

"Nice as I've ever seen." Banjo's eyes twinkled at Megan's enraptured exclamations over Bess.

"Oh, I've rolls in the oven." Megan lifted her wide skirt to free her ankles and ran lightly to the house. Banjo's chuckle followed her.

"We had some visitors while you were gone." Megan brought up the awful affair after the men had enjoyed a hot meal. They were relaxing over a second cup of coffee. "Beau Harrington and his hands."

"What did they do?" Steve sat up straight and stared at her, an unpleasant light in his eyes.

"They trampled the garden." She was worried by the thundercloud forming on Steve's face. "It wasn't as bad as I first imagined. I guess I stopped them in time."

"You what?"

"I took the rifle from over the fireplace and ran out and stopped them. I told them I'd shoot if they didn't go."

"They give you any trouble?" Steve's face matched the glowing embers in the smoldering fireplace.

"The red-haired one had his usual bluster, but the rest were ready to leave soon enough, I reckon."

"I guess they had good reason," Banjo said, dryly. "Facin' a man with a gun is one thing. Facin' a wrought-up woman with one is another'n."

Steve scraped his chair back and stood to his feet. "I'm going over there and have it out with Harrington."

His words were like a heavy millstone crushing the breath from Megan's lungs. "You'll be on their land," she protested. "There's no telling what may happen."

"This foolishness has got to stop, Megan," he insisted, clapping on his hat. "Harrington needs to learn a lesson. I reckon I'm the one elected to teach him." He flipped his gun belt around his waist and buckled it with a quick, practiced motion.

"Please, Steve," she pleaded, following him to the door. "They'll kill you if they get the chance."

"I'm going to put a stop to this kind of thing once and for all."

She reached for his arm, but he brushed her away and strode to the stable. In a few moments he galloped away on Caesar. Megan pressed her fist to her mouth to quench a silent sob as he disappeared into the trees.

Chapter 7

Banjo joined Megan in the doorway as Caesar's hoofbeats faded into the distance. "He's got to do it, you know."

"I know." Megan was still fighting tears. She was so afraid. "Are we going to win, Banjo? Do we have any chance of holding on to the Circle C against the Harringtons?"

Banjo didn't answer for a long minute. He stared across the meadow toward the setting sun. "Miss Megan," he finally answered, "I'm not a prophet like Elijah, so I can't tell the future for sure, but I will tell you this: The three of us are gonna make a brass-plated effort. That's all we can do. We'll have to leave it in the hands of the good Lord after we've done our best."

Without speaking any more, the old cowhand and the young wife lingered in the last light of day. Neither of them wanted to go back into the shadowy house.

"Did you have the safety off?" Banjo asked when the sky was indigo with a dull yellow glow rimming the mountains.

"The what?"

"The safety on the Henry. If you don't take the safety off, it won't shoot."

"I just picked it up and ran out, so I reckon I didn't."

"Ho, ho!" Banjo guffawed. "You chased those rascals away with the safety still on." He enjoyed a good chuckle then became serious. "You ought to learn to shoot. Most women out here do."

"Would you teach me, Banjo?"

"Well," he drawled slowly, "you'd best ask your husband first. If he doesn't have time, I'll be happy to."

Megan flushed, realizing her slip. Confused, she chose that moment to clear away the supper dishes, hoping he hadn't noticed.

                    ~

Megan was pacing the floor when Steve rode in late that night. Banjo had gone to his room in the stable. Steve's step was slow and heavy on the creaky porch.

"What happened?" she asked anxiously as soon as he stepped into the light.

"No one was there. Only one I could round up was the cook, and he said everybody was in town. By the time I got there I'd cooled off some. There was no good could come of going off half-cocked." He hung his hat and gun belt on their pegs and flung himself on the settee. "So I came on home."

"I kept some coffee hot for you."

"That would taste mighty good." He rubbed the back of his neck and stretched out his legs. "I guess we'll have to hold on and see what happens. Banjo's right, you know. With the law all the way in Denver, we'll have to fight it out ourselves." He took the steaming mug from Megan. "Thanks. That's exactly what I needed after a day like today."

"Will you teach me to shoot?" She sat in the chair near the fireplace.

"Teach you to shoot?" He looked up. "Sure. I was figuring on putting in some practice time myself." He sipped his coffee. "You've got to get the troops in order before you can go to war."

Megan tried to write a cheery letter to Jeremy the next day, but the words wouldn't come. She had been in Colorado for more than a month and still had had no word from Em. After several false starts she managed a bright description of the ranch and the garden. She described the four horses and Banjo's donkey in detail, knowing he would like to hear about them. With a heavy heart, she sealed the envelope.

Surely Jeremy wasn't worse. Could that be why Em hadn't asked someone to pen down a note for her? Tormented by doubts and fears, a dark cloud settled over Megan's spirit. Not knowing what was happening back in Baltimore was harder to bear than being there and facing the worst.

The days that followed were long and tedious. She spoke little and smiled less. Every rider that came into the meadow struck new fear in Megan's heart.

The afternoon a big palomino stepped into view, she was churning butter on the porch, hoping to catch a passing breeze. Instead of riding to the house, the tall stranger rode to the corral where Banjo was stringing barbed wire around a fence post. Megan was relieved to see Banjo raise his hand in greeting and straighten to talk. The rider stayed only minutes and rode away.

Brimming with questions, she took a cup of water out to Banjo later to give herself an excuse to talk to him.

"Who rode in this afternoon, Banjo? Did you know him?"

"That was Wyatt Hammond, Harrington's horse wrangler." He smiled at Megan's alarm. "Don't fret yourself. He's a fine young man. I knowed his folks. He's a different brand than that red-topped sapling. Wyatt was on his way to town and stopped to swap howdies.

"Somethin' troublin' you I could help with, Miss Megan?" He gave her a questioning, fatherly smile, his frayed felt hat knocked to the back of his head.

"It's nothing really, Banjo." She tried to smile back at him but only half succeeded. "I haven't had any word from my little brother, that's all. He's in a sanitarium in Baltimore with rheumatic fever. I guess I've been letting my worries show too much."

"That's what friends are for, you know, helping carry burdens." He hesitated a moment before adding, "I have a Friend who carries all my burdens."

Megan looked at him, waiting for him to continue.

"His name is Jesus. He's been carrying my burdens for almost fifteen years now."

"You don't have many burdens, Banjo. You are always so happy."

"You know what I said about being from Texas? My wife and I had a ranch a few miles south of the Red River. Purtiest little place you ever did see. We worked the land and ran some cows, kind o' like you and Steve. It was a good life. We had a son, a lively little lad. He used to foller me around like a little shadow." He cleared his throat.

"It was back in '58. I had to go away for a few days to take care of some business. While I was gone Kiowas burned the ranch. They killed Mary and took my son." His eyes filled with tears. He swallowed and went on. "Mary was a good Christian, but I wasn't, then. I wandered around for a while, not sure what to do or where to go. After a few years I joined Sheridan. I figured I didn't have much more to lose.

"A young preacher came out to the troops and held some meetin's. He preached right to me. I knew Mary was in heaven, and I wasn't goin' there. After one of the meetin's, I went up and talked with that preacher. He showed me how to make my peace with God. Jesus has been my best Friend ever since." He smiled gently. "I know He'd help you, too, if you asked Him."

His words came back to her later that evening. How could he be so happy not knowing if his son was alive or dead? *He must be a strong person,* Megan decided. *I don't have that kind of courage.*

⁀

Steve spent most evenings behind the corral practicing with his six-shooter. At first Megan jumped every time he fired a shot, but eventually she became accustomed to the noise. One day she ventured out to see if he would teach her how to handle a gun.

Surprise made her hesitate when she saw him. Instead of a pistol, he held a double-edged knife, poised to throw. He rose up on the balls of his feet, paused a second, and threw the knife into a straw target he had set up, a perfect hit. He walked over to pull the knife out and stopped short when he saw her.

"So you've discovered my secret weapon," he said, walking toward her. "When I was in the army, we'd practice throwing to pass the time. I was pretty good at it then. I'm a little rusty now."

"I'd like to learn to shoot."

"Oh, yes. I remember you mentioning it." He looked at his guns lying on a flat rock nearby. "Which would you prefer, the pistol or the rifle?"

"I don't know."

He picked up the pistol and handed it to her. "Try this and see how it feels."

"It's awful heavy," she said, holding it with two hands.

"See if you can raise it at arm's length."

Her arm wobbled as she struggled to keep the barrel up. "Let's try the Henry." He took the pistol from her. "You can use both hands to hold it and balance it on your shoulder." The rifle was awkward. She couldn't tell where to put her hands on it. Steve adjusted her grip. "Lift it shoulder high, and sight along the barrel. Aim at that tree trunk." He pointed to a pine thirty feet away. "Start at the base of the tree and follow it up."

Megan grasped the gun tightly, one hand on the trigger, one on the barrel. Taking a breath to calm herself, she lifted the rifle.

"Gently work the trigger. You feel the slack there?"

"Yes." She moistened her lips.

"Slowly take in the slack, and squeeze off a shot real gentle-like. Try for that slash in the bark about eye level. You see it?"

"I see it." Biting her bottom lip, she concentrated on that mark and squeezed gently, like he said.

BOOM!

The slam of the rifle against her shoulder made her step back. Her heel sank into a small hole, throwing her off balance. She sat down hard. Her shoulder was burning dreadfully. It must be black and blue.

"You hit it! You hit it!" He walked over to examine the tree. "A little to the left and a tad high, but you hit it."

"I think it hit me." She rubbed her sore shoulder. He was beside her in four strides. "Are you hurt?" He knelt down beside her, concern in his eyes.

"My shoulder's bruised, but besides that it's only my pride, I guess." She looked at him accusingly. "Why didn't you warn me?"

"About the kick? I guess I forgot. I'm sure sorry." He helped her up. "Don't rest the butt on your shoulder from now on. Hold it a little away if you can, or let it rest on top of your shoulder." He brushed dirt from her arm. "Do you want to quit for today?"

"I came to learn, and learn I aim to do." She straightened her skirt and picked up the rifle. "What were you saying about more to the left?"

With that, target practice became a daily ritual and, before many days passed, she could hit at leaf at fifty yards.

"You're a natural shot, Megan," Steve said after practice two weeks later. "You've got a steady hand and a keen eye. Just remember the Henry shoots a little high and to the left."

Megan thrived on these times of easy companionship with Steve. He was a patient teacher, and she liked to hear him talk. It gave her a contented, restful feeling to be with him and share things with him.

"I'm going to ride into town tomorrow," Steve said one evening in mid-July on their walk back to the house. "Is there anything you need?"

"You can mail a letter for me and check the post office," she replied quickly. "Besides that, there are a few groceries. A little sugar, molasses, things like that."

"Banjo will be around if you need him. I want to get some nails to repair the porch and some glass for the windows."

But the next morning, when Steve drove the buckboard around the meadow, a strange emptiness swept over Megan. It was odd she should feel that way since Banjo was still nearby. She tried to brush it away, but it kept creeping back.

Her spirits lifted later when her doggy friend crept to the porch to get a pancake lying on the ground near the steps. Megan had thrown it there to tempt him.

"Banjo," she called in the same voice she used when talking to the dog. "Banjo, come here."

Banjo appeared in the stable doorway. Megan placed a warning finger on her lips and pointed to the dog hungrily chewing the pancake. She threw down another when the animal looked up at her.

It was the first time she'd had a complete look at him. He was shaggy from his bearded cheeks to his feathery tail, a big dog, but not as large as some. His hips made bony points at his back end. He had black, brown, and white patches on his back and sides. The rest of him was the color of dirty mop water.

"Would you like a third?" she asked, holding up her last offering. The dog sat down, eyes boring into the pancake. "Here you go." She threw it to him. "I always was an easy mark for an empty stomach."

The dog seemed to sense there was no more food to be had. He picked up the pancake and trotted away.

"That's Cunningham's dog, all right," Banjo said, walking toward her. "Used to follow him everywheres."

"What's his name?" Megan excitedly voiced the question she'd wondered every morning these past six weeks.

"I don't know." The wrinkles in his brow deepened while he searched his memory. "I can't remember Cunningham calling him. I'm sure he must have, but it didn't stick with me." He grinned at her disappointed face. "Sorry, Miss Megan. Why don't you name him yourself? He'll pick up a new name soon enough, I reckon." He took off his hat to scratch the back of his head. "Do you mind me asking why you're so interested in a stray dog?"

"I can't really say, Banjo. I guess it's because he seems so alone. And he's starving. I guess I feel sorry for him."

"Keep workin' on him. He'll get used to you in time." He adjusted his hat and clumped back to the stable. Megan took a last look at the grass where the dog had disappeared. What could she name him?

Megan was knotting a rag rug to put in front of the hearth and thinking about dog names when she heard galloping hoofbeats. Dropping her work, she looked nervously out the window.

A large chestnut horse came at full tilt around the green field of knee-high corn waving gently in the breeze. A wiry man in a red plaid shirt and Levi's leaned over the saddle. Horse and rider slowed to a trot at the edge of the yard and came to a halt in front of the porch. The man swung down in an easy, lithe movement. Megan blinked her eyes and looked again.

Instead of a man, it was a tall, slim young woman wearing men's clothes, the same girl she had met in Harper's Emporium the day they arrived in Juniper Junction. Relieved and glad, Megan opened the door.

"Hello." The young woman took off her light brown Stetson, revealing her thick blond mane, full of strawberry highlights in the sun. "I'm Susan Harrington, remember?"

"Yes, of course." Megan smiled broadly. "Please come in." She was delighted to have feminine companionship. "Would you like some tea? I'll put the kettle on."

"How lovely!" Susan exclaimed when she entered the house. "I've always liked stone better than logs. And blue calico!" She gave the living room curtains a loving touch.

It was true the house had undergone a transformation under Megan's skillful hand. The floors shone with a coating of linseed oil. A blue checked tablecloth and matching curtains made the dining room a cheery nook. The kitchen range gleamed with a fresh coat of stove blacking, all signs of rust banished. A white gauze curtain dressed the kitchen window, and the stone floor, though worn smooth, was well-scrubbed.

"Please sit down," Megan said when she returned from the kitchen.

Susan perched on the edge of a chair, holding her hat in her hands.

"I came because"—Susan avoided Megan's eyes—"because I heard about what happened to your garden. I wanted you to know how sorry I am." She glanced at Megan. "I overheard some of the men talking when I was in the stable getting ready to ride this morning." She paused and drew in a deep breath. "It was Beau's doing. I know it."

"I hope the land dispute won't affect our friendship," Megan said sincerely. "I've thought about you several times since we met in Juniper. I was hoping we could get acquainted."

Susan's troubled face brightened. She watched Megan skillfully pour tea into two cups.

"Beau's always trying to prove something," she went on impulsively. "He scares me. If it wasn't for Wyatt—" She broke off and quickly sipped her tea.

"We didn't come here to cause trouble," Megan said, resuming her seat. "My husband has a deed to this land. It's his, and he wants to keep it, that's all."

"I wish Pa wasn't so set on having this place," Susan said, wistfully. "You aren't the only ones he's been against, believe me. A year ago he accused Jim Sanders of rustling. Elaine Sanders is one of my friends. I tried to tell Pa that Jim wouldn't do such a thing, but he wouldn't listen." She sighed. "Since Ma died, he won't listen to anyone." A brittle edge crept into her voice. "All he thinks about are his precious cattle." She shook her head and smiled at Megan. "Do you ride?"

"I used to when I was a child. I haven't tried lately."

"You should. We could go riding together."

"Do you always go off alone?" Megan asked wonderingly.

"Sure. No one will bother me. Unless I surprise some Indians or something." She laughed at Megan's alarmed expression.

"We haven't had Indian trouble for a year or so. Mostly they stay on the prairie these days. Anyway, I can shoot."

"I'd like to go riding," Megan admitted. "I'll practice a little, and maybe we can go." She looked at Susan's rugged costume. "I'll have to find something to wear."

"These are my brother's clothes. Most western women don't wear citified riding clothes, but you can if you want."

"I have an old riding costume that used to be my mother's. I do want to come."

"That would be nice." Susan set down her teacup and rose.

"I'd best be going. I'll come around after a while and see if you are ready to ride with me."

"All right." Megan walked to the door with the slim woman.

"I'm so glad you came. I was feeling a bit lonely today."

"And thanks for understanding about Beau." Susan turned impulsively and put her hand on Megan's arm. "I wish there was more I could do."

Before Megan could answer, Susan put on her hat, stepped across the sagging porch, and was gone. Megan gazed long at the cloudless blue sky, meditating on the visit. Poor Susan, living with a negligent father and a hot-tempered brother. At that moment Megan determined that no matter what the future held, she would try to be Susan's friend.

The hour drew late, and Steve did not come. Banjo sat with Megan in the light of two coal oil lamps while she read *The Pilgrim's Progress* aloud to pass the time. She forced herself not to look out the window, trusting her ears to tell her of Steve's arrival. Her nerves were frayed to a ragged edge when the hoofbeats she had been yearning to hear resounded in the dooryard.

"He's back." She dropped the book on the table and ran to the door.

"I'll take the hull off his horse." Banjo grabbed his hat from a peg near the door and was gone.

Megan stood on the porch, straining to see through the darkness. A wide, yellow crescent of light from the open door fell over Steve's face as he stepped up. The sight made her gasp.

Chapter 8

Both of Steve's eyes were black and blue, one almost swelled shut, and there was a wide, ugly gash over his left cheekbone. His lower lip was cut and puffy. He held his right arm close to his side, and that battered hand was twice its normal size. He made a rasping sound when he breathed. Like a sleepwalker, he shuffled over to the settee and sank to the seat as though the presence of the sofa was all that kept him from collapsing altogether. Several seconds passed before he could speak.

"Four or five of Harrington's men jumped me outside of Harper's." His voice was thick with pain. He grunted a little with each breath. "One of them clubbed me on the head from behind and knocked me down for the others to pound me. I couldn't see who they were, it happened so fast, but I heard that red-haired villain's voice." He stopped to take two ragged breaths. "I guess I passed out. When I came around it was almost dark. I wasn't in any shape to go looking for them, so I got the hostler to hitch the team for me and came home."

"You should have seen a doctor before you came out here." Megan stood near him, staring, shocked at the brutality of his injuries. She didn't like the sound of his breathing at all.

"Knew you'd be worried," he continued. "The doc might have wanted me to hang around, and I didn't want to." He grimaced in pain and held his side. "You got a letter." Fumbling, he pulled a wrinkled envelope from his shirt pocket and handed it to her.

Megan's heart lurched as she took the letter. She smoothed it lovingly between her hands before she laid it on the table and rushed to the kitchen for hot water and a towel. Gently, she bathed Steve's face and hand, cringing at what she found under the dirt and dried blood.

"I don't think there are any broken bones," she decided as he slowly moved his fingers. "At least not in your hand." She was thinking of his ribs and the sound of his labored breathing.

"The hand won't be any good to me for a while, though." He stared at the purple, swollen flesh. "Right now I'd like to be able to use an iron mighty bad."

"That cut on your cheek has to be closed," Megan went on, ignoring his remark. "It's lying wide open. I've got some tape in the kitchen."

"Mama and I patched up many a soldier when we were in Virginia," she chattered to ease the mood when she returned with tape and bandages. "There was a lot of fighting around Fredricksburg, you know." Her hands moved steadily, efficiently, as she talked. "We changed bandages, served meals, and did anything else that was needed in the hospital after our plantation burned. I guess we bandaged as many Yanks as we did Confederates." She pressed the last piece of tape on his cheek.

"Now let's take a look at those ribs."

"My ribs are all right," Steve protested, straightening.

"Yes, that's why you've been breathing so easily." Immovable as the rock wall behind the house, she met his eyes. "Let's have a look."

Never taking his eyes from her face, he slowly reached for his shirt buttons. In short order his ribs were bound tightly with a long, three-inch-wide strip of cloth. It was near midnight when he paused at the foot of the ladder to the loft. He put his foot on the first rung and paused, looking at her.

"Thanks."

"Get some rest," she replied lightly.

Bone tired though she was, she brought the treasured envelope close to the coal oil lamp and tore it open with shaking fingers. The words ran together when she tried to read. She squeezed her eyes shut, willing them to focus, and tried again.

Dear Miss Megan,
    Just wanted you to know we got your tellygram. Jeremy is doing good. Always talks about them horses you got. He can't git out of bed yet, tho. Doc says he'll be abed about two more months. Don't fret none. This was writ by my landlady, Mrs. Osgood.

                                    Sincerely,
                                         Em

After reading the note three times to wring every ounce of home from it that she could, she put the letter carefully in her trunk. She lay wide-eyed in the darkness thinking of Jeremy and Em and the home they used to share. She ached to put her arms around him once more, to see him smile, to hear him laugh. The lump in her throat choked her. She turned her face into her pillow and sobbed.

The next morning Banjo came to the house carrying a small pasteboard box. He tapped on the door and beamed at Megan when she opened it.

"Since when do you have to knock?" Megan peered curiously at the box. "What's that?"

"Look for yourself." He held out the box for her to take a look.

"Chickens."

Megan was too tired and emotionally spent to be excited at Banjo's announcement.

"Steve brought them. He brought a passel of other things, too. The wagon was loaded down." He glanced at Megan's serious face. "How is he?"

"Two cracked ribs, one of them may be broken. A horribly bruised hand and a beat-up face. I think he'll be all right, though, as long as those ribs heal without any trouble."

"I'll put up a coop for these pullets today. By the size of 'em, they should be layin' in two months or so. Haven't had an egg for purty nigh a year." He carried the box back to the stable.

"I bought them from a woman in town," said a voice behind her.

Megan whirled in surprise to see Steve at the top of the ladder.

"I've got a hankering for eggs myself." Slowly, carefully, he climbed down and eased into a chair.

"You ought to be in bed," Megan scolded mildly. She felt an almost physical pain at the sight of his swollen, shiny, purple-splotched face.

"Never stayed in bed a day in my life." He drew in a quick breath. "I don't aim to start now."

"Breakfast will be ready soon." She peeked at the biscuits in the oven and sliced some bacon. The frying pan was sizzling and popping when Steve called her.

"Come here, Megan. Banjo brought in something I bought for you in town."

Megan checked the biscuits again, wiped her hands, and wonderingly obeyed.

"I thought you might like this." He held up a large bolt of cloth. "You look mighty fetching in blue."

Stunned, Megan reached out for the powder blue fabric. She rubbed her hand over the lacy white print.

"That was kind of you," she faltered, her cheeks pink.

"I got the whole bolt so you can make a real nice one."

Her steps were light as she carried the bolt into her room, sampling the smooth weave under her hand as she went. In the bedroom she draped the end of the cloth over her shoulder and looked in the mirror nailed to her bedroom wall. That shade of blue was perfect for her hair and eyes. The roses in her cheeks and the glow in her eyes added to the picture. With deft movements she smoothed the fabric around the bolt and put it into her trunk. Going back to the kitchen, she avoided Steve's eyes as she passed, but inside she sang a soft, lilting, wordless melody.

Steve watched from the doorway when Megan took some scraps out to the dog after breakfast.

"I'm going to call him Lobo because he looks like a wolf." The object of their attention bolted down a scrap of bacon and two biscuits. "Banjo told me he used to belong to Cunningham."

"He must have been living off of field mice," Steve remarked.

"I haven't been able to get near him yet. It's taken six weeks for him to come this close."

Lobo sat on his haunches, watching Megan's face. He whined.

"All right, boy," she laughed, throwing him a third biscuit. "You always know when I'm holding out on you."

He picked up the biscuit and trotted off.

"That's it for the day. So far I've seen him only in the morning. He's getting braver, because usually he won't come near the porch if he sees one of you men around."

"He'll be protection for you when Banjo and I have to be away. I'll be glad if you can get him tamed."

"I feel sorry for him. He's been all alone for over two years. I wonder how he survived the winters."

"Probably holed up in a cave somewhere." Steve walked back into the living room and eased down on the sofa. "Hand me my gun belt, will you? I may as well clean my guns while I'm inside."

∽

It was early in August before Steve recovered enough to return to all his normal work. It took several days of painful practice to give him back his agility with a gun. Megan watched his recovery with mixed emotions. She was glad to see him strong again, but she knew each passing day brought closer another confrontation with the Harringtons. Someone was bound to be killed. Would it be Steve? She couldn't bear to voice the question even in her mind.

The hot summer seemed endless. Megan's face grew tan from long hours in the garden. She picked green beans until her arms and back groaned. She made catsup and chutney until the kitchen cabinets could hold no more jars. This in addition to her weekly chores of bread making, butter churning, and washing and ironing clothes made the days full indeed.

Late in the afternoons she often escaped the overheated house by doing target practice with Steve. When he hurled glass bottles into the air, she could strike them four of five tries.

"You stay at it, and you'll soon be better than me," he said one evening in mid-August. They were collecting guns and shells to go inside. "I've never seen the like. Have you thought of trying live game?"

"I don't think I could kill anything," she said, shaking her head. "I couldn't stand to." They meandered in the direction of the house.

"I would like to ride Candy," Megan said.

"We don't have a sidesaddle."

"I always rode astride when I was a girl. I can do the same now. Would you teach me to saddle her?"

"A saddle may be too heavy for a little lady like you, but you can try."

The saddle was heavy. The next day Megan gritted her teeth, took a breath, and heaved. The leather hit the horse's back a bit awry, but it stayed. Candy looked around and nuzzled Megan's hand. Megan patted her nose.

"Don't worry, girl, we'll do it yet." She turned to Steve, smiling triumphantly. "Now what?"

"Make sure you didn't wrinkle the saddle blanket. Her back will get sore if it's wrinkled." He lifted one edge of the saddle and pulled the blanket. "Fasten the girth tightly." He firmly punched the mare's stomach. "A canny horse will fill his belly with air so you can't tighten it right. Make 'em let it out before you cinch up."

"You can ride Billy or Star as well as Candy, but leave Caesar alone," he cautioned. "He's wild. He always tries to bite me when I saddle him. Don't ever turn your back on him."

Megan grasped the pommel with her left hand and stepped into the stirrup. Mother's dark green riding habit fit her to perfection after she had sewn in a few tucks. Instead of the ribboned bowler that was supposed to complete the outfit, she wore a dark green bonnet. The feel of the saddle and the movements of the horse brought back the carefree fun she had known in Virginia. With Steve on Billy, they cantered shoulder to shoulder in a circle around the meadow. When they got back to the yard, Megan's cheeks were flushed, her eyes shone. She felt the exhilarating urgency of a six-month-old fawn on a crisp fall morning.

"Let's do it again," she begged, "only faster."

Steve laughed out loud at her childlike enthusiasm. Without answering, he urged Billy forward, leading out at a moderate gallop this time. Candy lengthened her stride and stayed beside Billy's right hindquarters until they reached the curve in the field; then she was shoulder to shoulder with him for the rest of the ride. Megan would have gone for a third round, but it was not to be. Practicality won out. Supper must be cooked, and the hour was growing late.

After that day, Steve and Megan alternated riding and shooting in the late afternoons when they both were free. It was glorious to ride in the pine-scented air enjoying the country and their companionship. She was deeply in love with Colorado.

Often they rode south to the lake and strolled along its shore, charmed by a solitude that was interrupted only by an occasional bird call or the splash of a fat trout swimming under the surface. A thick grove of spruce blocked off everything but the sky. It seemed like she and Steve were the only people in the world when they were there.

"What was it like on the riverboats?" Megan asked one day as they rambled near the water's edge.

"At first it was exciting." Steve picked up a flat, smooth stone and skimmed it across the water. It hit three times and sank, leaving a spreading series of circles. "Bright lights, plush furnishings, elegantly dressed people." He glanced at her. "But when you probed beneath the surface, the picture wasn't nearly so appealing. It was there that I learned to use a hideout knife. It was that or risk being robbed every time I won a big stake." He selected another stone.

"Don't get me wrong. I enjoyed playing cards. It was intoxicating to be able to handle them and win." He shook his head. "But I learned those cards were a two-headed serpent. One bite and you were hooked. The second bite and they destroyed you." He flicked the stone with all his might. Five skips.

Megan watched his face as he spoke. It was the first time he had spoken of his past to her since they had met in the hotel in Baltimore. This time she caught a better glimpse of the person behind the handsome face.

"I saw men destroyed too often. When I felt myself withering inside, I had to get out. That's why I don't play anymore, even for fun. I don't want to give the serpent a chance to bite me again."

The sun's slanted beams sifted across the treetops. Steve measured their angle with a quick look and pitched one last stone. "It's getting late," he said, reluctantly. "We'd best get back."

In the passing days, Megan learned to read his mood by the turn of his head or the movement of his hand. His smile made the day full of sunbeams; his deep, resonant voice touched an answering chord inside of her.

⌒

"What is this?" Steve's clipped words, like stones thrown at a rock wall, brought Megan up short. She dumped the last pail of oats into Candy's trough and joined him beside the mare. He stood aside for her to see an ugly sore on Candy's back.

"You left a wrinkle in the saddle blanket." The hard set of his mouth condemned her.

"I was in a hurry to go riding with Susan when I saddled up." Megan avoided his eyes. Her tongue was suddenly thick and stupid. "I'm sorry."

He turned his back to her, folding the blanket with a snap.

She stroked the horse's neck. "I'm sorry, Candy. I didn't mean to hurt you. I'll be more careful after this." The horse lifted her head out of the feed trough to nuzzle Megan's shoulder. Megan rubbed the space between Candy's eyes. She gave the roan a loving pat and walked out of the stable.

"Megan," Steve called her back.

"Yes?" Reluctantly, she retraced her steps.

"I'm sorry I was hard on you." His mouth was still a thin, straight line, but his eyes were gentler than before.

"I shouldn't have been so careless. You were right about that." She met his eyes with a serious, steady gaze.

"Let's say we both fell short." The corners of his mouth turned up a little. "Care to go for a walk after supper? I'd like to look over our garden before it gets dark."

"Sure. I'll put the kettle on now so we can get an early start." She walked slowly to the house. It had been an unusual day, first a visit from Susan and now this interchange with Steve. Seeing that side of this personality was sobering and heartwarming at the same time.

Susan Harrington's visits brought sweet relief to the tedium of these days. If Megan had a few hours free, they would ride together. If not, Susan lent an extra pair of hands to Megan's never-ending chores.

"Everyone's going away for six weeks," Susan remarked later that week. They were sitting at the table shredding cabbage for sauerkraut. "Except me and three hands to watch over the ranch. All the hands are going on the cattle drive to Denver. It'll be a little lonely, but at least I'll have peace for a few days."

"You're always welcome here." Megan grinned. "Especially if you keep helping with all these vegetables."

"You've had a rest from their harassment, too," Susan went on, "with the roundup last month and all." She emptied her pan of shredded cabbage into the large crock on the table and picked up another cabbage. "I wish Pa would stay so busy he'd forget this land." She pushed the damp tendrils from her forehead with the back of her wrist.

"Oh," Susan broke out excitedly, "I almost forgot to tell you. The Sanderses are having a dance on September twenty-fifth. Elaine told me last week when I saw her in town. You haven't met Elaine yet, have you?"

"Not yet." Megan poured more brine into the crock. "I don't get away that much."

"I can't wait. I'm having a new dress made with a huge bustle and lots of ruffles."

Megan remembered the blue dress that hung half-finished in her closet. She had been so busy with the garden's harvest she hadn't been able to touch the dress for two weeks. With a few extra touches, she could make it into a party dress. Maybe she could get some blue ribbon if Steve went into town soon. Plans for the party captured their attention, and the basket of cabbage was finished in short order.

What good fun a frolic will be, Megan thought after Susan said good-bye and rode off. A party seemed especially exciting because she hadn't once been away from the ranch since they had arrived three months before.

She drew the unfinished dress from the closet, caressing the soft fabric and turning it critically in her hands. An extra ruffle here, some small embroidery there, and a little more fullness in the bustle. It would make a wonderful party dress. She held the dress under her chin and watched herself in the mirror, swaying gently to the music she could already hear.

The sound of horses in the yard shattered her daydream. She swept the dress back into the closet and scurried out to meet Steve and Banjo, back from a day of moving the longhorns to a new stretch of grass. Holding her skirt up, she ran lightly across the yard.

"Howdy, Miss Megan," Banjo said. His grin relaxed the tired lines around his mouth.

"What's got you so het up?" A faint grin hovered over Steve's features, a result of Megan's red cheeks and glowing eyes. "Who was here today?"

"Susan," Megan said breathlessly. She stood near Steve as he dismounted. "The Sanderses are having a frolic. Elaine Sanders is putting it on." The words spilled out. "Everyone's going to be there. Can we go, Steve?"

Steve stopped short, soberly regarding her hopeful face. Without answering, he pulled Billy's reins to lead him into the stable.

"Steve?" Megan took a step after him.

"We'll talk it over in the house," Steve said tersely over his shoulder.

Crestfallen, Megan looked at Banjo who, carefully keeping his eyes on Kelsey, followed Steve into the stable.

Megan stood still a moment, staring at the empty stable doorway. She was confused and hurt. Search her mind as she might, she could not understand Steve's reaction, nor Banjo's.

"About the frolic," Steve said after he had washed for supper. They were alone in the kitchen. "I'm not sure we ought to go." His voice was kind.

"Not go?" Disappointment fell on Megan with a thud. "Why not?"

Steve came near her, his face troubled. Megan had to lean her head back to look up at him, he stood so close to her. She noticed his lined brow, his set jaw, and she rebelled.

"Please, Steve." She raised pleading eyes to meet his. "It would be so nice to have some fun after working so hard. It would do both of us good to forget the ranch for a few hours. It wouldn't hurt to go, would it? I do so want to go."

He ran his hand through his freshly combed hair, looked away, and looked back again.

"It's against my better judgment, Megan, but if you want to go that much, I guess we can." He looked deeply into her eyes, hesitated, and was gone.

Chapter 9

I don't cotton to those parties much, Miss Megan," Banjo said to Megan's question the next morning. She had asked him to move a sack of chicken feed that had gotten wet on the bottom from a heavy rain the night before seeping under the stable wall and dampening the ground.

"A frolic means dancin' and likker. As a Christian I can't approve of either one." His voice was mild, but his words carried conviction.

"I can't see why Miss Susan is so worked up about goin' over there anyways." He eased the sack of cracked corn to dry ground a few feet away. "Her pa and Sanders had words a year or so ago. Jim Sanders is one to bear a grudge. When he first came to these parts, a man tried to push Sanders off'n his own range. Sanders killed him seven years later." He pushed his hat to the back of his head and glanced at Megan. "Oh, it was a fair fight all right. But Sanders had it in his craw the whole time. When men get their reason marred with drink, things start happenin'. No good can come of it."

Megan could not understand his reasoning because she had many happy memories of lively music and excitement before the war. The balls her mother had given! Megan used to stay up long past her bedtime to peer under the stair railing, hypnotized by the colorful, laughing, dancing crowd below.

Banjo is old, she decided on her way to the house. That must be it. *He's too old to enjoy those things anymore.*

That evening Steve's offer to take her to town with him the next day topped off her anticipation. Carefully counting her change, she mentally listed the things she would buy to complete her party costume.

The sky was cloudless, the sun strong on their ride to town. Megan raised her face and basked in the clear morning air. The tall, golden tasseled stalks of corn hid the house from view before they were halfway around the meadow. Megan watched the curling morning glory vines along the edge of the field. They made a carpet on the ground and wound around the first stalks of every row. Steve had eyes only for the promising crop. If all went well, they would reap far more than he had estimated.

With the eagerness of a six-year-old planning for a birthday party, Megan visited the only milliner's shop in Juniper Junction. After a long session of lip biting and toe tapping, she finally purchased a blue silk bonnet with fluffy white feathers on the left side tucked under the broad blue ribbon around the brim. Some extra ribbon for her dress was her next choice. As she was about to leave, a pair of long, white gloves caught her eye. She hesitated a moment, then impulsively nodded. Surely it wouldn't hurt to be a little daring. How many frolics would she get to out here in the wilderness? A thrill of expectancy passed through her as she gathered her parcels and stepped onto the boardwalk.

A letter was waiting for her at the post office. Impatient, she tore open the envelope the moment she was outside. Like a slow leak in a hot air balloon, her spirits sank. After two months Jeremy was still the same: no worse but no better. He was lonely for Megan, and would Megan please write him more often.

She stuffed the letter back into the envelope on her way to the hotel to join Steve for lunch. She tried to shake off her uneasiness and enjoy the rest of her special day, but the gloom clung to her, a nagging ache at the back of her mind.

A quiet meal at the hotel, a trip to Harper's Emporium for supplies, and they started the long journey home. They had barely topped the first rise when a group of riders came toward them on the trail. The party was led by a tall, broad man wearing a large white hat. He sat ramrod straight in the saddle with the unmistakable air of authority. The group split when they reached Chamberlin's buckboard, half on either side, and stopped. Each man except the leader was holding a weapon. Harrington's gun stayed in his holster.

"Chamberlin," the big man said, coldly, "you're a squatter. And more than that, you're a dirty rustler."

"I don't take that from any man." Steve's Winchester suddenly materialized in his hands.

"You'll take it from Victor Harrington." The big man's eyes narrowed. "I've lost a lot of stock ever since you moved on my land. Get out, or you'll pay the piper."

"I already gave your son my answer. I haven't changed my mind."

Megan couldn't take her eyes off Victor Harrington sitting so arrogantly on his giant black horse. This was Susan's father.

"You'll go, or I'll burn you out," Harrington persisted.

"I'll tell you this." Steve's knuckles were white on the rifle stock. He spat the words at his tormentor. "If you'd show a little backbone and stop hiding behind those toughs you ride with, I'd show you who you can run off. You probably haven't fought your own battles for years, Harrington. Are you afraid? We could settle it now, the two of us."

"I don't waste my time on vermin." Keeping his gaze straight ahead, Harrington prodded his horse. One by one his men followed.

Steve and Megan rode up the mountain in heavy silence. Megan secretly watched him. She was overwhelmed by the white hot temper she had witnessed, but at the same time she was glad Steve had talked straight to the big man. Harrington had trampled men underfoot for twenty years. It was time someone stood up to him.

As the frolic drew near, Megan pushed aside all thoughts of the Harringtons. Daydreaming of lively music and pleasant conversation, Megan stepped into the morning sunshine a week later. The glowing sun felt good after the chilly September evenings they were having. The stone house held the night coolness long into the day.

Humming softly, she took the feed pail from its peg and opened the sack of cracked corn. When she bent over the bag, a strange, acrid smell made her draw back. She wrinkled her nose and peered down into the almost empty bag. Rolling down the top of the sack so she could see better, she stirred the damp corn with the edge of the pail. A sticky film was over the grain.

Pulling her bottom lip between her teeth, she considered the unopened sack of feed Steve had bought on their last trip to town. He had told her to finish the old bag before using the new one. She'd better do as he said. He might be angry if she didn't. She scooped her pail into the corn and, holding it at arm's length, walked quickly to the hen yard. To her relief the six hens and two roosters attacked the feed with their usual energy.

Good, she thought. *If that's the case, why not give them the rest of the bag? Then it will be finished, and I won't have to handle the smelly stuff again.*

Holding it like an irritated mother holds a child's mud-covered shoes, she carried the offensive sack to the yard and shook it out. The greedy chickens scurried around clucking, fighting, and scratching frantically.

The unpleasant job finished, she took the empty sack back to the stable. By the time she went into the henhouse to gather the eggs, her mind had wandered again to the upcoming frolic and the dress she had almost finished. Her imagination could already hear the music and the laughter-filled conversations. The henhouse became a ballroom, and her gingham housedress was an elegant blue gown.

But when she returned to the henhouse door, the sight of the hen yard shocked her out of her fantasy.

One hen lolled her head from side to side and made a strange squeaking noise. Another walked in circles, her beak almost touching the ground. A rooster fluttered his wings and crowed, "Gobble-gobble-goo!"

Megan stared. She gasped when a hen fell to its side kicking convulsively.

"What did you feed them chickens, Miss Megan?" Banjo asked from the front of the stable. He propped a shoulder against the stable wall and looked on with interest, a smirk hovering about his face.

"What's wrong with them, Banjo?" She cried in alarm. She made a wide circle around the crazy chickens, watching them warily. "I gave them their corn a few minutes ago."

"That wet sack I moved for you a week or so ago?"

She nodded. Her dismay grew when the rooster flapped his wings for another crow and landed in a heap.

"They'll be all right by suppertime." Banjo chuckled softly.

"What's so funny?" she demanded, eyes flashing. "They might be poisoned. We could lose our eggs. I don't think that's anything to laugh about!"

"They're not poisoned." He chuckled at her indignation and succeeded in fueling it further. "They're drunk. Ever hear of corn likker? Home brew?"

"Drunk?"

Clucking, a hen walked head-on into the henhouse wall.

Megan's face was pink, her ears were hot, and she could hardly speak.

"This'll be a whopper of a story, Miss Megan," Banjo said, grinning widely and shaking his head. "A real whopper."

"Don't tell Steve," she begged, putting her hand on his arm. "Please, Banjo!"

"Don't tell Steve what?" a familiar voice asked.

She whirled around and there was Steve, his expression an identical twin to Banjo's. Face flaming, she looked from Steve's grin to Banjo's poorly muffled laughter and back again. Without another word, she did an about-face and marched to the house, her head held high and her back board straight.

She couldn't bear to look at either of them that night at supper. The thought of what she had done set her cheeks on fire. Both men were on their best behavior. They seemed completely unaware of her lingering embarrassment. By the time she served their after-dinner coffee, she was ready to believe they had forgotten all about the chickens. She breathed still easier when they rose to do the evening chores.

"Do me a favor, will you, Megan?" Steve said before following Banjo. His hand was on the latch as though he had almost forgotten to tell her something.

"Yes?" Puzzled, she looked at him. His face was expressionless except for the smallest hint of a twinkle.

"Don't ever feed the horses." With a friendly, teasing smile, he closed the door quickly behind him.

Her first impulse was to fling her coffee cup after him, but her temper quickly dwindled.

"He couldn't resist," she said aloud, chuckling. For some obscure reason she kept feeling an urge to laugh as she cleared away the supper dishes that evening.

The day of the frolic dawned dark and foreboding with the promise of heavy rain. With growing chagrin, Megan watched the sky. She hoped the rain would come and be done before too late in the day. She fairly skimmed through her housework that morning, wishing away the hours until time to dress, for her party gown hung in her room begging her to hurry.

With many anxious glances at the sky, she cleared away lunch dishes and prepared to take a short nap. The dark clouds continued billowing in growing mounds, swirling menacingly. Still it did not rain.

At last the hour arrived. Megan slid into the light blue swirl of ruffles, ribbons, and lace she had spent so many hours preparing. She set to work brushing her hair into a stylish chignon she had seen in Susan's copy of *Harper's* magazine. Frowning first in concentration, then in frustration, she rested her tired arms a moment and wondered if she would ever get it right. At last she slowly turned in front of her small mirror, satisfied.

Steve rose from his chair as the rustle of her skirt and gentle tapping of her shoes announced her arrival in the living room. His gaze lifted slowly from the wide ruffle brushing the floor in front and drawing up to join the cascade of ruffles descending from the bustle at her back, up, up to the halo of wispy ringlets that circled her face, and beyond to her rosy cheeks and starry eyes, devouring her face with his eyes. Megan was captivated by the power of his gaze. How long they stood motionless, she did not know. Suddenly, he looked down at his hat, held firmly in his hand. When he looked up his expression was closed, the same expressionless mask he wore so often these days except, perhaps, a little softened.

"Ready?" he asked politely.

"Yes." She pulled her mother's white silk shawl over her arm and swished through the door he opened for her.

Chapter 10

High above the horizon the sun peeked through a crack in the dark cloud cover when Steve and Megan left the ranch. Steve had placed a piece of tarpaulin in the back of the wagon to cover them in case it rained in earnest. Occasionally a drop fell on Megan's hand or face, and she looked anxiously at the black, billowing mass overhead, but it did not rain.

A carriage and two buckboards stood outside the Sanderses' barn when they arrived. Smiling excitedly, Susan was framed in the wide doorway when they pulled to a halt under a spreading cottonwood tree. She was lovely in a flowing, lacy yellow gown that brought out the highlights in her strawberry-blond hair.

"Megan," Susan called when they reached the door, "I'm so glad you came a little early. I want you to meet Elaine. You won't mind, will you, Mr. Chamberlin?" Assuming Steve's consent, she led Megan to the makeshift cloakroom and waited impatiently while Megan hung up her wrap and checked her hair. "There she is." Susan pointed toward a dark-haired young woman with olive skin who stood talking to a young man on the other side of the carefully swept barn. Elaine was petite and fine-featured, almost like a china doll.

After the quick introduction, Elaine said, "If we get a chance," she lowered her voice conspiratorially, "we must escape to the house for a chat. It's been ages since I've seen another woman."

"Elaine!" a man's voice called from the direction of the musicians.

"That's Ernie. He's one of the fiddlers." She put her hand on her silk shirt and pulled back slightly. "If you need anything, just yell *Elaine!*" With a tinkling laugh, she hurried away.

"Elaine's a world of fun," Susan declared. One of the fiddlers drew his bow across the strings. "They're getting ready to start. I'll see you later."

Working her way back to Steve's side, Megan wound her way through the milling crowd that had gathered since her arrival. She smiled and nodded a greeting to several people she recognized: Kip Morgan, who had been with them on the stage; Wyatt Hammond, Banjo's friend; and Mr. Harper, who bobbed his head absently in response to Mrs. Pleurd's chatter. Victor Harrington planted himself near the door, his henchmen nearby. The Hohner boys, Henry and Al, lounged near the refreshment table. They gawked openly at the young women, nudging each other in the ribs from time to time. Megan looked away when she passed them. Something about them made her feel unclean.

"I'm not much of a dancer," Steve said when she reached him, "but I'm willing to try if you are." Taking her hand and placing it on his bent arm, he led her to the dance floor to join the square dance that was setting up.

"I thought you said you rode the riverboats," Megan countered with a smile, "and you don't dance?" They were waiting hand in hand for the beginning chord.

"I stuck to the tables." He looked down at her with a teasing grin. "I always considered women to be trouble." His grin widened at her surprised expression, and they fell in step with the music.

"Swing your partner," the caller chanted, and they danced and danced until Megan's head reeled.

"I'd like to sit down," she said when there was a break in the music. "I'm a little tired."

"Having a good time?" Steve asked, handing her a cup of grape punch.

"Wonderful! I don't know when I've had so much fun." Still under the spell of the music, she sipped her punch and watched the dancers.

"I believe I'll check the horses."

Megan nodded to him, preoccupied with the scene before her.

A deep, prolonged boom of thunder, almost like a drum roll, interrupted the gay music. In minutes the deluge of rain hammering on the barn roof gave the fiddler competition.

"Let it pour," a man standing near her said loudly to his companion. "We can sure use it."

And pour it did. The roar on the roof made it impossible to continue dancing. The music could scarcely be heard. For fifteen minutes it lasted until, as suddenly as it began, the rain stopped, and the frolic resumed its breathtaking pace.

After a while it occurred to Megan that Steve had been away a long time. She was strolling leisurely in the direction of the door when he suddenly appeared through the crowd.

"I was beginning to wonder what became of you." Her smile froze when a woman's piercing scream shattered the gay atmosphere. Following Steve's gaze, she saw the cause of the confusion, and darkness closed in on her. For an instant she was afraid she would faint. Steve's strong arm was around her instantly, and she clung to him.

Outside the open door lay the body of a huge man. A knife was buried up to the long, black haft into the left side of his back. His out-flung hand gripped the door jam. Megan, transfixed, stared at that strong, calloused hand. She saw it slowly relax its grip and fall limp. Horror swept over her in great, crashing waves. She buried her face in the rough cloth of Steve's coat.

"It's Harrington," a man's voice called. "Victor Harrington."

"He's pulled leather," another voice added grimly.

"Get hold of yourself, Megan." Steve pulled her away from him and looked into her face. "Susan is going to need someone. He's her pa."

Megan drew a shaky breath and turned her face away from the scene in the doorway. She knew he was right. She ought to find Susan.

"Pa!" Susan's anguished, hysterical cry struck an answering chord in Megan. Her own feelings forgotten, she rushed to her friend's side.

Susan's face was white as chalk; her eyes were wide with terror. She stared dazedly at the body of her father.

Megan put her arms around the shaking young woman and pulled her away.

"Come," Elaine said softly in her ear, "bring her to the house."

Together Megan and Elaine half-carried the grief-stricken woman into the Sanderses' living room, and Elaine ran to the kitchen for some strong, sweet tea.

"Pa," Susan groaned between deep, body-shaking sobs.

Megan stroked her hand and tried to find something consoling to say, but she felt totally helpless. Nothing would bring Susan's father back. A hot, choking sob welled up in Megan's breast. She held it down, but it grew until it fairly smothered her. She understood Susan's loss. Hadn't she lost both father and mother as Susan had? What comfort was there?

None, her soul cried out. *No comfort. No comfort anywhere.*

She sat with Susan, hardly moving or speaking until Beau Harrington's slurred speech rose to a shout outside the Sanderses' door. It was past midnight.

"I want to see Susan!"

"Your sister is sleeping," Ruth Sanders, Elaine's mother, answered flatly.

Megan drew aside the curtain a fraction of an inch to see Mrs. Sanders barring Beau from coming up the porch stairs. Even from the ground the young man was taller than the little woman, but she seemed to tower over him, so great was the strength of her determination.

"She was hysterical," Elaine's mother continued, "so I gave her a little laudanum to calm her. She'll sleep for a long while. Why don't you leave her here tonight?"

Beau blinked stupidly at the commanding figure before him, apparently deciding his next course of action.

"Megan Chamberlin is with her now." Ruth Sanders took a step forward as though to force him back.

"Chamberlin!" He bristled, spitting out the words. "Don't you let any of that lowdown, murderin' bunch near Susan." He clenched his fists. "You get that squatter's wife out of there, or I'll bust in and take Susan home now." He scowled threateningly.

"How dare you say such a thing!"

"It was her husband killed my pa," Beau insisted. "He wanted revenge for

Pa trying to run him off."

Megan moved away from the window and sank into a chair. Leaning her throbbing head against the high back, she closed her eyes.

"You're drunk." Megan clearly heard Ruth Sanders's disdainful voice. "Go somewhere and sleep it off, or I'll have to call Jim from the barn."

Boots crunching on gravel was all the answer she received. Megan opened her eyes when she heard the front door open. Mrs. Sanders paused when she caught sight of Megan in the front room before deliberately closing and locking the front door. Even at this late hour, Mrs. Sanders showed no signs of strain or fatigue.

"You heard what he said?" she asked softly, coming near Megan.

Mutely, Megan nodded. After the strain of the evening, Beau's accusation was more than she could endure.

"You may as well know. Clyde Turner, Harrington's foreman, said he saw your husband outside right before the murder, and he knows your husband is good with a knife."

Megan pressed her temples.

"There wasn't enough evidence to pin Harrington's murder on your husband for sure, but there was quite a bit of arguing out there." She patted Megan's shoulder. "I'm sorry. You're new out here, and you'll have to get used to our ways. The law is a long way off in Denver, so the men have to settle these things themselves mostly. But with it being outright murder, they'll probably call in the U.S. marshal to investigate if he has time.

"Your husband's been waiting with the buckboard for over an hour. You're done in. Maybe you'd best go on home. We'll see to Susan."

Megan sat in silence for a long moment.

"Please tell Susan I'll do anything I can to help her if she needs me," she managed at last, getting shakily to her feet.

Steve was at her side the instant she stepped off the porch. He draped her shawl about her and handed her her bonnet. Helping her into the buckboard, he clucked to the horses as he gathered the reins, and they were off into the moonlight.

When the trees had closed around them, shielding them from the watching eyes of those still at the Sanderses' ranch, Megan's control disintegrated. She sobbed into her handkerchief, her shoulders heaving with every breath. Steve put his arm about her, but she barely noticed. The sympathetic moon drew a lacy cloud handkerchief across its face, darkening the night to hide her tears.

"It's all my fault," she murmured in an agony of self-reproach.

"What's your fault?" Steve demanded.

"I—I shouldn't have insisted on going to the. . .frolic." She sniffled, wadding her soggy handkerchief. "If we hadn't gone, they couldn't have accused you of. . . of. . ." A fresh storm of tears broke out.

"Wait a minute." His voice was stern. "Wait a minute. They could accuse me of coming around without attending the party, you know. Harrington was killed outside, remember. Someone could have been lurking in the darkness unbeknownst to anyone." He looked at her intently through a fresh stream of moonlight as the cloud covering passed on. "Who's been telling you things?"

"Mrs. Sanders."

Steve's gruff tone had calmed her emotional tempest somewhat. She stared at her hands, not wanting to meet his eyes, aware of the solid strength of his arm and the stiffness of his coat against her shoulder. Stumbling and groping for words, she told him of her conversation with Ruth Sanders.

"In the first place," Steve said quietly when she was through, "Turner didn't make a direct accusation. He made some pointed hints, and I'm sure every man there knew what he was getting at, but they're not going to string me up on that basis."

"As a matter of fact, I'm glad we were there. I had a chance to look around a bit after you left with Susan. I saw a few things that could mean somthin'." He reached inside his coat and handed her his handkerchief. "Here, take mine. Looks like yours is pretty used up."

Meekly, Megan wiped her face. She was a little ashamed of her outburst now. She felt herself relaxing as she listened to his calm voice, and she drew strength from his strength.

"It was a thrown knife," he was saying. "I went to the door after you went out with Susan. The downpour had wiped out all the footprints of people arriving. Harrington's prints were the only ones coming across the clearing in front of the barn. At one spot he stumbled. I figure that's where he was nailed. No one could have been close enough to reach him there."

"You can tell all that?"

"I learned many useful things in the Army of the Confed'racy, Miss Megan," he said, lightly. "I also located some boot prints under the shelter near the hitching rail. They had a star design in the heel. Looked like brand-new boots to me." Growing animated, he said, "Harrington's back would have been toward that person as he crossed the clearing, too. It seems pretty simple to me. Find out who's knife slick and wears those boots, and we'll have the murderer."

"Did you tell the men what you saw?" Megan held her shawl closely around her. She had begun to shiver.

"They weren't over-anxious to listen to anything I had to say," he admitted, reluctantly. "They don't know for sure I'm guilty, but they don't know for sure I'm not. And I'm a stranger. That's ten counts against me to start out." He paused, guiding the horses over the bank of the stream that circled the lower meadow.

"Try not to worry, Megan," he said after they were across. His voice was tender.

Chapter 11

Banjo was standing in the open doorway of the stable when they rode into the yard.

"Evenin', folks." He took the reins from Steve. "I'll tend the horses."

"We had some trouble," Steve said after he had helped Megan down. "Victor Harrington was murdered tonight. Stabbed in the back."

Banjo whistled softly. "You don't say. Any idea who did it?"

"Steve was accused," Megan blurted out. "Folks don't know whether to believe it or not."

"I found a couple o' clues." Steve told Banjo of his finds.

"Believe I'll ride over that way come daylight." Banjo rubbed his chin. "I'm a fair hand at readin' signs. Maybe I can come up with somethin' more."

～

The sun shone full in Megan's face when she opened her eyes the next morning. She blinked and sat up, disgruntled at having slept so late. This, along with the heavy feeling in her head and limbs, did nothing for her disposition. She put a weak hand to her head and pressed her eyes tightly closed. The terrors of the evening before rushed over her.

She ached afresh for Susan, left alone now to cope with her explosive brother. Megan hoped Susan wouldn't believe Steve was guilty of killing her father. How could she bear to lose Susan's friendship? She had come to love Susan like a sister.

Steve was not in the house when Megan came out of her room. She didn't feel like eating. Instead, she went out to her favorite haunt at the eastern side of the house. She walked off the porch to sit in the grass and look out at the rolling hills. She had been there for half an hour enjoying the breeze and the quietness of the landscape when she was startled by a stealthy movement beside her.

It was Lobo. He was lying about six feet away with his head on his paws, watching her.

"I forgot to feed you this morning, didn't I? I'm sorry, Lobo. I guess I had a lot on my mind this morning. Will you stay here if I go in for something?" She stretched her hand out toward the shaggy head. He didn't shy away. Edging a little closer, she let him sniff her hand without trying to touch him. "Wait here."

Moving quietly to keep from scaring him, she went inside and hurried back with a scrap of corn bread and a small dish of cold, congealed gravy.

She stood nearby while Lobo gobbled down the food. This time, instead of rushing away, he came to her and licked her hand. Megan knelt down in front of him. His gray face turned up to her face, his tail gave a short wag.

"Are you ready to be friends, Lobo?" she whispered. "I won't hurt you, you know." Gently, she touched his scruffy head, rubbing between his ears and long neck. "I'd like you to stay here with me and not run away every day. I'm lonely like you." She talked to him about Jeremy and how she hoped he would come to Colorado to be with them, stroking the dog all the while. His ears were pricked up, and his eyes followed her face. If she hadn't known better, she would have declared he understood every word.

They were still deep in conversation when Kelsey's lop-eared head appeared on the trail. Megan watched Banjo's progress around the meadow. When he came close, Lobo gave one short, sharp bark and ran away. Steve walked slowly from the corral to join them.

"Found a few things you'd be interested in," Banjo said, stepping from the saddle.

Steve stood without expression, waiting. Megan impatiently clenched her apron. Banjo seemed in no hurry. He ground hitched Kelsey and slowly perched on the edge of the porch.

"I found those boot marks you mentioned." He knocked his hat to the back of his head. "That feller stood there awhile like he was waitin' for somethin'. The ground was tramped down a good bit with his boot prints. He was wearing California spurs. The big rowels gouged into the dirt a couple o' times. He's about six feet tall judging from his stride."

He reached into his shirt pocket.

"I found somethin' else interestin'." He stretched his hand out to Steve, a small piece of wood in the palm. "Looks to me like the man we want has a habit of chewin' short, green juniper twigs with the bark peeled off. I found two o' these. Juniper has a powerful taste. Don't care for it myself, but this hombre must have a likin' for it."

Steve turned the twig in his hand, studying it thoughtfully.

"I talked with Ruth Sanders awhile this mornin'," Banjo continued. "The funeral is gonna be tomorrow at the Rockin' H. One of Harrington's hands went to Denver to get a parson. There's no parson in Juniper. A circuit ridin' preacher comes ever' three months or so, but he's not due for another month." He accepted the twig that Steve returned to him. "What I was thinkin' on was this: If Miss Megan would like to go to this here funeral on account of bein' Miss Susan's friend, I'd be willin' to go along. That is, if it's all right with you, Chamberlin."

"Megan?" Steve put the question to her.

"I'd like to go, Banjo. How is Susan? Did Mrs. Sanders say?"

"She's still with the Sanderses. Will be until the funeral. Miss Ruth says she's real quiet. Won't hardly talk to nobody, even Miss Elaine." He shook his head sadly. "I'm real sorry for the poor thing."

Megan climbed the porch steps with a tired tread. She put some soup on the stove to boil and went out back to the clothes she'd left soaking in the big tub overnight. She scrubbed and rubbed, squeezed and rinsed, puzzling over the clues Banjo had found, but her foggy mind could not make any sense out of them.

When Megan came outside after breakfast the next morning, Lobo was lying on the ground beside the porch steps watching the door. Wagging his matted tail, he stood up and met her at the bottom step.

"Here you go. Some bones from last night's supper. If you had come last night, you wouldn't have had to wait until now to get them."

The dog settled in for a long, ecstatic gnawing session.

"I've got to go out, so I can't stay to talk," she continued. "I wish you'd stay around."

He raised his head, swished his tail, and gave a short bark.

Megan laughed. "So you're talking back to me now. We're making progress."

Megan and Banjo set out after lunch. Megan's stomach was in knots. Not only did she dread the funeral itself, but she wasn't sure how Susan would act when she saw her. Megan's face was ghostly pale against the severe black broadcloth of her dress and bonnet, the same ones she had worn to mourn her mother.

The service had already started when they arrived. Crude benches had been set up in the yard beneath a dozen tall aspens. A slight breeze caused a faint whispering rustle among the leaves. The shiny, black coffin, a wreath of yellow flowers on the lid, was at the front. A short man with a dark complexion and a large, hooked nose stood behind the coffin, a black book open in his hand.

Banjo led Megan to a seat in the rear. Without turning her head, Megan looked over the grieving congregation. Susan, darkly veiled, sat with Beau near the front. Megan could see Susan trembling even at a distance. Beau looked straight ahead like a statue, oblivious of his sister's suffering.

The minister's high-pitched nasal voice droned on and on. Megan scarcely heard what he said, so caught up was she with the violence of her own emotions. The grim congregation, the coffin, and the minister reminded her with brutal clearness of her own bereavement. She wept soundlessly without trying to stop her tears. Occasionally she dabbed at her cheeks with a black, lace-edged handkerchief. She wept for Susan, for her own tragedies, for the feeling of utter hopelessness she felt in her soul. The parson's words were eloquent, but she found no relief in his message.

At last the assembly moved en masse to the gravesite, where the minister said a prayer and threw a handful of dirt on the lowered coffin. By twos and threes the mourners left the grave. From a cool distance they bowed in Megan's direction and nodded to Banjo, eyes averted. Susan, one of the last to leave, raised her head when she caught sight of Megan. She hesitated, glanced at Beau's back as he walked toward the house, and came over to grasp Megan's clenched hands in her icy, trembling ones.

Through the black veil Megan could see Susan's hollow, red-rimmed eyes and gaunt cheeks.

"I'm so glad you came, Megan," Susan whispered quickly. A smoldering fire burned from within her. Megan glimpsed it as she leaned forward. "I don't care what they say. I don't think Steve did it."

Tears streamed afresh down Megan's face. She couldn't speak.

"I'll be over when I can." A quick squeeze of her hand and she hurried to catch up to her brother.

Banjo took Megan's arm and walked with her to the buckboard. She couldn't stop crying. On the seat of the buckboard she held her handkerchief over her mouth and bowed her head until her face was all but hidden by the brim of her bonnet. Banjo called to the horses, and they set off.

"Miss Megan, Jesus would carry the load for you if you would let Him," Banjo said after several minutes had trudged heavily by.

"How could He help me?" she asked, looking up. Her eyes were red and swollen. Her chin quivered.

"Jesus said, 'Come unto me, all ye that labour and are heavy laden, and I will give you rest.' If you know you are a sinner and need Him to wash your sins away, He'll save you. The choice is as simple as that.

"I know there's plenty o' highfalutin' preachers who would like to make it seem harder than it is, but God's love is available to everyone. Even a child can understand it. God doesn't force His love on anyone. He lets each person choose for himself."

"How do I come?"

"Just pray and tell Him you mean business. Tell Him you know what you are and you want to claim His blood to wash your sins away. You know He died on the cross for you, don't you?"

"Of course." She remembered the camp meetings she had attended long ago in Virginia. The fiery preaching had made a lasting impression.

Was she a sinner? She didn't have to think about it long before she had to admit she was. She knew she had blamed God for her problems. She had never tried to live her life to please Him.

"Remember, God loves you," Banjo said, softly. "He wants to help you."

Megan squeezed her eyes shut. She poured out her tortured soul before the

Almighty. There was no lightning bolt, no crash of thunder, no audible voice from heaven, yet surely, definitely, Jesus calmed the churning, frothing sea that was inside her. Some sadness still lingered, but for the first time in her life she was at peace.

"I did it, Banjo," she said softly when she look up. "And God heard me. I know He did. I feel so quiet inside." She gazed into the distance examining the change within her like a mother examines her newborn child.

"That's the peace of God," Banjo said nodding. "It's one of the greatest blessings of being a Christian. As long as you obey Him, that peace will stay with you.

"Do you have a Bible?" he asked.

"Yes. I have one in my trunk." She thought of the old black Bible that had been a gift to her father from a beloved teacher. How glad she was she had brought it along.

"Read it every day," Banjo advised. "You'll get strength from it."

"I will read it," she promised. "I surely will."

And read she did. The words in that old Bible came alive as she read each morning, often before dawn. She grew to love its delicate ivory pages. It was marvelous the way its message met her heart's need every time. She never forgot the day she found the verse in 1 Peter, "Casting all your care upon him; for he careth for you." Knowing God cared for her gave her new strength.

It was good she had found new strength, for only a week later Banjo brought her a letter that caused her to cry out for still more.

Chapter 12

The letter read:

> Dear Megan,
>   I thought you should know Jeremy is having a time of it. The doctor says he has to go back to his bed again. His heart does git to racing when he sits up awhile. I visit him every day, but he misses you powerful. He loves your letters. Reads 'em till he has 'em down by heart.
>
> Love,
> Em

Megan sat on the edge of her bed, rereading the letter. How bad Jeremy really was she couldn't tell. She felt sick with longing to be with him, hold him close, and tell him she loved him. She knelt by the big bed and rested her head on the quilt to give her fears and heartaches to the One who had promised to care for her. An hour later a tender, sweet calmness replaced the fear and anguish. She washed the tears from her cheeks. Surely God would take care of Jeremy.

An idea came clearly as she patted her face dry with a towel. Jeremy had never heard that he could have his sins forgiven. She must write to him immediately and tell him about how she had found Jesus. And Em, yes, Em.

The letter was hard to begin, but once she found a starting place, her pen flew. There was so much to share of the joy and peace she had found and wished for her loved ones to find, also. Jesus was the answer to their devastating loss. He gave hope, blessed hope.

The letter was lying on top of her trunk ready for mailing the next morning when she went out to the henhouse. Steve and Banjo were working frantically to get the corn crop harvested for fear of a frost destroying it. When she finished her chores, she would help pick the fat ears while the men chopped the stalks for cattle feed.

The sound of the birds twittering in the branches of the oaks, the soft breeze flowing down from the mountain, even the familiar barnyard smells of earth and straw lifted her spirits. Something brushed against her skirt, making her turn around. It was Lobo walking behind her.

"Well, hello." Megan knelt down to rub his neck. He leaned into her hand a little, his head cocked to one side. "I hate to tell you this, but you do need a bath. I wonder what color you really are under all that dirt." She stood up. "I have to hurry. Steve needs me to help get in the corn." She continued across the yard, followed by Lobo. He went into the stable with her while she drew a pail of grain from the burlap sack.

"Chook! Chook! Chook!" she called to the clucking, scratching hens while she threw handfuls of cracked corn to the ground. Suddenly she stopped in mid-motion, staring at the side of the stable, the side not seen from the house. Scrawled on the weathered gray boards in large white letters was one word: MURDERER.

For a full ten seconds she stood there. She clenched her fists, pressing her lips so tightly they were all but invisible. Beau Harrington! It had to be Beau Harrington who did such a ghastly thing! She glared at the wall as though it were a living thing mocking her, mocking Steve, mocking their cause. Hadn't they done only what was right? Wasn't Victor Harrington wrong in trying to force them away? The pail of corn fell to the ground, forgotten.

"Well," she fumed, "he won't have the satisfaction of upsetting Steve with his malicious pranks. I'll scrub that wall before he sees it."

Shuffling her way through the mob of chickens looting the pail at her feet, she went through the rear door of the stable to fill a pail with water and get a broom. She scoured ferociously until the whitewash was nothing more than a gray smear.

Satisfied, she retrieved her empty feed pail and walked slowly to the corral to give Candy the carrot in her apron pocket and rest a minute to calm her shaken nerves. It wasn't until she got back to the house that she realized Lobo still followed her.

"Here, Lobo," she called holding out her hand. He trotted up and licked her hand. "You're a good fella." She scratched the ruff behind his neck. "Steve's probably wondering what became of me." She gave him a parting pat and then scurried inside to get a lunch packed and put on her bonnet.

After dark that evening the men had barely reached the house to wash up for supper when a wide, powerfully built man cantered in. He had a square face with a thick neck that seemed to be one with his wide chest. His silver badge reflected the lamplight streaming from the open doorway.

"Evenin', gentlemen," he said, holding his reins loosely on the pommel. "Is one of you Steve Chamberlin?"

"I am," Steve stepped forward from the porch. "What can I do for you?"

"I'm Ben Walker, the U.S. marshal. I'd like to ask you a few questions."

"Certainly. Come in and set a spell. We were just about to sit up to the table. You're welcome to join us."

"I'd be much obliged." The lawman dismounted. "Don't get much chance to eat home cooking in my business."

Megan, watching from the door, couldn't believe Steve's unconcern. How could he act so naturally when the marshal could be here to arrest him? She clasped her hands tightly together across her waist.

"We've a guest for supper, Megan," Steve called. "Set another place."

The fork and knife rattled against the enamel plate as Megan set them down. Taking a deep breath and biting her lip, she willed herself to calm down. Quickly, she set out a jar of her own bread-and-butter pickles for good measure.

"This is my wife, Megan," Steve said when they came inside.

"Ma'am." Walker took off his big hat and offered a polite smile.

"Hello." She smiled, but her cheeks felt stiff and heavy.

The man wearing the silver star was generous in his praise of the steaks and new potatoes baked with butter. He also commented on the bread while he was buttering his third piece.

"You're a blessed man, Chamberlin," he said, pushing back his chair. "I haven't had a finer meal in a coon's age."

Steve gave Megan that slow smile that made her glow inside. "I can't but agree with you, Mr. Walker," he said.

"What's on your mind?" Steve asked when the men were seated in the living room around the crackling fire. Megan, still clearing away the dishes, strained her ears to hear. Her hands moved automatically, for her mind was far from the chore at hand.

"I'm investigating the Harrington murder. I'm sure you know you've been accused in so many words. I must say there doesn't seem to be an overabundance of evidence against you, but four different people have told me you're an ace with a knife. I thought I'd come out and see what you had to say."

"I'll tell you all I know," Steve said easily. "Banjo can tell you some, too. He picked up some signs over at the Running M."

"What was your relationship to Harrington?"

Systematically, the marshal directed the questions until the entire story was told. Megan finished the dishes and quietly joined the men in the living room.

"What's your opinion of the folks around here, Banjo?" the marshal continued. "You've been in these parts long enough to know the lay of the land. Being from Denver puts me at a disadvantage. Who had a grudge against Harrington?"

"Most folks hereabouts," Banjo said after considering a minute or two. "Harrington pushed folks around to suit him. Offhand I'd say Jim Sanders, because of an old dispute, and Wyatt Hammond, because of Harrington's daughter. Then there's Logan Hohner, one of the blacksmiths in town. German man with two grown, no-account sons. He has a rawhide outfit north of here."

"What was Harrington's beef with him?" Walker asked.

"Accused him of rustlin'."

"He had a real imagination about rustlers, didn't he?" Steve asked quickly. "That's what he accused me of on the trail."

"I guess he's been losing cattle for four, five years from what Wyatt tells me. Never has been able to catch the rascals," Banjo said. His chair creaked as he changed position. "Then there's his son.

"I have my doubts Beau would have the gumption to do it, but he sure is a rebellious one. He could have gotten impatient to have the reins on the Rocking H himself." He paused. "I'm talking through my hat, Mr. Walker. I don't have any proof for that."

"I'm not saying I'm sorry Harrington's out of the picture," Steve admitted. "But I think it could have been handled better. You know, a fair fight. Whoever did it is a coyote. Not fit to live among decent folk."

It was late when the marshal left. Banjo went on to the stable when the big man rode away.

"Do you think Walker believes you did it?" Megan asked anxiously.

"Can't say for sure." Steve sat on a chair near her. "All we can do is wait for his decision. But he did say he'd be interested to hear of anything else we may learn in the meantime." He leaned slightly toward Megan. "I don't want you to make yourself sick by worrying over this thing. When a man's in the right, he shouldn't have anything to fear. Folks hereabouts are basically honest. They don't want to punish the wrong man any more than you or I do."

"It's hard not to worry, though." Megan looked down at her hands folded tightly in her lap. "There's so much at stake."

"You've been a real trooper, Megan. I'm glad you were the one I brought out here with me."

Megan glanced at him. He was watching her closely. She felt her face warm.

"I believe God will work everything out for the best." She wanted to tell him about her new faith but wasn't sure how to go about it.

"God?" Steve's eyebrows rose higher.

"I trusted Jesus as my Savior a few days ago." Once she had found an opening, she spoke with assurance. "The Bible says that He will give rest to people who carry heavy burdens. Since I trusted Him, I know there's a difference. You may not be able to see it outside, but I know it's there deep inside."

"If that makes you feel better, I'm all for it," he said awkwardly.

"Have you thought much about God?"

"Not much." He slammed the door on that subject and opened another. "The corn crop is excellent," he said abruptly. "I'm sure I'll be able to make four or five times what I spent for seed. If the frost holds off tonight, we'll finish getting it in tomorrow, and I'll take it to the mill the next day."

"I hope the other people around here don't convince the marshal you're guilty." She returned to the subject uppermost in her mind.

"I'm not worried about that." Steve relaxed, stretching his legs in front of him. "There is something that does bother me, though."

"What?"

"I've never held a knife around anyone in Colorado to my knowledge, except Banjo and you." He looked at his boots thoughtfully, pursing his lips.

"So?" His silence was maddening.

"So how does everyone know that I can handle one?"

Chapter 13

October days were busy. With Lobo trailing after her like a gray shadow, Megan followed the buckboard through the woods, picking up deadfall to fuel the stove and fireplace through the winter. Banjo butchered a fat, young cow and showed them how to jerk the beef and store it for the time when game was scarce.

Megan continued her target practice though her rides with Steve became less frequent. There simply wasn't time for both.

She held her rifle by the stock and gave it an excited shake the day she overlapped three shots in the center of a tin can lid at two hundred feet. Steve chuckled and shook his head when he retrieved the lid and examined it.

"I haven't seen many men who could do that," he said, giving her a wide, approving grin. She glowed under his praise.

Megan had conflicting emotions the day she watched Susan's boyish figure ride in. She was glad to see her friend, but she dreaded hearing the news Susan carried. Megan lay the heavy iron on the kitchen stove, hung up the shirt she had been ironing, and went out to greet her.

"Morning!" Megan called with a cheerfulness she didn't feel. Susan waved a greeting, ground-hitched the chestnut on the edge of the meadow where he could reach the rich grass, and came to the house. She seemed like a vacant shell of the vivacious, quick-smiling young woman she had been such a short time ago. Always slender, she was now gossamer-thin and pale to the lips.

"I had to get away from the ranch for a while," she said when they sat down. "I had to talk to somebody." Her face contorted, and Megan was afraid she was going to cry.

"I've been missing you, too," Megan said, trying to ease the tension.

"I'm so worried. I haven't been able to sleep or eat much the past two weeks. It's about Wyatt." Tears spilled over her cheeks and fell to her shirt. She pulled a handkerchief from her pocket and pressed it against her face. Her sobs were soundless, but they came from deep inside.

Megan didn't know what to say.

"Tell me about Wyatt," Megan prompted when the other woman's sobs had almost subsided. "You never have, you know."

Susan looked up from her handkerchief. "How do you know about Wyatt?"

84

"Banjo told me."

"Oh." Susan wiped her eyes. "That's right, Banjo would know." She drew a shaky breath and kept her eyes on her fingers twisting and wadding her wet, wrinkled handkerchief. "There's not that much to tell, really. He came to work at the ranch about two years ago. He works Pa's horses." She cleared her throat. "I like to ride, and I spend quite a lot of time at the stable. One thing led to another, and. . ."

"You love him, don't you?"

Susan nodded, tears falling afresh. "Pa said no when Wyatt asked his blessing," she continued in a moment. "He said no cowhand would ever marry his daughter. Wyatt was awful mad. He comes from a good family. Banjo can tell you that. They don't have much, like the Harringtons do." A bitter expression marred her pretty features for an instant. "Wyatt said he would have killed Pa if it wasn't for me."

"What?" Megan stared at Susan, instantly alert.

"He said he would have killed him," Susan repeated defiantly. She stared at the low embers in the fireplace. "That's what's got me so upset, Megan. Wyatt was at the party, and he's good with a knife. I've seen him."

"You think he did it?" Megan could scarcely believe what she heard.

"I don't know," she said in a small, tortured voice. "I don't know." She fell silent, staring at the floor, still absently snarling her handkerchief.

"Let me get you a cup of tea."

Susan had regained some composure when Megan returned.

"I'm not accusing Wyatt," Susan said after taking a sip. "I don't know what to think."

"I can understand that."

"Things have been awful since Pa's funeral. I don't know how I can bear to stay there much longer. Beau is more arrogant than ever, bullying me, trying his best to irritate me. And that Clyde Turner, the foreman. He doesn't seem to know his place anymore. I heard him talking to Beau last night, and it sounded like he was giving orders, not taking them." She shivered.

"Then yesterday the marshal. . .what's his name? Oh, yes, Walker. . .came to the ranch. He was there all morning looking around and talking to the men. He spent a long time talking to Wyatt before he left. It scared me something fierce."

"Have you talked to Wyatt?"

"No, I've been afraid to. I guess I'm being foolish, but I can't help it." Susan set her teacup on the small table beside her chair.

"Why don't you lie down in my room for a while?" Megan suggested. "You're all in. A quiet rest would do you a world of good."

"I ought to be getting back," Susan protested weakly.

"For what? There's nothing for you to do there except mope. Come along." She took Susan's arm. "Steve probably won't be home until shortly before dark, so everything will be quiet."

"I guess you're right." She allowed Megan to lead her to the wide, quilt covered bed.

"If you need anything, call out. I'm going to finish the ironing in the kitchen." Megan let down the curtain from its tie, dimming the room, and quietly went out.

Lifting the hot iron from its resting place on the stove, she thought about what Susan had told her. That Wyatt would murder the father of the woman he loved was inconceivable to Megan. If Wyatt killed Susan's father, Susan would turn against him, and he would lose the very thing he wanted.

Unless he lost his reason in a fit of rage.

She considered the possibility and rejected it. Maybe at the time Victor Harrington had humiliated him, but not months later. The problem weighed heavily on her mind long after Susan had returned home.

"I think a few strays have wandered out of the canyon," Banjo said when they sat around the fireplace after dinner that evening. "I saw some tracks leading toward Hohner's piece. I'd estimate there are probably less than ten cows, but I think it bears lookin' into. I didn't have time to do it today."

"Want to ride over that way tomorrow?" Steve looked up at Banjo from where he sat on the hearth plaiting a horsehair hackamore.

"Sure thing. It shouldn't take more'n half a day."

"Can I ride with you?" Megan asked impulsively. "It's been ages since I've been riding, and I'd like to get away from the house for a while."

"I guess it wouldn't hurt anything." Steve looked back down at his plaiting. "We'll leave at sunup."

Megan tingled with anticipation as she donned her riding habit the next morning. She could already feel the crisp autumn air and smell the pines. After all the heavy work of harvest time and the anxiety over the Harrington murder, she was ready for a change. She had been digging up vegetables, picking vegetables, canning vegetables, and jerking beef. She wanted to stretch her muscles, shake off the doldrums, and enjoy the day.

She packed a small tin with lunch, tied on her bonnet, and set off for the stable, Lobo close behind her. Whenever she stepped outdoors, he was always nearby.

Ears forward, head bobbing high, Candy was as eager to set off as Megan was. The strawberry roan nickered and nosed over Megan's clothes in search of a treat while Megan slid her Henry rifle into the saddle scabbard. She put her lunch tin in the saddlebag as she stood beside the mare to scratch under her mane before mounting up.

"Here's what you're looking for." Megan held out her palm, exposing a tiny mound of brown sugar. "You're a big baby," she said, patting Candy's nose affectionately. She stepped into the saddle with ease, enjoying the feel of the horse's movements beneath her, listening for the creak of leather.

"All set?" Steve called from the yard.

"Let's go!" Megan smiled happily and lightly squeezed her knees on the mare's sides. When she reached Steve, they set off together at an easy canter around the meadow with Banjo close behind.

They were halfway around when a rider came through the trees and trotted toward them. In the dim light of dawn it didn't take long to recognize Beau Harrington. He was alone.

"You still here, Chamberlin?" Beau shouted, menacingly. He drew his pinto horse to a halt near Steve. "I thought you'd have tucked your tail between your legs and run by now."

"Innocent men don't run," Steve said mildly, his hand resting on his thigh near his pistol. "What's your business, Harrington?"

"Thought I'd give you some friendly advice." He stared at Steve, hatred burning in his eyes. "The tin star had to go back to Denver. Seems he couldn't stay long enough to hang you. But don't you worry, the Rocking H can handle that job. You hang around asking for trouble, and we'll take care of you."

"That's the difference between you and me, Beau," Steve said. There was deadly stillness in his voice. "I don't ask for trouble. You came here looking for a fight. I'd hate to disappoint you."

Steve's hand shot out and grabbed Beau's shirt at the neck. He kicked the smaller man's boot from the stirrup and pushed him to the ground, falling on top of him. Caught off guard, Beau clutched frantically at the ironlike fist holding him.

Steve sat down across the smaller man's middle, drew back his free hand, and slapped Beau's freckled cheeks, back and forth again and again. Beau's red hair, now hatless, rolled in the dirt. A crimson drop oozed from the corner of his mouth.

Breathing heavily, Steve pulled young Harrington to his feet and backed away from him.

"You'd best get back where you belong before I decide to fight you like a man."

Beau's bruised lips drew back into snarl of rage. Livid streaks adorned both cheeks. He clawed for his gun.

Beside Megan's horse, Lobo growled deep in his chest.

"I wouldn't do that if I were you, Harrington," Banjo said in a conversational voice.

Megan turned around to see the big buffalo gun lying in the old man's hands like it had been carved to fit.

"This here's a Sharps .56. It takes soft nose bullets. It ain't purty what they'll do to a man."

Harrington stiffened and slowly turned his eyes toward Banjo. At the sight of that wide, black bore pointed at him, he raised his hands. Slowly, keeping his hands wide, he reached down and picked up his hat, set it on his head, and scrambled for his horse. He missed the stirrup on the first try, then mounted up. He jerked his horse around.

"We ain't done, Chamberlin!" he screeched. His face was the color of raw beefsteak. He gouged his spurs into the pinto's sides and galloped away.

When he had gone, Megan was shocked when she looked down to find that her rifle was in her hands, cocked and ready. She couldn't remember pulling it from the scabbard. She turned it wonderingly in her hands as though seeing it for the first time. Would she have used it? Her hands started shaking. The ague traveled up her arms until her shoulders were trembling. She slid the Henry rifle back into the scabbard and clenched her hands on the pommel. Sensing the change in Megan's attitude, Candy side-stepped a little.

"Are you all right?" Steve moved his mount close beside her. "Do you want to stay at the house?"

"No. I'll be okay." She moistened her lips, fighting for control. "I don't want to stay behind. Especially now. I'd spend the whole day doing nothing but worrying."

"If you say so," Steve said uncertainly. "If you feel too tired, let me know and we'll turn back."

"I'll be okay," she repeated as much to convince herself as to assure him. She gathered the reins tighter and straightened in the saddle. Steve gave her another searching look before leading out. Megan stayed beside him.

When they entered the woods, Megan fell behind Steve at the narrow spots, Banjo bringing up the rear. She studied her husband with new eyes. He could have drawn a gun on Beau Harrington and killed him. It would have been called a fair fight. She knew Steve had the coolness that comes with maturity. Beau was hot-headed, too rash. He would have probably spoiled his first shot and been easy pickings for Steve. But Steve hadn't taken advantage of the younger man's temper in spite of the trouble Beau had caused him. An icy hand squeezed Megan's heart. She knew Beau would be back for revenge.

"Would you really have shot Beau this morning?" she asked Banjo later as they rode together on the trail. "I thought Christians were suppose to be peaceful."

"Christians shouldn't hunt trouble," Banjo replied, "but the Bible teaches that folks are supposed to obey the law. There's no lawman here to make sure that they do, so it's up to us law-abidin' folks to see the law is kept. Otherwise, the outlaws would soon run the rest of us off." His mild blue eyes had that fatherly look again. "This is still a wild land, Miss Megan. When a peace officer comes to these parts, it'll be our Christian duty to let him do the keepin' of the law. Until then, we'll have to see to it."

"It scares me to think of what Beau will do next."

"Don't fret yourself," Banjo said. "Steve handled the situation this morning. He can handle it again." He drifted behind her. "Rock of ages," he sang softly, and Megan urged Candy forward.

With Lobo still on their trail, they picked their way across rocky slopes and skirted huge boulders. Though it was only midmorning, Megan's dress felt like it was pasted to her back. Her forehead and neck were clammy. When they reached the canyon where their cattle were pastured, Banjo moved around her and Steve to take the lead. Megan kept her eyes on Banjo when he leaned over Kelsey's gray shoulder to study the ground. Fifteen minutes of searching and he found the trail.

Chapter 14

The trail was easy to follow, and they moved along at a steady gait. They rode north over sagebrush-flecked hills, in and out of spruce and piñon pine, talking rarely, for almost an hour. The sky, full of great, billowing clouds when they left the house, had darkened to a muddy purple.

When they reached a large rock-strewn clearing, Banjo pulled up and dismounted. He knelt down, examining something in the dirt. In a moment Steve bent beside him. Megan came near enough to hear but kept her mount.

"The tracks join some others," Banjo remarked. "It appears some other cattle were drove through here sometime yesterday."

"Other cattle?" Steve asked.

"Not ours. They're coming from the wrong direction." He continued scouting around, his eyes examining every mound of dirt, every chipped stone.

"Well, looky here," he said at last.

Megan walked her horse closer and stepped down. Her curiosity grew by the minute. She looked over Banjo's shoulder. Lobo sniffled all around the tracks.

"See these horseshoes?" he said softly. "They have an *X* carved into them." Megan could see the print plainly. "That's the mark Logan Hohner puts on his own shoes."

"Logan Hohner? Whose range is this?"

"We're heading into a corner where the Circle C, the Rocking H, and Hohner's outfit meet up. I think we're at the edge of Harrington's range. If not, we're close to it.

"It wouldn't have been Hohner himself that came through here. He's always at the blacksmith shop in town. Must have been his boys." Banjo stood and knocked his hat to the back of his head. "I wonder what they was doin'."

A few drops of rain hit Megan's hand, and she looked toward the gray, swirling sky. Another drop hit her chin and another her cheek.

"There's a hollowed out spot in that boulder yonder." Banjo pointed to a rock face twenty feet high with a large stand of brush in front of it. "I've camped there a time or two."

Megan was surprised to see that behind the brush was an indentation in the rock about six feet by eight feet. They hadn't reached shelter any too soon. In seconds the rain was coming down like a heavy wind-blown curtain of water. From time to time a heavy gust blew some spray into the shelter.

Megan stood near the front watching the rain. Steve and Banjo moved inside to look around.

The remains of many campfires lay on one side with a little dry wood stacked not far away. "Look at this." Steve picked up something from the ground.

"What is it?" Banjo asked.

"It's a twig." He held it out between thumb and finger for Banjo to see. "See how the bark is stripped halfway off and one end has been chewed? It's not that old, either." He peeled a small piece of bark off. "See how much lighter the wood is under the bark? It hasn't completely dried out yet."

"Let me see that." Banjo stretched out his hand. "It looks mighty like the one I found at the Running M." He sniffed it. "It's juniper, too. It has a strong, sweet smell. It's a twin to the one I found after Harrington's murder."

"That's what I was thinking."

"Can I see it?" Megan asked, excitedly.

"Here." Banjo lightly tossed it to her. "Put it someplace safe." He turned back to the area he had been studying. "Let's look close. We may have hit pay dirt."

"This fire is only a day or two old," Banjo said, kneeling beside it. "Some of the coals are smooth, and some are jagged. The jagged coals are new."

"Let's quarter the area," Steve suggested. "I'll take the right side, Banjo." He held up a warning hand. "Don't come too close, Megan. You may ruin some good sign without knowing it. Stay where you are until we have a chance to look the place over real careful-like."

Leaning her shoulder against the rock, Megan fell into watchful silence. Lobo finally came in out of the rain. He sat by Megan's skirt, and she absently put her hand on his ruff. His fur was wet and foul. Disgusted, she looked at her grimy hand. It had a repulsive, wet doggy smell. She scrubbed at it with her handkerchief and made herself (and Lobo) an unspoken promise.

"Well, what do you know?" Banjo said in a half-whisper a few minutes later. "Here's a boot print. A clear one, not scuffed out like the rest. It looks like the ground was soft when he stepped here, and it dried without being disturbed." He knelt on one knee. "Old boots, I'd say. Run-down at the heel. And a big man. Two hundred pounds at least."

"Any idea who it may be?" Steve asked.

"There's quite a few big men hereabouts." Banjo shook his head. "I wouldn't want to venture a guess. You got anything else?"

"No, can't say I do." Steve carefully searched the ground at his feet.

Megan placed the twig in the pocket of her riding habit. She resolved again to watch for a man who chewed twigs. Many men she had seen chewed straws.

She couldn't remember anyone chewing a twig.

The rain had let up a little when Megan's stomach reminded her it was lunchtime.

"I'm hungry." Megan's voice sounded small. The men turned quickly. They had almost forgotten she was along.

"Let's eat." Steve walked toward her. "I could use a bit myself." He ran through the rain to retrieve the lunch tin from Megan's saddlebag.

"That Harrington boy won't soon forget the whoppin' you gave him this morning," Banjo said, helping himself to a second piece of corn bread.

Megan, already finished, idly twirled a yellow cottonwood leaf with brown edges, holding the stem between her thumb and forefinger. She glanced at Steve, who was wiping his mouth with the back of his hand, and waited tensely for his answer.

"I know it." He took a sip from his canteen. "He's a bully, but I don't want to kill him if I can help it, Banjo."

"I respect you for it, Chamberlin, but you'll have to be on your guard. I wouldn't put it past the young pup to burn the house around your ears if he happened to think of it."

The old panicky feeling came back to Megan in full force.

"What are you going to do?" she asked Steve. "Even Susan's afraid of Beau. He may do something terrible."

"You don't have to be afraid of the house burning. The sides and back are wood, but they're solid logs." Steve lay back on the grass, an arm under his head. "It would take a mighty big match to get them going. Now the stable would be a different story altogether."

"Maybe Banjo should start sleeping in the house—" Megan stopped in midsentence. She suddenly realized what that would mean to her and Steve's arrangement. She bowed her head, pretending to examine the leaf in her hand to hide the redness she could feel warming her cheeks.

"No, Miss Megan," Banjo said. "I need to stay in the stable to keep watch. Who will warn you otherwise?"

"If we do have trouble at night," Steve added, "Come to the house through the back door. Just bust in and get us up."

"I'll surely do that." Banjo rose stiffly to his feet.

"That was good, Miss Megan. I sure am glad I don't have to live with my own cookin' anymore. And there's always plenty. I appreciate that, too. There was times when I was so poor and hungry I had to cut my corn bread in half so I could get enough to eat."

"Cut it in half?"

"Yeah, so I could have two pieces instead of one." Chuckling, he peered outside. "Rain's stopped. We may as well move on."

Shaking her head, Megan smiled at the joke. She picked up the lunch tin and followed the men.

The shower had wiped away the tracks, but Steve led out in the direction they had been following before the storm. Ten minutes later they came on six young Circle C cows bunched together by a stream. It was short work to drive them back to the herd.

No one came to the clearing during the next week, not even Susan. The last of the canning was finished. The turnips were covered with straw so they wouldn't freeze in the ground and could be dug during the winter. Megan looked over her full cupboards with a deep sigh of satisfaction. The work had been hard, but now she was thankful.

She was pinning a last pair of jeans to the clothesline beside the house when she caught sight of Lobo lying on his back, legs spread-eagle, napping in the sun. Lobo was basking in the warmth, because the nights were windy and cold. The warm sunshine chased the gripping chill from his doggy bones. The smell of wood smoke from the fireplace and Banjo's potbelly stove in the stable made the air smell as well as feel like autumn.

Clothes basket in hand, Megan marveled at the change in the wolf-faced dog. His hip bones were no longer easy to see. He was quick to wag his tail and give short, happy barks when she played with him. He had lost his fear of Steve and Banjo but barked ferociously when a stranger rode in.

She set the laundry basket in the kitchen and went out by the spring to dump out the dirty wash water. She wished Jeremy could see Lobo. They would love each other. The warm, soapy water sloshed as she raised the edge of the tub. She was about to give the final heave but suddenly stopped.

Eyes on the few remaining soapsuds, she thought some more about Lobo.

"Lobo, my boy," she said aloud to herself, "today is a red letter day for you."

She opened the back door of the stable and called the unsuspecting dog. Tail wagging, tongue lolling, he trotted into the stable. He licked her hand once before sniffing her skirt, the ground, the doorway.

"Come on, boy." She led the way through the door with Lobo close behind. "I know you think I have something for you to eat. . . . Get down! I don't want your dirty paws on my skirt." She looked at the spot. "Oh, well, I guess it doesn't matter. Who knows what I'll look like by the time this project is over."

She led him to the edge of the tub. How to go about getting him into the tub was the next problem, after that how to keep him there. She put her forearms under his middle near his front and back legs. He licked her face and uncertainly waved his thick tail. Megan gasped when she hoisted him into the water.

"You certainly have put on weight," she panted, her hands holding him firmly. There was marked doubt in Lobo's eyes now. He sniffed the surface of the water and looked longingly at the stable door he had just come through.

"Be still, Lobo," Megan said, soothingly. "It'll all be over in a minute. Make that five or ten minutes. I promise to hurry." She picked up the bar of soap and rubbed it over his back.

The transformation took fifteen minutes. In that short space of time, Lobo's gray, matted fur turned ivory, the brown was rust-colored, the black, dark gray instead of soot. Megan, on the other hand, changed from a neat, albeit slightly damp, housewife to a dirt-smudged, gray-flecked, dog-smelling woman. When she set Lobo free, he gave his shaggy coat a healthy shake to further adorn his mistress.

"What happened to Lobo?" Steve asked her that afternoon on their way to shoot targets. "He have a fight with a scrubbing brush?"

"You could say that," Megan laughed. "I stuck him in my wash tub after I finished the clothes." She looked lovingly at the fluffy animal at her side. It was hard to see a wolf resemblance now. She reached down to scratch behind a pointed ear.

"Do you want to go with me to Juniper tomorrow?"

"That would be nice," Megan answered happily. "I have a letter to mail. I hope there will be one waiting for me, too." She broke open her rifle to check the load and then snapped it shut.

"What are we shooting today?"

Her hopes were fulfilled the next morning when the young postmaster handed her a small white envelope. She tore it open and scanned the contents. When she finished, the hand holding the letter fell limply to her side. She stepped outside and stood motionless on the boardwalk with the letter still crumpled in her hand. Jeremy had taken a turn for the worse. He was weak. The doctor was anxious.

Sheer willpower forced the tears back. Where could she hide to have a good cry?

"Megan!" Susan's voice startled her.

"Oh, hello." Megan shoved the letter into her skirt pocket.

"Bad news?" Susan asked, looking at her friend's strained face.

"Not really bad, just disappointing," Megan managed. "How are you?" She steered the conversation away from herself. If she had to talk about Jeremy now, she would burst into tears.

"Not too good." Susan stepped close to the wall of the postal station, away from easy view. "I saw what Steve did to Beau's face." She held up a hand against Megan's reply. "I'm glad, Megan. He needed someone to bring him down a notch. He wouldn't show himself outside the ranch until yesterday. I got him to bring me into town today." She glanced up the street. "I can't let him see me talking to you.

"Be careful." Susan was in dead earnest. "Beau says he's going to settle accounts with Steve, and he doesn't have any scruples. Tell your husband."

"Thank you, Susan." Megan clasped Susan's hand.

Tears shone brightly in Susan's eyes. She gave Megan's hand an answering squeeze and hurried away.

The letter in Megan's pocket had drained all the pleasure out of the outing. She was all in before Steve was ready to leave. The buckboard was parked in the shade of Harper's Emporium, so she put her few packages into the back and climbed heavily to the seat. Sitting in the shadow was much better than plaguing her shoe-pinched feet any longer. She laid her hand on her skirt and felt the paper crackle.

Poor little Jeremy. If only he could come to Colorado and play in the clear sunshine. She pictured him running free and strong in the meadow, romping with Lobo. Another crackle of the letter in her pocket and the picture shattered, leaving a painful emptiness in the pit of her stomach.

Did I make the right decision? In trying to give him more than I could afford, did I take away what he needed most: love, security. . .myself?

"Bad news?" Steve asked when he joined her.

"Jeremy is worse." She tried to say it without betraying her agitation, but her voice cracked. She pressed her arms against her sides and smoothed her skirt with small movements.

"Is there anything I can do for him? Does he have the best doctors?"

"The best the sanitarium has to offer, I guess."

"Let me get him the best one in Baltimore."

"Do you know how much that would cost?"

"I know. But it doesn't matter. I'll go to the telegraph office and send Tump my instructions."

"I appreciate what you're trying to do, but the doctor alone will take up more than all my wages."

"Consider it a gift. No strings attached." He jumped to the ground. "No more arguments," he said, firmly. "It's settled."

She was relieved Jeremy would be getting better care, yet she wasn't sure how to take Steve's offer. Or his insistence. Why was he doing this? In all their struggles against poverty, her mother had never taken charity. She didn't want charity either. Was that what Steve's gift was?

A flash of sunlight on silver caught her eye. It came from Clyde Turner, the Rocking H foreman, who was standing in front of the Red Rooster Saloon. He was wearing black pants with silver studs down the sides. On his black boots were huge silver spurs. The pants were topped by a silky black shirt with a gray kerchief. Fascinated, Megan watched him. She had never seen a cowhand turned out like that before.

Arms folded, Turner loafed against the hitching rail. He kept looking down the street like he was waiting for someone. Henry and Al Hohner shambled down the dusty street and walked up to talk to him. Glancing around secretively, he spoke a few words to them and strode into the saloon, causing the doors to swing to and fro several times after he passed. Al and Henry continued down the street in the direction of their father's shop.

"All set." Steve was at her side before she saw him. "I left instructions that we are to be wired of his condition within the week."

Megan drew a deep breath. There was nothing more to say.

Scraping the hoof of a horse, Logan Hohner stood outside his blacksmith's shop on the edge of town. He straightened and waved for them to stop when the buckboard drew near. Steve pulled up, and Hohner shuffled over to them.

"Gud afternoon, Mr. Chamberlin. Ma'am." The gap in his teeth was conspicuous when he smiled. His jaw was coarse with a thick patch of stubble. "I vanted to tell ye that I doan mind de gossips und all de slander dey be speakin' about ye. Ye can come to me any time to have work done." He leaned forward, speaking in a loud whisper. "Dey lie about my boys, too. My boys is gud boys. Dey never did no rustlin' in dere lifes." He leaned back an stuck his thumbs under his over-stretched suspenders. "So you cum to Logan Hohner if ye need someding."

Megan absently watched the Rocking H hands ride out of town.

"Thank you, Mr. Hohner, I'll be sure to do that." Steve clucked to the horses, and the buckboard jostled ahead.

When they were on the trail out of town, Steve cleared his throat. "I had an interesting conversation while we were in town. I saw Jim Sanders outside the emporium shortly before you came. As Banjo would say, he was as jumpy as a June bug at a poultry convention. He said not to worry, the gossip about Harrington's murder would die down before long. He thought Harrington deserved what he got. Whoever did it did a service to the community, so to speak. Then he left at almost a dead run." He shrugged. "I can't figure out why he was telling me all that."

"I saw something interesting, too." She told him about the incident between Clyde Turner and the Hohner boys.

"Most cowhands couldn't afford that getup," Steve agreed.

"He's foreman, though," Meagan reasoned. "And the Harringtons probably pay a pretty good wage."

"That Turner definitely reminds me of someone," Steve said. "The more I see of him, the more it strikes me. But for the life of me I can't put a name to him."

Suddenly a shot shattered the afternoon stillness. The four horses pulling the buckboard instantly bolted. They charged down the rough trail as though driven by an insane wagon master. Bracing her feet against the front of the wagon, Megan gripped the seat, her knuckles white, trying to stay aboard.

"Whoa!" Steve shouted frantically. "Whoa!" Raising the reins high, he leaned back on the lines with all his might, but still the horses ran. The rushing wind caught Steve's hat, sending it sailing. The plain was a brown blur. On and on the buckboard flew, bouncing, swaying, careening down the trail.

Frothing at the mouth, eyes wild, the horses bounded on. Megan's arms ached from clinging to the seat. She knew she couldn't hold on much longer.

The front wheel on her side slid to a small gully, and she felt the wagon tilt. Scrambling, clawing for a hold, she heard the splinter of cracking wood and the terrified scream of a horse. The buckboard fell heavily on its side, throwing her to the stony ground. She had the sensation of falling, felt a stabbing pain in her right shoulder, and everything went black.

Chapter 15

Megan? Megan?" A gentle hand touched her face. She raised her arm to touch the hand. The movement brought another stabbing pain to her shoulder, and she moaned.

"Megan?" It was Steve.

She opened her eyes to see him kneeling beside her, bending close to her face. "My shoulder hurts when I move it."

"Don't try to move until I check it out." He rubbed gentle fingers over her upper arm and shoulder. "Tell me when it hurts."

"Now." She winced.

"Move your fingers. Okay, now your lower arm."

She had to force herself to obey, clenching her teeth against the pain.

"I don't think it's broken, but it may be out of joint. I'm taking you back to the doctor in Juniper."

She looked at his scraped, dirt-covered face so full of concern for her. "You're hurt yourself," she breathed.

"Just a few scrapes." His jaw grew hard. "I wish I had the scoundrel who did this!"

"What?" His words frightened her.

"Someone burned Caesar's back with a bullet. That's what set the horses to running. You could have been killed."

He ran his hands through his wind-blown hair. "I've been a fool, Megan, thinking I could win against that Harrington outfit. We're bucking a stacked deck. I had no right to bring a woman out here in the first place." His eyes were windows to a tormented soul. "I think we ought to catch the next train back to Baltimore."

"But—" She tried to sit up, but the ache in her shoulder made her lie back. "We can't! Do you know what you're saying?"

"I can't stand to have them hurt you. Why can't they face me and fight like men?" He slammed an iron fist into his calloused palm.

Dr. Leatherwood, the new doctor in Juniper Junction, told them the shoulder was only badly sprained. He bound it up and put Megan's right arm in a sling.

"Wrap her shoulder in brown paper soaked in vinegar twice a day," he instructed as Megan prepared to go. "Leave it on for half an hour and then replace this binding." He was a young man, probably not much older than Steve. He was prematurely bald, and his nose looked like it had been broken more than once. In fact, he looked more like a boxer than a doctor.

"You'll have to rest the arm for at least a week. Ten days if it still pains you." He handed Steve a small brown envelope when they came out of the examination room. "Give her a little of this if she can't rest because of the pain. And feel free to call on me again if you have any problems."

"Thank you, Doctor." Steve gave Megan a relieved smile and opened the door for her.

"You've already got it fixed." Megan looked at the front rigging of the buckboard where it had cracked.

"I took it over to the blacksmith while the doc was looking at you. He did a smart job."

"I'll say." She supported the sling with her left hand. "I wasn't looking forward to limping home like we did to get back to town." Her arm ached frightfully from her elbow to her shoulder and neck.

"You think you ought to lie down in the back?" He looked anxiously at her wan expression.

"I think the jarring of the wagon would be worse that way than if I sat up."

"I'll try to take it easy on the ruts."

"Just get us there as fast as you can," Megan said through tense lips.

It was an endless, grueling journey. Every jostle was an irritation, every jolt an agony. Darkness fell before they had reached the stand of pines and oaks around the meadow. The pain was nauseating. White to the lips, she clamped her arm against her middle to keep it still.

"Why don't you lean against me?" Steve asked, sliding close to her.

Weakly, Megan laid her head against his shoulder and closed her eyes. The change of position did ease her arm some. She was weary beyond endurance.

"You were right back there when I was spouting off. I don't want to leave the ranch," he said at length. "It's more than my father's inheritance. I've come to love the place."

"I know," Megan said, softly. "It's so good to have open spaces and fresh air after living in the city. If it weren't for Jeremy, I wouldn't ever want to go back."

"You know what I said about putting down roots here?"

"Yes," she said, wincing as the buckboard bounced into a dry puddle.

"I want to do that. Stay here and work the land, raise some beef. . ." His voice drifted off, and they rode in silence the rest of the way home.

"Megan's been hurt," Steve told Banjo when they arrived at the stone house. "Ride over to the Rocking H, and see if you can talk to Susan without anyone knowing. I don't want to cause her more trouble. Just tell her Megan could use her help for a few days."

Ignoring her feeble protests, Steve carried Megan to the house and laid her on the bed. Tears of pain and exhaustion trickled down the sides of her face toward her ears.

"Here, take this powder. It'll help you sleep." He handed her a full spoon of powder stirred into a glass of water.

Raising her head off the pillow, she swallowed the medicine and shivered at the bitter taste. Steve took the glass from her hand.

"Thank you for looking after me," she said weakly.

"Don't talk." He turned down the lamp beside her until it was a dull glow. "I'll check in on you in a while."

The lamp was still glowing dimly when she awakened. A blanket covered her to the chin. She touched it, wondering how it got there. Sleepily pulling it aside, she sat up. She was thirsty. Thinking of the pitcher of water in the kitchen, she put her toes on the cold floor and realized for the first time that her shoes had been removed. She must have been sleeping like the dead to have stayed asleep when they were taken off.

Her shoulder still ached but not as sharply as before. Moving slowly through the gloomy room, she reached the open door of her room and paused. In the fireplace hot coals glowed brilliant orange, casting an eerie light over the room. When her eyes adjusted she recognized Steve's figure rolled in a blanket on the floor in front of the hearth. His back was toward her, but she could tell from his position that he was asleep.

Putting her hand out before her like a blind person, she started across the room. She had taken only three steps when Steve rolled over and came to his feet in one move.

"What are you doing up?" He blinked and peered at her through sleep-dulled eyes. "You should have called me."

"I wanted a drink." She felt like a schoolgirl caught passing a note.

"Go back and lie down. I'll fetch it for you."

"Banjo left a message for Susan with Wyatt," he said as he gave her a glass of cold spring water. "Hopefully she'll be here in the morning."

Megan drank long and deep. The cold water felt good on her parched throat.

"You shouldn't carry on about me so." She handed him the empty glass. "I'll be all right. There's nothing terribly wrong with my arm. It won't hurt me to move around some."

"Tomorrow you'll be sore in places you didn't even know you had. Take it from one who knows. You'll be glad I sent for Susan." He pulled the cover over her. "You need more of that powder to get back to sleep?"

"I don't think so." She yawned.

"Well, if you need anything else, give a holler. I'll be right outside."

⤚

The gray light of morning made a segmented square on the wall of her room. Half-asleep, she tried to roll over, and she felt a stab in her shoulder. The accident came back to her in the same instant. The creak of the opening front door had awakened her.

"How is she?" It was Susan's voice.

Steve replied, "She's sleeping. Seemed to rest fairly well through the night."

"What happened?"

Megan heard Susan's light steps cross the stone floor, and Steve told the story in five sentences. Susan, dressed in her black silk mourning clothes, was standing in the bedroom doorway moments later.

"Good morning." Megan tried to sound cheerful.

"I'm so sorry." Susan came to the bed and bent over her. "Does it hurt much?" She looked anxiously at the sling.

"Not so much now. It's a dull ache." She shifted her position on the bed. "Steve was right; I do ache all over this morning."

"You relax." Susan pulled off her black gloves. "I'll have you a nice, hot breakfast in no time." She was tugging at her bonnet strings as she went out.

"I've got some things to attend to on the range." Steve stepped into her room when Susan was gone. "I'll be back at suppertime." He came a step closer. "You be good and stay quiet."

"The way I feel, I can't do anything else." She tried to say it flippantly, but the words fell a little flat. Steve's expression unnerved her so much she couldn't think of anything else to say.

His face was full of compassion, but behind his eyes was something alive. He picked up her hand and held it between both of his. He didn't speak anymore, either, just stood there looking down at her. Megan felt strength in his gentle touch. She sensed fire beneath his tender concern. It gave her a sweet, warm feeling, but it frightened her a little, too.

He replaced her hand on the quilt like a collector setting down a rare piece of crystalware; he took a step backward and went out.

She wanted to analyze his expression, relive the sensation of his hand holding hers, but it was too tiring. She nestled her head deeper into the pillow.

Brilliant light cascaded over the bed when Susan tied up the curtain. Megan squinted against the glare. She must have fallen asleep.

"I've brought you some hot biscuits and tea," Susan said, placing a tray over her knees.

"Thanks." Megan slowly and painfully eased up into a sitting position and adjusted the sling around her neck. "I don't know what I would have done if you hadn't come over."

Susan's smile matched the sunbeams spilling through the window. "Wyatt woke me up last night. He threw pebbles at my window. It was very romantic."

"Really?" Megan came to life. "Did he say anything else besides Banjo's message?"

"That would be tellin'." Susan laughed lightly, and Megan noticed that though it was September, for Susan roses were back in season. "He said he would come over here if he got a chance."

"What did you tell your brother? About coming over, I mean." Megan took a small bite of a buttered biscuit.

"I left a note saying a friend of mine wasn't feeling well, and I'd be away helping her for a few days. What he doesn't know won't hurt him in this case."

"I hope you don't have any trouble because of me." The worried look returned to Megan's face.

"Never mind." Susan took the tray from Megan's lap. "Rest. You'll never get better if you lie there and fret. I'll have your brown paper and vinegar in a few minutes."

The stench of the vinegar was stifling, but it did seem to help the pain as it soaked into her sore muscles. Slowly, Megan moved her lower arm up and down.

"It's a miracle it wasn't broken!" Susan exclaimed when she saw the dark blue bruise on Megan's shoulder and upper arm.

"I've never seen a runaway horse before." Megan shuddered. "And when the wagon started tipping. . ."

"Don't dwell on it," Susan interrupted. "Let's get the dressing back on now, and you can have a rest."

"Would you like me to read to you, or do you want to sleep?" she asked when Megan was lying down again.

"I'll sleep. I'm worn-out. I can't believe how something so small can make me feel so tired."

Sometime later, the sound of the front door opening awakened Megan for the second time that day.

"Susan." It was a young man's deep voice.

"Hello, Wyatt."

"How's Mrs. Chamberlin?"

"She's resting." Light footsteps sounded on the stone floor. "Would you like to sit down?"

"I need to talk to you, Susan," he said, urgently. "Things are bad with you and Beau, aren't they?" Pause. "You don't have to tell me. I know they are. Why don't you come away with me? We can go to Montana or Oregon and start a life for ourselves. There's nothing left for us here."

"I wish I could, Wyatt, but it's impossible." There was frustrated longing in her words.

"What's the holdup?" he demanded impatiently. "There's nothing to stand between us now."

"I can't leave Colorado without knowing who killed Pa. After the murderer is caught and punished, I may consider it, but right now it's out of the question." She hesitated, then plunged on. "I've got to ask you something. Please don't be angry with me. I think I already know the answer, but I have to hear you say it."

"What is it?"

"Did you do it?"

"Kill your pa? Of course not!"

"I didn't think you did, Wyatt. I had to hear you say it." She sounded on the verge of tears. Megan sank deeper into her pillow and closed her eyes. She didn't like overhearing their conversation.

"He was a scoundrel," Wyatt went on, "and I have to admit I hated him, but I didn't kill him. I was tempted to the night he turned me down, but I knew you loved him. Not that I could understand why you did. I would never do such a lowdown thing to you as that."

"You don't know how relieved I am. I've wanted to talk to you a hundred times since the funeral, but I was too afraid of being overheard."

"To tell you the truth, I think a rustler killed your pa. While we were on the cattle drive, I heard him talking to his foreman and one of the hands. He said he thought one of the hands must be in on the rustling, because it's been going on so long. This was the fourth year the count was low. And this year it was worst of all."

"Do you have any idea who it could be?"

"It's hard to tell. There's quite a few of the hands may have done some underhanded things in their time.

"A person don't ask about those things. You know that." He paused. "Things are getting pretty rough at the ranch. Some of the hands are talking about asking for their wages. If it weren't for you, Susan, I'd pull out, too."

"Don't. Please don't leave me there all alone."

"I was sort of hoping you'd see it that way." His voice surged with a strong undercurrent. "You haven't given me much encouragement the last while. I was starting to fear you'd changed your mind about us."

"I could never change my mind, Wyatt." Susan spoke softly, intensely.

Boots scraped against the floor, and a chair creaked. Then silence.

"I can't stay too long. Turner'll miss me and ask me a lot of questions I don't want to answer. He sure has been on the prod lately. He's about as easy to work with as an irritated porcupine."

After a few minutes of silence, the door opened, and the clumping of heavy boots on the porch told Megan he was gone. Megan lay still, feigning sleep when Susan came in. She was happy for Susan, but even as she rejoiced, she wrestled another emotion: a strange, deep yearning. It was the sweet agony of discovering a deep, pure vein of gold at the bottom of a craggy cliff, a cliff so loosely seamed that one blow with a pick would bring the mountain crashing down on the miner's head.

It was the knowledge of something precious with no hope of having it for her own. She savored the new sensation and tried to understand it.

Chapter 16

"How are you comin' on, Miss Megan?" Banjo asked the next evening. He and Steve sat by Megan's bed for a chat after supper while Susan finished the dishes.

"Restless." Megan sat propped against some pillows. Her arm was still too sore to move freely.

"I rode back to the place where the horses stampeded," Steve said, "but I couldn't find a clue."

"Who would do such a terrible thing?" Megan asked, cradling her sling in her strong arm.

"Someone who wants to get rid of you folks mighty bad," Banjo offered.

"Wyatt was here today," Megan said. "He thinks Harrington had an idea that one of his own hands had a part in the cattle rustling."

"The Rocking H hands are a hard bunch, but I've my doubts that any of them would be a thief," Banjo said thoughtfully. "Course, there are a couple new ones I don't know so good."

"Wyatt said they've had cattle missing for four years now," Megan continued. "It would have to be someone who has been with them longer than that."

"I'd have to study on it awhile, I reckon." He shifted in his chair. "With your permission, Chamberlin, I'll ride over toward that corner of the range we were on a few days ago and have another look-see. I believe the man who stood under that shelter the night Harrington was killed is the same man who was in that cave."

"Shoo, you men," Susan scolded from the door. "Can't you see Megan's tired?"

"Susan's making herself right to home," Banjo said to Steve with an unusually serious expression. "Reminds me of a sergeant I knew in the Confederate army."

"Don't pay him any mind, Susan," Megan advised, smiling. "He's like a toothless lion, a big roar with nothing to back it up."

"Everybody around here knows Banjo," Susan countered, "and we make allowances for the aged and infirm."

"All right." Banjo chuckled. "I know when I'm bested."

Later that night Steve came into her room, closed the door, and made up his bed on the floor where he'd been sleeping since Susan came. He paused, blanket in hand.

"Still hurt bad?" he asked, referring to her arm.

"Not as much as at first, but it's still sore. I expect Susan will be able to go home day after tomorrow."

"I don't think she's in any hurry." He spread out the blanket and sat on it. "I feel for her, living with that hot-head brother of hers."

"So do I." Megan turned her face toward the wall and closed her eyes. She lay a long while half-asleep, missing Jeremy and Em, thinking of Susan and Wyatt, listening to Steve's deep regular breathing as he slept on the floor at her feet.

"I found it," Banjo announced the next day. The three of them sat around the table after Megan's first lunch outside her room. Susan had ridden home for some fresh clothing. "The purtiest little box canyon you ever did see."

"Where?" Steve asked.

"A little north of where we found the camp. It's Hohner's range. I'm sure of it. A hundred acres of nice grazing and a stream running through one end. Had maybe two hundred head of cattle. Good looking, young stuff. I'd say they're all two years old or less.

"I scouted around and found another camp near the stream. And get this"—he leaned forward—"it had the same marked horseshoe tracks and the same juniper twigs."

Steve whistled softly.

"Most of the cattle were too young to hold a brand, but I saw a couple of steers with a doctored Circle R. The top half of the brand was new, hadn't healed proper yet. It's my guess they're Rocking H cattle."

"What are you going to do?" Megan asked.

"Sit tight," Steve answered. "We don't know who's doing it yet."

"But it must be Logan Hohner." Megan persisted.

"Not necessarily," Banjo said. "I think someone is using Hohner's land without him knowing it." He paused and shifted his toothpick to the other side of his mouth. "Knowing Logan Hohner, he hasn't seen that canyon for a couple o' years." He shook his head. "His boys are probably in on it some way, but I think we need to look a little further before we can find the person behind it, the rottenness at the core."

"You think someone is putting Hohner's boys up to it?" Steve asked.

"That's about it. Those Hohner boys aren't smart enough for a long-term operation like this'n. Their boss has to make a slipup sometime, and with us knowing what to look for, we should be able to catch him."

In a few days Megan's arm was in working order again. It was weak, and she had to rest often, but she was able to carry out her household chores.

The promised telegram from the new sanitarium made Megan cry from glad relief. Jeremy was responding to the more expensive treatment. The doctor was encouraged by his progress in the few days he had been there. She hugged the news to her like a woolly blanket on a cold, wintry night.

"The circuit riding preacher is coming through next Sunday," Banjo said, pausing after breakfast. "I wondered if you were feelin' up to attending. I plan on going myself. A body don't get much chance to hear real preaching in these parts."

"I'd love to go," Megan said. "I'm sure Steve'll let us use the buckboard. Maybe he'll want to go himself. I'll ask him."

Steve shook his head doubtfully when she brought up the subject that evening.

"That's all right. You and Banjo take the buckboard and go," he replied. "I'll stay here and look after things."

She was disappointed by Steve's blunt refusal to join them, but the feeling was short-lived. She was too excited to let anything dampen her spirits. This would be the first church service she would attend as a Christian. She was looking forward to it even more than she had the frolic.

The buckboard rattled over the leaf-strewn trail on that fine, hope-filled Sunday morning. Only Billy and Star were hitched up today since they weren't going for supplies. It was a cool, crisp day. Megan pulled her white, knotted shawl closer around her pink dress with the starched white collar. She took a deep breath of the tingly breeze. Beside her, Banjo looked like a stranger in his carefully brushed black suit and black string tie. Without its usual growth of stubble, his face looked like a freshly skinned squirrel.

"Preacher Tyler is a young feller, but he can really preach." Banjo tugged at his celluloid collar. "He's been traveling through these parts for purty nigh three years. Don't have no real home. He keeps moving from place to place. Goes all the way from Montana to Texas, I hear." He glanced at Megan. "Don't expect no fancy sermonizing like that city feller from Denver who preached at Harrington's funeral. But you'll carry something home with you to hide in your heart against the hard places in life."

"Do many people come to the meetings?"

"Quite a few. Most of them because they go to every social gathering that comes along. But there are a few real saints in Juniper. I'll be proud to introduce you to 'em."

"I'm looking forward to it, Banjo."

The schoolhouse was half-filled when they arrived. The desks had been removed, and long, backless benches filled the room. They were crammed so closely together that Megan could barely get her skirts through the aisle. Banjo found seats for them near the center of the room. The seats near the windows were already taken, and the air felt stuffy. A hushed buzzing hovered over the group as folks chatted before the service. Megan recognized Mr. and Mrs. Harper coming in. They nodded, unsmiling, in her direction and found places on the far left. Elaine Sanders gave her a small noncommittal wave from across the room where she chatted gaily with a blond young man Megan didn't know.

A steady stream of people poured in until the room was packed shoulder to shoulder, knee to back. Megan's light cotton dress, so cool this morning, was becoming itchy with its high collar and long sleeves. Megan tried not to fidget, but she was impatient for the service to begin.

The sermon was simple and direct. In spite of the warmness of the room and the closeness of the congregation, Megan forgot all but the power of the message. The preacher's dark suit was shiny at the elbows and knees, and there was little to draw the eye to his rawboned, pock-scarred face. But Megan had never seen a man so completely absorbed in his message. She could tell he really believed what he preached.

"You must be born again," he urged, his voice quiet, intense, as he pleaded with the lost. And on he spoke, "Why call on the Lord and then not do the things He commands you to do?"

Megan's spirit was gripped. At the end of the message, she stood with others who wanted to surrender to God's will for their lives. Yet even as she stood, there was confusion and anxiety inside her soul. What of her marriage to Steve? What of her future?

She brushed her anxious thoughts aside to nod and smile in response to Banjo's introductions after the service. She especially liked Mrs. Stowe, a small middle-aged widow with wavy, chestnut brown hair and a motherly smile.

"Be sure to stop and have a cup of tea with me when you're in town," Mrs. Stowe urged. "I'd love to hear about Baltimore and the East. I'll pray for your brother, too," she promised when Megan told her about Jeremy.

Megan was touched by Mrs. Stowe's sincere kindness and promised to stop and visit the widow when she came to town.

The preacher's quick smile and friendly handshake were also encouraging.

"I'm glad to see you take your stand for Christ, Mrs. Chamberlin," he said. "I'll be sure to pray for you in the days to come. Satan would like to discourage you, but God is a strong tower. When you feel temptation, run to God and He'll keep you safe." He gave Banjo a friendly punch in the shoulder. "You can depend on Banjo to give you good advice if you need it. We go back a long way together. He prays for me. It's folks like him keeps me on the circuit."

It was an hour past noon when they set off on the trail out of town. They had barely passed the last frame building when Banjo untied his string tie and pulled off his collar.

"Excuse me, Miss Megan, but I can't abide this contraption any longer. Puts me in mind of being tied with a rope halter." He stuffed the black string and bit of celluloid into his shirt pocket.

Megan picked up the basket of food she had packed for their lunch and handed Banjo a thick beef sandwich.

"Much obliged," he said, taking a bite.

Lost in thought, she finished her lunch and packed away the leftovers. What about her marriage to Steve? What of the future?

Chapter 17

"There's power in the blood, power in the blood. . . ." Banjo's song reached far across the brown, evergreen-spotted hills. When they started to climb the mountain trail, he stopped singing. "I don't want to be buttin' in where I don't belong, but it appears to me something's troublin' you, Miss Megan," he said. "I don't want to know your business, but you know I'd do anything I can to help."

"I know you would, Banjo," Megan replied, carefully. "I'm thinking of the decision I made this morning and wondering what the future holds for me." She looked at her hands, clasping and unclasping them in her lap.

"It's Chamberlin, ain't it?"

Megan pressed her lips together and nodded. "You see, we don't have the usual relationship." She turned her head away from him, gazing out over the bare trees and rocks. Feeling a chilly breeze, she tightened the shawl around her shoulders.

"We're really married and all, but we're not. . ." She sighed. "It's hard to explain."

"I knowed it. I knowed it all along."

"You knew? How?"

"You told me yourself." He smiled at her doubtful expression. "Oh, not in so many words. But you didn't act like a young newly married couple. I'm no spring chick. I've been down the pike and across the river, you know. And one morning I came to the house early for breakfast, and I saw him coming down from the loft. It didn't take much figuring to work it out."

"I met him only a few weeks before we came here. He had to have a wife to fulfill his father's will. We have to live on the ranch for a year in order to collect his inheritance. He actually hired me to do it." She pressed her lower lip between her teeth, unable to go on.

"You did it for Jeremy, didn't you?"

Looking down at her restless hands, she nodded.

"He had to go to a sanitarium, and I didn't have the money. It is legal. The marriage, I mean. We didn't cheat on that."

"So what's got you so wrought up? You and Chamberlin seem to hit it off all right."

"Next May he's going to have the marriage dissolved, and I'll go back to Baltimore. I g–guess it shouldn't matter to me." She dabbed at the tears, blinking others back. "Jeremy is getting better, the doctor said. It's just that when I think of having to leave someday, I get all scared inside. I don't know what will happen to me."

"You're in love with him, aren't you?"

Megan stared at him. She wanted to cry out, "No, I'm not!" but her lips were silent. Was she in love with Steve? She couldn't say no. If she had said the words, they would have been a lie.

Like a priceless gem, she held the knowledge at arm's length and examined it against the light, marveling at its sparkling factets. It was too brilliant. Her eyes couldn't stand the brightness. She pushed the thought aside. Her future was too uncertain.

"I shouldn't have told you about the marriage," she said in a moment.

"You didn't tell me, remember? I already knew." The wagon paused on the edge of the stream. He clucked to the horses, and the buckboard rattled down the bank. "There's a verse in Proverbs says, 'Trust in the Lord with all thine heart; and lean not unto thine own understanding. In all thy ways acknowledge him, and he shall direct thy paths.' You've been trying to carry the load your ownself, Miss Megan. Give the problem to Jesus. The Lord will take care of the future."

Letting the Lord take care of the future wasn't always easy as windy and cold October became icy November. True, Jeremy was better. With the help of a kind nurse, Em sent glowing letters that thrilled Megan. Jeremy was able to sit in a chair for an hour at a time now. He gained strength by the day.

In spite of the good news, the feeling of emptiness lingered. Since her talk with Banjo, Megan was intensely aware of Steve. It was exhilarating torture. Secretly she scrutinized his every word, every expression, hoping vainly for a sign that he cared for her. He was polite, even deferential, but no more.

When the feeble light of a frigid November morning crept into the kitchen, she parted the curtain to see snow silently sifting down from a steel sky. The roof of the stable was covered in downy white, and little mounds were forming on top of each aspen post of the corral. Excited, she dropped the curtain and ran to the front windows to look at the meadow, fast disappearing under a fluffy, cold blanket.

"It's snowing!" she called to Steve when she heard the scuffling of his boots overhead. "It's snowing!" Happy as a child on Christmas morning, she skipped about the kitchen, popping a pan of biscuits into the oven, stirring the oatmeal with flourish.

The snow fell for three days, filling the meadow until not one nubby cornstalk could be seen and forming white winter blossoms on the trees. The house was tolerably warm as long as the fireplace blazed and the kitchen stove glowed. Megan despaired of ever being able to keep the kitchen floor clean with the constant tracking in of snow-laden boots from the stack of wood behind the house.

Because of the bitter cold, Lobo stayed in the stable with the horses and Banjo's potbelly stove, but every day Megan disappeared under wool wrap, scarves, and mittens to walk with him in the yard. She scattered crumbs for the ravenous birds and then knelt down to study their star-shaped tracks in the snow, wishing there was some way to preserve such pristine art. She and Lobo played and ran until numb feet and chattering teeth forced her back to the pulsating, enveloping warmth of the roaring fireplace.

On the morning of the second day, Megan was surprised when Steve came into the kitchen while she was washing the breakfast dishes.

"I want to make a built-in sideboard in the dining room. I was wondering where you want it."

She stood on the edge of the room taking stock of the oak table and the two windows.

"Why don't you put it in the corner? The depth of the corner would make extra storage space without taking so much space from the room."

"Good idea." He walked to the corner and spread his hands. "From here to here?" He nodded, considering. "And a small cabinet overhead with glassed-in doors for pretty dishes would be nice, too, wouldn't it?"

"That would be nice."

"I've been saving some wood for the project. It's in the stable. We may as well use up all this empty time doing something useful." Shrugging into their heavy coats, he and Banjo went out the back door and came back carrying some wide pine boards. They moved the table into the living room, and soon the air was filled with the rasping noise of sawing interrupted by loud pounding.

"Never use nails on furniture," Banjo said philosophically as he whittled a peg. "Like the Good Book advises, you don't put new wine in old bottles. Well, you don't put iron nails in good furniture."

"That your interpretation?" Steve asked, smiling.

"Sure, from the book of Banjo Calahan." Banjo chuckled.

"You know, Chamberlin, the Good Book does have plenty to say about life that's for our good. It's not just for women and old folks. Like in Isaiah, 'Though your sins be as scarlet, they shall be as white as snow,' or in Matthew, 'I am not come to call the righteous, but sinners to repentance.' "

Steve picked up the saw and drew it loudly across a board. Smiling to himself, Banjo picked up another scrap of wood to whittle.

"Haven't you ever thought about your soul?" Banjo continued when Steve laid down the saw.

"Not much." Steve gave Banjo a calculating look.

"You ought to. Young fellow like you has a long future ahead of him. Jesus can make all the difference as to how things come out."

"That your sermon for today?" Steve asked mildly, picking up the hand drill.

Megan heard their conversation from the kitchen. "Please, God," she prayed, "convince him that he needs you."

If only Steve were a Christian. Maybe then things would be different.

The men were still working on the cabinet when she sat down to write a letter to Jeremy. She wanted to tell him about the snow. If he were able to be here, he'd be rolling in the cold whiteness with Lobo, his cheeks ruddy with good health and a happy, secure life.

What would happen to them when she went back to Baltimore? Another squalid tenement house? She shuddered. How could she go back to the city now? "Oh, God," she prayed, "help me to trust and leave the rest to you."

The weather warmed up a little after two weeks of near-zero temperatures. The snow melted, leaving the ground soggy. Great puddle lakes lay across the meadow. Cold, damp, and miserable, Steve and Banjo slogged back to the house after the evening chores.

"I believe I like the snow better than the slush," Steve remarked, warming his hands before the fireplace. "This dampness goes plumb through a body."

"Soup's ready," Megan called from the kitchen. Hot food warmed their insides and cheered the men considerably. They were lingering over steaming cups of black coffee, enjoying the peacefulness of the evening when a commotion in the stable broke off the conversation. Lobo was barking frantically, loud, angry barks with no letup. A horse gave a piercing whinny, and there was the scuffing noise of pawing hoofs.

"Smoke!" An acrid smell and the scream of a horse reached Megan the same time as Banjo's cry.

"The stable! The stable's on fire!" Banjo overturned his chair in his hurry to reach the back door.

On the run, Steve grabbed his gun belt from its peg and followed him.

"Get the stock behind the house," Steve called as they banged out the back door. "And if Harrington's men are out there, heaven help 'em if I get my sights on one of 'em." The back door crashed closed, and they were gone.

From the kitchen window Megan could see smoke billowing from the far side of the stable. She grabbed the water bucket from the counter and ran to the back door in time to see Steve struggling to get panic-sticken Candy out of the stable.

"Steady, girl," Megan called, soothingly. "Steady, girl." She set down the bucket and walked slowly toward the horse.

"Tie her to the side of the springhouse," Steve called and ran back inside the stable. Banjo led Kelsey and Bess out as Megan drew Candy along. The presence of the other stock calmed the mare, and Megan was able to tie her without any difficulty.

Billy and Star bounded from the smoke-filled stable, their eyes rolling in terror, making it hard for Steve to keep them from rearing up. Tying them with hasty fingers, Steve raced back to the stable as Caesar's screams rose to a crescendo. Banjo held the horse's halter. He had to step nimbly to avoid the gelding's flying hooves.

"Megan, get in the house!" Steve yelled. He grabbed the halter on the other side so he and Banjo could force the horse into the fenced-in corridor. Thrashing and heaving, Caesar fought them. His front hoof caught Banjo on the leg, throwing him to the ground. Steve held on with both hands, talking, pleading with the horse. The fire roared higher behind them. Rearing high, Caesar raised Steve off the ground then bolted, dragging Steve along.

"Let him go!" Banjo shouted. "He'll kill you!"

Throwing himself clear, Steve fell into the freezing water of the stone basin. Caesar bounded forward toward the only opening he could see, and he galloped headlong over the cliff. His terrified scream turned Megan's blood to ice.

Teeth chattering, limbs shaking, Steve walked to the edge of the house and looked down. He stayed there only an instant.

"It's—s as black as pitch—ch down there," he stuttered, coming back. "I c—can't see a thing." He walked past Megan to where Banjo lay. The air was thick with heavy smoke and the hissing and popping of burning wood. Inside the stable a heavy timber crashed to the ground.

"You've got to get into some dry clothes or you'll freeze," Megan cried after him. She raised an arm to shield her eyes from the smoke, blinking as she peered after Steve.

"The f—fire will keep me from freezing. We've got to s—stop the flames from reaching the house."

"I'll help you tear down the fence." Banjo struggled to his feet.

"Chamberlin!" Beau Harrington's adolescent voice called from the darkness. "This is just the beginning, Chamberlin. Next it will be the house. Or better yet, we'll string you up to the highest cottonwood around. Won't we, Turner?"

"Turner!" Steve's voice bellowed above the roar of the inferno. "I know you, Turner. Come out in the open, you yellow dog, and fight like a man!"

"It would be your funeral, Chamberlin." A second voice called back. "No two-bit riverboat gambler could hold a candle to me!"

"Keep talking, Turner. I've almost got it."

"Got what?" The voice was edgy.

"Your real name. It'll come to me sooner or later."

The only answer he received was the volley of pounding hoofbeats retreating across the meadow.

Chapter 18

With strength that came from desperation, they tugged and tore at the smoldering wooden fence until there was a sizable gap between the house and the stable. Without a thought for her bruised and scraped hands, Megan worked on. Hauling bucket after bucket of water, they drenched the fence and the side of the house, praying all the while the wind would not blow in their direction.

"The chickens!" Megan cried. "What about the chickens?"

"I think the coop is far enough from the stable to be out of danger," Steve said, wiping his smoke-bleary eyes with his sleeve, "but I'll go open the door so they can get out just in case."

The roof of the stable collapsed with a jarring, scraping crash, sending a shower of sparks into the black sky. It startled Megan and broke the last thread of her endurance. She walked over to Candy and leaned forward, resting her head on the mare's neck. She didn't want Steve to see her, but she couldn't hold in tears any longer.

"Come." Steve's hand was on her arm. "Let's go inside. You're all in."

Megan washed the smeary soot from her face and set on the coffeepot. Steve climbed to the loft in search of dry clothes while Banjo hobbled in, painfully favoring his right leg, and sat down at the table.

"Is your leg okay?" Megan asked, worried.

"It will be in a day or two. It's just bruised. We can thank the good Lord no one was hurt any worse tonight. Trying to get a spooked horse out of a burning building is dangerous work. Your husband is a brave man."

Megan felt tears welling up again, hot, furious, revengeful tears. The hay and fodder they had carefully stored were gone as well as the buckboard and saddles. With six animals to feed through the winter, the loss was devastating.

"I could find it in myself to hate Beau Harrington," she said as she brought the coffeepot and three cups to the table. She sank into a chair and put her hands over her face.

"I know how you feel, Miss Megan," Banjo replied. "Just you remember, the Lord doesn't play any favorites when it comes to sin. Our sin is just as wicked in His sight as Beau's."

"I can't understand how anyone could be so vicious. We have a deed to this property. We've never done anything to hurt the Harringtons. We're right and they're wrong. So why are we the ones suffering?"

"I don't claim to understand it myself. All I know is that boy needs the Lord. Just the same as you and me."

"I guess you'll have to take the loft, Banjo," Steve said, later. "No doubt it'll be more comfortable than the stable was."

"I'm much obliged." Banjo said slowly. He bent over to rub a spot below the knee. "But I don't know if I can climb the ladder." He took two steps, testing his leg. "I'd best bed down in front of the fireplace tonight." He looked at Megan. "That is, if you all have an extra blanket."

"Oh, Banjo," Megan cried, "all your things were in the stable. You didn't even mention it. Of course I have a blanket. And anything else you need."

"Beggin' your pardon, ma'am, my Sharps was in the house, and Kelsey's safe out back. Long as I've got them and the Lord, that's all I need. The only thing I regret is my Bible. It's been with me since I got out of the army. I rode nigh two hundred miles to get it. But I'll get another'n one day." He sank to a chair, his face tense as he eased his leg.

"I'll get the blanket right away." Megan hurried to her room for the blanket, wondering at Banjo's matter-of-fact attitude through this entire ordeal.

"Why don't you let me have a look at the leg?" she asked as she arranged the blanket on the couch. "I may be able to do something for it, you know."

"Just let it rest tonight, Miss Megan."

"Megan's a hand when it comes to doctorin'," Steve said, coming to stand near her, close enough for his arm to brush hers.

"Tomorrow," Banjo insisted. "All I want now is a little rest." He lay down, rolled up in the blanket, and was still.

Megan rinsed out the coffee cups. Her mind was fuzzy with fatigue, her body weary beyond the point of exhaustion. She traced her way to her room hardly aware of her surroundings, but she turned around, startled, when she heard Steve follow her inside.

"How are we going to handle having Banjo in here?" he whispered after firmly shutting the door. He glanced at the floor. "I don't relish the thought of sleeping on the floor for the duration of the winter."

"I'm afraid I have something to confess." Megan avoided his gaze. She was afraid what she had to tell him would make him angry. "Banjo knows about us."

"What?" His brows drew together.

"He's all right. He won't tell anyone. I was upset one day, and he asked me about it. I guess I just blurted it all out." She turned away from his frown. "I know I shouldn't have. If it was anyone else, even Susan, I wouldn't have told. But Banjo's different."

Steve studied her a moment before his expression relaxed.

"I guess it's just as well under the circumstances. You're right on two counts. You shouldn't have told. And Banjo is different. I've never met anyone like him." He pulled his gun from its holster and checked the load. "I've got to see about Caesar. I can't let him lie down there with a broken leg or worse to suffer through the night." He put his hand on the door latch. "I couldn't rest if I did."

Megan crawled between the stiff, cold sheets and lay back with a deep sigh. Her eyes were so heavy she expected to drop off to sleep right away. Her eyes stayed closed, but sleep didn't come, for her ears were straining, her mind wondering what Steve would find at the bottom of the cliff.

She must have dozed, because the sound of a single shot jerked her awake and made her heart race. When the awful reality came to her, she turned her face into her pillow and wept.

Shivering with cold, Megan hurried into her clothes before dawn the next morning. With shaking hands she added small logs to the glowing orange coals in the kitchen stove and put on the coffeepot. Banjo hadn't moved when she tiptoed past, so she worked quietly, trying not to waken him.

She mixed the pancake batter, set it aside for frying when the men were ready, and sliced bacon into a pan. A quick glance out the kitchen window stopped her in midmotion and made her go back for a longer look. Before her lay the blackened, still smoldering remains of the stable. It was nothing more than a flattened heap of rubble with the old potbelly stove standing toward the back. Across the yard the chickens hopped in and out of the open door of the henhouse scratching and pecking about.

Megan tore herself away from the window when she heard Steve's tread on the loft ladder. She added coffee grounds to the boiling pot and set the cast-iron skillet on the stove.

"Sleep okay?" Steve pulled a chair from the table and sat down. Dark circles rimmed his bloodshot eyes.

"Well enough." She greased the skillet with a piece of bacon and poured on some pancake batter.

"I had to put Caesar away." He ran his hand through his hair. "Both front legs were broken."

"I heard." When the first pancake was done, she added a little cold water to the brewing coffee. Filling a thick, white mug to the brim, she set it on the table in front of Steve.

"I've got to ride over to Hohner's spread to see if he'll loan me a wagon and if he can sell me some hay for the stock. Buying feed is going to take most of our profit from the corn crop," he added bitterly.

"What about making a profit to meet the terms of the will?"

"We still have the cattle. If I have to, I'll sell them all in the spring. We'll still get by." He hit a hard fist on the tabletop. "If I had that Beau Harrington where I could get at him. . ." His eyes narrowed. "Not only him. That Turner fellow. I was awake most of the night trying to remember how I know him. I finally figured it out.

"He was in the Confederate Army. But his name wasn't Turner; it was Taylor. Charlie Taylor.

"He joined our outfit outside of Chattanooga. We used to pass the time playing poker for pennies when we had them, or else we used matchsticks. Anyway, we were having a friendly game and my friend Ted Miller was winning. The boys use to kid me about being a riverboat gambler and losing to Ted, who was a farm boy." He stared into space, absently running his forefinger along the rim of the coffee cup.

"Ted and Charlie were the only two left in the game when Ted showed three aces. Charlie was mad as hops. Stood up and called Ted a cheat. Well, Ted pulled a knife, and they set to. Like magic, Charlie had a knife in his hand, too. I never did figure out where he got it from.

"They came at each other, and Ted cut Charlie a bad one on his cheek. Ted stepped back, and about that time Charlie flipped that shiv to where he held it by the tip and threw it right into Ted's heart. Ted dropped like a stone. I don't think he even knew what hit him."

"What happened to Charlie?"

"They took him to the hospital. We pulled out shortly after that, and I never saw him again."

"Did he know you could use a knife?" She piled three pancakes on a plate and brought them to the table with a jar of sorghum.

"Come to think of it, he probably did. We used to practice pitching sometimes. He could have seen me. Offhand I can't remember ever holding a conversation with the man. That's why it took me so long to place him." He poured a generous amount of sorghum on the pancakes and ate like a man with an appetite.

"I'll ride Billy bareback to Hohner's," Steve said later as he set a pail of Bess's milk on the counter. "Should be back well before noon."

"Please be careful," Megan pleaded. "They'd have no scruples about ambushing you if they could."

"You watch yourself," Banjo called from the table where he was finishing a piece of bacon.

Later Megan was wrapping Banjo's bruised shin in brown paper and vinegar when the drumming of a running horse drew her to the front window. Riding a horse Megan had never seen before, Susan raced into the dooryard. She wore a brown coat and her Sunday bonnet.

Megan threw open the door to catch the panting young woman by the arm to draw her inside.

"What's happened?" Megan demanded, fear overtaking her.

"It's Beau," Susan gasped. "He's getting the men in town stirred up about Pa's murder. They're organizing a lynching party to come after Steve."

"Sit down, child," Banjo commanded. "Get hold of yourself so you can tell us the rest."

Susan pulled at the buttons on her coat until she managed to get it off and hand it to Megan. Her hands trembled as she struggled to untie the strings on her bonnet. She sat in a chair near the blazing fireplace. Her breathing was more regular, but panic lingered beneath the surface.

"Beau took some of the hands into town this morning. They kept laughing and saying they were going to celebrate. I couldn't understand it all." She clenched her white hands in her lap.

"I went along to see Mrs. Mullins, who has a new baby. I think the men had already been drinking a little from the way they were acting." She shuddered. "When I came out of the Mullins's house, I saw a commotion in front of the Gold Mine Saloon. Beau was standing on a barrel in front of the crowd. I walked close enough to hear him call out that Steve Chamblerlin had killed Pa. Clyde Turner got a rope off his saddle horn and held it up." She squeezed her eyes shut. "It was awful. When I saw what they were up to, I ran to the telegraph office and asked Tom to wire Denver for the marshal, then I ran back to Mrs. Mullins and borrowed a horse. I had come in with Beau in the buckboard."

"What are we going to do?" Megan asked Banjo.

"Sit tight until Steve gets back. He'll be here directly." He pulled the paper off his leg. "In the meantime, bring me my Sharps." He pulled down his pants leg and stood holding the back of the chair. "I'll set by the window and keep an eye on things."

"Mrs. Mullins loaned me a Winchester," Susan said.

"You wouldn't fight against your own brother!" Megan was horrified.

"Don't count on it." Susan's mouth was set in a hard line. "After all I've been through with him in the past few months, I'd be likely to do just about anything."

Megan dug every bit of ammunition from the kitchen cabinets and set the boxes on the sideboard. She took the Henry from the wall and laid it beside the bullets.

"May as well put on some more coffee and fix some vittles," Banjo said. "It's hard tellin' how long it'll take them to get here." Holding the rifle across his lap, he stared out the window. "They'll probably stop at the saloon and drink to their plan before headin' out. Bunch of coyotes."

"Here comes Steve in a buckboard full of hay," he announced an hour later. "Looks like he did right well for hisself. Hohner let him have another horse to help pull it."

Steve pulled the buckboard behind the standing length of fence. He climbed into the back of the wagon to throw hay to the stock before coming in the back door.

"Beau Harrington is stirring up a lynch mob in Juniper to come after you. Susan rode out to warn us," Megan blurted out from the back door.

"How many?" Steve asked, stepping past her into the house. He walked to the sideboard and looked at the weaponry spread there.

"Twenty-five or thirty if they all come," Susan said quietly.

"She wired for the marshal," Banjo said, "but it'll take him a day to get here."

"We'll have to stand them off." He loaded the empty chamber in his six-shooter, snapped the magazine shut, and replaced it in his holster. Striding to the ladder, he brought his other pistol down and loaded it. A strained, suspenseful silence saturated the room. Megan, preparing lunch, wondered how long she could stand the tension. Had the fire been only yesterday?

Chapter 19

Here they come!" Banjo's words late that afternoon brought everyone to their feet. Clutching her rifle, Megan took up her post by the living room window, heart racing, mouth dry. She looked past the edge of the window to see a small group of riders enter the clearing. They rode close together. Beau's pinto was in the lead.

"When they get in range, dust them," Steve ordered calmly.

Raising the window a small crack, Megan knelt and rested her rifle on the sill. To her, the men outside were no longer fellow human beings; they had become the enemy who wanted to destroy what she loved. Swallowing hard, she took up the slack under the trigger and waited. She heard Lobo's excited bark near the front of the house.

"Now!" A volley of shots rang out at Steve's command.

As one man the group wheeled and ran for the shelter of the trees. There were a few answering shots, then all was still.

"Don't let them fool you; they're still there." Banjo eased his leg as he leaned forward. "I wonder how cold they'll have to get before they give up."

But they didn't give up. After an hour of waiting, a thin plume of gray smoke rose above the trees.

"They've built themselves a fire," Steve commented. "Looks like they'll be staying awhile."

"Long's we've got food and ammunition, we'll be all right. The law will be here directly," Banjo said dryly.

"What if the marshal won't listen to us?" Megan spoke for the first time.

"He'll listen," Steve answered. "That Walker's a square dealer. He doesn't want to hang the wrong man."

"I hope you are right," Megan answered doubtfully.

"Let's take turns watching, Banjo," Steve said, stretching. "No need for all of us to watch all night. I don't think they'll be doing anything drastic right away."

Shortly after dark, Lobo's barking intensified. He was behind the house now.

"Call off the dog!" A young man's voice called from the stable ruins. "I'm coming to join you."

"It's Wyatt!" Susan cried, running for the back door. Megan was closer. She unbolted the door and called, "Down, Lobo!" Lobo growled softly, the fur on his back standing up. "It's okay. Wyatt's a friend." The canine trotted to Megan and put his wet nose under her hand.

Susan slipped past Megan and raced to Wyatt. She threw herself at him with such force he stepped back, off balance.

"Now that's what I call a welcome!" He put his arm around Susan's shoulder." And what, may I ask, are you doing here?" He guided her inside the house.

"I came to warn them this morning when I saw what Beau was up to."

"So that's where you went off to." He squeezed her gently. "I was powerful worried about you when you disappeared.

"Chamberlin," he turned to Steve, "I ride for the brand, but there comes a time when a man has to stand for what's right. What Harrington's doing is right low-down, and I can't abide it any longer." He looked down at Susan. "Are you with me?"

"I've always been with you." She smiled tremulously up at him.

"What are they planning to do?" Steve asked.

"The gang? They don't really have no plan. Just starve you out as far as I know. Beau and some of the hands were pretty bad off for liquor when I left. And the rest were getting tired. They'll probably sleep it off until early morning unless someone gets a bright idea before then.

"This place is a fortress. It's almost impossible to get within shooting range without getting shot first. I slid in on my belly right next to the rock face, but I doubt any of them are that determined. Might ought to keep a watch thataway, though."

"Lobo will keep watch," Steve replied.

Wyatt and Susan settled on the sofa in the flickering glow of the fireplace, the only light in the room. Steve relieved Banjo at the window, and Megan tried to keep from nodding as the heat from the fire relaxed her weary muscles. Hands clasped under his head, Banjo stretched out on his back before the hearth.

"This is cozy as a goose in a corncrib," Banjo drawled. "It'll be good havin' another man to spell us with the watching." He looked over at Wyatt. "Feel up to takin' the next round?" Suddenly his expression changed. He stared at Wyatt's feet stretched out, ankles crossed, before him.

"Sure, I can take it." Wyatt noticed Banjo's wrinkled brow. "What's the matter?"

"Where'd you get those boots?"

"Bought them in Cheyenne this spring. There's an old-timer up there who makes them." He looked down at the feathery pattern stamped on the light brown leather. "Why?"

"Were you wearin' 'em the night Harrington was killed?"

"I reckon." He sat up straighter. "I've worn 'em to all occasions since I got them." He stopped. "Wait a minute. Wait. . .a. . .minute." He stared overhead. "I didn't wear them that night. I hadn't intended on going because I was sick all day. Clyde Turner broke the heel off his good boots. We're about the same size, so I told him to go ahead and wear mine. Then I got to feeling better. I hated to disappoint Susan, so I shined up my old black boots and went anyway. I let Clyde have my new ones. I didn't want to take them back after I told him he could have them."

"I found those boot prints at the edge of the clearing where Harrington was killed," Banjo explained. "More than likely the man who wore them killed Harrington. The murderer stood there awhile, dropped a green juniper twig he'd been chewing, and stepped out like you do if you're throwing a knife."

"You mean Clyde Turner was wearing those boots that night?" Steve spoke from the window."

"Does he chew green juniper twigs?" Megan asked, now wide-awake.

"He chews some kind of wood. I don't rightly know if it's juniper or not. I never looked close." Wyatt looked around. "You think Clyde did it? Why would he do a fool thing like that?"

"We haven't put it all together yet," Steve said, "but I think we're finally barking up the right tree."

"Well, I'll be." Wyatt propped his right ankle on his left knee. "You may have a loop on the right steer at that. He sure has been coming off all high and mighty since Harrington died. Especially with the hands."

"He makes me feel creepy inside." Susan moved even closer to Wyatt.

Before daylight the next morning, Megan broke the thin layer of ice on her washbasin and bathed her face to drive sleep from her eyes. She had left Susan sleeping in the bedroom to stir up the fire in the kitchen stove, add a few small logs, and set on the coffeepot.

"Been a long night," Steve commented from his post. His face was grizzled, his hair tousled. Only his keen eyes seemed the same as they had been last night when she had finally gone to bed. Wyatt stretched out on the floor, and Banjo snored softly on the sofa.

"Coffee'll be ready soon." She pulled the flour bin from under the counter. "If that'll help." She smiled in his direction.

"Having someone to talk to helps." He leaned back, resting an elbow on the back of his chair. "I took over for Banjo about two hours ago. Nothing's moving out there as far as I can tell."

"I hope we don't have to pass another night like last night." She scooped some flour into a large bowl. "What are we going to do?"

"I'm not planning on being the main attraction at any neck stretching party. I can tell you that." He rotated his shoulders, working out the kinks. "If we have to fight, we'll fight. If the marshal comes and we can convince him I'm innocent, we'll do that."

It was a haggard crew that gathered at the breakfast table at dawn. Susan's face was strained; her eyes seemed too large for her thin face. She hovered near Wyatt, speaking little and glancing often toward the front windows. Megan bustled about setting on the oatmeal, biscuits, and bacon more from the need to stay busy than from any need to hurry.

"With your permission, Chamberlin," Banjo said as they sat down at the table, "I feel the need to ask the good Lord's help during this day. Would you mind if I said a short prayer before we ate?"

"Help yourself, Banjo. We can use all the help we can get."

Megan watched Steve closely to see if he was making light of Banjo's request, but his face was expressionless, his eyes serious. He bowed his head, studying the edge of the table while Banjo prayed.

"Dear Lord, we know You have a reason for everythin' that comes into our lives. I pray that You would watch over us today. Protect us from harm and teach us all to trust in You. Amen."

A dreadful lethargy caused by weariness and anxiety hovered over the stone house that morning. Conversation lagged. Everyone was too consumed with their own thoughts and fears for small talk. The sun was high above the horizon before the long awaited something happened.

"Chamberlin! Come on out. I want to talk to you. It's Ben Walker, the marshal."

"It may be a trick." Megan took a step in Steve's direction.

"That's Walker's voice all right." Steve peered out the window, keeping his body behind the stone wall. "I can see him. He's astride his horse to the north of the meadow. The gang is behind him."

"Yes, sir, Mr. Walker," Steve called back. "But I'm keeping my guns."

"Keep them. I only want to talk to you."

Megan could scarcely breathe as she watched Steve check his guns, slide them loosely into their holsters, and walk to the door. Putting on his hat and buffalo coat, he went out. Swiftly putting on her wrap and picking up her Henry, she shoved a handful of shells into her pocket and followed him. Banjo had already stepped through the door ahead of her, buffalo gun in hand.

Banjo stopped five yards behind and to the right of Steve at the edge of the dooryard. Megan stood a few feet from Banjo. She could feel her pulse pounding in her neck. Her eyes were riveted to the men in front of them.

Megan sensed someone walking up behind her. She turned to see Wyatt pass by her and stand a few feet to her left, his shooting iron ready. Susan stood on the edge of the porch huddled in her coat, looking small and helpless.

But the rifle she held was neither small nor helpless.

Chapter 20

There he is, Marshal! Take him!" His breath billowing out in white clouds as he spoke, Beau stepped his horse ahead of the ten to fifteen men behind the lawman. Their number had diminished considerably during the freezing night.

"That's high-handed talk comin' from a fellow whose sister stands with the other side," Banjo remarked dryly. His voice, though not loud, carried far in the icy air. "The rest of you brave hombres are hangin' far back for men acting in the cause of justice," Banjo continued, his voice thick with sarcasm. "You, Harper." The storekeeper jerked his head around at the sound of his name. "Are you here because you think Chamberlin's guilty or because it's Harrington money that keeps you in business?

"And Jim Sanders. If Chamberlin were hung for the murder of Harrington, it would take suspicion off you, wouldn't it?" Sanders studied the ground. "Everyone remembers the old score you had with Harrington." Banjo's eyes shifted to the two hulking figures in the rear.

"I can't say I'm surprised to see you, Henry, Al. You know where your bread's buttered, don't you?" As each man heard his name, there was a marked change of attitude. The thought uppermost in each man's mind was how to bow out without losing face.

"Marshal, I'd like to swear out a warrant," Steve said.

"You'd like to swear out a warrant?" Beau's look was lethal enough to kill a rabbit at twenty yards.

"Quiet, Harrington," Walker ordered. "Let him have his say."

"I'd like to swear out a warrant on Clyde Turner, otherwise known as Charlie Taylor, on suspicion of the murder of Victor Harrington."

Turner stiffened. He slowly took from his mouth the twig he was chewing.

"He's talking through his hat, Marshal," Turner said easily, back on balance again.

"Check that twig he has in his hand," Steve countered. "How many men do you know that chews juniper?" He reminded Walker of the twig found at the Running M after the murder and told him of the matching twig found at the campsite near the Hohner range.

In a furtive movement, Turner flicked the twig he held away from him.

Sanders saw what Turner was up to and slid from the saddle to pick up the twig. He handed it to Walker.

"You've got to be crazy," Turner said, angrily. "Why would I want to kill my own boss?"

"Maybe because he was getting too close to catching you rustling his cattle," Steve said. "Right, Henry?" Henry Hohner's jaw dropped open, his buckteeth sticking out. Seeing his reaction, Steve plowed on. "We found that pretty little box canyon on the Hohner range. The perfect place to hide stolen cattle until time to take them to the railroad. You boys had a real nice setup, didn't you?"

"It wasn't us!" Panic-stricken, Al spoke up. His eyes turned toward Turner. "All we did was pick up a few cows and keep them hid away. He did all the rest," he babbled, jerking his horse's head back as he sawed the reins.

"You idiot!" Furious, Turner railed at Al, the scar twitching as he spoke. "Don't you know what he's doing? He's trying to trap you into admitting something."

"Turner's knife slick, Walker," Steve continued. "I knew him in the war. His real name's Charlie Taylor. I saw him throw a knife and kill a man. It took me awhile to place him because of that scar. But I know him all right. If you look a little deeper, I believe you'll find he's been prodding young Harrington and fomenting the trouble we've had between us."

"He's right, Marshal." It was Curly, the bald, Rocking H hand that spoke up this time. "I've heard Turner making hints and pushing young Harrington. Us boys have had about all we kin take. I say he's your man." He walked his horse across the field to Steve and turned around, watching Clyde Turner carefully.

Slowly, thoughtfully, Slim and two others joined him.

"I don't know about the rest of you folks," Sanders said, turning his horse, "but I'm heading home. I can smell a polecat when I get next to one."

Turner cast an ugly glance in his direction.

Pointedly ignoring him, Sanders prodded his horse to a trot. The rest of the townsfolk followed, leaving Beau and Turner alone with Marshal Walker in the meadow.

"Stay where you are, Turner." The lawman's revolver was in his hand. "You're riding back with me. I'll get your accomplices by and by. Right now I want you." He took Turner's guns, pulled two pigging strings from his saddle, and tied Turner's hands to the pommel.

"I should have killed you, Chamberlin!" Stark hatred glared from Turner's weasel face. "I should have killed you when I first recognized you. You are the only one who knew who I was. I tried on the trail, but I missed. All I did was burn your horse and see if he'd do the job. If I had made that shot, I could have had it all. The Rocking H and everything that goes with it."

"Your days are over, Turner." Steve spoke without rancor. "There's no place here for your kind."

Beau had not uttered a sound throughout the unfolding of the facts about his father's death. He watched the marshal take Turner away as though he couldn't quite understand what was happening.

"Kill him, Beau!" Clyde Turner yelled in a desperate try for revenge. "Kill Chamberlin! He's the cause of all your trouble! Kill him!"

Marshal Walker silenced Turner with a lash of his quirt. He grabbed the reins of Turner's horse, and they trotted into the trees.

Absently looking at the spot where they disappeared, Beau was as still as though carved in marble. The four Rocking H hands slowly followed the marshal. Wyatt returned to Susan on the steps. Their footsteps and the creak of the door told Megan they had gone inside. Banjo relaxed, resting his rifle in the crook of his arm, barrel down. He stepped forward to meet Steve as they broke ranks. Megan, too, stepped forward. But a movement caught her eye. Looking back she stopped dead in her tracks, horror gripping her.

It happened in an instant, a split second. There was no time to cry out, no time to warn Steve. There was only time for action. Totally by reflex, Megan raised her rifle to her shoulder as Beau Harrington sighted his Winchester at Steve. Their shots, only a fraction of a second apart, sounded as one.

But Megan was too late.

Beau dropped his rifle and grabbed his right biceps, but Megan had already forgotten him. She had eyes only for Steve sprawled on the snowy ground before her, a thick red stain spreading from a point just above the knee of his left leg. Banjo already knelt beside him.

"Get a cloth to tie around his leg to stop the bleeding!" he ordered.

Megan pulled her handkerchief from her sleeve. Quickly Banjo tore the thin white cloth in half, tied the ends together, and wrapped it tightly around Steve's thigh. He and Wyatt carried him, half-conscious, to Megan's room, where they put him on the bed.

Steve's eyelids fluttered. He opened them wide and tried to sit up.

He fell back with a groan. "What happened?"

"That fool boy Harrington shot you in the leg," Banjo said between tense lips. He stepped aside so Megan could cut away Steve's trouser leg with a small pair of scissors. "Wyatt's going for Doc Leatherwood." He laid his hand gently on Megan's arm. "You know what to do. I'd best go have a look at the boy out yonder."

Megan didn't answer. She was only conscious that the bleeding must be stopped. She was terrified that the bone might be broken. She raced for a bowl of flour from the bin. Taking a handful of flour, she packed the wounds, front and back, and wrapped the leg tightly with a wide strip hurriedly cut from a sheet. Susan's sobs reached her from the living room, but she paid no mind. There would be time for Susan later.

Rushing to the closet, she found the paper of powder given her by the doctor for the pain in her shoulder. She poured a generous portion into a glass, mixed it with a little water, and held it to Steve's lips.

"What's that?" he grimaced, then shivered.

"For the pain." She smoothed his hair back from his pain-creased brow.

There's so little I can do, she agonized. *If something happens to him, how can I go on without him?*

She remembered the sound of his anxious voice calling her name when she was lying on the ground beside the overturned buckboard. She thought about his strong arm around her, supporting her on that torturous journey home. His insistence on getting Jeremy better care. Their quiet walks and talks beside the lake. He was security, comfort, and happiness to her as she had never known before.

With unspeakable dread she watched the crimson stain spreading over the bandage.

"Please, God," she begged with all her being, "stop the bleeding and let him get well. I know it may be selfish, but I can't face life without him."

Yet, even as she prayed, she knew she would face life without him next spring.

She walked into the living room when she heard the front door close.

It was Banjo. "How is he?"

"Dozing off and on. I gave him some of the pain powder I had left." She wrung her hands. "How long until the doctor can get here?"

"It could be another two hours; it could be tonight. There's no way of tellin'." He pulled off his coat and hung it on a peg. "Your brother's not hurt bad, Miss Susan." On the sofa, leaning against the back, Susan lifted a red, puffy face from her arm. Her breath came in ragged sobs. "He only got a flesh wound in his upper arm," Banjo told her.

"I didn't intend on killing him," Megan said reasonably. "I figured if I shot his gun arm, it would stop him."

Eyebrows raised, Banjo stared.

"You intended on shootin' his arm?"

"Yes. Why?"

"Well, I'll be a jackrabbit's hind leg. It must have been a hundred yards."

"Where is he?" Susan stood and leaned to look out the window.

"He was on the ground trying to get a grip on his Winchester when I went out. He was whining like a baby. Somehow he'd managed to get his bandanna tied around the wound. I tried to help him, but he swore at me and knocked my hand away. Didn't say where he was headed, but he was in a big hurry to get there."

"I'm sorry, Susan." Megan put her hand on her friend's shoulder.

"I'm not upset about that. Beau got what he's been asking for. It's hearing about Pa's murder that's got me upset. To think that Clyde Turner was the one. Just remembering all the times I was near him makes my insides turn over."

The doctor arrived shortly after noon. With haunted eyes Megan watched him unwrap the wounded leg.

"How bad is it, Doc?" Steve asked through thin, white lips.

"I've seen worse." After cleaning the wounds, Dr. Leatherwood made a close inspection. "I doubt that the bone is broken, but you'll have to take it real easy on the leg for a month or so." He smiled at Megan. "It's a good thing your wife knew how to stop the bleeding so soon. If she follows my instructions as well as that, you should be up and around before long." He rebandaged the leg, gave Steve another dose of powder, and stepped outside for a word with Megan.

"You did fine." He nodded appreciatively to Megan as Banjo looked on. "I'm glad the bullet passed clean through. The wound will drain better, and we won't have to go through the ordeal of digging out a bullet. Change the bandage and put on antiseptic twice a day to try to ward off any infection. That's the biggest danger. Infection. Here's some more of that powder. Don't give it to him unless he needs it, but he'll be needing it for the next two or three days." He put on his hat. "I'll be back around to see him day after tomorrow."

The doctor's words eased Megan's fears a little, but the possibility of infection was an ugly specter hovering over the injured man's bed. Megan had to force herself to leave him long enough to do a minimum of cooking and washing. She wanted to be with him every second.

~

"I've been a fool," Steve said tersely through the pain the next day.

Concerned, Megan felt his forehead before answering.

"No, I'm not delirious," he said, ruefully. "I'm thinking more clearly than I have for years." Beads of sweat stood out on his forehead. Megan wiped them away with a cool cloth. "A few inches higher and I'd have been a goner, Megan. It's put me to thinking about what my life means. If it's really important." He took a sip from the glass she offered him.

"You're tiring yourself by talking so much," she cautioned.

"I've got to tell you this," he insisted with an impatient wave of his hand, "so don't stop me." He paused while she pulled a chair close to his bed. "I guess I've been turning it over in my mind for a long time, but it never struck me as so important until now. I'm talking about my standing with God. Like you and Banjo have been trying to tell me. I want to make peace with God and let Him have what's left of my life."

Megan's hand crept to his brow again. It was cool and clammy.

"I don't think I'm going to die, if that's what you're thinking." He attempted a weak smile. "I want to be ready to live."

"I'll get Banjo." Forgetting her coat, Megan flew from the house to where Banjo and Wyatt were building a makeshift stable. "Steve wants you, Banjo," she panted. "Please come."

Banjo dropped the board he held and followed Megan. When they reached the house, she caught his sleeve.

"He says he wants to make his peace with God."

"What? Is he worse?"

"I don't think so. He says he wants to get ready to live, not to die, and he wants to live his life for the Lord."

"Thank God," he breathed. "If you'll get me your Bible, I'll go in."

Megan fetched the sacred book from her trunk and handed it to Banjo. She listened as Banjo explained the story of salvation in the same simple way he had told her.

"Just tell God you're a sinner and you want to claim the blood of Jesus to wash away your sin," he concluded.

Pain-wracked as he was, Steve's voice was strong.

"Lord, I want You to save me. I'm a rotten sinner. I know Jesus died for me, and I want You to take my life and make something useful from it. Amen."

Megan's eyes were misty when she looked up. She was surprised to see tears streaming down Banjo's face.

"I believe I could use some of that powder, Megan." Steve's face was ashen. His eyes closed as Megan scurried to bring him what he asked for. He swallowed the medicine without opening his eyes and sank back to the pillow.

Outside the bedroom door, Banjo drew a large red handkerchief from his pocket and loudly blew his nose.

"I tell you, seein' someone born into the family of God is almost as good as bein' born again yourself," he said, wiping his eyes.

"God sent you here, Banjo," Megan said with conviction, love welling up inside of her. "I'm so glad He did." Her voice quivered.

"Thank Him, not me." His voice was husky. "All I did was tell you. God made it real in your hearts."

⌒

The next evening Steve felt well enough to have Banjo visit for a few minutes.

"You wouldn't believe the shootin' that little lady did that morning," Banjo declared. "She saw Harrington draw and in one motion sighted and shot him in the arm. She hit what she shot at. Dead center."

"Is that right?" Steve looked over at Megan's faint blush.

"I did it before I thought." She was almost apologetic. "All I knew is that for some insane reason Beau had decided to kill you, and I had to stop him."

Steve grinned at Banjo. "I'm glad she's on my side." He shifted to a more comfortable position. "What happened to Beau?"

"He lit a shuck. Took some stuff from the ranch, and they haven't seen hide nor hair of him since. Miss Susan's taking it pretty good, considerin'. I guess she's glad to have some peace after all the trouble. She's got spunk, that one. She made Curly foreman and had a talk with the men, Wyatt tells me. They're all staying on."

The next long week, Megan nursed the man who was her husband in name only. It was gratifying to feel the closeness she sensed between them since he accepted Christ. They had quiet chats when he felt up to it, and she shared with him how God had given her peace she could not explain through the past months of hardship.

She was with him every available minute of the day, feeding him hot soup when he could swallow it, boiling water for preparing fresh bandages, changing linen, and doling out pain powder until she fought collapse.

"Megan." Steve caught her hand as she passed by. "You're pushing yourself too hard. It'll be no help to me if you wear yourself out to the point where you have to be cared for yourself." He had shown encouraging signs of improvement the last two days. "Go up to the loft and lie down. Banjo can get me anything I need when he comes in from choring."

"But—"

He waved aside her protest.

"Go. That's an order."

It took her last bit of strength to climb the ladder and lie down on Steve's cot. Her head hurt. Her eyes closed before she touched the pillow. The house had a tomblike silence, and it was fifteen hours before she opened her eyes again.

"It looks good," Dr. Leatherwood said a few days later as he replaced the bandage. "We want it to heal from the inside out, not close over too soon, or the wounds will fester." He winked at Steve. "You've got a good nurse there."

"I know it." Steve smiled at Megan. "She's done everything but pass her hand over the place and say, 'Be healed.'" Some of his original color had returned, though he still had spasms of pain now and then.

"How soon can I walk on it?"

"If you had a crutch, you could get up now." The doctor buttoned his buffalo coat around his thick neck. "But under no circumstances are you to put any weight on it." He picked up his bag. "And take it slow at first. Fifteen minutes, then twenty, and so on."

"Will do." Steve shook Leatherwood's hand. "And thanks.

"Thanks to you, too," Steve said to Megan when the doctor had gone.

"You're getting better. That's thanks enough." Confused, Megan picked up his water pitcher and carried it to the spring to refill it. She yearned to be near him, but she wanted to run away from him at the same time. She was afraid. Afraid he might not care, afraid she was reading things into his words that didn't exist.

"When Susan was here today, she told me she and Wyatt are planning a December wedding," Megan remarked to Steve as she sat by his bed the next afternoon. She was cutting bandages from a large piece of white cloth.

"So soon?" He looked up from the newspaper Banjo had brought from town.

"It's long enough, after all they've been through. I know it hasn't been a year since her father died, but she's all alone with Beau leaving her like he did. Folks should understand." She avoided his eyes, so probing and somehow close these days. "I got a letter from Em, too."

"How's Jeremy?"

"Out of the woods, thank the Lord. I can't tell you how relieved I am. Em says he may be able to leave the sanitarium in the early spring." A clammy hand squeezed her heart at the thought of returning to Baltimore. "I'll be back some-time around then."

"Will you?" Something in his voice forced her to look at him. His gaze pierced to the core of her being.

She didn't know how to answer his question. She knew she must go back East no matter how much she longed to stay. She must look after Jeremy. Tormented thoughts cascaded over her as she stared at him, her throat too tight to make a sound. She looked away, cutting blindly at the cloth, wishing she could hide from him. He was torturing her by looking at her like that.

"Megan." He laid the paper aside and sat up. "Megan, don't run away from me. I can't stand it any longer. Please."

Against her will, she raised her head and met those eyes again.

"I don't want you to go, Megan. I want you to stay." He searched her troubled face for the answer. "I know I'm not the greatest fellow that ever came along, but I love you, Megan. With all my heart and soul, I love you. All this"—a wide sweep of his hand included all that lay around them—"would be worthless to me if you weren't here."

Her lip began to quiver, and her eyes filled with tears. She pressed her eyes tight and looked down as the tears spilled down her cheeks.

"My dear." Anxiety clouded his features. "I'm sorry if I've upset you."

"No. It's not that." She shook her head, fumbling for her handkerchief. "I just. . .don't know what to. . .it's what I've been asking the Lord for ever since I've been saved. Of course I'll stay."

Sunbeams broke through the clouds like the first bright rays after a storm. He reached out and grasped her wrist, pulling her to him. Her scissors clattered to the floor, but no one heard.

"I can't believe it's true," Megan whispered in a moment. A lone tear trickled down her cheek, inconsistent with her glorious smile.

Steve took her handkerchief and dabbed at the spot.

"If you're happy, why do you keep crying?"

"I don't know," she said with a little laugh. "I can't help it."

"We'll send for Jeremy as soon as he's released."

"And Em," Megan added. "Don't forget Em." She nestled her head on his strong shoulder.

"Certainly Em. When you answered my ad, you were so scared and brave at the same time that it changed something inside me. I wanted to help you, to protect you from all the trouble you were having. That's why I was so anxious for you to come with me."

"Why didn't you tell me before this? There were times when I thought I'd die if you didn't care."

"When I got to know you, I saw what a conscientious, uncorrupted person you are, Megan. I'm nothing but a riverboat gambler. I couldn't ask you to stay with the likes of me."

Megan shook her head. "I never felt that way."

"Back then that possibility never occurred to me, but when I turned my life over to God, all those guilty feelings disappeared. I began to wonder if I may have a chance with you now that we share the same faith." He gave her a loving squeeze. "I want to build a new life, Megan. With you."

He tilted her chin up so he could look into her eyes. "There's only one thing I regret."

"There is?" Flickering doubt crossed her face.

"Yes. I can't ask you to marry me."

"Oh." The smile reappeared. "Well, you could say it anyway."

"Will you be my wife, Megan?" Infinite tenderness was in the question.

"Yes."

The fear, the empty longing, the anguish were rooted out and washed away by a flood tide of joy.

Whistling softly to himself, Banjo came into the house intending to ask Steve how he wanted the stable door set. When he reached the open door of Megan's room, he drew back. It took only a fraction of a second for him to realize how matters stood. Without hesitating, he tiptoed out of the house and quietly closed the door behind him.

When he reached the middle of the yard, he couldn't hold the joy any longer. He let about a thundering "Eee-hah!" and raised his hat in salute. A song gushed out with all his strength behind it:

> *"Praise to the Lord, the Almighty*
> *The King of creation!*
> *O my soul, praise Him,*
> *For He is thy health and salvation!"*

Megan heard his words, and her spirit joined in the benediction. She wanted to shout.

Em's Only Chance

Dedication

To my children:
David, Darrell, Miriam, Jonathan,
Nathaniel, Steven, and Jim.
Without you my life would be so empty.

Chapter 1

Em Littlejohn rushed to the open door of the cabin, where shouts of laughter and playful barks drifted in from the Colorado ranch yard. The broiling August sun made her squint and shade her eyes. In spite of the hurry, Em paused for a smile.

Eleven-year-old Jeremy Wescott rolled on the grass in a mock wrestling match with Lobo, the wolf-faced dog his sister had tamed.

"Jeremy! Come in this instant! You'se got to change now or we'se a-gonna be late for the barbecue!"

Lobo nipping at his heels, Jeremy trotted toward the cabin, his face glistening, his strawlike hair standing on end.

"Wash up in the spring out back," she continued. "I'se got your clothes laid out in the loft." The mouth-tingling aroma of freshly baked bread that filled the house touched her senses as she stepped back a pace.

"Is he coming, Em?" Megan Chamberlin, Jeremy's grown-up sister appeared in the doorway of the master bedroom. She smoothed the full skirt over her rounded abdomen. With the baby due in just eight weeks, this outing to the Rocking H would be her last for some months.

In answer to Megan's question, fifty-two inches of boy burst into the room. Pulling at his shirt buttons, he took a curved route past the two-person settee in the living room, around the gingham-covered dining table, and through the kitchen to the back door. His destination lay a wagon-length behind the house at a stone-lined basin where a spring flowed from a crack in the orange rock cliff looming five hundred feet above them.

Jeremy's words came from over his shoulder. "I'll be ready in a jiff, Em." The slam of the back door put a period to Lobo's final bark.

Tall and lean Em wore a new navy dress with gathered skirts and only two petticoats. The ex-slave's brown face had soft lines around the eyes, across the forehead, and beside full lips. Her cheeks had the texture of tissue paper, crumpled then flattened again. Black hair—gray strands woven through it—lay in shiny cornrows straight back from her forehead, ending in a knot at her nape. Tender devotion filled Em's wide-set eyes as she gazed after the boy. Her boy. As much hers as if he were her own flesh. For twenty-two years, Em had showered every ounce of her lavish mother love on the Wescott children, Megan and

Jeremy. At the end of Mr. Lincoln's War, the sobbing woman had begged Katie Wescott to let her stay with the family. Megan's widowed mother had hugged her childhood playmate, and with tears of her own, Katie had pledged that Em would always have a place with them.

Megan joined Em beside the dining table. Navy gingham curtains gently lifted in a soft breeze. "It's hard to believe, isn't it, Em? Fifteen months ago Jeremy could barely sit up. Often I thought that rheumatic fever would take him." She embraced the slim lady beside her. "I could watch him run and play from dawn to dusk just counting my blessings."

A lump tightened Em's throat. "You'se right about that, Miss Megan," she said huskily. "That boy's a seven day's wonder." She shook her head as though to shake off the sentimental mood and eased out of Megan's arms. "I'd best finish hookin' up these shoes. We'se a-gonna be late for sure." Three paces later, Em disappeared into her quarters—a new addition built off the dining area at the west side of the cabin, a narrow room with a plank floor, a cot, and four pegs on the wall.

A solid stone wall at the front and squared logs made up the rest of the Circle C cabin. Directly across from the front door, the master bedroom cut into the open living area, leaving an L-shaped space. The short section jutting toward the back was the kitchen. At the center of the front wall, smooth stones fitted closely together on the gray floor and on the gleaming orange fireplace. Two pegs over the thick mantel held the Henry rifle that dainty Megan Chamberlin could use to outshoot her husband.

The cabin was no bigger than a carriage house in the Old South where the Wescotts had their roots. The open-beamed ceiling over the front half of the cabin gave the impression of space. The floor of the loft—Jeremy's domain—formed a ceiling to the bedroom and kitchen at the back.

⌐

Twenty minutes later the buckboard lurched ahead with Joe Calahan—the Circle C's only hand—holding the reins. Known to everyone as Banjo, his innate kindness and good humor had won the hearts of Megan and her husband, Steve. The old cowhand had helped them find Christ last November.

As usual, Jeremy sat between Em and Banjo in front. After Jeremy and Em's arrival, Banjo had built a second seat on the buckboard. Steve and Megan always sat in back. Banjo called theirs the Lovers' Seat.

"Can I hold the reins, Banjo?" Jeremy raised his pleading face toward the grizzled cowpoke.

"Soon's we cross the creek, Jem," came the answer. "You remember the words to "Arise My Soul, Arise"? At Jeremy's nod, Banjo led out, his rough voice filling the air, "Arise, my soul, arise; shake off thy guilty fears. . . ."

The buckboard rattled around the tasseled, rustling cornfield, and the house was quickly hidden from view. Heat shimmered down from a merciless sun. A brown grasshopper surprised Em by jumping on her skirt. Grimacing, she quickly flicked it off.

Busily sniffing, feathery tail high, Lobo followed the wagon to the creek bordering the lower edge of the gently sloping field.

"Go home, Lobo!" Steve called, waving at the dog. Ears up, eyes watchful, Lobo stood on the edge of the trickling water, tail softly waving, until the wagon swayed over the creek, up the rutted incline, and out of sight.

Traveling southwest, the little party bounced along a rough trail through rolling hills randomly covered with towering firs and spindly pines. Beside wagon-driver Jeremy, Em let her body roll with the pitching wagon. Was it only twelve weeks since she'd walked garbage-laden streets filled with clanging trolleys, clomping horses, and clamoring newsboys? The stench of animal and human filth had shrouded everything.

Like overflowing buckets, Em's lungs drew up the pine-scented air. Her fingertips tingled. After scratching out a bare existence during the seven tedious years since the war, Em felt reborn. A thousand times she'd prayed for God to help her suffering family. Now that the blessing had fallen, she could hardly contain it.

When Banjo's song finished, the only sound besides Jeremy's shrill, excited voice was the sweet trill of a meadowlark. Before them lay a sparkling green and brown world with a wide blue dome for a lid. Fluffy, cotton-wool clouds floated from invisible threads.

Again Banjo lifted his voice toward heaven. "There is a fountain. . ."

The wagon's right front wheel dropped into a dry puddle. Em gripped the seat and blended her contralto with Banjo's bass.

The Chamberlin party arrived at the Rocking H an hour before suppertime. Five times the size of the Circle C, the Rocking H had belonged to Victor Harrington. After he'd been murdered, it had passed to his daughter, Susan, and her husband, Wyatt Hammond. Susan and Wyatt shared the running of the outfit. Married only eight months before, they were more than lovers. Wyatt and Susan were partners.

At the last rise, Rocking H buildings came in view. Banjo said, "Thanks, Jem. I'll take over from here." He retrieved the reins from Jeremy's fists and pulled the wagon to a creaking halt beneath a cottonwood on the edge of the compound.

The Rocking H sprawled before them—a circle of buildings around a center yard. The ranch yard looked like an ant hive today: women with baskets of food, a few men carrying sawhorses and boards to make tables, and others carrying benches. Sizzling beef sent up an odor that made all comers glance at the time, wishing away the minutes until time to dig in.

While happily greeting the guests around her, Susan organized the table quickly filling with baked beans, potatoes of every kind, vegetables, and mountains of biscuits. On the edge of the clearing, a black man tended the barbecue pit—a wide hole filled with glowing coals. Two feet above the heat source, a glistening side of beef turned slowly, skewered on a six-foot pole with a handle on one end. This was the source of that heavenly aroma.

Jeremy leaped to the ground the moment Banjo stepped down. He scampered across the grassy yard toward the beef, ready with fifty questions for the cook.

Banjo ambled around the wagon to help Em alight.

"Thank you kindly, Mr. Banjo." Her words had a soft, husky quality that was easy to listen to.

"Now, Em," Banjo playfully chided, "you and I've been gettin' on right fine, but that mister stuff has got to go, or we'll be fallin' out. Ain't nobody ever mistered me in my life."

She reached into the back of the wagon for the basket full of bread, baked that morning. "Yes, sir," she said, then halted when she saw Banjo's eyebrows raised in mock indignation.

"Yes, what?"

"I mean, yes, Banjo."

"That's better." Banjo's friendly grin summoned a wide smile from Em, showing glistening teeth.

Laughing, Em added, "You is a caution, Banjo. And that's for sure."

During Banjo's bantering with Em, Steve had carefully eased Megan down from the wagon. He placed her hand on his arm and covered it with his own. The foursome strolled toward the low, wide ranch house. Half a dozen men lounged on the broad porch, chewing tobacco and swapping yarns.

Striding shoulder to shoulder, the Rocking H foreman, Curly Hanna, and his boss, Wyatt Hammond, strode toward them, welcoming grins gracing both faces. Wyatt's new tawny beard gave him a jolly appearance. Shorter than long, lean Wyatt, Hanna outweighed his boss by almost sixty pounds. At the edge of his wide hat, bushy eyebrows contained every hair on Curly's bullet-shaped head.

Wyatt tugged the brim of his flat-crowned brown hat as he nodded to Megan. He punched Banjo's shoulder, then grabbed Steve's hand. "Good to see you folks! How's life treatin' you?"

"Couldn't be better." Steve clasped Wyatt's hand. He shook Curly's meaty paw. "How'd the cattle drive go?"

Curly's words came forth strident and loud, the voice of a man used to giving orders. "Great! We lost nary a head, found good grazing all the way, and didn't see hide nor hair of any Injuns. We got back three days ago."

Slim and girlish, her strawberry-blond ponytail gleaming in the late afternoon sun, Susan Hammond arrived ten steps after her husband. She put her arms around Megan. "Megan! How are you? It seems like weeks since we've talked." She glanced at Wyatt, Curly, and Steve jawing with Banjo. "Let's leave the men to talk about their favorite subject and find us a nice seat in the shade." She touched Em's arm. "I'm glad you came, Em." Arm in arm, Susan and Megan strolled to a bench beneath a wide oak.

Behind the younger women, Em took stock of the busy scene before her. The party atmosphere reminded her of another time, another life. She could almost hear the vibrant voice of Megan's young mother, the laughter of elegant guests, the slaves dancing in the moonlight after the white folks had gone to bed. Those days had ended years ago, but they lived in Em's memory as vividly as though it were yesterday.

She sensed the same spirit here. Yet she also felt a great difference. In Virginia she had been an integral unit of the plantation. Today, among strangers, she was a little afraid. How would these people react to a black woman, a former slave?

Em carried the basket to the food table. Two ladies arrived within seconds of Em. Neither looked at her. She might have been invisible.

Returning to the bench where Megan exchanged the latest news with Susan, Em's eyes sought out Jeremy. The boy stood before the busy cook, chattering and pointing. Curious, Em observed the dark man turning the spit. She had an urge to walk over to him.

Did he have a family? What had he suffered? How had he come to the Rocking H?

What's wrong with you? she scolded herself. *No one's introduced you to him. You may be more than forty years old, but that don't mean you can rush up to a strange man and ask him his life's story.*

During the next hour, she forced her attention away from the barbecue pit several times.

Suddenly she realized that Mrs. Pleurd—a barrel-shaped woman with quick, birdlike eyes—had stopped to greet Megan. The newcomer glanced at Em, acknowledged Megan's introduction with a noncommittal nod, and turned to Susan. "Are the Feiklins coming?"

"Here they are now!" At Susan's announcement, all eyes turned toward the wagons and carriages amassed on the eastern edge of the yard.

Curious about the newcomers, Em watched their approach with interest. Formerly from Texas, Sheriff Feiklin had brought his family to Juniper Junction only six weeks ago at the invitation of the town council. Rumors flew among the townsfolk that trouble with his oldest daughter had convinced the lawman to accept a position in a new place.

Led by Sheriff Rod and his wife, Sally, the four members of the Feiklin clan strolled across the clearing. A faint breeze rustled the leaves overhead. An irate jay scolded the rude humans below him.

Thick, wide, and strong, Rod walked in the loose-jointed gait of a man long in the saddle. He carried a hefty front paunch that lapped six inches over his belt. His booming voice cut through the hum. "Yes, Mama, Lisa has the basket."

Sally cocked her ear toward him, squinted slightly, and nodded. Eight inches shorter than her husband, Sally had been a beautiful teenager, but time and child-bearing had left her stout, with round, dimpled cheeks. Under his Montana-slope Stetson, her husband's hair was thinning and gray, but hers was thick and black, pulled into a fat bun.

Lisa and Jessica paced behind their parents. Nineteen-year-old Lisa, the elder girl, was a buxom lass with flashing black eyes. She stretched her neck, taking a tally of the guests.

Jessica jabbed her with a sharp elbow. "Lisa!" she whispered. "Don't be so shameless!"

"What's the matter, little sister? Afraid I'll catch a fellow's eye before you?" With long slim fingers, she raked through her thick mane, flipping her hand out as she reached the end.

"Lisa!" Jessica's firm mouth twisted in exasperation.

The pair seemed as unlike as two sisters could be. Lisa's curving cheeks softened her square features, and Jessica's high cheekbones gave the impression of flatness to her heart-shaped face. Lisa had flawless, milky skin. Jessica grew a crop of light freckles across her nose, and her cheeks always blushed.

Both girls had wavy hair that matched the color of a raven's wing, but bright sunlight brought out red highlights in Jessica's high chignon. Held back by two tortoiseshell combs, Lisa's mane cascaded to her waist.

"Afternoon, Mrs. Hammond." Rod Feiklin raised his battered hat. "Mrs. Chamberlin."

"This is Em Littlejohn." Megan stretched her hand toward Em. "Last May she and my brother came to join us from Baltimore."

Feiklin gave a short nod without looking directly at Em. His voice raised five decibels. "Sally, I'll leave you to gossip with the ladies."

His wife nodded. "Okay, Rod." Gathering her wide skirts, Sally settled onto the bench beside Susan. She waved at Lisa and Jessica as though shooing chickens. "Take the basket to the eatin' table and enjoy yourselves, girls."

Lisa hitched the basket closer to her waist and sauntered away. Casting a frustrated glance at her mother, Jessica's lagging steps trailed her sister.

Sally flicked open a fan and dove into the conversation. She squeaked like a young mouse. "How do you like Lisa's new dress? It's sprigged muslin. I finished the hem last night." She plowed ahead, hardly drawing a breath. "I tell you, I had the awfulest time with Rod this morning. The moon's waning, so I wanted him to help me turn our feather bed. Lord knows, it's too heavy for me or the girls." She sniffed. "He told me I'm silly and superstitious. I had to put my foot down. . ."

Em soon tired of the conversation and wandered toward the crowd around the table, hoping to lend a hand. She'd be more comfortable working than listening to Sally's prattle. Jeremy ran to meet Em in the center of the yard.

"Want to see the cow gettin' barbecued?" he asked, his brown eyes sparkling. "Chance is the cook. He let me turn the crank for him." He clutched her hand and pulled.

Em chuckled. "I'm coming, Jeremy. You don't have to drag me." Now that the moment for meeting the cook had arrived, she felt a little shy.

Chapter 2

"Chance, this is Em," Jeremy announced moments later. He might have been introducing the president.

Bent over the bubbling, seared carcass with a dipper of red sauce in his nimble fingers, the cook looked back over his shoulder. He stopped in mid-motion, eyes on Em. Slowly, deliberately, he returned his attention to the beef, poured on the remaining sauce, and straightened to his full height. Orange-red coals hissed as drips fell from the meat.

Though she was above average height, Em's head scarcely reached the bridge of the man's nose.

He ducked his head and said, "Glad to know you, Miss Em. You new in these parts?"

"Yes," Em replied. "I brung Jeremy to the Circle C three months back."

"He's quite a little fella." Chance's expression warmed as he smiled down at Jeremy. With skin the color of coffee mixed with a healthy dose of cream, his high cheekbones made him look almost Hispanic. Deep creases ran down the center of both cheeks and from the corners of his nose to the sides of his mouth. Fixing his gaze on Em, he said abruptly, "You workin' for his family?" He sounded gruff, suspicious.

It wasn't what Em had expected. Her chin rose. "I'm part of his family," she countered, matching stare for stare.

An instant later, Chance relaxed. A grin curved his full, expressive lips. "Where are you from?"

"Virginy." Em glanced at the sauce-smeared bowls set around the pit. "Can I help you with something?"

"Sure enough. In a few minutes I'll cut the meat off the bone. You can slice it into small pieces and carry it to the table." He paused, watching her closely as though trying to make a decision.

"Can I help, too?" Jeremy begged.

Chance chuckled, amused by the boy's anxious face. "Sure can, Jeremy. You hold the handle of the spit so the meat won't move while I'm cutting it." With deft movements his knife carved out a five-pound roast. Using a long fork and knife as pincers, he placed it on the platter Em held ready, then he reached for another from the stack on a stump nearby.

They worked in silence for twenty minutes, a silence punctuated with soft words like, "Move the handle a little to the right, Jeremy," and "Here's another ready for you, Miss Em."

Em looked up to catch Chance watching her again, that questioning slant to his brow. Her face suddenly grew warm. When the last meat plate lay on the table, people began easing toward the food like cows to the barn at milking time. Two barrels of water stood to one side with a dipper hooked over each rim. Bowls, plates, and pans covered every square inch of the table.

Wyatt and Susan stood together facing thirty guests. Wyatt raised his hand high and conversation died. He stroked his beard self-consciously. "We're mighty glad to have you folks with us today. If you don't get enough to eat, it's your own fault." Gentle laughter rose from the ranks.

He continued, "I suppose it's fittin' that we thank the good Lord for the food before we dive in. I'm not much of a hand at prayin', so I'll ask Banjo to do the honors."

Hat in hand, Banjo stepped from the ranks, head bowed. His graying black hair fit close to the scalp, a crease where his hat brim pressed.

Soon afterward Jeremy and Em loaded tin plates and located their family at one of four long tables lined up parallel to the vittles table in the center of the yard. When they arrived, Megan moved closer to Steve to make room for Em. Jeremy scooted in next to his pal Banjo. As the boy sat down, the light softened. Dusk lurked thirty minutes away.

"Where'd you two get off to?" Megan asked.

"I was helping Chance," Jeremy declared. "He let me turn the barbecue spit."

"Chance?" Megan glanced inquiringly at Em.

"He's the cook," Em replied, keeping her eyes on the beef, biscuits, and beans before her.

"Oh, yes. I know who you mean. I never knew his name before."

"He's real nice," Jeremy continued.

Banjo laid down his fork and grasped a tin cup of water, saying, "He's been here about five years, I reckon. Keeps mostly to himself."

"I like him," Jeremy declared. He picked up an ear of roasted corn and opened his mouth wide.

Rancher Sanders and his Mexican wife, the older Feiklins, and the Hammonds filled the remainder of the table. A few feet away sat Jessica and Lisa with their friend Elaine Sanders, an olive-skinned beauty with features like a china doll. At the opposite end of the girls' table lounged the Rocking H hands. Various visitors from town occupied the other two tables.

Twilight brought life instead of sleep—clattering forks on tin plates, teasing and hoots of laughter. Fireflies and crickets opened up for business. Darkness brought blessed relief from the day's sweltering temperatures. Mosquitoes came out to enjoy the cool night air. Two lanterns glowed on each table with more lanterns hung from nails on three trees and a post.

Chance had found a seat with the hands. Halfway through the meal, Em winced when a booming voice sliced the pleasant atmosphere.

"Hey, boy! Fetch me some water, will ya?" Holding his tin cup high in Chance's direction, a Rocking H puncher, Jake Savage, was the brawn behind the voice. Every ounce of 225 pounds, Jake looked fat, but his biceps didn't know it. Woolly black hair brushed his shoulders. "I say, boy! I'm talkin' to you!"

At the end of the table, Chance stabbed a morsel of beef and carefully placed it in his mouth. He chewed three times. Slowly facing Savage, his answer came out low and without expression, but the words carried far. "Get it yourself."

"Right, Savage." Curly Hanna spoke louder than Chance had. "Get it yourself."

Silence hung over the party for a count of three. Placing his palms on the table, Savage eased his bulk over the bench and trudged into the night. A sullen scowl twisted his wide, flat face.

Turning to Rod, Mrs. Feiklin asked loudly, "Why did Hanna say, 'Here's to your health'? Was he making a toast?" A relieved titter passed through the ranks. Normal noises returned. Soon afterward Em watched Chance lift his plate and leave the clearing, his bottom lip thrust forward.

Em met his eyes for a fleeting instant as he passed. She expected to see anger, hostility—and certainly, those emotions were present. But mostly she saw sadness. Hopeless sadness like she'd seen in the eyes of Megan's mother as she scratched out a living in the ghetto of Baltimore, leaning over a washboard and hot iron day after thankless day. The impression pierced her through. Shaken, she couldn't eat another bite.

⌒

After the meal, Sanders's pint-sized wrangler named Ernie put his chin on a fiddle and the young folks set up for a square dance. Lisa Feiklin crossed the clearing to latch on to Wyatt's newest hand, Brent Cavenaugh, a blond giant with a baby face and a strawberry mustache. He came willingly, his eyes admiring Lisa and at the same time challenging her. The only flaw to his perfect features was a brown, dime-size birthmark below his right earlobe. Rocking H men—Curly, Slim, and Amos—made up the rest of the form with Jessica, Elaine, and a stout, giggling girl from Juniper.

"Anybody for a man's sport?" Jake Savage bellowed when the music reached full pitch. "I'll take on any comers. Arm wrestling." He sidled onto the nearest bench, elbow resting on the plank table. His fingers looked like sausages, his lower arm like a ham hock.

"Ahm game," responded a muscular hombre sporting a sardonic grin. He sauntered up and claimed the place across from Savage. He had flat cheeks and a wide, flat nose, giving the impression that someone had pushed his face in.

Noting the man's southern drawl, Megan leaned toward Susan sitting beside her. "Who is that?"

"He's the new hostler in Juniper, Link Hensler. He's a good friend of Brent Cavenaugh, Lisa's dance partner." Em watched the contest from her seat at the next table, ten feet from the loud cowhand who'd tried to intimidate Chance. She hoped to see Savage get a setdown.

Savage leaned forward to clamp down on Hensler's hand. "Elbows stay down, left hand flat on the table," the big man growled, staring into the hostler's brown eyes. Savage's paw made the other man's hand seem slim as a girl's. Hensler had a jagged bumpy scar on the back of his right hand.

Faces grim, the combatants set to. Hensler's biceps bulged. His ruby red lips stretched tight as sweat rose on his forehead. Savage never changed expression. He coolly regarded his opponent as though he were a steer about to feel the lasso.

A dozen people left off watching the dancers and gathered around Hensler and Savage. Em left her seat to move closer. No one uttered a word.

At first locked hands stayed rigidly still. Soon, straining arms began to quiver. Hensler's yellow teeth showed as he grimaced, fighting to keep his hand up. Savage relentlessly pressed, the hint of a smile on his fat lips.

Quick as a rifle shot, Link's arm slammed to the table. Savage let out a victorious hoot. Hensler jerked his hand away, his breath coming in quick gasps. He wrinkled his nose, sniffing as though he smelled something foul, and strode through the circle of spectators.

Immediately, Kip Morgan, foreman of the Running M, filled Link's seat.

At the edge of the crowd, someone brushed Em's arm. She looked up to see Chance standing beside her, his eyes on Savage.

"He's a thorn in your flesh, ain't he?" she asked softly. The words popped out before she knew. Embarrassed, Em clamped her lips together; she drew a little away from Chance.

As his eyes burned into Savage, the black man's voice grated, low and intense, "He's just like all the rest of 'em. Fifteen years ago, he would have been a foreman with a whip in his hand." Abruptly, Chance about-faced and stepped away. Troubled, Em watched his back until he disappeared around the dancers.

At the table, Savage made short work of Morgan. The first dance over, Brent Cavenaugh and Amos McClintock tested their strength while the girls sashayed with another set of partners.

Brent lasted two minutes.

A Missouri farm boy built like a prize bull, McClintock gave Savage a run for his money.

The grin faded from Jake's greasy face. His shoulders bunched; cording stood out on his neck. Normally ruddy, his face looked like a tomato.

Amos's jaw jutted forward. Their clenched hands eased toward Amos, the farm boy. . .hovered. . .trembled. . .inched toward the top of the arc. Jake pulled in a bellyful of air and held it. Murder gleamed in his black eyes. Amos bent his head toward the table as though in prayer. A desperate battle followed with their hands moving only fractions of an inch. The spectators remained perfectly still; not a breath of noise disturbed the gladiators. Moments passed. The suspense rose to excruciating levels.

Sweat on his forehead and upper lip, Amos strained against Jake's mighty arm. Their arms paused at forty-five degrees.

Savage's arm struck wood.

A collective sigh went up from the group.

Hensler declared, "Weren't that a humdinger!"

Immediately, Amos grasped Savage's hand in a shake. "If you hadn't a-been tuckered out, I'd a been a goner, Jake. Next payday, I'll buy you a sarsparilla."

Reluctantly, Savage nodded, his jaw tight. "Sure, Amos. Sure." He unwound himself from the bench and lumbered into the blackness.

"It's about time we headed out," Steve said, lifting Megan's bonnet from the table and handing it to her. "I'll round up Jeremy." He lost himself in the gang headed for leftovers on the food table.

Anxiously scanning Megan's tense face, Em asked, "You okay, Miss Megan?"

Megan squeezed Em's arm. "Just tired, Em. I'm fine."

After saying their good-byes, Megan and Em found Banjo waiting for them beside the buckboard. From this distance, the lanterns looked like giant fireflies. As the untiring fiddle belted out a jig, Banjo handed the ladies up and climbed aboard. Jeremy in tow, Steve's tall form split the shadows. Seconds later the wagon lurched ahead.

"Nice party," Banjo offered as they left the clearing.

"It was grand!" Jeremy declared. "When will they have another'n?"

"Not till next year, Jeremy," Em said, slipping her arm around the boy's thin shoulders. Night breezes relaxed taut muscles; the smell of sweet sage soothed their senses. "But we'll be visitin' with Miss Susan and Mr. Wyatt before long."

"How about Chance?" Jeremy asked quickly.

"I suppose so," Em said softly.

"Unless I miss my guess, we'll be seeing Chance before the month's out," Megan announced. The laugh in her voice sounded rich. "Don't you think so, Em?"

Em cast a questioning glance over her shoulder at Megan. Faint moonlight showed only shadows, but Megan caught Em's movement.

"Don't be so innocent, Em. That man's interested in you."

"In me?" Em's expressive voice told that she doubted Megan's sanity. "That's fiddle-faddle!"

"No, it isn't. I saw how he looked at you."

"At my age? A man? You is out o' your mind, Miss Megan."

"Now hold on," Banjo intervened, chuckling. "I've got a mite o' snow in my hair, but I ain't dead yet. Neither are you."

Megan laughed, delighted. "I have a pink dress we could make over for you, Em, if you want."

"Land sakes, child! Let it rest!"

Megan's soft laughter graced the breeze, but she didn't say anymore.

Chapter 3

Three days after the party, Banjo slouched on the front steps with his left shoulder leaning against the porch railing. His hands worked nimbly over a hollow stick, whittling.

Em and Jeremy had finished the supper dishes an hour ago. Soon afterward Em, Jeremy, and Banjo had wandered outdoors to enjoy the twilight. Lobo lay, nose on paws, at Jeremy's feet below the steps. Weathered wood grain created a rough texture under the hand Jeremy leaned on.

"Is it almost ready, Banjo?" Jeremy asked, his face inches above Banjo's masterpiece.

Churning butter a few feet away, Em called, "Keep your nose out o' the way, son. You're 'bout to git whittled yourself."

"It's almost done, Jem." Banjo held the whistle toward him and rolled it over in his palm. "I may have it finished by tomorrow night."

"Will you teach me to whittle?" Jeremy's adoring eyes begged along with his words.

" 'Course I will. Next time you go into the woods, find you a chunk o' wood about the size of your fist." His knife moved in regular rhythm, peeling off short, paper-thin strips. He glanced at the boy, a twinkle in his mild blue eyes.

"I bet I can guess how old you are, Jem."

Jeremy straightened to attention. "How?"

"Stand on one foot," the old-timer commanded, pointing to the ground. "Right there."

Still watching the cowpuncher, Jeremy obeyed.

"Now hop around in a circle."

Looking skeptical now, Jeremy again obeyed. Em bit her cheek to keep from laughing. Eyes on his young master, Lobo raised his head, ears tilted forward.

With a serious, calculating expression, Banjo carefully monitored the boy's progress and continued staring at him after he'd finished the task.

Ten seconds later he declared, "You're eleven."

Jeremy scrambled up the stairs and dropped into his former seat, his face alive with curiosity. "How did you tell, Banjo?"

Thick hands sent another sliver of wood to the floor. "Miss Megan told me." He guffawed at the boy's I-can't-believe-you-did-that expression. Em's hearty laughter joined with Jeremy's.

A faint yellow light appeared in the open door. Megan had lit a lamp.

Steve called from inside the cabin, "Jeremy, come in now. It's time to wash up. Bedtime."

"Coming, Steve," Jeremy answered, still smiling at Banjo's trick. He brushed off the seat of his pants and trotted inside.

"That boy near worships you, Banjo," Em remarked. The handle of the churn made squish-thunk noises with regular rhythm.

"He reminds me of my own," Banjo murmured, turning the wooden cylinder in his gnarled hands. "Funnin' with Jem helps ease the empty place Todd left."

"I never knowed you had a son."

Banjo blew a wood chip from the whistle and placed the toy in the chest pocket of his overalls. He slid the knife into a sheath at his side. Of their own accord his eyes sought the mountain ridge where the orange sun sleepily nestled, but he looked far beyond boulders and sky and earth. His mind stared into another day, another life.

Em felt a story coming on.

He pushed up the front brim of his battered John B. Stetson until the hat rested on the back of his head. "I was twenty-six when I married an angel with hair the color of anthracite coal and a laugh that would charm the birds down from the trees. A year later God gave us a son. He had my eyes and his mother's smile.

"We owned a little spread near the Red River, ran a few cows and worked a garden. Much like Steve and Megan. My boy follered me everywhere, asking questions, anxious to help me in any little way he could." He paused. For a full minute he sat perfectly still. Drawing in a long breath, he went on.

"Back in '58, I left the ranch for two days to pick up a new bull, a big feller to strengthen my herd. When I got home the ranch was nothin' but a heap of ashes. They killed Mary and took my boy, Em. Kiowas." His eyes glistened. Blinking, he coughed. "I wanted to die, too, but somehow I kept on breathin'.

"I sold the ranch and rode the grub line for nigh on five years—mining here and there, hirin' on as a hand when the notion took me. In '63 I took up with Sheridan. To tell the truth, I still didn't give a hang if I lived or died. Fightin' for the Confed'racy seemed the best way to hang up my saddle.

"Spring of '64 my outfit camped in Mississippi. A young preacher rode out to give us a sermon. Most all of us went to hear him. There wasn't much else to do, and with the Pearly Gates loomin' up in front of us every day, we was ready to hear somethin' from the Good Book. After one o' them meetin's, I went up and talked to the feller. I knew Mary was in heaven, and I wasn't going there." Banjo glanced at Em, a keen edge to his look.

"I made peace with God that night, Em. Jesus is the only reason I can roll out in the morning. To this day I don't know if Todd's alive or dead. I don't even know which would be best. The thought of him livin' off white men's scourings on one of them filthy reservations. . .it's hard to take sometimes." His words faded away. Only the thumping churn handle broke the silence.

Em paused to wipe weary hands on her apron. She smiled, a knowing light in her eyes. When she spoke, Banjo looked toward her, surprised.

"I met Jesus when I'se a child, Banjo. At the Littlejohn house, us house slaves went to church with the white folks. Most o' the people there didn't pay us much mind, like as if we was part of the furniture or somethin'. But sometimes, a little old maiden lady with hair like combed cotton would take us children outside to teach us Bible verses and little songs. Miss Ida her name was." Em's face crinkled as she smiled. "I thought she was an angel come straight down from heaven. I loved her almost as much as I loved Miss Katie Littlejohn, Megan's mama, who was just about my age and my very best friend.

"Miss Ida was the one who told me about Jesus. Me and Miss Katie took Jesus on the same day after one of Miss Ida's classes." She shoved the churn handle down with energy. "One thing I regret, though. I don't know much Bible. I know some gospel slave songs but precious little more than Miss Ida's verses.

"When Miss Katie married Master Wescott, I went to live with them. We never went to church 'cept maybe to camp meetin' now'n agin. Master Wescott wasn't a believer."

Unaware that he was interrupting, Steve appeared in the open doorway. "Like to play me a game of checkers before turning in, Banjo?"

Banjo chuckled. "Does a chicken have lips?" He got to his feet and raised his hands for a stretch.

Em looked up, puzzled. "Chickens don't have lips!" she said.

He grinned at her. "Why, Em. You've been a city slicker too long. Check 'em out next time you feed them."

Steve shook his head. "If you believe that one, Em, he'll be sure to tell you another one tomorrow." Laughing, the men ambled inside.

Em pounded the thickening butter, lost in sweet memories, oblivious to hoofbeats and Lobo's bark announcing a rider. A tall bay gelding cantered into the yard. Startled, she looked up and recognized Chance astride the saddle. Instead of the white shirt and black pants he'd worn when cooking, he filled out a pair of scuffed jeans and a faded blue shirt. He prodded his mount close to the porch and pulled the flat-crowned black hat from his head. Lobo stretched out his nose for a wary sniff at the horse.

"Evenin', Miss Em." His words were friendly yet hesitant.

On the porch, Em stood almost at eye level with the caller. She found her tongue at last. "Steve and Banjo are inside. The door's open. You'se welcome to go right on in."

"I didn't come to see the men. . . I came to see you." At Em's bland expression, he hurried on. "That is, I was wonderin' if I could call on you sometime." He slid his fingers around the brim of his hat, around and around, but his eyes stayed steadily on Em. The last rays of the fading sun made his skin gleam like bronze.

Shock numbed Em's brain. "I reckon it won't hurt anything," she faltered. "Anytime."

Chance smiled, showing gleaming teeth. "I have free time two Saturday afternoons each month and all Sundays. I'll be seein' you." He bowed from the waist, his curls falling over his brow almost to his eyes. Moments later his horse's hoofbeats melted on the breeze.

Jeremy bounded through the door wearing a white knee-length nightshirt. His face glowed from scrubbing, his hair damp around the edges. "Who was that, Em?"

"Chance," Em stated briskly. She grasped the handle of the butter churn and *squee-lunked* it down. "He just stopped to swap howdies."

Jeremy studied her a moment, chirped, "Night, Em," and skipped back inside.

Frantic labor filled almost every waking moment of the next two weeks. Twice the size of last year's plot, the garden yielded bushels of beans, tomatoes, cabbage, carrots, potatoes, and turnips. Every member of the household went to bed with groaning muscles and a wearied mind. Megan tired quickly, so she took the lighter jobs like snapping beans or slicing cabbage.

Late in the afternoon on the thirtieth day of August, Em hurried outside to take the last of the washing from the line while biscuits baked for supper. A thick stew bubbled on the stove. Steve and Banjo looked like miniature cutouts in the garden plot down by the stream, hoeing and pulling out dry tomato plants.

Arms heavy with laundry, Em heard the faint drumming of hoofbeats. She stopped, straining her ears. Suddenly she wondered, *Is today Saturday?* A startled question on her face, she scurried for the house. Lobo, thinking it a game, barked after her.

Inside, she raced to her room to drop the clothes on the narrow bed and lean toward the window. A tall bay with a white blaze and one stocking bounded into the clearing. Em reached her bedroom door in five strides and spoke to Megan, who sat slicing cucumbers at the table.

"Miss Megan, someone's here. I'll be out in a minute." With that she flipped the door shut and pulled at the fastenings on the front of her dress. She grabbed a fresh dress from a wall peg and dragged it on. Dabbing at her hair with a brush, she muttered, "Em, ya knows you'se too old for this kind of foolishness. People your age shouldn't get so het up over a simple little visit. Fiddle-faddle, that's what it is."

A gentle tap on her door set Em's heart skipping faster. Drawing in a slow breath, she tiptoed over to open the wooden barrier a narrow crack.

Megan's sparkling eyes appeared around the edge of the door frame. "You've got company, Em," she whispered.

Em's face burned. A retort for Megan's teasing look sprang to her tongue, but Em held it in for fear Chance would overhear. Megan stepped away, and Em pushed the door open.

Chance stood in the living room, holding his hat by the brim. He had the look of a law student appearing for his first interview.

"Good afternoon, Miss Em," he said. "I was wondering if you'd like to walk out with me." He cleared his throat. "That is, if you're not busy."

"I suppose I could." She looked at Megan, as though asking for help.

Jeremy pushed through the back door, a basin of freshly scrubbed cucumbers in his hands. He set the basin on the table and glanced from Em to Chance and back to Em.

"Go ahead, Em," Megan urged. "You need a break. It won't hurt me to finish the pickles."

Chance opened the door, and they stepped outside. At the porch steps, Chance laid his hat under the railing. "I'll leave this here," he said. "There's a breeze, and I won't be able to enjoy it with my head covered."

Flat, wispy clouds reclined on a wide cobalt couch. Above their ethereal brothers, fat white puffs glided past. The northern sky had a darker cast. Shading his eyes, Chance stared at the horizon. "We'll have rain tonight," he predicted. "Lord knows, we sure do need it."

The couple strolled along the flat stretch in front of the stable, the corral—where four horses, Banjo's donkey, and Bess, the Jersey cow, milled about—on past the chicken yard and the bronze-colored cliff that acted as a backdrop to the Circle C homestead. Ahead of them, the ground sloped down to a winding stream that wove through a stand of pines.

"Been working hard?" Chance asked after a lengthy pause.

"Today we'se a-doin' pickles. Yesterday we canned a hundred quarts of string beans." Em heard herself talking as though from afar. A camp robber jay bounded for the sky, its beak full of pilfered corn, leftovers of the chickens. Em's skirt brushed a clump of baby blue-eyes. The tiny flowers bobbed in her wake.

She felt like a schoolgirl being courted for the first time, futilely trying to keep up her part of the conversation without giving away her nervousness. She hadn't stepped out with a man for twenty-five years.

Across the nearly dry creek bed, Chance leaned his back against a waist-high boulder. "How long have you been with Chamberlins?"

Em perched on a low, flat rock before replying, "In a way I been with them all my life. I'se born on Ebenezer Littlejohn's plantation. He was Miss Megan's grandfather. My mama was a field slave. She died in childbirth. Louisa Littlejohn, the master's wife, came to the quarters when my mama died. She took a shine to me and decided to bring me up by hand in the house. Miss Louisa had a girl two years older than me. That was Katie, Miss Megan's mama. Katie and I grew up together like sisters.

"When I got fourteen, Miss Louisa made me a housemaid. Later Miss Katie married, and I went to be her housekeeper. The war left poor Katie a widow. She had no home, no income, and two children to raise, but she let me stay when I begged to. She could have turned me out, but she didn't. She died two years ago. A few months later, Miss Megan came here with Mr. Steve. Miss Megan sent for me and Jeremy three months ago."

A movement caught her eye. "Look!" Pointing, she whispered, "An antelope with a young'un." The mother flipped her tail and bound into the trees, a baby at her heels.

Man and woman set off walking again. Spindly trees cast long, spiky shadows around them, and an aspen whispered a secret song.

Uncomfortable with silence, Em asked, "How long have you been with Hammonds?"

"A little over five years. After freedom came, I stayed one winter in Mississippi and came nigh to starvation. Every freed slave I knew almost starved that year. The next year I worked odd jobs tending gardens and digging ditches. No black man could get a decent job. Before the war the poor whites were fairly friendly. Afterwards they saw us as a threat. They thought we'd steal away their jobs. The third year I couldn't stand anymore, so I started hiking west."

They moseyed south across scrubby hillsides, winding around trees and brush until they reached a three-acre lake surrounded by thick spruce. Em knew this place from her walks with Jeremy. She loved the tranquil atmosphere in the quiet minutes shortly before dark.

Chance looked over the water with a knowing eye. "This place looks like a good fishing hole." He smiled. "I haven't been fishing since Georgia. I used to keep the plantation in carp and panfish. Sitting on the bank of a lake was the only way to get some peace in those days."

"Hammonds seem like good folks," Em commented as they paused at the still water's edge. The lake mirrored the trees, the hawk wheeling overhead, the clouds. Faint *ree-beeps* wafted from the other side.

"Hammonds are decent people," Chance confirmed. "Miss Susan's daddy,

Victor Harrington, was tough as an old corncob. Once he threw a plate of stew out the door because he got a piece of gristly meat." He chuckled, a mellow, musical sound. "I had to stay on my toes with him around." He swatted a gnat. "But the Hammonds are easy to please. Miss Susan's a jewel." Picking up a fat, round stone, he lofted it high and watched it plop. High circular ripples fanned from the spot. A dragonfly swooped lower to investigate.

Em found a fallen log to lean on. She said, "You know, you talk awful good. Almost like one of them city fellers."

Though the corners of his mouth turned up, bitterness gave the smile a bite. "I had a privileged upbringing. My mama was a housemaid." He bent over to pick up a twig. "My father was the master. I grew up in the house and had a white playmate like you. His name was Gregory. My half brother." He paused, his jaw muscle working in and out. He snapped the twig and threw it down.

"Gregory was as good as his father was wicked. We'd sneak outside with his schoolbooks and run down by the river so he could teach me his lessons from that day's school. It didn't matter to him that he was breaking the law by teaching a black boy to read." He snorted. "A black boy."

He glared at the ground. "Before my fifth birthday I didn't know people took me as being black. I knew Master Collins was my daddy. I lived in his house." He snatched a long blade of grass. "I wasn't allowed in the main part of the house, but I never wondered why. That was just how things were. One day I sneaked into the dining room, and Cook caught me. She grabbed me by the ear and hollered, 'Next time I catch you in heah, I'll warm your black hide!' " Chance's slim fingers split the grass and tore strips from it. "That night I asked my mama. I didn't believe it. . .but it was true."

"They treat you good?" Em asked. She couldn't keep her eyes from his sad face. In spite of wrinkles and signs of age, Chance was a handsome man.

"Two months after I turned twelve the foreman tied me up and took me to market. Like a hog. . .or a chicken. My mama screamed and cried. She begged Master Collins to let me stay. My daddy never looked at her or me. He got in his fine carriage and drove away.

"I never saw my mama again. She's probably dead by now. It's been thirty years. After the war I went back to Master Collins's place, but it was burnt, everyone gone. There's no way I could find her, Em. If she died, they sewed her in a canvas sack and dumped her in an unmarked grave. If she's living, where did she go?"

Though she'd heard this kind of story before, Chance's tale jolted Em. Her tender heart dreaded the rest of it, yet somehow she felt compelled to know. "Who bought you?" she asked.

"A small outfit in Mississippi by the name of Pettigrew. They only had a dozen slaves. Master Collins kept more than a hundred. While I was with my mama, I never saw a beating. They did happen once in a while but not out in public. Pettigrew beat somebody almost every week.

"I started out tending the garden and helping the cook. I was only twelve, remember? Because I'm light skinned, they wanted me in the house. Ten years later the cook had a stroke. I got his job."

"How long were you with Pettigrew?"

"Thirty-three miserable years. I cooked for twenty-three of them. The rest of the slaves got rest days—Sundays, a week at Christmas, and a week for the Fourth of July—but kitchen slaves had to work year around. People always have to eat."

With a parting glance at the water, they drifted back to the creek and along its edge to the wagon crossing. Six inches of water trickled around the mossy stones lining its bottom.

Em glanced at the lavender sky. "It's gettin' on to dark."

"Let's cross here," Chance said, pointing to three flat rocks. "We can step on those." He took two strides, balanced, and turned around to help Em, offering her his hand. As they approached the house, he asked, "What's your name?"

"Em."

"I mean your whole name. Emily?"

"Emma," she replied. "Emma Littlejohn."

"My mama named me Chance. Why, I don't know. I guess my last name should rightly be Collins, but I've never taken it. I'm just Chance." They paused beside the porch steps. He smiled into Em's eyes. "I've enjoyed the afternoon, Emma. Would you mind if I call again?"

Em heard herself say, "I'd be pleasured." At the same second she thought, *You must be tetched, Em. It's twenty-five years too late for these kind of goings-on.*

Chance scooped his hat from the porch and flipped it on. Fine white powder puffed around his head. It drifted over his face and hair to his shoulders. Coughing violently, he flung the black felt away. It tumbled to the ground in a cloud.

Em stared, horrified.

Chance brushed powder from his eyes and nose, punctuating the coughs with two sneezes. "What is this?" he croaked angrily. Creases appeared over his eyelids and around his mouth.

Em gasped. "What on earth happened?"

"Somebody put flour in my hat!"

Em covered her mouth to hide a smile.

"What are you laughing at?" he demanded.

"You look like a gingerbread man." Em chuckled. "Sugar frosting and all."

Chance's anger cooled as quickly as it had appeared. He grinned dubiously and reached in his back pocket for a handkerchief.

"I shouldn't have laughed," Em said, still smiling. "I'm awful sorry."

"You look sorry." He wiped his face and bent over to ruffle his fingers through his hair. A white cloud appeared for the second time.

"I'll find out who's responsible, Chance. I'm awful sorry."

"Don't keep apologizing. It's okay." He retrieved his hat, tapped the crown to shake out any loose particles, then pressed it on his head.

"Do you still want to come back?" Em asked, sobering.

"Of course. I'll see you in two weeks." With a nod and tug at his brim, he marched soldier-style to his horse, pulled out the picket pin, and stepped into leather—a futile effort to regain his dignity. A thoughtful, sweet curve to her lips, Em watched him trot around the meadow, a faint white mist surrounding him.

Chapter 4

Megan stood at the sink stacking soiled pans when Em arrived. On the counter beside her stood twenty-eight gleaming jars of dill pickles. An iron stewpot bubbled on the stove, sending up a luscious beefy aroma. Jeremy laid wide shallow bowls around the table. He looked up as Em entered.

"What happened, Em?" Megan asked the moment Em stepped into the kitchen.

"We walked to the lake," Em murmured, her mind preoccupied. She picked up the apron lying over the back of a dining room chair and slipped it on. "Chance had a hard life, Miss Megan. He's a sad man."

Sensing Em's sober mood, Megan plunged a kettle into soapy water and didn't press her for more details. Jeremy sent her short, inquiring glances throughout the meal. He seemed restive and unusually quiet, but the adults didn't notice.

Far into the night, Em tossed on her bed. Chance's story played through her mind again and again. What must it be like to cherish only a few spare memories of happiness in a life of almost half a century? She thought about her own past, crowded with people who loved her. Slavery hadn't meant cruelty and rejection to Em. She'd felt little difference after freedom. Chains of love had bound her to the Wescott family tighter than slavery ever could.

What had Chance known of love?

Embarrassed and unsure of her feelings, Em didn't want to discuss Chance with Megan yet. She kept her thoughts to herself until the following day when she met Banjo in the chicken yard.

After breakfast Em threw cracked corn to the chickens milling about her feet. In the yard Lobo clenched a short stick between his jaws.

Jeremy lunged for it. "Give it here, Lobo!"

Gripping hard, the dog backed away, shaking his head to loosen the boy's grasp. Jeremy laughed, captured the bit of stick, and tossed it far across the meadow. Lobo raced after it.

Banjo nailed a loose board on the chicken house, finishing with three hard whacks of the hammer. He fed the hammer handle through a thong on his pants and trudged over to Em. His heavy boots grated on the sandy ground. Removing his hat, he swiped a faded blue sleeve across his face. He adjusted the Stetson to its usual place, friendly eyes on Em.

"What's up?" he asked in his direct way. "You've been actin' like you're on your way to a funeral. When you don't scold me for eatin' five pancakes, something's wrong. Anything I can do?"

Em gazed at him an instant before chuckling. The creases around her eyes deepened. "I don't know if anybody can help me," she replied, shaking her head. "I don't rightly know what's wrong with me." She shook the last of the feed to the clucking, scratching hens. "Chance came a-callin' on Saturday."

"I heard about that," he said. "You like him?"

"I'm too old for this fiddle-faddle," she burst out.

"Now, Em." His tone was similar to that used by parents and schoolteachers. "We've been over that territory before." He repeated, "Do you like him?"

Em watched Jeremy and the dog chasing across the grass. She turned back to Banjo. "He's a fine man on most counts. But there's a hard core to him that worries me. I can't rest easy in my mind about him."

"Does he know the Lord?"

She shook her head. A dimple deepened on her right cheek—the one Megan called her worry mark. She brushed corn dust from her apron.

"He's mad at God." She sighed. "Likin' Chance ain't the issue, is it, Banjo? He don't know the Lord, and that puts a high wall between us." She tapped the empty feed pail against her leg. "I'm awful sorry for him, though."

"I'll be prayin' for you," Banjo promised. He let his eyes follow the romping dog and boy for a long moment.

"There's somethin' else, too," Em went on. She told him about the flour-in-the-hat incident. "I'm afraid Jeremy did it," she finished. "I don't want to tell Megan. She'd be awful crabbed. Her time's so close I don't want to make her fret." She shook her head. "I can't imagine why he'd do such a thing!"

"Should I talk to him?" Banjo asked. "We get along right well. I may be able to help."

"That's a temptin' offer, but I reckon I should be the one to do it," Em decided. She grunted, then laughed in a self-condemning way. "Not that it'll do any good. I can't bring myself to whup the boy no matter what he does. And he knows it. My scoldin' gets to him like rain on a duck's back." Mouth pulled down into a puzzled frown, she headed toward the house.

Banjo's face held a serious expression until Em disappeared through the door. When the door banged, his natural twinkle surfaced along with an amused grin. He muttered, "But I certainly can imagine why Jeremy would do such a thing." Picking up the shovel where it stood propped against the stable, he strode inside to clean out the stalls.

Em still hadn't resolved the Jeremy issue the following Friday.

Although September was only ten days old, Steve and Banjo smelled autumn while they saddled up by murky lantern light before dawn. Later that morning Megan—tired and uncomfortable—installed herself on the settee's tan and navy jacquard upholstery to embroider a tiny gown. Em booted Jeremy outdoors to romp with Lobo awhile before the family attacked a basket of late tomatoes for canning.

Em was examining the pantry and deciding on a lunch menu when Jeremy burst into the living room.

"A rider's comin'," he shouted. "I can't tell who it is."

Em met the boy at the door and looked out over his head. "It's a brown horse with black legs and a black tail. You know anyone rides a horse like that, Miss Megan?" She peered through the distance. "It appears to be a small man with a tan hat and a red plaid shirt."

Megan laughed. "That's not a man. That's Susan." She held the baby gown to her face and bit off the short embroidery thread. "Put the kettle on for tea, please, Em."

"I'll help her with the horse," Jeremy declared as the chestnut reached the yard. He strode across the grass in true cowboy fashion and stretched for the bridle far above him.

Watching him through the window, Megan smiled. Jeremy's restored health still brought her delight. She grasped the settee's cloth-covered arm, pushed herself to a standing position, and waddled to the door.

Pulling off her gloves and Boss Stetson, Susan tripped up the steps. She looked exactly as she had more than a year ago on her first visit to the Chamberlin home—thick strawberry-blond mane pulled back into a ponytail, light freckles across a pixie nose. Marriage hadn't changed her one whit.

"Susan!" Megan stretched out for a hug. "How nice to see you!"

Susan's tinkling laugh brightened the atmosphere. "I felt stifled at the ranch today. The men are on the range, Chance is out of sorts, and I felt a mood coming on. So I threw a saddle on Reggie and headed over here." She lifted her hat to a peg and set her gloves on the shelf above. "How are you, Megan?" Scanning Megan's puffy cheeks and tired eyes, she added, "Don't answer that. I can see you're worn-out." Concern clouded her eyes. "Maybe I shouldn't have come."

"Nonsense!" Taking her arm, Megan drew her to a chair. "Sit down and rest your bones. Em will have tea ready in a moment, and later we'll have lunch." Megan resumed her place on the sofa. "Lately my days are forty hours long. A body can only sleep so much. I'm glad you're here to make part of today fly by." She picked up the whalebone needle and a strand of blue thread.

"What are you making?" Susan asked.

Megan held up the pale blue gown, its yoke half covered with a spidery design in navy. "Another gown. This is the last one. I've got to stop playing and get to practical things, like diapers and bibs. I've got a bolt of gauze for the diapers, but so far I haven't made one."

Em appeared with a wooden tray. She set it on the small table beside Megan. "Good morning, Miss Susan," she said, her dark face beaming. "I sure is glad you decided to call. Miss Megan had a bad case of the blues this morning. You'll pull her out of it for sure." She handed Susan a cup of black tea.

"Why don't you sit with us awhile, Em?" Megan asked, accepting a steaming cup. "You're wearing yourself out while I sit here like a big. . .like a big. . ."

Em shook her finger at Megan like she was a naughty child. "Don't say it, Miss Megan. You'se doing the best work possible just now. After the baby comes, you'll be plenty busy, believe me." Em fetched a third cup, filled it, and found a seat next to Megan.

"The barbecue went off wonderfully, Susan," Megan said. "We had a marvelous time. Jeremy wants to do it again right away." She sipped tea. "You've hired four new hands. I've never met them before."

Susan's expression tightened. "I don't know how long they'll be with us. Last month we hired two: Brent Cavenaugh and Amos McClintock. A third man, Link Hensler, is always hanging around our place at night and on Sundays visiting Brent and Amos. He's the southern man who first took Jack Savage's challenge in the arm-wrestling contest. Hensler's not one of ours, but he's around our place so much some folks think he's on the payroll. Wyatt calls Cavenaugh, McClintock, and Hensler the three musketeers.

"Hensler is the new hostler in Juniper. No one seems to know anything about him. I have a bad feeling about him. About the others, too. They go on a drinking binge every time they set foot in town. Once Brent Cavenaugh asked Wyatt for an advance on his next month's pay. He'd gambled away his whole month's wages the very first day."

She shivered. "Brent's handsome in a saloon kind of way, but he's too vain for my taste. Wyatt says Brent's the only man he ever knew that could strut sitting down." She shivered. "Something about him gives me the willies."

Megan set her cup into its saucer. "Lisa Feiklin doesn't seem to agree."

Em's lips firmed together. "That gal's headed for trouble, Miss Megan. I can tell it just lookin' at her."

"There's another new man besides those three, isn't there?" Megan asked. "The big man who started the arm-wrestling contest?"

Susan nodded. "Jack Savage. He came six weeks before Brent and Amos. He's a hard worker, one of the best we've ever had." She paused, glancing at Em. "But he's got the nature of a loco longhorn. He constantly bullies poor Chance. It gets me riled enough to give him his walking papers. I wanted to, but Wyatt said we need him till winter."

Em froze when she heard Chance's name. *Does Miss Susan know about Chance and me?*

If she did, Susan didn't show it. She went on, "Chance, now, he's the best cook we've ever had. He looks for recipes in *Harper's Weekly* like he was a hotel chef. He makes some of those fancy fixin's, too."

Em clattered her cup to the tray and stood up. "It's nice to see you, Miss Susan, but I'd best call Jeremy and get started on them tomatoes. I'll set out some sandwiches in a little while."

Susan and Megan watched Em's thin back until she disappeared into the kitchen. Susan raised shapely eyebrows and looked a question at Megan as the back door banged.

Megan chuckled. "Did you know that Chance has been calling on Em?"

Susan's eyes widened. "No!" She leaned forward, speaking lower, her eyes dancing. "How long has this been going on?"

"Since the barbecue. Em hasn't said much to me, but she's been awful quiet, almost moody. They went for a long walk two weeks ago, didn't come back till almost dark." She ran her finger around the edge of her teacup. "What do you know about him, Susan? I'm a little anxious. Em's old enough to be my mother, I know, but I'd sure hate to see her wounded by a fellow with a smooth line and no scruples."

"You're describing Brent Cavenaugh, not Chance," Susan stated. "Chance is everything a house servant could be, Megan—honest, smart, not afraid to go the extra mile to make sure things are done right. Unfortunately, I don't know much more than that. He never talks about anything but the task at hand. He's polite but reserved in a way that keeps everyone at a distance.

"On his day off he rides out. No one knows where he goes. He doesn't go into Juniper and gamble, that's for sure." She reached forward to pat Megan's hand. "Don't worry, Megan. I think Chance is all right."

"I hope so." Megan's words held a thread of doubt.

Susan stayed an hour beyond lunch. After she rode off, Megan lay down for a much-needed nap. Half an hour later, window-rattling thunder awakened her.

Jeremy darted into the bedroom to hide his head in Megan's shoulder. She patted his hair. "Don't worry, Jeremy. The storm will pass in a few minutes."

"We never had thunder like this in Baltimore." The boy's muffled voice spoke close to her ear. Another crash split the air. The boy jerked, then snuggled closer.

"The storm is God's way of letting us know He's still there."

Em stepped inside the room, her worry mark showing. "I hope Miss Susan made it home okay. She's been gone less than an hour."

"She was raised here, Em," Megan replied. "If she gets caught in the rain, she'll know where to find shelter." She scooted over on the four-poster bed to make more room for Jeremy beside her.

"Jeremy bothering you, Miss Megan? You need to rest."

Megan patted the skinny shoulder next to hers. "Not at all, Em. Before long he'll be too big to want comfort from me. Let him stay."

"I'll fix hot chili soup for supper. Banjo and Mr. Steve are out there, too. They'll be soaked to the hide."

The storm raged through the night. Thick dark clouds scuttled across the sky Saturday morning. As the shadows began to lengthen, Em wore out the floor pacing in front of the front windows. Suddenly she realized what she was doing and rebuked herself for acting like a lovesick teenager.

Uneasy and vaguely worried, Em sat up late knitting a tiny sweater. Chance had told her he'd come. Why hadn't he kept his word?

Sunday dawned clear and cool. Em stirred the oatmeal and turned bacon in the frying pan while Jeremy helped Megan set the table. On the sofa, Steve studied the family's only Bible, preparing for the worship time he'd lead after breakfast.

A galloping rider shattered their routine and drew everyone to the porch. Banjo stepped from the stable, pitchfork in hand. Whoever the rider was, he had a reason to hurry.

The visitor swung from the saddle and, holding the reins, approached the house. Em recognized Slim Reilly, six foot four and built on the same lines as a pencil. This morning his thin, hatchet face bore marks of deep strain. His high-pitched voice puffed out in gasps. "Wyatt sent me to fetch Mrs. Chamberlin. Susan got soaked in Friday's storm. She took sick yesterday. This morning she's out of her head with fever. Amos rode to Juniper for Doc Leatherwood, but we need a woman to look after her, too."

Em received an unspoken message from Steve's lined brow and wise eyes. She reached a firm hand out to Megan. "Let me go, Miss Megan," she murmured. "You can manage here, but you're not up to nursin' anyone just now."

Megan nodded, regret tightening her lips. "I suppose you're right." She looked up at Steve. "I do wish I could go."

"It's good of you to offer, Em," Steve replied, slipping a protective arm about his wife's waist. "Banjo, will you hitch the buckboard and carry Em over?" He turned to Slim. "She'll be there shortly."

"Much obliged, Chamberlin." The cowhand took two steps away. "I'll cool off my horse a mite before I start back."

Jeremy skipped down the steps. "I'll do that for you," he offered hopefully.

"Come in for a bite of breakfast," Steve added. "The womenfolk were about to put it on the table."

Fifteen minutes later, Em sat beside Banjo on the front seat of the buck-board. Biscuit-and-bacon sandwiches lay wrapped in a cloth on her lap, a fresh dress in the carpetbag at her feet.

Megan came to the door to wave as the wagon passed the house. "Take good care of her, Em."

"Don't fret yourself, Miss Megan," Em called. "She's in the hands o' the good Lord."

Leading Slim's horse around the grassy yard, Jeremy looked after the buck-board with intent eyes.

Chapter 5

A hundred thousand acres of mountains, lakes, and forest surrounded Hammond's spread. The hub of the outfit lay twenty miles southwest of Juniper. From the final ridge, Banjo and Em could see that the buildings formed a ring—the sprawling house, the smokehouse, the corral, two twenty-horse stables side by side lying directly opposite Susan and Wyatt's home. The bunkhouse, a small blacksmith shop, and a tiny grove of oaks completed the circle.

Wyatt strode across the yard to meet them the moment the buckboard came to a halt. He had aged twenty years in twenty hours. His shoulders stooped, the flesh on his face had melted until cheekbones jutted harshly against the pallid skin above his beard.

Banjo helped Em climb down before turning to meet the desperate husband with the words on everyone's lips: "How is she?"

"The same," came the tortured answer. Wyatt stretched a bony, calloused hand to the dark lady standing shoulder to shoulder with Banjo. "Thanks for coming, Em."

"Miss Megan's gettin' too close to her time to come, Mr. Wyatt," Em said. "She wanted real bad to come herself."

"Chamberlin said to tell you they're prayin'," Banjo added.

They moved toward the house. "Doc Leatherwood hasn't come yet," Wyatt said. Shading his eyes, he strained to see as far down the trail as the mountain allowed. "No sign of him yet." Dropping his hand in a despairing gesture, he said, "Susan's sleeping now. Chance is with her. I didn't sleep nary a wink all night, and I had to get some air."

They stepped across the plank floor of the veranda and into the entry hall. Em glanced around as they moved through the living room and into the master bedroom.

Though not elaborate in any sense, the house had been built with skill and care. A mixture of lime and mud chinked the log walls. The boards in the wide plank floor were of varying widths, fitted together with expert precision. The living room was furnished with cowhide furniture and an Indian rug. Coal oil lamps adorned two small tables and the mantelshelf above a broad stone fireplace. On the right wall stood three doors.

The master bedroom lay behind the last door at the back corner of the house. Two-thirds the size of the large living room, it had wide windows on two sides. Ornately carved fronts adorned the chifforobe, chest of drawers, and mirrored dresser.

Em's attention immediately centered on the massive bed piled high with quilts. The prickly smell of sickness and the grating sound of shallow, raspy breathing gripped Em.

Susan's lips parted as she fought for air. Her beautiful hair lay matted against a ghostly pale face. Beside her, in a rocking chair, Chance got to his feet the moment Wyatt and Em entered the room. Banjo had stopped to wait in the living room.

Chance smiled when he caught sight of Em. "Mornin', Emma." He looked down at the patient, pity pinching his mouth. "She hasn't moved since you left, Mr. Wyatt."

Em moved around the bed and leaned over Susan. Her brown hand gently touched the sick woman's forehead. Hot and dry. Susan's lips were parched and peeling.

Susan stirred, mumbling under her breath. Her hands came up to push away the covers.

"While we'se waitin' for the doctor, let's make her more comfortable," Em said. "Chance, will you fetch me a fresh basin of cool water? Not cold, now. Cool."

Chance picked up the basin on the bedside table and headed for the door. Wyatt hovered at the end of the bed, tormented eyes on Susan.

Moments after Chance left, the door eased open, and Dr. Leatherwood stepped inside. Built like a professional boxer, the medical man removed his black felt hat to expose a shiny bald head. The baldness was a trick of nature, for the doctor had a mere five years' advance on Wyatt.

"Doc!" Wyatt reached out to grasp the doctor's hand like a drowning man reaching for a lifeline. "She's delirious. Is there anything you can do?"

Leatherwood shook Wyatt's hand briefly and shrugged out of his worn black coat. "Let me take a look at her, Hammond." His voice had the calm quality of a man in charge. "Step outside for a few minutes." He spoke to Em. "I'll need your help, ma'am, if you don't mind."

Fifteen minutes later, the doctor opened the bedroom door and called Wyatt inside.

"She's got double pneumonia, Wyatt," he stated.

Wyatt's face sagged. He seemed on the verge of collapse.

The doctor went on. "I've had some success with poultices in cases like this, but there's no way to tell how she'll respond." He spoke to Em. "I'll write down some directions for you to follow. The next twenty-four hours are crucial. I'll be back first thing in the morning to see how she's doing." He pulled a small pad and pencil from his pocket and sank to the rocking chair, talking as he wrote. "Do you have any onions?"

Anxious eyes on his bride, Wyatt stroked his bearded cheek with the back of his hand. "We have about a hundred pounds in the root cellar. We harvested them last week."

"Excellent." He held the page out to Wyatt. "Onion poultices are a lot of work, but I've had better luck with them than mustard plasters."

"Thanks, Doc," Wyatt said as Leatherwood reached for his coat and hat.

"That's what I'm here for," the doctor answered. "I wish I could do more." Putting on his hat, he picked up his black bag and left the room.

Em eyed Wyatt with the expression she used when reminding Jeremy to wash behind his ears. "Mr. Wyatt, this'll take all day and maybe all night. You get yourself to bed before we have to carry you there. Chance can read that paper and tell me what to do."

Wyatt shook his head, refusing though he seemed scarcely to hear. He knelt beside the bed and held Susan's limp hand to his lips. "Don't leave me, Susan. We've hardly begun life together. Don't leave me." He laid his forehead against the quilt.

Em squeezed his brawny shoulder. She resorted to pleading. "Please, Mr. Wyatt. You'll take sick your ownself if you don't rest." She drew the slip of paper from his fingers and pulled at his arm.

Like an aged man, he stood.

Susan turned her head to look at him with dull eyes. "Pa, my bridle's broken again. Can you fix it for me?" Her hand pulled from Wyatt's clasp and plucked at the quilt.

Head bowed, Wyatt plodded from the room in an exhausted daze. He opened the middle door off the living room and trudged inside. Two steps behind him, Em could see a narrow bed and chest of drawers before he closed the door behind him.

"I'd best be gettin' back, Em," Banjo said, rising from the sofa as Em reached him. "Here's your clothes case." He indicated the cloth bag beside the sofa. "Do you need anything else?"

"Only a miracle, Banjo," Em replied sadly.

"The Chamberlin house will be beggin' God for just that. Let's pray before I leave." Three minutes later he uttered a quick good-bye, pulled on his hat, and strode outside.

Walking through the hall running from the front door to the back of the house, Em stepped into a spacious square room, a place to feed many mouths. Chance met Em at the kitchen door. "What'd the doc say?"

"He said to follow these directions." She held up the paper. "Bring us some onions."

"How many?"

"All of them."

"All of them? There must be a hundred pounds in the root cellar."

"Read this."

Flattening the paper between his slim fingers, he glanced over it before reading aloud.

"It says, 'Slice onions and place in a frying pan with a little water. Stir and cook until the onions are transparent. Let cool slightly then place them in a clean cotton cloth and apply to the patient's chest and back. Put on fresh poultices every half hour until the phlegm breaks loose. This could take from ten to twenty-four hours.'" He laid the paper on the table, saying, "Looks like it's going to be a long day."

While he fetched the onions, Em lifted a square cast-iron skillet from a hook above the wide six-burner stove. A wall of cabinets covered the east wall. Opening doors, she found two pottery mixing bowls. Chance soon appeared with a fifty-pound sack of onions in his arms. He set it on the floor and turned back to the root cellar. "May as well get the other'n now while I have the strength."

"Wait a minute," Em called. "Where can I find some knives and cotton cloths?"

"Check those drawers." He pointed toward the counter on the left as he hurried away.

After a frantic rush to get started, the process became a monotonous routine. Rolling Susan over to replace the poultice under her back. . .bathing her face. . .stopping her from pulling off the covers. . .praying. . .praying. . .praying.

Wyatt slept until late afternoon. Deep black rings formed around his eyes, and he seemed glued to the rocking chair close to Susan's head, where he could hold her hand and speak into her ear. Em's heart ached for him as much as for Susan, for Em had felt the same pain many years before.

Soon after Katie Littlejohn had married Silas Wescott, Em had caught the eye of a young blacksmith named John Bob, a lighthearted, laughing creature with a strong, serious, sensitive soul. Bursting with happiness, Em confided in Katie, who rushed to Silas, coaxing and pleading until her defenseless new husband gave the slaves permission to wed. The law forbade slaves to marry, but regardless of that, Katie had the parlor decorated with flowers, and the family held a wedding ceremony. With Master Wescott officiating, the honored couple finished off their vows with the slave tradition of "jumping the broom."

In the truest sense, Em and John Bob had a common-law marriage. Em could not change her name.

Em had always lived with people who loved her, but those months with John Bob were a series of warm, rose-colored moments, a touch of heaven. Master Wescott gave them a private room in the slave quarters—a two-story dormitory behind the house. In spite of their bondage, John Bob and Em had bright hopes for their future in the Wescott household.

Eight months later a horse kicked John Bob in the head while he bent to nail on a horseshoe. He died the next morning.

Grief brought on preterm labor, and Em's tiny son never drew his first breath. The next day Em's dreams were sewn into the same canvas and covered with earth.

Wyatt's tears over his delirious bride put a fresh edge to Em's pain that had dulled to bearable levels twenty years before. She'd known deep sorrow several times since, but nothing to match the gut-wrenching agony of that day.

Tears filled her eyes and spilled over. She slipped from the room. The cowhide sofa seemed a good refuge. She sank into its comforting depths and covered her face with her calloused hands.

"What is it, Emma?" His voice heavy with concern, Chance knelt near her, a bowl of water for the sickroom in his hands. "Is she worse?"

Em shook her head. She'd hoped to be alone. How humiliating for Chance to come on her like this! She reached into her sleeve for a handkerchief to mop her eyes.

"No, Chance. Miss Susan's the same. It's me I'se a-cryin' for. Watching Mr. Wyatt with his poor, sick wife dug up some bad memories." Briefly, haltingly, she told her story.

"You'd best take that water to the bedroom, Chance," she said when she was through. "I'll fetch the next poultice." Stuffing her handkerchief into her sleeve, she trotted to the kitchen. She'd told Chance more than she'd intended. Action gave her an excuse to get away from the painful subject. She hadn't mentioned John Bob's name for fifteen years.

Though the whole house reeked of onions, pungent air slammed into Em's senses when she reached the kitchen. She wrinkled her nose, fighting against burning sensations on sensitive membranes. The first onion sack reclined, half-empty, on the floor, its untouched partner propped nearby. The skillet languidly steamed on the stove. Brown orbs adorned the massive work table in every form from half-peeled to sliced.

With shaky hands, Em picked up a cold poultice lying on the table and took it to the five-gallon bucket filled with cooked onions outside the back door. She was startled to see stars and a brilliant moon. All sense of time vanished in the sickroom.

She folded back the white cotton fabric and shook limp onions on top of their fellows in the pail. Spreading the cloth on the counter by the stove, she spooned hot stringy onions to the center and deftly folded it into a neat flat package.

Chance returned to the kitchen while she prepared the second poultice. He perched on the stool near the mound of raw onions and picked up a small knife. Feeling awkward after her unusual display of emotion, Em concentrated on her work. Inside the cookstove a pine knot popped. The fire made the kitchen warm and close on this mid-September evening.

Chance sliced the onions in even layers. His eyes were clear, unaffected by the tear-jerking vegetable before him. When he spoke it was as though Em's story had never happened.

"I meant to call on you yesterday, Emma, but Miss Susan felt poorly. I couldn't leave her with the kitchen work. It seemed like she got worse by the hour."

"When you didn't come," Em hurriedly replied, "I had a notion something had happened." She dropped two steaming poultices on a plate and hurried to the bedroom. Why did she feel all thumbs and left feet? Mentally, she shook herself. She'd come to the Rocking H to nurse Miss Susan, and that's all she'd think about.

Em slipped into the sickroom to find Wyatt just as she'd left him. Susan's face glistened, her face flushed from the heat of the onions.

"It's time to change the onion packs, Mr. Wyatt," Em said softly. "Can you help me turn her over?"

Awaking as a man from a dream, Wyatt put loving arms around Susan and pulled her straight up, her chin resting awkwardly on his shoulder. The movement sent a spasm through her thin frame. With a choking gasp, she coughed violently until tears streamed down her cheeks.

"Lean her over so she can cough it out," Em ordered.

Five minutes later Wyatt laid Susan back. She melted into the pillow, utterly exhausted. Em gently wiped the moist, sleeping face.

Wyatt relaxed into the rocking chair. His arms hung limply over the sides and toward the floor; his head rested against the chair's high back. "Does the coughing mean anything?" he whispered.

"It's a mighty good sign," Em announced, a weary smile on her lined face. "I don't think she's brought up enough to say she's out of the woods, but we'll keep workin' on her. Jesus will do the rest."

In the kitchen Chance heaved a relieved sigh when Em told him what had happened. "That's our first good news." He drew a red bandanna from his hip pocket to wipe his face. "I tell you, Emma, this is almost as much work as mining. And mining will kill a man if he doesn't pace himself."

"Minin'?" Em poured a glass of water from an enamel pitcher and perched on a stool across from Chance. An impatient rooster crowed. Em glanced at the clock on the shelf above the sink: 4:00 a.m.

Waiting for Chance to say more, she watched him slice through an onion with rapid, lithe movements. Eyes on his work, he spoke a moment later. "I've got me a claim ten miles northeast of here by Fox Hole Creek. Been working it every Sunday for the past year, some Saturdays, too."

"You find anything?"

"A little," Chance hedged, avoiding her eyes. "I've got a sack of silver nuggets. I'm not sure how much they're worth because I haven't turned anything in yet." He scooped the acrid pile before him into a glazed yellow bowl and picked up another onion. "I don't want the news getting out that there's silver in these parts. Every speculator for fifty miles would be up there in a day's time if I take the nuggets to town."

He paused, noting Em's absorbed expression. "I want to save enough money to buy a few acres and set up a farm. A small place with enough pasture to keep a couple of cows for beef and milk and some planting land besides. I could put in wheat or corn to sell." He grinned, a little sheepish. "You probably have me pegged for a dreamer."

"If so, you'se the good kind," Em said, warming to him. "I wish you well, Chance. I truly do."

A call from the bedroom brought Em to her feet.

"Em! Come quick!"

Em raced down the hall and through the living room, her heart keeping time with her feet. The sound of retching met her at the bedroom door.

"Keep her head down!" she ordered. She grasped Susan's forehead, supporting her. "This isn't pleasant, Mr. Wyatt, but it's just what she needs. I think she's gonna pull through."

Chapter 6

Two hours later Wyatt's insistent whisper brought Em's chin up from her chest. She sat in the rocking chair next to the sickbed. "Em! Go to bed. I'll sit with Susan."

Blinking, Em slowly focused on her patient. Susan's breathing came soft and gentle. She lay peacefully in normal sleep. Light penetrated the gauze curtains.

Wyatt hovered over Em's rocking chair. "Your things are in the front room," he said. "You haven't rested in over twenty-four hours."

Em looked up at the young husband. Her bleary mind suddenly realized that Wyatt wanted to be with Susan when she awoke. Em nodded. "That's fine, Mr. Wyatt. I b'lieve I'll do as you say."

Inside the small, unadorned bedroom, Em eased back on the goose-down pillow and pulled up the quilt. Her eyes drifted closed. The rope-hung mattress felt heavenly.

Em awoke to the tempting aroma of simmering beef. She stretched and relaxed, allowing herself the little-known luxury of quiet wakefulness. Her mind wandered from Susan's recovery to Chance and his confidences of last night. The man was much more complex than she had first imagined. Interesting. Intriguing.

Her gnawing stomach finally persuaded her to throw back the quilt and bathe her face in the basin on the dry sink. She drew a fresh dress from the carpet bag and smoothed a hand over her neat cornrows.

Wyatt held a finger to his lips when she peeked into the master bedroom. He nodded and smiled in answer to her questioning glance at Susan's sleeping form. Stepping back, Em gently closed the bedroom door.

Chance was scooping stew into serving bowls as she reached the kitchen. Seeing her, his drawn face lightened into a smile. All visible traces of their onion vigil had disappeared. Bubbling beef had banished the acrid smell.

"Good morning!" He glanced at the clock. "Or is it afternoon? Only two minutes' difference right now."

"What can I do to help?"

"Those biscuits need to come out of the pan."

With a broad knife she lifted hot biscuits from a pan on the counter and piled them on two plates waiting nearby. Shaking a finger that got too close to hot metal, she said, "I feel like a piker, going off to bed while you'se still working."

"I'll sleep after the lunch dishes are washed. It's not the first time I've worked the clock around. Won't be the last neither." He set down the stewpot and reached into a drawer for three giant spoons. "I've got some chicken broth simmering on the back of the stove for Miss Susan whenever she wants it." He picked up two steaming dishes. "You could get that door for me, if you don't mind." He bent his head toward the entrance to the north porch where the hands ate.

Em grabbed the remaining bowl of stew and hurried before him to open the door. The rumble of men's voices met her on the other side.

The porch was a narrow room tacked on the back of the ranch house. Ten feet wide, it ran behind the kitchen, dining room, and part of the master bedroom. Ten feet had been partitioned off the end behind the kitchen to make Chance's quarters.

The now-idle Franklin stove near the kitchen door heated this area built of bare board walls and floor. A plank table ran almost the full length of the room, though at this time of year it was less than half full at mealtimes. The only noticeable feature in the rough room were the windows, five wide ones across the back.

Curly occupied the head seat, flanked by Slim and Amos—who'd beat Jack Savage at arm wrestling. Beside slouching Amos, Brent Cavenaugh cut a fine figure. After six hours in the saddle, his black-checked shirt seemed freshly laundered, the black bandanna knot positioned exactly halfway between Adam's apple and ear. His shapely fingertips brushed the brown birthmark below his right ear as he talked to the husky farm boy next to him. Across from Cavenaugh hunkered Jack Savage, as vulgar in appearance as Brent was refined. Savage reeked of horses and stale sweat. Black wiry hair sprang from his skull at odd angles.

Deep in conversation, Curly and Slim leaned together. Curly's words, "beeves," "grazing," "box canyon," popped over the general noise like corn from a hot pot. Amos and Brent chuckled over a private joke. Savage morosely fingered his empty cup. Catching sight of the aproned black man's approach, Slim straightened. His voice cut through the hum. "Howdy, Chance. How's the missus?" All faces turned to catch the answer. The noise died.

"She's much better," Chance said, setting meaty soup at intervals down the plank table. "She passed the crisis about four this morning." A murmur of relief swept through the men.

The coarse voice of Jack Savage seemed almost indecent following so closely on talk of Susan's illness. "Who's your lady friend, Chance?" Savage thought he was laughing, but to Em's ears he brayed. She hadn't liked him the first time she saw him. She liked him less today.

The big man tapped the table with a chipped enamel cup. "Let's have some coffee, boy." When Chance didn't answer, Savage glared at him and spat out, "You understand me?"

The cook cast a lazy glance in his direction and drawled, "Yes, sir, Mr. Savage. I've been learning English since I was born and studying it ever since."

Snickers came from the hands. Savage glowered.

Avoiding Em's eyes, Chance turned toward the kitchen. Em set down her bowl and followed.

Using a dish towel to pad his hand, Chance grabbed the coffeepot and strode back to the porch.

When he returned, Em didn't comment on Savage's crudeness. Why bother? It was something to be endured and ignored. She remembered Susan's words to Megan about the man. Suddenly, Em's respect for the cook grew. Could she deal with Savage as well as Chance had? Her strong hands itched for a rolling pin or an iron skillet.

Chance set plates on the table in the kitchen and made a mock bow. "Care to join me for lunch, m'lady?"

Grinning at his playacting, Em perched on a stool. She watched Chance pick up his fork and stab a chunk of meat.

Quickly, she asked, "Don't you think we'd best pray before we eat?"

He looked up, startled. "Pray? What for?"

"To thank the Lord for bringing Miss Susan through her sickness and thank Him for the food."

"Emma." His words came out low but with a cold edge. "I've never prayed in my life. I don't intend to start now. If God's so good, why'd He treat us so bad?" Sad, smoldering eyes met Em's. He shook his head and lifted the fork. "You go ahead and pray if it makes you feel better. Don't ask me to."

Rebuffed and aching in her spirit, Em bowed with closed eyes. After a silent, ten-second prayer, she methodically cleared her plate. How could she share the gospel with him if he had that attitude?

In a few moments she carried a hot plate and a glass of water to Wyatt in the bedroom. When she came back, she pushed the exhausted king of the kitchen away from his dishpan. "Let me do that! You go and rest."

After a feeble protest, Chance dropped his apron across a stool and stepped inside his room off the back of the kitchen. Em rolled up her sleeves and plunged elbow deep in hot soapy water.

The clock on the living room mantel sounded two low gongs as Em opened the sickroom door. Wyatt was bending over Susan, lifting her so she could sip some water. He glanced up as Em stepped inside. His empty plate lay on the dresser.

"She's awake, Em." He laid his wife gently back and tenderly smiled down at her.

Susan's tired eyes sought out Em. She stretched out a limp hand. Em quickly clasped the weak fingers between her two sturdy hands.

"Wyatt told me what you've done, Em." Her voice had the quality of an aspen in a faint breeze.

"Don't wear yourself out talking, child," Em warned. "Do you feel up to taking some broth?" At Susan's nod, she placed the pale hand on the bed. "I'll fetch some straightaway."

"I'll feed it to her," Wyatt said, reaching for the mug and spoon when Em returned.

"After she rests again I'll bathe her and get her into fresh clothes," Em said. "Would you like me to sit with her for a while?"

"No, thanks," came Wyatt's quick reply. "Seeing her get over that fever is better'n steak and apple pie to me. I don't want to leave her." He carefully raised half a spoonful of broth to his wife's parched lips.

That evening, after supper, Susan slept deeply, comforted by a warm bath, a fresh gown, and new linens. Wyatt stretched out in the middle room, napping. Em softly rocked in the chair beside the sick woman's bed. Her eyes wandered from Susan to the big windows that met at the corner across the room. With silent tread, she stepped closer and peered around the curtain.

Twilight crept over the landscape, turning the mountains into giant black mounds against a mauve sky. Ridges and crests had distinct outlines as though cut out with an engraving tool.

If Susan keeps gainin' strength, Em thought, *I'll go home in the morning. Megan will be needin' me.* When Wyatt came to relieve her at eight, Em strolled out to the front porch to rest her weary mind in the cool night air. Sinking to one of four wooden rockers, she watched the darkness. Faint creaks marked her back-and-forth motion. Across the yard, light from the bunkhouse stabbed three yellow beams into the night. In a moment the door opened, letting out an oblong splash, blocked an instant later by the figures of three men passing through. Resting her head against the chair's back, Em lazily observed their course across the yard. They perched on the empty hitching rail thirty feet from the house. Matches flared as two of them lit cigarettes.

"Hensler, nex' time you come over, bring me a pouch o' tobaccy." The Missouri drawl belonged to Amos McClintock. Em's eyes strained to make out their shadowy forms as smoke reached her nose. These must be the three musketeers, as Wyatt called them.

"If Ah remember, Amos," came the answer from the center man. "Mah memory ain't always the best, ya know."

Brent chuckled. "You don't have any trouble if there's whiskey, women, or money in it for you."

Hensler snickered. "Ah kin handle the important stuff. It's the details Ah mess up on." He drew on the cigarette, making a red glow. "You hopped on the trail of that Feiklin filly quick enough, Cavenaugh."

"Lisa's wild as a yearling. She needs to be halter broke."

"Watch out," Link's sarcastic voice warned. "She may halter break you."

Cavenaugh laughed aloud. "No chance of that, Hensler. It's been tried before."

"How 'bout some poker?" Amos asked. "We kin play for matchsticks."

"Sounds good by me," Brent agreed.

The smokers ground out their cigarette butts, and the troop sauntered across the yard. A flash of light, the bang of the door, and the night resumed its cricket chorus.

Em rocked gently.

Sensing a stealthy motion beside her, she jerked around.

"Evening, Emma." Chance's deep, mellow tones wafted through the evening air. "Sorry if I scared you." She peered toward him. Light from the window shone on his shirt as he walked toward her.

She faltered. "I must have dozed for a minute there." Instinctively, her hand touched the knot behind her head, though she knew he couldn't see her clearly.

"I thought I'd come out and rest my nerves a few minutes before I turn in," he said. "I didn't know you'd found my favorite night spot."

Em sighed. "It's mighty peaceful out here. I can hardly believe I'm out of Baltimore. Have you ever been to a big city, Chance?"

"I passed through St. Louis on my way west. I can't say I was tempted to settle there."

"In Baltimore we roasted in the summer and froze in the winter. Inside the apartment, I mean. The city was crowded and filthy. I can't hope to tell you how relieved me and Miss Megan are to be away from there. Poor Jeremy, too." She laughed softly. "You should see him a-runnin' with that dog."

"He's a fine boy, Emma. You raised him, didn't you?" It was more of a statement than a question.

"His mama died when he was nine. Up until then her and I shared the motherin' of him." She paused. "I love him like he's my own, Chance. Megan, too. I never had any young'uns but them."

They sat in silence, soaking in the night.

"When are you going home?"

"In the mornin', if Miss Susan's gainin' strength."

"Okay if I call on you Saturday?"

"Why, surely."

"Long as there's no more trouble, I'll be there."

After breakfast Slim brought the buckboard around to the front door.

"A million thanks to you, Em," Wyatt said.

"That's what neighbors is for, Mr. Wyatt." Em picked up her carpetbag and stepped off the porch. She'd already said good-bye to Chance in the kitchen. "If you need me again, I'll come right away."

An hour later Megan met Em inside the Chamberlins' front door. "How is Susan?" she asked as she placed her cheek next to Em's.

"Mendin'," Em replied. She set down her case and returned the embrace.

Jeremy rushed up for a hug. "I'm glad you're home, Em," he said. "Megan's been awful tired since you left."

Megan made an effort to smile. Shadows rimmed her eyes. Her silky brown hair lay in wisps about her face. "I was tired before she left, Jeremy, so that's not really news."

"Take this bag to my room," Em said to Jeremy, "and I'll get started on the washing right away."

"Not so fast!" Megan protested, pulling Em's arm toward the settee. "First, you have to tell me what happened at the Rocking H."

Em gave a two-minute description of onion poultices and late nights, ending with, "Miss Susan slept all last night and ate some solid food for breakfast." She made to stand up, but Megan held her back.

"What about Chance?"

"Chance? Why, he's fine, Miss Megan. He warn't sick a bit."

Megan looked toward the ceiling in mock disgust. "I know that, Em. I want to know if you talked with him."

Em studied her work-hardened hands for a moment. "We did talk. I got to know him better."

"You're troubled about something, aren't you?"

"He said, 'If God's so good, why'd He treat us so bad?'" Her worry mark deepened as she looked into Megan's brown eyes. "He's a fine man, Miss Megan: honest, hardworking, smart. But if he's mad at God, I can't hope to see any tomorrows for him and me."

Megan nodded. "You're right about that, Em."

"It's like he's wrapped in a cocoon of bitterness and hate," Em went on. "He can't cut himself loose. I can't cut him loose neither. Only Jesus has the power to snip those threads." She shook her head in a disheartened gesture. "How can I convince the man of that?"

Chapter 7

At nine o'clock Saturday morning, Em was hanging freshly boiled white clothes on the line when Lobo began barking and making short sprints toward the trail.

"Look, Em," Jeremy called from the porch steps. He had a thick piece of pine and a short knife in his hands. "A buckboard's coming."

Em walked to the end of the row of newly sewn diapers flapping in the gentle breeze. Before her a field of corn stood browned and dry, days away from harvest. The sun shone brightly; the breeze had lost its torrid feel. Em savored the coolness on her face as she gazed along the edge of the cornstalks. A water-wrinkled hand shading her eyes, she suddenly stiffened.

The wagon driver was Chance.

Why had he come so early in the day? Why in the buckboard?

Quickly she returned to her laundry basket to finish pinning up the final two shirts before he reached the yard. Two horses paced past her as the wagon clattered into the yard, Lobo yapping at its wheels. Lifting the empty basket, Em turned to greet her visitor.

Jeremy called, "Here, Lobo!" from his seat on the steps.

Chance swept off his flat-crowned black hat. "Mornin', Emma. I'm on my way to town to buy supplies. Mr. Wyatt doesn't want to leave Miss Susan, and the rest of the hands are working the range." He glanced at the crowded clothesline. "I was hoping you could ride into Juniper with me if you're not too busy."

Quickly, Em mentally ticked off the chores she'd mapped out for the day. None were essential.

"Give me a few minutes to set supper on the stove and change my dress. I'd like to come along."

A few minutes past ten, Chance handed her up to the buckboard seat and climbed aboard himself. Em wore her new navy dress with a matching spoon bonnet. She'd finished covering the bonnet form with fabric only last evening.

"Be good, Jeremy," Em called to the solemn urchin leaning on the porch rail, "and I'll bring you a peppermint stick!"

Jeremy's dour expression brightened by half, but eyes half closed, he cast sideways glances at Chance every five seconds.

"Enjoy the day!" Megan said, smiling and lifting her hand as the buckboard moved away. She placed her arm around Jeremy's sagging shoulders and squeezed. Looking down, she asked, "Why so glum? You've got the whole day to do nothing but play. Want to take Lobo down to the creek until lunch?"

"Okay," he murmured. He slid the knife into its sheath and stuffed it and the wood into his spacious overalls pocket. "Come on, Lobo." With a final look at the retreating wagon, he set off jogging across the yard, the wolf-faced dog at his side.

Em looked back in time to see boy and canine leave the porch. The sky directly overhead gleamed clean and bright, but to the west a dark mass hid the mountain peaks.

"I hope that storm doesn't move this way," Chance said. "If it does, we'll be in for a wettin'."

"Let's not borry trouble before it comes. It's a lovely day." She retied her bonnet strings. "What's your chore in town?"

"I've got a list to fill at the general store." He smiled at her. "And I'd like to buy you lunch."

She beamed. "That'd be nice, Chance."

The buckboard rocked through dry puddles, across mounds and rolling hills, around giant orange rocks. Soon frost would wipe out the straggling clumps of blue chicory and black-eyed Susans that had survived the dry heat of late August and early September. Sage and pine tingled their noses.

They talked of canning, crops, and Susan's steady recovery as the wagon wound around a long, straight family of Douglas fir interwoven with scrub oak. Before they were ready, Juniper lay before them, nestled between two low hills, a rifle shot from the endless prairie to the east. Chance guided the wagon to a small space along the populated boardwalk near Harper's Emporium. Saturday was a busy day in Juniper.

The dim interior of Harper's seemed crowded when Chance and Em stepped inside. A bell on the door announced their arrival. Three ladies turned to see who stood at the door. Each glanced quickly away without so much as a nod or smile of greeting. Em had seen similar expressions on white faces thousands of times before: a mixture of fear and distaste.

She glanced at Chance, standing close beside her, hat in hand. He avoided eye contact with anyone and studied the stocked shelves behind the counter.

The door behind them jingled as two men stepped inside. One drew up short then edged around the black couple leaving a wide girth. The second man paused near Chance.

Harper—the thin gray man behind the oak counter—busily filled orders alongside a young clerk with pock-scarred cheeks. When the storekeeper finished with someone, he'd say "Who's next?" and another customer would step to the front.

While they waited, Em looked around the small store. The smell of new leather, fresh-ground coffee, and tobacco filled the air. In the left corner near the door a table held two new saddles, some bridles, and spurs. A dozen leather belts hung on the wall above. Three copper-bound barrels—pickles, crackers, and coffee beans—sat in a triangle shape at the far left of the counter, just below the coffee grinder. Most of the merchandise lay on neat shelves covering the wall behind the counter. Harper and his clerk scurried back and forth plucking items from these stacks and dropping them into burlap sacks.

Last in the line of ladies, Mrs. Pleurd collected her change, picked up her sack, and passed within inches of Em, eyes averted. She must have forgotten their introduction at the barbecue.

"Who's next?" Harper asked, scanning the faces of the men. Grasping an empty potato basket, the clerk stepped through the curtained doorway to the rear in search of a refill.

Chance raised a finger and began to step forward. Ignoring him, Harper turned to the cowhand on the right.

"What can I get for you, Jensen?"

"Half a pound of tobaccy and twenty-five rounds of .44's," the short cow-poke drawled, digging into his jeans for a coin.

Em felt Chance tense, saw his jaw clench. Otherwise his placid expression remained intact.

"Grover?" Harper's attention centered on the man beside Chance, a muscular hombre wearing buckskins and a drowsy expression.

"These folks were ahead of me, Harper," the big man announced. His words were slow and cool, like small stones thrown in a quiet pond.

The storekeeper's eyes wandered in Chance's direction. "What can I get for you?"

Em looked up at the man called Grover. He had kind blue eyes that weren't afraid to meet hers. He allowed himself a small smile and nodded politely.

Chance handed the list over the counter. "Mr. Wyatt said to put these things on the Rocking H bill. He'll settle with you when he comes to town. And," he placed a penny on the counter, "I want a bag of peppermint sticks."

Harper nodded, scanning the paper in his hand. In three minutes he held out a bulging burlap sack along with a small paper bag.

"How long you stayin', Grover?" Harper asked as Chance grasped the rough cloth.

"I'm passin' through to Texas, Harper. I've been trappin' with the Arapahoe this year, and I'm on my way to sell the pelts."

Chance hefted the heavy load and headed for the door, Em behind him.

Noonday sun clawed at their eyes when they reached the boardwalk. Em waited in the shade of the store's awning while Chance set the groceries in the wagon.

Sheriff Feiklin strode past, heavy boots thumping the boardwalk. He didn't hesitate or speak when he overtook the black couple, but Em saw his eyes. Icy blue, they flicked from her to Chance with a hard, calculating gleam. Em swallowed, suddenly nervous. Why did she suddenly feel guilty for standing on Main Street? Uneasy, Em watched the lawman's back until he ducked into his office farther down the street.

A steady stream of people filed by. If possible, they would have walked straight through her. These people were no different than the white folks in Baltimore: After taking her labor for a few pennies, they'd acted as if she was deaf, blind, and without feelings.

She gazed at the stage station across the street where she'd arrived three months ago. At that instant she decided she wouldn't be coming to Juniper often.

"Ready for lunch?" Chance asked brightly, offering Em his arm.

Shaking off gloomy thoughts, she smiled. "Surely," she replied, slipping her hand under his elbow.

They strolled ten paces down Main Street to a two-story wooden structure with a giant sign. In green and gold lettering it proclaimed BENSON'S HOTEL AND WORLD FAMOUS RESTAURANT.

"Let's see how famous the food is," Chance said, grinning, as he opened the door. His gleaming hair hung in loose curls that brushed the tips of his ears and the edge of his collar.

A red-haired girl in a white bib apron met them just inside.

"We'd like a table, please," Chance told her.

The girl's cheeks flushed. She cleared her throat. "This way, please." Turning, she led them through the room filled with chatting, chuckling people to the farthest dark corner of the dining room. The noise swelled and faded moment by moment.

Set close together, a dozen tables made up the restaurant. They were cut from the same mold: a thick square of wood with four Windsor chairs each. The plank floor added scuffling, tramping noises to constant chatter and clatter of cutlery.

"We have steak, fried potatoes, beans, and biscuits. Apple pie for dessert," the waitress droned. "Or vegetable soup with light bread if you'd rather."

"We'll have steak, beans, and biscuits?" Chance waited for Em's approval. At her nod, he finished with, "Coffee, too, please."

"You come to Juniper often?" Em asked when the waitress left.

"Twice a year, usually," he said, relaxing in the chair.

"That seems like plenty often to me."

"You noticed the friendly welcome?" Chance's sardonic smile had that bitter tinge.

"Why can't they understand that we'se just people like them? We want a family, a decent place to live, and a future for our children. What's so wrong about that?"

"You've just asked a whopper of a question, Emma. The man who comes up with the answer should have a marble likeness of him set in Washington." Shrugging, he changed the subject. "Tell me, do you ever use saleratus when you're cooking beans?"

They continued trading culinary secrets, discussing the merits of sourdough over yeast, an hour later as the buckboard moved south on Main, headed for home. They passed Hohner's blacksmith shop, and the horses picked up their pace.

"I feel guilty leaving Megan again so soon," Em said. The light took on the soft, clear quality of twilight when the sun has sunk behind the mountain yet indirect light still reaches the earth. Today, though, black clouds hid the sun, only an hour past its zenith.

"Did Megan say anything against you coming with me?" Chance asked, suspicion in his voice.

"No. She almost ordered me to go."

"In that case, do you feel too guilty to take a little detour with me before we go back?"

Surprised, Em asked, "Where?"

Chance laughed. It was a soft music that Em loved to hear. "My mining claim. It's three miles west of here." He scanned the sky. "I hope we don't get caught in the rain."

"I don't have to be back till supper, so I reckon I can come along." Em was enjoying herself. If only her nagging doubts about Chance would vanish. She liked his company more than she'd let herself admit. The buckboard lurched off the trail and bounced toward the hills. Em gripped the seat. Her hands ached, then felt numb.

The sky boiled with angry clouds. A chill wind cut through her thin dress, but she was afraid to let go of the seat long enough to pull her shawl about her.

"I'm sorry about the rugged trail, Emma. I usually ride Po'boy over here. It's almost too rough for a buckboard, but we're almost there."

Em drew in a relieved breath when he finally pulled the horses to a stop under a giant cottonwood. "It's over that mound. We'll walk from here."

Grateful to be on solid earth again, Em picked up her shawl and followed him through sagebrush and around wide firs for a hundred yards, watching carefully so she didn't snag her skirt.

"Here it is!" Bending, he pulled away some dry bushes to expose a deep hole in the side of a hill.

"A cave?" Em stepped closer, the worry mark showing. "Ain't it dangerous digging under the ground? The whole thing could fall on you."

"This is a natural cave. The actual mine isn't all that deep. Besides, I'm bracing it with timbers." He stepped inside. "Come and see." Scrabbling around on a ledge, he found matches and a hobo lantern made from a rusty tin can with holes punched in the side. It held a stub of candle.

Feeble light cast long flickering shadows on the inky interior. Em felt a creepy cold shiver that didn't come from the approaching storm. Slowly, like stepping on thin ice, she eased inside, her eyes wide. In the shadows to the left, she made out a bundle of clothes and a wheelbarrow with a pick and shovel lying inside.

"Here's the vein." Holding the lantern high, he pointed to the right, shoulder high. Em came close, peering at the dark streak. It was as wide as a pencil and led into the uncut earth ahead.

"That's silver? It's black."

"It has to be purified in a smelter before it'll shine." He ran a long finger along the wide line. "It's silver all right. A rich strike." Letting his hand fall to his side, he turned toward her. "In six months' time I should have enough for a nice piece of land and a small house."

A deep rolling boom reached them from outside. Em hustled twenty steps to the opening and peered out to see rain pelting the landscape. She heard Chance's footsteps behind her. When he spoke, she forgot the storm.

"I brought you here for another reason besides seeing the mine, Emma."

A spasm flitted through her stomach. Turning abruptly, she watched him, fearing his next words.

He set the lantern on the ledge and drew near enough to see the curly fringe around her dark eyes. "These past five years I've planned and schemed how I could get a place of my own and be independent—my own meat, crops, a steady income from a farm. I've had it in my mind that I'd be alone there."

He swallowed. "Then I met you." He inched closer. "During our first walk I realized that being alone isn't what I want after all. I want to share life with someone."

Em stared at him, transfixed.

Deep longing on his face, he said, "It's you, Emma. I want to share it with you."

Em's throat tightened until she feared she'd choke. She backed away from him, from his lonely eyes, from the spell he cast over her. Her emotions ran hither and yon like a rabbit seeking a way out of a hunter's well-laid trap. Was this where she'd gotten herself by spending time with a man who didn't know Jesus? No wonder God warned against being joined with unbelievers. It had seemed so natural to be with Chance, but she hated the thought of hurting him. But could she put Chance above God? She felt her pulse jumping in her neck.

She croaked, "I can't, Chance. You paint a pretty picture. . .but I can't."

"Why not?" he demanded, disappointment and hurt clouding his eyes.

She hurried on, "In the first place, I can't leave my children. Megan's about to birth that baby. She needs me. Jeremy needs me." She remembered the boy's prank and his sullen mood whenever Chance came around.

"That's not a good reason, Emma," he retorted. "It'll be another year before I've got a place ready with a house and all. By then Megan's baby will be crawling around getting into mischief."

"I'm too old!" The words gushed out unbidden.

Chance stepped toward her, grasped her shoulders, and pulled her toward him. His lips found hers for an instant.

She wrenched away. "No!"

"Am I so disgusting?"

"No! It's not that." She was trembling.

"I know what it is!" he barked, his temper flaring. "You've held on to your masters for security all these years, and you're scared to break away. That's it, isn't it?" He made it a statement, not a question.

"No!" she protested, her volume rising. "I stayed because they were my family."

Chance's firm lips twisted in disdain. "White folks?"

Indignation tightened her words. "They were my family, Chance. I didn't have no other'n. Can't you understand that?"

"No, Emma, I can't."

Em's voice grew lower, but her words shook with emotion. "I can't marry you because you aren't a believer. I'm a Christian. I can't join my life to someone who scorns the Lord. It wouldn't work."

"Show me a preacher, and I'll join the church."

"That's not what I mean. Being a Christian is a commitment of the heart, not just joining something like you'd join a political party or a posse. It's asking God to take away your sin and make you His child. When you do it, you have to mean it with all your heart."

Jaw hard, eyes glinting, Chance stared at her. A cool damp wind blew inside and put out the light. "We'd best be getting back," was all he said.

The rain stopped as quickly as it came. It left behind chilly breezes and the flavor of freshly washed air. Flipping the warm shawl about her shoulders, Em followed Chance into the light. He stayed ahead of her on the trail back to the buckboard. The journey home was long and cold and silent.

Chapter 8

Two weeks overdue, first frost arrived on the last day of September. Thus, the opening day of October marked the beginning of corn harvest. Banjo rode to several ranches and through the town seeking idle hands to join the work. The following day, a Thursday, the Circle C would host a work day—food, fun, and a fiddle provided when the sun sank below the mountain peaks.

Digging a pit for roasting the young cow Steve had butchered, Steve and Banjo labored until stars twinkled above them. In the center of the yard, Jeremy had carefully teepeed long branches for a wide, high bonfire.

Em slid her first six loaves into the oven half an hour before dawn showed its sleepy face above swaying prairie grass. Wives and daughters would accompany their menfolk to help cook lunch and supper as well as work in the field, but Em wanted to get the baking out of the way before they arrived. A work-hungry man could eat half a loaf without knowing it.

On the kitchen floor stood two bushel baskets: one of corn in the husk ready for roasting and another of fresh apples from the orchard of the Running M, Sanders's outfit.

While the second set of bread baked, Em whipped up a dozen eggs. Bacon sizzled and popped in the frying pan. Jeremy crept up behind her and wrapped his arms about her slim waist.

"Good mornin', child," she said, dropping her fork to put an arm around the boy's shoulders. His hair looked like a new rag mop. "I'll have you a plate ready by the time you wash up. Don't forget. . ."

". . .to wash behind my ears," Jeremy finished, giving her an impish grin. He banged out the back door and returned in two minutes, dragging a black comb through blond tangles.

"Who's comin' today, Em?"

"I don't rightly know, Jeremy." She lifted the last crispy strips from the pan and poured some grease from the skillet into a clean tin can. Clanging the frying pan back to the stove, she poured in a small circle of eggs. "Mr. Wyatt said he'll encourage his hands to come, though the Lord knows cowboys do hate farm work. Miss Susan may come, too, if she's feeling up to it. She won't be doin' any work, though. She and Miss Megan will sit on the sofa and visit."

"Can I have an apple?" he asked, looking over the juicy specimens before him.

"Sure thing, child. Pick out one for yourself."

He lifted two for inspection before deciding on a third. "Here, Em." He held the red fruit toward her. "I want it bald-headed."

Em smiled. "Lay it on the counter, and I'll peel it while you eat."

He scooted into a chair at the table, cocked his head at her, and asked, "How about Chance? Is he comin'?"

Em tried to act normal, but she felt her face growing tight. "I don't know about Chance, Jeremy. I haven't seen him for two weeks, since I went to Juniper that time."

Leather hinges on the front door groaned as Banjo came through. Glad for a diversion from Jeremy's quizzing, Em added more eggs to the hot pan and picked up a clean plate.

She was pulling the last loaves from the oven when the Feiklin family arrived. Draped over the kitchen counter were several snowy dish towels. On them lay twenty golden loaves in close rows. Beside the bread stood six dried-apple pies she'd prepared yesterday.

With cheeks and eyes glowing in anticipation of feminine company, Megan opened the door for Sally, who bustled in carrying a cloth-covered basket, Lisa and Jessica close behind her. Through the window, Em noticed Rod Feiklin heading for the cornfield, scythe in hand. Steve, Banjo, and Jeremy were already pulling fat ears from crackling brown stalks. They'd chop the bare corn plants and store them in bins for cattle feed against the coming winter.

"Good morning, Miz Chamberlin." Sally's brassy voice filled the house. "Are we the first ones here?" She set the basket on the table and swiveled her head toward Megan to catch the answer.

Megan glanced out the window. "I believe the Sanders family has just arrived."

Sally leaned toward Jessica. "What did she say?"

Her younger daughter leaned toward her, forming the words carefully, "She said the Sanders family is here."

Sally beamed. "Wonderful. I haven't spoken to Ruth since the barbecue." She picked up the saltshaker and threw a shower of salt over her left shoulder. "We'll need some luck today." Setting the tin container down, she snapped the cloth from the basket. Inside lay two paper sacks and a large bowl stacked with sweet rolls.

Em brought the coffeepot and a nest of cups as Sally placed the sweet rolls in the center of the table, a light breakfast for the ladies. Later, one of the girls would carry cold water and buns to the field for the men.

Within the hour the modest home seemed crowded. Elaine Sanders and her mother, Ruth, sat with the Feiklins at the table while they all peeled potatoes.

"Did I ever tell you about the time a young fellow sent me a poem every Sunday?" Sally chirped. "He'd tie the paper to a stone and throw it through my bedroom window."

"Do you remember any of the words to them?" Elaine asked.

Lisa laughed. "She's got them all in a cigar box tied up with red ribbon."

Sally singsonged, "Sally, I love you. You are my turtledove, you. Your face is a dandy. Your lips as sweet as a gum drop."

Listening from the sofa, Megan winced.

When the titters around the table died down, Ruth spoke. "What happened when the weather turned cold and you had to close your window?"

"Oh, before the summer was over, he pitched one rock too hard and cracked the mirror on my bureau. Daddy made him quit throwing stones. After that he'd slip his poems into a crack on our porch swing and stand outside my window making noises like a hoot owl. That way I knew to go downstairs and look for it." The pudgy woman smiled, remembering. "He did that till he got his feet frozen one night in a heavy snow."

"Didn't you feel sorry for him?" Elaine asked.

"I guess I did," Sally replied. "I've been married to him for twenty-one years."

Astonished looks were followed by another round of merry laughter. Chuckling over the story, Em stepped outside to check the roasting beef in the yard.

She was turning the spit when the Rocking H crew arrived. Wyatt and Susan sat in the front of the buckboard with Brent, Amos, Curly, and Chance in the wagon. Em watched Chance lift a stack of bushel baskets from the buckboard and trudge toward the field. He glanced her way but made no sign that he saw her.

Would he speak to her today? Besides a gruff good-bye when he left her two weeks ago, he hadn't said a word to her since they'd left the cave.

Why did she feel so low when she'd done the right thing?

"I'll turn the handle awhile," Lisa offered at her elbow.

"Thank you, Miss Lisa. My arm could use a rest." For the first time, Em noticed that Lisa had left her hair down.

Not very practical, the older woman mused. Releasing the makeshift spit handle, Em trudged toward the house.

Across the yard, Brent arrived at the Rocking H buckboard for his second load of tools. He lifted a scythe and paused, calculating eyes on Lisa.

Em's lips pursed thoughtfully as she watched Brent saunter in Lisa's direction. Lifting the door latch, Em stepped inside.

Beside the fireplace sat Susan, a mite thin but with roses faintly blooming in her cheeks. Across from her, Megan wove a three-inch strip of lace to put on the edge of a crib coverlet. Susan's smile widened when she saw Em.

"Miss Susan!" Em hurried over to clasp the young woman's hand. "It's good to see you lookin' so well."

"I'm almost back to normal, Em," Susan said. "I still have to nap in the afternoon, but otherwise I'm fine. There's no way I can thank you for all you did."

"That smile is thanks enough!" Em exclaimed. "You all have a nice visit while I look after the food." She bustled into the kitchen.

Potatoes peeled, the teenage girls joined the men pulling corn in the field. Sally tended the beef while Em stirred together a rice pudding and Ruth laid corn in the coals under the roasting cow.

Backs ached and feet felt like lead by the time darkness ended the workday. By twos and threes dusty, weary people trudged into the bonfire's light. Lisa, Elaine, and Jessica arrived together with smudged cheeks and bits of brown husk in their hair. Fatigue hadn't dulled the fire in Lisa's eyes. The girls joined the line in front of the full barrel beside the stable to share a common ladle. The water was cold, freshly drawn from the mountain spring behind the house.

The work lay half finished. Tomorrow Steve, Banjo, and Jeremy would finish the rest with three hired men from town.

Ernie perched on an upended log, tuning his fiddle. Tonight his bow would earn him three dollars.

Chairs from the house stood in the yard for the ladies. Steve and Banjo brought the settee to the porch so Megan and Susan could enjoy the music. Several people found logs to sit on. The rest lounged on the grass or the porch steps.

Ruth and Sally filled the sawhorse table with sliced bread, mountains of potatoes, and long pans of rice pudding dotted with raisins. Em stood beside the sizzling brown beef, cutting out hefty chunks and placing them in a bowl at her feet.

"Need some help?" a mellow voice asked.

Em faltered. "You've been working all day, Chance. Sit down and rest yourself."

"I'd rather help you." Gently, he plucked the long fork and knife from her hands. He worked without talking, but it was a different kind of silence from what they'd shared on their ride home from Juniper.

Lifting another long fork from a platter, Em dug corn from the ashes in the pit. The blackened husks crackled as she rolled them out and scooped them into a bowl. Jeremy appeared from the darkness, Lobo at his heels. He jogged past the black couple without stopping to say hello.

After prayer, folks lined up to pass by the food.

"Well, looky here." Banjo's voice rose above the rest. "Step aside, folks, and let me at the spotted pup," he said, eyeing the rice pudding. "I love that stuff almost as much as I love Kelsey, my long-eared donkey."

"There's apple pie for dessert," called someone who'd reached the end of the table. "I'm glad I'm ahead of you all." Chuckles and smiles flitted through the ranks.

Dinner was a festive affair, though it had a different flair from the barbecue. Tired and bedraggled though they were, the laborers found enough energy to play awhile before they scattered across the hills to their homes. Jeremy and Lobo sprawled side by side on the grass beside the porch steps. Ears high, the dog watched for frequent offerings thrown him by his young master.

Em sat on the steps, an empty plate on her lap. Behind her, Megan said, "Susan, are you sure you're not too tired?"

"Don't fuss over me," the young woman replied, laughing lightly. "That nap will hold me till we get home."

The Sanders family left as soon as they finished the meal. They had the longest distance to travel. Em tensed as Chance strode purposefully in her direction, glad he'd come yet wishing he'd go away.

He said, "Would you like to walk awhile?"

Her feet groaned, but Em ignored them. She couldn't bear the tenseness between them, and they needed to talk. Handing her plate to Megan, she stood. "That'd be fine, Chance."

Slowly, aimlessly, they strolled away from the garish light of the fire and a rollicking rendition of "Old Dan Tucker." The sweet odor of cut cornstalks came in waves on the breeze. When her eyes adjusted to the gloom, Em saw two forms ahead of them in the darkness and made out a riotous mass of curly hair—Lisa Feiklin with a man.

"How have you been, Emma?"

"Same as always, I guess," Em answered. "Since the canning got done, things have been quiet around here till today. I'll be pullin' corn tomorrow, I reckon." She searched her mind for a safe topic. "Miss Susan's looking right fine."

"Another week and she'll be riding again, I expect." Chance dismissed the subject and groped for another.

The moon shone like a brilliant silver dollar, shedding smooth, gentle light on the party. It was a hayride moon, a hunting moon, a lover's moon.

When he spoke, his words seemed impatient, as if he wanted to get them over with. "Look, Emma. Do you think we could go back to the way things were before? Before the cave, I mean? These two weeks I've whipped myself day and night for being a brass-plated fool. Can you forgive me?"

Maybe they could salvage a friendship out of this, even if marriage was out of the question. "Surely, Chance. I'd like to forget it ever happened."

He drew a deep breath. "So would I."

Jeremy and Lobo passed them, brushing Chance's elbow.

"Jeremy! Watch where you'se a-goin'," Emma called.

"It's a miracle he can still run," Chance remarked, "after the backbreaking day we've had."

Emma chuckled. "It's a miracle all right." She told him about Jeremy's battle with rheumatic fever.

They walked past the corral and the chicken house before circling back. A chilly breeze skipped through but quickly left to find other sport. Em wished she'd brought her wrap.

"Would you mind if I still call on you sometimes? As a friend? That is, if you don't mind being friends with an old heathen like me."

"I'd like it fine, Chance. That's what I wanted all along." She drew in a breath of clear air. Oddly, she didn't feel nearly as tired as she had twenty minutes ago.

Out of the darkness, racing Jeremy knocked Chance full in the back, almost knocking him down. The boy fell back, bounced up, and kept running.

"Jeremy Wescott!" Em cried. "What's got into you?" Mortified, she said, "I'm real sorry, Chance."

He worked his shoulders as though stretching. "Nothing's broken, I guess." His expression changed from concern to alarm. Clutching at his back, he twisted around, his movements becoming more frantic by the second.

"What is it?" Em demanded.

"Something's crawling down my shirt!" He slapped behind his shoulder blade.

"Is it stinging you?"

"Not yet." He tugged frantically at his buttons, noted Em's anxious eyes, and turned his back toward her. "I apologize, Emma. I can't abide crawly critters. Never could." Slipping out of his shirt, he shook it—then held it up, catching the firelight to check for residents.

The ludicrous situation made Em smile. Chance glanced over his shoulder.

"For shame, Emma! You laughed at me when I had that tomfool flour in my hair, and now you're about to do it again."

"I'm afraid Jeremy's up to something," she said, biting her upturned lips. "I'll speak to him about it."

"As Mr. Wyatt says, I'd be much obliged." A hint of sarcasm came through. An instant later Em's snickers died.

The glow of the flames reached Chance's bronze back. Instead of the firm, smooth flesh she expected, the thick skin was creased, puckered. Pale lines crisscrossed from shoulder to shoulder, from neck to waist. Scars. Deep, hideous scars.

Tears welled up before Em could stop them. She put out her hand and touched a white streak.

Chance froze. Slowly he turned and looked at her. Em's swimming eyes gazed mutely into his. He looked away and shrugged into his shirt.

Fastening the buttons, he spoke deliberately. "I took *Clark's Grammar* from Master Pettigrew's library. The foreman found it in my bedding. I didn't steal it. I used to take it every Saturday night to study while the others slept."

Tears spilled over one by one and slid, shining, down Em's brown cheeks. Naked pain lay grimly detailed on the man's taut face. His lips twitched.

For the first time in twenty years, Em listened to her heart instead of her head. She stepped into his arms.

One wounded creature reaching out to another, they held each other and shared the anguish, the agony that only those who know like affliction can fully understand.

"Forgive me," Em whispered into his shoulder.

"For what?"

"For acting like your past was no account." She drew away and lifted her wet face to him. "I don't know all the answers, Chance. Fact is, I don't know half as many as I thought I did ten minutes ago." She pulled in a shaky breath. "But I do know that Jesus can help you. If only I could explain it to you better."

He placed a finger on her lips, his voice thick with unexpressed emotion. "Let it lie, Emma. Please."

Closing her eyes, she nodded. He lifted her hand and placed it inside his crooked elbow. They took one more slow turn around the yard, not talking but sensing deeper companionship than mere conversation could provide.

Near the fire, Ernie was sawing out "Buffalo Gals" when Wyatt's voice sliced through the music. "The Rocking H wagon is pulling out. Everybody get aboard."

"Okay if I come by next week?" Chance asked.

The woman by his side smiled softly. "I'll bake a cake."

"Gingerbread with icing sugar?"

They laughed. It had an infectious, warm sound. He touched her chin lightly before he turned away.

Em watched him stride toward the stable, where Wyatt and Susan waited in the buckboard. Brent and Lisa lingered beside the wagon, waiting for the last passenger to climb aboard before they said good night.

After the buckboard vanished, Em scanned the yard—now occupied by the Feiklins, Banjo, and Steve—seeking a small boy. Ernie scratched away at the last verse of "Good-bye Ole Paint, I'm A-Leavin' Cheyenne," the usual signal that the party was breathing its last.

On the steps Em collared protesting Jeremy and hauled him into the house, shushing him as they moved so he wouldn't bother Megan, who had already retired. A lighted lantern rested on the mantel shelf.

"Now then, Mr. Jeremy," she whispered fiercely when they reached the empty living room. "What's this about tormenting poor Chance? First flour in his hat and now a bug down his back." Her eyes skewered him. Jeremy stood before her, carefully inspecting his bare toes.

"What's got into you, child?"

Finally, he blurted out, "He's gonna take you away, ain't he, Em?"

"Take me away?" The weary woman repeated. She grasped the boy's shoulders. He looked up at her, the corners of his mouth pulled down. Leaning toward him until her nose came inches from his, Em said softly, "He's not gonna take me away, Jeremy. You're my boy. Nothin' could ever change that, you hear?"

Jeremy threw his arms around her middle, squeezing the breath out of her. "I couldn't stand it if you went away, Em."

Em pressed him tightly to her heart. *Lord,* she prayed, *this knot's got to be untangled. And You'se the only One who can do it.*

Sunday morning the Chamberlin family lingered around the breakfast table, relaxing their aching joints and heavy heads. The last of the corn had been bagged and—with the last chopped stalks—had been loaded into the barn at midnight. That was eight hours ago. Every man and woman was anxious for a quiet, restful day.

"Six hundred bushels from twenty-five acres ain't bad, Chamberlin," Banjo remarked.

"A bumper year," Steve agreed, stretching back in the chair, legs straight out before him. "Let it rain buckets now. The better to sleep by."

Beside him Megan chided, "Now, Steve. You've never slept in the daytime in your life."

"I feel like today'd be a good startin' place." He sipped his third cup of coffee.

"A rider," Banjo announced, leaning back to look out the window. "Looks like one of Hammond's men."

"I hope Susan's not sick again," Megan worried. "I'm afraid she overdid herself by coming Thursday."

Jeremy scampered out the door without closing it behind him, hoping to take care of the man's horse. The rider turned out to be Wyatt himself. He tossed the reins to Jeremy and strode to the house. Hat in hand, the rancher stepped inside.

"Mornin', Wyatt," Steve called from his seat. "Come on in and take a chair. We're actin' like rich folks over breakfast. Been sittin' here for an hour or more. Care for some coffee?"

"That would hit the spot." Wyatt took a place next to Banjo and reached for the full cup Em offered. He took a long sip and sighed. "The field looks good. You finish last night?"

"At midnight," Steve said. He handed Wyatt a plate with two biscuits left on it.

"How's Susan?" Megan asked.

Their guest split a biscuit and smeared it with freshly churned butter. "I left her scrubbing breakfast dishes. We had us a full-fledged squall this morning.

Chance didn't come back after his day off, and she insisted on cooking for the hands." He chuckled softly. "When a woman gets her dander up, Chamberlin, there's no talkin' her down."

"Where's Chance?" Megan asked, impatient for news.

"Nobody knows. To make matters worse, we got a visit from Sheriff Feiklin at first light this mornin'. Late Friday night some hombre robbed the stage to Cedar Grove. He got away with ten thousand dollars in coin and silver nuggets. Witnesses say the robber was a black man."

Chapter 9

Em laid aside her dishcloth and stood beside the table near Megan's chair while Wyatt continued his story.

"Feiklin searched Chance's room and found a sack filled with silver nuggets. Three thousand dollars worth, according to him."

Em interrupted. She couldn't bear to hear more. "Chance got those nuggets from a mine in the hills. He took me there on our way back from Juniper. Chance would never steal!"

"Susan and I agree with you, Em. That's why I rode over. I knew you and Chance have been friendly, and I was hoping you could give me a clue where Chance might have gone."

"Why didn't he come home last night?" she asked.

"The sheriff told us that Chance showed up in Juniper on Saturday afternoon. He went into Harper's store and bought a shovel. Somebody saw him ride in. They rounded up a posse to shanghai Chance when he came back into the street.

"When Chance realized what the gang was up to, he knocked down two of them with the shovel, cut open a third man's head, and lit out on Po'boy. Two of the jaspers found a couple of empty saddles and took out after him. They lost him in the hills. No one's seen hide nor hair of him since." Hammond drummed his fingertips on the table. "Unfortunately, the sheriff takes that as a sign he's guilty."

Em's worry mark widened. She pulled out a chair and plopped into it as though her knees had given out. Four pairs of eyes watched her. Four pairs of ears waited for her to speak.

She stared out the window. A brown sparrow walked across the outer sill, head bobbing forward at each step. When it reached the edge, it leapt into the air, body curved, tail spread, and wings wide. Em sighed twice. Finally, she faced Wyatt. "If I tell you where he is, what will you do?"

"Just talk to him, Em. If he gives me his word that he didn't rob the stage, I'll believe him. But remember, whether he's guilty or not, the safest plan is for him to surrender to Sheriff Feiklin and stand trial. Then his name will be cleared."

"What if he don't agree to that?"

"I won't force him to do anything, Em. I can't force him."

"You could turn him in."

Wyatt's eyes crinkled as his words intensified. "That's the last thing I want to do. Please believe me."

Em searched his open, concerned face for a long moment.

Banjo leaned forward, his forearm on the table. "Chance needs some friends right now, Em. Who else will help him if we don't?"

"Will you go along, Banjo?" Em asked.

"Be glad to."

She turned back to Wyatt. The lines on her face had deepened. Her eyes were pools of pain. "I want to go, too."

"That's okay by me," Wyatt said, stroking his beard.

Megan and Steve were solemn spectators to the drama unfolding before them. Megan reached out to clasp Em's hand as the troubled woman spoke.

"He's probably in the cave near Fox Hole Creek where his mine is. I saw some food and clothing stored there. The cave's hidden, so he'd likely think it's the safest place."

Banjo asked, "Can you find it again?"

"I reckon so. At least comin' from Juniper way I could."

Megan squeezed Em's hand and said, "I'll take care of the house today."

Steve intervened, his expression a mixture of love and resolve. "You mean Jeremy and I will take care of the house, little lady. You didn't sleep till way past midnight last night."

Megan ruefully smiled at her second mother. "I couldn't get comfortable. I feel like a lumpy sack of potatoes these days."

"I hate to leave you, honey," Em said.

Banjo stood and scraped his chair back. "If the cave's between here and Juniper, we shouldn't be gone long, Em."

Megan reached out to Em for a hug. "Go ahead with the men. Steve will take your place bossing me today. You can have your turn when you get back."

Em gave Megan a squeeze and got to her feet. She headed into the kitchen to pack some food. Chance would surely be hungry by now.

In the buckboard, Banjo and Em crossed the creek with Jeremy and Lobo trailing behind it. Wyatt rode his sleek palomino, Ben. Boy and dog stopped for a rough-and-tumble before racing back toward the house. The cornfield lay full of awkward stubbles.

Few words passed between them on the journey. Em twisted her hands together and focused on the horizon, oblivious to the sharp-edged smell of autumn, the brown foliage razed by frost. Only the firs and pines remained clothed in deep green—like soldiers in proud uniform.

"It was somewhere in here," Em decided a little more than an hour later. She peered west, straining to find a familiar boulder or tree. "There it is! See the spot where the trail widens?"

The buckboard rattled and jolted around the turn.

Beside her, Banjo remarked, "With this racket, he'll light out before we get there."

"We'll have to walk a good ways," Em said. "I doubt he can hear the wagon from where we have to stop."

The closer they drew to the cave, the more anxious she became. Would Chance trust Wyatt and Banjo enough to let them help him?

"We walk from here," she announced ten minutes later. The cottonwood's spreading limbs held limp, drab scraps of what had been brilliant gold only two weeks ago. A few more days and all its leaves would lie scattered about the hillside.

Em gnawed her lip. Her face was seamed with worry as she stepped to the ground. "How about if I go up first and talk with him alone?" she asked.

"You're calling the shots, Em," Wyatt said. His proud stallion stood ground hitched nearby. "If that's what you want, we'll wait here. Give a holler when you're ready for us." The men followed her for a dozen paces then turned to the left to rest on a fallen log.

Heart thumping dully, Em slowly wound around the sage-strewn incline. Thirty feet from the cave entrance she stopped and called, "Chance! It's Em! I need to talk to you."

Heavy silence answered her. Listening to her own breathing, she waited.

Ten heartbeats later, his uncertain voice called, "You alone, Emma?"

"Look outside and see for yourself," she called. "I came because I want to help you, Chance."

"Come on in." He spoke like a condemned man waiting to hear his sentence.

Em reached the door of the cave and pulled a small crackling bush from the edge of the mound before her. Chance's strong hands reached out to widen the gap for her.

She stepped inside, peering at his gaunt, weary face through the dim light. "You okay? You gave me the scare of my life."

"I gave you a scare? I haven't been sittin' up here enjoying the scenery."

To the left lay a rumpled coat that looked as if it had been used as a blanket. The hobo's lantern lay cold and dark on its shelf. A tall bay gelding stood hobbled and snubbed up short by the far right wall.

"I came to hear your story," she told him. "Mr. Wyatt rode in this morning to tell us what happened. He thinks you're innocent, Chance. He says he wants to help you."

"You sure he isn't just trying to find out where I am so he can tell Feiklin?"

Em studied his haggard face before saying, "Mr. Wyatt's your boss man. You'll know the answer to that if you study on it awhile."

The gelding stamped and sidled away from the wall. His saddle lay on the ground a short distance away.

Bottom lip thrust forward, Chance said, "If somebody would let me prove where I was when the robbery happened, I might be able to clear myself." He shrugged. "Maybe. I don't even know when the holdup happened."

"I know someone who wants to hear what you have to say."

"Who?"

"Banjo and Mr. Wyatt." Em's chin came up. "They're waiting outside." She raised her hand. "Simmer down, Chance. They want to help you."

Chance grimaced. "Sure." He sounded anything but sure.

Em's temper blossomed. "Use them smart brains in your head, man! While you're thinking, think about this: If they don't help you, who will? You can't hide here all winter. You'll freeze. And what'll you eat?" She held out the sack of food in her hands. "I brought you this, but it won't last over two days."

Immediately, he lost interest in the argument. Taking the sack, he peered inside, holding the wide mouth sideways to catch the light. "You're a saint, Emma," he murmured. He lifted out a slab of beef and bread wrapped in a light cloth and, setting the canvas aside, lost half his face in the sandwich.

Em's heart twisted. The man must be half starved. While he ate, she took stock of her surroundings. A dented pail, pick, and shovel lay inside a wheelbarrow. Two empty tins and a canteen lay beside the rumpled coat, but she could detect no traces of a cooking fire.

Swallowing the last crumb, he said, "I've had two cans of peaches, some cold beans, and two hard biscuits these past two days. At night I sneak down to the creek to fill my canteen."

She pushed away the sentimental feelings gripping her. She must talk reason to him. Her question had a hard edge. "You think things'll get easier from here?"

His shoulders sagged. "Bring the men in."

Em gripped his arm, her expression softening. "You won't be sorry, Chance. Banjo and Mr. Wyatt are right as rain."

"I feel like a rat in a barrel. I don't even have a gun."

Three minutes later Em entered the makeshift doorway with two men ducking in behind her. Chance stood five paces back in the darkness of the cave, his jaw hard, his eyes narrowed.

Banjo paused a moment, squinting his eyes trying to adjust to the dimness. He stepped forward, hand outstretched. "Howdy, Chance. You're a sight for sore eyes. For a while there, I was afraid you wouldn't talk to us."

Chance shook Banjo's hand and quickly dropped it.

The old veteran went on, "We want to help you. Both Wyatt and I can read signs, and we thought we may be able to pick up some clues the sheriff won't find."

Of course they could read tracks. Why didn't I think of that before? Em wondered. Hope rose in her heart.

Banjo went on, "Feiklin's honest as the day, but he's always in a hurry. If he's satisfied that he knows who's guilty, he won't look any further."

Wyatt added, "We want to hear what you have to say, Chance. Susan's worried half to death about you."

At the mention of Susan's name, the black man relaxed a little. "How's Miss Susan getting along? I'm sorry to have to leave her with the cooking."

"She's in fine fettle," Wyatt said, grinning. "We had a big ruckus this morning. She insisted on cooking for the men. I tried to talk her out of it, but short of dragging her out by the hair, I couldn't make any headway." He chuckled. "She finally picked up a cast-iron spider pan and chased me out of the house. Said not to come back till I found you and did something to help."

Chance drew in a long breath. He wanted to go home. "Let's sit down," the wanted man said, moving two steps toward the front, where more light trickled in.

Perched on the hard-packed earth, Chance rubbed his face with both hands in an agitated gesture. Wyatt and Banjo sat across from him, but Em remained standing. She refused to soil her dress by sitting on the ground. The horse swished his tail and blew.

"When did the robbery happen?" Chance rasped out.

Wyatt answered, "Friday evening after sundown. The holdup man stopped the stage where the road to Cedar Grove cuts through the woods. The road runs along our south property line at that spot."

The hunted man gazed into the middle distance, considering. "I'd turned in by that time, I reckon. Miss Susan gave me the whole of Saturday off. I wanted to head out before first light, so I went to bed right after the supper dishes."

Banjo grunted. "That cuts out an alibi. Where did you go when you left home?"

"Up here. I worked till past noon, when my shovel hit a stone and a big piece of metal chipped off. I rode into town to buy another one. When I came out of Harper's store, a bunch of men tried to jump me. They said I'd robbed a stage and called me some names I'd rather not repeat. One of them shouted that they ought to string me up." He paused, sweat beading on his forehead.

Em's throat tightened. She hid her trembling hands in the pockets of her skirt.

Chance went on. "I guess I panicked. I swung at them with the shovel, knocked a couple down, and ran for Po'boy. That horse has bottom, I tell you. He lit out of there like a jackrabbit with his tail on fire and didn't quit till we got to Fox Hole Creek.

"I circled wide around and came back here. I've been here ever since."

"Who jumped you?" Wyatt asked. "Did you know the men?"

"Link Hensler was the ringleader. He was the one promoting a necktie party. I've seen the other four a few times, but I don't know their names."

Banjo spoke up. "Where'd you get them silver nuggets?"

"You're looking at the place. I've been working this mine for more than a year. I haven't turned in any ore because I was afraid there'd be a run on the area if the news got out that I'd made a strike."

"Sheriff Feiklin found your nuggets, Chance," Wyatt said. "He took the sack with him as evidence."

Chance's head jerked around. His nostrils flared out. "Evidence! Evidence of what? That silver cost me sweat and blood." Chest heaving, he glared at the bearded man across from him. "What right did he have to take my silver?"

"The stage carried ten thousand in coin and silver nuggets," Wyatt continued calmly, "so finding a sack of nuggets in your room looks mighty bad." He scratched the back of his neck. "I wish you hadn't kept your mine a secret, Chance. But it's all water over the dam now. We'll have to go on from here."

Em's voice made them crane their necks upward. "Can you all do anything to help him?"

"We can try to track down the guilty cuss," Banjo replied grimly. "The thief was no stranger to Juniper. How many folks know that the Rocking H has a black cook, that the road to Cedar Grove passes by the backside of the ranch, and that the stage was carrying so much money?"

Banjo got to his feet and dusted the backside of his pants. "We'd best be movin' on. I'd like to ride into Juniper and talk to the stage manager, Buckeye Mullins. He's a friend of mine."

Em stepped closer to Chance as he stood up. "Is there anything you need?" she asked.

"A couple blankets and some hot food. I'm afraid to build a fire in case someone comes nosing around." He turned to Wyatt. "Can you take my horse home? I can't keep him. There's no food for him here."

Banjo spoke up. "How about if I turn him into the box canyon with our beeves? Feiklin will be less likely to find him there."

"I'm obliged," Chance said shortly. His attitude had improved slightly, but he wasn't bursting with warm friendship. He strode to Po'boy, speaking softly as he untied the knots.

"Chance," Wyatt said, grasping Po'boy's bridle, "we'll do what we can."

Banjo lifted the saddle. Men and horse slipped through the doorway, but

Em waited. She wanted to say something comforting before she left. But what?

Finally, she blurted out, "Take care of yourself. I'll see you in a couple days."

He stared. His face turned hard and cold. "If they put out a reward on me, I'll swing from a rope. Maybe it's just as well. From where I stand, living isn't such a treat. I'm tired of being kicked around. Go on home, Emma. I'll be just fine. And you can tell your friends I'm not worth helping. Not that they intend to help me anyway."

Chapter 10

After Banjo and Wyatt carried Em back to the Circle C, Banjo saddled Kelsey. The men paused long enough to swallow a sandwich and a bowl of Megan's turnip soup before dusting off to Juniper.

Em scarcely touched her lunch. She stared glumly at the blue gingham hanging beside the dining room window.

Gathering, scraping, and stacking dirty plates, Megan asked, "Are you okay, Em? You haven't said three words since you came home."

Em laid her spoon on top of Megan's pile. "I keep seeing Chance standing in that dark cave. He looked like he'd lost his last friend. I reckon he thinks he has, Miss Megan. He don't rightly trust Banjo and Mr. Wyatt." She sighed. "Even if those fellers find the real thief, Chance is so bitter and twisted up inside that I doubt he'll ever turn to the Lord."

Megan pulled out the chair next to Em and sat. Eleven days from the projected end of her vigil, her movements were awkward, her face puffy with added pounds. She reached for Em's strong hand lying limply on the oak table. "Things look bad, Em. But I know God can turn it around for good. Let's pray about it right now." She closed her eyes.

Em dipped hot water from the reservoir at the back of the stove and poured it into a basin. Megan trundled to the bedroom for her prescribed afternoon nap.

A few moments later, a shout drew the weary black woman to the window.

"Anybody home?" It was a resonating voice, as if it came from the inside of a cracker barrel.

Em felt close to panic when she peeked through the window and recognized Sheriff Rod Feiklin. He stood at the porch steps. His horse, a blue roan with an apron face, cropped grass ten feet behind him. The lawman held his tan Montana Slope, and wisps of gray hair lay plastered across his pink skull. Like his jeans and blue flannel shirt, his hat showed plenty of mileage.

"Chamberlin!"

Like a young'un expecting a lickin', Em moved to the door and gently lifted the latch. "Miss Megan's restin'," she said, stepping outside. "Mr. Steve is on the range today."

Five feet eight and two hundred pounds, the man before her stood wide in the body, thick in the neck, and deep in the chest. His round florid face hung down in big jowls with a permanent five o'clock shadow. He wore a scuffed cowhide vest sporting a shiny silver star.

Feiklin didn't smile or greet her. He merely grunted, "I reckon it's you I want to talk to anyway."

Em trod to the top of the stairs. She rubbed the inside of her fingers with a nervous thumbnail.

"I saw you walkin' out with Hammond's cook at the corn harvest. One gets you fifty, you know where he ran off to." He stood with his shoulders thrown back, his feet planted, and his jaw tilted upward. His large, lumpy nose had red veins crisscrossing it.

At porch level, Em stood far above the lawman. She unwound her fists, making a conscious effort to look at ease.

"If you know his whereabouts," he went on, "you'd do him a favor by tellin' me. He'll get a fair trial."

Em could hear Chance's sarcastic voice answering, *Sure.*

"He didn't do it," Em managed to croak. "He's been minin' silver for over a year. Them nuggets was his."

The sheriff barked, "He's the only black man for twenty miles, and he left a trail a fresh fish could follow. It made a beeline for the Rocking H."

"He didn't do it, Mr. Sheriff," Em repeated. "That's all I can tell you."

Feiklin eyed her, cold suspicion drawing up his lips. "I've got a posse scouring the hills. If they find him before he turns himself in, they may just have to shoot him for resisting arrest. I'm puttin' a five-hundred-dollar ree-ward out for the thief. Dead or alive."

Em clenched her teeth. She didn't make another sound.

Her tormentor pinned her under a killing stare for a count of ten before grabbing the trailing reins of his roan and heaving his bulk into the leather. "You think it over. I'll be back."

Weak as a newborn kitten, Em stepped inside and closed the door. She sank to the settee, bowed her head on her hands, and sobbed.

⌒

Unaware of Em's despair, Wyatt and Banjo enjoyed a pleasant ride. Though afternoon, the air still held that gentle nip, that subtle coolness craved by mountain folk and city dwellers alike. Summer had finally cashed in her chips.

Banjo resettled his ragged hat and glanced at his companion mounted on the handsome honey-colored horse with satiny white mane and tail. "What do ya think?" he asked.

"About Chance?" Wyatt replied. "He's innocent, Banjo. I knew that before I left the house this morning."

"That's what I figured, too. I wish Feiklin wasn't so quick on the trigger."

"I tried to tell him," Wyatt said, "but he wasn't havin' any."

In Juniper they tied their mounts to the hitching rail in front of the tiny stage station. Except for a plump housewife walking down the boardwalk with a basket on her arm, the town looked dead.

Inside the station the men removed their hats and glanced around. They smelled raw tobacco. The stage depot measured half the size of Harper's store. A short backless bench lay tucked against the right wall as they entered. To the left hung a cork board covered with a schedule, various notices, and a freshly printed wanted poster. The men paused to read it: "$500 REWARD FOR THE MAN WHO ROBBED THE CEDAR GROVE STAGE." It didn't mention Chance by name. Four strides from the door sat a man behind the counter, a short, leathery gent with a handlebar mustache and a scar on his left jaw. The black mustache twitched into a smile when he saw Banjo.

"Well, howdy, Banjo, you ole sidewinder. I haven't seen you in a coon's age. . . Wyatt. How's it goin'?"

Wyatt nodded a greeting.

"We've been gettin' in the corn crop and reddin' up the place for winter," Banjo said, his manner relaxed and friendly, "so I haven't been in town for a while. I hear you've had some excitement hereabouts." He leaned an arm on the polished walnut surface between him and Buckeye Mullins.

"Don't you know it." The mustache drooped back into place, and Mullins shifted a wad of Bull Durham tobacco to the other side of his mouth. "First time one of my stages has been hit. I'd like to tie the thievin' hairpin to the nearest tree."

"Any idea who did it?" Banjo probed.

"Black man, six foot tall, give or take an inch, medium build. He wasn't wearing a mask. He rode a tall bay with a white blaze."

Not good. Po'boy was a tall bay with a white blaze.

"What did the hombre look like?"

"Look like?" the stage manager barked. "What does it matter? They all look alike. Ain't that many black boys in these parts." He squinted at Wyatt. "Matter of fact, your cook is the only one I know of."

Wyatt's lips tightened.

Banjo quickly asked, "Who was on the stage, Buckeye? Anyone I know?"

Mullins grasped a giant black ledger and pulled it toward him. Flipping it open, he ran a wide finger down the page. "Byron Cotton had a ticket through to Colorado Springs. And A. J. Kinny of Cedar Grove." He closed the book. "Just them two. The driver, Shorty Gates, drives through to Colorado Springs. He'll be back tomorrow night."

They chatted a few minutes about the frightening increase in crime before

Wyatt and Banjo broke away and stepped back into the sunshine.

"I know Kinny, one of the passengers," Banjo told his friend. "He works in a blacksmith shop fixin' pots and coffee grinders. Let's ride to Cedar Grove and have a little talk with him."

Wyatt nodded. "We can check out the site of the robbery when we pass it. But first, let's cross over to the livery stable. I'd like to hear what Link Hensler has to say for himself."

Across Main Street and two places north, Benson's Livery was owned by a man with the girth of a fifty-gallon drum. He spent his days in a chair beside the wide double doors. Whether he sat inside or outside depended on the weather, but he always occupied his place. Benson found it easiest to hire passing saddle bums and youngsters to muck out the stalls and dole out grain.

Today, the doors stood wide, the sun reaching far inside to chase away the morning's chill. Banjo paused only long enough to say, "Hensler around?"

Benson jerked his meaty head to the left. "He's on shovel duty inside. Help yourself."

The stable reeked of manure, hay, and horseflesh. Only three residents filled the ten slots lining the back of the wide room: a bay, a paint, and a buckskin.

Wyatt cast an appraising eye over the horses. "That's Hensler's horse," he told Banjo in low tones, indicating the buckskin. Pausing a brief moment, the men took in the long deep ridges streaking the horse's belly and sides. Wyatt's jaw hardened. Evidently Hensler frequently gouged spurs to his mount, a practice that Wyatt, a former wrangler, despised.

"Ya lookin' for something?" Hensler's drawl sounded out from the end of the building.

"Howdy, Hensler," Wyatt called. "We came to ask you about Saturday." He led the way toward the hostler.

Hensler leaned a grubby shirt sleeve on a spade handle, dark eyes on his callers.

"When you came on Chance in Juniper, I mean," the blond man finished. "What exactly happened?"

Banjo sized up the man while Wyatt talked. Five foot eleven and one hundred sixty pounds, Link Hensler had a thin, flat frame that matched his flat face. His thick red lips pursed as he considered Wyatt's question. Was that suspicion lurking behind his eyes?

The hostler waited a moment before answering, "The sheriff and Buckeye Mullins had told a bunch of us at the restaurant how a black man had robbed the stage. Well, you and I both know they's only one hombre in these parts who fits that description." He scratched his belly with broken, black nails. "Me and some fellows—Tom, Jim, Joey, and Abe—were moseying down the street on Saturday just mindin' our business when that black boy stepped out of Harper's holdin' a new shovel. Well, we all looked at each other, and someone said, 'Let's take him. He ain't heeled.'

"So we all cat-footed up behind him. He saw us before we could grab him, and all of a sudden he turned into a wild man. Knocked Jim and Tom down and cut open Abe's head. The thievin' galoot jumped into the saddle and lit out like the devil himself was on his tail." Hensler shrugged. "That's the last we saw of him."

Banjo spoke, "Did anyone mention hangin' him?"

Hensler's grin had a wicked curve. "Now that you ask, I reckon someone did. But nothin' came of it. He got plumb away before we could lay hands on a rope."

Noting Wyatt's set look, his tight fist, Banjo said, "We'd best be headin' out, Wyatt." He caught the young rancher's eye. "We've got some ridin' to do."

He turned to the hostler. "Thanks for the chin music, Hensler. We heard Chance had been in town, and we wanted to hear about it."

"There's a posse out today," the shovel-wielding man volunteered, "but I couldn't go. I hope they get him quick. He deserves to get his neck stretched. A body won't feel safe till he's behind bars at least." He leaned over, thrusting the blunt end of the spade along the ground.

Five minutes later donkey and horse cantered out of town, humble Kelsey keeping time with elegant Ben. Slowing to a walk as a grove of pines and scrub oaks closed around them, Banjo leaned forward, studying the ground.

"The trail's a day old already, but we haven't had any rain. We should still be able to find. . ." He drew up on the reins. "Eureka!" Quickly, he swung down. Wyatt followed suit but stood well back, his eyes on the soil at Banjo's feet.

Chapter 11

B anjo squatted beside the road, pointing. "Here's the stage tracks. They have narrow wheels, too fine for a buckboard. Yesterday's stage cut through them. The horses must have been nervous during the holdup because the wheels of this coach rocked back and forth a few times. See it?"

"I'm following ya."

"There's a nice boot print on the side. Must be the driver's. The thief stayed mounted." He moved off the trail into softer earth. "Here's some horse tracks." Wyatt circled around to join Banjo without stepping on the marks in the dirt.

"Those aren't Rocking H shoes," the young rancher declared. "They're too heavy. Slim uses a lighter shoe. He does all our smithing."

Banjo glanced at the sun, glowing high in the sky. "We have a little time. Let's see where he went."

They quartered the roadside, searching for a trail away from the robbery. Fifteen minutes later, Wyatt raised his hand. "Over here! He cut away south then turned back north into our land." He squinted at the sky, figuring the direction. "He headed straight for the ranch if he stayed on course."

They wound through the trees, studying the ground, before mounting up and quickening the pace. A quarter of a mile later, a small stream cut across their path. The muddy edge was trampled, a mixture of boot prints and horseshoes.

"Well, looky here," Banjo said, stepping down. He peered at the tracks, memorizing the details. "He has a bit of a drag on the left leg. Probably not noticeable to someone watching him walk."

Wyatt scanned the opposite bank. "He crossed over. Still headed for the ranch." He stroked his beard. "Why would he come to the Rocking H? He ought to be running for the hills."

"Feiklin has seen these same tracks, Hammond. No wonder he thinks Chance is guilty. Our good sheriff has quite a case." Banjo stared at the tracks across the stream, lips pursed. "I think somebody's runnin' a blazer, deliberately pointing to Chance."

"What a lowdown trick!" Wyatt wasn't surprised that they might be up against a con artist's hoax, but it didn't increase their odds of catching the villain.

Banjo's features hardened. "We're gonna nail his hide, Hammond. I'm promisin' you that." He picked up Kelsey's dragging reins. "Let's go."

The thief's trail led through the yard of a dilapidated line shack with a sagging roof and straight into the Rocking H yard. He'd tethered his horse to the hitching rail beside the bunkhouse. Scouring the ground, Wyatt found several older tracks nearby. Evidently, the guilty man frequently visited the Rocking H.

Or maybe he worked there.

Wyatt pulled off his brown, flat-crowned hat and scratched his head. "Let's say howdy to Susan and get a drink before we move along."

Banjo rubbed his stomach and said, "I'm agreeable. Maybe she's been baking pies or bear sign."

Wyatt chuckled at Banjo's use of that name for doughnuts. "After this morning, she'd probably throw them at me."

The men walked around the house to enter through the back. Giving Banjo a watch-this expression, Wyatt eased the kitchen door open twelve inches. "Should I throw my hat in first?" he called.

Susan's saucy voice came back, "Wyatt Hammond, what are you up to now?" Her slender hand pushed the door open; her slim form filled the doorway. She ran lightly toward Wyatt, aimed for his arms. Catching sight of Banjo at the last minute, she drew up short, cheeks flaming. "Banjo! How nice to see you!"

Banjo's stubbled jaw widened into a grin. "We thought we'd wet our whistles while we're close."

Wyatt slipped his arm about his wife's waist, laughing eyes looking down at her. "A sandwich or two would hit the spot. We may not be back till late."

"Welcome to my parlor," Susan laughed, stepping back to let them in. "I've got two steaks in the frying pan. You caught me cooking lunch. The beans are already finished."

"If you weren't already employed, I'd hire you," Wyatt teased, tweaking her ponytail as she hurried away. The men found seats at the kitchen table.

"Did you find Chance?" Susan asked, forking mansize steaks onto plates.

"He's safe," her husband said. "We talked to him."

"Come on, Wyatt," she urged, "don't quit now. What did he say?" She dished up beans and set the food before them. Grabbing two cups, she poured coffee.

Wyatt quickly told her of Chance's silver mine and Banjo's theory that someone had framed the cook. "We're on our way to Cedar Grove to talk to one of the stage passengers who saw the thief," he finished.

Chewing a juicy bit of beef, Banjo noted that Wyatt hadn't mentioned the trail that led to their ranch. Swallowing the last of their coffee, they reached for their hats.

"Thanks for the meal, Miss Susan," Banjo said. "It's good to see you lookin' so fit."

Susan's bantering mood faded. Absolutely serious, she gazed from Banjo to

Wyatt and back again. "Help Chance, Banjo," she said. "For Em's sake. Help him."

"We're givin' it a brass-plated try," Banjo replied.

"Don't worry if I'm late," Wyatt said, planting his hat above his ears.

They rode into Cedar Grove as the light faded to dull gloom. At the northern edge of town, the blacksmith shop had its doors locked. Closed for the day.

"There's a light on at the sheriff's office," Banjo said, prodding Kelsey forward. "He'll know where Kinny lives."

Following the white-haired lawman's terse directions, they stumbled up the dark stairs outside the general store. The moon had not yet risen, and they didn't have a lantern. Kinny lived in an apartment above the store.

Banjo knocked loudly, calling, "A. J. Kinny? It's me, Banjo Calahan."

The door creaked inward. From the semidark interior a scratchy, deep voice boomed, "What're you doin' in this neck o' the woods, Banjo, you old hooligan? Come on in. Who's yer partner?"

The tall man with his hand on the door was bacon thin, with the stooped shoulders of a man who'd spent years bending over a worktable. His ruddy face looked like a rubber ball squeezed in the middle so that the top bulged up. His forehead stretched more than four inches from deep-set eyes to a close-cropped shock of brown hair.

Banjo stepped across the sill. "Meet Wyatt Hammond, owner of the Rocking H spread. This is A. J. Kinny. We used to work together on the Lazy R." He playfully punched Kinny's chest. "That was at least a century ago, eh, A. J.?"

"Maybe two from the looks of you." Kinny *haw-hawed*. He stretched a big bony hand toward the table and chairs in the center of the room. "Light and set."

Each chose a straight-backed chair around the yellow glow of a single lantern in the center of the square table. The room was clean but spare. No curtains. No rugs. No woman's touch.

Banjo got right to the point. "You were on the stage that got robbed Friday night."

"For my sins." Kinny's unsightly mug waited expectantly.

"The sheriff of Juniper thinks a friend of ours held up that stage, A. J. We need to know exactly what the robber looked like. It could mean an innocent man's freedom."

"He was a black man on a tall bay."

Banjo glanced at Wyatt and waited. When Kinny didn't volunteer more details, Banjo's eyes bored into the lean man. "Surely you can tell us more than that. What was his hair like? Did he wear a mask? How tall was he? What build? What about his clothes? Did he have a gun?"

Kinny held up a hand as though warding off a blow. "Okay. Okay. I've got you in my sights." He coughed and shifted in the chair, making it creak. With hair like that, he might have just stepped in from a gale. Each short brown strand stood on end, but few went in the same direction.

The gangly man cocked his head, remembering. "We'd been in the stage for about an hour when a shout made me and Cotton look out. Cotton was the other passenger.

"The coach drew up real quick like. Outside beside the driver was this black man mounted on a bay and wavin' a hogleg like he meant it. I heard him say, 'Hand me the strongbox and no funny business.'"

Banjo interrupted. "What was his voice like?"

Squinting, Kinny paused. "He sounded like a gent from Dixie. Took twice as long to get those words out as you or I would."

Banjo leaned a forearm on the table, concentrating on the man's words.

"His hair touched his shoulders. It was coal black and woolly comin' out from under his Stetson. Looked like he forgot how to use a comb.

"Once he'd set the strongbox in his lap, he prodded his horse over to the door of the stage and told us to hand out our cash."

"What about his skin?" Banjo prompted. "How dark was it?"

"When I said black I meant it. Now that I think about it, he looked a little strange, that black face with fat red lips. Night was coming on, and his lips was about all I could see in the bad light. I remember thinkin' how shiny my gold eagles looked in his coal-black palm."

"What kind of gun?"

"A Colt, I guess." He paused. "No, wait a minute. It was a pepperbox, a twelve shot." He grinned but without humor. "That bore looked big as a cannon pointin' my way." His rough voice became tense, impatient. "Anything else you want to know?"

"Think back real close," Banjo said. "Did you see any marks on him? Anything besides his skin color that would set him apart?"

Kinny relaxed in the hard chair, eyes gazing dully into a dark corner. His visitors didn't move a muscle. Silently they willed him to recall some vital tidbit that would buy Chance's freedom.

Suddenly Kinny's face took on a surprised look. "Yes, by jingo," he said. "A jagged scar on the back of his gun hand, his right. It's an ugly thing. Raised and bumpy."

Banjo thumped the table with his fist. "That's the ticket."

Kinny's good humor reappeared. "Now that you've pumped me dry, would you like some coffee?" Banjo shoved his chair away from the table and stood. Wyatt followed suit.

"Wish we had time, A. J.," the old-timer said, settling his stained Stetson in place. "But we've got to mosey along." He shook the blacksmith's carbon-stained hand. "We'll have to get together and swap yarns sometime. I owe you one, A. J. Call on me anytime."

"I'll do it." Kinny followed them to the door and shut the travelers into the night.

The journey home seemed double long as the hour approached midnight. "Rock of ages. . ." Banjo's low voice drifted on the breeze.

When he tired of singing, wild night sounds closed about the riders. Banjo yawned. "If I'd brought my blanket roll, I'd sleep under the stars tonight. I'm plumb tuckered out. Maybe I should fix myself a Scotch hammock."

"What's that?"

"They're easy to make." The puncher pulled Kelsey closer to Ben to make talking easier. "First, you find two trees about six feet apart. Ya nail the south end of your longjohns to one tree, then ya stretch yourself over and nail the north end to the other'n." Hammond's long, echoing laughter ricocheted from boulders and rocky hills. Banjo's sandpaper voice joined him.

Wyatt waved a good-bye and split off when Rocking H range met the trail, leaving Banjo to his own thoughts until he reached the Circle C.

Kinny's description of the thief didn't come close to matching the light-skinned cook. Why hadn't someone thought of that before?

Chapter 12

Em woke to brilliant sunshine the next morning. In spite of the light, to her the day had a dreary cast from the moment she opened her eyes. She performed a hasty toilet, shrugged into yesterday's work dress, and trod to the kitchen.

What had Banjo learned in Cedar Grove? Why had he come back so late? She'd waited up until past ten. Weary and utterly discouraged, she'd turned in only to toss for two more hours.

Her thoughts wandered to Chance, cold and hungry in that dark hole. *Please, God,* she prayed, *bring him safely home and safely to You.*

Fumbling flour into the mixing bowl, she dropped the scoop on the floor. White powder covered her dress, the cabinet front, and the floor. Em stared at the mess, thoroughly disgusted.

"What'sa matter, Em?" Jeremy's shrill voice startled her.

"I'm all thumbs and elbows this morning, Jeremy," Em retorted. "Now look what I've done."

"I'll help you." The child ran for a damp dishcloth.

Em took it from his hand. "Thank ye, child, I'll be needin' a broom, too." She dabbed at her skirt while Jeremy skittered to the back door.

Despite the accident, breakfast was a tasty treat delivered on time. Steve greeted Em with the words, "Megan had a bad night. She's sleeping now, and I didn't want to wake her."

Steve and Banjo piled biscuits and bacon on their plates, covering the whole with Em's salty milk gravy. At the far end of the table, Jeremy finished his third biscuit with sorghum. Before him was a half-empty glass of Bess's milk. Eyes wide, he listened to the men talk.

"How was huntin' yesterday, Banjo?" Steve asked after he'd tasted his coffee.

Bit by bit Banjo relayed the many events of his travels. "I feel certain some palooka's trying to buffalo the law," he concluded. "If Chance was guilty, he'd have covered his tracks. The jasper didn't even wear a mask, for pity's sake."

Across from Banjo, Em's plate was still clean. "Feiklin rode in after you left," she announced listlessly, sipping black coffee. In two sentences she described the sheriff's words and attitude. "I didn't tell him anything, but I feel certain sure he'll be back." She turned haunted eyes toward Steve. "What'll I say, Mr. Steve?"

"You'll have to tell the truth if he keeps after you." He took in Em's unwilling frown. "You'll have to tell Chance to go someplace else and not tell you where. That's the only way I can figure it."

Banjo added, "If we knew he'd get an honest trial, there'd be no problem. But with Hensler puttin' fuel to the fire every time he can, I'm afraid the townsfolk will be dressin' Chance in a California collar." He used a scrap of biscuit to mop up the last drops of gravy.

In a moment he went on. "Kinny said the thief had coal black skin. That lets Chance out by a country mile. The robber rode a horse that wasn't shod at the Rocking H. Wyatt confirmed that. Another thing, the holdup man talked with a slow southern drawl. Chance comes from Georgia, but he talks like a lawyer from Philadelphia." Banjo grinned at Em. "He's right uncanny, is your Chance."

Em straightened. "My Chance?"

Ignoring her, Banjo said, "Let me see your hand."

Studying his face, Em stretched out her fingers, palm up.

Steve watched the interchange closely, curiosity openly displayed on his features. Banjo nodded. "That's what I figured."

"What is it?" Steve demanded.

"Her palm is tan, not much darker than mine." He laid his own calloused hand next to Em's slim one. "Kinny said his gold eagles glowed against the thief's black palm." He leaned forward excitedly. "That proves the thief wasn't really a black man. He was a white man runnin' a blazer, trying to make out like he was black to bring the law on Chance."

Em's waning strength drained away, leaving her limp. "Who would do such a devilish thing?" she whispered, horrified.

His lips tightened. "That's what I aim to find out. As soon as I can figure out how." He paused at Em's disheartened sigh. "Now, Em, when trouble comes, there's three things you can do: go to pieces, go to drinkin', or go to God. The first two don't accomplish much, so let's take hold of the third."

The anxious woman managed a weak smile. "I'se a-tryin', Banjo."

He relaxed, glancing at Steve. "What's on the work list for today?"

Steve set down his cup. "I figure we need to get some logs split and stacked. Jeremy and I hauled in three loads of wood yesterday. One of deadfall and two more from the trees I cut last week."

All heads swiveled east as the bedroom door creaked open. Deep circles under her eyes, Megan waddled toward the table. "I don't want to scare anyone," she said, "but I've been having pains every eight minutes for the last half hour."

Steve bounded from his chair to take her arm. He led her to the table and pulled out a chair at the corner between his seat and Em's.

"You feelin' hungry?" Em asked.

"Only thirsty," Megan replied weakly. "I'd like some cold water."

At Steve's nod, Jeremy left his chair to fetch a clean glass and head for the spring.

"I'll get the maul and start on that wood," Banjo said, rising. He tramped outside, boots thudding against the wood floor. Jeremy set a glass of water before Megan and ran after him.

"Are the pains bad?" Em asked. She touched Megan's cool forehead and smoothed back her hair.

"Not really painful, just uncomfortable. I was having them last night. That's why I couldn't sleep."

"I'll make you some tea, and then it's back to bed with you, little lady," Em announced. She turned to Steve, hovering anxiously nearby. "It ain't the real thing yet. Just a practice run." She placed a loving arm around Megan's shoulders. "But it's a good sign we won't have too much longer to wait."

Megan laid her head on Em's shoulder. "I wish it were over already. I'm so tired. Every day is so long."

After settling Megan comfortably, Em went through her chores with automatic hands. She ran Banjo's news through her mind, wondering who could be so evil as to try to hurt honest Chance.

Later in the day Megan stepped out to the spring where Em bent over a washboard. "I feel much, much better, Em," she said, smiling. "Steve finished the cradle last night. I think I'll stuff the mattress for it this afternoon. That is, after I find something to eat. I'm starving."

The sight of her happy face brought Em a surge of energy. "That's fine, Miss Megan. The ticking is in the sideboard drawer. I cut it out last night." She slapped the cloth in her hands. Suds flew up. "I'll be done here in a little while." Megan disappeared inside as Em attacked the soiled bedsheet. The new arrival would certainly be soon. Megan had started feathering her nest.

The next morning Em packed a basket with jerky, canned peaches, sandwiches, biscuits, and a covered dish of hot stew. Banjo carried the food out to the buckboard while Em fetched two wool blankets. The sun had hardly cleared the horizon when they pulled away from the house. Oatmeal and biscuits sat hot and ready on the back of the stove for the Chamberlin family to help themselves when they roused. Em and Banjo were on their way to visit Chance.

"Have you thought up any new ideas for smokin' out that lying robber?" Em asked.

"Been beatin' my brains to a pulp," he answered, shaking his head regretfully. "Maybe talkin' to Chance will give me some fresh ammunition."

"Somethin's gotta happen soon. I'se afraid Sheriff Feiklin will come on

Chance in that cave."

"Just you remember," Banjo warned, "the good Lord sees Chance. He knows all about this trouble."

"Sometimes I get so tied up, I can't remember anything except that poor man hidin' in a dark hole, afraid for his life."

"We've got to pray that hombre into the kingdom." The force of Banjo's words brought a questioning look from the woman beside him. "You've got a bad case of Cupid's cramps, Em. Like it or not. The only answer is to pray a certain dark gentleman into the family of God."

With a sudden absurd impulse to give way to tears, Em stared straight ahead. She didn't say another word until they reached Fox Hole Creek.

Chance stood waiting in the door of the cave when they arrived. His face was gaunt, his eyes sunken. Em thrust the basket into his hands and followed him inside, Banjo trailing close behind with blankets tucked under his arm.

"Has anyone come around here?" Em asked anxiously as Chance plopped to the floor and dug into the basket.

Shaking his head in answer to her question, he lifted out the bowl of stew. "Pardon me, Emma. As Amos says, I'm as hungry as a woodpecker with a headache." He dove into the beef and potatoes.

Banjo placed the blankets on the rumpled coat beside the cave wall. The wheelbarrow and tools sat in a new place. Dirt crusted the pick and shovel.

"Sheriff Feiklin has a posse combin' the hills for you," Banjo said. "He tried to get Em to tell him where you are."

Em added, "I didn't tell him nothin', but I'm afraid he'll come again." She paused. "I can't lie to him, Chance."

The starving man finished the last bite of beef and reached into the basket for a sandwich. "I haven't seen anyone." He got his mouth around the first sandwich, chewed, and swallowed. "They got a reward out for me?"

Em nodded sadly. "Five hundred dollars." She stood in front of Chance so she could watch his expression.

He stopped chewing to stare hard at Banjo. His jaws moved twice more before he swallowed. "Why didn't you turn me in? That's a fair amount of money."

"I wish you'd believe we want to help you," Banjo said, sitting down near him.

Puzzled, Chance eyed the man beside him a moment longer before chomping down more bread and meat.

"Wyatt and I did some scoutin' where the robbery happened," Banjo continued. "And we talked to a man who was sittin' in the stage." He related Kinny's account. "The way I see it, a white man got himself up to look like a black man. He left a trail a mile wide heading straight back to the Rocking H. It was a put-up job."

Chance's expression changed from watchfulness to sullen calculation. He said, "There's more than one man on the Rocking H who's onery enough to do that to me. Jack Savage lives to put me down. Doesn't he, Em?"

"He's right, Banjo," Em confirmed. "I'se seen him ride Chance more than once."

"The thief had thick, black hair reaching to his shoulders," Banjo said, slowly. "That matches at least."

"The three musketeers aren't above it either," the accused man added. "They've been in more than one scrape since they came around. Gambling. Chasing calico. Guzzling whiskey. You name it."

Banjo knocked the tattered Stetson to the back of his head. "I've been studyin' on it till my head aches. Somehow we've got to smoke the thievin' galoot into the open."

"What did he do with the strongbox?" Chance asked, wiping his hands on dusty pant legs. "It must be somewhere around the ranch."

Banjo scratched his days-old stubble, considering. "You might have something there. The strongbox must weigh a good thirty pounds. Set in front of him like that, it wouldn't ride easy. Either he dumped it someplace along the way or he took it to the ranch and hid it there. He wouldn't carry it anywhere folks would see it, that's sure."

Em picked up the basket and unpacked the rest of the food items, placing them on a new shelf Chance had carved from the hard earth wall.

Banjo stood. "I'll ride over the thief's trail again today. Who knows? I may find something else this time. It's happened before." He glanced at Em. "I'll mosey on down to the wagon, Em. You come when you're ready." He ambled out the small opening and disappeared.

Chance got to his feet and came near Em. "For the first time, I can see why you like him, Emma."

"He's a Christian, Chance. A real Christian looks beyond the color of a man's skin. Jesus died for us all, you know."

He smirked. "You sermonizing at me again?"

The worry mark deepened. "I can't help preachin' sometimes!" she exclaimed. "Jesus can set you free like no man or no man's law can ever do. I wish you could believe that."

He grimaced. "Freedom?" He walked a step beyond her. His next words came from over his shoulder as he stared at the inky back of the cave. "We laughed and shouted and danced back in sixty-five, out of our minds with joy because we'd been set free. What foolish children we were!" He jerked around to face her. His eyes were glowing coals. "Now I know a black man can never be free. Not really free like other folks are."

"Chance. . ." She touched his sleeve.

He shook her off. "Save it, Emma!" A second later his face softened. "Forgive me. I didn't mean to shout at you. I just can't abide any more preaching." He dug into his pocket for a match.

"I've been busy since you came last time." He picked up the bachelor's lantern, and the match flared to life. "Come with me."

Light held high, he led her toward the mine shaft. Only now the tunnel was no more than six feet deep. Em leaned forward, peering closely at the mound of loose dirt that reached within two feet of the ceiling.

"It's a false wall," he explained. "I dug out the back of the shaft and piled the dirt here. If anyone does find me, I'll crawl in here. . . ." Stooping, he set down the lantern to tug at a knee-high stone. Splotchy brown, it was pitted and rough. "This looks heavier than it is. It's limestone. I found it in a pile near the creek last night and rolled it up here." With a little effort the rock came out of the hole in the dirt wall. Behind it Em could see a cavity.

"What's that? A little tunnel?" She squatted beside him.

"It's a big hollow log." He moved the candle flame closer. "I mean, it's hollow at this end. The top end is two feet thick.

"I've been scouring the country just before dawn and at the edge of dark, looking for something to make me a hidey-hole. I spent two hours brushing out the track from dragging this piece of cottonwood up here." He pointed upward inside the hole. "It goes up about four feet. If I squeeze, I can get in there and pull the stone after me."

"Chance! You'll stifle in there!" Em's face mirrored her alarm.

"You're good at praying," he replied. "So pray I won't have to use it." He got to his feet.

Em stood also. "I best be goin'," she said. "I'll be back day after tomorrow." She paused. "I know you put a lot of sweat into that little place, but you really ought to find another cave or something. Someplace I don't know about." Her voice caught, then she plunged on. "I can't lie for you, Chance. Much as I want to help you, I can't lie." She snatched up the empty basket and headed out the door.

Stumbling ahead, she blinked away hot tears. When she reached the wagon, her cheeks were dry, but she was still weeping in her heart.

Banjo was lounging in the buckboard when she arrived. He helped her aboard and shook the reins. The horses, Billy and Star, jolted into motion.

The sun slid beneath a billowing gray cloud. When they reached their own creek bed, the first smattering drops hit Em's hand. The brown hides on their horses became splotched as the rain increased.

Shading her eyes, she looked up. It seemed all nature wept with her.

Chapter 13

Splitting wood under an oak on the east side of the house, Wyatt didn't act surprised when Banjo rode into his yard in time for lunch that same day. The shower had passed, leaving in its wake a clean, sharp smell. Hammond lowered the ax long enough to raise a wide hand in greeting.

"I see you under that Stetson, Banjo. You caught me chorin' like a sodbuster. Chance usually splits the kitchen wood." He thunked the ax into the much-scored stump acting as a chopping base. "What's up?"

Wearing a rain slicker and slouching in the saddle, Banjo told him about his visit to Chance that morning. "We've got to find that strongbox, Wyatt. It must be stashed around here somewhere."

"Around here?" Wyatt repeated, scanning the circle of buildings before him. He stroked his beard, lips pursed. "You do have a point. He must have ditched it soon after he left the stage." Bending to fill his arms with wood, he said, "I'll take these in for Susan. We'll take a gander around the bunkhouse while the hands are settin' up to the table."

Banjo tied Kelsey to the rail beside the bunkhouse. He pulled off the slicker, tied it behind the cantle, and strode into the left stable. He looked down the line of horses: Susan's chestnut gelding, Wyatt's palomino, two roans, and two duns. He strolled to the next stable and counted three buckskins, four duns, and a paint. Ten horses wandered about the box-shaped corral spreading behind the stables and up one side of the yard. Not a single bay in Hammond's remuda. Unless one worked on the range.

When Wyatt joined him at the corral fence, Banjo asked, "You got any bays in your string?"

"Yeah, a small mare. She's combin' the brakes with Slim today."

Banjo pulled off his John B. and scratched his head. "I wonder where the thief got his horse. It was a tall bay with a blaze, like Po'boy."

"This thing's gettin' downright spooky," Wyatt declared. He glanced toward the house where the hands were eating. "Let's take a look in the bunkhouse while we can." He led the way. The hands' quarters ran at right angles to the west of the stables. Hammond pushed open the door and stepped inside.

Built like a railroad car, the doghouse—as the hands called it—contained ten sets of bunks in close regimentation. More than half of these were unoccupied at this slack time of year. The beds were in varying degrees of disorder. In the front area stood a blackened stove, a table of rough lumber, and six chairs. A lantern and a disheveled checker game graced the tabletop. Assorted clothes and bits of tack hung from nails on the walls.

Wyatt knelt to look under beds while Banjo moved along feeling wool blankets and hanging clothes. Beside the back door at the opposite end of the building stood a small table with a pitcher and basin. A roll towel hung above it. Nothing there.

Banjo scanned the ground along the wooden structure, seeking freshly dug earth. Nothing there either.

Wyatt's scuffling boots announced his arrival. He swung open the back door and stepped out. "Looks like we've struck out here," he said. "Want to try the haymow?"

Banjo nodded. "That's as good an idea as any, I reckon."

Fifteen minutes of concentrated searching yielded no results. Back at the woodpile, Wyatt pried the ax away from the stump and sat down where it had been. He said, "So much for that bit of genius. He must have dumped off the box before he got here."

"Let's ride back the way he came," Banjo suggested. "The tracks are long gone by now, but we know his trail. If he buried the box, we should be able to see where."

"I'll saddle Ben," Hammond said and strode away.

Banjo claimed Wyatt's empty seat and snatched a brown grass straw to chew on. Suddenly, the porch door slammed back and the hands poured out.

"Hey, you old souwegian!" Curly belted out when he reached the woodpile.

"Howdy, Curly," Banjo replied, chuckling. "How's life treatin' you?"

The foreman replied, "Not bad if a body don't mind chasin' cantankerous cow young'uns out of the brush. That's where we're headed now."

"You takin' Cavenaugh along?" Banjo joked. "By the looks of him, I'd say he's headed for a church social."

Jake's laughter shook the trees.

Brent pulled out his most winning grin and said, "Everybody couldn't be handsome, so God picked out just us few."

"Now, Brent," Amos drawled, "you know I'm just as good-lookin' as you."

That brought a hoot from everyone, and the hands moved on. Curly paused a moment longer than the rest.

"One good thing about Cavenaugh," Banjo told the foreman, "he's hardly ever talking about other folks."

Curly grinned. "Take care of yourself, old-timer," he said and moved away.

Halfway across the yard, the bald foreman met Wyatt with Ben's reins in his grip. They stopped for a word. Banjo fetched Kelsey.

Hammond and Banjo rode past the hitching rail and into the trees. Brown leaves and pine needles littered the ground, making their quest more difficult. Once out of sight of the ranch, they slowed to a crawl, eyes on the ground. Twice Banjo dismounted for a closer look, then mounted again and moved on.

At the old line shack they dropped their reins and scouted around the rickety building. The house seemed boarded shut, but on closer inspection, the board over the door was only propped in place.

Banjo tugged at it. The wood came off easily in his hands. "Well, looky here," he drawled. "Somebody's been in here. And not long ago."

Wyatt peered through the door. "Let's take a gander inside." The interior of the house was much like the bunkhouse, small and bare with two sets of bunks, one on each side, and a fireplace covering most of the back wall. Musty odors clogged their noses. Banjo peered overhead. The roof showed spots of sky at irregular intervals.

An iron grate and pot hovered over the dead fire, testifying to a thousand meals eaten and forgotten. In the center of the room, two benches formed a V before the hearth, a small stool that doubled as a table at the apex.

Peering under beds, running hands over the rotting straw mattresses, the men scoured the room. Banjo stirred a half-burned stick around the inside of the cooking pot, and Wyatt tapped the mud chinking.

On the thick mantel shelf resided a lantern, a large rusty can, and a tin of matches. Wyatt lifted the can and reached inside. He pulled out a cloth bundle and took it to the door for better light.

"What do you know about this?" He held the open cloth toward his partner. On his palm lay a stump of burnt cork, a bag of white lime, and a homemade horsehair brush. "That's not all," Wyatt announced, handing the items to Banjo.

He reached into the can again and pulled out a wad of black fibers. Shaking the packet loose, it became a black woolly wig.

"Great sand and sagebrush!" Banjo exclaimed. He stepped back and found a seat on the nearest bench. "What do you make of that?"

"Our man stopped here long enough to hide his costume," Wyatt said. "Burnt cork to black his face, a wig to hide his own hair. . . See that lime? If he mixed it with a little water, he could use it to paint a blaze on his horse."

"He made himself a little brush to do it with." Banjo held the horsehair brush aloft before handing it back to Wyatt. The rancher stuffed the objects back into the can. "He must have hid the money here, too."

"Wyatt," Banjo said suddenly, "say we do find the money. How will we know who buried it?"

The blond bearded gent stared at the can in his hands, considering.

"We can quit lookin'," Banjo announced, excitement in his voice. "If we draw the hairpin out of hidin', he'll lead us to the money and nail himself at the same time."

"Keep talkin'," Wyatt invited.

Head cocked, inner wheels turning, the veteran leaned forward and spoke in low tones.

An hour after Em left him, Chance hunkered down near the mouth of his cave, ears straining. The clink of a horseshoe on stone had fine-tuned his senses to an excruciating pitch. He peered through a thin spot in the dry brush piled before the entrance. Fine misty rain clouded the air.

Did friend or foe lurk outside?

With frantic haste, he gathered the food Em had brought. Stuffing the jerky into his jeans pocket, he dropped the cans and biscuits on his blankets. Bundling them together, he threw the whole into the darkest corner of the room. He grabbed a handful of sticks from the brush at the doorway to scuff out his footprints as he backed up to the false wall. His heart was pounding so loudly he feared his pursuers would find him by its traitorous clangor alone. He crayfished into the hole and strained to roll the stone into the opening.

His knees nudged his chin. Dirt fell into his eyes.

How long could he endure the log's squeezing him? It had looked so wide before, but now he felt as if he sat in a vise.

Already his heaving lungs cried for more air.

Would someone come?

Pressing his eyes closed, willing his breathing to calm, he slowly counted to five hundred. Twice more to five hundred and he would move. He must.

Sweat trickled into his collar.

A skating stone made him lose count.

"Hey! What's this?" someone called. Scraping wood and snapping twigs.

The brush at the entrance, Chance thought.

"A cave!" Was that Feiklin's resonant voice?

"Shall we look around, Sheriff?" a high-pitched nasal voice asked.

"Looks empty," Feiklin stated. Boots crunched on the dirt floor. "Relax, fellows. We may as well wait out the rain in here."

"Someone's been here," the shrill voice said. Chance tagged this one as Mousy and cursed him for his keen eyes when he said, "Look! A shelf and the lantern!"

"Someone's been minin'," a third husky voice offered. "See those tools in the wheelbarrow?"

Feiklin said, "Let me see them, Tom." A short pause. "This shovel's brand new. It's not even rusted."

Mousy exclaimed, "That black rascal had a new shovel with him. He used it against us outside Harper's. I had a headache for two days after he walloped me."

Chance swallowed convulsively and sank his head lower between his knees. "Light the lantern," Feiklin commanded.

In a moment Tom announced, "A blanket roll. . .and food. Two cans of peaches. Fresh biscuits, too. Ummm. . .good ones."

"Find a squirrel?" asked a new man, unheard until now.

Feiklin answered, disgusted, "Looks like he's already taken to tall timber, Abe. You see any tracks outside?"

"Only to the creek and back here. I saw a wagon's tracks come up to the big cottonwood a few times in the last week. Someone might have taken him away."

"Look in the back of the cave, Tom," the sheriff ordered. "There may be another chamber. . . . And, Tom, if you see him, haul iron. No sense givin' him the first shot."

Chance's breath left him as heavy boots grated close.

"Hey, Abe," Tom called, "hand me that shovel."

In a moment, Chance felt the jarring of the shovel on the dirt somewhere above his head. A shower of dust fell. The shovel struck twice more.

God, Chance prayed, *if You're really there, please make him stop. He'll bury me alive.* A sharp pain stabbed his chest. He fought off faintness.

More footsteps and Tom's voice called, "Nothing there, Sheriff." The words came more muffled than before but were still clearly audible.

"The rain's let up," Feiklin said. "Let's check further up, and then we'll head home. I'm feelin' narrow at the equator. It's past noon." Feiklin's equator was anything but narrow.

"No sense wastin' these vittles," Tom said. "Want a can o' peaches, Jim?"

"Throw her here," Mousy answered.

The rustle of dry branches and fading footfalls told Chance that they had gone.

Every impulse told Chance to break free of the wooden shroud that crushed him like a giant python. He fought for control. He must think.

Had the posse really gone? Was someone waiting in the darkness, stalking him?

Despite numb limbs and aching lungs, he waited. He counted his heartbeats to five thousand and then waited some more. When he finally moved, his legs were dead. He shoved the stone away with the last strength in his trembling hands and crawled from his prison on elbows, dragging his nerveless feet.

Outside, he lay on his side gasping. Weak tears dripped to the ground.

God, he prayed again, *I don't know if what Em says is true or not. But one thing I do know. You're there.*

Chapter 14

Banjo and Wyatt carefully restored the line shack to its original appearance. They parted ways there, so Wyatt rode back to the ranch alone. In a thinking mood, he returned to the woodpile and split enough wood to last the week. The sun was at half-mast when he filled his arms the final time and headed for the kitchen.

"You sure are ambitious," Susan commented wonderingly. She looked half her age, enveloped in a red gingham bib apron, her ponytail bobbing as she spoke. "I declare you haven't filled the woodbox all the way to the top since we've been married."

"Got any coffee?" her husband asked, dropping into a chair beside the table. "I'm powerful thirsty."

"One barefoot cup of coffee comin' up," Susan chimed, reaching for a tin cup. "Supper's almost ready." She picked up a dish towel and folded it several times. Using the cloth to pad her hand, she lifted the dented blue coffeepot.

Wyatt sipped the strong, black brew and watched his wife's graceful movements around the kitchen. He couldn't have told which he enjoyed more—the brew or the view.

"I'll serve the hands tonight," he announced when Susan had filled a platter with steaks. Ignoring her dubious expression, he grabbed the plate and headed for the back porch.

The hands were in their usual places, jawing and joking. Their talk died when they caught sight of their waiter. Slim drawled, "Got yourself a new job, Boss?"

"I always fancied myself a dough puncher, Slim," Wyatt joshed. "I've just kept it well hid till now." He kidded and laughed at their banter, but his keen eyes stayed busy. Three trips to the kitchen, and his duties were through.

Wyatt stayed with Susan through the dishwashing routine, drying and stacking for her. He loved to watch her smile as she talked to him. The memory of those terrifying days of sickness still were fresh in his mind. Dishes done, they moved to the front porch to rock and chat till crickets and coyotes had taken over the still air.

" 'Bout time to turn in, don't you think?" Susan asked, stifling a yawn. "I have to be up by four to start breakfast."

"You go ahead." Wyatt stood and stretched. "I've got to ride out."

"At this time of night?" she asked, a fearful look appearing on her face.

"Come inside and I'll explain." Rising, he took her hand and walked with her into the house. In the privacy of their living room, he pulled her into his arms, enjoying the scent of her hair.

She submitted to a short kiss before demanding, "Where are you going at this hour?"

"Banjo and I have a plan to trap the stagecoach bandit." As her mouth opened to protest, he hurriedly said, "I'm sorry, sweetheart, but I have to go. You were the one who made me promise to help Chance, weren't you?"

"Yes. But I didn't expect you to go off and get yourself killed doing it."

"If I see any flying bullets, I'll duck." He kissed her again and left quickly before she could argue anymore.

Stepping off the porch, he strode across the dark yard to the stable. Saddling Ben, he led the animal away from the bunkhouse to circle the yard and end up ten yards into the trees. Snubbing the stallion to a tree branch, he found his way back. Light from the three bunkhouse windows guided him the last few feet. Finding the latch by instinct, he stepped inside.

Hunched over the small table, Curly, Slim, Jake, and Amos each held a handful of cards. Brent looked into his polished brass mirror, combing his hair. He was dressing to go walking out with Lisa. Link Hensler leaned against the first bunk, cleaning his nails with a Bowie knife.

"Howdy, Boss," Amos drawled. He was the first to see Wyatt.

"What's up?" Curly asked.

"I came to let you know there'll be a change in the work we laid out for tomorrow," Wyatt said, catching up an empty chair and turning it around. He straddled the backward chair.

"First off, we're gonna scrub Amos's eyeballs with a toothbrush."

Loud hoots and wild laughter crisscrossed the room.

"That'd be your second job," Amos drawled, a slow grin on his heavy face. "The first one would be catching me."

More laughter.

"Actually," their boss man said, "I've decided to fix up that old line shack south of here. I want Slim and Amos to ride over there and start emptying the stable so we can tear it down. It's about to fall in." His quick eyes surveyed the men before him. No one seemed more than mildly interested.

"I'm going over after breakfast, too." He paused. "I'm thinking I'd like to enlarge the corral, so we'll dig up the posts. I'll show you that when the time comes." He glanced around. "Any questions?"

No answer.

"I'll see you in the morning, then."

He flipped the chair back to its original position and strode into the night to find Ben where he'd left him in the trees. Mounting, he held the beautiful animal to a slow walk, hoping to muffle the sound of his passing.

The night had a half-grown moon that filtered through the trees like splashes of gold on black velvet. He let the horse have his head for a short time, knowing that Ben's night sight was better than his own. Once a small branch smacked his head, almost knocking off his flat-crowned hat.

The line shack loomed up, eerily speckled and shadowed with moonlight. He skirted the small clearing that served as a front yard to leave Ben fifty yards away, beyond sight and sound of the house. Stepping from the leather, he wrapped the reins around a branch without tying them. The tension alone would keep the well-trained animal from moving.

Wyatt paused long enough to dig his Peacemaker Colt and gun belt from the saddlebag and buckle them on. He hadn't wanted to frighten Susan by wearing them, but common sense told him that he'd need a weapon when dealing with a desperate outlaw.

Edging back the way he'd come, Wyatt found a small dry ditch and followed it to the appointed meeting place, a stand of young aspen across from the front door. Soft-footing across leaves and twigs, the sound of his movements seemed like the arrival of a freight train to his tense mind.

At the edge of the copse he whispered, "Banjo? You here?"

"In the flesh," the coarse voice answered. "I been here an hour already."

Wyatt sidled between the saplings and squatted beside the broad shadow that was Banjo. The thin strip of blackness beside the grizzled jaw was his Sharps .56, a wide-bored buffalo gun with a roar like a cannon.

"I laid out the bait real thick," Hammond said. "Told 'em we're gonna tear down the stable and dig up the corral posts. If one of 'em knows the box is buried around here, he'll be almighty anxious to get it out."

Wyatt moved ten feet further toward the cabin and hunkered down on some wet leaves, ears alert, eyes adjusting to the darkness. Half an hour later, he felt the urge to close his eyes. He rubbed his face, fighting sleep, and kept watching.

A few moments later, hoofbeats from the north brought him to full alertness. A horse and rider broke into the clearing and disappeared around the back of the house. Keeping to the trees, the stalkers moved around, carefully placing each foot to avoid a rustling leaf or stick.

Wyatt knew that Banjo was circling in the opposite direction to catch the crook between them. He lifted his shooting iron from its holster and gently replaced it to have it loose and ready. Drawing in a chestful of air, he slowly released it, demanding steadiness from his high-strung hands. Somewhere west of them, an owl demanded, "Who–o–o–o? Who–o–o–o?"

The lanky rancher paused in the shadows at the edge of the corral. Their quarry must have time to find the evidence and condemn himself. He heard scuffling noises inside the stable, then the groaning stable door opened. A feeble lantern glowed next to a pair of legs and the handle of a shovel.

The faceless man didn't hesitate. He strode to a back corner of the corral next to the stable wall and set the lantern on the ground. A dozen thrusts of the shovel and he cast the tool aside. Kneeling, he stretched downward.

"Hold it right there!" Banjo barked. "I don't want to trim your ears, but I will if you move."

Cold steel felt clammy in Wyatt's hand. With nerves taut as a bowstring, he edged around the fence line. Intent on the prey, he stepped through a moonbeam.

With a quick, swift lunge, the outlaw rolled and kicked the lantern to kill the light. In the same instant he fired. Wyatt reacted by instinct rather than design. He felt the Colt buck in his hand and a fiery pain stab his biceps.

From the black depths of the corral came a gasp and soft thud.

Was the man hit? Was he conscious? Was he still armed?

Wyatt swallowed the fear and pain that washed over him. His arm felt warm and sticky from shoulder to elbow. Holstering his gun, he fumbled for his kerchief to staunch the bleeding, thinking, *Won't Susan be in a flap when she gets an eyeful of this!*

A low moan crossed the night air. Was it real or a trick to get the hunters to show themselves?

Wyatt gritted his teeth. *This is a pretty pickle,* he told himself.

A different sort of owl gave a low hoot. Wyatt crept along, knees bent, toward the sound. That night bird wore a ragged Stetson and packed a Sharps.

Wyatt almost bumped into the old-timer before he saw him. "What'll we do now?" he whispered. "He may be layin' for us in there, playin' possum."

"We need some light," Banjo said, stating the obvious.

"Let's set fire to the stable," Wyatt suggested. "It's about to fall in anyway. That'll give us enough light to see him plain as day. A lantern will only draw his fire and likely kill one of us.

"I'm hit," Wyatt added, as an afterthought. "He nicked my arm." Weakness and nausea washed over him. "Go ahead and fire the place, Banjo. We just had a good rain, so the grass won't go. Let's get this show over with." He eased into a sitting position on the ground, head hanging low.

Banjo disappeared inside the stable. He was back in three minutes.

"I put a match to some straw up next to the wall on that side," he whispered. "Everything inside's dry tinder. It won't be long."

A brief flicker grew into a glow then a gleam of orange and yellow light.

Acrid smoke pricked their senses.

From the shadows, Banjo and Wyatt watched the corral light up before them. Next to the freshly dug hole lay a prone figure, gun arm outstretched. A pepperbox revolver lay two feet from lifeless fingers. Nimble for his years, Banjo skipped over the fence to retrieve the gun. Wyatt climbed across the boards to reach the scene as Banjo grasped the unconscious man's chin and brought his face into view.

Link Hensler.

A sticky red smear half covered his bald spot. Bending over him, Banjo examined the wound.

"Looks like you creased his scalp," he decided. "He'll probably come around after a while." Gripping the man's right wrist, he held it toward the light. A jagged, bumpy scar crossed the back of his hand.

Banjo straightened and pulled a wad of rawhide string from his pocket. "We'd best tie him tight. This hombre can make a powerful lot of trouble for us when he wakes up." Working over him like a rodeo contestant on a calf, he bound Hensler's hands in front of his belt buckle.

The stable was blazing beautifully now. Shooting flames rose thirty feet in the air. Inside, a timber crashed to the ground, shaking the earth.

Hensler moaned and turned his head. His eyelids blinked sleepily. Bleary eyes focused on the men above him. Both Banjo and Wyatt backed out of range of the wounded man's boots.

"Give it up, Hensler," Banjo advised. "You'll only hurt yourself more if you try anything. Wyatt, here, is gonna hold his hogleg ready. If you give me any guff, he'll nail you."

Stark hatred twisting his features, Hensler didn't move. His slack lips spouted words he hadn't learned in Sunday school.

"On your feet now," Banjo commanded. "If you need help, I'll give you a hand." He glanced at Wyatt. "Don't give him an inch, son. He'll kick both of us into next week if he sees a weak spot."

Hensler rolled over to a hands-and-knees position and slowly pulled his feet under him. Panting, he rested his forehead on the ground for a count of ten. Finally, he got erect, weaving slightly. Banjo came behind him and placed strong hands on the wounded man's shoulders.

"Let's find your horse, young fellow. I'll help you mount up."

"Where to now?" Wyatt asked. "We need to get him into town."

"And you need to see Doc Leatherwood," Banjo added. "Let's fetch your buckboard. I'll drive it for you."

The house was dark when they returned to the ranch. While they hitched two buckskins to the buckboard and transferred Hensler to the wagon's back,

Wyatt debated whether to wake Susan or not. He finally decided to let her sleep. He was leading the horses across the yard when the front door burst open and Susan, in a dark robe, came running toward them with a glowing lantern swinging from her hand.

"Wyatt! Are you okay?" She grasped his arm and recoiled in the same move. "You're bleeding!"

"It's just a scratch, Susan. Nothing to fret about."

She looked over Wyatt's head. "What's that orange glow in the sky? I woke up and smelled smoke. Then I saw the light above the trees, and it frightened me."

"We set fire to the stable behind that old line shack east of here. It's okay. I woke up Slim and Amos, so they can make sure it doesn't travel. Banjo and I are on our way into Juniper to turn Hensler over to the sheriff."

"Hensler!" Susan's blue eyes widened. Lifting the light above her head, she peered over the side of the wagon at the bound man lying in back. As an added precaution, Banjo had roped the outlaw's feet to the side post of the wagon. Her eyes narrowed. "To think of all the times he's eaten our food and taken advantage of our hospitality!"

Holding the light to advantage, she inspected Wyatt's arm. "You sure you're okay?"

"I'm fine. When we get to Juniper, I'll get Doc Leatherwood to look at it. The sooner we get goin', the sooner I'll be back." He looked at the moon. "At this rate it'll be dawn before you see me again." He stooped to kiss her. "Go back to bed and don't worry."

"You may as well tell a meadowlark not to fly." She squeezed his hand and released it. "Take care of him, Banjo," she called to the still form waiting on the buckboard seat. Banjo's Kelsey and Hensler's buckskin stood tied to the back of the wagon.

"I'll make him behave, Miss Susan," the veteran called. "Good night to you."

Wyatt watched his wife enter their home before he weakly climbed aboard. "Don't waste no time getting there, Banjo," he said. "It's been a long night."

Chapter 15

Five minutes of pounding brought Dr. Leatherwood to his door. His thick face and broken nose looked sinister in the wee hours.

"What is it?" he asked, holding the door wide and staring into the darkness outside the door.

Banjo prodded Hensler inside. "There's been some gunplay. This man," he pointed to the hostler staggering before him, "robbed the stage." Quickly he told of the evening's events. "If you'll look after the wounds," he finished, "I'll round up Sheriff Feiklin."

The doctor grunted. His bare head reflected the light of the coal oil lamp. "The sheriff won't be in a good mood at this time of night." He turned to Wyatt. "You got a gun?" At Hammond's nod, he said, "Lay it on the table where I can reach it. Hensler, sit in that chair. I'm going to look at Hammond's arm first. Then I'll take care of you."

Leaving the doctor to his business, Banjo stepped into Oak Street, a residential lane running parallel to Main. He traced his way to the end of the dusty road where Feiklin's house lay a stone's throw behind the sheriff's office on Main Street.

Halfway there, he stopped in the middle of the road to take off his hat and rub sleep-hungry eyes with his shirtsleeve. Now that the pressure was off, he suddenly felt exhausted.

A lamp sprang to life seconds after Banjo's knock.

Feiklin's wide jowls jutted through the doorway. He growled, "Can't it wait till morning?"

"Sorry, Sheriff," Banjo said, hat in hand, "but we've brought in the thief who robbed the Cedar Grove stage. He got his head creased when we took him. Doc Leatherwood's tendin' to him."

Immediately interested, Feiklin straightened. "You don't say. Give me two shakes to fetch my hat." He disappeared. Banjo stepped away from the door. The sheriff was beside him in minutes. Side by side they strode down the street. "Where'd you catch him?" Feiklin demanded. "We found the cave where he's been hiding, but we missed him. He'd lit a shuck for parts unknown."

"He's not Chance." Banjo's words came out low, distinct, and definite. "He's Link Hensler."

"Hold on!" The lawman stopped short. "You leadin' me on a wild-goose chase?"

"Hensler rubbed burnt cork on his face and hands. He wore a black wig so folks would think him a black man. He found a tall bay horse somewhere and painted a blaze on it to look like Chance's horse."

"A tall bay?" Feiklin demanded. "I keep a bay at the livery stable." His eyes burned with indignation. "You think he used my horse to pull off the robbery?"

"Where else would he find a horse the right size and coloring? There's no doubt he buried the strongbox and rode to the Rocking H to make his trail end there. How could he know where the money was hid except that he hid it? When he thought Wyatt Hammond was gonna dig up that old corral, Hensler made tracks right to the spot and commenced to diggin'." The old cowpoke stepped into a patch of moonlight and stood still, unrelenting eyes on the man at his side. Banjo pushed on. "Why didn't he wear a mask during the holdup?"

Feiklin didn't answer.

"I'll tell you," the old-timer grated out. "He was already wearing one. His black face was a mask. Hammond and I found the makin's of his costume. It's in the buckboard now. Hensler shot Wyatt in the shoulder and got a furrow in his own skull for his trouble."

He paused to draw in a breath. "You had your mind made up from the time you heard about the color of the man's skin. If you'd checked further, you'd have learned that the thief had skin the color of coal. He couldn't have been Chance, Feiklin. Not in a hundred years."

The big man didn't say more, but his curt attitude simmered way down. When they stepped through the doctor's door, Leatherwood was putting a final layer of cloth over Hensler's pate. The wounded man looked as if he wore a white cotton nightcap. On the sofa Wyatt sat with his arm in a sling, the Colt gripped in his uninjured hand.

"Howdy, Sheriff," Wyatt called. "Welcome to the party."

"I hear you fellows had some excitement," Feiklin drawled. His voice practically echoed in the small room. "Hensler, what do you have to say for yourself?"

"Nothin'." The guilty man stared at the floor. "I'm gettin' me a lawyer before I say a word."

"You'll have awhile to wait then," the sheriff said. "The circuit judge isn't due for two months. I suppose we'll ship you to Denver. The big boys can take care of you."

He turned to Wyatt and Banjo. "I guess you boys can split the reward money. I'll write up a promissory note. You can cash it at the bank."

"We'll pick it up later, Sheriff," Wyatt told him. "At the moment home means more to me than any amount of money." As an afterthought he added,

"We'll tie Hensler's horse to the doc's hitching rail. You can get him later."

"Let's go," Feiklin said to the guilty man. He glanced at Banjo. "I'll return your rawhide later. This turkey had best stay trussed." Drawing his six-shooter, he marched Hensler outside.

"Thanks, Doc," Wyatt said, standing. "We'll leave you to pound your pillow. There's a whole hour till dawn."

"I slept through the night at least five times last month," the doctor said, grinning wearily. "Seems like every baby within thirty miles wants to get introduced to the world by candlelight."

Firm knuckles outside the door brought concern to the good man's face. Breaking away from the conversation, he pulled up the latch.

"Can you come, Doc?" Steve's white face appeared in the doorway. "Megan's gonna have that baby tonight."

"I'll be right there." Leatherwood grabbed his coat from the tree by the door and scooped his black bag from the table. "Sorry, gentlemen. We'll have to make it a short good-bye."

"Banjo!" Steve exclaimed. "What brings you here?"

"We brought in Hensler. He held up the stage and framed Chance. He shot Wyatt's arm, so we stopped in to see the Doc."

The nervous father interrupted Banjo to say to Leatherwood, "I've got the buckboard, Doc. You can ride with me." He held up his hand, palm out, toward his friends. "We'll talk it over later, Banjo. Em's watching over Megan, but I've got to get the Doc there pronto."

Banjo chuckled. "Take it easy, old man. Babies are born every day."

"Not mine!" Steve retorted, rushing away. He clambered into the seat beside the black-coated medical man, released the brake, and slapped the reins. Billy and Star jumped into a brisk trot, trace chains jangling.

Wyatt and Banjo paused on the street in the damp coolness of the morning.

"We'd best let Chance in on the good news," Wyatt said, easing the sling where it bit into his neck. "He can ride home with me in the buckboard."

Banjo stretched widely and ended by swinging his arms back and forth. "I believe I'll wake up, directly." He stepped to a full water barrel at the corner of the doctor's house and splashed his face. His black bandanna acted as a makeshift towel. Kelsey's head was drooping when they reached the buckboard. Banjo gave the faithful donkey a slap on the rump, bringing the animal's head around. "We're almost home, pal." He untied the weary palomino, led him to the water barrel for a drink, and carefully tied him in front of the doctor's house.

Wyatt climbed into the wagon and sank back on the hard bench. "Go ahead and drive, Banjo," he said through tense lips. "This arm's throbbin' like the dickens."

"Hi-yup!" Banjo called, easing off the brake. The gelding set out as if he smelled water. In minutes Juniper faded into the distance behind them.

A faint ochre gleam surged above the dark horizon. It moved upward, becoming an orange strip with a burst of yellow on top. Orange and yellow widened—pushing, pushing the indigo sky until light conquered the night. Gradually, yet somehow suddenly, the sky was azure, and the sun blithely floated free of the land.

Tired as he was, Banjo felt the wonder of a fresh, new day.

The wagon creaked to a halt under the giant tree, and Banjo wound the reins around the whip stand.

"I'll wait here," Wyatt said. "You don't need me no how."

Above the lone walker, a flock of honking geese cut a V in the cloudy sky. A lizard skittered out of the trail, avoiding heavy boots.

Twenty paces up the hill, he paused and cupped hands to his mouth, "Chance! It's me, Banjo! I'm comin' up!" Was the hunted man still in the cave? Feiklin said he'd left. If so, where had he gone? Five more paces and Banjo helloed again. Dry bushes rustled in the mouth of the cave. A bushel-size piece fell away. Relieved, Banjo hurried forward.

Before him stood a shadow, a shell of the person he'd seen twenty-four hours before. Thick dust covered Chance's face and hair. Ground-in dirt stiffened his clothes. Wrinkled and drawn as a man twice his age, his cheeks sank in. The black man's frame seemed almost skeletal.

"Good news!" Banjo announced by way of greeting. "Last night Wyatt and I caught Link Hensler red-handed digging up the strongbox stolen from the stage. He's sweatin' it out in the calaboose right now. You're free. You can go home."

Shock blanked out Chance's expression for an instant before his eyes crinkled in disbelief. "Hensler?" He stepped back to let Banjo enter. "I thought sure Savage was the man."

Again, Banjo told the story. "Wyatt took a bullet in the arm. He's waiting in the buckboard. Doc Leatherwood just patched him up."

Chance raked trembling fingers through his gritty hair. "I've died a hundred hideous deaths since the sheriff came up here yesterday. I'd just about decided I have only two choices: hanging or starving. If I had a six-gun, I might have taken a third way out."

Chance shied away from his visitor's kindly look. How could he face Banjo after he'd doubted the old man's integrity, scoffed at his sincerity?

"You and Mr. Wyatt risked your lives for the likes of me. Why?"

"Can we sit down?" Banjo asked.

They sank to the hard earth. Bottom lip thrust forward, Chance stared at the ground, waiting.

Banjo's rough voice softened to a low pitch. He spoke slowly, choosing his words with care. "You've endured more grief than most men, Chance. I know a small bit of what you feel." He told the story of his wife and son. "I've felt my insides churn with grief so thick, so hard, I thought I'd die. I wished I could die.

"I despised those Injuns. I used to dream of how I'd ride into their camp and get revenge. Hate was eatin' me alive.

"What I'm trying to tell you, Chance, is that I understand. I know what it means to hurt.

"If I can only make it clear." Banjo's lips puckered as he groped for words. "Those men who put your people into slavery, those Kiowas who murdered my Mary, didn't cause that pain because of their skin color. They did it because they were wicked.

"There's still plenty of that brand around, too. I don't have to tell you that. The Good Book says, 'The heart is deceitful above all things, and desperately wicked.' That applies to everyone the world over. And folks can't straighten themselves out. The only way a lost man can get straight is in a coffin. Jesus alone can change an evil heart." Chance raised his head and stared at the square of light in the doorway.

Banjo went on. "You were surprised because Wyatt took a bullet to help you. I know someone who went even further. He died a horrible death for you. It was Jesus. He wants to take away your pain. But you must give it to Him. Give Him your pain. Turn loose of your grief. Salvation means a life of joy and peace like you've never imagined.

"It's a gift, Chance. Will you take it?"

The atmosphere thickened with the weight of that question. Chance studied his soil-caked boots, Em's voice echoing in his ears, "A real Christian looks past the color of a man's skin. Jesus died for all of us, you know."

Finally, the haunted man spoke. His voice creaked. "When the posse came into the cave, I crawled into my hole and pulled the stone in after me. One of them walked into the tunnel, looking for me. He took a shovel and dug at the false wall." Chance drew a trembling breath.

"I've never prayed in my life, but I prayed then." He rubbed his face with stiff fingers. "You know what happened? That man quit digging and walked away. Five minutes later the posse walked out of here and didn't come back." He swallowed hard.

"At that moment, I knew God is real." His voice cracked, but he kept talking. "That was the first time since I left my mama that I really felt someone care for me."

Banjo started to speak, but Chance waved him off.

"You folks cared, too. I see that now, but I didn't believe it then." For the first time, he looked directly at the man sitting beside him. "I can't keep going on like I've been. I want what Em has, what you have."

Banjo placed a calloused hand on Chance's sagging shoulder and closed his eyes, saying, "Let's pray."

Hands up to shade his eyes, Chance stepped into the light of day. He clutched a bundle of blankets and a filthy coat in his arms. With Banjo, he strode across the hillside toward the buckboard where Wyatt lay on the seat dozing.

At the crunching of boots on gravel, the wounded man sat up and scratched his beard. "I was wonderin' if you-all had decided to camp out a few days longer."

"Sorry to keep you waitin', Wyatt," Banjo called. "We had some things that we needed to talk out."

Wyatt took stock of Chance's appearance. "Howdy, Chance. Looks like you could use a hot tub and a plate full of biscuits and gravy."

Chance nodded and managed a tired smile. "Not in that order, I hope." He threw the blankets into the back of the wagon and climbed in after them. "I could put away a cow and a half about now."

They hit the trail, and Banjo let the buckskins have their heads. Sailing breezes whistled through the clothes of the three men. They felt the chill, but it gave them pleasure, quickened their weary blood.

"Before the throne my surety stands. . . ." Banjo's music reached far across the rolling hills as they headed toward the mountains.

Stretched out in the back, Chance closed his eyes, savoring the song and the deep peace within him. After he cleaned up and filled his gnawing stomach, he'd sleep for about two weeks. Then he'd pay Emma a visit. He smiled.

"Here's where we part," Banjo announced, pulling up the reins. "Get yourself home, Wyatt, and let Susan fuss over you."

"I'll enjoy every minute of it." Wyatt laughed. "Be seein' you, Banjo. You ever need a job, look me up."

The grizzled cowpoke chuckled. "I'll do that."

He swung his legs over the side of the buckboard, pausing to say, "We'll get together for some Bible study, Chance, once you rest up. I'll be over to see you."

Chance climbed into Banjo's seat and lifted the straps of leather. New light glimmered in his eyes as he said, "God bless you, Banjo. I thank you."

"Thank the Lord, my brother," Banjo responded warmly. "He's the One who should get the praise."

Wyatt heard their conversation with growing interest, a puzzled wrinkle to his brow. Banjo trod back to untie Kelsey and step into the saddle.

Noting Wyatt's expression, Chance told him, "I found Jesus today, Mr. Wyatt. Have you ever met Him?"

Kelsey turned down the trail toward home. When Banjo looked back, the buckboard had lurched ahead with Chance and Wyatt in serious conversation.

The Circle C seemed quiet when Banjo arrived. Something about the scent of woodsmoke from his own chimney gave him a glad, satisfied feeling. Leading the tired donkey into his stall, Banjo saw to the animal's needs and headed through the stable's back door to the spring behind the house. He paused long enough for an icy drink from the tin cup hanging from a rawhide cord before opening the kitchen door.

At the stove Em fried eggs, a plate of steaming steaks on the counter beside her.

"Dish me up half a dozen of them steaks," Banjo ordered, his twinkle showing, "and a dozen eggs."

Em's head jerked around, her eyes wide. "Where you been, Banjo? We'se all wonderin' what become of you."

"Well, first off, me and Wyatt caught us a holdup man named Link Hensler. As I speak, your friend Chance is on his way home."

Em raised her face toward heaven, eyes closed. "The Lord be praised," she breathed. Her round eyes were moist when she opened them, and she wore a brand-new smile. "Well, come on in and have a seat. Things have been happenin' here, too. Looks like nobody in this family got any sleep last night. Except'n Jeremy, that is!"

"How's Megan?"

"Sleepin' like the baby beside her," Em announced happily. "The most beautiful little girl you ever laid your eyes on, Banjo.

"Mr. Steve's snoozin', too, but he said to wake him up when breakfast is ready."

Jeremy burst in the front door. A brown smudge already colored his nose. "Did you catch him, Banjo?" he demanded, claiming the seat next to his hero.

"Sure did." He ran through the much-told tale yet another time. "The Doc bound up Wyatt's arm. It's not serious, but it's givin' him some double-distilled pain at the moment."

Em set two plates on the table. "I'm startin' you out with two steaks and four eggs, Banjo. The biscuits will be ready in two minutes." She chuckled. "If you want more, just holler." She headed toward the bedroom door. "I'll fetch Mr. Steve."

In a moment she returned with Steve two paces behind her. Thick stubble coated his jaw, and his eyes were bloodshot. He paused outside the bedroom door to massage his face.

Banjo jumped to his feet to shake the weary man's hand. "Congratulations, Chamberlin!"

Fatigue forgotten, Steve's grin split his face. "I'm a rich man, Banjo. Richer than Vanderbilt." He sank into the chair at the end of the table and watched Em lay a plate in front of him.

"Em!" A call came from the bedroom. Em hurried to Megan's side and closed the door.

"How's Chance?" Steve asked, attacking the steak.

"Headed for home. He received the Lord this mornin'. I didn't tell Em. I reckon it's his news to tell her with what's taken place between them."

The events of last night provided much conversation with Jeremy, jaws in motion, hanging on every word. They lingered over second cups of coffee, relaxing tired muscles and weary minds.

"Want to see the baby, Banjo?" Em asked, appearing in the bedroom doorway. "Megan says you can come in now."

"Does a chicken have lips?" the cowhand retorted with a smile.

Jeremy slipped a small hand into Banjo's wide, hard palm. They approached the room with quiet reverence, Jeremy's eyes as big as teacups.

Under the wedding-ring quilt lay Megan with her hair cascading over the pillow. A peaceful glow surrounded her weary face.

Smiling softly, she said, "Come and see what I've got, Jeremy." Near the side of the bed, she held a closely wrapped bundle in the crook of her arm. Jeremy peeked over the edge of the white flannel blanket, intensely curious yet awed. He froze, cast an incredulous look at Megan's face, and leaned forward for closer inspection.

Tiny fists grasped the blanket's border. Snuggled against her mama's safe warm side lay a ruddy munchkin face crowned with curly black hair. Still grasping Banjo's hand, Jeremy stretched forth a finger to stroke the tiny cheek.

"When she wakes up, you can hold her," the new mother promised the little boy.

"Congratulations, Miss Megan," Banjo breathed. He glanced at Steve, hovering at the end of the bed. "You're right, Chamberlin. You're a mighty rich man."

Steve looked at his wife, and a wide soft arc of joy and love passed between them.

Jeremy wiggled an index finger under the baby's hand. The movement caught Megan's eyes.

"Her name is Katie," she told him. "After Mother."

Jeremy burst out, "When can she play with me? Will she be able to catch a ball?"

They stayed three minutes more, answering Jeremy's questions, listening to his observations, until Banjo tugged at the boy's hand.

"We'd best let Miss Megan rest, Jem," he said. "She was up most of the night, and she's awful tired."

Jeremy looked at his sister for confirmation.

Megan nodded. "You can help Em give Katie a bath later, honey. There'll be lots of time to play with the baby."

From that point on, the Chamberlin household took on certain aspects of heaven: relief, rejoicing. . .and no night there. Little Katie loved the midnight watches. Unless hunger was the problem, Em sat up with the baby to let the exhausted young mother sleep. Normal routine blew to the four winds, and Em lost complete track of time.

Chapter 16

The morning Chance rode in, he found Em sweeping the porch. Broom in hand, she stared dumbly at his approaching horse, wondering, *What day of the week is it? Saturday?*

Megan and the baby slept. Jeremy had ridden into the woods with Banjo and Steve to collect yet more firewood. Em propped the broom against the house and waited on the top step. Now that Chance had come, she was eager to hear his version of his fearful escapade. She noticed that he still looked thin, though not nearly as haggard as before.

Chance dropped Po'boy's reins and strode toward her, his face alight. Em observed his long stride, the tilt of his head, his keen eyes.

Something's changed, she thought. *Would having his name cleared make him look like that?*

"Good morning, Emma!" Even his voice had a different ring.

Em smiled widely. "Is it mornin'? That new little girl has kept me a-goin' so much, I don't know which end's up." She put out her hand. "I'se mighty glad to see you, Chance. How are you?"

"I've never been better." He squeezed her fingers and didn't let go. "Do you feel like walking?"

"The fresh air will do me good, I reckon." She stepped down to his level, and they headed toward the stable and beyond.

"Banjo told me what happened to you. . .about Sheriff Feiklin comin' to the cave and all." She shuddered. "I'm mighty glad it's all over."

Chance chuckled. "Miss Susan about smothered me when I got home. She fed me steak and beans until I couldn't hold another bite. While I stuffed myself, she heated about ten gallons of water so I could take a bath while Slim buried my clothes. Since then, she's only let me sleep and eat. Tomorrow I start cooking again."

He changed the subject when they had crossed the stream. "How's the new mother getting along?"

In few words Em listed the goings-on of the past four days. "Megan and the baby are right as rain. God has been so good to us."

"He sure has," Chance agreed, his voice strangely quiet.

Em stared at him. "Something about you has changed. I knew it the first I laid eyes on you, Chance. What's happened?"

He smiled and a soft light turned on within him. "I found Jesus, Emma. Or maybe I should say He found me. Banjo talked with me in the cave, the morning he and Mr. Wyatt brought in Hensler.

"It was amazing how it all took place. You see, God already had my attention." He told her of the man digging into the false wall.

"So when Banjo laid it out for me clear and plain, I knew I had to surrender." He laughed softly. "When God's got you covered, you better come out with your hands up."

"Praise be to Jesus!" Em's face took on a glory light of its own. "You don't know how many nights I laid awake prayin' for you."

"Banjo called on me yesterday," his deep voice continued. "He brought his new Bible. We're reading through the Gospel of John together." He stooped to pick up a large pinecone and toss it into the stream. "I'm going to get me a Bible, Emma, if I have to pay two hundred dollars and ride two hundred miles."

She clapped her hands together. "Wouldn't it be passin' wonderful to hear you a-readin' it!"

Chance grasped her arm and stopped their progress. They stood among the pines at the bottom edge of the empty cornfield.

"Emma, can I make you change your mind about marrying me?" He took a step forward and turned to face her. "Please think it over, Emma. Now that I'm a Christian, I see that my dreams have been nothing but an empty shell. Things can never make a person happy. Only God can do that." He stepped closer, speaking softly, gazing into her eyes.

Em stood stock-still. This time she couldn't break the spell, didn't realize it even existed.

The man continued, speaking intensely. "You thought you were coming to Colorado to help Miss Megan, but I believe that God brought you here for me. We both love Jesus. If we love each other as well, the circle's complete." That sad look—the one that first reached out to Em—showed itself again. He stood as though frozen, waiting for the verdict.

His appeal squeezed Em's heart. How could she turn him away?

Tears spilled over. "Yes, Chance," she whispered. "I will marry you."

In an instant he folded her into the safe shelter of his arms. Em squeezed her brimming eyes tight and knew that this was where she was meant to be.

They stood together for a moment before he released her and caught her hand. She stuffed her damp handkerchief into the pocket of her work dress. Without making a conscious decision, they veered toward the lake. An irate squirrel chattered from a pine bough, its cheeks bulging.

They spoke of life and love and the surprising turns that God brings people through.

"The sheriff came yesterday to return my silver nuggets," the man said when they reached the edge of blue water. "He had a slip from the assayer's office saying it's worth $2,750. That ought to be enough to get us started. Next week I'll go to the land office and see what's still open in these parts.

"He also apologized." Chance grimaced. "After a fashion."

Em looked up at him, surprised. "What did he say?"

"He told me he should have done more checking before telling the town it was I who robbed the stage. He said he'll be more careful in the future."

"Well, I guess that's some comfort."

"I wouldn't count Feiklin a heartfelt friend, but at least he was man enough to say what he did." They walked in the mottled shade near the water. A fish splashed on the surface and disappeared. A woodpecker's tattoo echoed through the mountains.

"How about a Christmas wedding, Emma, if we can find a preacher? With some help, I can put up a small log cabin in a few days. We'll add on a room or two as time goes by. Wouldn't it be grand to snuggle in together and wait out the winter?"

As though waking from deep sleep, Em exclaimed, "Oh! What am I gonna do about Jeremy? It was him that played those tricks on you, Chance. He was scared you'd take me away." The handkerchief reappeared. "Now it looks like the boy was right."

"Would Miss Megan let him stay with us?" Chance asked. "Jeremy's a fine boy. I know we could be friends."

"I'd have to talk to Miss Megan. I don't know how she'd feel about that."

"Would it help if I talk to him?" he asked.

"Maybe." She shrugged. "I've been prayin' about it, Chance. But so far, I don't have no answers."

Perched close together on a flat rock, they talked and planned for another hour.

"I've been thinking, Emma. When a man marries, his wife takes his name." He looked at her, an amused expression on his features. "I seem to be lacking something essential there."

"That don't. . . ," Em began, but he cut her off.

"What do you think of taking Calahan for our last name? Banjo's my father in the Lord. I think it would be fitting."

"That's a wonderful thought! I'd like to be with you when you tell Banjo." She laughed. "I can see his expression now."

With much regret they retraced the path toward the house. The sun beamed on them from high above.

"I'd best go to Miss Megan," Em said when they reached the porch steps.

"You think she'd let me see the baby?"

"Why, sure! I'd have asked you myself if I thought you'd want to." She climbed the stairs and opened the door, Chance close behind her. "Let me see if they'se still sleepin'."

Megan was sitting up when Em peeked inside. The baby lay on the bed, waving little hands.

The lean woman stepped through the door. "Is it okay if I take Katie out so Chance can see her?"

Two minutes later, holding the wiggling bundle in tender arms, Em joined Chance on the sofa.

"Her name's Katie after Miss Megan's dear mama." Em smiled into the wide blue eyes, so serious. She looked up to her guest. "Would you like to hold her?"

Grinning, Chance reached for the flannel parcel. He gently cradled the tiny girl, touched her hair and her hands. She stared into his eyes with the wise expression known only to newborns.

"What do you know?" he exclaimed in muted tones. "My first granddaughter. Who would have guessed she would be a white child?" He laughed, an infectious sound. Em laughed, too, her heart so full she had to keep dabbing her eyes.

The mantel clock had passed noon before he said good-bye and rode away. Carrying Katie back to her mama, Em entered the bedroom.

Wearing a soft blue gown, Megan sat on the edge of the bed. By doctor's orders, she wasn't allowed to get up for ten days. Em laid the sweet bundle on the bed.

"What happened, Em?" Megan asked. "You look like the cat who swallowed the canary."

"He received the Lord, Miss Megan. We'se gettin' married." She paused. "It would have broke my heart to turn him down again. I couldn't say no."

"I thought so!" Radiating happiness, Megan held her arms out for a hug. "I'm so glad for you." She squeezed Em hard.

Em clung to her. "I don't want to leave you, Miss Megan. Or Jeremy. I feel like I'm being cut in two." She straightened. "Chance needs me. But so does Jeremy. How can I tell the child?"

Megan stared at the floor, considering. Baby Katie let out a wee cry. "Don't tell Jeremy yet, Em," she said, reaching for her daughter. "Let's pray about this awhile."

Prayer was about all Em accomplished through the next two weeks. Her emotions ran up and down so quickly, most of the time she didn't know whether to laugh or cry.

Chance appeared at odd times, whenever he could spare a couple of hours from his duties. His warm looks and broad smiles made it no secret that he was as much in love as a boy of eighteen. Whenever he appeared Megan and Steve shared a secret smile, but Jeremy's countenance resembled a thundercloud.

A few days later, Chance arrived to find the boy sitting on the top step of the porch, his determined hands gripping a piece of pine and his new knife. As always, Lobo hovered nearby. Chance had become such a regular guest, the dog merely sniffed his cuffs.

Jeremy gave an up-from-under glance at the man, expecting him to pass by. This time, however, Chance sat on the step beside the child.

Jeremy's chin sank lower. He continued scraping at the wood, sending irregular chips to the floor. The pine resembled a half-eaten ear of corn.

"What are you making?" Chance asked, hoping to break the ice.

The answer was barely audible. "A dog." Shrinking away, he scored the lump of wood with vengeance.

Chance saw that the only way to begin his speech was to begin it. He plunged ahead. "Jeremy, I want to tell you that I don't plan to separate you from Em. I know you love her. She loves you, too."

Jeremy's hands became still. He stared at his handiwork.

The adult rubbed nervous hands on his pant legs. "I'm going to buy property as close to the Circle C as I can." He hesitated, then rushed ahead. "Em and I are going to get married and live there. We want you to be with us, Jeremy. You can visit often or even come to live with us if Miss Megan will let you." Chance was running out of ammunition, and he wasn't sure if the battle was over yet.

"You're a great lad, Jeremy. If I'd had a boy of my own, I would have wanted him to be like you. I wish we could be friends."

The towheaded child turned toward him. "Do you know how to fish?"

Taken aback, Chance replied, "Why sure. It's one of my favorite ways to pass an afternoon."

"Banjo and Steve don't take to fishin', and I wish I could learn how."

"Would you like to go tomorrow? After lunch?"

The dark look disappeared. In its place came a cautious acceptance, a tentative approval. "Okay," he said quietly.

"We may not get much fishing done the first day," Chance told him, relaxing a little. "We'll have to find some good poles and fix a line. I have some hooks. I made them myself." He gave Lobo a friendly pat. "We'll go at the warmest part of the day. To the lake. Okay?"

"Maybe Em'll pack us some sandwiches," the boy added hopefully.

Chance chuckled. "I'm sure she will. She thinks I'm about to fade away from starvation these days." He stood up. "I'll see you tomorrow, then," he said.

Jeremy's knife gouged at the figure, sending a chunk to the floor.

Megan sat with Em in the living room the next afternoon while Chance and Jeremy were on their fishing expedition. The boy had been too excited to eat lunch. Em wrapped sandwiches and placed them in a tin to carry along. She shared a secret smile with Chance before the twosome set off.

Megan sat on the sofa, folding diapers, while Em bounced Katie on her knee. "Have Chance come for supper Friday night," Megan suggested. "That will be November first."

"He's planning on comin' over then anyways, Miss Megan." She broke off to make some absurd clicking noises into the baby's face and was rewarded with Katie's studious expression.

Em looked at Megan to ask, "What do you want to have for supper that night?"

"Barbecued steaks and baked potatoes. Wyatt and Susan will be coming, too."

"You sure you aren't oversteppin'?" Em asked, eyebrows raised. "You still ain't too strong."

"I'll be fine. Just invite Chance for the meal when he and Jeremy get back." She picked up a wrinkled diaper and snapped it loudly.

Friday evening Chance rode in alongside the Rocking H buckboard. Susan wore a long black coat with a large stiff bonnet against the cold night air. After they stepped down, Banjo helped Wyatt unhitch the horse, Jeremy following every move.

Susan carried a large basket into the house. She set it on the kitchen counter. "Don't touch that, Em," she said. "I'll take care of it later."

Em bent over the oven, basting the steaks. "Okay, Miss Susan," she said, straightening. She inspected the cloth-covered wicker, her curiosity piqued. *What's goin' on?* she wondered.

Chance stood inside the door, hat in hand. As a guest, he didn't feel he should join Em in the kitchen, yet he didn't want to stay far away from her in the sitting room either. Em noticed his predicament and called, "Come talk to me while I finish, Chance."

Relieved, he slipped his hat on a peg and strode to her side. In a moment he laughed when she dropped a piece of meat on the open oven door. He grabbed a fork to help her retrieve it.

Jeremy skipped through the back door and straight to the man in Em's kitchen. "Look at this, Chance," he chirped, holding out a stick. "Should I notch it here to hold the string? See where I trimmed down the end? I wanted to make a better rod for the next time we go to the lake."

Dropping the steak to its platter, Chance straightened up to regard the boy's masterpiece. He picked it up for a better look. "Nice job, son. If you notch it here"—he pointed—"the string will grip good and tight."

Jeremy took the rod and, pulling his knife from his overalls pocket, headed for the porch steps.

Baby in arms, Megan entered the living room.

"How's the new mother?" Susan asked, approaching Megan. "Mind if I hold her?"

Megan relinquished her burden and found a seat on the sofa. "I'm starting to feel like myself again, thank the Lord."

"We had some startling news this morning," Susan said, choosing a perch on the chair. She laid Katie on her knees, both hands cupped under the tiny head—the best position for a chat.

"What's happened?" Megan asked.

"Brent and Lisa eloped last night. He left a note for Amos. Amos brought it to Wyatt this morning."

Megan's face drew into a frown. "Will they come back to Juniper? What about his job?"

"Your guess beats mine," Susan replied sadly. "The Feiklin family has a lion's share of heartaches today. I guess everyone does at one time or another." Turning to the sweet bundle on her lap, she cooed, "Hello, little lady."

Wyatt stepped through the front door and drew up short. "Careful, Susan," he warned. "I hear that womenfolk catch a strange fever from holding a tiny bundle like that."

Entering behind him, Banjo chuckled. "That's a fact, Hammond. I've seen it happen."

"You men go chase your cows or something," Susan retorted. "Let me have some peace." She smiled down at the infant.

At the meal, Megan seated wondering Em with Chance at the head of the table. Steve remained standing when everyone had found a chair.

"We're gathered together today to honor a special couple who are about to enter the blessed state of marriage."

Embarrassed, Chance and Em shared a startled glance. Em's eyes widened as she stared at Megan's wide smile. Jeremy beamed along with everyone else.

Steve continued his speech. "We want you, Chance and Em, to know that we wish you a long and happy life together and to pledge our help as neighbors whenever you may need us." He bowed his head saying, "Let's ask God to bless this new family."

His heartfelt prayer touched Chance like nothing else could. Under the table he squeezed Em's hand.

After the food disappeared, Susan fetched the mystery basket from the kitchen. She laid aside the towel covering and drew out a white sheet cake.

"No wonder you chased me out of the kitchen this morning," Chance said, laughter in his voice.

As Susan picked up a knife to cut the cake, Steve half rose to thrust a folded paper at Chance.

Em peered over her intended's shoulder at the maze of lines and letters drawn on it.

"It's a surveyor's map," Chance told her. He looked at Steve. "What's this?"

"See the red plot beside the lake?" Steve asked. "That's yours. A wedding present from Megan and me. Forty acres of grazing or farmland opening on the water."

Astonished, Chance stared at Steve, then pored over the map. He looked up. "I'm not sure I should take this," he stammered.

"It's a selfish gift," Steve added quickly. "We wanted to keep Em close enough for Jeremy to visit her every day. Please take it, Chance. I've already got my lawyer drawing up the deed."

Wyatt leaned over to pull a small sack from under his chair. "This is from Banjo and me," he said, handing the clinking leather pouch to Chance. "It's the reward money for catching Hensler."

"Use it to get you through the winter," Banjo added. "You'll need feed for your horse and all."

Chance balanced the money in his palm. He swallowed the lump rising below his Adam's apple. "There's no way to thank you all," he managed.

"Be happy," Megan said, eyes shining. "That's the very best way to thank us."

"Would you mind if we eat that cake later?" Chance asked Susan. "We've got an hour till dark, and I'd like to see the land." He squeezed Em's hand. "Want to come?"

"Does a chicken have lips?" she replied, drawing a chuckle from Banjo.

Taking down her wool shawl, she followed her man outside.

"If we step smartly, we can walk over," he said. He slipped a firm arm about her waist. "Emma, my love, let's take a look at the home place."

Lisa's Broken Arrow

Chapter 1

When the final rays of twilight melted into night, Lisa Feiklin realized that Brent Cavenaugh had deserted her. She was stranded in Silverville.

Lisa stared out the diner's window at the shadowy silhouettes of horses and their riders as they ambled down the mining town's dusty main street. Sipping cold coffee from a blue enamel mug, she idly twisted a long lock of wavy black hair around a slender finger and pondered her predicament. What should she do now?

Her thoughts drifted back to the first time she had laid eyes on Brent—last summer at the Rocking H barbecue. If she had known then that her taunting looks and teasing glances might lead her to this place, she most certainly would have run the other way. Nevertheless, his dandified ways and angelic good looks had instantly captivated her. He'd looked so sleek in his sharply pressed cowboy garb, a black silk bandanna knotted exactly halfway between his Adam's apple and his ear; his strawberry-blond mustache twitching upward with his smile.

He had noticed her, too, and stood opposite her in the square dance. She could still feel the tingle that his touch produced when he had taken her hand to lead her in the promenade.

Later, in the line of people easing toward twin tables loaded with bread and beans and beef, pies and tarts, Lisa whispered to her year-younger sister, Jessica, "Did you see Brent? He's the one in the red-checkered shirt."

"I saw him, sure enough," Jessica hissed back, her heart-shaped face showing disapproval. "You'd best stay away from him, Lisa. He's trouble."

Flipping fingers through her glossy black waves, Lisa chortled. "He's my kind of trouble, Jessica child. When you grow up you'll understand."

Just two weeks after their first meeting, Brent started spinning rosy dreams of marriage and a cabin in the mountains where they would always be together. He called on Lisa every Saturday night, squeezed her hand during long, moonlit walks, sent her love notes tied with red ribbon.

Never had one of Lisa's many other beaux been so romantic. Gazing into her mirror, she daydreamed of her new love by the hour.

At the end of Brent's fourth visit, Lisa's father, the stocky sheriff Rod Feiklin, pursed his lips and stared after the suitor's cantering palomino. "Lisa, I'm not so sure about that hombre. He's too polished. Something's mighty suspicious about him."

She slanted her eyes at him. "I like him, Daddy."

"He's turned your head with pretty talk, I'll bet." He shook his head in a warning. "Next time he comes around here, tell him to keep riding."

Turning her head away, Lisa did not answer him. After that, she met Brent by day in a copse of trees near the river. When he tried to kiss her, she'd laugh and push him away, exhilarated that he found her appealing, intoxicated with her own feminine powers.

In late October Brent touched the tiny mole at the corner of her lips and sweetly pleaded, "Come with me, Lisa." She watched his hazel eyes search her face before fixing upon her lips. "We'll go to South Dakota and find a preacher. I can't live without you any longer."

Mesmerized, she breathed, "Tonight. After midnight."

Like a knight rescuing a maiden from an evil baron, Brent waited under her window astride his palomino stallion. Instead of his usual Stetson and jeans, he wore a tailor-made black broadcloth suit and black bowler.

In Denver the runaway couple boarded a stage heading north. Brent's arm stayed protectively around Lisa, and she felt secure and relaxed against his shoulder. However, when his grasp on her tightened and his hand found her waist, she began to squirm, wishing she could put some distance between them. After all, they weren't married yet. They would have a leisurely honeymoon in a plush hotel following the wedding. She would have time to warm up to him then. Sitting tight against him on a stage filled with strangers made her feel cheap. She glanced at his round cheek next to hers. Why couldn't he understand how she felt?

They had to wait a day for the next stage in Laramie. That evening, Brent stepped, uninvited, into her tiny hotel room. "Come here, Lisa girl." He smiled like a fox in a chicken yard.

She stepped away from his groping fingers, arching her eyebrow in hopes of hiding her dismay. "Let's get some supper, honey. I'm worn out and hungry."

He dropped his hand, but the glint never left his eyes. Lisa, her heart pounding, swished past him and yanked open the door. Brent followed her with the air of a man biding his time.

This was not the first time Lisa had attempted to elope with a man. She and Hank Penbrook had been boarding the stage when her father caught up with them and forcefully carried her home. Afterward, she had sobbed and blamed her father for interfering. Now she yearned for him to appear again and rescue her. Brent made her feel hunted.

The cat-and-mouse game lasted for more than a week. As Brent's advances became more insistent, Lisa frantically searched her mind for ways to delay a showdown with him. A dozen times a day, she asked when they would stop to find a preacher. Brent remained vague, unresponsive.

For the first time in her life, Lisa regretted the haughty, flippant attitude that caused her to toss her head at her mother's warnings and her father's rules. More than anything in the world, she wished the scarlet Concord stage was headed toward Juniper Junction again.

In the Black Hills of South Dakota, Lisa's time ran out.

During a stagecoach stop, Brent escorted her into Silverville's solitary shack of a diner, and they found seats at a rough plank table. The dining room's four other tables stood empty, except for the clutter of crusty, half-eaten dinner plates and half-drunk coffee cups. There was no waitress in sight. The smell of old grease hung heavy on the air.

Grabbing a chance to speak unheard by others, Lisa asked, "When are we going to stop traveling long enough to find a parson, Brent?"

He stiffened, then relaxed. He slowly brushed a forefinger over his strawberry-blond mustache as he studied her. When his hand glided down to the table, his slack mouth turned hard. "I'm tired of playing games, Lisa." He let out an exasperated breath. "After the way you led me on, I never dreamed you'd be such a Polly Prude." His head tilted forward. His hazel eyes bored into her. "If you play by my rules, I'll consider buying you a ring and calling on a preacher to do the honors someday. If you tilt your nose in the air, I'll dump you here without a penny."

Clenching her hands around her empty purse, Lisa swallowed and gulped for breath. "You promised to take care of me, remember, Brent?" Her pleading tone turned accusing. "You said we'd be together always, come rain or shine. What about your duty as a gentleman?" Lips tight, she gazed from his perfect hairstyle to his impeccable mustache, and a fresh realization dawned within her. "You can't act like a gentleman because you aren't one. You're nothing but a double-dyed fraud." Her chin came up. "I'm staying here."

"And do what?" He spoke low and intense. "You don't know a soul here, and you haven't any money. Where will you sleep? What will you eat?"

Black eyes flashing, she forced her jaws to relax enough to speak. "I wouldn't go another mile with you, Brent. Even if I have to sleep on a bare floor and eat sawdust."

A slim, graying waitress slapped a pencil-scribbled menu card down on the table between them. "Here's today's grub. I'll be back in a minute." She marched to the kitchen without waiting for an answer.

Brent patted at his coat pockets and stood, reaching into them. "I've dropped my wallet. I must have lost it on the stage." His longs legs stretched toward the door. He stood aside for an elderly couple to enter, then disappeared into the afternoon. The biting chill of late autumn reached Lisa from across the room as the door *whooshed* shut.

When the waitress returned, Lisa smiled nervously and tapped long, slender fingers on the wooden table. "My friend will be back in a moment. I'll wait for him so we can order together."

"How about a cup of coffee meanwhile?"

"Thank you."

The coffee came soon afterwards, but Brent did not appear. Lisa fidgeted and stared out the smudged window. Her stomach rumbled. She smoothed down her lavender skirt, anxiety mounting every minute. More than an hour later, the last rays of an orange sun vanished from the rooftops across the street.

What shall I do now? The question echoed through Lisa's thoughts.

The waitress returned. "Looks like he got held up," she said with a small, cautious smile. As she spoke, she swept from her cheek a strand of gray hair mixed with blond, an unusual color. Yet her hair was her best feature. She had a flat, long face with a straight nose. A curved scar circled her left cheekbone, giving her a harsh look, but her eyes were kind.

Lisa pulled the corners of her full lips into an upside-down smile. "I can't order until he comes back." She ran fingers along the strings of her empty purse. She ought to leave, but where could she go? With nothing to eat since breakfast, she was starving.

"It's okay, honey. We're not busy, so you can sit tight. I'll warm up your coffee." She brought the pot and poured. "My name's Bess."

"I'm Lisa. Thanks very much."

"Don't mention it." Bess hurried to serve the other table and didn't return for an hour. Lisa gnawed her lip and fought back tears. Resting her chin on her hand, she closed her eyes.

"You okay?" Firm fingers touched her shoulder.

Lisa jerked erect and stared at Bess. The older woman slid into the seat across from her. "You're in trouble, aren't you?"

Forcing her lips into a small curve, Lisa nodded. "My gentleman friend left me stranded. I don't know what to do. I don't have any money." She ran a thumb over the handle of her coffee cup. "Would the boss let me clean the kitchen in exchange for supper?"

Bess looked at the younger woman's ruffled cuffs and embroidered bodice. "I reckon he might, but you wouldn't be much good in that getup."

"My suitcase is at the stage station. I have other clothes in it."

Bess watched her, considering. "I suppose he may give you a try. The girl who used to be our waitress and dishwasher moved to greener pastures last week. I've been doing triple duty for five straight days. I'm the cook here. . .for my sins." She stood. "I'll bring you a hot meal and send a boy to the station for your things.

Now let me go and mention you to the owner." She hustled back to the kitchen and returned five minutes later with a short, round man beside her. He was bald except for a fringe above his ears.

"This is Lisa, Mr. Brockwyn," Bess announced.

He let his eyes trail down Lisa from her crown to her fingertips. "This ain't no society parlor. She looks like she's never done a day's work in her life." Brockwyn was a full inch shorter than Bess, but he moved with a swagger and his fleshy lips held a cynical twist.

Lisa met his disdainful black eyes. She wanted to tell him what she thought of him, but desperation pinned her tongue.

"Please give her a chance, Mr. Brockwyn," Bess said. "I can't do everything myself for much longer. If she don't work out, you can always let her go."

Brockwyn spoke like a Gatling gun. "You will wait tables. Wash all the dishes and pots. After closing time, mop the floors. If Bess needs help, you do as she says. Report at six in the morning. Leave at eight at night. Salary's five dollars a week."

When Lisa nodded, the manager trundled into the kitchen and let the door bump closed behind him.

Five dollars a week. Could she even afford a telegram to let her parents know she was safe?

"Thank you!" Lisa called after him.

"Save your thanks," Bess replied, shaking her head. "The job is no prize, believe me."

Lisa pulled in a sharp breath. "I forgot to ask him when I get my first pay. I'm starving."

Bess reached into her apron pocket and pulled out some change. "Here." Gold and silver coins clanked onto the rough table. "Consider this a loan until you get paid." She hurried away and returned carrying a heaping plate.

Beef and beans never tasted so good. Relief made Lisa almost giddy. With a job, she would be able to get a room somewhere nearby. A nagging voice asked her how soon she would get home, but she pushed the thought aside. One problem at a time.

In a chilly storage room, she changed into her drab brown work dress and forced the lavender frock into the suitcase. Twisting up her black tresses, she pinned her hair into a high bun, ignoring the wisps around her face.

Rolling up her sleeves, she summoned up enough grit to plunge her soft pink arms into an iron sink filled with cold, greasy water thick with stale food particles. She bit the inside of her cheek to hold back the disgust rising in her throat, then began to pull out stack after stack of plates and cups. Finally, she reached the bottom and yanked the drain plug. Water chugged into a bucket under the sink.

Bess called to her from the rusty stove three strides away. "Dump that waste bucket outside on the ground. I've got hot water in the stove reservoir for new wash water." Piquant wood smoke drifted upward as Bess lifted a heavy iron circle from the top of the stove to add another small log.

A few minutes later, Lisa panted as she set down the pail of filthy water and tipped it over onto frozen earth. She paused, enjoying the frigid air on her burning cheeks. Already exhausted, she had yet to wash a single dish.

"Where are you from?" Bess asked half an hour later. The dining room had closed, and she poured leftover beef stew into a wide bowl.

Lisa looked up from the sudsy dishpan. "Juniper Junction, Colorado."

Bess replied over her shoulder, "Never heard of it."

"I never heard of Silverville either, until the stage drove in this afternoon."

"I've been in South Dakota for five years," Bess told her, setting the dented soup pot on the counter near Lisa's arm. "I used to work in Deadwood, but when I heard about the silver strike, I decided to come over here and get in on the excitement." She shrugged. "Didn't take me long to see that this place is just like the last one. You get up and go to work, you eat and you sleep, and you start all over again the next morning."

Lisa kept her eyes on the dishpan. Is that all she had to look forward to as well?

"You can bunk with me if you'd like. I have an extra bed. The waitress that left used to be my roommate."

"Thanks." Lisa straightened and drew in a slow breath. At least she wouldn't be sleeping in the icy storage room.

No thanks to Brent Cavenaugh. Now that her initial fears had calmed, hot anger rushed in. She scoured a pot with vengeance. Men were beasts! She'd had enough of them to last a lifetime.

Chapter 2

By lantern light, Bess's cabin looked as dismal as the diner's kitchen. Nestled in a grove of cottonwoods one hundred feet from the kitchen's back door, the structure's half-peeled logs rose two feet taller than Lisa's head with a bark-shingle roof on top. Lisa studied the oiled-paper windows while Bess groped for the door latch. With a scrape and a groan, the door swung open, and they stepped inside.

Across the room, the flame of a burning log in the stone fireplace had smoldered down to a dull orange gleam. Bess waved a hand at the only chair, a crooked, handmade affair that tilted slightly to one side. "Have a seat while I stir up the fire."

She set the lantern on a scarred table and bustled out the back door. In a moment she returned with three wedges of wood in her arms. "You can split logs before breakfast," she said, dropping her burden and lifting a poker to stir the coals. "I have to start work before dawn. You've got an extra hour before you have to be there."

Lisa nodded, her heart sinking. Did anyone ever sleep in this town?

The fire blazed higher, slowly warming the room. Nothing within the cabin's four walls looked appealing. The floor resembled a washboard, and the mantel shelf had one end broken off. Shivering inside her coat, Lisa noticed a ragged curtain on the west end of the room.

"That's our sleeping quarters," Bess offered, nodding toward the scrap of gray muslin hanging from two nails in the ceiling. "You can take the left cot."

Sick with exhaustion, Lisa pushed aside the curtain and lay down on the narrow rope-strung bed. A lump in the bare straw mattress gouged into the small of her back. A rotten smell pricked her nose. For the second time tonight, she swallowed back the revulsion tightening her throat and pulled the only blanket—a thin bit of stained wool—over her middle.

She closed her eyes and saw her mother's seamed face, haggard with worry over her rebellious daughter. How long until Lisa saw that dear face again? Tears of loneliness and despair seeped from the corners of her eyes. Utterly spent, she let them flow.

⌒

From December to late March, Lisa worked from dawn until far past dark, six days out of seven. Her once-buxom figure grew slim and hard. Her hands developed calluses. Her hair lost its wavy sheen. She paid the milliner two bits for a scrap bag and used its contents to stitch a quilt. Stuffed with chipped corncobs, the cover wasn't exactly eiderdown, but at least it covered her from chin to toes. If she spread her coat on top of it and wore her shoes to bed, she felt almost warm.

After paying rent and buying her meals at the restaurant, she had only pennies left each week. The stage to Juniper cost twelve dollars.

Shortly after Christmas, she swallowed her pride and wrote to her father, asking him to come and get her. A month later, a letter arrived from him. Lisa's heart sank as she studied the familiar scrawl: *You have a job and a place to live. When you save enough money for the stage, you'll be welcome home.*

As the winter days hinted of spring, Lisa's desperation to return home became an almost living thing. A deep, wrenching despair coated her spirit like thick wax. She moved through her days as though sleepwalking. Speaking little. Thinking less. Her only goal—to survive another harrowing day, another frigid night.

During the coldest part of February, a tiny green bud of hope sprouted in her soul when a letter came from Mother. *Daddy will travel by stage to bring you home soon after the warm chinook winds.*

Smiling, Lisa folded the pages. Mama had finally worn down his resolve. Still, Daddy had gotten his way. Little Lisa had learned her lesson well this time.

In the dead of the night on March 28, the drumming of horses' hooves on frozen earth jarred Lisa from her sleep. Her heart thumping, she stood and gathered the quilt around her shoulders. As she stumbled through the dark, she banged her shin on the end of the bed and let out a sharp gasp. Bess's cot squawked when she rolled over, but she did not waken.

Lisa hesitated in the living room, pausing near the fireplace. Although tempted to open the door, she balked at the thought of facing the bitter cold. Perhaps the stamping sounded only in her dreams and the horses ran only in her mind. Just outside the cabin a whinny set her pulse racing. For a full two minutes, she waited for a knock on the door, but the knock never came.

Scolding herself for her fear, she lit the rusty lantern with a flaming stick and pulled up the latch. An icy gust tore through her, but the sight outside her door drove all thoughts about the cold from her mind.

Two horses stood near the log cabin's front wall. The black carried a lumpy pack. A man slumped over the saddle of the bay.

Not wanting to spook the horses, Lisa set the lantern on the ground near the door and tiptoed forward. "Easy," she said, keeping her voice low and calm. "Easy, boy." She touched the bay's nose and ran her hand down his gaunt neck toward the man, murmuring softly all the while.

Was the rider dead?

"What's all the commotion?" Bess appeared in the doorway, swiping the sleep from her eyes with a leathery hand. Her hair fell loosely about her shoulders. Her coat tented over a ragged flannel nightgown.

"Someone's hurt." Lisa felt the man's icy hand. "Maybe he's dead. He's sure enough froze."

Bess stepped forward, slipping her arms into her coat sleeves and buttoning it around her as she moved. She grabbed the horses' reins and tied them to a nearby bush. Reaching for the man's dusty, jeans-covered knee, she said, "You'd be cold, too, if you were out here all night."

The man moaned softly.

"See here," Bess said. "Let's get his boots out of the stirrups so we can ease him down."

While Lisa pushed him upward on one side, Bess stood on the other to break his fall. He almost knocked her over. "He's been shot in the head," Bess panted. "It's a miracle he's still alive." She leaned over to grasp him under the arms. "Here, grab his boots. He's a heavy dude. I wish he'd laid off the grub awhile before he did this."

With a good deal of huffing and tugging, the women dragged the two hundred pounds of dead weight over the threshold. After they had situated the unconscious man on Lisa's cot, which she'd hurriedly pulled in front of the fire, Bess forced frozen boots off frozen feet, coaxing all the while as though scuffed leather could hear her.

Lisa draped her rustling coverlet around his chin, then tucked it under him and down both sides. Swinging an iron pot away from the fire, she poured steaming water into a basin and added cold water to cool it down. She found a cloth and began sponging the man's filthy, blood-streaked face. Fine dirt filled the tiny weblike lines around his eyes and the creases in his neck. Not grime acquired over a long time, but dust as though he had been digging or maybe plowing behind a horse for days.

Things didn't add up. He wore a bandanna, jeans, and narrow-toed boots. Cowboys despised farming.

"I wonder who's after him," Bess said in a few moments. "What if they trail him here?"

"We can't leave the man out in the cold to die."

As the crusty flecks of dried blood dissolved and the dirt washed away, he looked painfully young—in his late twenties at the most. He had a Roman nose and a full, firm mouth. The left side of his short, dusty hair lay darkly matted to his skull.

"Look at this!" Bess said. His feet were swollen and raw around the toes and heels. The wounds had festered. "Looks like he hasn't had these boots off for a long time. Otherwise, he wouldn't have been able to put them back on."

"How did that happen, Bess?"

"You've got me. A cowboy would sooner saddle up to cross the street than use his shoe leather."

"He had two horses. Why would he walk far enough for his feet to look like that?"

"When he comes to, he'll probably tell us a good long tale."

"Should we do anything to his head?" Lisa asked, glancing at Bess as she gently eased a warm, wet cloth over his icy feet.

"Let's get him warmed up first," she replied shortly. "Throw some more wood on the fire. I wish Silverville had a doctor."

After several long minutes, his cold body turned warm, then feverish. The bullet had creased his scalp, leaving a wide gash in its path. Lisa cleaned the wound and bound his light brown hair with a few of the multicolored cloth strips from her ragbag.

Though he never opened his eyes, he sometimes moaned or moved his hand. For the next four days, Lisa ducked out of the diner up to ten times a day to check on him and try to force some broth through his clenched teeth.

The stranger's horses stood tethered in the lean-to where Bess stored her firewood. The same dusty earth that had caked the man also covered the hides of both horses. The outline of ribs shadowed the animals' skin. Pooling their funds, the women purchased three bales of hay and a quart of oats from the livery stable. Neither broached the subject of what they would do when that ran out.

Lisa spread a pallet on the floor close to the warmth of the fire and near the cot so she could hear if he awakened during the night. She felt a keen understanding of his desperate circumstances and knew she must help him. Gazing at his still face in the flickering firelight, she wondered if he were an outlaw. He didn't look like one, but what did looks really show?

On the evening of the fourth day, Lisa jerked awake when a hand trailed along her arm. Eyes wide, she sat up and edged away from the sick man's cot.

The touch had been a glancing one, because the hand moved up to touch the green cloth binding the wound. The man's eyes squinted and blinked and turned toward her. Piercing blue, they seemed to look at Lisa from far away.

"W—w—what happened?" he muttered with a thick tongue.

"Someone shot you." Lisa knelt beside him.

He looked toward the ceiling, his eyes wide with fear. "He's coming after me. I've got to hide."

"You're safe here." She reached for the dipper hanging over the edge of a tin bucket on the table. "Here, drink some water." Supporting his shoulders, she held the drink to his lips. "That's enough for now." She gently eased him back onto the cot.

"I've got to get out of here," he said, his eyelids lowering. "He's after m. . ." He was asleep before his lips formed the last word.

Lisa returned to her pallet and tried to sleep. In less than two hours, she must rise and face another backbreaking day. Finally, she rose to stoke the fire and put on coffee, her eyes constantly straying to the quiet form nearby. His relaxed posture told her that he was sleeping comfortably.

Her lips formed a half smile. Soon she would hear the answers to the dozens of questions now obsessing her.

If he wasn't an outlaw, why had someone shot him? Why was someone chasing him? She glanced at his pack propped in the corner, so heavy that Bess had to struggle to get it inside.

When Lisa left for work that morning, he was still asleep. She set the water pail near his hand in case he awoke while she was out.

At lunchtime Lisa saved some of her stew to carry to the cabin. When she crossed the clearing, a fresh warm breeze stroked her face and ruffled her hair. Pausing, she lifted her cheeks toward heaven and closed her eyes. The chinook. Daddy might be here within the week.

Wearing a wide smile, Lisa opened the door to the cabin and found her patient alert, one arm tucked under the back of his head.

"Well, you decided to wake up, did you?" she asked, a new light in her eyes as she closed the door firmly behind her. "I brought you some food."

"Thanks. I'm famished." His voice sounded raspy. "I've drunk almost all the water in the pail, and I'm still thirsty."

She smiled. "It's been four days since you had a proper drink."

"Four days?" He tried to sit up, blinked, and laid back down. "The room's spinning."

"You'd best take things easy for a while. The scrape on your head went pretty deep." She pulled the chair closer and sat near his shoulder. "Here. Try some." She lifted the spoon to his lips.

"My horses."

"They're out back, safe and well."

He opened his mouth for the spoon.

"Who is after you?" she asked when he finished chewing.

"I can't remember. Somebody was trying to kill me." His breathing quickened. "He was chasing me full tilt, blasting at me with a rifle." Beads of sweat formed on his brow. "I've got to get away."

Lisa reached for a damp cloth on the edge of a basin on the hearth to wipe his face. "You've been here four days and no one has come. Surely they would have found you by now if they could."

He relaxed a little, but his expression remained taut with anxiety. His hands clenched the sides of the cot.

She fed him the rest of the stew in silence, not wanting to push him for more answers, afraid her questions would upset him again.

As she rose to leave, he said, "Say, what's your name?"

"Lisa. Lisa Feiklin." She touched her limp, knotted hair, suddenly aware of how frightful she looked.

"I'm John Bowers." He pulled the quilt higher and rolled onto his side as his blue eyes drifted closed.

Lisa shut the door behind her and paced down the path toward the restaurant, a troubled frown tightening her features. If John knew his name, he did not have amnesia. So why didn't he know who wanted him dead? Was he lying?

Chapter 3

John sat on the edge of the cot when Lisa returned that evening with beef and beans for his supper. His lips formed a soft smile when she eased into the chair across from him and held out the plate.

"Thank you kindly." He centered his full attention on the food while Lisa focused on him. He had broad shoulders and moved with the grace of a strong man. A sandy brown lock fell over his forehead almost to his eyebrows.

When he handed her the empty plate, he asked, "Who all lives here?"

"Bess Johnson and I. We work at the Silverville Restaurant just over there." She pointed toward the door and beyond.

"So that's where you're getting the food?" he eyed the plate and looked into her face. "Must be costing you. I don't want to be a burden to you ladies." In a lithe motion he pulled a wide belt loose from his waist and turned it over.

Digging a finger into the folded black leather, he drew out a gold piece and pushed it into her hand. "Bring me back a steak with all the trimmings when you get off tonight. Get one for you and your friend, too." He lay down, and his eyes drifted closed. "Oh, and get some hay for the horses. Please don't mention to anyone that I'm here. I'm a goner if that scoundrel gets wind that I'm here."

Tucking the coin deep into her coat pocket, Lisa closed the door softly behind her and trotted toward the kitchen. John wore old boots and scuffed jeans, so why did he have a loaded money belt around his middle?

Lisa moved in a daze the rest of the afternoon. When she confused three orders in a row, Bess said, "Whatsa matter with you? You sick or something?"

"No. It's John," she replied, her hands moving through hot dishwater with practiced rhythm. "He gave me a gold eagle and ordered three steak dinners, one for each of us."

Bess's eyes widened as she smiled. "Well, I'd have never guessed it. Looks like we had a stroke of luck, him riding in like that."

"His horses were starving. Where did he get so much money?"

Bess lifted the lid off a pot of beans that had started bubbling over on the stove. "Maybe he's a miner."

"He's a cowboy. You know that."

"His boots were coated with dirt, as was the rest of him. That don't sound like a cowboy, no matter what kind of clothes he had on." Bess forked thick steaks onto

263

two plates and added a scoop of beans to each. "But you know the saying about looking a gift horse in the mouth. Let's just be glad he can help us." She laid wide slabs of corn bread beside the meat and turned toward Lisa. "Here's your order. Smile pretty and maybe they'll leave you a dime."

Lisa's lips tightened. "Those cheapskates never leave me anything. It's Ben Hardy and his brother, Al, from Sandusky Mine. They're filthy rich, too." She lifted the plates and headed toward the dining room.

"Howdy, Lisa, honey," Ben Hardy said. With his bristly hair and husky build and long, puffy face, he resembled a brown bear, right down to his slow expression.

His brother, Al, was slim and mean-looking with a missing front tooth and a blue-black shadow on his jaw. He kept his eyes on the food, never once looking at the pretty girl carrying it.

"How about walking out with me after you get off?" Ben said, giving her a wolfish grin. "I know a quiet spot down by the river where we could look at the stars."

"Sorry. I'm busy," Lisa said without a moment's hesitation. Ben asked her the same question every Wednesday and Friday. He never thought of a new place to go and never grew discouraged by her answer.

She offered a pasted smile as she served the meal, then hurried back to her dishpan, anxious to leave work early tonight. Maybe, if his head was clear and his stomach full, John would loosen up and tell her more about himself.

John pushed his empty plate away from him on the rugged table. "It's strange— how I can remember bits of my past but not everything. I never heard of someone losing half his memory before."

"Where do you live?" Lisa asked from her seat on the hearth.

He pushed the lock of hair from his forehead and stared into the blazing fireplace. The flames made dancing shadows on the planes of his face. He did not answer for several minutes. "I'm not sure. All I know is that it's in a grassy canyon with sheer rock cliffs on three sides. She's a beautiful little spot in the spring, with a stream rushing by and trees sprouting leaves." His blue eyes turned toward her. "What about you? Where are you from?"

"Juniper Junction, Colorado," she said softly.

From the other side of the hearth, Bess added, "It's a hole-in-the-wall town somewhere north of Denver." She stood and stacked her plate on top of Lisa's empty one. "Thanks for the fine supper, John. I'm going to turn in." She shoved aside the curtain and let it fall behind her.

"You miss your home, don't you?" John asked, moving to his cot and lying down.

"I'd give my eyeteeth to get back there."

"Why did you leave?"

She turned away. "Well, that's a long story." She hastened to change the subject away from herself. "Don't you remember anything about who did this to you?"

His face tensed. "Whenever I think on it, my insides turn to jelly." He pulled in two deep breaths. "I haven't always been such a coward, Lisa. I've faced down gun-toting four-flushers since I was knee-high to a pony. But for some reason. . ." He paused then suddenly burst out, anguished, "Maybe I've lost my nerve."

"That kind of a wound would take the fire out of anyone for a while," Lisa murmured, wishing she could say something more to comfort him. She knew the same anguish in her own heart, only her pain came from a different source.

"I'd have died without the help of you and Bess," he said.

"We only did what was right." She stood and gathered the dirty dishes. A part of her felt sorry for John, wounded and scared like he was. Yet another part of her wondered if she could trust him. Would she ever trust a man again?

When she had dried the last plate, Lisa turned to look at John. He slept with one hand hanging down to the cold floor. Lisa picked it up and tucked it under the quilt, noticing a deep scar around the base of his callused thumb. The flesh wound looked rough, like a rope burn. Lying down near the fire with her coat pulled over her, she slept.

"Lisa? Are you awake?"

Her eyes flashed open at John's voice. "What's wrong? Are you sick?"

"Why are you sleeping on the floor?"

Her face flushed. "We only have two beds."

He sat up and swung stockinged feet off the cot. "I'm not having you sleep on the floor because of me."

"You're sick. You need a bed."

"I'm not sick anymore." He eased down to the floor. "Get in the bed."

She sat up, blinking at him, her brain working at half speed. "You'll catch cold."

His face stayed calm, but his intense look told her that he meant what he said. His voice stayed low. "Get in the bed, Lisa."

She pulled off her coat and handed it to him. Without a word, she lay on the straw mattress and pulled up the quilt. The cot felt wonderfully warm from his body heat. Her eyes drifted closed.

When Lisa awoke, the cabin was silent and bright sunlight gleamed against the oiled paper. She sat up, whipping off the quilt. She was late.

Running a comb through her hair, she twisted and pinned the limp tresses up into a bun. Where was John? Raising the curtain, she saw him on Bess's cot, sleeping soundly. She watched his rhythmic breathing a moment longer, then rushed out the door and up the narrow path, bushes tugging at her skirt as she brushed past them. Bess would be at the end of her tether if she had to serve tables.

She burst into the restaurant kitchen as her housemate laid biscuits on six plates loaded with eggs, bacon, and fried potatoes. Bess jerked around. "There you are! I was beginning to wonder if I'd have to send Mr. Brockwyn after you."

Lisa grimaced and reached for three breakfast orders, balancing one of them on a bent elbow. "Sorry, Bess. I don't know why I slept so late." She hustled into the dining room and faced her workday at a breakneck speed. Yet no matter how hard she worked, she could not seem to make up for the first hour she'd lost.

That evening after work, Lisa carried two covered plates out of the restaurant. Bess carried a third. When the weary women reached their clearing, they paused a few feet from the house, shocked to see glass panes winking at them instead of oiled paper. They glanced at one another, then hurried to the cabin.

When they burst through the door, John sat near the fire. Lisa's cot was no longer in the living room. He looked up, smiling widely at their surprised faces. "What's wrong? The restaurant on fire or something?"

"The windows," Lisa said.

"I got the boy from the livery stable to buy them for me after he delivered the hay. My way of saying thanks." He rubbed open palms on his knees. "When my head quits hurting, I'll tighten this place up to keep out the drafts."

"We didn't intend to make you work for your keep. You just need to get to feeling better," Bess told him. She took a plate from Lisa and handed it to John.

"I have to do something to fill my days. I may as well make myself useful." He reached for the fork Bess handed him. "This beef stew smells great!" He hesitated. "I've been too sick to think of this before, but would you ladies mind if I thanked the Lord for the food? Sayin' a grace has always been a custom at my house."

"Help yourself," Bess said. "Praying never hurt anybody."

From her place on the hearth next to John, Lisa bowed her head while he spoke in low tones.

"Father, thank You for protecting me against my enemies, just as You did for Your servant David. Thank You for the hospitality of these two ladies. Bless them for helping me, Lord. Thank You for the food we are about to eat. Use it to give us strength to serve You. Amen."

When he finished, Lisa kept her head down and speared a fat potato wedge. His prayer had sounded so humble, so earnest. Yet doubt continued to tug at the back corner of her mind. Was he pretending so that they would lower their guard?

"I went outside to see Molasses and Ginger this afternoon," John said between bites.

"Molasses and Ginger?" Bess repeated, laughing. "Sounds like a gingerbread recipe."

John smiled. "That's the idea. Those horses were born within a week of each other. It was spring, and I'd just bought a cask of molasses and a sack of ginger. When one foal was black and one brown, I got the idea to name them after the fixings for my favorite cake."

"Is Ginger spicy?" Lisa asked, her sober mood forgotten.

"Actually, Molasses is the spirited one. I usually ride him and let Ginger carry the pack." A startled look came over his face. "Speaking of my pack, where is it?"

"Under that gunnysack," Lisa said, pointing to a back corner of the cabin. "Bess took it off the horse and put it there until you woke up."

Setting down his empty plate, John stood up. He blinked hard and touched his bandage. "I guess I moved too fast that time."

Lisa rushed to take his arm. "You'd best get back to bed."

"No." He gently brushed her away. "I'm all right now. I want to look in my pack."

Pacing forward, his expression showing his concentration, he knelt down and unfastened a buckle. Lisa sat and picked up her fork, still watching him. He reached inside the worn leather pouch, pulling out a handful of something before he stood. "I want you to have these." His open palm held a dozen dirt-crusted rocks.

Bess glanced at them, looked at Lisa, and turned to John, her face blank from shock. "Gold?" she gasped.

"Turn them in at the assayer's office and get yourself some decent furniture and some blankets." His hand began to waver as he held it out. "You saved my life. This is the least I can do."

Lisa's cheeks felt warm. "You don't need to pay us for helping you."

"You know we can use the money, Lisa." Reaching out, Bess took the nuggets from him and stood to drop them into the pocket of her faded green skirt.

John returned to his seat on the hearth and picked up his coffee cup. "Pretty soon I'll be able to split wood." He paused. "That is, if you don't mind my staying on for a few more days."

Bess smiled. "Stay as long as you like."

Lisa stabbed a morsel of meat and slowly raised it to her mouth. The more she learned about John, the more of a mystery he became.

⌒

Two more weeks passed, and Lisa's father still had not come. Lisa awoke each morning thinking, *Surely, this is the day he will come for me.* But each night she was disappointed. On Monday of the third week, she started to worry. Seven days later, she wondered whether he had met with an accident or had changed his mind and decided not to come after all.

She nibbled at her food. Her face became gaunt and drawn. Finally, Bess gave her four bits to send a telegram asking if he had left Juniper Junction yet. Three days later the answer came: He had taken the northbound stage the day after Mother wrote her letter to Lisa announcing that he would come after the chinook.

Lisa wept into her pillow. If not for her rebellion, her father would be safe at home instead of lying in the wilds with a broken leg or worse. Someone had to do something to find him. But who? She'd never felt so alone in her life.

As his strength returned, John took over Lisa's job at the woodpile, and he built a new cot. His hair grew long—over his ears and onto his collar—until one night Lisa offered to cut it for him. Every few seconds she would stand back to eye her work.

"I think I've cut it higher over your right ear than your left," she said with a giggle as she peered from one side to the other. "Let me trim the left side just a bit more." She snipped the scissors.

"Oh, no. Now that one's higher."

"Hold on," John said, laughing and raising one hand when she came at him again. "Let's just leave them uneven, okay? If you keep going, I'm liable to end up with a mohawk."

Her cheeks turned pink. "I'm awful sorry, John. Before we started I told you I'm no hand at this."

He gently plucked the scissors from her hand. "I'm not worried about it in the least. As long as my hair's not swishing around my ears, then it's fine. I just can't abide feeling like I have a feather duster on my head." He grinned. "I'm much obliged for your help."

She reached for the broom, trying to ignore the tongue-tied, all-thumbs feeling she got when he looked at her with that laughing light in his eyes.

The next day Bess purchased two ladder-back chairs and three eiderdown quilts at the mercantile. She filled her few shelves with canned goods and salted meat.

The cabin became snug under John's painstaking labor. Yet, even while enjoying these creature comforts, Lisa's misery continued to grow. What had happened to her father? Why had he not come for her?

Two weeks later Lisa carried a dish of stew to the cabin for John's lunch and found him pacing in front of the fireplace. He lurched around, aiming a shiny Colt revolver at her head as she stepped through the door.

She screamed and dropped the bowl.

"Shut the door—quick!"

Her shaking hands fumbled with the latch. When it slid into place, she leaned her back against the door, watching him with wide eyes.

"Sorry, Lisa," he said, dropping the gun into its shiny leather holster. "I just got spooked in town, and now I'm kind of touchy." He swallowed and touched the gun at his side. His hand shook like a leaf in a strong breeze.

"What happened?"

"I went to the assayer's office to change in my nuggets for cash. When I came out, I saw a fella across the street. He was wearing a black jacket and black flat-crowned hat with a yellow band around it."

"Who was he?"

"I don't know. I'm not sure I've ever seen him before." His brows drew together. His breath came fast and shallow through his open mouth.

"Why are you so scared if you can't remember ever seeing him?"

He looked at her, panic in his eyes. "Sometimes I think I'm going insane." He reached his pack in three strides. "I've got to get out of Silverville. If someone's after me, next time I may not be lucky enough to escape with my life." He lifted the leather bag to the table and began stuffing it with the food on Bess's shelves. "I'll leave Bess some money to replace this. I am no thief, Lisa, but I have to go. Now."

As Lisa's shock wore off, her mind began to function at quick speed. "Why don't you take me to Juniper Junction? You can get a job on one of the ranches around there and lay low. No one around here will know where you are."

He paused to look at her. "The trip is a hard one for a man on horseback, much less a woman. That must be three hundred miles."

"I can make it."

"Have you ever ridden all day on a horse?"

"Once, while picnicking in the mountains." Her chin came up. "I can manage, John. I must get home to my mother. My father is out there somewhere—maybe dead—because of me."

"What do you mean?"

She blurted out the story of her elopement and the disaster that followed. Her voice grew shrill and intense. "Please take me with you. We saved your life. How can you turn away and leave me here when I'm so desperate to go?"

Jaw clenched, he drew in three long breaths as he looked into her pleading eyes. Finally, his shoulders relaxed. "Get your gear together," he said tersely.

"What about Bess?"

"Leave her a note, letting her know that we're leaving. But don't mention where we're heading."

Lisa scrambled to her room and tugged her suitcase from beneath the cot.

Dumping its contents onto the quilt, she pulled out a single change of clothes and a comb. The rest she left for Bess. Rolling her few belongings into her corn-cob quilt, she ran out the back door in time to see John tightening the cinch on his saddle.

"I've only got one saddle," he said. "We need another saddle and a third horse if we're going to make any kind of time."

"I'll ask Joe at the livery stable," Lisa said, dropping her blanket roll.

John said, "Stay here. I'll ask him."

"What if somebody sees you?"

"I'll go the back way." He ducked out from under the lean-to's low roof and jogged out of sight.

Lisa patted Ginger and counted her own breaths, willing John to reappear.

Twenty minutes later he came around the corner leading a saddled bay mare. "Mount up while I tie on your blanket roll. No time to talk now."

Keeping the horses to a slow trot, they headed straight into the trees behind the cabin and circled wide around the town. Shivering with excitement, Lisa sucked in the sweet scent of pine mingled with the tingling aroma of freedom and home. She wanted to laugh, wanted to cry from sheer joy. When she reached Juniper Junction, she would never leave again.

Chapter 4

Three days later Lisa again felt like crying. But not from joy. She was raw from the saddle and weary beyond endurance. Aching for a sip of fresh, cool water, she gazed overhead at the stars and wondered how she had gotten herself into another unbearable situation. Juniper Junction seemed ten thousand miles away.

On the other side of their campfire, John snored softly. Lisa glared at him, irritated. The rocky terrain and incredible thirst didn't bother him. He listened to her complaints without responding—and without slackening their pace.

The night before, they had camped in the center of a thick aspen grove, safe from the eyes of anyone who might pass by. Utterly exhausted, Lisa fell asleep the moment she lay down. Her eyes flew open hours later, wide awake, her heart pounding. Over the constant chatter of crickets and night frogs, a moan, then a cry, came from the darkness. A man's deep voice turned shrill.

Had John's enemy found them? If she made a noise, she would be found out, too.

Straining her eyes, she tried to see through a darkness so thick she could almost feel it.

A tortured cry stopped her breath. "Mama, run! Don't let him get you!"

John was having a nightmare.

Lisa unwound the blankets from around her and, hands skimming the ground, crawled toward him, murmuring, "John, wake up." She found the edge of his blanket and followed it upward toward the sound of his voice. "John, wake up."

He gasped and lurched away from her hands. "Who's there?"

"You're okay. You were having a bad dream."

He lay back, his breathing quick. "Lisa? Are you all right?"

"Besides being scared half to death, I'm fine."

"Sorry."

"What were you dreaming?"

"Renegade Indians were after my mother. They were twelve feet tall with bear claws for hands."

"Did you have Indian trouble on your ranch?"

He grunted. "That's strange. No, we didn't. The Indians had already gone when we came."

271

Lisa sat on the corner of his blanket and wrapped her arms around her knees. "Tell me about your family, please."

He hesitated, then spoke slowly. "My father was a sharecropper in Georgia when I was born. He and Mama worked from sunup to sundown trying to scratch a living from the soil. When the cotton crop came in, they had to give half of their harvest to the landholder. Finally, Pa saved enough money to travel to St. Louis and join a wagon train. When he saw the green Wyoming hills, he decided to stay there instead of going on to Oregon."

"Where are your parents now?"

"Dead. They both died of cholera three years ago, shortly before I turned twenty-five. I've tended the ranch alone ever since." He shifted onto his side. "Say, that's more than I ever remembered before. I wish I knew where my ranch was. I'd light a shuck and go searching for it this moment."

"After you take me home, you mean." She shivered. "I'd best get back under my blanket. I hope I can find it again."

"Straight ahead about three paces."

Bent low, she kept reaching out until her hands touched the corncob quilt. "Found it." She arranged her skirts and pulled the cover around her. "Didn't you have a brother or a sister?"

"Nope. Only me."

Lisa's thoughts turned to her younger sister, Jessica. "You've not missed much by being an only child. My sister and I, well, we never did get along. All our lives, I was the one constantly getting into trouble, and she loved to brag about how she never did."

He chuckled softly. "I can believe that."

"What?" She sounded defensive.

"That you always got into trouble. Look where I found you."

"Thanks for the compliment."

"You're welcome. Now get some sleep." After a rustle of his blankets, he lay still.

Lisa pulled in her bottom lip, wanting to defend herself, but unable. Suddenly, she remembered that John was in trouble this minute. Was it of his own making?

Pulling the bumpy quilt over her head, she snuggled down and let sleep black out her thoughts.

On their fifth day out from Silverville, Lisa stayed in the saddle by sheer force of will. She hurt in places she had never thought about before. Her skin had fried in the sun and wind. She touched her peeling nose and wished again for a wide-brimmed hat. Would her face ever be the same?

After their short conversation in the darkness, John had returned to his usual silent self. Several times Lisa tried unsuccessfully to draw him into conversation.

When his headache returned, he tried to ease the pain by tying a damp bandanna around his forehead.

"Let's stop for few days," Lisa begged at noon when they paused just long enough to chew some hardtack for lunch. "You're in pain and so am I. The horses need a break, too."

He handed her his canteen. "If we can find a place with grass and water close by, we'll hole up and sit tight tomorrow."

Three hours later they found the perfect spot—a meadow surrounded by firs. A swollen stream cut across one corner. Unsaddling the horses, John let them roll in the tall grass, then picketed them while Lisa gathered branches for a fire. In order to disperse their smoke and screen their fire, they set up camp among the trees.

"I'm going to make biscuits with the last of the flour," she told him when he returned.

"Fine. We'll stop in Laramie for supplies in a couple of days." He took out his knife to shave off some wood slivers, added bark fibers, and then lit it with a flint. In minutes they had a crackling flame.

Lisa formed biscuits between her hands and dropped them into a tiny iron skillet, watching John out of the corner of her eye. Of all the men she had known in her life, she had never met anyone like John Bowers. Not that her observations mattered. When they reached Juniper Junction, he would get a job, and she might never see him again.

Setting a tin plate over the skillet, she laid it on the fire and scooped coals on top of it using a long, wide stick. "When those are done, I'll fry some bacon."

He stretched out his legs and leaned on one elbow. "Too bad we can't milk a horse. I'm hankering for some pan gravy on those biscuits."

She grinned. "I believe there's a tin of peaches in the pack. Maybe that will do instead. I'll get it."

Sitting on opposite ends of a short log, they ate near the fire. The meal fell far short of Bess's cooking, but it eased the knot in Lisa's stomach and made her drowsy. Before the last rays of sun disappeared, she had rolled herself up in her blankets and nodded off into a deep sleep.

When she opened her eyes the next morning, John was gone. The horses lazily cropped grass while a meadowlark chirped overhead. When Lisa moved, the bird flew up and away.

She stretched, enjoying the quiet, grateful that she did not have to move.

The next moment John stepped through the trees. "Here's breakfast." He held up two limp prairie chickens.

"I didn't hear a shot."

"I don't want to use my gun if I can help it. You never know who may be around to hear. I killed these by throwing a stick. It's not hard if you know how." He glanced toward the fire. "Before I left this morning, I put on a pot of water to boil. Now I can scald and pluck these birds." Turning toward the fire, he plunged each one into boiling water and then laid it on the ground to rake off feathers. The smell made Lisa wonder if she was hungry after all.

She covered a yawn, then said, "You can fry them in the bacon grease from last night."

"Me?" He glanced at her, his left eyebrow raised as he pulled the last pinfeathers from the second hen.

"That's right, you." She slid deeper under the covers. "I'm on vacation today." He watched her without blinking.

Lisa tried to ignore him.

Finally, she flung back the blanket. "Oh, all right! I'll cook them." She groaned as she rose to her feet, stifling the urge to massage the places that hurt the most.

"Say, are you okay?"

"I'm fine." She grabbed the chickens out of his hand, picked up his knife, and headed toward the nearby stream to finish cleaning the birds. Fresh, rippling water skipped from rock to rock and left a wake of white foam. Lisa paused to bask in the beauty around her. She would have a bath and fresh clothes today, even if she had to blindfold John and tie him into his bedroll.

The smell of bubbling coffee greeted her as she made her way back to camp. When she reached the fire, John handed her a steaming cup.

She took it from him, then set the brew aside to cool. No sense adding a scorched tongue to her woes.

While the chicken fried, she reached her hands toward the sky and bent over backwards. At last her muscles were starting to loosen up a little, and the stretching felt so good. She suddenly wanted to move and have some fun.

John, his hat over his eyes, lay sprawled on the ground with his shoulders against the log.

On impulse Lisa grabbed the hat and slapped it across his face. He yelped and reached to recover it, missing by a fraction. Laughing, she hiked her skirts and dashed into the meadow.

He clambered to his feet. "Are you crazy?"

"You're an old sobersides, John Bowers. You need to lighten up a little."

He followed her to the edge of the meadow, wearing an expression that was half amusement and half irritation.

"Well, what are you waiting for?" she taunted, twirling his hat on one finger. "Come and get this old thing if you want it."

He stooped to pluck a grass stem and stuck one end between his teeth. "Lisa, you're acting like a twelve-year-old."

Backing up, her left foot sank into a gopher hole, and she felt herself losing her balance. Her arms flew out, and she sat down hard. . .right where it hurt.

Her face pinched into a grimace. "Ohhhh."

John dashed to her. "Are you all right? Did you hurt your ankle?"

Lifting her hand for a pull up, she let out a soft gasp as she got to her feet. "Not my ankle, no." She took a painful step. "That's what I get for trying to act like a kid when I'm pushing a hundred."

He chuckled and retrieved his hat from her hand.

Trying to pretend as though nothing had happened, she resumed her cooking, keeping her face turned away so he would not see her burning cheeks.

Unruffled as always, John sauntered back to his spot and sat down. He ate his fried chicken and rewarmed biscuits without speaking, then lay down on his bedroll to nap.

"John?"

"Ummm?"

"Stay put until I get back, okay? I'm going to wash up."

He reached for his Stetson to bury his face. "No problem. Just let me know when you get back."

Digging into her pack, Lisa found fresh clothes and headed upstream. The water, a few degrees cooler than lukewarm, felt wonderful. An hour later, she slid between her blankets and gladly forgot the world.

Chapter 5

The next two days passed in agonizing monotony. After her initial soreness, Lisa's aches began to disappear. However, she still felt unspeakably tired. She daydreamed of her four-poster bed at home, laden with down-filled tick and fluffy pillows.

When they rode into Laramie, they stayed only long enough to replenish their food supply. As they headed down the narrow main street, Lisa gazed longingly at three false-fronted hotels.

"Can't we stay just one night?" she asked, turning to the man beside her.

"Lisa, I can't take the chance." Beneath his hat brim, he scanned the boardwalks on either side. "If only I knew what he looked like. The way things are, any gun-totin' cowboy could be the fella who's after me."

Easing her gritty collar away from her neck, Lisa sighed and squirmed uncomfortably in her saddle.

That night she went to sleep without eating. Her head was simply too heavy to hold upright a moment longer.

Before dawn the next morning, she felt a rough glove on her shoulder. "Lisa. Wake up. It's time to hit the trail."

"Leave me alone!" She rolled away from him.

"We have to go."

"I want to stay here another day." Her eyes drifted closed. The next moment she felt the blanket jerk away. Tepid water splashed her face. She screamed and sat up, hands raised to protect herself.

"How dare you!" She glared at him, fists clenched, wishing he were close enough to reach.

"We've got to go," he said mildly. "Now."

She stood to be at eye level with him. "I told you I'm not going. I need another day to rest." Staring him down, she took a step forward. "I'm not getting on that horse today; you hear me?"

Lips pursed, his blue eyes watched her. "I didn't want to scare you, but you leave me no choice. We are being followed. I've seen dust behind us since we left Laramie."

"Well, whoever it is surely can't be chasing you," she declared. "If he knew where you were, why didn't he come for you at the cabin?"

"Who says he followed us from Silverville? He may have spotted us in Laramie."

"Not likely."

He took a step backward, that haunted, wide-eyed look taking control of his face. "We've got to move. I can't risk finding out that it's him."

The fire of anger left Lisa's eyes as quickly as the blaze had erupted. She realized afresh the severity of John's predicament and his hidden terrors. Protective instincts overcame her desire for rest. Lowering her face, she turned away. "Give me a few minutes, and I'll be ready." She touched her hair. No time to comb the snarled mass again today. Did it really matter?

John poured her a cup of hot coffee and forked bacon onto the one tin plate they shared. Lisa ate hungrily, picturing in her mind scrambled eggs, fat sausages, and pancakes smothered with sorghum.

"Somewhere ahead is the Colorado state line," John said as he tied Lisa's bedroll behind Ginger's saddle.

Lisa grimaced. "That's been true since we left Silverville." Since the hat episode, she had baited John every chance she got.

"I meant," he said quietly, "we should reach the border today."

Who is the real person hiding beneath that shell? Each passing day this question grew more important to Lisa. She had made a personal game of learning the answer. Yet it was a difficult game to master.

He moved to the campfire to gather up their few dishes while Lisa retired to the bushes to rub witch hazel on her healing wounds. Thank goodness she had remembered to bring the smelly stuff along.

"What was your mother's name?" Lisa called out an hour later as they cantered shoulder to shoulder across the plain.

"Martha."

"What was she like?"

He looked at her, irritated. "Why all the questions?"

"I'm trying to help you remember."

He pulled his horse away from her. "Don't trouble yourself."

She called across the widening gap between them. "If you remember who's chasing you, you won't have to run from every shadow!"

He urged his horse ahead of her without answering. They rode the next two hours in a silence that grated on Lisa's raw nerves. Riding with John Bowers was like keeping company with a stuffed owl.

At noon they stopped under a wide rock overhang behind a copse of trees. Unsaddling the horses, John took his Winchester and set off in search of meat.

Lisa dug a frying pan and a packet of bacon from the saddlebag. Gathering twigs and small branches, she shaved off some wood slivers and tried to start a fire with the flint, as she'd often seen John do. She worked over it for the next hour. Gnats buzzed around her eyes. Mosquitoes swarmed every square inch of exposed flesh.

Finally, she'd had enough. Pent-up emotion from the past weeks and months swirled together until she felt she would smother under its weight. In a burst of red-hot fury, she slammed the flint to the ground, grabbed her head with both hands, and screamed out her frustration. Pausing long enough to draw in another full breath, she screeched again. Her shrieks ricocheted off the mountains.

Covering her face with her hands, she plopped down on a wide rock. Why had she done something so insane?

A few minutes later, John bounded into the clearing, his lips white. "What happened? Are you hurt?"

"No." Her face flamed. She tucked her chin onto her chest. "I lost my temper. I can't start the fire."

He stared at her, his eyes blue chips of light. "What are you doing trying to start a fire out here in the open with someone on our tail?" Toe-to-toe with her, he glared into Lisa's eyes. "I've put up with your bellyaching from morning to night. I've coddled you and lost time for you. Now this! You may as well run up a flag and ask that guy following us to come on over." He lifted his open palm, put it down, and raised it again.

Whirling, he stomped off into the brush. "I'll start the fire when I get back."

Lisa clapped her hand over her mouth. A giggle, then a chuckle came out. She leaned over, caught in a wave of helpless laughter. Stonefaced John finally got ruffled. He actually wanted to spank her. As if he could.

Wiping tears and chuckling, she scouted around for some bone-dry branches, then moved behind high, leafy brush that leaned over to touch the rock face about five feet up. She picked up the flint and started the fire on the third try. Adding wood carefully, keeping the flame low, she ran out of the tiny shelter to fetch the frying pan.

Bacon sizzled and popped when John returned with two skinned rabbits in his hand. Lisa hid a smile as he sat beside her.

"Got a blaze going after all, I see," he said, glancing at the bush above them. "Not a bad setup."

"I'll get the hang of things after a while." She held the fork and stared at the frying pan. "I'm sorry I scared you. I didn't mean to."

"I reckon I'm over the fright by now." He deftly carved a rabbit into quarters and threw the fresh meat into the pan. "Just don't pitch such a fit again."

A giggle escaped, and he sent her a calculating look. "What's so funny?"

She tried to straighten her face. "I've never seen you so riled over anything before."

He grinned. "I reckon I'm just naturally easygoing. Always have been." He breathed in the aroma of frying meat. "That sure does smell good."

"Wish we had some potatoes to go with it."

"Lisa, you'd get along a lot better in life if you'd thank the good Lord for what He's given you without thinking about what He hasn't done yet." His hand stretched toward the fire, his scar a wide white streak on his palm. "We've got shelter, a beautiful sunny day, good food, and quiet. What more could we ask for?"

His soft words gentled her like a kind touch settles a nervous mare. She sat next to him while they ate, enveloped in a calmness she had never before experienced. When he stood, she reached out her hand for him to give her a pull up, then she stood before him.

"You're an unusual man, John Bowers," she murmured. "I've never met anyone like you before."

He grinned, but his eyes remained serious. "I could say the same about you."

She wanted to say more, but she forgot how. Her world centered on the deep pools in his eyes, his strong jaw, his quiet strength.

She did not want to travel any farther. But this time, her reluctance wasn't due to sore muscles and weary limbs. She wanted to stay here and bask in his comforting presence forever.

He took a step back and cleared his throat. Looking at the blue dome of sky overhead, he said, "We can make ten more miles before dark. We'd best mount up and ride."

Since they first left Silverville, they had ridden in tight formation, but now they seemed even closer somehow.

Two days later Lisa felt a sense of loss when Juniper Junction appeared on the horizon.

⌒

"Lisa, baby!" Sally Feiklin cried when she saw her daughter in the doorway of their home. She threw her pudgy arms around Lisa.

Blinking back tears, Lisa hugged her mother, so glad to be home.

"Where's your father?" Sally asked, peering past John, who stood just outside the door, to the tiny front yard where the white gate stood closed.

Lisa said, "Daddy never came." Fear formed a lump in her throat as she watched her mother's round face turn into a picture of worry.

"He took the stage a month ago to come for you," she gasped, panic in her eyes. "He said the stage would be easier on you, so he left his horse here."

Lisa heard John's boots on the plank floor. She felt his presence behind her as she replied, "We didn't hear about any accidents. I was hoping that he had returned home for some reason. What could have happened?" She looked over her shoulder at John. "Where is he?"

"He must be somewhere between here and there," he said, his dusty hat in his hands. "We didn't see him because we left the trail."

Lisa said, "Mama, this is John Bowers. He brought me home."

Sally glanced at John and nodded absently, her eyes reaching for the open door as though her husband would step through the gate at any moment. A dimpled hand pressed her cheek, and she cried, "What happened to Rod? He was on the stage."

Smaller and slimmer than her older sister, Jessica Feiklin stepped into the front room. Her dark hair had auburn highlights that matched the smattering of freckles across her nose. "What is the matter, Mama?" she asked anxiously, darting a short glance at Lisa.

"Daddy's lost," Sally sobbed, pulling a cotton handkerchief from her sleeve. "Lisa hasn't seen him."

John touched Lisa's arm as tears filled her eyes. She turned to face him. "What happened to him, John? He must be hurt, or he would have come to me."

Jessica hurried to her mother. "Come and sit down, Mama." She put an arm around Sally and urged her to the green camelback sofa. Blinking tears, she glared at Lisa. "If it weren't for you, Daddy would still be here."

Lisa froze. She and Jessica had never been close, but this was more than she could bear.

Jessica hugged her mother, and both women sobbed.

Tears coursed down Lisa's face. She ran to her mother and knelt on the hooked rug to lay her head on the apron across her mother's wide waist. Sally reached down to cradle her wayward daughter.

The room filled with sobs and sniffles. A warm breeze lifted white lace curtains to brush twin Windsor chairs and the small table nestled between them. Sunlight reflected in two glass lamps on the mantel.

Sometime later Lisa remembered John standing awkwardly near the door. Wiping her face, she slowly stood and moved toward him. "It is my fault," she sniffed.

"I'm going after him."

She peered at him through bleary eyes. "John, you're not well. You can't turn around and go back."

"I'm in no shape to fight about it now. I've got to find a place to sleep before I fall over."

She rubbed open palms over her burning cheeks. "You can stay here."

He glanced at the distraught women on the sofa. "I don't want to trouble your mother at a time like this. I'll get something; don't worry."

Her eyes lingered over his tousled, dust-colored hair, the dark stubble on his cheeks. She hated to see him go. "Take care of yourself," she murmured.

He touched her chin. "You do the same." He lifted his hat and settled it onto his head as he went out the door.

Lisa followed to close the latch behind him, her heart aching in a new way. What a pity she had given up on the male gender.

"Lisa, you must be starving." Sally's ragged voice broke into her daughter's thoughts.

She turned back into the room. "My stomach feels sick. I'm not sure I can eat anything."

"I've got some bean soup on the stove. Maybe that will make you feel better."

"I'll fetch some hot water first," Lisa said, heading toward the kitchen at the back of the house. "I can't sit down to eat until I've had a bath."

Lifting a pail to the top of the iron stove so she could dip water from the reservoir, Lisa held a pain-filled numbness inside. *Daddy,* she cried in her spirit, *where are you?*

John stalled his horses at the livery stable, then paced down the central street of Juniper Junction like a man walking in a deep sleep. He checked into the town's only hotel, a two-story building with a wide porch, to take a hot bath and sleep until suppertime. With a thick steak and a mountain of potatoes warming his middle, he returned to his creaky bed until breakfast.

Back in the dining room, he shoveled in a man-size stack of hotcakes without looking up. Standing to dig two bits from the pocket of his jeans, he glanced up and caught the eye of a lowbrowed man with curly black hair and a furtive crinkle about his eyes. The stranger instantly turned his attention to four fried eggs on his plate. John paid his bill and stepped into the morning light, his hat brim low over his brow.

Digging into his saddlebags, John took stock of the meager remains from their journey, then strode toward Harper's Emporium. He needed supplies before he hit the trail. Twenty strides later, he pushed open the shop's door and heard a tiny tinkling bell.

Small windows kept the interior of the store dim despite the brilliant sunlight outside. Harper's smelled of freshly ground coffee and new leather. Three barrels containing pickles, crackers, and coffee beans made a triangle at the left end of the counter near the coffee grinder. The back wall held shelves laden with canned goods, ammunition, and ready-made clothing for men and boys. A dozen bolts of dress goods lay stacked on the right end of the counter.

Edging between tables of shoes and woven baskets on his way to the back counter, John spoke to the slim, graying man standing under a sign marked POST

OFFICE. "A pound of beef jerky, a dozen potatoes, and five pounds of flour."

"Sure thing, mister." He picked up a scoop and lifted the lid on the flour barrel. "You passing through?"

"I reckon so. I'd thought about looking for a job, but now I'm not sure that I'll be around long enough to take it."

"The Circle C is looking for a cowhand who's not afraid to do a little farming on the side."

"Where is that?"

"Due west of town. About five miles."

"Add a pound of bacon and a hundred rounds of forty-fives to that, will you?"

Ten minutes later John stepped out of the store with his saddlebags over his shoulder. He turned toward the livery stable, thinking that he would leave the bay here and fetch it when he returned.

Flipping a silver dollar at the livery man, he slapped the saddlebags over Molasses and hit leather. On his way out of town, he stopped at the Feiklins's whitewashed house, pretty as a painting with its white picket fence and tiny yard.

When Jessica answered the door, he lifted his Stetson. "May I see Lisa?"

She paused, sizing him up before answering. She had wide eyes, a serious mouth, and flat-planed cheeks. "Lisa's upstairs. I'll get her."

John stared after Jessica. He could imagine her at six years old, singsonging to Lisa, "I never have to stay after school and write sentences like you do."

Light steps sounded on the oak floor, and his jaw went slack. Before him stood a lovely lady with glossy dark waves held back by two tortoiseshell combs as it flowed down to her waist. She wore a powder-blue morning dress with tatted lace about the throat. She smiled, delighted.

"John, come in. I'm glad you came."

He swallowed. His thumb felt the grosgrain ribbon on his hat. He could not take his eyes off her. "Lisa. . .I hope I'm not disturbing you."

She laughed. "Of course not." She sat on the sofa and patted the seat next to her. "Where did you sleep?"

"I stayed in the hotel last night." He paused, trying to remember what he had come here to say. "I'm riding out to find your father."

"Today?" Worry creased her brow.

"Right away. When I get back, I'll look for a job."

"Mama sent word to the sheriff in Denver that Pa was missing. The law will go after him. You don't need to go."

"I want to."

She put her hand on his sleeve. "Please don't put yourself in jeopardy, John. I couldn't live with myself if something happened to you because of me."

He covered her hand with his. "I'll stop here as soon as I get back." His eyes scanned her face, amazed that this was the same girl he had known for almost two months. Her nose was still shiny red from sunburn, but she was the prettiest thing he had ever seen. And she smiled at him like she meant it.

Gulping, he stood. "Good-bye, Lisa. I'll come back as soon as I can."

At the door she gave him her hand. "Stay safe. Please," she murmured, and stood waving as he rode away.

Turning west on Main, John caught sight of the dark stranger from the restaurant standing on the boardwalk. When John drew near, the man turned to look into the window of the milliner's shop and kept his back toward the road until John had passed him.

Glancing back a few yards later, he saw the dark stranger reach for the knob of the shop and push the door inward. Drawing in a shaky breath, John kicked Molasses into a canter.

A hundred emotions swept through John as he left Juniper Junction behind, most of them painful. He followed the trail heading west of town, intending to turn north when he found a likely spot. No sense making things easy for his pursuer. If such a man did exist. Again he glanced behind him, wondering if his imagination was playing tricks on him.

Suddenly, a gunshot split the quietness of the morning. John jerked as a searing pain cut into his shoulder. Gasping, he bent low over Molasses's neck and urged the mustang to a gallop. They veered off the trail and through a stand of pines, on and on until John lost track of his direction. The front of his shirt felt hot and sticky. His senses began to spin. A moment later, everything faded into darkness.

Chapter 6

When John opened his eyes, a balding man with a broken nose was bending over him, creating a block of shadow from the blinding sun. "Glad to see you're coming around, young man. I had to dig a bullet out of you, and you lost a lot of blood." The timbre of the stranger's voice sounded deep, throaty. His gentle hands bound a strip of white cloth about the injured shoulder.

John squeezed his eyes closed against searing pain. He groaned.

"I'll take him to the ranch," a rough voice said. "It's closer than going back to town. He may not make it that far."

The first man nodded toward the speaker then said to John, "You have family around here?"

Sick with pain, John shook his head. He tried to speak, but his tongue would not cooperate. Turning his head, he realized that he lay in the back of a wagon.

A grizzled old cowhand wearing a stained hat stood nearby with his forearms resting on the wagon's side. "Good thing we were passing at just the right time, Doc. This hombre would have been swapping howdys with St. Pete in another hour or two."

The doctor swung his legs over the buckboard and slid down. The bouncing of the boards below John sent white-hot needles of pain through him. Tree branches overhead swayed into a crazy green blur, and blackness closed in.

⁓

When John awoke he lay on a narrow bed in a quiet room with a quilt pulled up to his chin. His eyes drifted to the long window across from him where puffy cloud shapes drifted across a cobalt sky.

Unfinished wood formed the walls and floor of the room, which was about half the size of Bess's cabin. John's clothes hung from two pegs near the door. Two straight-backed chairs stood close to the bed with a small table nearby. John's eyes drifted closed. Far away, he heard a baby's gentle cry and the barking of a dog.

Sometime later the door eased open, and John awoke to see a slim black woman wearing a brown gingham dress covered by a long, white apron. She had graying cornrows straight back from her brow. She paused inside the door when she noticed him looking at her.

"Well, you decided to wake up, did you?" A soft smile warmed her seamed face. She had a kind light in her eyes and spoke with a thick Virginia accent.

His voice dry as crackling paper, John whispered, "Where am I?"

She stepped closer. "This is the Circle C. Banjo brought you here five days ago." She touched his forehead. "Praise to Jesus. It's cool. You was out of your head with fever, son. We's been a-nursing you day and night."

"We?"

"Me and Miss Megan, the lady of the house. I am Em Calahan. My husband, Chance, and I live on the other side of the meadow."

John watched her, trying to absorb her words. Suddenly he remembered something important. "I've got to go." He tried to sit up. "I've got to find Lisa's father."

Em gently pushed his good shoulder down. "You ain't a-goin' anyplace for a couple of weeks at least. You'll kill yourself if you try."

"But Lisa's father. . ."

She leaned closer, her tone like a mother to a stubborn child. "You'd best stay put. You'll not be any good to anybody passed out along some trail, will you, now?"

He closed his eyes. The ache in his shoulder made him want to grind his teeth.

"I'll fetch you some hot soup." Em bustled out, and John drifted into a pain-filled daze.

It seemed he had scarcely closed his eyes when a spoon nudged his lips. "Here you go. Open up now."

Warm chicken broth reminded his stomach that he had not eaten in days. He peered at Em. "That tastes good. You don't have to feed me. I can feed myself."

"Is you left-handed?"

John flexed his right arm under the bandage and felt a stab. Stifling a groan, he winced instead. He turned toward her and opened his mouth.

As the last drop of soup left the bowl, a slim cowhand with a weather-beaten face appeared in the doorway, the man who had stood beside the wagon. "Jem told me he's awake, Em. Mind if I come in?"

"The door's open," Em replied with a smile. She spoke to John. "This is Banjo. He and Doc Leatherwood found you on the trail with a bullet in you."

"I'm much obliged," John said weakly.

"Just being neighborly." His twinkling blue eyes sobered. "When I saw you laying there, it struck me that God had sent us along to find you." He pulled a chair close to the bed. "Who did this to you? Are you in trouble?"

John let out a tired sigh. "It's a long story. I don't have the strength to tell it all now."

"Let him rest, Banjo," Em scolded. "There'll be plenty of time for jawing later."

"What's your name?" Banjo asked.

"John Bowers."

"I'm Joe Calahan, but most folks call me Banjo because I'm always making music." He chuckled.

"You play the juice harp?"

"No. I sing."

Em laughed. "Croaks is more like it." She waved both hands at him in a shooing motion. "Out, Banjo. The boy needs some rest."

He grinned. "You win, you ol' drill sergeant." Standing, he said, "I'll come by tomorrow, John. Maybe you'll feel more like talkin' then." He strode out, boots loud, spurs jingling.

Em held a glass of clear liquid toward John. "This has laudanum in it to make you sleep."

He drained the glass, then grimaced. "I'm not sure which is worse, that or the pain."

Em picked up the soup bowl. "Sleep, Mr. John. I've got to get myself home now. Megan will be in to check on you after a while."

"You don't live here?"

She chuckled. "This used to be my room before I got married. As I said before, Chance and I live in a cabin down the hill. Steve and Megan Chamberlin own this place."

"I thought I heard a baby cry."

Em beamed. "They have the cutest little girl you ever did see. Her name is Katie, and she is six months old. I've been a-comin' up days to help care for you, but now I've got to see to Chance's supper. He's been out plowing since before first light." She stepped toward the door and spoke over her shoulder. "Megan will be in after a while."

The medicine took effect, and John slept.

⌒

Night had fallen when he next awoke. A coal oil lamp cast a yellow glow over his portion of the room and lit the way for a serene young woman with light brown hair drawn back in a bun. She carried a tray. Beside her, a fair-haired boy about twelve years old brought a pitcher. His eyes danced, alive with curiosity.

"Feel like some supper?" she asked. She had the same southern accent as Em, but more refined.

John tried to smile. "I could eat a steer all by myself."

"That's a good sign." She set down the tray and eased into the chair. "I'm Mrs. Chamberlin. You can call me Megan. And this is my brother, Jeremy. His nickname's Jem. I'd introduce you to my husband, but he's in Denver taking care of some business. Won't be home till next week."

"I'm obliged to you for taking me in like this."

"We're glad to do it." She took the blue enamel pitcher from Jeremy and poured a glass of water. "Can you handle this?"

John reached for it with his left hand, sloshed a few drops, and brought it to his lips. The cool liquid made his parched mouth ache. "Say, this is cold."

Eager, Jeremy said, "It comes from a mountain spring behind the house."

Megan lifted a spoonful of chopped beef mixed with broth. "Jeremy will be your helper while you're recovering. Just call him when you need him. He'll stay nearby."

The boy hooked his thumbs under the straps of his washed-out overalls and grinned, his hair sticking out at odd angles like straw on a scarecrow. He had the unusual combination of blond hair and brown eyes.

"I'm obliged, Jeremy." John took another sip and handed the water glass to Megan. She fed him steak and potato stew until he held up his hand, palm out. "Thanks, ma'am, but I can't hold another bite."

For the next few days, John lay on the narrow bed, sleeping most of the time. In his waking moments, he worried about Lisa and her father, but he had no strength to hurry the healing process.

Jeremy never seemed to tire of sitting beside John, whittling at a fistful of wood and chattering about ranch life.

"We have a dog named Lobo," the boy said one afternoon. "He used to belong to the man who owned this ranch before we came along. He had gone wild, and Megan tamed him. She named him Lobo because he looks like a wolf."

With his strong arm under his head, John gazed at a dark oval knot in the ceiling plank over him. "I used to have a dog named Shep," he said. "He got killed in a buffalo stampede when we were on the Oregon Trail. I was about six years old."

Jeremy's eyes widened. "You came over the Oregon Trail?"

"That's not so special. Thousands of folks did the same thing. We didn't go to Oregon, though. We stopped in Wyoming."

The boy's eyes narrowed. He leaned forward to study John's lean face. "Are you a brave man?"

Startled, John tried to decide how to answer. He did not want to lie to the boy, but could he bear to tell the truth? Waiting for a count of three, he said, "Why do you ask?"

"Em always says that a coward has a thousand lives but a brave man only one. So I was wondering if you have any lives left."

Despite his discomfort, John chuckled.

Jeremy lifted the piece of wood and gouged off a thick chunk. "Do you still live in Wyoming?"

"I guess so."

"You don't know?"

"I had an accident and hurt my head. I can't remember some things."

Jeremy stopped whittling to stare at him. "I heard of a man one time who forgot who he was. He couldn't remember his name or who his wife was or anything."

"I know who I am. I just can't remember some details like where I live." John's eyes felt heavy. "Would you mind going out for a while? I'm tired."

"Yes, sir." The barefoot boy scooted toward the door. He dropped his carving, stooped to pick it up, then let the door close behind him. Top-heavy and sagging on leather hinges, the wooden door always flopped open or closed.

That evening Banjo came to sit with John. His gray hair had a crease where the hat clamped his head. He wore a faded flannel shirt and jeans. A barnyard smell came along with him. "Howdy, John," he said, clumping across the floor. "How's the shoulder?"

"Sore. Doc Leatherwood came out this morning. He says I can't move it for another three days. He's afraid the wound will reopen."

Banjo turned the chair around and straddled it, his arms across the back. "Hey, enjoy the easy life while you've got it. Two nice ladies to fuss over you. Nothing to do but rest. What more could you ask?"

John grinned. "I guess it all depends on how you look at it. Last week I was half dead for want of sleep and wished I could stay in bed for two straight days. Now I'm taking it easy and wishing I could ride." He eased his forearm across his chest. "I never thanked you proper for helping me. You saved my life."

"That wasn't anything I did. The good Lord brought me along at the right time and sent a doctor with me to see to you."

John peered at the old cowhand. "You're a Christian?"

"I reckon I am. What about you?"

"Yes, sir. That's one thing about myself I remember for sure."

"Jem tells me you've lost your memory."

"Only some parts of it. A bullet creased my skull about a month ago. It was past midnight when my horse stopped beside a cabin where two women lived. One of them woke up and found me before I froze to death."

Banjo leaned forward, his face concerned. "Are you in trouble, son?"

John sighed. "I wish I knew. That part is a big black hole in my mind."

"How did you come to Juniper?"

"I brought Lisa Feiklin home."

"Did you now?" Banjo sat up straighter. "She eloped with a hand from the Rocking H last—let's see—last October."

"He dumped her in Silverville, South Dakota," John told him. "She was one of the women living in the cabin."

"And she got you to bring her home?" When John nodded, Banjo said, satisfied, "I'm glad you did. She must have suffered a lot these past months. I wonder that her father didn't go and fetch her back."

"He tried to, but he never made it to Silverville. He's disappeared. That's why I've got to get out of this bed. I promised Lisa that I'd look for him."

Banjo rubbed his prickly jaw. "What was Sheriff Feiklin riding when he left town?"

"He took the stage."

"The stage?" His bushy eyebrows reached for his hairline. "What could have happened to him on the stage?"

"It's a puzzle. And that's not the only one. I don't know who wants me dead bad enough to follow me clear across the territory." John let out a long breath. "You may as well know the rest. I've lost my nerve. My insides turn yellow every time I think about that hombre who shot me." His eyes felt heavy, and he let them close.

Banjo stood and turned the chair back around. "I'll come again tomorrow evening. We'll talk some more then." He trudged out of the room and let the door fall closed, leaving the room in shadows.

John lay in a pool of cold misery, alone and afraid.

Chapter 7

The day after John told Lisa good-bye and rode away, she answered a knock on the door and found a tall stranger wearing an immaculate tan suit with a black string tie. He had on a white ten-gallon hat and the star of a U.S. marshal. When he saw her, he swept off his hat. His mouth widened into a gleaming smile.

"Yes?" she asked, her heart thumping. Did he have news about her father?

"Good morning. I'm Marshal Chandler Brinkman. Are you Mrs. Feiklin?" His mellow voice had a deep quality that made it easy to listen to.

"My mother is lying down. Can I help you?"

"Someone told me that the sheriff lives here. I was wondering if you may have a room I can rent for a week or so as a friendly gesture to a fellow lawman." He took half a step forward. "I'm on an important secret mission and need to stay out of sight as much as possible. I can't stay at the hotel."

Wide-eyed, Lisa stepped back, holding the door open. "Please come in. I'll fetch Mama."

Shoulders back in military style, the marshal eased across the threshold, his eyes moving left then right over the modest furnishings.

"Please sit down," Lisa told him, waving a hand at the sofa. "I'll be back in a moment." She paced sedately toward the side hall. Once out of the marshal's sight, she broke into a run, keeping to her toes so her shoes would stay silent, and burst into her parents' room at the back of the house.

Her mother lay under a wedding-ring quilt on a wide iron bed, her hair in tangles about her shoulders, her puffy eyes closed. She had not eaten anything solid since she had learned that her husband was missing.

"Mama! A marshal's here," Lisa said when she had shut the bedroom door.

Sally gasped and sat up. "A marshal? Has he come about Daddy?"

Lisa plopped down on the edge of the bed, making the springs groan. "No, it's not about Daddy. He said he's on a secret mission and needs a private home to stay in for about a week."

"A secret mission in Juniper?" Sally's mouth formed an oval. "What's the world coming to?"

Impatient, Lisa stood and tugged her mother's sleeve. "He wants to see you about a room."

Sally pulled away. "I can't go out there, child. It'd take half an hour to get myself dressed and fix my hair." She ran a pale hand over her fleshy, mottled face. "Go back out there, and tell him he can have the loft room for two dollars a week. Ask him to give us an hour to get it ready for him."

Already at the door, Lisa said, "I'll get Jess to help me clean it up." She stepped into the hall. Closing her eyes, she drew in a deep, slow breath then exhaled with a long puff, trying to calm herself. Marshal Brinkman had a shining lock of black hair that fell across his forehead and a gleaming smile that took her breath away. The sight of those chiseled features, that broad build, revived old feelings that she thought Brent had killed forever.

Wetting her lips, she waltzed down the hall to the sitting room, mentally practicing her answer to him.

She reached the doorway in time to see Jessica hand their guest a tall glass of tea, then sit on the opposite end of the sofa and smile sweetly at him.

"Thank you kindly, ma'am," he said. "I've been riding since dawn this morning, and I'm bone weary." Lowering the glass after a long drink, he caught sight of Lisa. "Your sister was kind enough to get me a drink, Miss Feiklin."

Darting a glance at the glowing Jessica, Lisa paused, shocked at the change in her normally sullen sister.

"Can your mother see me?" Marshal Brinkman asked.

Lisa tried to pull her thoughts together. "She said you can have the loft room for two dollars a week. We'll need a couple of hours to get it ready for you."

"May I see the room?" He finished the last of his tea and handed the glass to Jessica as he stood. "A wonderful refreshment, Miss Feiklin. Thank you kindly."

Jessica stood. "I'll show him the room, Lisa," she said, staring squarely into Lisa's face.

"Mother asked me to," Lisa said lightly. "Step this way, sir."

Leading him toward the narrow stairs, Lisa said, "My father hasn't been seen for almost a month. My mother is taking his disappearance hard. She rarely comes out of her room these days."

"That's too bad," Brinkman said, close behind her. "Where was he when you lost him?"

"Somewhere in Wyoming, we think. We sent word to the sheriff in Denver about it, but we haven't heard anything yet."

"If I can be of service, please let me know."

At the head of the stairs, she turned toward him. "That's kind of you."

He smiled. "Just doing my job, ma'am." He stepped up to her level. His eyes drew close.

Flustered, Lisa paced to the door at the far side of the short hall. "This is the room. The ceiling and wall are slanted on one side because of the eaves of the house. That's why we call it the loft room." She flung back the door and stepped aside so he could enter first. A faint dusty smell seeped into the hall.

Two dormers formed small openings in the slanted wall. A wide four-poster bed filled most of the room, with a narrow dresser and a single chair the only other furniture. A worn rag rug lay near the bed.

"Mighty nice," he said, turning around to take in every angle. "I'll take it."

"I'll tell Mama that you'll stay, Marshal Brinkman," Lisa said.

He moved toward her, still smiling. "Please call me Chandler."

"I'm Lisa." She felt her cheeks warming. "If you'd like to relax in the sitting room for a while, Jess and I will clear out the dust for you and change the linens."

"I need to tend to my horse first," he said, extending a spotless tan coat sleeve, indicating for her to precede him down the stairs.

Lisa kept her eyes on the stairs below her, attracted to the man who followed close behind her, caught by an impulse to hook him with her teasing eyes then carefully reel him in. She had done it so often, it would be easy. But this time she felt a strange uneasiness that held her in. Something inside her had changed—just what, she wasn't sure.

∾

A few minutes later, Lisa carried a broom and a duster into the loft room with Jessica following, her arms full of linens.

"How old do you suppose the marshal is?" Lisa asked, propping the broom beside the door.

"Thirty at least," Jessica answered shortly. Her brown eyes had a watchful expression.

"He's mighty handsome," Lisa said, flicking the duster over a windowsill.

Jessica sniffed. "I knew you'd think that."

"You weren't exactly blind to the fact while you were serving him tea."

"I'm not man-crazy like you are, Lisa."

Lisa dropped the duster and stepped toward her sister, a hard light in her eyes. "Take that back."

"I won't." Jessica stood with hands on hips, leaning slightly forward, her lips tight. "If you hadn't gone chasing after that dandified cowboy, Daddy would still be here."

Hand raised to slap her sister, Lisa stopped in midmotion. The truth of Jessica's words jolted her. With a sharp cry, she ran out of the loft room, across the hall, and into her own bedroom.

She slammed the door and leaned against it. Her anger turned inward toward herself. Much as she hated to admit it, Jessica was right.

∾

That evening Jessica fried steaks and baked potatoes for supper. She put a fresh tablecloth on the table and pulled good china from the glass-fronted hutch in the dining room. When Lisa offered to help, she abruptly refused to let her.

Lisa shrugged and wandered to the sitting room where Chandler Brinkman sat smoking a pipe and peering through the gauzy curtain facing the street.

He looked up when she came in. "Good evening, Lisa. Would you like to help me?"

Arranging her navy skirt, she perched on the sofa. "If I can, I'll be glad to."

"I'm looking for a man in his midtwenties, about six-two, two hundred pounds. He rides a black horse."

"What's he done?"

"He stole a Wells Fargo shipment of gold nuggets about a month ago in South Dakota."

Her mouth turned dry. "What part of South Dakota?"

"A few miles west of Tombstone."

"Are you sure he's in Juniper?"

"I trailed him and a companion all the way from Wyoming." He looked closer at her pale face. "Do you know someone like that?"

"Not. . .not that I can think of." She touched the lace collar brushing her chin. "If you'll excuse me, I'll help my sister in the kitchen." She made a graceful exit, took a wide circle around Jessica at the stove, and stared out the glass in the back door.

Was John an outlaw? She could not believe that he was.

She glanced at Jessica. If Chandler mentioned his quarry to the younger Feiklin girl, would she tell him about John? Lisa chewed her lip, trying to think. Asking Jessica not to mention John may cause her to do just that. Better not say anything and hope Jess hadn't noticed enough about John to connect the two.

John Bowers was no thief. He couldn't be.

⁓

For the next three days, the marshal left the house before dawn and returned at dusk, his wide smile always intact. Lisa eyed his city-style clothing and wondered where he spent his time.

She figured that John should be in Wyoming by now. If Marshal Brinkman was indeed on his trail, he had lost the scent. The longer he stayed in Juniper, the colder that trail would become.

Smiling into the lawman's eyes on the evening of the third day, Lisa swept into the kitchen to fetch him a cool drink. She was playacting—a distasteful job—but if, by distracting the marshal, she bought John a few hours' time, it was worth the effort.

"I'll take that to Chandler," Jessica said when she saw Lisa pouring tea into a tall glass. The younger girl's chin jutted forward; her eyes flashed fire then grew cold. "You always shove me aside when a handsome man comes around. Well, you're not doing it this time." She grabbed the glass from the porcelain tabletop and reached back to touch the French twist she had perfected that afternoon. Drawing in a deep breath, she held herself erect and minced into the dining room.

A corner of her mouth quirked in, Lisa edged to the kitchen door to peek through the dining room and into the living room where Jessica perched on the sofa beside Brinkman.

What disgusted Lisa most was the realization that she saw herself in Jessica's movements, her practiced smiles, the provocative tilt of her head. What had happened to the prudish girl Lisa had left behind a few months ago?

Piling fried chicken, boiled potatoes, and peas on two plates, Lisa carried them through the back hall to eat supper with her mother. Since the marshal arrived, Jessica had made it plain that she wanted him to herself. Tonight Lisa could not face the overt snubs of her sister at the dinner table.

Lisa sighed. Jessica had turned a deaf ear to her advice. She would have to learn the hard way.

The next morning Lisa strolled down Main Street's boardwalk to Harper's Emporium with the handle of a large basket over her arm. She put her hand out to open the door when a thin, wiry man with a prickly gray beard called her name.

Turning toward him, a question on her face, she waited.

"Howdy, Miss Lisa," Banjo said, removing his hat. "I was just about to call on you at home. Do you know a man by the name of John Bowers?"

Her heart took a dive. "Yes."

"He's at the Circle C with a bullet wound in his shoulder. He's asking for you."

"Is he. . . ?" She could not say the words.

"He's going to be all right, Miss Lisa," Banjo told her, grinning kindly. "He's worried about your father, and he wants to talk to you."

She touched the gingham-covered basket. "I've got to fetch some things for Jessica, then I can come with you."

"I brought the buckboard. I'll drive you over to your house."

She swallowed back the panic pressing her throat and forced her voice to be calm. What if the marshal was watching their house? Would he follow her to John? "No, thank you, Banjo. I'll meet you in front of the hotel."

His shaggy brows drew down. He studied her a moment, then said, "That's fine, Miss Lisa. I'll meet you there."

Lisa rushed home and entered by the back door. She dropped the basket on the table and told Jessica at the sink, "I'm going out to the Circle C with Banjo Calahan."

Her sister spun around, shocked. "Just like that? What's happened?"

"I met Banjo in town, and he asked me to ride out. He'll bring me home by evening time."

Jessica's face creased into a teasing smile. "Isn't he a little old for you?"

Lisa picked up a damp dishcloth and flung it at her. "Very funny. Don't wait supper for me." She hurried to the door and glanced back to see a satisfied smile on her sister's face.

Banjo gave her a hand up to the buckboard seat and climbed aboard himself. "He'll be mighty glad to see you, Miss Lisa." He chuckled. "He's a fine young feller, John is. Fits into the family like he was born to it."

"What happened to him?" Lisa asked. "The last I heard from him, he was leaving to find my father."

"He got as far as the trail west of town. Somebody drygulched him. Doc Leatherwood and I heard the shot and found him a few minutes later. . .right about there." He pointed at a clump of trees fifty yards ahead. "He was unconscious and losing a lot of blood. If we hadn't happened along, I'm afraid to say what would have become of him."

"He was already weak from his head wound," Lisa said, shading her eyes to stare at the place where John had lain.

"How much do you know about him?" Banjo asked over the grating of the wagon's wheels on sandy soil.

She told him about waking up to find John wounded outside the cabin, about the gold nuggets, and the dirt covering him and his horses.

"Maybe he was mining," Banjo said, "and had a good strike."

"He was wearing cowboy clothes."

"Maybe he's a cowboy who decided to stake a claim and didn't want to spend money on a new outfit. I did some mining my ownself in my younger days. I didn't always dress the part."

"He had a money belt full of gold eagles, too." She sighed. "I believe he's honest, Banjo. He prays."

The old-timer adjusted his hat and squinted at her. "One thing I do know; he's bound and determined to find out what became of your father."

He flapped the reins, propped one boot on the front panel of the wagon, and bellowed out a verse of a hymn, "Arise, my soul, arise; shake off thy guilty fears. . . ."

Letting her shoulders sway with the jouncing of the buckboard, Lisa listened to him sing and wondered at her own soul's answer to his musical plea.

Chapter 8

When the buckboard broke through the last stand of piñon pine, Lisa saw the Circle C ranch house at the top of a rising meadow. The stone-fronted cabin had a wall of orange rock behind it and a wide expanse of sky to the east. A stable and chicken coop lined up along the rock face as well.

For fifteen minutes the wagon rattled over a well-traveled trail toward a swollen stream.

"We just finished this bridge," Banjo said with a satisfied nod at the wide strip of planking before them. "We'll put up some rails soon's Chamberlin gets back."

Lisa gripped the edge of the seat as metal-strapped wheels rumbled over bare boards. She could see straight down into the water by her side, no planking in sight.

Banjo chuckled. "Don't worry, little lady. We used to just roll across the stream, water up to the axles, this time of year."

Lisa let out her breath and nodded. The trail rose before them in a wide circle around a misty green field.

"We planted corn a week ago Saturday, and it's already sprouting. Good soil."

Lisa smiled. "You sound like you own the place."

He grinned. "I don't have a deed, if that's what you mean, but I belong to the land." He glanced at her. "For years I rode the grub line or hopped from one mining camp to the next, no place to call my own. The Chamberlin family needed help when no one else would lend a hand, so I pitched my tent here, thinking that when their trouble was past, I'd move on."

He took off his hat, pressed a sleeve to his brow, and set it back on. "Then Jeremy came out from the East." He chuckled. "That little feller staked a claim around my heart the first minute I laid eyes on him."

"He's a bundle of energy," Lisa said, smiling. "I remember him running around at the corn harvest last fall. He never quit."

"Would you believe that two years ago he was stretched out in bed, his heart so weak the doctors wondered if he'd live?" His twinkling blue eyes darted toward the cabin as a blond boy burst out the door and into the yard, a wolf-faced dog at his heels. "Just look at him now. There's no way to explain that except'n that God did it."

Lisa nodded, but her mind had already reached into the house where a man lay on another sickbed.

Holding her spoon bonnet in one hand, Lisa appeared in the bedroom doorway with Em a few minutes later. John's head rose from the pillow. His face was chalk white, his mouth tense.

Em entered first. She lifted the blue enamel water pitcher and strode out as Lisa crossed the room and sat beside him. "John, what happened? Was it the same man? Did you see him?"

"The last I remember I was riding west of town, then I woke up here. I never knew what hit me."

Liquid pools formed in her eyes. "You've got to stay hid away. He'll kill you next time."

He tried to smile. "I'm not checking out of here before the good Lord allows. Soon's I'm fit, I'll be riding out to find your pa. Just like I said."

She pulled at the strings on her purse. "I've caused you nothing but trouble since we left Silverville."

"I wouldn't say that." He clasped her hand. "Please don't fret. I didn't ask you to come here to make you feel bad."

"If I. . ." She sniffed and pulled a handkerchief from her pocket. "If I hadn't run away, Pa wouldn't be out there hurt. . .or. . .or dead. And now you get yourself wounded again because of me." She shook her head, and one comb slid lower over her ear. "Jessica's right, John. I'm no good."

She pulled her hand free and covered her eyes with the thin cotton cloth. John's quiet voice cut though her misery.

"No one's good, Lisa. Not me, not Jessica, no one."

She lowered the handkerchief, blinking salty, burning, swollen lids.

"Jesus forgave my wickedness when I was six years old. He can forgive yours anytime you care to ask Him."

"What if my daddy's dead?" she breathed. "How can I ever forgive myself?"

His mouth softened; his eyes looked deeply into hers. "Let's leave tomorrow in the Lord's hands. He's big enough to carry it until we get there. Don't you think so?"

Nodding, she dabbed the soggy cloth against her eyes and drew in a shaky breath. "Now that I'm here, how can I help you?"

"Your being here helps me," he murmured. "Until now I haven't had the will to fight, to get back on my feet. I feel weak as a newborn calf."

She tucked the handkerchief into her pocket, her eyes on his navy-colored sling. "Let me stay here and take care of you."

His expression stiffened. "What about your mother? Isn't she ill?"

"Not physically. She took to her bed because she is worried about Pa. Besides, Jessica can see to her. Please let me stay." Her eyes darted about the sparsely furnished room. "I'll sleep on the floor if I have to."

The door scraped against leather hinges as Em stepped in carrying the pitcher. She paused, a puzzled look on her face. "Miss Lisa, why would a fine lady like you want to sleep on the floor?" Em asked, glancing from her to John.

Lisa's face felt as if it were on fire. "I was telling John that I'd like to stay and take care of him even if I have to sleep on the floor."

"Why, Miss Lisa, Miss Megan would never allow that. Besides, they's plenty of room. We could put Jeremy out in the stable quarters with Banjo so's you could have the loft. I know Miss Megan would be glad to have you."

"I'm not convinced that you ought to," John said. "Your family may not like it."

Lisa suddenly smiled, her spirit returning in a rush. "You're not in any shape to stop me, are you?"

His eyebrows lifted. "And here I thought you'd turned over a new leaf."

She stood and took off her wool shawl. "A new leaf, maybe, but the tree's still the same." Turning to Em, she said, "Would you mind showing me where to leave my things?"

Em's face wrinkled into a pearly white grin. "Sure thing, Miss Lisa."

Pausing long enough to send John a look that said, *Try to stop me,* Lisa left the room.

Outside John's door in the dining room, Em took Lisa's bonnet and shawl. "These can go on the shelf by the door." She turned to Megan, who sat in a wooden rocking chair before the living room fireplace. A flannel blanket covered her shoulder as she nursed the baby. "Miss Megan, Lisa would like to stay on to help care for John."

Megan's smooth features beamed a welcome. "Why, surely, Lisa. We will be delighted to have you. Please consider this your home."

"I'll tell Jeremy to move his things out with Banjo," Em said, her leather soles slapping against the stone floor. She stepped outside and called loudly, "Jeremy! Come to the house!"

"Sit down, Lisa," Megan said, reaching a hand toward the blue settee across from her. "I'm so glad you've come back to Juniper. Your mother was very worried about you."

"My father traveled north looking for me. He hasn't come back," Lisa said, sinking to the soft seat. "I can't sleep for blaming myself. And now John's been hurt because of me."

"Because of you?" Megan reached under the blanket, lifted the tiny dark-haired girl to her shoulder, and patted the baby's back. The child immediately lifted her head and stared at Lisa, a thin stream of white drool trickling from her delicate mouth. Megan touched the baby's lips with a snowy white cloth. "Surely, John wasn't shot because of you."

"Someone's been chasing him for months. If he hadn't set out to look for Pa, they may not have found him again."

Megan nodded. "John told us about that." She smiled into her daughter's eyes then turned her attention to Lisa. "He's a nice young man."

"Why would someone want to hurt him?" Lisa said. "He can't remember anything about it. I know John wouldn't hurt a soul. Why would anyone be so determined to kill him?"

"You ought to get Banjo to help you. He's pretty good at following a trail."

"After two months? It would take a pretty good tracker to find a trail that old."

"Katie, would you like to say hello to Lisa?" Megan cooed. She turned the baby to sit on her knees, facing Lisa. Katie *goo-gooed* and waved her hands as her mother gently bounced her.

"She's adorable," Lisa murmured, smiling gently.

"The apple of her daddy's eye."

The door burst open, and Jeremy bounded in. He reached the loft ladder in three strides and scurried to the top. Em chuckled as she closed the door. "You would think that I just give that child a peppermint stick; he's so excited."

"Banjo's his favorite," Megan said. "They'll have some good talks out there in the quarters."

"I get the top bunk," Jeremy called from above.

Megan laughed. "I don't think Banjo will argue over that."

"Let me show you around, Miss Lisa," Em said, moving into the living area. The spacious main room of the cabin lay in an L shape. In front of the door was the living area with a dining room adjoining it. The back leg of the L was a narrow kitchen with cabinets on both sides and a large black stove ten feet from the dining room table. From the stone fireplace to the corner hutch behind the table, the marks of a craftsman were evident everywhere Lisa looked.

"There's a spring outside the house." Em led the way through the kitchen and toward a path out the back door. Lisa kept pace behind her.

Out back, between the cabin and the towering rock wall, lay a corridor fifteen feet wide and forty feet long. A high board fence stretched from the house to the stable. Across from the back door, a thin stream spurted out of a crack in the rock and into a stone-lined basin that overflowed into a narrow, man-made stream and under a springhouse. The water disappeared at the edge of a sharp drop-off on the east side of the house.

"Stay back from the edge," Em warned. "I's pulled Jeremy away from the lip of that cliff so many times, I's lost count." She chuckled. "He sure does keep me on my toes." Pointing to the left, she said, "That's the new stable down yonder. They had a fire here about two years ago that destroyed the old one. Now, in bad weather we can get to the stock through here—behind this fence and out of the wind."

She turned back inside. "They's a hot-water reservoir in back of our cookstove, if you need some. I tore up an old sheet for bandages. They're in here." She pulled out a drawer in the kitchen. "And there's alum powder in this little tin to sprinkle on the wound. I haven't changed his dressing yet today."

Lisa lifted a rolled strip of cloth from the drawer. "I need to get word to my mother that I'm staying here," she said. "She'll be worried if I'm not back by nightfall. I'll need a few clothes, too. Maybe I can send a list to my sister."

"I'll ask Banjo to ride into town," Em said. "He was planning on taking you back anyway." She pulled out a second drawer. "Here's a pair of scissors."

"Thanks, Em. You've all been so kind."

"You's welcome, Miss Lisa. I's sorry you're having so much trouble. If you need anything more, just give a holler."

Her hands full of supplies, Lisa returned to John's room. "Time for a bandage change," she said brightly.

He grimaced. "Not my favorite part of day, I'm afraid."

"I'll be gentle." She moved to the chair and lay the supplies on her lap. "Now, let me see what you've got there. I'd just gotten used to bandaging your head, and you had to switch places on me."

"Sorry to trouble you. I should have had him shoot me in the head again."

She gasped then giggled. "I can tell you're feeling better already." Lifting the scissors, she said, "Tell me when it hurts, and I'll quit."

"Thanks a bundle."

⌒

Two days later Dr. Leatherwood announced that John could get out of bed as long as he took it easy and made no sudden moves. "Great, Doc," John said, grinning. "I'll be riding again in no time."

The doctor, built like a boxer, shook his head, his face serious. "Not for another two weeks, you won't. You've had a big hole gouged into your shoulder. A gunshot won't heal over in a few days like a cut would." He snapped the clasp on his Gladstone bag and lifted his black hat. "I'll come around in another week and see how you're doing."

John held out his left hand. "I'm obliged, Doc."

Briefly grasping his hand, Leatherwood said wryly, "Next time you see a bullet coming at you, do me a favor and duck." He nodded to Lisa and stomped out of the room.

John swung his legs over the edge of the cot. Lisa stood close and gripped his strong arm. He looked up. "What do you think I am, an invalid or something? I can stand without help."

She turned loose of his arm. "Sorry."

He eased his weight onto his feet and straightened his knees, lifting himself erect. An instant later he swayed. "Whoa!" He blinked, and Lisa grabbed him. "I guess I'm weaker than I thought."

"I think you've had enough for one time." She held on to him until he sat down. "Rest a couple of hours, and we'll try again."

His eyes drifted closed. "I think I'll sleep awhile."

"Good. I'll go out back and do some washing. If you need anything, just call."

He didn't answer, and she soft-footed out the door. Two hours later, she returned to check on him. He lay still, eyes closed, so she hesitated near the door.

Suddenly he looked at her and said, faintly accusing, "I've been waiting for you to come back."

"I've been scrubbing clothes—mine and yours. They're hanging out to dry." Stepping toward him, she said, "I have work to do, you know. Do you expect me to spend every second with you?"

He cocked his head on the pillow, his expression vaguely amused. "Lisa Feiklin, you're like a wild pony. You need taming."

She sat down and leaned toward him. She meant to speak with an arched tone, but her words came out breathy and soft. "You think you're man enough to do the job?"

His left hand flicked out and grasped behind her head. Before she realized what was happening, he pulled her down and kissed her.

Chapter 9

Lisa jerked back. "Why did you do that?" she demanded, her heart pounding. John gave her a slow grin. "It seemed like the thing to do at the moment." When she didn't answer, his expression sobered. "Maybe I was mistaken."

He raised up on one elbow. "I'm sorry. I was out of line."

She leaned against the back of her chair and swallowed hard, staring at her hands tangled in her lap.

Her voice sounded husky. "You're a fine man, John. The best I've ever met." She paused. "I'm not good enough for someone like you."

He laid his hand over hers. "You're wrong there, Lisa. I know you've made some bad blunders, and you've been deeply hurt, but there is an answer for that."

She looked up. "You're talking about God, aren't you?"

"He's real, Lisa. He cares for you so much that He sent His Son to die for you."

That truth pierced to the marrow of her being. Unconditional love was something she had never experienced yet longed for with all her soul.

"Just tell Him that you know you need Him," John murmured. "Ask Him to forgive you and make something new of your life."

Turning her hands to hold John's in both of hers, she pressed her eyes closed and poured out her heart to the God she'd known only by name until now. She had always feared His holiness; now suddenly she felt His love, warm and full, flowing through her.

She blinked at John, who was peering at her with an intensity that she could feel. "He is real," she murmured.

He lay back, his face glowing. "You know what this means?"

She waited for him to go on.

"You've got a clean slate. No more kicking yourself over what happened last month or last year."

She raised his fingers to her lips, then her cheek, her heart too full to speak.

Jeremy burst through the partially open bedroom door. Lisa dropped John's hand and pressed the left comb more firmly into her hair.

"Mr. John, want to see my horse?" Jeremy held out an oblong lump with four sticks coming down from the corners. It looked like something Lobo had chewed.

"Let me see that," John said, smiling. He held the piece and turned it over.

"Much better than your last try. You need to work on making the neck curve a little."

Jeremy took the carving out of his hand and dropped it into a massive front pocket of his overalls.

"Jeremy, since you're here," Lisa said, "will you help me get Mr. John out of bed. Last time he almost fainted."

"Fainted?" John demanded. "My head got a little dizzy, that's all. I didn't almost faint."

Lisa ignored him. "Jeremy, if you'll stand on his good side, I'll take the other one." She turned to her patient. "Ready?"

Three days later John and Lisa strolled around the front yard in the cool of the evening, enjoying playful breezes and the warmth of a late sun. The orange cliff glowed bronze behind the house, and two hawks played tag above its rocky summit. The cornfield below had turned a deep leafy green, its fledgling plants swaying gently.

Behind Lisa and John, Megan hung diapers on the clothesline, and Jeremy rolled a wheelbarrow out of the stable. Ears up and tail high, Lobo trailed his every step.

"Next week this time, I'll be able to ride out," John said, reaching up to brush back his hair from his forehead. It was getting shaggy again.

"Why do you always spoil a good time by talking about leaving?" Lisa asked, her hand resting on his arm. "The sheriff from Denver is looking for Pa. I don't want you to go, too. If you're hurt again, a guardian angel may not find you next time."

He laughed. "Banjo's a funny-looking angel. I'll have to tell him you said that."

She nudged him in the side with her elbow. "I was talking about myself. I found you first, remember?"

He touched her hand with his fingers that showed at the edge of his sling. "That's one thing I hope I never forget."

She smiled up into his blue eyes. "Speaking of forgetting, have you remembered anything more about who's chasing you?"

Gazing toward the east at silver-green prairie grass rippling in the distance, he drew in a deep breath. "I keep having a nightmare about a big man with a whip. I can see his white shirt and his hairy hands, but his face stays in the shadow of his Stetson." His jaw muscles worked in and out.

"You think that man is real?"

He glanced at her, his face showing pain. "I don't know. I always wake up shaking and cold, like I just came out of a fever. My insides turn to applesauce whenever I dream of him."

They roamed about the yard for another ten minutes, then slowly strolled toward the cabin. Once inside, John returned to his cot while Lisa helped Megan put supper on the table.

"I suppose I ought to be going home soon," Lisa said, holding a cloth-lined basket of rolls. "John won't need me much longer."

Brushing a strand of honey-colored hair back to her fat bun, Megan smiled softly. "You're welcome to stay as long as you like. It's been nice having another lady in the house again. I've been lonely since Em married and moved to the other side of the property."

"You've been awfully good to John and me. Especially after the scandal I caused last fall."

Megan set a wide bowl of chicken and dumplings on the table. "You've suffered enough over that episode, Lisa. It's not our place to add to your sorrows."

Katie's lusty cry in the bedroom cut off their conversation. Untying her apron on her way to her daughter, Megan said, "Call Jeremy and Banjo, won't you? I'll change the baby and be right there."

Lisa strode to the porch to shout, "Supper's ready!" then returned to the table to fill enamelware cups with water. Over the past week, John's appetite had returned twice over, and he could manage a fork with his weak hand. She stepped to his door and pushed it open.

From the doorway she asked, "Do you feel up to coming to the table tonight?"

He passed a hand over his forehead. "Sorry. I'm feeling kind of tuckered after that walk. Would you mind bringing me a plate?"

"Coming right up." She let the door close and returned to the table. Filling a bowl with thick chicken soup, she pushed open the door with her shoulder. It gave against her pressure, then banged shut after she passed through.

"Here's supper," she said with cheerfulness she did not feel. Just a few more days and he would saddle Molasses and canter away—maybe forever.

"I'm starved," he said, sitting up and reaching out for the bowl. He lifted the spoon and tasted. "Great soup. Just like my mother used to make."

Lisa paused beside him, wanting some space for her confused emotions. "Would you mind if I eat at the table tonight rather than in here?"

He looked up, puzzled. "Is something wrong?"

She avoided his eyes. "I'd like to visit with the family. I've hardly spoken to them since I arrived almost a week ago."

"Go ahead. I don't mind." He swung his legs to the floor and plunged the spoon into a fat dumpling.

Lisa reached the table as Banjo slid into his seat. Megan came out of the bedroom with Katie on her hip. The baby wore a navy gown with white smocking on the bodice, her bare toes sticking out from under the hem. Jeremy darted in the back door, his slicked-down hair standing up at the crown.

"Banjo, look at my horse." He pulled his creation out of his pocket and thrust it at the cowhand.

Banjo took it and turned it over in his palm. "You've been working hard at it, Jem," he said, blue eyes twinkling. "What you have here is the rough shape. Now you need to work on the curves. You do that with tiny smooth cuts. I'll show you how after supper." He handed the wooden lump back to the boy.

Jeremy set it beside his plate next to Banjo and flung himself into the chair. "I want to make a figure of Lobo next."

Banjo chuckled. "That's the mark of an achiever, son. Always thinking ahead."

Megan sat at the head of the table, the baby in her lap. "Banjo, would you thank the Lord for the food?"

Lisa bowed her head while he prayed a short, simple prayer ending with "Bring Steve home safe to us, and heal that boy in the bedroom yonder so's he can go about the business You've given him to do. Amen." He lifted his head and reached for the serving bowl to hand it to Lisa.

"Thank you," she said, filling her bowl. She handed the food to Jeremy, her attention on Banjo. "What did you mean when you said, 'The business You've given him to do'? I hope you don't mind my asking."

"Not a bit. I was talking about John's trouble. Surely you know all about it."

She nodded. "I know as much as he does anyway."

Banjo leaned his forearm on the table, his voice low. "He's got to go back and face his enemies, Lisa. Something has him scared spitless. He's got to go back and face his fear or give up his manhood."

Something squeezed in her middle. "I'm so scared. Every time he gets on the trail alone, someone shoots him. Next time they'll likely kill him."

"I know how you feel," Megan said, mashing a bit of potato with a fork while dodging Katie's chubby, grabbing hands. "Steve and I went through some trouble when we first came here. I thought I'd die when he rode out to face Victor Harrington." She shivered. "I still get the willies thinking about it."

Smiling, Banjo reached out to touch the baby's waving hand. Katie gave him a wide-lipped grin that showed a single tooth.

Lifting a tiny spoonful of potatoes, Megan found Katie's open mouth. "Steve will be home tomorrow. I can't wait."

"Maybe he'll bring me some peppermint," Jeremy said between mouthfuls of thick broth.

"Don't get your hopes up, buddy," Megan told her brother. "Steve may not have thought about satisfying your sweet tooth."

Jeremy's last dumpling disappeared in three bites. He scraped his plate clean and lunged to his feet. "I told Em I'd come over after supper." Dashing to the door, he pulled it open, calling, "Lobo! Here, boy!"

Her mind still on John's dilemma, Lisa said, "I don't think John's strong enough to go alone." Her eyes pleaded with Banjo. "Won't you please try to talk him into waiting a couple more weeks?"

Banjo's expression turned thoughtful. "What about your father? I'd think you'd want John to look for him."

"If John gets himself killed, he won't be able to help my father. Besides, the sheriff. . ." Her voice trailed away. She was beginning to wonder what had become of Denver's sheriff. All this time and no word had come. Would Jessica let her know if she heard something?

Confused and hurting, Lisa finished her meal without saying more. She knew Banjo well enough to know that he was trying to help her. But his kind of help didn't go down any easier than a helpful dose of cod-liver oil.

A few minutes later, a volley of horses' hooves in the yard drew everyone from the table and to the front door. Megan had a look on her face that spoke of her hope that the rider might be her husband.

Leading a bay mare that carried a side saddle, a slim young man slid from the back of a glossy blue roan, his legs reaching for the porch steps while his fingers pulled a slip of paper from the pocket of his blue flannel shirt. Lisa recognized her teenaged neighbor, Jimmy Bledsoe.

"Hi, Jimmy," she said, worry in her voice. "Did Mama send you?"

Flipping off his hat, he handed the paper to her. His voice sounded too deep for his small size. "Miss Jessica sent this to you."

Lisa's mouth felt dry. She unfolded the page and read, *The sheriff came back empty-handed. Mama's inconsolable. Please come home.*

Chapter 10

John spoke from the open door behind her. "What is it, Lisa?"

She turned and held the paper out, her brow puckered with worry. "I've got to go home."

Megan said, "We're still at the table, Jimmy. Would you like a bite of supper?"

"I'd be obliged." His stiff boots sounded on the porch steps.

Lisa pushed past John and, holding her skirts to one side, climbed the loft ladder. She stuffed clothes into her carpetbag without bothering to fold them. How could she face her mother? If she hadn't run off with Brent, this wouldn't have happened.

John was waiting at the bottom of the ladder when she came down. "I need to talk to you," he said.

She stared down at the bag in her hands, painfully aware of Megan handing Jimmy a plate and Banjo drawing out a chair next to his own for the boy to sit down. Her feelings ran too deep to be hauled out and discussed in front of everyone.

John glanced toward the dining room. "Let's go out to the porch," he whispered.

Outside, he eased down to sit on the top step and reached for her hand, tenderly pulling her down beside him. She dropped the carpetbag and sat. The warmth of the sinking sun could not melt the icy knife of fear that pierced through Lisa.

John's voice made her turn toward him. "There's no one left to help your father. No one but me."

"If the sheriff didn't find Daddy, he's most likely. . ." She could not force herself to say the word. "He's not there to find."

She latched onto his arm. "Please don't go out there and get yourself killed."

He picked up her hand and held it like he would a wounded bird. Leaning close enough for her to see the gold flecks in his eyes, he murmured, "I hate to leave you." His glance wandered from her hair to her brow to her lips. "You've become very special to me, Lisa." Suddenly, his expression changed. He pulled away, dropping her hand. "I'm sorry. I shouldn't be saying such things to you."

Lisa found her breath and asked, "Why not?" a catch in her voice.

"I'm a broken arrow. Good for nothing." He looked down at his worn boots.

"Your wound will heal in time."

"I'm not talking about my shoulder." His voice became angry. "I'm yellow, Lisa. I never dreamed I would end up like this, but I have to face it. I'm yellow to the core."

She touched his cheek, and he looked at her. "If you're afraid, why do you insist on going?"

He gazed toward the eastern horizon, across miles of tall grass swaying in the constant breeze. After a long moment, he said, "I guess I want to prove to myself that I can still be a man."

Without looking at her, he reached out and claimed her hand again. "After my folks died, a big rancher to the west of us thought he'd run me off. I wasn't much more than a kid, alone. . .scared to death. He brought four of his hands over to my place late one afternoon just as I was heading to the house to cook me some supper." The fingers in the sling curled together, forming a loose fist.

"They called me out and beat the fire out of me. Left me on the ground and rode away laughing."

Lisa swallowed, the sound loud in the heavy silence between them.

"I crawled inside the house and doctored myself as best I could." He glanced at her. "It took me two weeks to get over that beating."

"What did you do then?"

A half grin formed on his lips. "I started sleeping and eating in a tight stand of aspen on the hillside above the ranch yard. I picketed my horses in a cave way off yonder. I knew those men'd be back. They wouldn't have such an easy mark the next time.

"Every day I changed my schedule in case they'd started watching my place. I never took the same route to the barn or the well. They came about a week after I got better. This time they had torches and a keg of dynamite."

Lisa watched his jaw move as he talked. He had a shallow cleft on the side of his chin.

"One of 'em rolled the keg onto the porch while the other lit a torch and headed for the barn."

"You just stood there and watched them?" Lisa breathed.

He glanced at her. "I was bellied down on the hillside with my Winchester. I nailed the one carrying the torch before he took three steps. He squalled and lit out for his horse. About that time, the man with the dynamite changed his mind, left the keg, and jumped into his saddle on the run. I took a shot at him, missed, and hit the keg instead. That hombre landed halfway up the hill with his back against a fir tree."

"Was he dead?"

"Naw. But I suspect he had a dislocated shoulder and a bear of a headache." He grinned. "And little green needles sticking in him from hoof to hindquarters." He turned serious. "That wasn't the last of 'em, but I kept my place. I finished proving up the place and got a deed."

His eyes found hers again. "It's not just finding your Pa that's driving me. Something happened to me somewhere around Silverville. I've got to find out what it was and why I shiver in my boots whenever I think about that place. I'd be better off dead than the way I am. Can you understand that?"

She searched for her voice. "I've known a lot of men, John. They all turned out to be nothing but selfish beasts." Her voice wavered. "You're different from them. You're honest and caring and. . ." Biting her lips, she blinked hard. "What will I do if something happens to you?"

He dropped her hand and stretched his arm around her. "You've given me a good reason to come back with a whole skin." There were those gold flecks again. "I love you, Lisa. And I will come back. That's a solemn promise." He gently kissed the corners of her glistening eyes, then reached down to her lips.

She clung to him, feeling completely protected for the first time in her life. He pulled her into a warm hug and said into her hair, "When I come back, will you marry me and come to the Lazy B?" He gasped. "I remember! My ranch."

Lips parted, Lisa looked up into his face; the wonder in his expression matched the joy cascading in her heart.

"It's about twenty miles west of Silverville, before you get to Sundance. I can see the fork in the trail where you cut off to go to the house." Almost nose to nose with her, his brilliant smile warmed Lisa. "After the explosion, I built a new cabin with three bedrooms and the biggest kitchen north of Laramie." He pulled her closer, her head nestled against his shoulder. "Will you go there with me when this is all settled?"

"I give you my solemn promise."

He kissed her again then turned her loose and grinned. "I'm going to hold you to that promise, Lisa. Don't even think of changing your mind."

The front door opened, and Jimmy Bledsoe stepped out. Lisa and John widened the gap between them, both turning to see who was there.

"Ready, Lisa?" the dark-haired youngster asked, glancing from her to John.

Lisa got to her feet and reached for her bag. "Send me word when you can, will you?" she asked John.

"Will do." He stood and moved onto the porch so Jimmy could pass. "I won't be leaving for a few days."

She mounted the mare and waited for Jimmy to tie on her bag. The ride home seemed doubly long and ten times as lonely as the trip to the Circle C she had taken ten days before.

From astride a trotting buckskin, Steve Chamberlin hailed the house as he arrived the next day after breakfast. From his window, John saw the tall, lean rancher hug his wife and lift Katie from her arms. Banjo came from the corral to slap his boss's back and swap howdys while Jeremy and Lobo did a happy dance around them all, the dog yapping and wagging his whole body.

Lying on his bed, his good arm under his head, John watched the happy family in the yard and felt a comfortable glow. One of these days he would have a home like the Chamberlins. He held the thought close, warming himself.

Half an hour later, Banjo knocked twice on his door and stepped through, bringing with him the mouth-tingling aroma of baking bread. His faded blue eyes seemed to laugh at some private joke. This was the first time John had seen him without his stained and weathered Stetson. "I've got a proposal for you, young man," he said, letting the door bump closed. "How would you like a riding partner?"

Head tilted, John watched him, waiting for him to explain.

"Yesterday, young Jimmy said that he don't have a job lined up for the summer yet, so I asked Chamberlin if Jimmy can stand in for me until we get back."

John sat up and eased the sling around his neck. "You're serious, aren't you?"

"Serious as the apoplexy." Banjo stumped farther into the room and rested his bones on the chair. "The question is, how soon will you be able to travel?"

Lifting his weak arm, John used his other hand to pull the sling's knot over his head and remove it. He flexed his elbow. "I reckon it's about time to do some finding out."

They left three days later at the first light of dawn.

Chapter 11

"Ever been up toward Silverville?" John asked Banjo when they stopped for a nooning near a sloshing, stone-filled stream. The men sat on either side of a tiny campfire where a coffeepot bubbled and four thick strips of bacon sizzled in a pan.

"Not for almost ten years," Banjo said, fork in hand. He eased the holster away from his jeans and stretched out one leg. "I did some mining in the Black Hills awhile back but never found much. If I'd only tried a few miles north, I might have made the strike that caused so much commotion in those parts last summer."

John worked his stiff right arm in and out. "You just said a miner's favorite words: 'If I'd only.'"

Banjo chuckled. "You've got 'em pegged all right. Mining is as close as I ever come to gamblin' in my life." He forked two pieces of meat onto a plate and held them out to John. "I've been meaning to ask your advice on a biblical question that came to me recently," Banjo said, filling his own plate.

Puzzled, John asked, "What is it?"

"You think there's anything wrong with me marrying my widow's sister?"

John paused, uncertain about what kind of answer Banjo expected of him. "I reckon not," he said finally.

The old-timer laughed deep in his belly. "Sorry, son, but I'm afraid I have to disagree. I could never marry my widow's sister because I'd be dead."

Looking skyward, John grunted and shook his head. "You got me fair and square." He chuckled and dug into his lunch.

When he finished, he picked up his coffee cup. "Before I left Juniper I saw a man—just a glimpse of him—but I can't get him out of my mind. He was on the boardwalk in Juniper. A few minutes later, I was laid out on the ground with a bullet in my shoulder."

"You think he's the gent who drygulched you?" Banjo asked.

"I can't say for sure, but he sticks in my mind—a dark fellow with kind of a squashed-down face. His hair started growing just above his eyebrows." He took a bite and chewed slow. "I keep having a nightmare about a man with a big whip. He's standing over me while I'm on the ground. I never get a look at his face."

"You ever get bullwhipped?" Banjo lifted the coffeepot and refilled the two tin cups.

311

John's cheeks billowed out as he exhaled, thinking hard. "I want to say no, but something won't let me." He looked at Banjo, fear in his eyes. "Sometimes I wonder if I'm going crazy."

"Simmer down, son. You're as sane as I am." The old-timer chuckled. "Some folks would say that ain't much comfort." Lifting his cup, he slurped coffee. "How long did the ride to Juniper with Lisa take you?"

"A week. We had to move slow there at the last and ended up stopping a day for Lisa to rest. The trip was real hard on her."

Banjo stood and kicked dirt over the fire. "We'd best put some miles behind us. Chamberlin's waiting for me to get back."

Standing, John murmured to himself, "Chamberlin's not the only one waiting." He swallowed a grin and settled his hat.

Banjo mounted his lop-eared donkey, Kelsey, and sang, "Alas, and did my Savior bleed. . ."

When they cantered away from the clearing, John was humming along.

⌒

When Lisa reached home she found her mother lying on her bed moaning. Tears of exhaustion streamed from her eyes and trickled toward her ears. Jessica sat beside her sobbing into a handkerchief. When they heard the bedroom door open, both women turned to see who had come in.

"Lisa!" Sally wailed. "Your father is dead."

Lisa ran to her mother. "Don't say that, Mama!" She flung herself across Sally's prone form, hugging her and crying into her shoulder. "He can't be."

"He is," Jessica gasped. She gave a sobbing hiccup. "Indians got him, I bet."

Lisa raised up and glared at her sister. "You're not helping, Jessica. Keep your horrid guesses to yourself."

Jessica's heart-shaped face looked like a strawberry, puffy and red. She opened her mouth to reply, but Lisa cut her off. "If you say it's my fault, I'll whip you right here. You know I'll do it, too."

The younger girl covered her face with a damp handkerchief and wept in earnest.

Sally sat up, effectively putting Lisa aside, and reached for Jessica. "Now, now, dear. Don't take on so." She glanced at Lisa. "Make us some tea, will you, honey?"

Lisa stood frozen to the floor, her heart feeling as though it would explode. Remorse, sorrow, and fear swelled and swelled until her chest was a pain-filled mass. Pulling in a sharp breath, she rushed to the door and closed it behind her.

Her hands shook so badly that she could hardly fill the copper teapot. A fire still smoldered in the kitchen stove, so she added a small log through the round opening on top and replaced the cast-iron circle lid. While the pot heated, she reached into the cabinet for the square tin of black tea.

Her father was dead. She was slowly accepting the fact. If he was alive, he would have contacted them or come home by now. More than a month had passed since he left Juniper on that stage.

She ran stiff fingers across her scalp, dislodging her combs but paying them no mind. How could she live with herself?

Several minutes later she remembered why she had come to the kitchen. Filling the metal teaspoon with dry leaves, she clipped the tin shut. She moved the steaming pot from the hot circle to a cool one, opened the lid, and propped the spoon inside.

She opened three cabinet doors before she found the wooden tray in its customary spot. Then she reached to the shelf above for three cups.

"Well, look who came home," a smooth voice said from the doorway.

Lisa whirled to see Marshal Brinkman grinning at her. He smelled strongly of sweet cologne.

"Mama sent for me," she told him. "The sheriff from Denver has given up searching for my father."

The marshal's chiseled features turned sympathetic. "I'm sorry to hear that. I'd offer to look for him myself if I weren't already on another case."

Reminded of her fears about John, Lisa turned back to the tray. "I need to get back to my mother. She's overwrought." Quickly filling the cups, she lifted the tray. "Excuse me, please."

"Certainly. I'll rest my weary limbs in the living room." He stood aside for her to pass. She could feel his eyes on her until she turned the corner into the hall.

Her mother and Jessica seemed calmer when Lisa arrived. Sally reached for her tea and sipped it, her face so swollen that it looked painful. Jessica took her cup from the tray and held it in her hands. She didn't look at Lisa.

"Marshal Brinkman just came in," Lisa said, watching Jessica.

"Get him a drink, will you, Lisa?" Jessica said, patting her fiery cheek. "I can't let him see me like this."

Feeling like she was on the outside of their grief, Lisa carried her untouched cup back to the kitchen. She saw the back of the marshal's sleek black head from his spot on the sofa. He had his head angled back as though deep in thought.

She poured her cup of tea back into the pot, swirled the teaspoon to get more flavor from it, and poured the steaming liquid into a wide bowl so that it would cool. Adding some sugar, she carefully emptied the bowl to half-fill a tall glass then topped it off with cool spring water and carried the drink to the living room.

"Would you like some tea, Marshal?" she asked when she reached the sofa.

He smiled up at her as he took the glass from her hand, his fingers brushing hers. "Why, thank you, Miss Lisa. And please call me Chandler, remember?" He touched the seat beside him. "Won't you join me for a few moments? I'd like to hear more about your father."

Her mind too numb to think up an excuse, Lisa sat. How could he be so callous as to want to talk to her at a time like this?

"There's nothing I can tell you about Daddy. He left here on the stage and disappeared somewhere in Wyoming. That's all anyone knows."

"Where have you been for so long?" he asked gently. "I've missed seeing you around."

Lisa swallowed and touched her mouth. "I was helping a sick friend."

"You're a lady of many talents, not only beautiful but compassionate as well."

Intensely uncomfortable, Lisa stood. "Please excuse me. I've got to see to my mother."

He tucked his chin down and leaned slightly forward. "Certainly. Give my condolences to your mother and your sister."

When she reached the bedroom, Lisa found Sally alone with her eyes closed. Not wanting to disturb her sleep, Lisa trudged up the stairs to her own room. She locked the door behind her, lay across the faded quilt, and buried her face in her pillow.

Lisa walked through the next three days in a thick fog. She prepared small meals and worked hard at staying away from Jessica's reproachful eyes. Her mother and Jessica had not appeared in the main part of the house since Lisa's return. If not in her mother's room, Jessica stayed locked in her own. Lisa worried that they would break down, but she couldn't convince them to do otherwise.

Surprisingly, the marshal became more relaxed in his manner and suggested that he eat with Lisa in the kitchen. He dried dishes for her twice. Not wanting to offend their guest, Lisa reluctantly allowed him to help, but she feared that Jessica would suddenly decide to come out and stumble into what appeared to be a cozy tête-à-tête. Worse, the younger girl would never believe Lisa's explanations.

While Lisa and Chandler lingered over a second cup of coffee on Friday evening, a knock at the back door made Lisa start. She hurried to open it while Chandler watched from his seat at the table.

The Bledsoe boy stood outside, his face flushed with exertion.

"Jimmy, what's wrong?"

He pushed a slip of paper toward her. "I just rode in. John asked me to give this to you."

"Thanks. Would you like a cup of coffee?"

"Can't," he said, stuffing hands into the pockets of his jeans. "Mama will want me to come home right away." He stepped off the back stoop, and Lisa closed the door.

She opened the page and read: *Banjo and I are going north. Won't be back for a while. Don't worry. John.*

"Bad news?" Chandler asked.

"Uh. . .no." She shoved the note into her skirt pocket. "It's nothing, really." Returning to the table, she asked, "Would you like more coffee?"

"I've had plenty, thanks." He stood and gathered plates. "I'll help you with these dishes, then maybe we can play some checkers. What do you say?"

"I suppose so." She picked up her plate and glass and turned toward the counter. Chandler moved in the same direction, his coffee cup in his left hand. They collided. The coffee cup skimmed off the saucer and shattered on the floor.

"I'm terribly sorry," he said, kneeling to pick up the pieces.

"It was my fault as much as yours." She set down her dishes and hurried for the broom.

"I'm not usually so clumsy," he said when she returned. "I'll replace the cup, of course, if you'll tell me where your mother purchased it."

"It came off Harper's back shelf. It's nothing special, believe me. Don't trouble yourself."

Three minutes later she left the kitchen to fetch her mother's dirty dishes. Jessica had refused to eat tonight.

When she returned, Chandler had his white sleeves rolled to the elbow and was pouring hot water into the dishpan.

"I'll wash," she said, unbuttoning her cuffs.

Throwing a dish towel over his shoulder, he made a small bow. "Whatever m'lady desires." His gentle laugh should have warmed the atmosphere. Instead, it sent a surge of distaste through Lisa. She wished that Jessica did not find him attractive either.

Arms deep in sudsy water, Lisa rubbed a cloth over plates and cups while Chandler rambled about his case.

"The man I'm after seems like a nice fellow to those who don't know him. He's got an innocent face and likes to talk religion." He shook his head, deeply regretful. "It's a shame he's got such a black heart."

He glanced at Lisa's tight face. "I apologize. I'm boring you." Reaching toward the pan of clear water beside her, he seemed to lose his balance and knocked against her.

She lurched back, indignant.

He laid down his towel. "I don't know what's wrong with me tonight, Lisa. I think I'd best sit down for a while."

"Are you sick?" she asked, watching his face. His mouth drooped at the corners, and his eyes seemed a little unfocused.

"I don't think so," he passed a hand over his forehead. "I'll sit down awhile, though. I feel a little weak." He ambled out of the room, reaching out to touch the corner of the door and the back of a dining room chair as he passed them.

Lisa finished scrubbing the last pot and set it to drain on a towel. She stopped in the kitchen doorway, shocked to see Jessica on the sofa beside the marshal.

"Forgive me for neglecting you," Jessica was saying to him. "My father and I were very close."

Chandler leaned toward her. "I've been worried about you, Jess. You don't know how badly I feel about your father. I wish there were something I could do to help."

She sighed. "Your being here is a comfort, Chandler. I just had to come out and see you for a while."

Lisa edged around the dining room table toward the hall and solitude. Relieved that Jessica would take the marshal off her hands for the evening, she was also troubled at the relationship that seemed to be developing between them.

She reached her room and pressed fingertips to her throbbing temples, trying vainly to put two thoughts together in her grief-muddled brain. She had to break Jessica away from that man.

She reached into her pocket and drew out John's letter. Holding it to her lips, she sat on the bed to read it through again and kiss the signature. *Please, God, protect him and bring him back to me.* The page still tight in her hand, she lay down and stared at the ceiling.

Chapter 12

The next morning Chandler Brinkman appeared while Lisa was frying eggs. Brilliant sunshine and the aromas of baking biscuits and bubbling coffee made the kitchen an inviting place.

"Good morning, Lisa," he said, pulling out a chair at the enamel table.

A metal spatula in her hand, she looked up, surprised. "Good morning. What keeps you in today?"

He smiled. "Would you like to take a buggy ride with me later?"

She turned her attention to the eggs bubbling in the pan.

"How about a picnic?" he went on. "I found a small lake just north of town. We could ride out in time for lunch."

Lisa turned her back toward him, trying to think. She did not want to go, but maybe this was a chance to divert his attentions from Jessica.

Lifting four sunny-side-up eggs from the pan, she slid two on each plate and cracked four more into the skillet.

"I'll pack a basket," she told him, her voice casual. She had planned to scrub some clothes this morning. Maybe she could still do the washing if she hurried.

A nagging voice told her she should not be going out while her family was in mourning. She considered the thought, then pushed it away. It was more important to protect Jessica from that man than to follow a tradition that might not apply to them. They could not even hold a funeral until they were sure Daddy was really gone.

Lisa was puffing from exertion but ready when Chandler drew his horses to a halt in front of the house shortly after eleven o'clock. She breezed into her mother's room, where Jessica sat in the rocking chair and read aloud from *Harper's Weekly* to her mother on the bed.

"I'm going out for a couple of hours," Lisa said, pulling on her white gloves. "I've left fried chicken and boiled potatoes on the back of the stove whenever you're ready to eat."

"Where are you going?" Sally asked. Sitting up, she let the counterpane fall away from her cotton nightgown.

"Is it Chandler?" Jessica demanded. "You've been spending a lot of time with him lately, haven't you?"

"Why not? You've been hiding in the back of the house."

Jessica took a step forward, her finger marking her place in the magazine. "Keep your claws out of him, Lisa. He's mine."

"He's no good for you, Jess. I know he is as handsome as a Greek god and he knows how to make a girl feel special, but he's trouble. Believe me."

Her sister's eyes sparked fire. "You're trying to put me off so you can have him to yourself, aren't you?"

Unwilling to get into a scene with Jessica, Lisa drew back. "I'll be home by midafternoon." She pulled the door shut and hustled to the living room where Chandler waited with the loaded picnic basket over his arm.

"All set?" he asked, looking her over from crown to flowing skirts.

She lifted her yellow calico bonnet from the shelf by the door. "Ready," she said and swished past him. She had worn an extra crinoline today, making her pink skirts billow. Laying the bonnet over the braided double crown on top of her head, she tied the ribbons.

Outside, she paused when she saw the black surrey, a bobbing fringe around its flat roof, the sides open to catch the breeze.

"How lovely! Wherever did you find it?"

Chandler chuckled. "I rented it from Mr. Harper at the emporium." He held out his arm. "May I?"

"Thank you," she said, suddenly glad she had come. Chandler may not be her first choice for a companion, but the fresh smell of timothy and sage wafting down from the hills made her want to spread her wings.

With practiced ease, Chandler handed her up to the carriage seat. Pulling her skirts inside the half door, she glanced toward the house. Was that Jessica's face in the window?

Before she could tell for certain, Chandler sat close to her on the leather seat and shook the reins, leaving the house far behind.

"What a beautiful day!" Lisa exclaimed when the buggy left the last of Juniper's buildings behind. Ahead lay rolling hills with spruce and pine clumped between rocky boulders. A chipmunk darted up a scrub oak as they passed. It paused on the trunk to look back and flick its stubby tail before scampering to the safety of the top.

"I know how to pick them," Chandler said. "A day and a girl."

She chose to ignore his meaning. "How far is the lake?" she asked.

"Just over that hill." He pointed far up the trail. "I found it last week and spent a solid hour just sitting there and feeling the quiet. It's a perfect spot for a relaxing afternoon."

"It sounds wonderful."

They drove for several minutes in silence. At the crest of the hill, Chandler tugged the reins, and the horses turned off the trail onto a rutted lane.

Lisa tried to lean and sway with the surrey, but several times she had to hold on to the side to keep from slipping off the seat. The wheel on her side slid into a hole, and she felt the jarring thump all the way up her backbone. "How much farther?"

"The place is just behind those trees," he said, an unusual suppressed excitement in his voice. Screened from the road by a long line of spruce trees, the horses slowed their pace and stopped, the harness creaking.

Tall grass dipped and swayed around them. On the other side of the carriage stretched a broad expanse of bare earth dotted with scrub brush.

"There's no lake here," Lisa said sharply. "Why did you stop?"

The marshal reached under his jacket and pulled out a Colt revolver. His voice sounded flat. "This is where we get out." He aimed the gun at her middle and looked her full in the face, his handsome features slanted into something cruel. "You heard me. Get out."

She felt for the latch on the door, still watching the black bore in the gun. "You hurt me, and this country won't be big enough to hide you."

His lips formed a wicked grin. "Don't worry. You're only the bait to catch a bigger fish. If you're the praying kind like your milksop boyfriend, pray he'll come and rescue you."

Her jaw dropped until her mouth came open. "How do you know about him?"

"I followed you here from Laramie. This marshal badge was just to get your confidence. I knew if I waited long enough, you'd lead me to him. And you did."

Aghast, she cried, "I did not."

"I picked your pocket last night, my dear. Uncle Gil knows all."

"Who's Gil?"

His smile had a mean curve. "Yours truly." He waved the pistol. "Now get down."

Wishing she were dressed to run, Lisa jumped to the ground. Wearing button-up shoes and four crinolines, she would not get three yards before he caught her.

He followed her down and pulled two strips of rawhide from his pocket.

"My folks will miss me come nightfall," she said, her eyes darting left to right, desperate for a way out. "They'll send someone after you."

He chuckled. "You took care of that for me." Moving toward her, he wrapped the strip of leather around one wrist and reached for the other. "I left a note saying that we'd eloped. From what Jessica told me, that's nothing new for you."

She wrenched away from him and beat his chest with her fists. "How dare you!"

Laughing aloud, he caught her and threw her to the ground. Like a cow-puncher working over a calf, he tied her wrists and ankles in less than twenty seconds, using his knee to hold down her kicking legs. "No sense screaming, Lisa," he said when she stopped to catch her breath. "Nobody can hear you."

She cried furious tears while Chandler unhitched the horses and pulled two saddles from the back of the buggy. Sitting up, she tried to wipe her sticky face on her skirt but had little success. She could feel bits of grass and twigs in her loosening braids.

Pausing before her, he smiled broadly, pleased with himself. "On the trail from Laramie, John always managed to stay far enough ahead of me so I couldn't get a shot at him. Then when I did get a chance, that meddling cowhand came along before I could finish him off.

"I spent days watching that cabin to see if I could catch him alone outside, but he never moved out of the house without someone around."

He leaned close to her face. "But with you as my hole card, I'll get him all right. He'll beg me to take him and let you go."

After saddling the horses, Brinkman opened the picnic basket and filled his saddlebags with cold chicken, biscuits, and a tin of molasses cookies.

"Harper won't miss his surrey until late tonight," he said. "It'll take him awhile to find it here. We'll have plenty of time to get away." He closed the leather flap and flipped the bags across his shoulder. "Okay, mount up," he said abruptly.

"Where are you taking me?" Her voice was ragged.

"Don't you know?" he mocked. "Back where you came from—Silverville. You're going to catch John Bowers for us."

"No!" She lunged at him again, straining her bonds until she tore her flesh.

Brinkman stepped back. He laughed when she landed facedown at his feet. "If I weren't such a gentleman, I'd give you a swift kick to teach you some manners. Now get up, you wildcat. We've got to ride."

Moaning out her frustrated rage, Lisa moved to the strawberry roan he had tied to a tree. Untying her ankles, he gave her a leg up to the stirrup. Her skirts lay around her in a jumble when she found a seat in the saddle, and she could not do anything to fix them. "I'm not exactly dressed for an afternoon ride," she called angrily as he mounted the bay.

He did not bother to answer. Looping the reins of her horse to his saddle, he set off at a canter.

⌒

Less than a day's ride ahead of Lisa and her captor, John and Banjo rode into Laramie shortly before sundown of their second day on the trail. A booming metropolis compared to Juniper Junction, Laramie was a hub for soldiers, pioneers, and merchants. It had several wide streets and two private schools—one Baptist and one Catholic. A blacksmith's rhythmic hammering and tinny saloon music sounded above the rumble of wagons and clopping of horses in the street.

The men tied their horses in front of the stage station, a squat building with tiny windows and a bench leaning against the outside wall. Above the door a tiny sign said simply, STAGE.

Seated at a low table with a long cash box on one side, the attendant—an obese man with a greasy face and red stubble on his three chins—looked up when they walked in. "Howdy, gentlemen," he wheezed. "Have a seat."

Hats in hand, Banjo and John sat in wooden chairs in front of the table, the only furniture in the room.

The stench of the man's unwashed body was stifling. Banjo spoke first. "We're looking for a man who came through here about six weeks ago, a sheriff named Rod Feiklin."

The fat man pressed an arm against the table and stretched out a leg so he could lean forward. "Never heard of him. Lots of men come through here. I can't remember all of them."

"Feiklin stands about five feet eight, weighs over two hundred pounds."

The attendant chuckled deep in his chest. "A little guy, huh?"

"He's about fifty years old and has a big red nose," Banjo went on. "He would have been wearing his tin star."

Impatient to get back into the fresh air, John tapped his fingers against his knee while the big man considered.

"Come to think of it, maybe he did come through here." His eyes folded into half-moons as he squinted at the ceiling. "He bought a ticket for Silverville, I think it was. Impatient as all get out, he was. He acted like I could make the northbound stage leave the following day instead of at its usual time on Wednesday."

"Thanks for your help," Banjo said, standing to shake hands.

"Anytime," he replied, shaking hands with John next. "Pardon me if I don't stand up. Bad knees."

John and Banjo paused outside the door, settled their hats above their ears, and paced down the dusty street, nearly deserted this late in the day. Across from the bank, a three-story house had the roof and sides on, but the empty windows and doors showed an unfinished shell.

"I wonder whose mansion that is," John said, pausing for a closer look. "It's got to be the biggest house in Laramie. Going up fast, too. I didn't notice it the last time I was here." He walked on. "There's no sense leaving right at dark. We may as well take advantage of being in town." He stopped beside the street and looked both ways. Pointing to a restaurant, a bathhouse, and a hotel, he said, "I only want three things—a six-inch steak, a hot bath, and a soft bed."

Banjo chuckled. "You and I'll get along just fine. Lead the way."

Five minutes later they ducked through the low doorway of Sal's Kitchen to trade their money for what their empty stomachs were crying for.

⁓

The next morning when he awakened, John's head had a pounding pain so fierce that he could not eat breakfast.

"We'll stay here a day," Banjo said, staring down at his friend on the narrow bed. There was a decisive note in Banjo's voice.

"I can ride," John insisted weakly, his eyes closed.

Banjo chuckled. "You can't hardly lift your head." He drew a chair near the window. "Lie still and catch about eighty winks. Then we'll talk about riding."

The next thing John knew the sun was setting on the horizon. His head felt some better, but the hour was too late to head out. After another steak-and-potato meal, he took a long soak in a galvanized tub of steaming water and fell into bed for six more hours of oblivion.

Well before dawn, the two men were already five miles out of Laramie and heading due north. A chill wind blew down on them from the mountain peaks, causing them to turn up their collars and hunch their backs. The horses felt it, too, and eagerly picked up the pace.

By midmorning the temperature rose until John took off his coat and laid it across the saddle in front of him. He spotted a ten-point buck in the distance, a majestic shape against the darkness of a stand of fir trees.

"Looky there," he breathed to Banjo, pointing.

The old-timer nodded. "Nice rack," he said. "I haven't seen one that big since sixty-eight down near San Antone. I was riding point for a cattle drive at the time and couldn't take off after that one either."

John grunted as the buck bounded into the trees. "There's more to life than having a big rack on your cabin wall."

"Yeah, like having a beautiful girl in your kitchen." He sent John a meaningful look and urged his donkey ahead.

Red around the ears, John grinned and fell in behind him.

The closer they drew to Silverville, the more tense John became. Fifty miles north of Laramie, he suddenly drew up, his face covered with sweat. "Hold on, Banjo," he called. "I need a breather."

Kelsey's head reached toward the sky as Banjo turned him back and rode close to John's mount. "What's wrong? You sick?"

John lifted his blue bandanna to wipe his face. "I don't think so. All of a sudden I felt like someone dumped a cold bucket of water over me." He took off his hat and ran shaky fingers through his hair.

Banjo scanned the area. "That rock face over yonder looks like a likely spot for a cave. Let's take a look. It's late enough; we may as well camp." He urged the donkey forward.

John slowly followed. A cave was exactly what he did not want to find. The thought of sleeping in a black hole made his face tingle and his stomach feel tight.

Unaware of John's agitation, Banjo moved along the side of the flat-topped orange boulder. "Nothing here," he said in a moment. "Maybe on the other side."

"Forget it," John croaked.

"What?"

"I'm not sleeping in a cave. I'll sleep in the open first."

Banjo cocked his head, studying the younger man's ashen face. "What's gotten into you, boy?"

"I don't know. But I'm not sleeping anywhere closed in like that."

Without further comment, Banjo found four beech saplings close together and tied a corner of his massive poncho to each, forming a makeshift roof to cover their bedrolls. "If it rains hard, we'll still get soaked to the hide," he said, "but it's better than nothing, I guess."

Moving slowly, John took the saddle off Molasses and let him roll in the grass. He dropped his gear under the poncho and sat down to lean against his saddle and hold his head in both hands. He felt like the sky was a top, spinning round and round above him.

Banjo knelt next to him. "Say, you are sick. I hope we didn't jump the gun and leave the ranch before you were ready."

"No," he shook his head like a drunken man. "It's not that. It's my mind. All of a sudden everything went out of kilter." He looked across the meadow beside them, intent, watchful. "Something happened here. Something bad."

"This is the middle of nowhere. What could have happened?"

John's face turned red. He shouted, "If I knew that, I wouldn't be in this shape, would I?"

Banjo drew his face back and squinted at John. "Where did that come from?"

"Just leave me alone for a while, will you?" he said gruffly. He slid down until his head rested against the saddle. Turning on his side, he drew his knees toward his chin and closed his eyes.

Chapter 13

When John awoke, darkness had fallen. A tiny glow to the right showed him the source of a wonderful smell: camp stew. Pulling his feet under him, he stood and shambled to the fire where Banjo sat with his back against a log, whittling at a stick.

The old man looked up when John reached the light. "Well, howdy. Feeling any better?"

John sank to the ground and rubbed his face. "To tell the truth, I'm not sure how I feel. It's sort of a cross between getting back on a horse after you've been throwed and working up the nerve to ask a girl to a church social. Kind of excited and terrified at the same time." He glanced at Banjo. "I'm sorry I got so rough with you awhile ago. I don't know what came over me."

"Don't fret yourself, son. You've been under a lot of strain." Handing him a bowl of beef and potatoes in thick broth, he said, "I scouted around some while you were asleep. It looks like there's been quite a bit of traffic over yonder on the other side of that big rock. Not a trail exactly, but a lot of riders coming and going." He picked up his own bowl and lifted his spoon. "Come morning, I'll branch further out."

The stew tasted salty. John savored each bite. "We're at least twenty miles south of Silverville."

Banjo nodded. "The stage comes along here if I'm not mistaken."

"That's right. The only trail from Laramie to Deadwood is just across that rise. That's the same stage the sheriff was riding on his way to fetch Lisa."

"Is that a coincidence or a clue?" Banjo asked. He poured himself a second cup of coffee and held out the pot to refill John's cup. "I wonder when the next stage is due."

"That's one question I can't answer." John turned his attention to the food and finished the stew. "Did you find any water close by?" he asked when his plate was scraped clean.

"About fifty feet over yonder." Banjo pointed with his chin. "It's too dark to see to the dishes now. We'll catch them in the morning."

John handed the plate to Banjo and aimed through the brush toward the stream, finding his way by moonlight and sheer instinct. When his toes sank into damp earth, he sank to his haunches and felt ahead of him until his hand splashed into cool water. Leaning forward, he washed his face then cupped his hands and drank deeply.

An owl hooted and John looked upward. A crescent of bright moon shone behind the dark web formation of cottonwood branches intertwined with pine. In a moment he bent and drank again.

Back at the campfire, he told Banjo, "I'm tuckered. See you in the morning." He untied his bedroll from the cantle, lay down, and immediately sank into deep sleep.

⌒

"I think we should change our tactics from here on," Banjo told John the next morning while they ate the last of Megan's cold biscuits for breakfast. "We've got to start playing like Injuns. I'm not a spooky man, but something about this situation gives me the by-jimminies. I couldn't sleep last night. I kept waiting for a bogey man to jump outta the bushes."

John didn't know whether to laugh or not. "Are you joshing me?"

"I'm dead serious, son. Something evil's around here."

John swallowed hard. "I sure am glad you came along. If I were alone, I'd probably be hiding with my tail curled up between my ears." He shook his head, disgusted.

"You've got just as much grit as the next man," Banjo said gruffly. "Whatever's got you buffaloed, it's more than just a little nick on the skull." His bushy eyebrows twitched. "If you're too stubborn to believe that, you've got your head in the sand and the wrong part of you is sticking up."

Grinning, John reached up to adjust his hat. "I'm not sure if that makes me feel better or worse." He cleared his throat. "What makes you so sure you know what's going on inside my brain?"

"If I was a woman," he said, chuckling, "I'd call it intuition. Since I'm not, you can choose whatever name you want."

Swallowing the last crumb of his breakfast, Banjo reached for his saddle. John did likewise. Keeping their mounts single file, they stayed close to the flat-topped boulder.

"Here's the spot I was talking about," Banjo said, kicking his boots from the stirrups and swinging down. "Lots of traffic but no real trail. Does anything about this place ring a bell with you?"

John paused in the saddle to take in his surroundings. They stood in the middle of a dusty stretch behind some trees with hills rolling away to the east, the boulder south of them now. Below them, a rutted trail wound away to disappear in the distance. Dropping to the ground, he squatted next to Banjo to study horseshoe prints scuffling the dirt.

"These are two, maybe three days old," Banjo said. "See how the edges are blown away? None of them are sharp anymore."

Circling slowly, scanning the area, John froze for an instant, then leaned forward until his face was a foot from the ground. "Look at this one," he said, pointing to a horseshoe print with a V notched on one end. "I know that horse."

"Who owns it?"

He looked at Banjo, shocked. "I do."

The old-timer knocked his hat to the back of his head. "You don't say."

"I had three horses when I came to town that day—Molasses, Ginger, and. . . Sally." He spoke slowly as though pulling the words from deep inside a barrel, leaning over to grasp each one. "Sally's a black with a white chest and one stocking. I bought her for thirty dollars from a stranger in Sundance. He wanted the money to stay in a poker game."

He reached over to touch the print. It crumbled.

His gaze sweeping the ground, Banjo swung north looking for more prints. "There's another one, heading northeast. Let's see where they lead."

Stopping often, they inched along until noon. At one o'clock the trail died.

"Wouldn't you know it?" John said, his voice showing frustration. "We're finally getting somewhere and—poof—they disappear like someone in a side-show act."

Banjo rubbed his jaw. "They must have taken the main trail for a ways. We can take it, too, and see where they turned off."

John massaged his sinking stomach. "How about some grub first?"

The old-timer grinned and reached for his saddlebag. "Today's menu is beef jerky with jerky for dessert." He threw a strip to John, bit off a chunk of his own piece, and stuck the rest in his pocket.

Keeping an eye out for other riders, they rode north on the trail for almost a mile. Finally, John said, "I hate to admit it, but my head feels like a blacksmith's anvil on horseshoein' day. Can we find some shade and rest for a while?"

Banjo squinted at the sky. "I'd say we're about an hour away from suppertime. I'll stir us up some flapjacks and fry some more bacon."

"Sold," John said. He pointed toward a stand of piñon pine to the northeast. "How about there?"

Trotting easy, they entered the trees and soon found a narrow stream just deep enough to fill a coffeepot without letting in sand with the water. Banjo led Kelsey across the stream and staked him where he could drink and find grass.

Knowing how Molasses loved an open space to stretch, John let the horse drink then unsaddled him and let him roll in the grassy meadow for a while. He would stake him later.

John gathered sticks and built a fire while Banjo dug the makings of supper from his saddle. The cowhand ambled to the stream with a cup and his cooking pot turned mixing bowl.

Two minutes later John heard a boot snap a twig behind him. He whirled, gun in hand, and found himself between three men—one tall and fleshy, one scrawny, and one short. Each held a Winchester, his face hard, his eyes flat.

The blood rushed to John's temples. For an instant he thought he would pass out.

"Stand up, partner," the smallest man said in a shrill, harsh voice. Shorter than the others by at least five inches, he seemed to be the leader. "Drop your hogleg, and we won't put a bullet in you."

"Yet," the slim man on the left muttered, his face tilted back, his expression taunting.

"Wh–what do you want?" John stammered.

"We want you," Shorty said. "Come along peaceful-like, and you won't get hurt."

"Where's your saddle?" the third man asked. He had bristly brown hair and a long, puffy face with a bearlike body to match.

"Yonder by that pine tree." John kept his eyes away from the area where he had last seen Banjo, hoping the men had not spotted him.

Hairy arms big as ham hocks lifted the saddle while the slim man caught Molasses and brought him in.

John stood like a statue, praying that Banjo would not stumble into the hornet's nest that had suddenly swarmed around him.

"Tie him up, Ben," the leader shrilled. The big man pulled a piggin'-string from John's saddle and lumbered toward him, a mean smile showing the wide gap between his front teeth.

"Welcome to the Sandusky operation, mister."

Those words sparked across John's brain in a flash of white light. He saw the rawhide tightening around his wrist, smelled the foul odor of the man binding him. Suddenly, a rush of violent emotions and soul-crushing memories took away his breath. The next instant, the world spun, and everything went dark.

Unaware of his friend's predicament, Banjo knelt by the stream and stirred his flapjack batter. A moment later he dipped up more water to add to his pot, moving in practiced silence. He never made noise in the woods. Long years of living by his wits, in a land filled with renegades and outlaws, had made the habit a vital part of his life.

Moving his spoon through the pale yellow mass, he added a few more drops of liquid and suddenly stiffened.

Men's voices drifted toward him, the words unintelligible. Who had come into camp? Setting down the pot, he crouched lower into the bushes, setting down his feet with special care.

He eased back down the trail toward camp and dropped to his belly when he heard a shrill voice say, "Tie him up." The camp came into view as John collapsed on the ground.

"Put the bag on his head," the short fellow said, "in case he wakes up before we get there."

"This guy looks familiar, Andy," the slim man said, glancing at the leader.

"Al's right," the bruiser panted, raising John's limp body to his shoulder like he was a sack of grain. "This guy looks like the man we're hunting. Some luck, huh? Finding him like this?"

The small man holstered his gun. "Tie him to his saddle, Ben. We'll deliver him to Hogan before we put him on a team. He may have sent Gil on a wild-goose chase."

Al hooted. "Hogan never makes mistakes. You know that." They all laughed, a harsh, mocking sound.

"In his dreams," Ben added.

Banjo eased back to the stream. Out of sight, he crossed the water and grabbed Kelsey's reins. The donkey made a rasping noise. Banjo clamped a hand over his nose and waited.

When he heard the sound of pounding hooves, he leapt into the saddle with surprising agility for his years, urged Kelsey across the stony stream, and held him to a slow walk on the trail.

He reached the clearing in time to see four horses disappear into the trees on the other side of the meadow. A big man held Molasses's reins and did not seem to notice that John's head sagged hard to one side of his saddle.

Banjo circled the clearing at a trot and followed them a few yards to the right of their trail, keeping track of them using his ears instead of his eyes.

When they reached another clearing, he again veered right to stay within the trees. He didn't intend to catch up to three armed men for a showdown. He would wait until they stopped and watch for a chance to split them up or catch them by surprise.

After three miles, Banjo ran out of good cover. He drew up under a wide cottonwood and watched his quarry ride into a small settlement. A long narrow building that looked like a bunkhouse stood on the east of the yard; a wide stable and corral on the south and a tiny clapboard house on the west all appeared gray in the late afternoon sun. He blinked and took a second look. The windows of the bunkhouse were all boarded over, as were a few on the house, as well. What was this? A deserted ranch? An outlaw hideout?

Leaving Kelsey under the tree, the old cowhand pulled his Sharps .56 from its scabbard and walked close enough to see sunlight reflecting in the remaining windowpanes of the house. He dropped to a belly crawl until he reached the last bit of scrub brush before the yard. There he froze.

Ten yards ahead of him a potbellied sentry wearing filthy mining garb and carrying a Henry rifle ambled from the bunkhouse to the main house and about-faced.

Moisture sprang up on Banjo's brow. This was a heap more than he had bargained for.

About that time, a troop of at least twenty men marched in single file from the north. Each man had a long rope around his left elbow, joining them together. Shoulders slumped, covered with grime, they kept their eyes on the ground in front of them as they trudged ahead.

Banjo squinted. What were they? Convicts? There was not a jail of any size from here to Laramie.

John Bowers was nowhere to be seen. Two of the four horses Banjo had trailed here had also disappeared. Easing his Colt from its holster, Banjo settled down for a long wait.

Chapter 14

Still a day's ride behind John, Lisa gritted her teeth against the pain that had become her constant companion. Her wrists had deep abrasions from the rawhide's constant friction against her soft skin. Old wounds from her initial ride over this rugged trail had reopened with searing vengeance so that contact with the saddle meant sheer anguish. This time she had neither witch hazel along to relieve her distress nor a sympathetic companion to give her time to rest.

Her pink dress lay in ragged tatters around her ankles, her crinolines torn beyond repair. She had not washed her face or combed her hair since the day she left her mother's house for that bogus picnic by the lake.

"We'll camp here," Chandler said, swinging down from his horse. He let Lisa stay in the saddle while he scouted around for sticks to build a fire. Chin resting on her chest, she stared straight ahead, her mind a muddle of agonizing sensations, her prayers mainly for the safety of a tall, sandy-haired man with calm blue eyes and a gentle touch.

A gruff voice broke through her stupor. "Okay, missy. Time to light and set." The deep mellow tones he had used in Juniper had disappeared altogether. The real Chandler Brinkman—known to his friends as Gil Harris—was no gentleman.

He tugged at her elbow, and she slumped to the ground. Her legs were nothing but twin pillars of pain. Pulling her up by the shoulders, he half-carried her to a nearby pine and set her down beside it. "No sense tying you up anymore," he mumbled. "You can't run no way."

Lisa leaned against the rough bark and let her eyes drift closed. If only she was just pretending that her legs wouldn't work. If only she could run like the wind and lose herself in the woods, where the breezes flowed cool and soft and there was plenty of water rushing down from the mountains.

Gil pulled a greasy paper filled with salted meat from his pack and sliced off a couple of thick slabs with a dirty pocketknife. The evening after they had left Juniper, he had carefully packed away his tan suit and changed into greasy overalls and a flannel shirt with a hole in the elbow. His white hat he slipped into a cloth bag and tied behind his saddle, exchanging it for a flat-crowned hat the color of mud. The transformation was miraculous. Gil had missed his calling. He could have starred in a traveling drama troupe.

The smell of frying meat brought Lisa to full awareness. Her mouth tingled at the aroma rising from that dented skillet. Her last full meal had been breakfast the morning before her capture.

Gil pulled her tin of cookies from his pack and popped off the lid. He glanced at Lisa. "Here, have some supper," he said, tossing two of them onto her soiled dress.

Pulling her legs around, she winced and swallowed hard. "Could I have some water?" Her voice was raspy and weak. She felt almost surprised at the sound of it.

Gil nodded absently and lifted his canteen by its canvas strap. He stood briefly to swing it over beside her and resumed his cooking.

Licking her lips, Lisa stretched her bound hands toward the canteen and lifted it, unscrewed the metal cap, and raised it, shaking, to her mouth. The tepid liquid trickled across her tongue and down her dry throat. She gulped greedily.

"Hey!" Gil jerked the canteen away from her, jarring her teeth. "You'll get yourself sick drinking that way." He picked up the cap where it dangled from a tiny chain around the canteen's neck and screwed it on.

Revived somewhat by the water, Lisa held the cookies and stared into the fire. She had been on the trail for four days. It seemed an eternity. In the saddle before sunup, riding until dusk with no midday break. How much more could she stand?

"How long until we get there?" she asked suddenly, her voice cutting through the noise of crickets and cicadas stirring in the night.

Gil waited to finish chewing his bacon before he said, "We'll be there tomorrow night. Probably after dark." He grinned, his teeth gleaming in the firelight. "Just think, you may be able to sleep on a real bed." He chuckled as though he had just told some kind of private joke.

Ignoring him, Lisa ate the first molasses cookie with the haste of dire hunger. The second she consumed in small bites as though savoring it would unwind the knot in her stomach. She had no hopes that Gil would share his meat with her. He hadn't thus far. Why would he change now?

The pins holding up her hair had fallen out two days ago, leaving two prickly braids that brushed her neck and caused constant irritation. When one of them caught on the tree bark, she reached back and pulled it forward, snapping the thread at the bottom and combing it out with her fingers. Soon the second braid also lay loose about her shoulders.

She raked her hands across her scalp, pulling out leaves and twigs and longing for a hot tub of water and a cake of Octagon soap. Her first chance, she would get some of the expensive, scented soap that Harper kept under the counter for his special customers.

Gil unrolled his blanket near the fire. As talkative as he had been at the Feiklin house, he wasted few words on his captive. Picking up a strip of leather from his pack, he came toward Lisa and knelt before her, his hands nimbly working the strap around her ankles. "Just in case you recover your strength after that hearty supper." He paused long enough for a mocking smile. "Sleep well, little princess."

Lisa clenched her hands, fighting the urge to strike at his grinning face. The last time she hit him, he hadn't given her a drink for half a day.

Sensing her desire to lash at him, he chuckled as he stood and walked away.

Pulling her hair over her shoulder to keep it out of the dirt, Lisa lay on her side on the hard earth. Her eyes closed and weary tears sprang from their corners. *John,* she cried in her heart, *where are you?*

John woke up to find himself strapped to a wooden chair in the middle of a bare room with the windows boarded over. A glimmer of light came under the door, and some men argued in the next room.

"I say we kill him!" Andy said.

A calm, well-modulated voice replied, "Why didn't you do it when you found him then?"

"We wanted to see what you thought first, boss," Al replied.

Andy added, "He's already escaped once. Why should we give him another chance?"

"Because we're short of men. We lost three more this morning." The head man paused. "I agree that he must be disposed of, but we can put him to use while we do it. Give him half rations and put him on the digging crew."

Squinting, John stared into a black corner, memories washing over him. He had come to town with twenty beeves to sell in order to buy spring supplies. At Silverville, he had made the sale, filled his pack saddles, and gone on his way. Ten miles south of town, the same three men had kidnapped him and brought him here.

Over several weeks, he had taken gold nuggets from his digging and dropped them down his shirt. With the help of several other prisoners, he had escaped during the weekly camp cleanup. Through sheer brass and dumb luck, he had retrieved two of his horses and his pack before he fled.

Twenty minutes out of camp, someone had come galloping after him on a palomino with plenty of bottom. There had been a mad chase covering five miles with several shots fired at him. John headed for Silverville, hoping to get some help. That is when he must have been wounded, because the next thing he remembered was waking up at Lisa's cabin.

The door to the dark room flung back, and a bulky figure appeared shadowed in the light from the next room. "Okay, Bowers. We're taking you to the bunkhouse. You're lucky. You can have your old cot back. The guy who got it after you just kicked the bucket."

From behind him Ben tugged at the straps that bound John's arms to the chair, then pulled his hands toward his back and tied them together. "On your feet now."

Feeling dizzy, John hesitated and got a slap on the side of his head.

"I said, on your feet!"

Blinking, John staggered after his tormentor to a door at the back of the room and found himself outside in the moonlight. He stumbled once, then ducked to avoid a second blow.

In the yard the fat sentry paused to watch them cross. Rattling a key in the lock, Ben flung back the door of the bunkhouse, shoved his prisoner inside, and slammed it shut again.

Squinting to see through the dull glow of a single lantern hanging from the ceiling, John leaned back against the rough-hewn door. Swallowing, he fought back a rush of despair. After all he had been through, to end up where he had started. How could he bear it and keep his sanity?

Someone pulled at the rope on his hands, and it came loose. John rubbed his wrists. Before him stood two rows of bunks with a center aisle the width of a broom handle. Hollow-eyed faces covered with whiskers and a thick coating of dust stared at him, waiting for him to move or speak.

"Hey, John!" A dull voice came from his left, about halfway down the row. "Over here. It's me, Charlie. You can have the bunk next to mine again."

"Charlie Randolph?" Like a man in a nightmare, John lurched down the center aisle, touching each bunk for support as he passed. He licked his thick lips. "Charlie, I need a drink."

"Get him a drink," someone called from the end of the line. A gray-whiskered man with skeletal cheekbones came toward him with a tin cup clenched in a wavering hand.

John emptied the cup in three gulps and handed it back. "Thanks." He met Charlie at the next bed.

"Welcome home," his friend said with a poor attempt at a smile. "We've been lonesome around here without you."

John placed his palms on the top bunk beside Charlie but was still too shaky to heave himself up. Hands reached out to help him.

When he lay back on the bare mattress, Charlie's gaunt face came toward him, his nose like an eagle's beak. "John? What happened to you, boy? I thought you were going to get us some help."

"They followed me out of here and put a bullet in my head. It only creased me, but I lost my memory. I couldn't remember where I'd come from or why." He scanned the anxious faces surrounding him. "I'm sorry, men. I let you down."

"How's your head?" Charlie asked.

John touched his temple, suddenly aware that he had lost his hat. "It's a mite touchy. I still get powerful headaches sometimes, but I'll live, I reckon."

"Not if you stay here too long," a slow voice drawled from somewhere in the back of the crowd.

"How'd you get caught?" someone asked from the darkness.

"I met a girl."

Somebody whistled. Another man gave a low hoot.

When the noise died down, he said, "Her father's missing. I came to look for him."

Charlie asked, "What's his name?"

"Rod Feiklin. He's a sheriff."

"Hey, Feiklin," Charlie hollered. "John here's been a-lookin' for ya."

John rose on one elbow and tried to focus his eyes to see through the faint light. In a moment he saw a wide shadow that slowly formed into a man who had once been husky. He had a bulbous nose and thin, wispy hair. His jowls shook when he spoke.

"You've seen Lisa?" His voice had a firm resonance that came from somewhere around his knees.

"She's at home with your wife, Sheriff. I found her in Silverville and took her home to Juniper Junction."

"How's Sally?"

John hesitated. "She's taking it hard, your being gone and all. The girls are a mite worried, too."

Feiklin thumped a shaky hand against the wooden bunk. "We've got to bust out of here!" He glanced around. "Look at us, a bunch of tough men acting like kids afraid of a mean schoolmaster." He ran a trembling hand over his face. "God help us. We've got to get out."

John sat up. His head felt clearer than it had since he woke up. "Listen," he whispered, waving them closer. The men gathered near until he could feel their breath and smell their desperation. "I've got a friend on the outside, an ol' codger named Banjo."

"Hot diggety," Feiklin said, glancing around. "I know him. He's a salty old cowhand. He packs a Sharps .56 and always hits his target."

Muted excitement swept through the twenty men huddled close.

"We'll help all we can," Charlie said, "but we don't have much strength left. After another escape attempt last week, they cut our rations again." He ran a trembling hand over his spiky hair. "That Gil knows a dozen different ways to kill a man."

John grunted. "So do I. After the first time." His voice grew stronger. "We'll need some kind of weapons."

"Let's break apart one set of bunks to use for clubs," Feiklin said. "If Banjo doesn't make his move tonight, a couple of us can double up, small guys like Peterson and Smithy, until he does. This place is like a fortress. Banjo may need to size up the territory before he makes his move. He can't see much in the dark."

Several of the bigger men began tugging at the last bunk near the back wall. Five minutes later, the splintering of wood told of their progress.

Lying on his back, John closed his eyes. Banjo had better be out there. If not, they were sunk.

Chapter 15

After the initial excitement died down, the men returned to their bunks wide-eyed and waiting until, one by one, they fell into troubled sleep. John lay awake until dawn. Now that he knew what he was afraid of, his fear had turned from sheer, numbing terror into a galvanizing dread that would give him the strength to fight back. He clenched and relaxed his right hand. It felt good. Almost the same as before he was injured.

He must have dozed. When the front door slammed, he sat up, blinking and dazed. Harsh sunlight streamed in for an instant before a big man stepped through.

"All right, on your feet! File out for the grub line!" It was Ben with a wicked gleam in his slow-moving eyes.

Charlie nudged John. "Better move quick. Ben's looking for trouble this morning."

John slid his feet to the floor and stayed close behind his friend. When they reached the doorway, Ben stared at John. "Thought you'd run, did you? Well, look at you now. You ain't so all-fired smart."

Forcing his eyes to look straight ahead, John kept a lid on his temper. To lash out now would only make matters worse.

Standing at the steps to the main house, Al had a long-handled ladle in his hands beside a tall pot. The men filed toward him and waited while he slopped some kind of brown porridge into wooden bowls and handed them out.

When John reached him, he tipped the ladle and dumped most of its contents back into the pot. What landed in John's bowl would not fill three good-sized spoons. "Eat hearty," Al said, his lips pushed out, his eyes mocking.

Following the others across the yard to lean against the outer wall of the bunkhouse, John glanced furtively around, wondering if Banjo were there or not, wishing he knew a way to communicate with him.

Tipping up the bowl and raking porridge out with his fingers, Charlie eyed John's portion. He licked his fingers and said, "Here, take some of mine. You won't last two days on that kind of feed, you just wounded and all."

John covered his bowl with his hand. "Thanks, Charlie, but you need it more than I do."

A few minutes later, Al came along with the empty pot in his hands and each man dropped his bowl into it. When Al shambled back to the big house, they turned as one man to face the yard, each holding out his left arm. A hank of rope over his shoulder, Ben progressed down the line, binding elbows with the smooth, quick movements born of long practice, and the group moved toward the northern rise.

John glanced back and saw Ben bringing up the rear, a long bullwhip in his hand.

At the top of the hill, he saw a small shanty three hundred yards ahead near the base of a mountain. A few yards away, a black, timber-outlined hole told why they were here. The Sandusky Mine, the richest strike since the Comstock Lode, lay just ahead.

A lanky man with a Winchester leaning on his shoulder unlocked the shanty and began throwing shovels and picks to the men. Grimly, without speaking, they trudged ahead into the gaping mouth of a living death—no light and no breeze to cool their sweaty faces and brighten their weary minds.

At the entrance to the cave, John stiffened. The old, nameless terror came at him with a rush. His feet froze in his boots. He could not move.

"You there!" Ben bawled. "Get on in there." He cracked the whip.

"John!" Charlie said, shaking his arm. "Snap out of it."

White and shaking, John drew in two deep breaths and rolled his head from side to side, like an angry bear. Finally, he lifted his right foot and stepped inside. When he felt the darkness swallow him whole, he broke into a sweat. "I can't go on," he murmured. "I can't."

Feiklin stepped back two paces and paused beside him. "What's the trouble?"

"I can't stand closed-in places," John said. "Never could. I've got to get out. I can't breathe."

Feiklin jerked him around. "Get a grip on yourself, boy! You've got to go ahead. If you go back outside, they'll kill you, sure."

John swallowed. "It was bad when I was here before, but this time I can't make it. I feel like my chest's caving in."

"What about us?" Charlie demanded. "You're the only one strong enough to attempt another escape." He grabbed and shook John's wounded shoulder.

The pain shocked John out of his panic. Drawing in a loose-lipped breath, he knocked Charlie's hand away. "Okay. I'm all right. Let's go." Letting his mind go blank, he found his place in the row of men digging at the end of the tunnel. Moving in rhythm, he worked the stiffness out of his shoulder until he hardly felt any pain at all.

⁓

The sun's final rays flickered above the horizon as Banjo watched Ben hustle John across the yard and lock him into the bunkhouse.

When the last light of day disappeared, so did Banjo's hope of getting John out before tomorrow. Moving in darkness was difficult when a body knew where he was headed. Trying such a feat on new ground was nothing short of foolhardy.

Edging back to Kelsey, he turned the donkey away and rode for half a mile to a thick forest that sloped down into a lush valley. Within the safety of dense darkness among the pines and junipers, Banjo spread out his blankets and slept for six hours.

Morning light found him back at the camp with his shirtfront dug into the dirt, watching for signs of life. He kept his position when the men filed out for breakfast and when they headed off for parts unknown in the north.

Still on foot, he circled wide, out of sight of the camp. He came closer on the north side until he stopped, his target in view—a mine with men swarming over it like so many ants and armed guards out front, one of them with a bullwhip.

Lying flat in the dust until noon, he pulled some jerky from his pocket and sipped water from his warm canteen, ignoring the soft rumble of his neglected stomach. The workers before him did not slacken their pace for the noon hour or the supper hour either. As twilight approached, they plodded back to camp. Banjo stayed behind them long enough to see the guard click a large padlock on the shanty and turn his duties over to another man.

Banjo reached the shelter of his lookout post near the yard just in time to see the last few prisoners drop their empty bowls into Al's pot. They then proceeded wearily into their bunkhouse prison. Now that he knew the routine and the lay of the land, a plan took shape in his mind—fairly simple, but with the Lord's help, it just might work.

While Banjo watched, a husky guard paced from the clapboard house to the makeshift jail, his Henry rifle aimed at the ground. He turned and retraced his steps, taking his time as twilight turned to dusk. A full moon, already high in the sky, gave an eerie cast to the landscape, where shadows covered the hollows and moonbeams made white stones glow.

While the guard's back was to him, Banjo left the security of his bush and, bent over at the waist, ran for a depression near the bunkhouse. Holding his Sharps away from his body, he flung himself down, pulled off his hat, and raised his head enough to get a look at the guard.

In the center of the yard, the sentry suddenly stopped. He turned full circle, peering through the moonlight as though he could feel Banjo's stare from the shadows. Finally, he stretched his arms wide, arched his back, and loudly yawned. He shifted the Henry to his shoulder and continued his rounds.

Easing his legs to a more comfortable position in the shallow ditch, Banjo hunkered down, watching for a chance to overcome the guard.

Two men stepped out of the house, one wide and tall, the other slim. They paused to speak to the sentry, then mounted and rode out, passing ten yards from where Banjo lay.

Time was running out. That guard would need a replacement soon.

Tense as a bowstring, Banjo felt around on the ground for a fist-sized stone and waited, his breath keeping pace with the guard's footsteps. At the bunkhouse door, the man turned. He was humming "Old Susanna."

Three paces later Banjo sprang like a cougar after a rabbit. The guard collapsed. Pulling him close to the back side of the bunkhouse, Banjo dug a couple of rawhide strings from his pocket and tied him, hand and foot. He stuffed a dusty bandanna into his mouth for good measure.

Returning to the ditch for his rifle and hat, Banjo circled wide to the north.

Across the rise, he squatted behind a cedar tree and saw the dim form of the small tin-roofed shanty near the mouth of the mine. He hesitated, his ears alert for a human sound. There it was. The soft grating of boots on earth.

When the lanky guard reached the back of the shanty, Banjo hoofed it to the next patch of brush. He played the game until he was close enough to hear the man's gentle cough and make out the outline of his Montana Slope Stetson against the sky.

Inching forward another three feet, he crouched behind a boulder that reached to his chest, waiting for just the right moment to spring.

"Say, Tom!" a shrill voice shouted from the darkness.

Banjo jerked like he had been struck. He huddled close to the rock, his face peeking around the side of its cool surface.

A short, slim man's form strode over the rise. "Got any rolled cigarettes with you?"

"Yeah." Tom propped his rifle against the shanty while he held the bottom of the pocket and pulled a package out with his other hand. He dug a forefinger into it. "Here's one." He held it out. "That makes four you owe me. Ask Roger next time."

Grabbing the cigarette from the guard's hand, the man headed back without saying so much as a thank-you.

Banjo closed his eyes and prayed. On his way back to the main house, would the borrower notice the absence of the other guard? A moment later the door to the house slammed, and Banjo let himself breathe a little.

Tom shook his head at his friend's rudeness, then hunched over with his hands cupped around a flaming match to light a smoke for himself. He stood about six feet from Banjo, facing away.

The old man came to his feet and reversed his hold on his Sharps rifle. Swinging it by the barrel, he caught the man on the side of the head with a thunk that sounded like a melon falling off a wagon.

The guard tumbled sideways and lay still, the match flung harmlessly away. Banjo picked up the man's Winchester and propped it against the rock beside his Sharps. He took the revolvers from both of Tom's holsters and stuffed them behind his own waistband.

Taking hold under Tom's arms, Banjo dragged him about two wagon lengths to the left and into the mine entrance, his boots making twin trails in the earth.

Banjo pulled off the man's belt and boots, looping the belt around the guard's knees and pulling it tight. Then he folded back the strap of leather and tucked under the end—not hard to loosen once the man came around, but he wouldn't be doing any running with his legs asleep.

Returning to the shanty, Banjo used a large stone to hit the padlock and knock it loose. He scraped a match on the corner of his boot sole, and raised it high to see what the storage room held.

Against the back wall stood six crates marked "Dynamite." Three tall cans of kerosene were nearby. Against the left wall hung several tools: hammers, a wide crosscut saw, a small handsaw, crowbars, and a length of rope. Below them lay two dozen shovels and several pickaxes. Two stacks of dented, galvanized buckets almost reached the ceiling on the right.

The match went out, and Banjo stood in the dark, his mind cataloguing the items he had just seen. This was the hand he had been dealt. Now how was he going to play it?

Pulling out his knife, he cut off a length of rope and returned to the mine to tie the hands of the unconscious guard.

Fifteen minutes later, he made another wide circle around the compound. This time the bunkhouse was his objective. Besides the two rifles, he carried a coil of rope and three pickaxes, which made quiet movement a challenge.

The moon shone too brightly for Banjo's comfort. A gentle breeze felt damp against his face. Now that both hands were occupied, his nose began itching like mad. He raised one shoulder and bent his face toward it. Not very satisfactory, but that would have to do for now.

The sound of two horses approaching from the south sent Banjo down on his belly. He lay in a shallow depression in the darkness, his Sharps tight in his right hand, the other weapons close by on the ground. One of the Colts in his waistband gouged into his stomach. He reached under his shirt to adjust it.

The horses halted across the yard near the main house where the light splashed from a window. One of the riders dismounted. He walked around his horse, out of sight. A few minutes later he reappeared, his arm around the shoulder of a smaller companion who seemed to have trouble walking.

The door opened, flooding them with light as they moved inside. Banjo blinked. He would know that long wavy hair anywhere. The small rider was Lisa Feiklin.

Banjo lay there for a full five minutes without moving. He had known the same sensation as a boy when he fell off a tree limb and landed flat on his back. Like then, he had to take a few minutes to catch his breath.

What was Lisa doing here of all places?

Loud angry voices came from an open window in the main house. "Why did you bring her here? We've already got Bowers. You know what they do to a man who hurts a woman? Gil, your head is like a gourd, full of nothing but air."

"How was I to know you had him?"

"Whether we had him or not, you shouldn't have brought her here. We can't just turn her loose now, can we? Ever think of that?" A door slammed and the conversation cut off.

His face grim, Banjo rose to a crouching walk and approached the bunkhouse. He tapped lightly on the back door and prayed there was no guard posted inside. The Sharps held ready, his mild eyes continually scanned the grounds around him.

"Yeah?" a weak voice called.

Banjo backed up to the door and angled his mouth close to the splintery wood. "It's Banjo. I need to talk to John." He swallowed. Each second seemed like hours.

"Banjo?" John's low voice vibrated with hope. "Can you get us out?"

The old-timer spoke into a crack around the door frame. "I've got some weapons for you. The third window down from here has a crack in the boards big enough to pass a revolver through. I've got three here. I'm leaving a rifle and some picks by the back door, too."

He moved down and handed the weapons inside. Invisible fingers caught them. "John?" he whispered.

"I'm here."

"The minute you hear a big explosion, blast away at the lock to the back door, and everybody pile out. We'll meet south of here in the woods. I left Kelsey over there."

"What about horses?"

"When you pass the corral, take them with you. Tell the men to ride out like their tails are on fire. Then you meet me behind the house."

"What do you have in mind?"

"I just saw Lisa ride in with a big hombre. They've got her in the house."

"What!"

"Simmer down, boy. You'll be no good to me with your brain in a stew."

"Sheriff Feiklin's in here."

"Well, what do you know?" Banjo passed a hand over his leathery face. "I'd best be going. Get yourselves ready in there."

Familiar with the ground now, Banjo bent low and crab-walked through the darkness. The journey back to the supply shanty took less than fifteen minutes. Easing the door open, he lifted a can of kerosene and unscrewed the top.

A heady smell filled his nose and throat as he backed out of the door and off to the left thirty paces, letting the liquid slosh out of the can in an unbroken line. When he figured that he'd gone far enough, he hustled back to the doorway and lay the can on its side, in line with the damp streak at the door. Kerosene *glug-glugged* out.

Banjo scampered back toward the end of the line. Halfway there, the moon went behind a cloud, and he could not see the trail. He dropped to a crouch, his eyes squinting toward the heavens. In a moment the billowing mass of gray moved on and a beam of light shone down upon him.

The damp trail looked like a giant black snake. Banjo lit a match and dropped it on the reptile's head. With a whoosh and a flash, the fire zipped along the ground. Banjo raced to dive behind the boulder, his hands over his ears, his eyes squeezed tight.

Ka-boom!

Through his closed eyelids, he could see surging brilliance. He smelled the inferno, felt the heat. A few seconds later, bits of metal and wood fell around him.

Chapter 16

Inside the bunkhouse John blasted the lock on the back door the moment he heard the explosion. Three shots and the door swung free. Instantly, a wall of club-wielding men pressed forward, shoving John aside in their haste. When the last one passed him, John looked over to see Sheriff Feiklin beside him, a pistol in his hand.

"Let's go. Lisa's in trouble."

They stepped into the night, their eyes already accustomed to the gloom. Instead of heading for the corral, the mob in front of them ran toward the main house, shouting and waving their sticks.

"What are they doing?" John cried. "They're going to get killed. All of them."

"Let's go around back of the house," Feiklin said, stepping forward.

John caught his sleeve. The door to the house opened, and a tall man shoved Lisa outside ahead of him, a black ropelike noose looped around her neck. Behind him came two men with rifles aimed at the crowd.

"Come any closer and this little girl pays," the big man shouted.

John felt a physical stab in his middle. He stared at Lisa's form outlined in the door and recognized the object around her throat. A bullwhip.

That voice pulled up every nightmare that John had agonized through these past months. The man with the whip had Lisa.

Hidden by deep darkness beside the bunkhouse, John waited for his insides to quiver and melt. Instead, they pulled together into an iron knot. He cocked his pistol. "I'm going after him," he told the sheriff.

"She's my daughter," Feiklin wheezed. "You'll have to shoot me to keep me from coming along."

Turning, John ran on his toes until he reached the back of the bunkhouse. He found the empty ditch and dropped into it. Grunting, the sheriff landed beside him.

John whispered, "We'll crawl on our bellies until we get past those guys' line of sight, then we'll bust into the house the back way and surprise them."

"Just get me close to that man who has Lisa." Feiklin's voice was hard. "I'll take him with my bare hands."

John licked his lips and moved down the ditch. *Not if I get to him first.*

On the steps the two men with guns pressed forward. Andy shouted, "Throw down your weapons or somebody's going to die. Do it before I count five, or I'll shoot the closest man to me."

A few men threw down their clubs. The mob lost its heart and became a milling, confused crowd.

"Now get back into the bunkhouse. All of you." Andy started down the stairs as John rounded the corner of the house, heading toward the rear. With the sheriff breathing down his neck, he cocked his revolver and tried the back door. It was open.

The room inside was dark, but light from another area came through the doorway. Taking wide steps, John stepped across the bare pine floor and peeked around the doorjamb. The next room, a kitchen, stood empty as well.

Keeping close to the wall, John headed toward the front of the house. At the door to the sitting room, he stopped and stared at the back of a wide pair of overalls and a flat-crowned hat. He knew that man. It was Gil Harris, the cruelest of the gang.

In an instant, he stood behind Lisa's tormentor with his gun pointed at the man's neck. "Turn her loose."

Harris stiffened.

In one movement, he flung Lisa away from him and dropped into a squat. Moving like a frog, he bounced up, his shoulder knocking John sideways.

Clawing for a hold and finding none, John fell off the step, his gun flying out of his hand. The big man moved to the side of the step where the light spread out the door and onto the ground. The end of the long bullwhip flipped at the ground by the big man's ankles.

On his back, John looked up at the man in his nightmares—Gil's face hidden by the shadow of his hat.

"Whatsa matter, Bowers?" Gil asked. "You look a little down in the mouth." He chuckled and popped the whip. "It's about time you learned a lesson."

Using his heels, John scooted away and tried to roll out of his reach. Before he'd moved far, the whip caught him around the waist and spun him back.

From the place she had fallen, twenty feet away from him, Lisa screamed, "John!"

Gil let out a harsh laugh and pulled back for another lash.

Chest heaving, John watched the lithe movements of his opponent. *Get ahold of yourself, Bowers. Use your brain instead of your brawn.*

The second lash caught him across the chest, making him cough. Only two blows and he felt like his torso was on fire.

Bracing himself, John stayed still, his mind focusing on the movements of the other man. When Gil drew back for a third strike, John watched for the moment his arm began the arc downward.

The same instant, he raised his left arm high across his body. The whip caught him just below the elbow and wrapped three times around. When it was tight, John jerked with strength born of desperation. The whip flew from Gil's hand.

John flung the weapon away.

Though it seemed like a century since Gil had released Lisa, mere seconds had passed. Sheriff Feiklin and Banjo leapt from the shadows and got the drop on the two men pointing guns at the crowd.

John saw them, but Gil didn't notice. He jumped from the steps, intent on his prey.

"John!" Lisa called again, struggling to get up. "Watch out. He's the man who kidnapped me. He's brutal."

Lisa's words lit a fire in John's brain. He got to his feet.

"Whoa, there!" Banjo called. "We've got everything under control. There's no need to fight him, John."

"Let him come, Banjo," John said. "We've got something to settle here." Elbows bent, hands loosely clenched, he moved lightly on his feet, waiting for his chance.

"What do you think you're doing, Bowers?" Gil taunted, his fists high in front of his face, bearing down on John like a train engine. "You're yellow as a canary. You know you are."

John's senses tensed to an agonizing pitch—screaming for action. He lunged in as his fist came up and caught Gil just below the breastbone, a pile driver with every ounce of his strength in it.

The big man crumpled to his knees, his hands covering his belly, then fell on his side in the dirt.

"Don't count your canaries before they're hatched, Gil," he said, stepping back. He waited for his shoulder to ache, but the pain never came.

Turning toward the crowd, he searched for only one face. He saw her hair instead—a massive tangle with bits of twigs in it. She lay tight in her father's arms, her head pressed to his chest. She seemed to be sagging against him.

As John reached her, she said to her father, "I'm sorry I've caused so much trouble, Daddy. If anything had happened to you, I'd never forgive myself."

His voice unusually husky, he said, "When I was a youngster I had to learn my lessons the hard way. I reckon you're like your old dad." Bending down, he kissed her cheek.

John came near.

"Lisa, honey, I think someone wants to see you," Feiklin said.

She lifted a tear-blotched face and saw John. Sobbing, she held out her arms to him. He pulled her to him and realized that she was dead weight in his arms.

"What's wrong, Lisa?" he cried, swinging her up into his arms as though she were a small child. "What did he do to you?"

"He made me ride until my legs were raw and bleeding. He only had one bedroll, so I had to sleep on the ground. And he gave me hardly anything to eat." Bright tears glimmered in the light of the lantern. She tightened her arms around his neck. "I thought he was going to kill you."

Holding her close, John laid his cheek against hers, and she dampened them both with fresh tears.

The sheriff touched his daughter's hair. "I take it you kind of like this fellow."

Turning toward him, she nodded, a new glow on her face.

Sheriff Feiklin's slow grin made his jowls quiver. "I'm glad you finally learned what a real man looks like." He said to John, "Let's get these varmints to the closest jail and head home. I'm hankering for some of Sally's dried-apple pie."

They looked up to see Banjo stride out of the house with his Sharps pointed at a spectacled man wearing a black suit. "Hey, Feiklin," Banjo shouted. "Recognize this hombre? It's Patrick Hogan, from the assayer's office in Laramie. He weighed out my diggings many a time. He's the brains behind this two-bit outfit."

"Then those slimy brothers, Ben and Al Hardy, must have been the brawn." Lisa nodded toward the two as several of their previous captives shoved them into the center of the yard. A shiver of revulsion raced down Lisa's back as she recalled Ben Hardy's frequent invitations for an evening stroll during her weeks at the Silverville Restaurant.

Feiklin threw a length of rope to Charlie, hovering nearby. "Hog-tie 'em till we can deliver these rogues to the marshal in Silverville."

Charlie pulled the hemp tight between his fists and approached the unhappy outlaws. "It'll be a pleasure."

While the freed workers headed to the corral to find their horses, John pulled Lisa into the shadows beside the house and held her close. "I thought my heart would stop when I saw you here," he murmured. "I wanted to charge across the yard and knock Gil flat for daring to lay his filthy paws on you."

His lips met hers for a long moment. Then he spoke into her hair. "You haven't changed your mind about marrying me, have you?"

"Not a chance." Snuggled in his arms, she reached over for another velvet kiss. For the first time in her life, she knew exactly where she was meant to be.

"John?" Banjo called a few minutes later. "Where are you?"

Loosening his hold on his intended, John stepped into the light from the still-open door. "Here we are."

The old-timer strode toward them. "We're going to ride into Silverville to turn those hombres over to the law. Then we'll head south. Some of the men have already cut out for home." He glanced at Lisa and grinned. "For someone in such a misery, you sure do look happy." To John, he said, "I take it congratulations are proper?"

"Yes, sir." John's expression matched Lisa's.

Banjo chuckled. "I'd shake your hand, but both of them seem to be occupied." He turned back the way he had come. "It's time to mount up."

"How will I get back?" Lisa asked. "I can't ride anymore."

"You can sit sideways in front of my saddle. Silverville is only a few miles from here. Don't worry; I'll hold on to you." He gave her a little squeeze.

Lisa leaned her head closer to his ear. "While we're on the subject, there is one thing you've got to agree to before I'll stand before a preacher. Cross your heart."

He smiled into her eyes. "Anything your heart desires."

"Buy me a carriage. Once we get to Silverville, I'm not sitting on another horse for as long as I live."

Banjo's New Song

Chapter 1

Dust rose thick and warm toward the brilliant Colorado sky where two dozen men on horses and donkeys sashayed and swayed among a sea of bawling cattle in a wide canyon. It was August 4, 1875, and not yet eight o'clock in the morning, but these men had been working for nearly four hours. Although this was the first official day of the Juniper Junction roundup at the bottom of the foothills west of town, the men had been putting up corral fences and getting ready for nearly a week.

Joe Calahan—known to all as Banjo—laid a loop around the neck of a wild-eyed yearling and cinched it down. He urged the longhorn toward a smoldering fire manned by two men: his boss, Steven Chamberlin, and an extra hand Steve had hired for the roundup and cattle drive, an hombre with a gray beard.

In seconds Steve wrestled the yearling to the ground, tied his own rope on the steer's legs, and pulled Banjo's loop loose. Steve had been in the West for only four years, but he was a seasoned rancher now.

Winding up his lasso with automatic movements, Banjo squeezed his knees against his donkey's sides and urged him into the herd. That made fourteen brands for him this morning—not bad for the first few hours' work.

At noon the men gathered around the chuck wagon to pick up tin plates of beans and biscuits from Chance Calahan, a cook by trade and a farmer by choice. His wife, Em, basted a roasting cow on a spit nearby. Chance and Em were freed slaves who had chosen to take Banjo's last name when he led Chance to Christ.

"How's it goin', brother?" Banjo asked Chance, reaching for a loaded plate. He glanced at the mound of pinto beans. "This smells good enough to eat."

Chance's seamed face broke into an easy grin. "You can quit while you're ahead, Banjo," he said. "I've only got four dried apple pies, so sweet talking the cook won't help you."

"You're breaking my heart," Banjo shot back, moving on. He stepped beyond the chuck wagon, then turned and looked up as three riders approached. They were riding herd on two dozen cows. Their leader was small and wiry, a natural rider whose body moved in unison with his lively dun mustang. He wore tan buckskin breeches and a cowhide vest. The hands bunched the cattle near the edge of the canyon while their boss approached the chuck wagon.

Banjo balanced his plate on the tongue of the wagon and strode toward him, studying hard, trying to place him. Banjo knew most everybody in these parts, but he'd never met this gent. When Banjo drew near, the rider swung his leg over the saddle, slid down in a single lithe movement, and stepped toward him.

Banjo drew up and stared. That walk wasn't the usual cowboy stride. The next moment he gazed into a pair of wide-set blue eyes above high cheekbones and full, rounded lips. The rider was a woman. Her skin was tanned, and she'd seen some hard times, but she was striking. He blinked, trying not to stare but failing miserably.

His normal "howdy" died in his throat.

" 'Morning," she said, all business. "My name is Sally Newcomb. I'm looking for the Bar N outfit. Do you know my son, Jake?"

Banjo pulled off his stained Stetson and scratched the creased ridge at the back of his gray hair. "I reckon I do, ma'am," he said, still a little off balance. "I know your husband, too. What's happened to Mickey?"

She tensed. "He died in an accident last spring."

"I met him and your boy last year in Juniper. We ate a steak together at the hotel. I'm real sorry, ma'am."

She cut him off. "I need to find our outfit," she said. "On the way here we found some cows hiding in an arroyo, so we stopped to gather them up. Jake's probably worried to death because we're late."

Banjo turned north and pointed. "Head that away, and you'll come to him. When I saw him this morning, he was holding a branding iron. We swapped howdies yesterday, but he never mentioned your husband." Banjo glanced back at the eight Circle C hands gathered around the chuck wagon. "If you need more help, give a holler, and we'll cut someone loose."

"Thank you, Mr.—" For the first time, she looked into his eyes. Her gaze seemed to come from far away.

"My name's Banjo, and I'd be obliged if you didn't hang a mister on it."

She nodded. "I'm happy to know you, Banjo." She turned back to her horse. With another agile move, she slid into the saddle. "Thank you," she said, and her mount stepped away.

Banjo stood in his boot tracks, staring after her. He'd never seen anyone like her, and he'd been down the pike and up the river. Sure, many a widow kept going after her husband died, but this was the first time he'd seen one suited up like a cowhand and bulldogging cattle like a pro.

He turned back to the chuck wagon, paused, and glanced again at the dun mustang moving the cattle toward the north.

"What's the matter, Banjo?" a deep voice asked behind him. "You look like a calf staring at a new gate."

Banjo shook his head and adjusted his hat. "Steve, that was Sally Newcomb,

Mickey Newcomb's widow. She's ramrodding the Bar N, an outfit a couple of hours west of here. Looks like she's doing a fine job of it, too."

"You mean a widow's bulldogging for the roundup?" Steve stared after the mustang.

The men ambled back toward their food, and Banjo went on. "I met Mickey Newcomb last year. He'd been in this area about two years then. I've never seen his spread, but I hear it's a pretty place in the hills." The men reclaimed their dinner plates and found a place on the back of a nearby buckboard.

"Did she say what happened to her husband?" Steve asked, lifting a biscuit.

"An accident." Banjo forked beans into his mouth and chewed. He swallowed and said, "Mickey Newcomb was a good man—honest, hardworking, and all—but he was hardheaded as they come. Treated his son like he was a dumb houseboy."

"If you notice that Widow Newcomb needs help, we'll send Hank over for a few hours," Steve said.

"Right, boss," Banjo replied, grinning. "I already told her."

Steve laughed. "If you hadn't, I would have been surprised."

Banjo finished his lunch in silence, the Newcomb family still on his mind. Always on the alert for people in need, he had a gut feeling about that widow and her boy. Maybe the Lord wanted him to help them until they got on their feet again. He had a hankering to ride on up to the Bar N this fall and offer his services. Steve could get another hand for a couple of months before winter. Still distracted, he mounted his donkey, Kelsey, and went back to work.

The rest of the day passed in a dusty cloud of activity. Only darkness brought riders and ropers back to their campfires for a well-earned meal and rest. They had to be back in the saddle in seven short hours.

The next morning Banjo was on the job before the last twinkling star had vanished overhead. He felt good. Roundup was the highpoint of his year. He enjoyed it all: the bawling cattle, the dust and the heat, the jokes over a hot plate of beans.

Not long after dawn the next morning, he met Jake Newcomb while combing the dips and gullies for strays. About fifteen years old, Jake had been a boy when Banjo saw him last year, but he was a grown man now. His growing spurt and taking on his father's duties had made a big difference in Jake's looks, but Banjo knew there was still some of the little boy left inside that muscled body. There always was. Tight muscles filled out his blue-checkered shirt. His dark hair formed a fringe under his black Stetson. At Banjo's wave, Jake rode to meet Banjo beside a lone cottonwood.

"How you doing, Jake?" Banjo called when he drew near. "I've been waiting for a chance to speak to you."

"Yeah?" the young man muttered. His high cheekbones and blue eyes gave him a strong resemblance to his mother, but his face was sullen. He watched Banjo, waiting for the older man to speak.

"I met your mother yesterday," Banjo went on. "Y'all been having a time of it, haven't you?"

"We do all right."

"If you ever need any help, give me a holler. I'm at the Circle C, but I can cut loose if I want to."

Gazing at the ground, Jake nodded. "Thanks for the offer. I'll tell Ma," he said and turned away.

A moment later Banjo spotted a long brown horn sticking up above a wide bush and set Kelsey after the stray. He worked without a break until near noon when he heard a man shout, a harsh sound that meant trouble. The noise came from a small stand of cottonwoods near a stream.

Banjo urged Kelsey into a gallop. Seconds later he saw a mossy-horned outlaw bull bearing down on a paint horse and its rider. It was Jake Newcomb. The boy had a loop over one of the bull's horns. His pony backed up, trying to pull the line taut, but the bull kept heading for him, pawing and snorting.

Banjo spurred his mount forward, lasso at hand. Before he could get close enough to throw, the bull rammed the pony's front quarter and threw rider and horse to the ground. Jake screamed in pain.

Banjo's loop slid over the bull's neck as the crazed animal circled for the kill. Bawling, the bull lunged into Banjo's rope, but Kelsey held fast. Banjo guided his mount to a tree and quickly circled it. He tied off the end and moved away, leaving the angry bull to work out his frustration on the cottonwood.

By the time Banjo reached the fallen rider, the downed mustang had scrambled to his feet. Jake's hat was off, and blood smeared the side of his head. His right leg lay at an odd angle between the knee and thigh. Jake gripped the wounded limb and moaned. "It's broken!" His head rolled from side to side, his eyes half closed. "I know it's broken."

Chapter 2

"Hold on, partner," Banjo called, sliding to the ground. "Hold on." He knelt beside the injured man. The leg was surely broken, one of the worst Banjo had seen in his thirty years of ranch work. "I'll git Doc Leatherwood. He's at the Sanders' camp." He reached for a stick and tied his red bandanna to it. Riding Kelsey to the rise above the roundup, he waved the flag back and forth in quick strokes. Within seconds, hawk-faced Hank Andrews rode up, and Banjo called, "Jake Newcomb has a busted leg. It's bad. Get the doc!"

Hank's mustang set off in a cloud of dust.

Riding back to the injured boy, Banjo pulled the bandanna from the stick and pressed it to Jake's head. The cloth was soon saturated. All Banjo could do was press and wait. . .and pray.

Dr. Leatherwood was an old friend of the family. Over the past four years he'd patched up more than one broken body at the Chamberlin home. He'd delivered the Chamberlins' two children, as well. Thickset, with heavy features and a broken nose, Dr. Leatherwood resembled a boxer more than a medical man, but his rugged face was compassionate, and his thick fingers were gentle.

The doctor reached them about fifteen minutes later. Instead of his usual black broadcloth suit, he wore jeans and a leather vest. Holding his black bag, he slid to the ground beside the wounded man. Right behind him, Hank arrived with Steve and several other riders.

"His name's Jake Newcomb," Banjo told the doctor.

Leatherwood took hold of Jake's face to turn his head for a better look. "Jake?" he said, his voice firm. "Jake? Can you hear me?"

Scowling as though angry, the young man tried to pull away from the doctor's grip. His eyelids fluttered, but he didn't answer.

"Looks like he may have a concussion," the doc said, tilting Jake's head back to look into his eyes. "Keep holding that rag on his cut, Banjo. I'd best set that leg right away before it swells too much." With quick, sure movements, he felt the limb. He glanced up. "Men, take a strong hold on his body for me, will you?" Six pairs of hands reached for Jake's shoulders, arms, ribs, and waist. Leatherwood gave the leg a sharp yank.

Jake screamed and fainted.

"That was a mercy," Leatherwood said, feeling the break and nodding in satisfaction. "He probably won't remember this." He looked at the crowd that had gathered around them, some on horseback and some standing. "Someone fetch me two flat sticks from the bundle tied behind my saddle," he called.

No one spoke except in hushed tones as one of the men got the requested equipment.

"Jake!" a woman's husky shout rose above their quiet voices. "Jake!" Sally Newcomb flung herself from the saddle and would have thrown herself at her boy's body, but Steve caught her and held her back.

"The doc just set his leg, ma'am," Steve told her. "You'd best let him be until they can get a splint made."

At that moment Chance and Em Calahan arrived in a buckboard. Em was a seasoned nurse and always eager to help.

Totally focused on her boy, Sally's face was an agony of fear and grief. "He's passed out!"

"He fainted when I set the leg," the doctor told her. He reached into his bag for a wide roll of cloth and went on, "He hit his head when he fell, so I think he may have a concussion." He glanced at the frantic mother. "We'll have to keep him quiet for a couple of weeks, ma'am." With Banjo's help, he bound the cloth around the splints and the injured leg.

"You can bring him to our house," Steve told Sally. "My wife, Megan, is good at nursing folks. We live about half an hour over that rise. It's the closest ranch."

Pulling off her gloves, Sally passed her trembling hand across her mouth. She stared at Jake, tears streaming down her cheeks.

Em Calahan stepped close to her. "Me and Miss Megan will take good care of y'all," she said. "We used to patch up the soldiers at Fredericksburg, honey. He'll be in good hands." She kept talking, her voice soothing and low.

The doctor finished splinting the leg and put three black stitches across the cut on Jake's head. Someone brought some blankets and spread them in the back of the buckboard. The men gently lifted Jake and laid him on the blankets. Sally climbed in beside him.

"Banjo, go ahead and take them home," Steve said. He turned to Sally. "I'll send one of my men to help your hands," he told her. "We'll see your cattle are taken care of." She nodded as though hardly hearing him.

"I'll come along home," Em told them. "Megan will need me." She looked at her husband. "Jeremy can come back to help you with the cooking."

Jeremy was Megan Chamberlin's fourteen-year-old brother. Since both of their parents were dead, Jeremy had come to live with Megan and Steve shortly after they married. Em came, too. When the slaves had gained their freedom, Em had begged Megan's mother to let her remain with the family. Love kept her bound to the family with greater chains than slavery ever could. Even her recent marriage to Chance hadn't taken her far from her "children."

Chance nodded and gave Em's shoulders a gentle squeeze. "I'll be praying," he said.

Banjo stepped closer. "Chance, I'd appreciate it if you'd ride Kelsey back to camp for me. I'll be back in a couple of hours." He looked at Em. "I guess it's you and me again, Em."

She shook her head, her seamed face full of concern. "I wish it weren't like this, Banjo," she said.

He helped her into the buckboard and shook the reins.

The roundup was located in a canyon a few miles west of Juniper Junction, Colorado. Juniper sat on the edge of the plain—a brown lump on a swaying green landscape. As the foothills of the Rocky Mountains rose toward the skies, small valleys and canyons appeared. For the roundup, the men had chosen a large canyon, actually a section of the plain that had been partitioned off by an upthrust of soil and rock—a handy spot to keep the cattle until they could be sorted, branded, counted, and herded south to the railroad in Denver.

On the ride higher into the hills, Em turned often to see if Jake had come around, but he hadn't. Sally didn't speak once. She just sat beside her boy and cried.

Steve Chamberlin's ranch wasn't far as the crow flies, but crows can climb thousands of feet with a few flaps of their black wings. The buckboard had to gain altitude through the sheer muscle power of two horses that leaned forward into their harness to pull the buckboard up a trail that circled hillsides and looped around giant brown boulders. As they moved upward, the rocks became smaller, the aspen and pine groves became thicker, the constant breeze became cooler.

When they topped a rise, the Circle C ranch house came into view. It stood in front of a massive rock cliff at the top of a hill that was just a few feet shy of being a mountain. The original cabin made from stone had a newer log addition on the west side. The horses picked up their pace as they headed down the well-worn trail toward a wide stream. The wagon wheels rumbled over the half-log planks forming a crude bridge, and they began the final climb to the house.

A field of swaying corn covered the thirty acres between the stream and the ranch yard. Thousands of yellow-brown tassels bowed with a gentle rustle as the wagon passed.

When the buckboard neared the edge of the yard, a gray and white dog with a wolf-like face came from the barn to bark. Steve's wife, Megan, soon appeared on the porch. She wore a dark dress with a white apron, her honey-colored hair pulled back into a bun. She twisted her hands inside her apron, and her face was full of dread. A tiny girl with dark pigtails stood beside her mother, her brown eyes wide, her index finger in her mouth.

When the buckboard pulled to a halt, Megan cried, "What is it, Em? Who's hurt?"

"It's Jake Newcomb," Em told her, climbing down. "He took a fall. His head's cut, and he's broke his leg. He and his ma live a good distance away, so Steve sent him up here." She glanced toward Sally. "This is his ma, Sally Newcomb."

Megan let out a quick breath then swallowed convulsively. "I was afraid it was Steve," she said, her shoulders sagging. She moved to the back of the buckboard and peered over the low side. "I'm so sorry, Mrs. Newcomb," she said. "You're welcome to stay with us. We'll do all we can for your boy."

Sally dabbed the back of her hand across her swollen red eyes. "Thank you," she whispered. The spunky woman who had ridden into the roundup that morning had disappeared, leaving a bent and grieving mother in her place.

"We'll put him in the children's room," Megan told Em. She turned to Banjo. "I'll change the bedding on Katie's bed while you get him inside." She gazed at the barn. "Jeremy!" she called. "Jeremy, come here!" She turned to Banjo. "He can help you get the boy inside." Looking at her daughter, she added, "Come along, Katie," and hurried inside, the little girl close behind her.

As Banjo watched them leave, he noticed Jeremy emerge from the barn's wide doorway. When the boy saw the buckboard, he set off running, the wolf-faced dog bounding up to meet him, then following him back.

Letting down the back of the buckboard, Banjo told Jeremy the story of Jake's accident, ending with, "You'll have to help me carry him in."

"I can help," Sally said. She stood up in the buckboard then paused to gaze at her son as though she'd forgotten what she'd meant to do.

"Fetch me a board from the ones stacked in the barn," Banjo told Jeremy. "We'll lay him on it and carry him inside."

The straw-haired boy dashed away. "C'mon, Lobo," he called to the dog. Moments later he reappeared dragging a long piece of dark wood.

Banjo helped Sally to the ground, then he and Jeremy laid the board beside Jake. Taking a firm grip on the blanket beneath the injured boy, they had Jake on the board in one smooth motion. Then they began the slow move into the house.

The Chamberlins' home was simple and square, with one room cut out of a corner on the east side of the house, leaving an L-shaped space that served as the living room, dining room, and kitchen. A wide, stone fireplace filled much of the front wall. The floor was also stone, smooth and carefully crafted. An open loft under the rafters was Jeremy's domain. Steve and Megan's children occupied the newer addition on the western side of the house, and it was toward that room that Banjo and Jeremy carried Jake.

Em and Megan were already there, working with the speed of women who are used to being together. On the other end of the narrow room stood a crib containing Megan's sleeping baby boy, about six months old. His sister, Katie, stood near the head of the bed, watching every move the two women made.

"Why are you changing the covers, Mama?" she asked, her voice lilting and shrill.

"The sick man will have to use your bed for a while, Katie," Megan said. "You can sleep with me and Daddy."

"I can?" she asked, swinging on the headboard. "Goody! Goody!"

"Shh," Em said, grinning at the little girl. "You'll wake Stevie." From the day Megan and Jeremy had been born in Virginia, Em had been a second mother to them. Now she was like a grandmother to Megan's children.

Banjo backed into the bedroom, one end of the stretcher in his hands. Jake's head lolled to one side. He seemed in danger of falling off the board. "Hold tight there, Jeremy," Banjo said. "Just a few more steps."

The women had the sheets changed by the time the makeshift stretcher arrived.

Katie ran to Em and threw her arms around Em's knees. The dark-skinned woman lifted the little girl and moved over to the window to give room for the stretcher to pass her. Megan stood at the head of the bed, hands ready to help. Sally hovered behind Jeremy. She was white to the lips.

When Jake was settled into the bed, Em set Katie down and left the room.

Sally grabbed Megan's hands. "Thank you for helping us," she said. "I don't know what I would have done. . ."

Megan drew the distraught woman into a brief hug. "That's what neighbors are for." She turned toward a rocking chair in the corner. "Here. Let's pull this closer so you can rest yourself."

A rustle and a small cry from the crib caught Megan's attention. "It's time for Stevie to wake up from his nap," she said. "He's hungry." She went to the crib and scooped up her son. He nestled his head under her chin and sucked his pudgy thumb, his eyes still closed.

"I guess I'll go," Banjo said, his hat in his hand. "Okay if I take Jeremy along to help Chance?" he asked Megan.

Immediately, the boy's face lit up. Banjo grinned. He knew that Jeremy had wanted to go to the roundup in the worst way, but Steve had said he ought to stay home to do the chores.

"Of course," Megan said. Stroking her baby's soft head, she smiled at her younger brother. "We'll manage for a few days. Em's here now."

Jeremy scooted out the door and almost ran into Em, who held a basin of water in her hands.

"Land sakes, chile!" she gasped, drawing back. Shaking her head, she moved forward to set the basin on the narrow chest of drawers near the window.

Banjo knelt beside Sally in the rocking chair. Flipping his hat gently between his hands, he asked, "Would you mind if I say a prayer for him before I go?"

"I'd be grateful," Sally murmured. "I know the good Lord says that He won't give us more than we can bear, but. . ." Tears welled up, and she couldn't go on.

Banjo bowed his head, and the three women closed their eyes. His gruff voice rang out. "Father, I'm asking that You watch over Jake and make him well. You know that Miz Newcomb just lost her husband. We ask that You spare her son. But above all, I pray that Your will be done."

He stood, and Sally held out her hand to him. He clasped it gently in his calloused paw. "Thank you, Banjo," she said, focusing on him for the first time since the accident. "I'm grateful to you."

He cleared his throat, tried to think of something to say, and failed. Finally, he remembered to let go of her hand. "Chance'll come home tonight to check on things here," he said. "The doc will be by later on." With the jingle of spurs, he strode out.

As though from a distance, Sally watched Megan and Em follow Banjo out of the room. Pulling off her Stetson, she leaned back in the rocking chair. She wanted to climb onto the bed and hold Jake like she'd done after he'd fallen off the corral gate and cut his forehead when he was four years old. Then she'd bandaged his face, and he'd cried himself to sleep in her arms. Two days later, the accident was almost forgotten.

Watching Jake's still form, she knew it would be weeks before he recovered from this. Maybe he never would. *What if he can't walk once the leg heals? What if he. . .*

She shuddered and drew in a quivering breath. When Mickey died, she had cried. But she'd also felt a little relieved to be free of his strict control. Mickey had watched her portion out sugar as though it were gold dust. He'd insisted that Jake wear his shoes until they were worn-out, even though the stiff leather pinched the toes of their growing son. Mickey had been hardworking and honest, but he hadn't been easy to live with.

Jake was an entirely different matter. Since Mickey had died, Jake had become more than a son for her to nurture. He was her ranching partner, her strength, her reason to go on in this pain-filled life. How could she go on if he was taken from her? Fresh tears slid down her cheeks.

The door to the room creaked open, and Megan's gentle voice said, "Here, Sally." She handed Sally a few clean handkerchiefs. "I've got plenty of these. You may keep them."

"Thank you," Sally said. She wiped her face. Blinking hard, she tried to pull herself together.

"Would you like to bathe his face?" Megan asked, moving to the enamel bowl. "Em brought some warm water." She squeezed out the cloth in the basin and handed it to Sally. "Here's a towel, too."

Taking the cloth and towel, Sally glanced down at her dust-covered buckskins. "I'm sorry about my clothes. My kit is at the roundup, and I didn't bring a dress along with me. I figured I wouldn't need it."

Megan smiled. She had a gentle, comforting way. "When you're ready to wash up, I can loan you a clean dress. You're at home here, Sally. Please let me know if you need anything at all." She moved to the door. "I'm going to start supper. If you need someone to sit with Jake a spell, just let us know." She opened the door and went out.

Later that evening Chance arrived with Sally's bag. He helped Megan move the crib into the master bedroom, stayed for an hour to visit with Em, then left. After dark Dr. Leatherwood came to check on Jake. Concerned that the boy was still unconscious, the doctor left some pain powder in case Jake woke up. Closing his bag, he promised to return the next evening.

By the time Megan had the evening meal prepared, Sally was dizzy with exhaustion. She ate a few bites of beans, then lay down on the pallet Em had spread for her on the floor near the bed. Instantly, she fell asleep.

⌒

Em filled the chair beside the sickbed through that first night. Shortly after dawn, Megan stepped into the room with Stevie in her arms.

"Get yourself some coffee, Em," she whispered. "I've got some fresh and hot on the stove."

Jake groaned and moved his head. Watching him, Megan and Em leaned closer. "Ma?" he rasped. "Ma? I need some water."

Em leaned forward. "I'll get you some, son," she said. The chair continued swaying when she darted out of it and left the room. In seconds she was back with a tin cup in her hand.

"What is it?" Sally asked, sitting up. She squinted toward Jake.

"He wants some water," Megan said.

Sally was on her feet in one movement. "Jake?" she cried, bending over the bed. "Can you hear me?"

"Water," he rasped.

Em handed Sally the cup then moved to the head of the bed to support Jake so he could drink. Sally held the cup to his lips, and he sipped.

When he lay back, he moaned, "My leg! It's hurtin', Ma!"

"You fell off your horse," Sally told him. She handed Em the cup and leaned close to her boy's face. "You broke your leg. The doctor left you something for pain."

Em was already stirring powder into his water. She handed the glass to Sally.

"Get him to drink all of it," Em said. "It'll make him sleep."

After several attempts and a few spills, the tin cup was finally empty. A few minutes later, Jake was dozing, and Sally was alone with him again.

Sinking back into the rocking chair, Sally sighed and pushed at her scruffy hair. With automatic movements, she began removing the pins holding her black knot of hair on top of her head. Wearing a Stetson over her high bun let her ride herd on cattle without fear of her hair coming down and getting tangled by the wind. Wishing for a hot tub and some strong soap, she pulled at the thick strands, trying to smooth them out. Her brush was in her kit, but she was too tired to fetch it.

A few minutes later, Megan came in holding a tray containing a plate of eggs and buttered toast. A steaming mug of coffee gave a warm aroma to the room.

"I filled the water reservoir on the back of the stove," Megan told her. "When you're ready to wash up, just let me know."

"You are so kind," Sally said, watching her with wonder. "You don't know me at all, but you treat me and Jake like we're family."

"I had a lot of trouble myself when we first came here," Megan replied. "God has been so good to me. Sometime I'd like to tell you the story of how I came here, and what God did for Steve and me. Then you'd understand why we're anxious to help others." She set down the tray. "I'll bring you a fresh change of clothes."

Jake didn't awaken again until the doctor arrived late that afternoon. "How bad is it, Doc?" he asked between clenched teeth. His face was white, his eyes wandering over the ceiling, across their faces, and back again.

"It was a bad break," Leatherwood said, shaking his head. "But I think I got to you soon enough that you'll heal up good as new. The danger with a break like this is that the swelling will prevent the bones from going back together right. I think we got you fixed up just fine."

"How long until he can ride?" Sally asked. "We've got to get back to our ranch."

"It'll be at least six weeks until he can put any weight on that leg—at least six. We'll have to wait and see how he gets on before we can know for sure."

She wilted into her chair. "Six weeks? We can't impose on these good people for that long. It's too much to ask."

Megan clucked her tongue. "Don't even say that, Sally," she said. "I told you that you were welcome here, and you are. Any rancher in these hills would do the same." She touched Sally's shoulder. "You've got enough on your mind without worrying about us."

Doc Leatherwood promised to come back in two or three days then hurried back to the roundup.

The next morning Sally stood at the bedroom window and watched Banjo ride in on Kelsey. A few seconds later, he tapped on the bedroom door. Sally opened it, and he motioned for her to step outside. She moved into the dining room and closed the door behind her.

"I come to see what you had planned for your stock," he said, his voice low. "We put Hank to work on your brand, but your hands weren't sure of what to do about the drive. None of them cottons to the job of ramrodding the outfit."

Sally hesitated. She didn't want to leave Jake for any reason. But the sale of those cows meant survival to the Bar N. Someone had to take the final responsibility of getting her cattle to market in Denver. She didn't have a foreman to organize the men for the two-week drive and then handle the business of selling the cattle once they arrived at the holding pens beside the railroad.

"Why don't you let us move them with our herd?" Banjo asked, tilting his head a little and gazing into her eyes. "We'll tally them up when we get there and bring you your portion." He paused. "That is, unless you have someone else you'd rather have."

She still hesitated, trying to think but too tired to feel certain about any decision.

His stained hat in his hands, Banjo waited without saying more.

Searching her weary mind for an answer, Sally glanced from Megan, who stood at the stove stirring something in a large iron pot, to Em, who sat in the living room folding diapers. Sitting on the floor near Em, Katie was arranging clothespins into the shape of a house and singing, "Good-bye, Old Paint."

Finally, Sally looked at Banjo and said, "I don't like to put you out, but if you could take my cattle to Denver, I'd surely appreciate it. There's no one else I can call on. Our spread is so far back in the hills that we haven't made the acquaintance of many folk. Just our one neighbor, and he's no friend." She felt her face tighten at the thought of the man and tried to cover it up with a smile. "Thank you, Banjo. You've been a godsend to Jake and me."

He cleared his throat. "It's only fittin' that we should help. Everybody needs a hand sometime or another. This happens to be your time. You'd do the same for us if need be." He lifted his hat to his head. "I'll get myself along then. Bye, Miss Megan." He paused beside Em and added, "Chance said to have a big plate of biscuits for him when we get back."

Em grinned. "You can tell him I'll have two plates filled and ready. And a gingerbread cake besides."

Katie stood and held up her arms for Banjo to pick her up. He lifted her, planted a kiss on her forehead, and gently set her down. "Bye now, honey," he said. "When I get back, I'll whittle you a whistle." He stroked her hair once. The

363

next moment he was gone.

"He's a fine man," Sally murmured, moving to the window to watch him ride away.

"He's fine as silk," Em said, nodding. She laid a folded diaper on the stack.

Megan chuckled. "Rough silk, but pure through and through."

Eighteen days after Jake's accident, Steve and Banjo returned to the Circle C with Chance and Jeremy. The moment they appeared on the horizon, the house came alive with excitement.

Little Katie bounced on the plank flooring of the porch and squealed. "Daddy! Daddy!" Lobo ran toward the horses and buckboard, giving short, shrill barks, his tail swishing back and forth like a ship's sail on stormy seas.

The baby on her hip, Megan ran out into the yard with Em. They waved, stopped a moment to hug each other, then waved some more. Sally watched from Jake's window. She wore a deep blue dress of Megan's. Her hair lay in soft waves over her ears and wound into a wide bun at the base of her neck.

"What is it, Ma?" Jake asked. He was sitting up, a two-year-old copy of *Harper's Bazaar* in his hands. He wasn't strong enough to whittle yet, so he was leafing through old magazines and glancing at the drawings, his least favorite pastime since he couldn't read.

"The men are back from the cattle drive," Sally told him, still watching the horses approach the house. "They made it home safe."

"I wish we had," he grumbled. He threw the magazine to the floor. "I wish they had a decent picture book. Even baby stuff would be better than these sissy magazines. This morning, Mrs. Chamberlin actually asked me if I'd like to read her Bible." He shook his head, disgusted. "I've got to get out of this bed or I'm liable to start chewing the bedpost and kill myself swallowing the splinters."

"Jake! Hush!" Sally said, not paying attention to his rambling. His pain had made him so irritable that she was growing tired of listening to him.

Half an hour later, Megan came in to prop open the bedroom door. "Why don't you join us at the table tonight, Sally?" she asked. "We can keep this door open so Jake can feel like he's part of the family, too. The table is just outside his door."

"That's okay. You can go ahead and close it," Jake said. "I'm tired, and I'd like to take a nap."

"Thank you, Megan," Sally said, frowning toward Jake. "I'd be honored to join you. I hope you'll forgive Jake. He's still in a lot of pain."

He lay back and pulled the covers high under his chin. Eyes closed, he pretended to sleep, but Sally saw his eyelids twitch and knew better.

"I'll bring you a tray in a while," Sally told him and followed Megan out the door. She desperately needed a break from Jake's dour mood. Part of her pitied him for his constant agony, but another part of her was growing impatient with his self-centered attitude. It wasn't like her Jake to be so grumpy.

The long table was set with blue enamel plates and tin cups. A large pewter platter of steaks and a bowl of mashed potatoes sat in the center flanked by green beans, shredded cabbage in a vinegar brine, and hot rolls. It smelled heavenly.

Holding a dish of pickles, Megan asked, "Sally, you've met my husband, Steve, haven't you?"

"Just for a second after the accident," Sally replied. She held out her hand. "Thank you for your hospitality, Mr. Chamberlin," she said.

"It's Steve," he replied, clasping her hand for an instant. "We don't cotton much to mister around here, do we, Banjo?"

The cowhand chuckled and rubbed the gray bristles on his chin. "Mister's one handle I can't carry," he said.

Sally held her hand out to him. "Thank you for your help, too, Banjo," she said. "I don't know what Jake and I would have done without your kindness."

"I'm only glad I was nearby," he said.

After Megan introduced Chance to Sally, Steve handed Sally a worn saddlebag. "Here's your take from your herd," he told her. "I paid off your hands so they could be on their way. You had 142 beeves at $6 a head. That came to $852. I paid the four hands $40 apiece. That left you $692."

She blinked. At first she thought there must be a mistake, but he'd said 142 beeves, and that was the number of cattle she'd sent to market. She smiled and said, "That's almost one hundred dollars more than I'd hoped for." She took the leather bag to the bedroom and told Jake the good news. He lay still with his eyes closed as though he hadn't heard. Sally stood near him for a moment, wondering if he was asleep or in one of his moods. Finally, she decided it wasn't worth finding out and returned to the dining room.

Everyone found a place around the table. Steve offered thanks for the food and for their safe return from a dangerous journey. When he lifted his head, he sent his wife a warm smile. "I've been waiting for this meal for nearly three weeks. Pass those steaks."

Banjo picked up the bowl of potatoes and handed it to Sally. "How's your boy coming along?" he asked.

She took the bowl and said, "He's at that awful stage where he feels better but still can't do anything."

"Now that Jeremy's back, maybe they can play checkers or something," he replied, winking at Jeremy. "This boy's gotten to be a champ at checkers since I've been schoolin' him at it."

"I can beat him three times in five," Jeremy announced between bites.

"Jake used to play checkers with his father. He's pretty good at it."

"I'll get the board after I wash up," Jeremy said, reaching for another roll. "It'll be good to have some competition for a change."

Banjo laughed. "See how much respect I get around here?"

The talk turned to the cattle drive and getting in the corn crop. After the meal, Chance and Em set off for their cabin across the meadow, and Sally lent a hand with the dishes. A few minutes later, Jeremy came in from the spring behind the house wearing clean pants and a red flannel shirt. His hair was wet and plastered down. He skittered up the ladder to the loft and reappeared holding a homemade wooden checkerboard and a small box.

"You reckon Jake would like to play?" he asked Sally, who was drying the last of the dinner dishes.

"Ask him, Jeremy," Sally said, putting away the yellow crockery bowl and draping her cloth over the edge of the counter. "If he's not too tired, I know he'll be glad to play. He loves the game."

Jeremy dashed away.

Sally moved to the bedroom door to watch Jake sit up and reach for the wooden tray he set his meals on. "Would you like some supper now?" she asked him.

"After we finish a game," he said, not looking at her.

When Jeremy laid the checkerboard on the tray, Sally let the door softly close. What a relief to have Jake occupied for an hour or so.

"I believe I'll get some air," she told Megan, who was nursing baby Stevie on the settee near the dark fireplace. His tiny fingers pressed at his mother's mouth.

"Don't hurry back," Megan said, lifting her head away from Stevie's hand. "If Jake needs anything, Jeremy can fetch it for him. You've earned some time to yourself." Still nursing, the baby kicked out, and Megan cradled his foot in her slender hand.

The evening breeze was still warm, but it had lost the searing heat so common to late summer in Colorado. Sally let her hands hang free and tilted her head back to enjoy the wind on her face and in her hair. She strolled along a well-worn path that went along the rocky cliff behind the house and sloped down to a stream. She'd been here several times before. Now that Jake had company, she wouldn't have to hurry back.

Carefully lifting her skirts, she hopped from stone to stone across the swift water. The air above the stream felt cool, and she paused near the center to enjoy it for a moment longer.

"Howdy!" A gruff voice behind her startled her.

Her arms flew out, and her skirt was instantly soaked. Lifting it to free her feet, she skipped from one stone to another and landed on the other side, shaken but still partly dry.

"I'm sorry," Banjo said, grinning. "I didn't mean to scare you."

She drew in a quick breath and tried to settle her jumping nerves. "That's all right," she stated. "I may get startled, but I never fall."

He stepped across the stones. "You sure can ride," he said as he moved. He was surprisingly agile. When he reached dry ground, he went on, "I never did see a woman ride like you."

"My father was head boy at a rich man's stable in New York while I was growing up. I started exercising horses when I was six. My sister helped Ma in the house while I worked in the stable with Dad." She set off down the path toward a waist-high flat rock where she could sit and watch the rushing water.

"You don't sound happy about that arrangement," Banjo said, falling into step with her.

She shrugged. "I guess I've always wished I was better prepared to be a housewife. Mickey always complained about my cooking, and I've burned more shirts with a hot iron than I can count."

"You ought to let Miss Megan and Em show you a few things while you're here. It's never too late to learn, you know."

She pulled at a piece of tall grass beside the path. "I reckon," she said. She gazed upward at the orange cliff, brilliant in the setting sun. "That stone face almost looks like it's on fire."

"I love this place," Banjo replied. "While I rode the grub line, there was another hombre here, and he'd hire me time and again. I stopped in to see if he needed a hand and found the Chamberlins had just moved in. The place had been empty for a while, and it was in pretty bad shape."

"What happened to the other family?"

"The wife died in childbirth, and the man went back East. I guess he'd had enough of the wide open spaces."

She turned her back toward the wide flat stone and heaved herself up to sit on it. It was high enough to cause her feet to dangle. Banjo leaned against it next to her. "I had to come down here and find out something," he began. "I hope you won't mind me asking you."

Wondering what he was getting at, Sally turned to watch his face. He had deep-set blue eyes that seemed to twinkle even when he was serious. For the first time it occurred to her that this man was more than the average cowpoke.

"Are you a believer?" he asked, turning to look her in the eye.

She stiffened. "What do you mean?"

"Have you ever put your faith in Jesus Christ?"

"Yes. I did that when I was about twelve years old." She looked away. "I haven't thought about it for a long time though." She glanced at him. "Mickey wasn't a Christian. He didn't like churches or preachers. I never went to meeting after we started going together."

"Was he from New York, too?" Banjo asked.

She shook her head. "When I was fourteen, my family moved to Missouri. Dad had an idea about going to Oregon, but once we got to St. Louis, he decided to stay there and sell horses to the travelers passing through. Mickey was a buyer for one of the wagon masters. That's how we got acquainted. We'd only known each other for three months when we got married. Soon after that the wanderlust struck Mickey, so we packed up two wagons and started for Denver. We had a place in Wyoming, but Mickey got tired of the dust and heat. Finally, we moved on and staked a claim to a pretty place in the hills west of here."

She sent him a sideways glance. "I never wanted to be a rancher's wife," she said. "Mickey wanted it, and I had to help him do what he wanted. It was my duty."

"Why did you stay on after he passed?"

"Since Mickey died, I've had a couple of offers for the ranch. Every time I've told myself to take it, but I just can't. Maybe I'm too stubborn to admit I can't handle this life. Maybe I've put so much into the place that I can't bear to leave it. I'm not sure why I haven't sold it. Maybe I still will. . .especially now." Her voice held a sour note.

She drew in a breath and smoothed her hair. "When we head home in a couple of weeks, I'll have to make up my mind. Right now the only thing I can think of is getting Jake well again." Her voice broke. "I can't bear to lose him, Banjo. Mickey and I weren't close, and it was hard enough losing him. If Jake. . ." She swallowed and went silent. Even in her mind she couldn't finish that sentence.

"The good Lord will see you through, no matter what," Banjo told her, his voice gentle. "I know whereof I speak. You see, I lost my wife and my boy on the same day."

"How awful!"

He nodded. "It knocked me down right and proper. It was in the mid-fifties, almost twenty years ago, but it seems like just yesterday. I had a small ranch in Texas, the purtiest place you've ever seen. We ran a thousand head of longhorns. I was away from home on business when Kiowas burned my ranch, killed Mary, and took my boy. I've never learned what became of him." He drew in a breath. "It's the not knowing that's worse than anything. When I think that Todd may be locked in some filthy reservation, I want to beat something with my bare fists."

"How old was he?"

"About ten."

They sat in silence for a few moments watching the water and listening to the call of a meadowlark.

"What hope is there in this life, Banjo?" she murmured. "Every time a person turns around twice, there's some new grief stabbing him like a jagged knife. What good is it going on?"

"Now, don't go talking like that, missy," he said. "There's all kinds of good. Being able to help you and Jake has been a good thing for me. It brings joy to a man's heart to know he's put a little light into someone's dark day. Look at little Katie and that little boy of Steve's. Don't they make you smile?"

Looking at the ground, she nodded. "I guess so. It's just hard for me to see things straight right now."

A tepid breeze caught her dress and flipped up a corner of the damp hem. She slid off the stone. "We ought to get to the house," she said. "It'll be dark in half an hour."

They walked back in quiet companionship. "How soon will Jake be ready to travel?" Banjo asked.

"The doctor said he won't be able to sit astride a horse for another month or so." She sighed. "With him down, I'll have to hire a hand for the winter months. We'll get by somehow."

They said good-bye near the barn, and Sally returned to the house. Walking across the yard, she wondered about Banjo. He looked like a man with the bark on, as Mickey used to say, but underneath his gruff exterior lay warmth that surprised her. He was different from any man she'd ever met.

Lost in thought, she climbed the steps to the front porch and went inside the house.

Chapter 3

Over the next three weeks, the Chamberlin household bustled with activity. Corn harvest was one of the busiest weeks of the year. The harvest party meant hours of cooking and preparation for the women, and Sally helped as much as she was able. On the big day, Megan's friend Elaine Sanders came to the house when her father headed for the field to help the men. Dressed in a tan work dress, Elaine wore a green sunbonnet. She had a tiny figure and moved with natural grace.

"Good morning!" Megan said, opening the door. She hugged Elaine. "It's been ages since I've seen you. You'll have to fill me in on all the latest doings around these parts." She took a covered basket from Elaine's hand. "What did you bring us?"

"Doughnuts," Elaine said with a tinkling laugh. "I've got to score as many points with the fellows as I can, don't I?" Elaine was the most popular girl in those parts, yet she was still single at age twenty-two. She constantly joked about it. "Oh," she said, reaching into her dress pocket. "Pa picked this up in town yesterday. He told me to give it to you." She handed a thin yellow page to Megan.

Megan glanced at the folded paper. "It's a telegram for you, Sally." She looked at Sally, who was in the kitchen with her hands in the dishpan.

Sally looked ready to cry. "Those things give me a sinking feeling in my stomach. They always bring bad news, it seems." She dried her hands and reached for the page. After unfolding it, she squinted at the words. In a moment she returned the sheet to Megan. "Could you read it for me? I can read a little, but this is beyond me. It's something about my brother, Jimmy."

Megan took the page and read:

Jimmy Hodges and wife drowned in boating accident STOP Left child—Carey, age twelve STOP Must go to orphanage STOP Will send Carey to you if will accept STOP Augustus Tillman, attorney at law.

Sally sank into a chair beside the table. "I can't believe it's true," she gasped, reaching into her pocket for a handkerchief. "They were married just before we came west." She wiped her eyes. "As soon as we finish the corn, I'll have to go to town and send an answer." She reached for the telegram. "I never knew they had a son. Jake would be so glad for some company, and Lord knows we could use the help on the ranch."

She sent Elaine a watery smile. "Thank you for bringing the telegram to me," she said.

Megan spoke to Elaine. "Have you met Sally Newcomb? Her son broke his leg at the roundup, and they've been staying on while he mends."

Elaine nodded. "I heard about that. How is he doing, Miz Newcomb?"

"Please call me Sally. Jake's leg is getting better, thanks. We're hoping to go home soon. Please excuse me while I tell Jake about this." Tilting her chin, she blinked away her tears and took the telegram to Jake. He was sitting up in bed, looking through the window at the field of working men. He had a sour look on his square face when his mother came through the door.

"Your cousin is coming to live with us," Sally told him, holding up the telegram. "He's my brother Jimmy's boy."

She suddenly had Jake's full attention.

"He's twelve years old," she went on. "He'll have to go to an orphanage if we don't take him in." She squinted at the page. "The date on this is August 18, two weeks ago. He's probably at the orphanage right now."

"What kind of a kid is he?"

She folded the page and slid it into her pocket. "I'm not sure. I didn't even know that Jimmy had a son. We haven't kept in touch. He's from St. Louis. That's all I know about him."

"A city boy?" He quirked in one side of his mouth. "How will he make it out here?"

Sally said, "My dad sold horses, and Jimmy loved them, too. If Jimmy took Dad's business when he passed on, Carey may not be as dandified as you think." She headed back toward the kitchen. "I'm going to send word that he should come."

The Chamberlins' corn harvest was a rousing success. The workers got in about two-thirds of the good crop. For two days following the big event, Sally worked in the field pulling the last fat ears from their stalks. After that, the men took care of chopping the stalks for winter cattle feed.

The day after the hard work was finished, the family sat at the breakfast table, lingering over coffee and enjoying a rest for tired muscles and weary minds. Katie ran from one person to another, passing out clothespins. On her next round she'd collect them again.

"I need to go to Juniper," Sally said. "I've got to buy supplies and send a telegram."

"When would you want to go?" Banjo asked as he handed Katie his wooden pin.

"Tomorrow."

He looked at Steve. "Mind if I ride along with her?"

"Help yourself, Banjo," Steve replied. He drew in a deep breath and leaned back in his chair. "We're going to take it easy around here until Monday anyway."

Sally asked, "Harper's open on Saturdays, isn't he?"

" 'Til noon," Banjo replied.

"Tomorrow will do, then," Sally said. "I want to leave for home next week sometime."

"Next week?" Megan asked, pulling Katie into her lap. "That's awful soon."

Sally sipped coffee. "There's a lot to do before winter. We can't wait much longer."

"Take the buckboard," Steve said. "We won't need it here."

"Bring me a peppermint!" Katie cried, turning her shining brown eyes to Banjo.

He chuckled. "I guess I've been told!"

Megan made a shushing noise at the little girl. "Mind your manners, Katie," she scolded.

Banjo reached out and patted Katie's shoulder. "I'll see if I can dig out a penny, honey," he confided, winking. "Will you give Stevie a taste if I do?"

She nodded, an intent expression on her face.

"That's my girl!"

Jeremy broke in to ask, "Can Katie and I go out to play now?" At Megan's nod, he rose from the table and skipped toward the door. Katie scooted down from her mother's lap and dashed after him. Outside, Lobo's happy barks greeted them.

Banjo laughed. "Oh, to be a kid again. Jeremy worked alongside the men from dusk to dark for three days straight, and he still has energy to run with that dog."

Megan nodded. "I wish I could bottle that kind of liveliness and sip on it when I've been up with the baby all night."

◠

The next day Sally set off in the buckboard with Banjo to purchase her winter supplies in Juniper. The air felt crisp. The breeze had that tang that said fall would soon come. When they had crossed the stream and topped the rise, Banjo said, "So tell me more about your life before you came west."

"There isn't much to tell," Sally said. "I spent my days with my dad training the horses, exercising them, doctoring them. . ." She spread her hands, palms upward. "Horses were my life. I had no interest in book learning or housekeeping or anything else."

"Things are sure different for you now."

"You said a mouthful there. Our ranch work deals mostly with cows. They're such dumb beasts. I get tired of them." She smiled wryly. "That sounds ungrateful."

"No, it sounds honest. That's what I like in a person."

They rode into Juniper just before noon and stopped in front of the emporium. Just as Banjo got down from the buckboard to tie one of the horses to the hitching post, a lady wearing a navy coat over a ruffled blue silk dress passed him on the boardwalk. She had on a navy hat with the brim swept upward on the left side, giving her a dashing appearance. With a cold smile for Sally and a stiff nod to Banjo, she swished down the sidewalk.

He stepped to the side of the buckboard to help Sally down. "Do you know who she is?" he asked, gazing after the lady.

"That's Mrs. Virgil Ganss, the new banker's wife," Sally told him as she stepped to the ground. "I met her once when Mickey and I came to town to make a loan payment. She was in her husband's office when we arrived."

"She sure stands out in a place like Juniper," he said. He looked at Sally. "Would you be offended if I offered to buy you lunch at the hotel after we finish at Harper's? They make a right juicy steak."

She smiled. "That sounds wonderful. We've plenty of time to get home before dark."

When they'd filled Sally's shopping list, they strode across the street to the hotel. While they waited for their meal, Banjo said, "When I was a young fellow, I always dreamed of having a ranch of my own. Well, I got one, and I found out that it's a good life. A hard life but a good one." He smiled at Sally. "Then I lost my place and started working for other people. You know what I learned?"

"What's that?"

"I learned that a man can have a good life at just about anything he does that he enjoys. It's not the place or the job. It's what's in here"—he tapped his chest—"that makes the difference. I've seen men with spreads the size of a small state with cattle galore, horses and all." He shook his head. "But they're just as sour and dry as a crab apple in July."

"What do you want now, Banjo?" she asked, watching him carefully.

He rubbed his stubbled jaw. "I don't rightly know," he admitted with a sheepish grin. "When I find it, I reckon it'll hit me between the eyes."

They finished their meal without hurrying. When they left the restaurant, Banjo crossed the street to the Emporium while Sally stepped into the stage station to send her reply to Attorney Tillman. She returned to the buckboard as Banjo loaded a sack of beans.

"That's everything on your list," he said.

"I'll just look around the store for a minute," she told him. "I won't be long."

Fifteen minutes later, Sally came out holding a small sack of peppermints, and they set off.

As they topped the first rise, the urge for a song came over Banjo. He glanced at Sally. "Do you know the tune to 'Trusting Jesus'?"

Her brow creased for a moment, and then she slowly nodded. "I seem to recall it from my days in New York. I don't think I can remember the words."

He grinned and settled himself back on the seat. "This is a good time to learn it. Just follow me. We'll sing it a few times through:

"Simply trusting every day
Trusting through a stormy way. . ."

They sang all the verses until they arrived back at the Circle C at dusk. "Thanks for a memorable day," he said as he left Sally off at the house.

She gave him a broad smile. "Thanks to you, Banjo, it was a good day."

He pulled at the brim of his Stetson, then rustled the reins, and the buckboard moved toward the barn. The supplies would stay in the wagon until they loaded them onto several mustangs from Sally's string of horses for the trip home.

Over the next week, Jake's leg made steady improvement. He still had spasms at times, but the constant agony of the break had disappeared. In the early afternoon of September 8, Dr. Leatherwood gave permission for Jake to travel. "But don't put any weight on the leg whatsoever for another month," he told the boy.

Jake's lips curved downward. "I think I'll die before I can get on my feet again," he complained. "I can't stand this bed no more!"

Dr. Leatherwood turned to Sally. "Maybe you can get someone to make him some crutches," he said. "He could get around on those." He looked at Jake. "Just take it easy, son. When you get tired, go and rest. Your body will tell you when you're doing too much."

He smiled at Sally, and they shook hands. "Thank you, Doctor," Sally said.

"My pleasure." He cocked his thumb and pointed at Jake as though aiming a pistol. "Don't give your ma too much trouble, boy," he said.

Jake gave a reluctant grin.

Leatherwood put on his black hat and stepped out of the room.

"When can we go home?" Jake asked. "I'm so tired of being here."

Sally sank into the rocking chair and sighed. "I know. We've got to get back and get in some hay for the winter. There's no telling what our troublesome neighbor, Douglas O'Brien, has been up to since we've been gone." She searched Jake's face as though looking for an answer. "Maybe we ought not go back. Maybe we should head to Grandma Hazlet's place in New York. I could get a job. You could, too."

"You mean stay locked up in the city?" Jake demanded. He lay back on his pillow and stared at the pine-board ceiling. "I'd curl up and die in a month."

Sally rubbed her forehead. "What are we going to do? We can't afford to hire a hand. Even at thirty dollars a month, by spring almost half our money would go for wages."

He turned toward the wall. "My leg aches," he said. "I'm going to sleep."

She sat in the chair, quietly rocking, trying to pray but not sure how. After all the years of struggle and pain, she couldn't see any way to keep the ranch. Should she sell the land? She'd had an offer. Or maybe she should marry again. She'd had an offer for that, too. Only she didn't care for the gentleman much. Sick at heart and exhausted, she laid her head against the high back of the rocking chair and dozed.

The room was gray with twilight when she awoke. Jake lay on his back, mouth sagging, in deep sleep. Sally blinked and smoothed her hair. It must be near suppertime. She got up and went to the dining room.

Megan was setting the table. Katie stood beside her mother with several spoons in her chubby fist. Megan looked up at the sound of the bedroom door closing. "Feel better?" she asked. "I looked in on you awhile ago, and you were sleeping in the chair. I figured you must need the rest, so I left you alone."

Sally glanced at the simmering pots on the stove. "You should have called me to help with supper," she said. "Is there anything I can do?"

"It's ready," Megan said. "Em went out to call the men."

"I'm helping!" Katie announced, giving the spoons to her mother.

"I see that," Sally said, smiling. "You look like a big girl in that pink dress."

Katie beamed and held out her wide, gathered skirt for Sally to admire. "G'ammy Em made it!"

"It's lovely."

"What did the doctor say?" Megan asked. She set a plate of hot corn bread on the table.

Sally lost her smile. "He said that Jake can get around on crutches if we can find someone to make him some."

"No need for that," Megan said. "Several years ago Banjo made a pair for Steve. Jake can have those."

"But you may need them again," Sally said. "We'll be leaving soon."

"Then we'll just make another pair." She paused to look at Sally. "Please don't fret yourself, Sally. I want you to have them. What good are they doing hanging in the barn loft?"

The front door opened, and Jeremy burst in. "Megan, Bessie's going to have her calf," he announced. "It'll be tonight, maybe."

Megan looked at Steve, who was coming through the door.

He nodded. "She's calving."

Banjo said, "I'll look in on her a few times through the night." He chuckled. "Her bedroom is practically beside mine."

Megan set a large pot of beans on the table, and everyone found his place. After Steve thanked the Lord for the food, Megan began filling plates.

"How's the boy?" Banjo asked Sally as he handed Megan his blue plate.

"The doctor says he can walk with crutches now."

"I told her that he could have Steve's old crutches," Megan said, ladling up red beans for Banjo.

"Are you sure you won't need them?" Sally asked. She handed Megan a plate. "This one is for Jake," she added. "He'll have to wake up, or he won't sleep tonight."

"Go ahead and take the crutches," Steve said. "We can always make another pair if we need them."

"I'm everlasting grateful to you folks." She placed two pieces of corn bread on the beans and stood to take Jake's supper to him. "There's no way I can ever thank you enough." Feeling awkward, she hurried to her son and set his food on the dresser. "Jake! Wake up!" she said, touching his shoulder. "Your supper's here. You need to wake up."

He shrugged and opened his eyes. "What is it?" he asked, sitting up. "I'm starving."

Sally handed him his plate and a spoon. In the dim light she found a match on the dresser and lit the coal oil lamp. "Do you need anything else?" she asked.

He shook his head as he shoveled beans into his mouth.

When he didn't speak, she waited a moment then left the room and let the door close behind her.

Back at the table she said, "We need to be getting home. Winter's coming on, and there's hay to get in for the stock."

Banjo spoke up. "Jake won't be able to work for a couple of months. Do you have a hand to help you?"

She scooped three beans onto her spoon and stared at them. Finally, she murmured, "We've never been able to afford a full-time hand. Jake and I do whatever needs doing."

"You can't get in hay by yourself," Banjo told her. "No one could do it."

"I'll get by." She laid down her spoon and reached for her tin cup. Keeping up a brave front came naturally to her, but her stomach felt like she'd swallowed a cannonball. What was she going to do?

Banjo turned to Steve to discuss plans for the Circle C's preparation for winter, and Sally managed to finish her supper.

When she rose to help with the dishes, Megan shooed her away. "Why don't you go on out for a little walk in the yard before bedtime? You've been in the house all day. Some fresh air would do you a world of good. Jeremy will help me here." She tossed her brother a dish towel. He caught it and pretended to flick it at her.

Sally fetched Jake's empty dish and brought it to the kitchen. She set it on a stack near the sudsy pan of water and walked past the men seated in the living room. They were still deep in discussion about how much hay they should cut this year. Pulling her shawl from its peg near the door, she stepped onto the porch and filled her lungs with the cool night air. This time of year, she could stand outside and just breathe for pure enjoyment. Nothing matched the scent of pine and sage on an autumn breeze.

The stars made a pattern overhead like diamonds scattered across black velvet. Sally held on to a tall porch post while she bent her head far back to gaze overhead and locate the constellations she'd learned from her father.

"Purty, ain't it?" a deep gravelly voice asked.

Gasping, she jerked around. "Banjo!"

"Sorry if I scared you." He chuckled as he looked at her shocked expression. "I don't wear my spurs when I'm farming, so you didn't hear me."

She looked overhead again. "I was trying to find ten constellations. I've only got seven so far."

"Let's walk out and look behind the cliff," he said. "You'll see the rest of them and more."

She moved down the steps and backed away from the house with Banjo beside her.

"There's Orion!" she said, pointing. "He's my favorite. The Little Dipper, Big Dipper!" She let her hand fall to her side. "That's ten."

"See there? I knew you'd do better out here." He glanced toward the barn. "I'd best go and check on Bessie. You want to come?"

"Sure." She fell into step with him.

"I wish she'd waited until spring to have another calf," he said. "I'm not sure how she got crossways on her timing." He pulled open the door and found a lantern on the shelf just inside. Drawing a match from a packet in his shirt pocket, he lit the wick, and a dim yellow glow seemed to open the area around them. Holding the lantern high, he moved toward a stall on the right.

Sally stayed close to him and peered over the top rail into the enclosure. Bessie stood toward one side. She turned to give them a slow stare. Standing on shaky legs beside her, a damp calf nosed around her hindquarter. His little tail quivered when he found what he was looking for.

"Isn't that sweet!" Sally whispered.

"It's a miracle," Banjo's husky voice replied. He reached out to pat Bessie's rump. "That was a great job, old girl! I'll bring you some oats and a bucket of water when I come in later."

They stayed a few minutes longer, then moved back into the yard. Reluctant to go in just yet, Sally drew in another cleansing breath and pulled her shawl closer.

"Sally. . ." Banjo hesitated until she looked at him. "Sally, I want to help you this winter." Her happy expression tightened, and he rushed ahead. "Steve can get Chance to help him finish up here. There's not that much more to do."

"Much as I'd like to, I can't pay a hand, Banjo."

She kept watching him with that blank expression, and he started to sweat. He fully believed that God wanted him to help these people. Convincing this independent woman of that was harder than he'd expected. "You could put my wages on account and pay them whenever you have the cash. I'm in no hurry."

She began to walk, and he fell in step beside her. "I've got to make some decisions about the ranch, Banjo, and soon. I've had a couple of offers that would solve everything." She raised both hands, palms upward. "The thing is, Jake won't be happy with either one of them. That's why I haven't made a decision yet. It would be best for Jake if we stay where he's used to being."

The tree frogs and crickets filled the night with constant chatter. Sally and Banjo walked a dozen paces. Finally, she went on, "I'm embarrassed to even say this, but how about if I pay you ten dollars a month?"

"On account," he said, relieved. If she'd offered him fifty cents, he would have taken it. "Don't give my wages a thought until your next cattle drive."

She turned to shake hands with him. "I'll give you a hundred dollars from the next cattle drive," she said.

He gripped her firm hand in his calloused paw. "Fair enough." He suddenly felt like singing. "How about a walk?" he asked. When she moved out beside him, he went on, "My real name's Joseph Calahan, but folks call me Banjo because I'm always making music. Lately, we've had so much on our minds here that I haven't done much singing. If you'd call it singing," he added, chuckling. "Do you have any hymns you like in particular?"

"I don't know too many, I'm afraid," she said. "Maybe you can teach me some. I like singing, but I haven't had much of a chance to learn anything besides 'Oh, Susanna' and 'Good-bye, Old Paint.'"

They set off in a circle around the ranch yard, and he belted out "Amazing Grace."

When he finished the first verse, she asked, "How can you keep going on, Banjo? It seems like every day is a hundred years long."

"I keep my eyes off the clock and off my troubles when I put them on the Lord. He has given me a new song, set my feet on a rock, and established my goings. He has seated me in heavenly places and sealed me by His Spirit. What can hold me down with that kind of pedigree?"

She smiled. "I see what you mean." They walked a few steps, and she spoke again. "I haven't been to church since I left New York. It's been so long. . .too long. I don't read too good. I don't have a Bible anyway."

"You don't say! We should get together of an evening and read the scriptures together. I used to read to Em before she married. We had some good times together."

She nodded. "Let's do that, Banjo. I'd like that."

"How about starting tonight?" he asked. "We could set in the living room. Steve and Megan won't mind. They may even join in."

"Do you go to church in Juniper?" she asked.

"There's no church in Juniper. We've been praying for a steady preacher to come here. Up to now we get a circuit rider through here about every three months or so. He's a good fellow, steady as they come. I just wish he could stay on." He stepped toward the barn. "I'll fetch my Bible and meet you inside," he said and hurried away.

The next day Banjo rigged a sling to support Jake's leg so it wouldn't swell so much while he was riding. Using an old piece of canvas and a couple of lengths of twine, he made a sort of hammock that looped around the base of the mustang's neck and hooked onto the cantle of the saddle. It was an odd-looking affair, and Jake's expression turned doubtful when he saw it.

Sweating and panting, Steve and Banjo managed to heft the boy into his saddle. He winced and shifted a couple of times, trying to find a comfortable position. "It hurts like fire," he said. "I don't think I kin do it."

"Not right now, you can't," Banjo told him. "We'll have to give you a couple of days to get used to it. You've been abed nigh onto a month. You'll have to build yourself up." He held out his arms to the boy. "Let's get you down now. Tomorrow we'll work at this some more. Now that we know how to get you astride the saddle, things'll be easier."

Every day for the next week, Banjo worked with the boy until Jake felt comfortable. Then they worked with Jake's horse, Haney, until the horse grew accustomed to the awkward pull of Jake's weight in that position.

On Sunday night Jake and Sally were in their room while Sally packed their gear. They planned to leave in the morning.

"It's only three hours ride from here," Sally told her son. "We can do that and still be home by nine in the morning."

Jake wasn't convinced. "Three hours in pain may as well be three months," he retorted. He stared at the plank floor for a moment then looked up at her, his brow puckered. "What if I can't make it?"

"We'll stop and rest awhile if you can't make it all the way. Banjo is trail wise. He can even make us a camp where we can spend the night." She shoved a shirt into the bag. "If you have to stop, just give a holler." She reached for a pair of socks.

Jake slid farther down to stretch out on the bed. He turned his back to her.

Sally finished stowing their things into the bag. She was dreading the trip almost as much as Jake was. She sighed and stood to spread out her buckskin outfit. She'd have to return her borrowed clothes tomorrow. A tiny thrill went through her as she set her riding boots near her breeches. It would be good to get back in the saddle again. She hadn't ridden her horse, Joey, for any length of time since last month, far too long.

The next morning the Chamberlin household was awake an hour before dawn. Megan made biscuits and bacon while Steve and Banjo loaded the pack horses with Sally's supplies. Sally helped Jake dress and finished packing away the last of their belongings. After a quick breakfast, Megan handed Sally a tin can with a handle on it. Inside were more biscuits and bacon wrapped in a cloth for their lunch.

Sally took the can and hugged Megan. "There's no way I can thank you," she said, her eyes filling as she looked at her dear friend.

"Take good care of Banjo," Megan said, beaming at him. "That's all the thanks I'll need."

Banjo stepped forward for a quick hug. "You take good care of these babies until I get back." He leaned down to lift Katie high and plant a kiss on her cheek.

"Are you going, too?" Katie asked Banjo, sneaking a glance over his shoulder at Sally.

"I'm afraid so, honey," he replied. "I'll be back come spring or summer, though." He set her down. "Take good care of Stevie for me, and tell him I'll sing him a song about Woody, the mixed-up crow, when I get back."

Nodding, Katie backed into her mother's skirt and held on to it.

Quite adept at using his crutches now, Jake headed out the door. Jeremy had the horses waiting near the porch steps. Steve and Banjo had Jake in the saddle in ten seconds. Sally and Banjo climbed aloft, gave a final wave, and set out around the stubbly cornfield. Behind them, tied together with a long rope, came eight horses—the Newcomb's remuda. Five of them carried pack saddles holding Sally's winter supplies.

Sally felt a little sad. Her time at the Circle C had begun in a traumatic way, but the ranch had become a peaceful haven to her. It was time to go back to her world, and she didn't want to face it.

"You're mighty quiet," Banjo said, riding near her. "Are you happy to be heading home?"

She pulled in a corner of her mouth. "I was just thinking about that. To be honest, I'm not sure. The Chamberlins' home is so peaceful. I'm going to miss it."

"With Jeremy around?" Banjo laughed. "That young'un has more energy than a sack full of stray cats." They rode in silence for a few moments, then Banjo said, "Tell me about your spread, Miz Newcomb."

"Call me Sally," she countered, slanting a look of mock irritation at him.

"Yes, ma'am," he replied, stifling a smile at the sudden fire in her eyes.

They reached the rise and continued down the trail heading northwest. The sky turned a bluish-gray, and birds twittered among the aspens and pines around them. Already Banjo felt the inside band on his Stetson growing moist. The sun was going to be a scorcher before long.

"We have two quarter sections," she told Banjo. "One section is mostly timber with a few patches of pastureland. The other section has a canyon with a nice stream running through it. Our place is in the back of that canyon." She smiled. "From a distance it's the purtiest place you ever did see."

"From a distance?"

Her voice grew tired. "Once you get into the dooryard, you can tell that the porch roof sags on one corner, the corral needs mending, the barn—"

"I get you," Banjo said. "That's why I'm coming along."

"Tell him about O'Brien," Jake called from behind them.

Glancing back at her son, she didn't say anything.

"You may as well give me the bad news," Banjo told her. "I need to know the lay of the land."

"It's my neighbor, Douglas O'Brien. Since Mickey died, O'Brien's constantly making all kinds of trouble for me. I think he wants to drive me out."

"Has he offered to buy your place?"

"No. Once, I went over to talk to him, to ask him why, but he ran me off with a shotgun."

"Did you have trouble with him before your husband passed away?"

She shook her head. "Never. He wasn't overly friendly when we happened to meet, but he was a good neighbor. We never saw all that much of him."

Jake said, "He's a—"

"Jake! Don't say it!" Sally cut in.

"Let's start at the beginning," Banjo said. "I want to hear every detail."

Chapter 4

I t started about two weeks after Mickey died," Sally said. "It took about two weeks for Jake and me to get set up to take care of the ranch. Up to then we just did the chores and didn't leave the yard. On our first ride around our spread, we came on a cut fence."

"Barbed wire?" Banjo asked.

"Right. It was cut and bent back. There were plenty of cattle tracks coming in through the opening, so we followed them."

Jake spoke up. His voice was harsh. "They went right through our best watering hole. It was a muddy mess."

"A week passed before it ran clear again," Sally said.

Jake added, "It took us two days to get O'Brien's cows back on his side, too."

They rode a few minutes in silence. Usually when he was riding, Banjo passed the time with music, but today he didn't sing or speak. He was waiting for them to go on.

Jake said, "Tell him about the remuda."

Sally glanced at her son and back to Banjo. "Shortly before the roundup, someone opened the corral gate and set a beaver loose in the middle of our horses. They stampeded to the four winds. It was three days before we got them all corralled again. And then they were worn-out when we started for the roundup." She patted her mustang's neck. "Joey didn't run, though. Did you, boy?" She rubbed his smooth coat. "He got out of the gate and came to the porch to wait for me."

"We were short on calves, too," Jake added. "We should have had twice as many as we did."

"Are you certain of that?" Banjo asked. "Did you keep count?"

Sally nodded. "On such a small outfit as ours, we know most of the cattle by name. I keep a record in my tally book when a cow drops a calf. We should have had sixty calves, and we only had twenty-eight."

Banjo lifted his canteen from where it hung beside his saddle. "Now that's a hanging offense." He took a long drink and recapped the metal container. "Are you sure it's O'Brien who's doing it?"

"Who else would be so hateful?" Sally demanded. "We don't know anyone else."

"Hold on, Ma," Jake said. "You didn't tell him about Mr. Ganss."

"Oh!" she gasped, looking back at her son. "I forgot all about him." She turned to Banjo. "Virgil Ganss is a banker in Juniper. We saw his wife wearing a silk dress when we were there. You must remember her. Have you ever met him?"

"Not that I recall. Which bank?"

"Colorado Bank and Trust, next to the stage station."

Banjo shook his head. "I don't believe I've been there. My money never finds its way into a bank. Once those hombres get a man's folding money, it takes too much trouble to get it out again."

"Mr. Ganss is their newest partner. He came from Cheyenne last winter. He puts me in mind of a snake-oil peddler. He has a kind of weaselly face, and he smiles too much."

"He's got big white teeth," Jake put in, "and he likes showin' them off."

"He's offered me two thousand dollars for the ranch," Sally said. "He's been out to the place twice since Mickey died. Last time he said he's not giving up."

Banjo said, "That doesn't make much sense. Why does he want your place when he's got a soft job in town? Is he a rancher, too?"

She shrugged. "He said he wants the ranch for investment purposes. He'll hire someone to run the place and split the profits. He said he'll hire us if we want to stay on."

"Share the profits!" Jake spat out. "What profits?"

"You're right. It sounds plumb loco," Banjo told him. "No one buys a struggling place as an investment. They'd have to be touched in the head to do that."

"Ganss must be powerful stupid then," Jake said. "He's as hungry for our place as a lobo wolf in the dead of winter."

"Call him Mr. Ganss!" Sally told him.

Jake retorted, "Mr. Ganss is a rascal. I know it."

"We don't have any proof of anything," she told Banjo. "It's just this feeling we get when he comes around."

They came to a wide stream, and Banjo moved to the back of the remuda to urge the horses across. He didn't like the sound of what Sally and Jake had told him. Something was simmering below the surface. Why would O'Brien want to run them off when he didn't want their place? Why would a banker who was money-smart want a ranch that was about to go under? Was O'Brien working through Ganss to get the Bar N? Nothing made sense.

Once the pack horses were across the stream, Banjo urged Kelsey forward to join Sally and Jake at the head of the line. Jake's face was drawn, his mouth tight.

"I'm afraid I'll have to rest," he said. "My leg's paining me something fierce."

Immediately, Sally rode close to his wounded side to look at his leg. "It's swelling bad," she told Banjo. "We'll have to let him rest and prop it up."

"Let's find a good spot, and we'll stop. I think there's water and shade up ahead."

They rode for another twenty minutes before they found the right place—a narrow creek with tall grass and a stand of aspens nearby. Banjo dismounted and kicked at the grass, matting down a spot for Jake to lie on. He moved to the remuda to untie the crutches from the back of a deep-chested bay.

With many tense glances at Jake's pale face, Sally hurried to help Banjo.

"Okay, son," Banjo said, reaching up to Jake on the mustang. It was a good thing that the paint horse was fairly small. "Let's get you down."

Sally moved to the sling holding the injured leg. "We've got to get you out of this." She tugged at the canvas. Jake moaned as the leg fell free.

Sally hurried to stand beside Banjo. "Take it slow and easy, son," she said. "Let us have time to bear your weight."

He leaned forward and let his injured leg slide over the horse as he moved toward his mother and Banjo. It was an awkward descent, but he made it safely to the ground, and Banjo handed him the crutches.

Moving slowly, Jake reached the tramped-out stretch of grass and sank to the ground. Sally brought a folded blanket and placed it under his swollen knee. "Lie back and let the leg rest," she told him. She glanced at Banjo. "While we're here, we may as well stretch out and rest, too. There'll be plenty to do once we get home."

Banjo checked the horses, refilled the canteens, and joined the others. The grass felt like a springy mattress beneath his back. Overhead, tiny clouds formed a dotted pattern across a brilliant sky. The air smelled of sweet timothy. Could life be better?

With his Stetson on the grass beside him, Jake lay still, seemingly asleep. Sally had lain down near him with her eyes closed as well. Stiff buckskins covered her from chin to ankle, but she was still very much a woman. Banjo had never met anyone like her, so independent and determined. Yet she showed a subtle vulnerability that he couldn't quite explain.

She stirred and opened her eyes. She blinked and turned toward Banjo. She looked so young.

"How far to your place now?" he asked.

"Another hour or so."

Jake spoke up. "I don't know how I'm going to make it. We should have waited another week!"

Sally sat up and placed her hand on his shoulder. "I'm sorry, Jake. I wish we had waited, too. We thought you'd be able to make it okay." She looked at Banjo. "What are we going to do?"

"We could camp here tonight and go on in the morning. After a night's rest, he should be able to sit astride for another hour. Let's make camp," Banjo said, standing up. "I'll scout around and try to find us a grouse or a couple of sage hens for the noon meal." Since the ride was only three hours, they'd originally figured to be at the Bar N well before noon.

"We still have the biscuits and bacon Megan sent."

"We'd best save them for the morning." He paced along the edge of the stream until he found a stick about the length of his forearm. Then he stepped off into the aspen grove.

After Banjo disappeared from view, Sally sat beside Jake for another moment. "I'd be grateful if you'd show Banjo a little respect," she told her son. "He's doing us a great favor. What would we do if he hadn't come along?"

After a moment he muttered, "Banjo's fine. There's no problem about him. I guess I'm just mad at the world."

"Life hasn't exactly been candy sticks and roses," she said, "but we've got to make the best of things." She squeezed his arm, then got up and moved toward the stream, looking for deadfall. They'd need a cooking fire and enough fuel to keep it going through the night to keep coyotes and wolves away.

One good thing, the pack horses carried enough beans, bacon, coffee, and other staples to last them through the winter. Even if Banjo didn't find a wild chicken, they would still have plenty to eat.

When the fire was crackling, she dug a coffeepot out from one of the packs. She had ten pounds of coffee beans but no grinder. Well, maybe she could find a stone and smash enough of them to make a small pot of the black brew. After filling the pot with water, she found three wide flat stones from the stream and a smaller rounded one with one flat side. She positioned two of the wide stones in the coals to set the pot on. The third flat stone became her millstone. Using the rounded stone, she crushed a small handful of coffee beans against the larger stone. In a few minutes she had a tiny mound of brown bits. It smelled wonderful.

The heady aroma of simmering coffee filled the air when Banjo returned an hour later carrying two sage hens. He handed them to Sally for cleaning and cooking, then he began the long job of settling the horses for the night. He unloaded all five pack horses. Tying two riatas around four trees, he formed a makeshift corral. Once secured, the long hemp ropes created an area where the horses could roll and rest. They'd already had their fill of grass.

When he finished, Banjo sat next to Jake. "How's the leg, son?" he asked.

"It still hurts some," Jake replied, his voice low. He cleared his throat. "I'm sorry I've been such a whiner about everything. It wasn't nothing against you."

Banjo reclined next to Jake, his right arm under his head. "Tell me about your ranch, Jake," he said. "Your ma did most of the talking on the way here. I'd like to hear your point of view."

The boy rubbed his calloused hand across his dark hair as he said, "It's a purty spread. Lots of trees and timothy with some clover mixed in. Pa built the cabin in the back of a small grassy canyon with a fast creek alongside the cabin. I like to lie up in the loft and listen to the water running. You kin hear it through the chinking in the logs."

"How many cows are still running there after the ones you sold?"

"Close to a hundred, I reckon. Good young stock, all cows except for two bulls. The old one is Samson, and the other'n is his son, Red Neck. Red Neck is a spooky yearling with no good sense. Ma and I are hoping he'll quiet down after a while. If not, he'll make some good steaks come spring."

Banjo chuckled. He let a few moments pass then asked, "Why do you think Douglas O'Brien is on the prod? Most people looking for trouble have a good reason."

Jake grunted. "He's just poison mean, that's all."

"Did anything happen between him and your ma after your pa died? Did they have words or anything?"

"Just that time she went over to see him, and he run her off."

"Were you with her?"

"Naw." He looked disgusted. "She took off without telling what she was doin'. If I'd a been there, O'Brien wouldn't have gotten away with a fool thing like that."

"Tell me about your grazing land and your timber," Banjo said. "I want to know everything."

Jake settled back with his good knee slightly bent, his eyes half closed. He talked for a solid thirty minutes. He knew the land, and he knew cattle. Banjo stretched his legs and let Jake talk himself out. By the time Jake finished the report, Banjo was properly impressed with the young man. He was canny, energetic, and outspoken—qualities Banjo admired. The next thing he knew, Sally's voice brought him out of a light doze.

"You fellows hungry for some lunch?"

Banjo came into a sitting position and glanced at Jake beside him. Expressionless, the boy watched him.

"I reckon I could eat Kelsey without stopping to sip water. My stomach's wondering if my throat's been cut," Banjo said grinning. "Those chickens smell good."

They didn't have proper plates, so Sally passed around the partially cooled skillet and let them take out a couple of biscuits each. The chickens hung from a stout branch over the fire, handy for pulling off a piece.

"Ow!" Banjo howled when he reached for a drumstick. "I'd best put on my riding gloves to get hold of my lunch! My poor fingers is goin' to be smoked sausages in no time."

Jake snorted and tried to hide a grin.

Banjo laughed. "Just funning, Sally," he said. He chewed a bite of chicken and nodded in satisfaction. "This beats Aunt Josie's parlor food, in my book."

They finished the noon meal and stretched out to rest in the shade for the remainder of the afternoon.

As the sun sank low over the horizon, Banjo found a piece of string and a hook in his saddlebag. "I'll find a quiet spot and see if any granddaddy trout are hiding near the bottom of the stream," he said and set off again.

"See what I told you?" Sally told Jake. "He's a handy hombre to have around."

Jake tipped his hat down to cover his eyes. "He'll do," he said.

The sun sank low in the sky, and the air had a warm, lazy feel that naturally made a person drowsy. As darkness moved in, Banjo returned with four large trout, and they ate their fill.

When they finished, he hefted his saddle nearer to the fire and used it to lean his back against. Sally and Jake stretched out on blankets.

They enjoyed the silence for a few moments, then Banjo rubbed the back of his neck and drawled, "A couple of days after Mary and I were married, we got on a stage for a little wedding trip to Dallas. I'd saved for most of a year to make that trip with her. We'd talked about it ever since we got engaged."

He stretched and looked around to see that he had the full attention of the others.

He went on. "We put up in a high-class hotel with a couple of bathrooms where a person could soak in a hot tub of water for as long as he wanted. They had a fancy restaurant there and all. It was a high old time.

"Only thing was, the place had three stories, and all of them looked exactly alike—same kind of wood fixtures, same lamps, same everything. The first floor had the bathrooms, the restaurant, and a couple of bedrooms. The upper floors was all bedrooms.

"My wife decided she wanted a glass of sarsaparilla on a hot afternoon, so she left me in our room to go and fetch us some from the restaurant. She never was good at directions. On the way back she got confused, thought she saw our room, and turned down the first-floor hallway." He chuckled. "She knocked on the door and said, 'Honey, let me in!' I didn't answer, so she called again, louder this time. A minute later, this deep man's voice called out. 'Madam, this is a bathroom, not a beehive!' "

He laughed. "She was so embarrassed that she wouldn't go out of the room without me from then on." He shook his head, sadness creeping into his voice. "She was a sweetheart, Mary was."

Sally had tears in her eyes. "You still miss her, don't you?" she murmured.

He nodded. "Sometimes when I'm at the Circle C, I look up and expect to see her at the stove, but it's Miss Megan instead. Megan has the same gentle way that my Mary did. Maybe that's why I like being at the Chamberlin place so much." He got to his feet. "I believe I'll get a drink at the creek," he said and ambled away.

Mary hadn't been so clear in his mind for five years or more. The sharp memory sent a stab to a place deep within him. It was a familiar pain, but that didn't make it hurt less. That kind of agony didn't lessen with the years; it just got set back a ways where it was harder to reach.

When he came back to their campsite, Sally and Jake were asleep. He rolled up in his saddle blanket and was soon asleep as well.

Jake did better on his second day of travel. The three travelers were singing "When I Survey the Wondrous Cross" as they rode into the Bar N canyon shortly after dawn the next morning. They kept a leisurely pace, and Banjo got a good look at the spread. It was a quiet place with plenty of grass. A couple of cottonwoods near the house gave shade from the worst heat of the day.

"You've got a mighty nice place here, Miz Sally," he said, still looking around. "You could run two hundred head of cattle in this canyon alone." He looked overhead. "Have you been up on the rim?"

Jake said, "Pa and I rode up there from time to time. There's a gap in the rock where a horse can squeeze through to go straight to the top. I'll show it to you once I get back to riding natural again."

Banjo nodded. "We'll do it."

As they approached the ranch yard, Banjo realized that Sally had told him right when she had described the place. It did need shoring up. He drew up when he saw a broken window.

Sally gasped. "Someone's been here," she cried and urged her horse ahead.

Jake shouted after her. "Watch yourself, Ma! They may still be here."

Shattered glass, broken pottery bowls, and feathers from a mattress ticking covered the yard. Sally leapt from her horse and ran into the house. A second later, she screamed.

Chapter 5

Sally's scream was a shrill cry of anger and despair. A second later she reappeared in the doorway. "They've ruined our cabin!" she shrieked. "They've been here and hacked up my chairs, my cooking bowls, everything!"

She bent over to pick up a broken chair leg lying beside her on the porch and heaved it through what remained of a windowpane, spraying bits of glass into the house.

Banjo leapt off Kelsey and hurried after her. He reached the door in time to see her smash a battered coffeepot against the stone fireplace.

"Sally!" he bellowed. "Stop it!"

She lifted an enamel dishpan and flung it against the log wall. "Those rotters!" she cried. "I wish I could a been here to shoot every last one of 'em!" She reached for the black poker and began to beat at the thick oak table, leaving ragged scars in the stained wood.

"Sally!" Banjo shouted. "Stop it! You're making things worse!"

She held the poker in both hands and hacked at the table, sobbing and screaming with every blow.

Watching the poker with a wary eye, he came up behind her and waited for the right moment to grab her. His arms circled her shoulders, so she couldn't lift her arms.

She dropped the poker and swung around, causing him to lose his grip. "I shouldn't 'ave come back!" she shouted into his face. "I was a crazy fool to come back here. I hate this place!" She raised her fists and swung at him. He stepped back, arms raised in a defensive stance, watching for a chance to grab her wrists.

"Simmer down, Sally!" he cried. "You're out of your head. Simmer down!"

"I am out of my head! I was out of my head when I came back here." She stepped toward him, a gleam in her eye. "And you were the reason I did. If you hadn't come to help me, maybe me and Jake would have gone on to St. Louis, or anywhere out of this. . .awful pit." She let out another cry that sounded like a panther in pain and swung at his chest.

When the blow landed, Banjo grabbed her right arm. The next instant he had her left. She yanked hard to free herself, bending at the waist to writhe and turn. When she saw there was no use struggling, she tilted her head back and let out an agonized wail that sent a shiver through him.

She sobbed, "God, help me! What am I going to do?" and he caught her as she collapsed. She moaned against his chest. Her head lolled to one side. Her eyes were half closed.

With her head still against his chest, Banjo eased her to the floor. At that moment, Jake came through the door on his hands and knees. Somehow he had managed to get out of the saddle alone. "Ma!" he cried, fear contorting his face. "Ma!" He crawled beside her and grabbed her in an awkward hug. "Don't cry, Ma! Don't cry!" Tears streamed down his cheeks. "We'll make it. Don't cry."

Sally's hand came up to touch his face. She coughed and struggled to sit up alone.

Watching her closely, Banjo stepped back.

"I'm s—sorry," she stammered, wiping her eyes. "I don't know what came over me. I've never had hysterics in my life."

"It's understandable," Banjo said, clearing his throat. "Both you and Jake have had your pockets full of troubles."

"We'll get by," Jake told her. He held her hand to his cheek.

She drew in a deep breath and pulled her hand away from him. Leaning over to kiss him, she got to her knees and then to her feet. With shaking hands, she wiped her face again and pushed at her hair. She righted the only chair still in one piece and sat in it.

"Just give me a minute to fetch Jake his crutches," Banjo said, heading for the door. "Once I get back, we'll take stock of the place and decide what to do."

A few minutes later, Banjo helped Jake to his feet and handed him the crutches. He fetched Sally a cool drink from the pump in the yard, and the three of them sat in silence for five minutes trying to muster the courage to begin a long, hard task—Sally in the chair and the gents on the hearth.

The cabin was divided in two parts. To the right stood a small bedroom with a double bed and a single window. The remaining area held a cast-iron cookstove and a long table with one of its four chairs remaining. That was all the furniture in the house. A loft ladder on the dividing wall hung just inside the front door and led to an open loft that topped the bedroom. Long wooden pegs on all four walls held various garments and items for cooking or washing. The windows had no curtains.

Banjo looked around at the mangled cabin and felt a hot ball rise in his chest. Whoever had done this would pay. He'd personally see to it.

Finally, Sally set her empty cup on the table. "We've got to get this mess cleaned up," she quavered.

"I'll unpack the horses," Banjo said, "then I'll give you a hand." He stepped outside to haul several burlap sacks to the cellar at the back of the house. For the first time, he wondered what he was doing here. He wondered what Sally and her son were doing here. This sure was a pretty place, but it was more than one man and one woman could handle if they had enemies as determined as theirs seemed to be.

He took a moment to send up a fervent prayer, then he unloaded a lumpy sack holding supplies for the house and set it inside the door.

When he stepped inside, Sally was sweeping glass and bits of chipped enamel into a pile on the plank floor. She bent over to pick up a bent tintype. "Look. My only picture of Jake when he was a little boy." Fresh tears sprang up.

Jake moved to his mother. "Let me have it," he said, holding out his hand.

She let him take it from her. Sniffing, she touched her nose with the back of her hand and continued sweeping.

Banjo examined the broken chairs and decided which ones could be repaired. The others he took outside. When he returned, Jake was seated at the table with his bad leg resting across the tabletop. He was flattening the tintype under his hand, examining it closely. "You can still tell it's me," he was telling his mother. "We can keep it. I'll whittle a new frame for it."

An hour's work had the place in fair shape, though they would spend days putting things completely to rights.

Finally, Sally reached for the lumpy sack Banjo had left by the door. For the first time her grieved expression softened a little. "I'm so glad I picked up these things. At the time I felt guilty for spending the extra money, but now I think it was the good Lord telling me to get them."

Banjo grinned. "That's the way He works, Sally. Most times we can't even see His hand in things until later."

She set the bag on the table and opened it. First out was the coffeepot they'd used on the trail, followed by a cast-iron skillet, two bowls, and an enamel wash-basin. A fat bundle of green calico came last. "That's for curtains," she said, feeling the fabric. "I'll sew them up of an evening." She took the calico to the bedroom and returned right away.

"I need to put some food on the stove before I go out to see about the barn," she said, hurrying toward the stove. "I'll mix us up some corn bread."

"I'll do that," Jake said, looking up. "Just set the stuff here on the table, and I'll do the rest." He laid the picture aside. "You've already got the fire made, so there won't be anything to it. I can carry the bowl over there to fry us some corn cakes."

She hesitated, watching him. "Are you sure you're up to all that?" she asked. "You've just come through a long ride, Jake. I don't want you getting down again."

He waved her away. "I've got a busted leg, Ma. I'm not half dead."

Banjo let them decide the details and set out to get the pack horses taken care of. He grabbed the bridle of their leader—the deep-chested bay gelding— and led them to the pasture. Ground-hitching the bay, he left them tied together and went to check out the corral. He couldn't turn the horses loose until he was sure the fence was tight.

The vandals had knocked it down in a couple of places, but he should have it fixed in no time. Looking for tools, he went inside the small barn. The structure wasn't a showpiece, but it was tight and strong. To the left he found a tack room with a ball peen hammer and a post-hole digger. Several fence rails lay piled up against one wall, probably left over from the original work and saved for an emergency. Well, this qualified.

Sally arrived as he set the first post upright in a new hole. The post had been shoved askew, not broken.

"How can I help you?" she asked. Her chin was up, and she had life in her voice again. She reached for a fence rail and shoved it into the bottom slot on the post. Banjo picked up the other end and slid it into the next post. In thirty minutes they had the fence in good shape again.

"Whoever did this was in a hurry," Banjo said. "He didn't take the time to destroy the whole fence, just knocked it around a little."

"I wonder why he didn't burn the place," she said. "That would have been easier than all this."

"That's a good question," he said. He leaned his back against a post, pulled off his hat, and wiped his brow on his sleeve. "That would bear studying on."

Jake called from the house, "Grub's ready!"

Banjo grinned. "He's singing my song!" Replacing his hat, he said, "I'll turn the horses loose in here before I come inside."

Sally stepped closer to him. "There's no way I can ever thank you," she said.

His eyebrows went up. "I thought I was to blame for helping you come back here."

She blushed. "I feel like a fool for acting that way. I don't know what came over me. You must think I'm a silly female the way I've been carrying on since we got back. It's just. . .I'm so tired of all this, Banjo. I want some peace."

"You're only a human being, Sally," he said. "Don't let it get you down. Look at what happened today. You got upset, but a few minutes later you pulled yourself together, and now you're back to fighting. You're a strong woman, Sally. Don't ever tell yourself that you're not."

She watched him a moment, her face still, then strode to the house, the fringe on her jacket whipping with the breeze.

Banjo spent the next few days repairing broken furniture and cleaning out the barn. Time was a-wasting. They had to start cutting hay lickety-split. But first, he had to ride along the property's fence line to check for breaks.

He had just saddled Kelsey and led the donkey out of the barn when a big black stallion pranced into the yard. In the saddle sat a tall slim man wearing a black broadcloth suit and a flat-crowned hat. Before Banjo could reach him, Sally appeared on the front porch. She was smiling wider than Banjo had ever seen her smile before. She waved as she hurried toward the stranger.

"Hello, Pastor Monaghan," she said. "We weren't expecting you back so soon."

He slid from the saddle, a thick black book in his hand. "Good morning, Mrs. Newcomb," he replied, his voice smooth and deep. "I'm on my way to Denver, and I remembered how good your cooking is. I hope you don't mind if I impose on your hospitality again so soon." He grinned down at her.

Banjo felt a tightening in his chest as he stepped closer. Did he have that feeling because of the man's manner or something else? Whatever it was, he took an instant dislike to the parson.

"Oh," Sally said, turning to Banjo. "Pastor Monaghan, this is our new hand, Banjo Calahan."

The preacher nodded and shook hands. "Good to know you," he drawled. He might have come from Texas.

"Howdy," Banjo replied. He sized up the man from his black eyes to his beaklike nose and narrow chin.

The preacher reached behind his saddle for a black traveling bag tied there. He pulled it off the horse and turned to Banjo. "Turn my horse into the corral, will you?"

With a brief nod, Banjo reached for the horse's bridle and led him away as the preacher went inside with Sally.

"Tell me about your travels since you were last here," she said as they turned away.

Banjo unsaddled the stallion. Then he unsaddled Kelsey. Suddenly he didn't feel inclined to be away from the ranch all day. He mucked out a few stalls and fed the stock. At noon he went inside.

The preacher sat at the table with Jake. Without his hat on, he looked even thinner, sort of like a plucked chicken. Sally set a pan of biscuits on the table. She had fried some thick bacon and made a pot of beans. The table was set for four, but there were only three chairs.

When he stepped inside, Sally turned to Banjo and asked, "Would you mind fixing your plate and sitting back since the pastor is here? I'm sorry, but there aren't enough chairs anymore."

"Of course," Banjo said, but he wasn't sure he meant it.

"Pastor," Sally said, "would you thank the Lord for our food?"

"Let's pray," Monaghan said. He bowed and his voice boomed, "O God, we thank Thee for Thy bounty. We thank Thee, O God, for Thy goodness and Thy holiness. Help us to follow Thy ways, and bless us, we pray. Amen."

When he finished, Banjo spooned beans onto his plate, picked up a biscuit and a couple of pieces of bacon, and found a place on the hearth with his back to the fireplace.

During dinner the preacher held Sally and Jake spellbound with tales of his travels through the Rockies from Montana to Texas. Banjo munched bacon and listened without commenting. He did plenty of thinking though.

When the meal was over, the preacher pulled out his big black Bible and opened to a passage. "Let's have a little Bible reading before I head out," he said.

"You're not staying over until morning?" Sally asked, disappointed.

"I'm afraid not, Miz Newcomb," he replied. "I've got to be in Denver tomorrow." He turned a few pages. "It says here in Isaiah 45:22–24:

"Look unto me, and be ye saved, all the ends of the earth: for I am God, and there is none else. I have sworn by myself, the word is gone out of my mouth in righteousness, and shall not return, That unto me every knee shall bow, every tongue shall swear. Surely, shall one say, in the Lord have I righteousness and strength: even to him shall men come; and all that are incensed against him shall be ashamed.

"God's word is righteous," he went on. "It's that righteousness that we must strive for every day."

Banjo kept his seat. As the preacher spoke, Banjo watched his face, his eyes. Something about Parson Monaghan didn't set right with him, but exactly what it was, Banjo couldn't tell. Jake seemed to feel the same way. He didn't look at the preacher once during the hour-long sermon that followed.

Shortly after he finished, the preacher got ready to leave, and Banjo went out to saddle the stallion. Pastor Monaghan soon had his hands full with his bag and Bible, so Sally opened the door for him.

After they'd stepped outside onto the porch, Pastor Monaghan moved closer to Sally, his gaze intent and intimate. "Sally," he said, "I've been hoping for a chance to speak to you."

She stared at him, vaguely alarmed because she knew what he was about to say. He'd said it twice before.

"You're a fine woman," he went on. "I've come to have the deepest regard for you." He cleared his throat, and his Adam's apple bobbed. "You'd do me the greatest honor if you'd agree to be my wife. You don't have to give me an answer now," he rushed ahead as the barn door creaked open, and Banjo appeared. "Pray about it some more. We can talk more when I come back through."

Grasping for composure, she nodded. She didn't know what to say to him. Marrying the preacher would provide a home for her and Jake, but she wasn't sure that a roof over her head was all she wanted from a marriage. She sighed. Still, she felt an overwhelming impulse to leave the ranch forever, no matter how.

When Banjo reached the porch, Sally's cheeks looked flushed. He handed the reins over to the parson and climbed the two steps to stand next to Sally.

"Thank you kindly for the meal, Sally," Monaghan said when he was in the saddle. He lifted his hat to her.

"Please stop in whenever you're passing through," she replied with a smile.

"I'll do that." He glanced at Banjo. "Thanks for seeing after my horse, Benjy," he said and rode away.

Banjo stared after him for a full minute before he realized that Sally still stood beside him. She was also gazing after the rider, a nervous twist to her mouth.

Banjo glanced at the sky, figured he had a good eight hours until full darkness fell, and strode back to the barn to saddle Kelsey. He still had time to do some fence work. He might as well get started on it.

As he cinched the saddle down, he said, "Kelsey, don't ever get tangled up with no pesky female. She'll have you turned inside out before you know what hit you." He flipped the stirrup down and climbed aboard. "Funny thing is, I still can't figure out what's going on. . .with me or with her." He tightened his knees around the donkey's ribs and set off at a trot.

An hour later he was on the other side of the canyon when he heard a rumble like distant thunder. Kelsey's ears pricked up. He hee-hawed with a squeaking noise. Banjo wheeled around to see fifty cows stampeding toward the ranch. Their heads down, they moved in unison like some deadly machine set for demolition with no brake to stop it.

This far away, there was nothing Banjo could do but ride after them. He'd never reach them in time to turn them or stop them from charging through the ranch yard. Sending a quick prayer heavenward, he kicked Kelsey into a gallop.

Five hundred yards from the cabin, he watched the corral fence buckle and flatten under the tremendous power of two hundred hooves. The horses in the corral joined the stampeding herd. The porch swayed, and one end broke loose from the house. The dust swelled until the house and barn looked like two roofs above a gray cloud. The noise was deafening.

In seconds, the herd passed through the yard and down the edge of the canyon. Banjo pulled Kelsey to a halt beside the porch, leapt across the slanting boards, and yanked at the cabin door. "Sally! Jake! Are you okay?"

Sally was kneeling beside Jake's chair. They had their arms around each other. When she saw Banjo, she stood and threw herself into his arms. "I thought we were goners! I thought you were. . ." She burst into tears.

He moved closer. "The house and barn are okay. They roughed up the porch some, but I can fix it. It's the corral that got the worst of it."

"I can't take this any more, Banjo," she gasped. She moved away from him, lifted her open hands to shoulder level, and shook them in the air. "We've got to leave here before somebody gets killed!" She paced to the stove and back to Banjo. "Pastor Monahagn just asked me to marry him," she said. "I'd best take him up on it before he changes his mind."

Chapter 6

But Ma!" Jake cried. "You don't have to do that. Sell the place to Virgil Ganss. Two thousand dollars will go a long way to setting us up again."

Sally's voice rose. "I'm tired of being alone, Jake. It's so hard when you're a woman and have no man to take care of things."

"I'll take care of you!" he declared. "Just give my leg time to heal, that's all. I'll do it!" He looked at Banjo. "What about our horses? Did they get trampled?"

Banjo shook his head. "They just ran off with those loco cows. They'll be back once they run themselves out." He scratched the hat crease that ran around the back of his hair. "One good thing about living in this canyon—there's no place for the animals to run to unless they find the opening on the other side."

Sally pulled a chair away from the table and sat down. She looked like she'd aged twenty years in the last twenty minutes. "I'm serious about not going on," she said. "I was crazy to think I could handle this place alone, just me and Jake."

"You're not alone now," Banjo told her. "I'm here to help you, remember? I'm going to backtrack those cows and see if I can figure out what spooked them." He headed for the door. "I may not be back until dark." With that, he went outside and stepped into the saddle.

Following the trail back to where the stampede began was childishly simple. The ground had been churned, the grass obliterated in a path fifty-feet wide across the canyon. Banjo shook his head, disgusted at the grass destroyed by those cattle. Sally needed that hay for winter feed. At least the meadow was large and thickly grown. Soon as he finished checking out the fence line, he had to get out here and start cutting hay.

Moving at a moderate pace along the edge of the turned-up earth, Banjo reached the end of the path and paused to look carefully around. He stayed in the saddle, letting his gaze cover the area with patient care. Finally, he spotted something that intrigued him. He dismounted.

Fifty feet away, a long straight stick lay on the ground. It didn't seem like much at first glance, but when Banjo turned it over, he spotted two white threads caught in a rough spot where a twig had been recently broken off. He stood with the stick in his hands, tapping it against his palm, and turned his attention back to the ground.

Ten feet away, he found what he was looking for—the track of a shod horse, fresh and sharp. Kneeling beside it, he studied the clear imprint for several minutes. Hard clay covered the bare spot, the reason no grass grew there. The horseshoe print was so clear that the shoe must be new. He stayed there for nearly half an hour, moving around the area in ever-widening circles, looking for a clue to identify the man, but he found nothing. He pulled out his tally book and made a note of the date the stampede had occurred.

Finally satisfied that he'd seen all there was to see, he tied the stick to the cantle behind his saddle and finished the day outside the canyon, riding the Bar N fence line. He only got about a tenth of it covered before dark, but it looked fine.

Sally had supper on when he returned. It was the remainder of their noon meal warmed over.

"That looks good," he said, hanging his hat on a peg beside the door. He carried the stick in his hand. "I'm hungry enough to eat bear tracks and coyote howls."

Jake stared at him, a question on his face.

Banjo chuckled. "Never heard of such?" he asked. He took a seat at the table. "Well, you're not alone. Neither have I."

"Did you find anything this afternoon?" Jake asked.

"Sure did, son," Banjo replied, handing him the stick. "That's it. Someone tied a handkerchief or a piece of sheet to it. A white cloth flapping in the wind will make a wild-eyed steer stampede every time."

"Red Neck was leading the pack," Jake said. "No doubt about it. Maybe we should butcher him now before he can cause more trouble."

"Who would do such an awful thing?" Sally demanded. "Anyone in the yard would have been killed."

"It appears to me that someone wants your ranch, ma'am," Banjo replied. "Someone wants it mighty bad."

Sally sat down at the table, and Banjo offered thanks. When he finished, he lifted a biscuit from the plate in the center of the table. "Would you be offended if I gave you a couple of pointers on making these things?" he asked, eyeing the lumpy mass in his hand. "I'm a hand at cookin'."

Jake let out a loud laugh.

Sally turned pink. "Banjo, I'd be thankful if you would. Mickey and Jake were always tormenting me about my cooking. I've been too embarrassed to ask help from any womenfolk."

"When we get a chance, we'll do it," he said, dipping the stiff biscuit into his beans to soften it up. After a few bites, he asked, "When did all this interest in the Bar N start? Was Ganss after Mickey to sell, too?"

Sally laid down her fork and leaned back. "Virgil Ganss was the banker who loaned Mickey the money to improve on the place. We staked claim to these two quarter-sections under the Homestead Act then borrowed the money to build the cabin, the barn, and the corral. Mickey paid off the note about three months before he died."

"You can thank the good Lord for that," Banjo said.

She nodded. "I do. We'd have been destitute but for that. The bank would have taken our place by now."

He turned his attention back to the meal. In a moment he said, "You're having too much bad luck around here for it to be just happenstance." He looked into her eyes. "Promise me one thing, will you?"

"What's that?"

"You won't pack up and leave until I can get to the truth. I've got a notion that someone wants you off this land for a mighty big reason. Don't light a shuck for the hills until we can find out why. Deal?"

She slowly nodded. "I'll try, Banjo," she said. "But I've a mind to sell the place one way or the other."

"Suit yourself. Just don't get cheated in the process."

They finished the meal, and Banjo fetched his Bible from the corner of the mantel shelf where he'd been stowing it lately. Tonight he read from Psalm 18:16–19:

> "He sent from above, he took me, he drew me out of many waters. He delivered me from my strong enemy, and from them which hated me: for they were too strong for me.
>
> They prevented me in the day of my calamity: but the Lord was my stay. He brought me forth also into a large place; he delivered me, because he delighted in me."

"Read that again," Sally said.

"I like it better when you read," Jake said as he stared at the fire. "When the preacher reads, it makes me feel bad."

"Jake!" Sally scolded. "Don't talk that way."

"That's not necessarily a bad thing, Sally," Banjo said. "Sometimes we have to feel bad before we come to getting right with the Lord." He read the passage once more, led in a short prayer, then stood. "It's time for me to turn in. Good night to you," he said and reached for the ladder.

Later, in the quietness of the loft, Banjo tossed on his straw mattress. His mind kept working long past his normal sleeping time. His thoughts ran from the massive job of cutting hay this late in the year, to the white threads caught on a stick, to the flashing glint in a woman's eyes.

Riding the fence line the next morning, Banjo topped a rise to see the neighboring ranch house off in the distance. He watched a small spiral of smoke rising from the chimney atop the house. Reaching for his canteen, he took a long pull of tepid water and screwed the metal cap back on. "C'mon, Kelsey, old boy," he said, urging the donkey ahead. "Let's be neighborly for an hour or so."

The donkey shook his head and set off down the trail.

When he reached the ranch yard, Banjo shouted, "Hello," in the general direction of the house. A few minutes later, a broad, red-haired man in worn jean coveralls came from the barn, a pitchfork in his hand. Banjo let Kelsey amble forward until they reached speaking distance. "Howdy," he said. "Mind if I stretch my legs for a minute?"

The other man watched him, suspicion on his wide face. "Suit yourself." He had a tinge of the Irish in his speech.

Banjo stepped out of the saddle and shook hands. "I'm Banjo Calahan. I'm new to these parts and stopped in to swap howdies."

"Douglas O'Brien," the rancher said. He still held the pitchfork. "Where ye be staying?"

"I'm the new hand at the Bar N," Banjo said, keeping his tone casual. "I was riding the fence line, checking for breaks, when I spotted your place. I thought I'd mosey on over and introduce myself."

O'Brien's face turned red. "You'll do yourself a favor and get back on your donkey," he said. "We don't keep no truck with the likes of them Newcombs."

Banjo looked surprised. "Any reason why not?" he asked. "Like I said, I'm new to these parts. If there's a feud going on, I'd like to know about it."

With the tines pointing upward, O'Brien shook the pitchfork. "Get on your mount," he ground out. "Those Newcombs are cutting my fences and driving their cattle through my watering hole. They cull out my calves and take them when they're scarcely weaned." He spat on the ground. "That Mickey Newcomb was a backroom gambler who welshed on his debts. Nobody in these parts liked him. We felt sorry for his wife, but since he died, she and the boy have turned mean. They're a no-good lot, man. You'd do yourself a favor and keep on riding when you leave here."

"Would you mind showing me where your fence was cut?" Banjo asked, keeping his tone calm and unconcerned. "Someone's cutting the Newcombs' fences too. Maybe it's the same person."

"Take a look for yourself," he said, nodding toward the north. "Beyond the mesa you'll see a pine grove. That's the place."

Banjo's boot found the stirrup, and he heaved himself into the saddle. He pulled at his hat brim. "I'm obliged to you, Mr. O'Brien," he said. "Good day to you." With that he turned Kelsey and trotted out of the yard, not too fast so O'Brien wouldn't think he was afraid but fast enough to keep from pushing the angry man into a rage.

So O'Brien thought Sally and Jake were cutting his fences. This was an interesting turn.

Banjo rode north until he spotted the mesa O'Brien had mentioned. In ten minutes he found the mended section of fence and stepped out of the saddle. Leaning over, he swept aside the grass below the fence and soon found something unexpected: red flecks of paint.

He reached into his coat pocket for a little wad of paper he'd put there before and opened it up. Carefully lifting a few fragments of the red paint from the ground, he dropped them onto the paper and held them to the light for a closer look.

As far as he could tell, they were the same color. In a part of the country where a tool was used for decades, a new wire cutter with red paint on it was a rare item.

He twisted the paper together and put it away in his pocket for a future time when it might come in handy.

Banjo spent the rest of the day checking the rest of Sally's fence. By the time he rode into the ranch yard, the edge of dark covered the house and barn. Over supper he told Sally and Jake about his visit to O'Brien's ranch. "What did he mean when he said that you were cutting his fences and tramping cattle through his water?" he asked them.

"We never!" Jake ground out. "He's a liar."

Banjo drew back, dismayed. "You'll keep that kind of talk to home, son, if you know what's good for you. You spout off like that to a man's face, and you'll likely pick up a bullet or two."

"There's nothing to what O'Brien said," Sally told him. "Neither of us have been over there since Mickey died, right Jake?"

Jake stared at the tabletop and didn't answer.

"What is it?" Banjo asked him. "You know something."

"I went over there onc't," he muttered. "I wanted to warn him to keep off our place. I didn't even get off my horse."

"I did the same," Sally said. "He ran me off with his shotgun."

Banjo chuckled. "He had a pitchfork this morning, but I'm not sure that was any safer. He was so mad, he was chewing iron and spitting nails when he found out I work for you." He sipped coffee. "How was he before Mickey died? Was he this angry?"

Sally shrugged. "He was never overly friendly, but he wasn't as mean then as he is now. He was polite to me the two times we met on the trail to town."

"He didn't like Pa," Jake said. "He'd turn his head whenever they met."

"When did you meet up with him?" Banjo asked.

"We was in the back room of Red Rooster Saloon. Pa was playing poker, and

O'Brien was in on the game."

"You were watching him gamble?" Sally demanded, shooting Jake a scorching look. "When did this happen?"

Jake wilted. "About six months before Pa died."

"That was the time when we ate together at the hotel, right?" Banjo asked.

He nodded. "After we ate, Pa and I went over to the Red Rooster and stayed until late that afternoon."

"And you never told me!" Sally burst out.

"Pa would have tanned my hide," Jake cried. "All I did was sit in the corner and watch them play. I didn't do nothing."

"I don't care. Just taking you there was wrong, Jake! If Mickey were here, I'd speak my mind to him." She grabbed their plates and cleared the table. The dishes thumped and clacked as she stacked them.

"Was your Pa in debt from his gambling?" Banjo asked Jake.

The boy nodded. "He owed a couple of people."

"Do you remember who?"

He shrugged and shifted in his chair. "Barney Sykes, Hank Andrews, Douglas O'Brien. . ." He paused, then said, "I can't think of anyone else. I didn't always go with him, so there's no telling who all may hold a—"

"How much did it amount to?" Banjo asked.

"I don't know. I can't remember." Jake turned to stare at Banjo. "Why? Do you think that may have something to do with our trouble?"

"That's hard to say. I'm still trying to figure it all out."

Sally slid the stack of plates and cups into her dishwater, left them soaking, and returned to her chair. "To be honest, I've always wondered about Mickey's accident," she said. "It didn't strike me right from the first day."

She had Banjo's full attention. "What happened?" he asked. "Tell me every detail."

"Mickey didn't come in for supper," she said. "He'd been riding the range, looking for weaned calves to bring into the holding pen. I last saw him around midafternoon when he brought in two little heifers. He waved to me and set off for the edge of the canyon again. I didn't think any more about him until it was getting dark and he didn't come back."

"I was cleaning out the barn," Jake added. "If I'd a been riding with him, it may not have happened."

Sally said, "Me and Jake set out with a lantern when it got real late, but we couldn't find him. When we got back, his horse had come in with an empty saddle." She shivered. "I walked the floor for the rest of the night, waiting for dawn to break so we could look for him. I couldn't stand to think of him out on the cold ground with a broken leg. . .or. . ." She couldn't go on.

Jake picked up the tale. "We found him the next morning. He'd fallen off the rim above the canyon."

"How did he get there?" Banjo asked. "It seems strange that he'd get off his horse and step so close to the edge that he could fall."

"I thought so, too," Sally said. "He had a fear of heights that usually kept him away from the rim. I don't know what would have possessed him to get down from the horse and walk to the edge."

"Can you think of anything else that was different from usual?"

Jake said, "Someone had built a fire there. I always wondered why Pa would build a fire. It was May, and it wasn't terribly cold that afternoon. Even if it was, he wouldn't have stopped to build a fire. He would have come to the house if he needed to warm up."

"Maybe someone else was there," Banjo said. "Did you see anyone else around?"

They shook their heads. Sally said, "We were out there just after dawn, and there wasn't a soul around then."

Banjo drained his cup and set it down. "Tomorrow's the Lord's Day. Would you mind if we read some from the Good Book after breakfast?"

"That would be nice, Banjo," Sally said.

"Maybe we can work on those biscuits tomorrow, too," Banjo said. "I usually like to take a rest from heavy work on Sunday."

"Sounds good to me. I could use a quiet day," Sally said, smiling at him.

He pushed his chair back from the table. "I'll see you folks in the morning then." He paused at the foot of the loft ladder. "I'm nigh on to certain that all of this is tied together, Sally. I'll keep my ears open and try to put things together for you."

She nodded and moved to the dishpan. Enamel plates made a scuffling noise as she scrubbed them.

Sunday morning after the chores, Banjo joined Sally in the kitchen. She had a bowl of flour on the table, a small sack of salt, and a crock of lard.

She flushed when he stepped inside. "I'm as nervous as a fifteen-year-old at her first box supper," she said with a little laugh. "It's ridiculous."

He chuckled. "Let me wash my hands, and we'll get started. This'll be much easier than breaking a yearling colt, believe me." He looked at the table. "Have you got any sour milk?"

She nodded.

"That'll make some great biscuits."

"I'll get some from the springhouse." She hurried away.

By the time he'd finished washing his hands, she was back with a small jug in her hands. "I use this for corn bread, too," she said, setting it on the table.

He dried his hands on a flour-sack towel and strode to the table. The bowl seemed small under his big calloused hands. "First you need to add a healthy dose of salt and saleratus," he told her.

"Saleratus?"

He nodded. "That's what Ma called it. I guess folks nowadays call it baking soda."

She handed him a small tin. "Here it is."

He opened the lid and used a spoon to sprinkle some of the white powder over the flour. He repeated the action with the salt. "Now here comes the important part," he told her as he mixed the flour with a large wooden spoon. "Cutting in the lard makes a big difference." He used the wooden spoon to scoop out a large lump of rendered pork fat and showed her how to work it into the dough until it disappeared.

Sally poured in the sour milk and watched Banjo deftly stir it in. The flour soon became a smooth, light dough. "Handle the dough gently, and you'll get a flaky biscuit," he told her. "Pretend it's a French pastry, not a mud pie." He winked at her.

She grinned.

He shoved the bowl toward her. "Stir it a few times to get the feel of it."

She picked up the spoon and dabbed at the dough. "That's wonderful. I can't wait to eat these." She handed the bowl back. "Do you roll them out? I've never been able to get the knack of that."

"I don't roll them," he said. "I think that makes them tough. Remember, if you handle the dough very gently, the biscuits will come out tender." He looked around. "Fetch me a small bowl of flour, and I'll show you how I do it."

She reached up to a shelf for a yellow crockery bowl with two blue stripes on it. "Where did you learn this, Banjo?" she asked.

"I had a mother who didn't think that kitchen work was only for women," he replied. "So many times I've wished I could thank her for that. Her lessons have given me many a good meal, I'll tell you."

She smiled as she handed him the flour. "That's certain." She watched him dip flour out of the bowl, hold it in his hand, then drop a spoonful of dough into his floury palm. Sprinkling more flour on top, he held the ball of dough over his small bowl and flipped the biscuit back and forth, forming it into a smooth ball. He dropped it onto the baking pan and gently pressed the top down to make it flat.

"That's different from anything I've ever seen before," Sally exclaimed. "Let me try it."

"Get a spoon," he said, grinning.

Favoring his bad leg, Jake appeared in the bedroom door and gripped the doorjambs for support. Banjo had hauled Jake's cot downstairs to Sally's room until Jake mended enough to climb the loft ladder. "You've got flour on your jeans, Banjo," Jake called. "You should have worn an apron." He chuckled.

His hands still in motion, Banjo looked up at him. "You'd do yourself a favor if you came down and learnt a few things, young feller. This is more fun than the time a mouse ran up Grandpa's pant leg."

Jake gave a hoot and disappeared back into the bedroom.

A few minutes later, Sally slid the pan into the oven. She and Banjo met over the wash basin to scrub the gooey bits of dough from their fingers.

"Thank you," Sally said. "Jake will thank you, too, once he tastes them."

Banjo smiled into her eyes. "I've enjoyed it. I ought to be thanking you."

She smiled, flushed, and turned away to reach for a towel.

Monday morning Banjo and Sally were hard at work in the meadow when a piebald mare rode into their canyon. The rider rode close, and Banjo eyed the horse's Spectacles brand on its flank. The Bar N had more visitors than the local grocer these days. Who was it now?

Sally stood up from tying a bundle of hay together and said, "Hello, Mr. Ganss. What brings you out here? I'm still not ready to sell the ranch."

He had a forced smile pasted on his weasel-like face. "Good afternoon, Mrs. Newcomb. It happens that I've brought you a telegram." He reached into his vest pocket and pulled out a yellow page.

Sally reached for it, glanced at it, and handed it to Banjo. "Read it for me."

Banjo read, "Carey arrives by stage October 15. A. Tillman." He looked at Sally. "That's four weeks away."

Sally had her arms folded across her middle. "Thanks for bringing that out. I'd invite you for supper, but Banjo and I are mighty busy here, and Jake's the cook."

"I'm here to offer you twenty-three hundred dollars," Ganss said.

"Is that right?" Banjo asked, eyeing him closely. The banker's blue pinstripe suit wouldn't last long on the range. Banjo turned to Sally. "Do you mind my asking him a few questions?"

"Of course not," Sally said. "Ask anything you like."

Ganss forced a chuckle. "Don't get too personal, please. My sensibilities are easily offended." He laughed at his own joke.

Banjo didn't smile. "Exactly what is your interest in the Bar N?"

"I'm looking for investment properties," the banker replied. He looked toward Sally. "You can't refuse my offer. It's twice what anyone else would give you."

Sally sent Banjo a glance that he couldn't read. She hesitated a moment, then said, "You'll have to give me a little more time, Mr. Ganss. At least till spring. You wouldn't want to take possession of the ranch this time of year anyways." She lifted her ball of twine and unrolled a section. "Why don't you ride to the house? Jake will give you some loaf bread and coffee before you head out."

"Twenty-five hundred dollars," he said. "That's my last offer."

She shook her head. "Come back in the spring," she repeated. "I don't want to move at this time of year. It's too hard with winter coming on. You never know. We could get stuck in a blizzard just trying to get back to Juniper with our wagons loaded."

When the banker set off for the house, Sally sent an irate glance after him. "That fellow is starting to irritate me. Nobody in his right mind would offer that kind of money for a no-account place like this. We haven't turned a profit once in four years. Why is he so determined to buy it?"

"That's what I'm wondering," Banjo said, leaning over to swing the scythe. "You just hold on, Sally. We'll unwind this tangle after a while."

Lifting a bundle of hay, Sally heaved it into the wagon and reached back to tie another one.

Chapter 7

Over the next two weeks, Banjo and Sally finished cutting and binding the hay. They hauled in the last load late on Saturday night, the twenty-sixth of September. Parson Monaghan rode in the next afternoon.

"Howdy," Banjo said, coming from the barn to take the man's horse. Because of the preacher's position, Banjo forced himself to be friendly, but it was a strain.

"Thanks," Monaghan said, handing Banjo the reins. "He'd like some oats if you have some."

"I'd like to oblige you, Parson, but we've got a little corn, and that's all."

"Put him out to graze then. That will be fine."

Banjo nodded and led the stallion to the pasture behind the small barn. At the gate he pulled off the saddle and let the horse go. The black stallion lifted his tail and sprinted toward the other horses gathered in the far corner.

Banjo took the saddle to the tack room and draped it over a sawhorse. A strange mood settled over him. He finished shoveling silage into the feed bins and greased the wagon wheels. That preacher had come just over two weeks ago, and he was already back. He'd probably come to press Sally for an answer. Was he planning to set up residence here after a while?

As Banjo was wiping the grease from his hands, Jake called, "Supper's on!" and Banjo headed for the house. Sally's husky laugh met him at the door.

"Pastor Monaghan," she said, drawing in a breath, "you tell the funniest stories for a preacher."

"What? Are preachers some sort of strange breed that doesn't know how to laugh?" he asked grinning. "If they are, I'm in the wrong business."

Banjo wanted to say, *You're in the wrong business, all right,* but he held his tongue. Picking up his plate, he dished up beef stew and palmed two yeast rolls. Sitting on the floor near the hearth, he waited for the blessing.

"You feeling okay, Banjo?" Sally asked. "You're awful quiet."

"I'm fine," he said shortly. "Have you had grace yet?"

"Pastor, would you pray, please?" Sally asked sweetly.

Monaghan bowed, and his voice rang out for what seemed to Banjo to be an eternity. Finally, he said, "Amen," and they dug into the food.

Scraping up the last bit of broth with his bread, Banjo asked, "Where are you headed next, Parson? Have you got a meeting tomorrow?"

"Not until tomorrow night," Monaghan replied. He smiled at Sally. "I figured we could have a little service here in the morning if it's okay with you, Sally."

"That would be wonderful," she replied.

Banjo felt a tiny twinge of guilt. He should be glad about the service. They had precious few of them in these parts. Usually he was glad to hear a new preacher, but somehow he just couldn't get excited about this one.

The next morning Pastor Monaghan turned up for breakfast with his suit brushed and his hair slicked back. He was handsome in spite of his beak nose. Banjo brought his Bible from the loft. For the service Banjo took Monaghan's chair at the table while the preacher stood near the fireplace, his open Bible in his hand.

"Let's read today from Isaiah 51:4–6:

"Hearken unto me, my people; and give ear unto me, O my nation: for a law shall proceed from me, and I will make my judgment to rest for a light of the people.

"My righteousness is near; my salvation is gone forth, and mine arms shall judge the people; the isles shall wait upon me, and on mine arm shall they trust.

"Lift up your eyes to the heavens, and look upon the earth beneath: for the heavens shall vanish away like smoke, and the earth shall wax old like a garment, and they that dwell therein shall die in like manner: but my salvation shall be for ever, and my righteousness shall not be abolished.

"God's wrath will not wait forever," he intoned. "His fury will pour forth upon all who do not follow Him in righteousness." The parson belabored that point and three more like it for the next twenty minutes.

Jake kept his head down and didn't move for the entire time. Banjo waited for the end of the message, hoping for a word of hope, an explanation of redemption and forgiveness, but it didn't come. Finally, Pastor Monaghan closed in prayer.

Five minutes later he gathered his belongings. In the hearing of them all, he said, "Thanks again for the hospitality, Sally." He sent her a warm look. "I'll be back before too long. I wish you'd think about my question a little more. I'm still waiting for your answer."

Sally blushed.

Banjo glanced at Jake and noted the boy's sullen expression. Jake hadn't worn that look since they'd come home three weeks before.

During the weeks after the preacher rode out, Sally never mentioned him. Banjo kept an eye on the lower pasture for days. He had an idea that the man would be back before long, but he didn't come. Just the idea of his return kept Banjo on edge.

The day before Carey's arrival, Banjo had built a crude cot, and Sally had filled a clean mattress tick with fresh straw. They'd wrestled both up the loft stairs that night.

Jake lay down on the loft floor to lean over the edge and pull from above while Banjo heaved from below. Sally giggled when the cot fell back for the fourth time.

"What is so powerful funny?" Banjo demanded.

"You look like a ripe tomato," she said. "I've never seen anyone get so red." She pulled out a chair. "You'd best sit down awhile."

"I'm okay," he insisted, heading for the door. "I'm going to fetch a rope from the barn. We'll have it up there in two shakes." The door banged as he went out and banged again when he returned. He tied the rope around a joining on the headpiece, and Jake heaved the cot up. The mattress soon followed.

Sally said, "I'll make the bed up—"

"In the morning," Banjo finished. "I'm beat, and I'm turning in." He climbed the loft ladder. "See you in the morning. I'm leaving before first light," he called down.

"Why are you so grumpy?" Sally demanded. "What's gotten into you, Banjo?"

Without answering, he stretched out on his cot and closed his eyes. *What has gotten into me?* he wondered, but he was too tired to worry about that now.

⌣

Before dawn on what had turned out to be a frigid day, Banjo hitched two horses to the buckboard. He'd soon be on his way to fetch Carey Hodges from the stage station in Juniper. Just before he set out, he shoveled some coals into a steel pan and wrapped it with a thick quilt to keep his feet warm. In October the cold took a firm hold on Colorado and didn't let go until May.

By the time Banjo rode out, Sally had gotten Jake out of bed, and he was busy helping her clean the loft. The upper quarters of the house would be crowded with three fellows up there. Banjo and Jake had been comfortably set until now, but another bed left little room for moving around.

The buckboard was bouncing down the trail by the time the sun peeked over the rim. Once again Banjo tried to figure out what had come over him recently. Banjo Calahan was never cynical or short-tempered or depressed. For some reason he'd been all three for the past few days. He pulled his Bible out of a canvas sack at his feet. Maybe he'd better get into the Good Book more often. His spirituality was running a might thin. The thing was, he couldn't for the life of him figure out why.

He reached Juniper Junction a couple of hours before noon and stopped at the stage station. As usual, Buckeye Mullins sat behind the counter. He was stroking his handlebar mustache and playing solitaire with a deck of torn cards.

"When's the stage from Denver due in?" Banjo asked from the open door. He wanted to get to the hotel and buy a cup of coffee. He was frozen plumb through.

Buckeye looked up. "Well, hey, old-timer. What're you up to? I ain't seen you in a coon's age."

Banjo stepped inside and closed the door behind him to keep out the chill. The stage station's potbelly stove did precious little to keep the inside temperature above freezing.

"I'm picking up a kid coming in from Denver today."

"You don't say." Buckeye moved a card and told him, "The stage is due in around three this afternoon. Could be an hour early or an hour late, depending. Check back in a while. I should get a telegram giving me the time they left."

Banjo stepped to the door. "Will do. Thanks." He moved down the boardwalk and stepped into the hotel restaurant.

The dining room was empty except for old Joe Harper, owner of Harper's Emporium across the street. The shopkeeper was bent over an empty plate and a tin coffee cup. His shoulders were bony and bowed down, as if he carried an enormous burden.

Mr. Harper looked up when Banjo stepped closer. "Howdy, Banjo," he said, straightening. "What brings you to town?"

"I'm picking up someone on the Denver stage," Banjo said. He took off his hat. "Mind if I join you? I need a cup of coffee and a piece of bread in the worst way."

"Pull up a chair," Harper said, motioning toward the wooden chair across from him. He waited until Banjo sat down and the red-haired waitress had taken his order. "Who's coming in?" Harper asked.

Banjo got comfortable in the seat and said, "A young relative of Miz Newcomb at the Bar N. An orphan. Miz Newcomb is taking the child in."

"Nice of her," Harper said. He sipped his coffee.

"Say, did you know Mickey Newcomb?" Banjo asked. "Did he come into town much?"

Harper looked wary. "You might say that. He was here about every other Saturday, near as I can tell." He leaned forward. "He was a big gambler. Spent almost every minute of his time in the back room at the Red Rooster playing five-card stud." Harper glanced around, then leaned in. "I heard he was into Pike Ludlow for a couple of hundred dollars."

"You mean Pike of the Rocking Chair Ranch?"

"The same. He's a mean hombre. I wouldn't want to tangle with him."

Banjo's coffee and sweet roll arrived.

"I'd best get back to minding the store," Harper said. He stood and dropped two bits on the table. "Nice seeing you, Banjo," he said and trudged out of the restaurant.

Banjo finished his late breakfast and strolled over to the Red Rooster. The place wouldn't be open for business until later in the day, but the bartender would probably be sweeping out last night's dirt and setting up for tonight's crowd. Banjo used to punch cows with the man—a tall hombre by the name of Rance Holcomb. He had a black beard and arms like timbers.

Rance was sweeping the boardwalk in front of the saloon when Banjo arrived. "Howdy, old-timer," Rance called, his words coming out in white puffs. "How's life treating you?"

"It'd be better if I was propped up by a stove," Banjo retorted. He was getting tired of being called *old-timer*. His last birthday had made him fifty-seven, but he wasn't ready for a lap blanket and a rocking chair yet. He rubbed the stubble on his chin. Maybe a shave would peel off some years.

"Come on in," Rance said, striding through the saloon door. "I put a good-sized shovel of coal in the stove before I went outside to sweep."

Banjo followed him in and perched on a stool while Rance moved around the counter to wash a stack of glasses sitting beside a dishpan of soapy water. For a big guy, the bartender's hands moved with a gliding grace. "Want some coffee? I've got some on the stove."

"No, thanks. I just came from the hotel restaurant."

"I hear there's a silver strike northwest of town in the hills," the bartender said. "I'm not sure if it's a hoax or not." He chuckled. "I guess time will tell."

"That it will," Banjo said. "I try not to get too het up over that kind of news. I spent some time in the mines some years back and learnt that digging for gold is backbreaking work. You earn every penny you may find, believe me." He leaned his forearm on the bar. "I need some information," he said. "It's about Mickey Newcomb."

The bartender paused as he looked up. "He was a bad egg," he said and reached for another dirty glass.

"He died last spring. Did you know it?"

Rance nodded. "I heard about it from Virgil Ganss."

"I hear Mickey was a real gambler."

"He was here a couple of times a month," Rance said.

"He win or lose?"

"He lost mostly. Once he won a pile and paid off the mortgage on his ranch. But the next time he was back to losing and never won again that I heard of."

"Did he have any enemies?"

Rance reached for a gray dish towel. "He owed Pike Ludlow quite a bit, I hear.

Pike's a mean cuss. He threatened to take the debt out of Mickey's hide."

"You think he did?"

Rance shrugged. "I wouldn't want to guess."

"Why didn't Pike come to the Widow Newcomb to ask for his money?"

"Pike's tough as a cob, but he's not cruel to womenfolk. He'd be rode out of town on a rail for the likes of that." Rance set a glass on the shelf. "There is someone else who had more reason than Pike." He hesitated, considering. "I'm not sure I should tell you about it."

"Rance, Mickey might have died because of a swift push from someone he knew. Mickey was honest and hardworking, but he wasn't a model citizen. It's his wife and boy that I'm concerned about. Someone made a widow out of that young woman and left her boy without a dad."

"Ivan Tucker," Rance said. "Newcomb set Ivan's boy, Tyler, to gambling. The kid's here most every night. His folks are frantic, but the boy's of age. There's nothing they can do about it."

"You're joshing me."

"I wish I was. Mickey Newcomb was not a good man, no matter how hardworking he was. Who knows how many others around these parts had good reason to settle a score with him?"

Banjo slid off the seat. "Thanks, Rance." He held out his hand to shake. "Take care. I'll see you around."

Back on the boardwalk, Banjo hesitated. He had some errands to take care of before the stage arrived. He'd best see to them. On the way to the Emporium, he stopped at the stage station and learned that Carey would arrive in Juniper around three o'clock.

He still had two hours to wait. He spent thirty minutes buying a Colt revolver and two boxes of shells. He picked up a nice piece of dark-green dress goods and a new harmonica. Maybe he could teach Jake to play. They'd have a lot of fun with two harmonicas of an evening.

He bought everything on Sally's list and carried all of it out to the wagon. Then he stopped in at the barbershop next to the hotel. "I want a shave and a haircut—the works," he told the man behind the chair.

Half an hour later, he stepped out of the shop and rubbed his chin. He felt kind of naked with a smooth face. Oh well, he'd get used to it. He crossed the street and returned to the hotel restaurant. He was nigh onto starving. He might as well get a hot meal and have them pack something for the boy.

After his talk with O'Brien, Banjo had suspected that Mickey wasn't the kind of man who collected a lot of friends. But what he had learned today was more than he'd figured on. Poor Sally, saddled with someone like that. Then again, she probably didn't know the full story about her husband. That was a mercy. Banjo certainly didn't want to be the one to tell her.

His plate came piled high with two steaks and fried potatoes. He sprinkled on some salt from a tiny dish on the table and applied his fork to the food. Chewing, he stared out the window at people moving down the street, all of them huddled into their dark woolen coats with hats pulled low over their ears.

He couldn't figure out why anyone would want to run a poor widow and her boy off their range. The land was paid for. Mickey had been something of a rascal, but Sally was as fine as they come. She didn't have any personal enemies in these parts. She couldn't. There had to be another reason.

He was finishing the last chunks of potato when the stage rolled in. Looking up, he caught the attention of the red-haired waitress. "Could I have the other dinner I ordered?" he asked. "I've got to go."

She hurried into the kitchen and returned with a thick, rolled-up newspaper. "Here it is, Banjo," she said, handing it to him. "That will be four bits."

He handed her two quarters and took the newspaper-wrapped bundle. After thanking her, he set out for the stage station. His buckboard was still in front of Harper's, so he wouldn't have far to carry the boy's bags. Moving quickly, he stashed the newspaper bundle under the buckboard seat and headed for the stage. Two men and three women stood on the boardwalk. They were talking together, stopping often to hug each other and pick up their chattering again.

To the side of the stage stood an olive-skinned girl with brown braids showing beneath her navy bonnet. She wore a well-cut navy coat that brushed the tops of her buttoned shoes. She carried a thick book in her hands.

Banjo looked past her to peer inside the open door of the stagecoach. The red velvet seats were empty. He went inside the stage station and found only Buckeye Mullins and the stage driver. Puzzled, he stepped outside. "Has anyone seen Carey Hodges?" he asked.

"I'm Carey," the girl replied.

Chapter 8

Banjo's eyebrows rose to meet his hatband. He took in the girl's erect carriage and solemn face, her citified clothes and direct gaze. Scrambling for his manners, he tugged at his hat brim. "Well, howdy do, Miss Carey?" He pulled off his right glove to shake hands with her.

She clasped his hand with a firm grip, like a banker sealing a deal. "Are you my aunt Sally's husband?" she asked. Her face suddenly came alive. "I've never met Aunt Sally. She left St. Louis before I was born. She and my dad were brother and sister. Daddy was younger than she was by four years. He told me that once when we were out riding."

Banjo waited for her to draw a breath. "I'm Banjo Calahan," he said, grinning down at her. "I work for Sally Newcomb, and she asked me to come and fetch you." He looked at the baggage piled on the boardwalk. "Which of these is yours?"

"That one," she said, pointing to a large leather trunk. "And that one." A smaller suitcase stood near it. "The big one is for my clothes, and the small one is for my books. I got the best books from my mama's collection." Her mouth twisted. "I couldn't bring them all, so I had to pick my favorites. I could only fit in twenty-five of them. It was such a shame to send the rest of them to the public library." She lifted her shoulders in a dainty shrug. "Other people will be able to read them in the library. I guess that's good, though."

While she rattled on, Banjo heaved the trunk to his shoulder and started across the street to the buckboard. For such a little girl, she had a lot of clothes—heavy clothes. In a moment he came back for the suitcase—which was even heavier. Carey followed him this time.

She walked directly to the horses, in front where they could see her past their blinders. She stroked the nose of the bay mare. "Hello," she cooed. "I'm Carey. What's your name?"

"Sassy," Banjo replied. "The other one is Haney."

She moved to the black and stroked his nose. "Hello, Haney. We're going to be great pals." The horse nuzzled her face. She giggled. "See? He likes me already." With a parting pat, she came around to Banjo. "I love horses," she said. "Daddy and I went riding every Saturday."

"That'll get you a head start here," Banjo said, grinning at her. "Anyone who loves horses will settle into western life mighty quick." He helped her up to the seat.

"How far is it to the ranch?" she asked, shivering. "I'm almost frozen from the ride in the stage."

"We've got nigh onto four hours' ride." He remembered the dinner he'd bought and reached under the seat to pull it out. "Here's some supper for you," he said, handing it to her. "That will warm you up a little. I've got two buffalo robes here to put around us, too." He untied the horses and got to his seat.

The metal box at his feet was icy cold, the coals long dead. Before heading out of town, he stopped at the blacksmith shop and paid a nickel to have him shovel glowing embers into the box. Carey moved closer to him so her feet could feel the warmth, and Banjo wrapped both buffalo robes around them.

"This feels good," she said munching fried potatoes. "I was so hungry my stomach was a knot. We ate cold ham and dried apples at the stage station before we left Denver. The train ride lasted forever and then some."

"How long were you on the train?"

"Three days. Mr. Tillman gave me a hamper full of food for the trip—" She gasped. "I left the hamper on the train! I never thought of it until just now!"

Banjo chuckled. "It's a little late to go after it now, missy. Someone else will enjoy using it, for sure."

She pulled her shoulders into that delicate shrug again. "I'm always forgetting things. Mama said it was my Achilles heel."

"Your Achilles what?"

"My Achilles heel. You know, the Greek myth about the man who was invincible except for his heel." She glanced up at him.

Banjo shook his head. "That's a new one on me."

"You never heard of Achilles?" She stared at him for a moment then returned to her meal. Moving closer to Banjo, she leaned against his side and began, "Achilles was a hero. . . ."

The story lasted until the wagon began the long climb into the hills west of Juniper, then her voice trailed off, the empty wad of newspaper fell to the floor of the buckboard, and Carey's bonnet rested against Banjo's shoulder.

Banjo pulled the buffalo robe closer around the two of them and settled a strong arm around the little girl to keep her from falling off the seat. With a sigh, she shifted to a more comfortable position against him and slept. He hummed a soft tune to himself all the way home.

Night had fallen by the time the buckboard pulled into the ranch yard. Banjo stopped the horses beside the porch steps, and Carey sat up, rubbing her eyes. "Are we there?" she asked.

The cabin door opened, and Sally came out with a lantern. "Hurry inside," she called. "You must be two icicles sitting up there."

"We ain't warm, and that's a fact," Banjo said. He jumped down, ignoring the twinge in his stiff joints, and reached up for Carey. The buffalo robe fell aside, and Carey let him set her down.

Stunned, Sally peered at the little girl.

Banjo grinned and said, "Sally Newcomb, meet your niece, Carey Hodges."

"Well, I'll be!" Jake said from the door.

Sally glanced at Banjo then looked at Carey. The girl stood on the porch, looking around, her face alive with curiosity. "Come in, child," Sally said. "You need to get by the fire and thaw out." She put an arm around the girl's thin shoulders and drew her inside.

Jake stepped outside and closed the door after them. He came up to Banjo. "What kind of doings is this?" he demanded. "That's no kid boy to help us with the chores."

Banjo laughed. "You're a mighty smart fellow, Jake." He turned toward the buckboard. "How about helping me unload her things? We'll set them on the porch and unhitch the horses. Your mother's going to have to figure out where to put Carey tonight. She sure can't sleep in the loft with the likes of us."

"What's wrong with us?" Jake demanded.

"It's not us that's the problem," Banjo retorted, reaching for the suitcase. "It's her. She may be little, but she's every inch a lady."

Jake took another look at Banjo. "Say, you look like a skinned rabbit."

Banjo busied himself lifting Carey's suitcase and didn't answer.

With another glance at the house, Jake pulled the trunk to the edge of the buckboard and swung it to the porch floor.

Inside the cabin Sally helped Carey take off her coat. She pulled a chair close to the fireplace. "Here, sit down and stretch your feet to the fire, dear. You've got to be exhausted."

"I slept most of the way here," Carey said. "Have you got a buttonhook? I'd like to take off my shoes, but my hook is in the trunk."

Sally shook her head. "I'm afraid I don't. Banjo will bring your things inside in a minute."

Carey stretched her hands toward the fire. "He's a nice man. He got some coals to keep our feet warm and bought me some supper, too."

"Now there's something we're agreed on," Sally replied with a chuckle. "He's helped us out a lot since he came here." She pulled a chair closer. "Please tell me about your parents, honey. What happened to them?"

Carey's expression tightened. "They went out in a rowboat for an afternoon ride. It was a special outing for their anniversary. Mama loved the coolness of the water in the summertime, and Daddy wanted to do something extra nice for her." She looked down. "I'm not sure what happened, but the boat tipped over, and they both drowned."

She looked at Sally. Her eyes were full of tears. "They left me at Mrs. Tompkins's house for the day. A policeman came to the door to tell us." A tear slipped out. "I didn't know what to do. Mrs. Tompkins kept me there for a whole week, but she couldn't keep me forever. She's an old lady with a bad hip and crippled hands. Mr. Tillman told me that he'd have to send me to the orphanage until he could find you." She was crying in earnest now. "I was afraid he wouldn't be able to."

Sally drew the child into her arms. As Carey sobbed against Sally's breast, something warmed inside the woman. She'd always wanted a daughter after Jake was born. This poor little girl needed a family in the worst way. Sally closed her eyes and hung on to the weeping child. Carey had just come home.

By the time the men came in, the ladies had dried their eyes, and Carey was sipping a cup of hot water with some molasses added for flavoring.

Jake hefted the suitcase inside and set it down. "What're you carrying in that? Anvils?" he asked gasping. His cheeks were pink from the cold air and exertion.

"No. Books," Banjo told him. "Carey's a bookworm, right?" He looked at the girl.

"I suppose you could say that," she replied. She spoke with the precision of a lawyer or a judge.

Banjo tried to size her up but found himself at a loss. Sometimes she acted like a twelve-year-old child; sometimes she was too grown up for her own good.

"You can read them if you want," she offered, watching Jake.

His mouth pulled in. "I can't read nohow," he retorted. "Never learnt."

Carey stared. "You never went to school?"

Sally spoke up. "There are no schools all the way out here, honey. I don't read well enough to teach Jake anything, and his pa didn't neither."

Carey looked at Banjo. "Do you?"

"Read?" he asked. "A mite. I do all right with the Bible."

While Carey absorbed this, Sally said, "Put her things in my room. I've got a double bed, and she can bunk with me."

Jake picked up the suitcase. "I guess we went to all that trouble for nothing."

"Not for nothing," Banjo said, following him with the trunk. "I plan to trade out beds every other night. No sense wasting that new tick." He chuckled. "Of course, you could have it if you want. We could move it out to the barn for you. You could have the stall next to Haney."

Jake snorted, and Banjo laughed.

The next morning, Carey came to breakfast in a brown dress with puffed sleeves and an enormous gathered skirt covered by a wrinkled white apron. She kept smoothing at the white organdy as though trying to iron it with her palms.

"Have some griddle cakes," Sally said, handing the girl a platter filled with cornmeal flapjacks. "We eat them with sorghum."

Carey placed one on her plate, and Banjo handed her the cup of syrup. "What are we doing today?" she asked, looking at Sally.

"I've got washing to do. You can help me with that," Sally replied. "Have you ever used a scrub board?"

Carey shook her head. "My mama always did the washing. I helped her hang up the clothes, though."

"If you could rinse and hang out the clothes, that would be a mercy to me." Sally glanced at Banjo. "What about you?"

"I'll make us a bench for the table today," he said. "With another body to set at the table, we need one in the worst way."

Jake forked another corn cake onto his plate. "I'll curry the horses. They haven't been done for a while."

"Can I help?" Carey asked. She glanced at Sally. "After the clothes are done?"

"You go ahead after breakfast," Sally said. "It'll take me awhile to set up the washtub and scrub enough clothes for you to get started. I'll call you when I'm ready."

After breakfast Carey skipped out to the barn with the men, her face eager, her eyes shining. In the tack room, she picked up a wide brush with worn black bristles. "Can I use this?" she asked.

Jake grinned at her. "You ever done this before?"

She nodded. "My Dad and I went riding every Saturday. We had two horses in a riding stable on the edge of town. Afterwards, we'd curry the horses."

"What happened to them?" Banjo asked.

Her smile faded. "We had to sell them to pay off the debts. Mr. Tillman said that there was just enough money left to pay my way out here." She turned the brush back and forth in her hands. "Mine was a little sorrel mare named Sookie. She used to lick sugar out of my hand."

Jake looked at her, new interest in his eyes. "Would you like to take a ride this afternoon when it warms up some? You could ride Mitsy. She's a paint pony Pa won last year." He glanced at Banjo. "Ma thinks Pa bought her, but I saw him win the pony at the Red Rooster."

"You mean we can ride?" Carey hopped from one foot to the next. *"Eh bien!"* she exclaimed.

Jake looked at Banjo, and Banjo shrugged. He had no idea what she had said either.

Jake bore down on Carey. "What's that?" he demanded.

"What?" she asked, her expression blank.

"A bean, or whatever that was."

"Eh bien?"

"Yep."

"That means 'Oh, good!' It's French. My teacher used to say it all the time." She headed for the door. "Let's get started. Aunt Sally's going to call me pretty soon, and I'll have to go in."

Banjo watched the youngsters go out. He shook his head, and a wide smile came across his face. That little young'un was going to liven things up around here, for sure. She was like a sunbeam on a cold, damp day.

Belting out "I Sing the Mighty Power of God," Banjo picked up a couple old boards that were lying in a stack near the wall. He had a happy, satisfied feeling that he hadn't felt in a long time. It lasted until Pastor Monaghan rode in around suppertime.

Chapter 9

Jake and Carey were still out on the range when Banjo heard a call from the yard. He laid down the peg he was whittling and headed out the wide doors to see who had come. These days a body never knew if a visitor meant friendship or trouble.

Still in the saddle, Pastor Monaghan was talking to Sally beside the porch steps. He noticed Banjo, stepped from the saddle, and led the stallion toward the barn. "Here, take care of him, will you, Benjy?" he asked.

"Banjo," the cowhand replied, watching the preacher closely. What was it about the man that made the hair on the back of Banjo's neck stand up? Banjo had never found it hard to be sociable with a man of the cloth before this. Clamping down on his jaw, he led the horse to the barn. *Don't let your fool notions trip you up, Joe Calahan,* he told himself. *You'd best do some extra praying and read a couple more chapters before bed tonight. You're getting pretty sorry.*

Just then Jake and Carey rode up, their faces shining with exhilaration. "That was first rate!" Carey cried. "Let's go again tomorrow!"

Jake laughed, and Banjo looked up. He'd never heard the boy laugh aloud before.

"If the weather's fine, we'll go," Jake told her. He slid out of the saddle with practiced ease. He complained about his leg aching from time to time, but he was able to get around almost perfectly now.

Jake helped Carey down, and they led their mounts around the corral to cool them down. Lifting the preacher's saddle from the stallion's back, Banjo hung it over one wall of the stall. He paused to watch the youngsters through the window, marveling at the change in Jake, and sent up a prayer for the boy's salvation. Pouring corn into the bin, he prayed for Carey, too. That little girl had seen her share of heartache. He only hoped that this would be a happy chapter in her young life.

Returning to the job at hand, Banjo tapped the last of the pegs into the bench, his ear tuned to hear the call for supper, his mind on the preacher and the boss lady inside the house. One time he thought he heard Sally laugh, and he felt his insides tighten. What was so splendidly funny?

✐

In the house Sally placed a cup of coffee on the table in front of the preacher and pulled up a chair to join him. "That was the funniest story I've ever heard," she said, still laughing. "Did you see the preacher actually run out of the baptizing pool?"

Monaghan nodded. "For a fact. He'd had a fear of snakes all his life. When he saw that stick bobbing toward him, he thought his time had come." He smiled and leaned closer to her. "Have you thought any more about my question?"

She grew serious and shifted in her seat. "I have thought about it, Pastor. . . ."

"Call me Garrett," he interrupted with a soft smile. "In private, of course."

Looking away from the closeness of his gaze, she went on as though he hadn't spoken. "It's so soon after Mickey's passing that I just don't feel right about it. I've given it a lot of thought. Honest, I have."

He patted her hand. "I'm not giving up so easy," he said. "You've got all the time you need. I'll wait five years if I have to."

"It's so soon after Mickey. . ."

"That's just what I mean. You have all the time you need."

She got up to stir the stew pot, bending away from him to hide her dismay. If she had so much time, then why did he keep pressing her for an answer? This was the third time he'd been here in six weeks.

She pulled a pan of biscuits from the oven. They were smoothly formed and golden, just the way Banjo loved them. "I'll call everyone for supper," she said as she set the pan on the table.

When Banjo heard her call, he picked up the bench and was out the door before the sound had died on the breeze. "How's this look?" he asked Sally when he reached the porch. "I figure it's big enough for two people, so we can all set up to the table tonight."

"It's beautiful, Banjo," she said, looking at the planks laid side by side to make the seat. He had planed them so they fit together perfectly.

Carey skipped up the steps and followed the adults inside. Taking his time, Jake came in last.

"Good evening, Parson," Banjo said, setting the bench in place. "What brings you through these parts so soon?"

"I'm on my way to Salida to preach a camp meeting," Monaghan said. "I'll be there for two weeks."

"This time of year?" Banjo asked. "It'll be mighty cold for folks traveling to the meetings."

Monaghan's cheeks flushed. "The church is in town, so it's not far for the townsfolk to travel."

"A camp meeting in town?" Banjo persisted. "I thought camp meetings were in the country."

"Well, it's more like a revival meeting," Monaghan said. He cleared his throat and touched his string tie. "I must say, the food looks delicious, Sally," he said, smiling at her.

She gave him a polite smile. "I hope it tastes good, too," she said.

A sudden look crossed the preacher's face. "I forgot to give you a letter someone gave me in town," he said, reaching inside his coat pocket. He took out a tan envelope and handed it to Sally.

She opened it and held it out to Banjo. He glanced at it. "A gentleman wants to make sure you haven't forgotten his offer," he told her.

Nodding, she looked at the paper again and returned it to its envelope. She laid it on the mantel shelf. "Will you thank the Lord, Pastor?" she asked, returning to the table.

Monaghan stood, and his voice filled the room. "We thank Thee, O God, for Thy bountiful blessings. Help us to keep in the narrow way. Hold back Thy wrath and remember mercy, O God. In the name of Thy dear Son. Amen."

Banjo picked up two biscuits and dipped one of them into his stew. Now that he was at the table, he'd much rather sit beside the hearth. Sitting so close to Preacher Monaghan wasn't too comfortable, especially with him sending Sally those calf-eyed looks. Keeping his head down, Banjo chewed and swallowed his way through the meal.

Half an hour later, the preacher stood. "I hate to be rushing away, Sally, but I've got to head on down the trail. I just stopped in to rest awhile and deliver that letter." He glanced at the mantel shelf. "I believe it's from Virgil Ganss at the bank. I ran into him while I was in town yesterday." He glanced at the shelf again and hesitated.

Sally stood and sent him a polite smile. "Thanks for bringing it out to me," she said.

He picked up his hat. "I probably won't be back through here until the spring thaw," he said. "You folks take care of yourself. Let's pray for each other until we meet again."

Banjo stood to shake the preacher's hand. "I'll fetch your horse," he said and strode to the barn. A few minutes later, he smoothed the saddle blanket over the black stallion and settled the saddle over its back. Well, at least the preacher wouldn't be back until spring. That news was one good outcome of this visit.

Leading the horse to the porch where Pastor Monaghan stood talking with Sally, Jake, and Carey, Banjo looked up and saw the sun glinting against Sally's glossy black hair. At just that moment, she laughed at something Carey said.

Banjo felt a shock in his chest. His boot caught on a stone, and he almost stumbled. Jake turned to stare at him. Taking a firmer hold on the preacher's horse, Banjo felt his face grow warm.

Without looking directly at anyone, he reached the steps and handed the reins to Monaghan. With a nod to be polite, he turned and headed back to the barn.

You are a brass-plated idiot, he scolded himself. *You're old enough to be that woman's father. You can't be in love with her!*

October faded into November, and life settled into a gentle routine. Banjo and Jake worked hard chopping trees, cutting logs, and splitting a mountain of wood. Carey stacked most of it herself. She was a plucky girl and fit into the family like she had been born to it.

One evening near the end of November, they sat around the fire after dinner. Sally was mending Jake's socks. Banjo lay on his back in front of the fire, his eyes closed, while Jake practiced reading from *Great Expectations*—one of four Dickens novels Carey had brought with her. The young people sat close together at the table, Jake with his finger following the lines, and Carey watching closely as he read.

"An eper. . ."

"Epergne. That's a pretty silver container," she told him.

He went on, "An epergne or centerpiece of some kind was in the middle of this cloth; it was so heavily overhung with cobwebs that its form was quite indis. . ."

"Indistinguishable," she said. "Take the word one part at a time, and you'll be able to figure it out."

"Indistinguishable; and, as I looked along the yellow expanse out of which I remember its seeming to grow, like a black fungus, I saw speckled-legged spiders with blotchy bodies running home to it. . . ." He glanced at Carey with an awed expression, then bowed his face closer to the page. "And running out from it, as if some circumstance of the greatest public importance had just transpired in the spider community." Holding his finger at the place, he leaned back. "The old lady's got her hairpins crossways," he said, smiling.

Banjo chuckled. "She's got more than that crossways, son."

Jake continued reading for another thirty minutes. Finally he sat back and rubbed his eyes. "I'm seeing blurry," he complained. "That's all I can do tonight."

Carey marked the spot with a bit of string and closed the book. "You catch on quick," she told Jake with an admiring smile. "It took me three years to learn to read. You've only been at it for a few weeks."

He grinned, pleased with himself.

Sally spoke up. "Banjo, read to us from the Bible before we turn in."

Banjo sat up and found the black book on a low table near the fireplace where he'd laid it after their morning study. Flipping it open, he asked, "Any favorite passage you'd like to hear tonight?"

"Read a story," Carey said. "I like the one about Mephibosheth."

"Mephibosheth?" Jake stared at her. "Is that a real name?"

"Of course it is. He was Saul's grandson. When he was a little boy, his nurse dropped him, and he was lame of his feet. But David loved him anyways and brought him to live in the palace."

Banjo focused on her. "You've been to church, haven't you,?"

She nodded. "My mama took me to Sunday school every week." She glanced at Jake. "I took Jesus as my Savior last May. It was just before my. . ." Her voice faltered.

"Trusting Jesus is the best step you'll ever make," Banjo told her. "I lost my family too, honey. I almost gave up, but Jesus saw me through." He flipped to the front of the Bible. "Let me see if I can find that story about Mephibosheth. It's one of my favorites, too." He turned a few pages. "Here it is in 2 Samuel 4:4: 'And Jonathan, Saul's son, had a son that was lame of his feet. . .'"

He glanced up from the page for an instant and met Sally's gaze. She had a sweet, contented expression that warmed him clear through. Forcing his attention back to the printed page, he read to the end of the story.

As the weather grew colder, the wind harsher, the family huddled together in the cabin. Snow covered the ranch with a thick coating. Jake and Banjo stayed busy stoking the fireplace and the cookstove, yet the family still wore thick woolens to stay warm.

One evening near the end of November, Jake brought a wooden cigar box from the loft and set in on the table. Its paper label was almost worn off, and the corners were scarred.

"What's in there?" Carey asked. She laid her embroidery on her lap and reached out to touch the smooth wood.

"This is my treasure chest," Jake announced. "I keep all kinds of things in here."

"Nothing alive, I hope," Banjo drawled from his place on the floor in front of the fireplace.

Sally chuckled. "I hope not, too."

Jake opened the lid. "This is the first candy wrapper I ever got. It was around a fat peppermint stick Pa bought for me while we were in town." He lay the strip of paper aside and reached into the box. "This is a piece off the old plow point. I was plowing when it broke." He pulled out a rock. "Here's the stone that broke it."

"What's that shiny white thing?" Carey asked.

"I don't know." He held up a flat triangle made of mother-of-pearl. "I found it at the campsite where Pa died."

Banjo sat up. "Can I see that?" When Jake handed it to him, Banjo turned it in his hands several times then gave it back. He stretched out before the fire and closed his eyes while Jake continued his inventory for another hour.

"It's December," Carey announced one morning. "When do we cut down a Christmas tree?"

"You have the funniest notions," Jake said. "Whoever heard tell of that?"

"It's a tradition," Sally told him. "Your pa never liked the fuss, so we never had much for holidays like most folks do."

"Can we have one?" Carey asked, hope making her face glow.

Sally smiled. "Why not?" She looked at Banjo. "Would you mind going for one?"

He gently tugged at one of Carey's dark braids. "Want to come with me to pick one out?" he asked.

She bounced on her toes. *"Eh bien!"* she cried.

He turned to Sally. *"Eh bien!"* he said, winking. To Carey he added, "Get on your warmest woolen underwear and two sets of thick clothes. It's sunny out there, but that wind will take your breath away."

Carey ran to the bedroom, and Banjo said, "I know where there's a stand of Douglas fir trees not far from here on the edge of the canyon. We won't be gone long."

"I'd best stay here," Jake said. "That cold will gripe my leg something awful."

"We'll have to clear a place for the tree," Sally told Jake. "You can help me shift the furniture around to make room." She looked at the fireplace, the stove, the table, and added, "Don't get a big one, Banjo. It won't fit."

He laughed. "We can take the table out, can't we? We hardly ever use it."

At Sally's disbelieving look, he laughed louder. "I'm joshing you. We'll get a small one."

A few minutes later, Carey bounded out of the bedroom. She looked like a padded doll with a tiny head on a big body. Sally helped her fit her puffy arms into her coat sleeves. Then Carey tied a gray woolen scarf over her head and wound it around her neck.

Banjo pulled on his heavy wear, and they set out. "Let's take us some horses," he told her. "There's no use freezing our feet on this cold ground. Besides, we'll need Haney to pull the tree back for us." With their faces bent low into their scarves, they set out for the barn.

While Banjo saddled up, Carey asked, "Are Jake and Aunt Sally Christians?"

"Your aunt Sally is," Banjo replied, tightening a cinch strap. "Jake isn't, I'm afraid."

"I was worried about that," she said. As she watched him, she set her tiny buttoned shoe on the bottom rail of the stall and stepped up, her arms over the top rail. "He never wants to read out of the Bible when we practice our lessons."

Banjo moved to Penny, a copper-colored pony that was Carey's favorite. He flung the saddle on the horse's broad back and said, "Jake's pa wasn't a Christian, honey. He took Jake places a boy should never go and talked bad to him about religion. We'll have to pray hard for Jake. He's had a hard time for such a young fellow."

He led the horse closer to her. "Here, mount up. I'm getting cold already."

He tied an ax to the cantle, looped a hank of rope over the saddle horn, and they set off across a field of powdery white. The snow barely covered the horses' hooves along their path. The wind swept the snow from this portion of the canyon, so the ground on this side stayed fairly clear.

When they reached the stand of fir, Carey pointed at a tree near the front. "Let's take that one!"

Banjo dismounted, looped the rope over his shoulder, and retrieved the ax. He paced around the blue-green trees. "We'll have to get one that's shorter than me," he said. "That one is way too big. We won't be able to get it through the door." He chuckled. "Aunt Sally will have our hides if we bring back a giant with big hairy arms."

She laughed. "How about that one?" she asked, pointing.

He stepped up to the tree, snow crunching beneath his boots. "This one just may do," he said, circling it. "The back is a little bare, but we'll set that side against the wall." He lifted the ax and swung hard again and again. The tiny trunk splintered at the base and fell over.

Banjo strung the rope through the branches and backed the horse to the tree's spiny top. He tied it on and got back into the saddle. "Let's go," he said, pulling his chin down toward his coat collar. "I'm about to freeze."

Carey's teeth were chattering. Her nose was rosy.

Fifteen minutes later, they arrived at the front porch. Banjo helped Carey down and sent her into the house. The next moment Jake appeared, still buttoning his coat.

Banjo's gloved hands fumbled with the rope. "Give me a hand here, will you, son?" he asked. "Your hands aren't numb with cold like mine are."

In short order they had the tree on the porch. Banjo looked inside the cabin door. "Where do you want this?" he asked Sally.

She nodded toward the corner near the fireplace. "Over there. How are you going to stand it up?"

"I'll get a bucket and fill it with rocks and sand," he said. "We can add water to it to keep the tree from drying out too bad."

"I hope it's not too wide," she said, edging by him to peek out the door. Her face was inches from his.

She had a womanly smell that hit him hard. Her dark hair curved over her ear in a fascinating way. He swallowed hard and moved into the house.

"I'll warm up a mite, then go out for those things," he said, clearing his throat. He winked at Carey, who was seated beside the fire with her coat still on and her feet near the fire. "We'll have it up in two shakes."

Jake came inside, and a cold gust followed him.

Shivering, Sally closed the door. "What are we going to put on it for decoration?" she asked. "I don't have enough candles, and besides, they're dangerous."

Carey reached for her coat buttons. "I have some hair ribbons in my trunk. And some little lace whatnots. We could put those on it."

"I've got some red calico scraps I've been saving for a quilt," Sally added. "Maybe we can tie them onto the branches like little bows."

Banjo reached for the coffeepot bubbling on the stove and poured himself a cupful. "It sounds like you've got everything under control, ladies," he said. He only wished he did.

Chapter 10

The day before Christmas, Jake and Banjo were at the woodpile when Jake slipped and landed hard on his bad leg. "O–ooh!" he gasped. His face turned white.

"Are you all right?" Banjo asked. "Here, sit down on the chopping block a minute."

Jake eased himself down to the crude seat, his hands covering his thigh. He closed his eyes and drew in a couple of deep breaths. In a moment, he said, "It's passing. It was a spasm, I guess. This cold makes them worse."

"Jake, do you mind if I ask you something?" Banjo asked. He sat down the split log he was holding and propped his boot on it. "What would have happened to you if that horse had fallen on your neck instead of your leg?"

Jake tensed. He turned away. "I would have been kilt, I guess," he said, looking over the snowy field.

"What then?"

He glanced at Banjo. "What do you mean?"

"Where would you have gone if you had died that day? I'm asking you a serious question now, son. Think on it a minute before you answer."

After a long pause, he replied, "I reckon I don't rightly know, Banjo."

"Mind if I tell you the straight of it?"

He shrugged. "It's your breath. You can use it as you like."

Banjo's voice dropped to a softer pitch. "There's only two kinds of people in this world, Jake—those who've taken Christ for their Savior and those who haven't. We're all wicked sinners. We're born to that, and we can't change it. The good news is that Jesus took our place on the cross so we could be forgiven. That's the difference. A person who accepts Jesus' sacrifice becomes a child of God and goes on to heaven. A person who refuses to take Jesus stays in his sin, and he'll have to suffer for it when he passes on."

Jake continued staring across the field. He didn't move for the space of ten breaths. Banjo watched him carefully but saw nothing in the boy's face to give a hint of what lay beyond.

"Will you think about what I've said?" Banjo asked.

Jake's head dipped in a quick nod. "I reckon it won't hurt nothing." He stood and brushed off the seat of his pants. "Let's get inside," he said, bending to pick up a log. "My sitter's frozen from being on that stump too long." In three moves he loaded his arms and set off for the house, limping a little.

Banjo picked up six pieces of wood and followed him.

Inside, Sally had three pots bubbling on the stove and floury dough spread out on the table. Carey stood beside the table with a small knife in her hand, cutting fat snowmen from rolled-out cookie dough. Three apple-shaped cookies already lay on the wide pan, ready to bake.

Jake dropped his logs into the wooden box near the fireplace, and Banjo did likewise. Jake stepped to the table and pressed his hands across his stomach. "I'll never be able to wait until tomorrow to eat all those goodies!" he said. "I'm so narrow at the equator that my belly button's kissing my backbone."

Carey giggled. She reached to the other end of the table and lifted a golden cookie shaped like a heart. "You can have this one," she said. When he took it, she wagged her finger at him. "But that's all until tomorrow."

He tweaked her braid and laughed when she swatted at him with her floury hands. Fine powder flew toward him, but he escaped unscathed. He made his way up the ladder to the loft and disappeared.

In a moment his voice drifted down, "These are good! I'll take another one!"

"You'll not!" Carey called. She took a broom straw and carefully made a hole in the top of each unbaked cookie.

"What're you doing that for?" Banjo asked, sitting near her.

"That's to put a string through so we can hang them on the tree," she said. She let out a sad sigh. "My mama used to make sticky popcorn balls for the tree. We'd wrap strings around them and tie them to the tree, too." She blinked hard at the broom straw in her hands.

Banjo leaned down for a closer look at her work. "These are very well done for not having a pattern," he said. "Look, that snowman over there is perfectly round. I don't think I could do that, honey. You have talent for this." He patted her shoulder then moved to the fireplace to add a few more logs.

Despite Jake's declarations about his soon-coming starvation, Christmas morning dawned with the young man still intact. Sally had coffee and biscuits ready before dawn. Soon after that a wild turkey roasted over burning logs in the fireplace. While their dinner cooked, Banjo read the Christmas story as written in Luke 2 in his black Bible. He led in prayer to thank God for His Son, who came to die for lost sinners.

Afterward, Sally grabbed Carey in a big hug. More handshaking and hugs followed. Wiping her eyes, Sally hurried to the stove to stir the simmering food.

Christmas turned out to be one of the warmest, most satisfying holidays of Banjo's life. The gifts were simple: an embroidery needle for Carey so she and

Sally could work on a white-work bedspread together and a Bowie knife for Jake. Carey handed Jake her copy of *Great Expectations* and said, "This is for you. I hope you'll like it as much the second and third time you read it."

Jake's face grew still. He stared at the book in her hand, then glanced at her face. "That's from your parents' library," he protested. "You sure you want me to have it?"

She touched the cover to his hand. "It's Christmas. I want you to have it. You can read it to me sometime if you'd like."

Jake took the book and ran his hand over the stiff black cover. Opening the book, he paged through it and didn't say anything more for five full minutes.

"This meal is present enough for me," Banjo said, pulling a chair up to the table as Sally placed the roasted turkey in the center of it. Much as he would have liked to, he hadn't given Sally a Christmas gift for fear it might add strain to their relationship. Sally was already dealing with one suitor. She might flare up at the prospect of a second one. That was the last thing Banjo wanted.

Everyone gathered around the table. Banjo thanked the Lord for His goodness, and they dug into the turnips and onions, corn bread and gravy, and the succulent meat.

After the dishes were dried and put away, Banjo lay stretched out in front of the fireplace, his favorite spot. Jake was in the loft with his book. Sally hung up the dish towel and came to sit at the table. She crossed her arms and stared into the fire.

A small noise caught Banjo's attention. He opened his eyes and turned his head to see Carey standing near him, looking at the Christmas tree, her eyes shiny with unshed tears. He sat up. "What is it, child?" he asked.

"We used to play games on Christmas afternoon, Ma and Pa and. . ." Her lips puckered.

"Come here," he drew her onto his lap as he sat on the floor. Her head found the gentle curve of his shoulder, and she turned her face toward his flannel shirt. He held her close until her shoulders stopped shaking, then he gently rocked her back and forth.

At the table Sally's head rested down on her crossed arms so he couldn't see her face. A soft gasping sigh and a sniff came from her, and Banjo felt a lump rise to his throat. He rested his cheek against Carey's soft hair and closed his eyes. They'd all lost someone dear to them. They'd all felt the hopelessness that came with facing a lonely future. By His grace, as only He could, God had brought them together. One day soon, they'd sing a new song.

A low rumble started deep in his chest. He hummed a few bars then softly sang:

"Simply trusting every day,
Trusting through a stormy way. . ."

Sally lifted her head and sang with him in a wavering voice:

"Even when my faith is small,
Trusting Jesus, that is all.
Trusting as the moments fly,
Trusting as the days go by. . ."

Soon Carey began to sing along. Jake's face appeared over the edge of the loft floor. He was lying on his stomach, peering down at them. He didn't sing, but he didn't scowl either. He just watched.

"Trusting Him whate'er befall,
Trusting Jesus, that is all."

Their voices grew stronger with each line until the cabin resounded with the glory of the Lord. When they finished, Sally said, "I love that song."

"Do you know more songs?" Carey asked Banjo. When he nodded, she cried, "Let's sing more!"

He belted out "Amazing Grace," and they sang for a solid hour. After that, the gloom was gone, and peace settled over the Bar N.

All too soon, Christmas was over. The year 1876 came in with a blizzard that kept the family inside the cabin for weeks. At the first sign of snow, Banjo tied a rope from the house to the barn and from the house to the woodpile so he and Jake wouldn't get lost in the swimming white cloud that settled over them for two days. When the weather cleared, the entire ranch lay under four feet of snow. They had to shovel the doorway clear so they could get out. At the edge of the barn, the snow had drifted seven feet high.

"We could make a snow cave," Carey cried, looking out the window at Banjo and Jake shoveling a path to the barn. Their heads had completely disappeared, but small clouds of snow from their shovels flew up over the sides of their path. "Me and Jake could dig one out."

"I wouldn't try that," Sally said. "It could fall in on you, and you'd suffocate. More than one young'un has been lost that way." She picked up a tiny ball of white thread. "Let's start on the bedspread while we wait for the men to come in. They'll be at least an hour yet."

They sat side by side at the table. Sally showed Carey how to mark the cloth using a pot lid to define a circle.

Holding up her needle to admire the thread dangling from it, Carey gazed at Sally and smiled. "This is fun!" she said. "Where do I start first?"

That bedspread became the ladies' evening occupation for the rest of the winter. Carey tied off the last piece of thread the day yellow daffodils opened up to show their white throats.

The next day Banjo decided he'd best go to town for supplies. They discussed it over lunch.

"I'll leave Tuesday morning," he said, sipping his coffee. "Jake and I will check the fence line when it quits raining, and then I'll go." He turned toward the front windows where sheeting rain blocked out the light.

"I wish I could come," Carey said.

"What would you do there?" Jake demanded. "You can't load the wagon, and that's all there is to do in Juniper Junction."

"No, it isn't!" Carey declared. "I could watch the ladies walking along, and buy some penny candy, and. . ."

Banjo chuckled and tweaked her ear. "I'm afraid it's still too cold and muddy for a pleasure trip now. Maybe at roundup time you can come into town with me. We'll see." He looked at Sally, and she smiled. Next week was Carey's thirteenth birthday, a promising event at the Newcomb household.

That afternoon, Banjo saddled Kelsey. Jake saddled Haney to ride the canyon perimeter with him. The last time they'd ridden out to check the herd, a bitter wind had come from the west. It was time to size up the herd for the year, steer the male calves, and take a tally. They also wanted to check for new breaks in the canyon wall that might have been caused by the four-month freeze. Winter came in hard and lingered long in this part of the territory.

A hundred yards from the ranch yard, Banjo stood in the stirrups and squinted into the distance.

"Not many cattle about," Jake said, turning to peer around the edges of the canyon pasture. "I see a handful of them that away." He pointed.

Looking concerned, Banjo settled into the saddle and rubbed his smooth chin. "Let's see what's outside the canyon," he told Jake. "Maybe they found a depression to hunker down in while it rained." Kelsey broke into a trot with Haney beside him.

Ten minutes later the men cleared the canyon's entrance and pulled up. Not a single cow in sight.

"Let's go over by the water hole," Banjo said.

They topped a crest to see two dozen cows and five calves near the swollen pool.

"There ought to be fifty cows here, at least," Jake said. He swung his mount around and gazed into the distance in all directions. "There are a few to the south," he said.

Banjo pulled in a slow breath. He didn't want to speak the words that were going through his mind. He pulled out his tally book and made a note. "Let's go ahead and ride the fence line," he said. "We'll come across the rest of the herd somewhere along the way."

The farther they rode, the more Banjo doubted his prediction. The fence looked fine, but only a few cows grazed along the way.

"What's that?" Jake asked, looking ahead. Suddenly, he swore.

"Whoa!" Banjo said, sending him a shocked look. "Watch yourself, son."

"Look!" Jake shouted. Haney broke into a gallop and left Banjo's mount behind. Kelsey picked up speed and stopped beside a wide gap in the barbed wire. Both ends were bent far back.

Banjo's boots slid down to the soggy ground. "Wait!" he told Jake. "If you get down, you'll spoil the sign. Stay put while I look around a mite. I know where to step." He bent over to study the ground around the last post with wire attached to it. "Nothing here. They must have done this before the rain."

A low mumble came from Jake's direction, but Banjo ignored him. His sole attention was focused on the mat of wet brown grass under his feet. A few paces out, the grass disappeared, and bare earth stretched to where the fence began again. Not a single track.

Banjo let out a deep sigh and raised his hand to signal for Jake to come. "The rain wiped everything out," he said when the younger man reached him. "All I know is that many a beef passed through here a short time ago. Look at the ground. The grass was trampled out."

"What are you talking about?" Jake demanded. "Rustlers?" His face grew red. He whirled around as though trying to spot the criminals behind a fence post or a bush.

Banjo leaned over the cut ends of the wire and spotted a tiny speck of red on two of them. The same red as the paint chips he had found months before at O'Brien's. But how could he prove anything by just a few paint chips? They were too small to be of much use except for their color.

Banjo's chin jutted forward. His lips formed a tight circle. Hooking his thumbs into his pants pockets, he paced back and forth across the mud a dozen times, staring blindly at his boots slogging through the gray sludge. How was he going to tell Sally? She was depending on the next cattle drive to cover her costs for the next year.

Who would have done such a thing? He thought of O'Brien. "C'mon, Jake," he said heading for his donkey. "I doubt that O'Brien would be dumb enough to pull a stunt like this, but we have to make sure." He got in the saddle and waited for Jake to do likewise. Before they moved, he grabbed hold of Haney's bridle. "Don't go off half-cocked," he said. "We've got to think hard and move slow. If you act like a young fool, you could get us killed. You got that?"

Staring at him with hard eyes, Jake gave a quick nod and backed his horse away until Banjo lost his grip on the bridle. He kept his distance as they moved into O'Brien's field.

"You quarter that area," Banjo said, lifting his chin toward the south. "I'll take the east. We'll meet by that black rock yonder."

"If O'Brien catches us at this, we'll be full of buckshot," Jake said and rode away before Banjo could answer him.

They worked their way across O'Brien's property for more than an hour, but every cow they spotted had O'Brien's brand.

"What now?" Jake demanded when they met up.

Banjo pulled out his tally book and made a note. Shoving it back into his pocket, he said, "I guess we'll have to go back and tell your ma." He felt like he carried a lead pack on his pack. "I'd rather take a whipping with a new rope." His knees gripped Kelsey's sides, and the donkey set off at a canter.

Instead of heading for the barn, the men ground-hitched their mounts beside the porch and went into the house, pausing beside the door to pull off their muddy boots before entering. The ladies looked up when the men came in. Sally was ironing. Carey was folding clothes.

"What is it, Banjo?" Sally asked, alarmed. "You look like death."

"Rustlers!" Jake declared, stepping inside behind him. "They cleaned us out."

She dropped the iron to the top of the stove and rushed to Banjo. "All of them?" She grabbed his arms. "Tell me!"

"They left about three dozen cows and a handful of calves," he said, gazing into her frightened eyes. He wanted to fold her into his arms and promise her everything would be all right. But he couldn't. He had to stand there and watch her suffer.

Sally drew herself up and her expression cleared. "We'll have to think this through," she said, pacing to the fireplace and back to Banjo beside the door. "What about tracks?" She stopped to look at him. "Can you tell who did this?"

He shook his head. "Nary a one. They must have taken the cows before the rain."

She paced another round then darted into her bedroom. A moment later she reappeared holding a tan envelope. She shook it at Jake. "I'm going to accept this offer from Virgil Ganss. We'll clear out of here and get a new start in St. Louis."

"Wait a minute!" Jake cried. "Don't you see? It's Ganss that's been causing all the trouble. He wants the land, and this is his way of running us off!"

Sally stared at him. She turned and looked at Banjo. "You think Ganss did all this?"

Banjo slowly shook his head. "I'm not so sure," he said. "Ganss is a city man.

He lives in Juniper, and he has a steady job. How could he get out here to cause all this trouble?"

"He could hire some rowdies to do it," Jake said.

Banjo pursed his lips, considering. "Before I hang all that on a man, I'd like to get more proof."

Sally raised her eyebrows. "You've seen his wife. Why would he want to bring a girl like her to a place like this? It doesn't make sense."

Jake snorted. "She wouldn't last one day."

"Then why does he want to buy the ranch?" Sally went on. "He won't live on it, and selling it wouldn't make him any money."

Banjo added, "There's no crops nor cattle to make it worth hiring someone to tend the place neither."

"Crops!" Sally cried, flinging the letter to the table. "There's time to buy seed and prepare the ground for a late crop. What do you think of that?"

"We could put in some corn," Banjo told her. "Steve Chamberlin's had good success with his corn."

"Farming?" Jake demanded. "I can't abide walking behind a plow anymore. My leg won't stand it."

Sally's shoulders sagged. She gazed at Banjo, defeat in every line on her face. "What am I going do?"

In his mind Banjo cried out, *Marry me, and let me take care of you!* But he couldn't say the words. There was too much separating them.

"I wish I could give you some advice," he said, avoiding her eyes, "but this has to be your own decision."

Sally's face twisted. Her hands curled into fists. "I'm so tired. I wish I could leave this place and never come back!"

Carey's small voice came from behind her. "But Aunt Sally, I love it here. It's the best place I've ever been. Do we have to go when I just got here?"

Sally turned and looked at Carey's pleading face. With an anguished cry, she dashed into her bedroom and closed the door with a bang.

The young people turned to Banjo as though expecting him to say something. He hesitated a moment then opened the front door to slip into his boots on the porch. "Let's get the horses unsaddled," he told Jake. "They need hay and water."

While Jake pulled on his boots, Banjo drew in a cleansing breath of cool air. What could he do to make things come to rights for Sally? He didn't have enough money to buy more cows. Even if he did, they'd probably disappear like the other ones had. It looked like the Newcombs were sitting ducks in the bottom of this cracker keg, just waiting for the final spray of buckshot.

Jake didn't utter two words as he took care of his horse. Leaving the barn without a parting word, he headed for the house. Banjo took his time over Kelsey, running the events of the past seven months through his mind. He had his tally book in his pocket. It was as good as a diary, but what did it tell him? Almost nothing.

Someone had cut those fences. That was a fact. Unfortunately, all he had for proof were those paint chips tucked into a paper wad inside his coat pocket, and they were well nigh worthless.

Chapter 11

The next morning before dawn, Banjo and Jake set out for Juniper with two pack horses. It was a cool, quiet ride with each lost in his own thoughts.

They rode into town at near nine in the morning. The town was in full swing. Three buckboards waited outside of Harper's. A dozen horses stood at various hitching rails along the main street.

Tying their mounts to the rail in front of Harper's Emporium, Banjo and Jake set off across the muddy street to the hotel for some coffee and breakfast.

"This one's on me," Banjo told Jake. "Get whatever you want. We'll set back and take our time for a change."

They pushed through the door and found the dining room was three-quarters full. Edging between chairs, Banjo waved and spoke to half a dozen people before he reached an empty table near a window.

"Three eggs and fried potatoes with plenty of biscuits," he told the red-haired waitress. "And bring a coffeepot."

"I'll have steak and eggs," Jake said. "Six eggs, scrambled."

While they waited for their food, Banjo leaned his elbows on the table and said, "Listen, Jake, I've been worried about you."

The young man stiffened. "We're going to make it. One way or the other."

"Now hear me out," Banjo went on. "Everyone has hard times. I've had 'em. Carey's had 'em. Folks all over these parts has had 'em. Some get sour, and some get mean. Others get wise. They develop a soft spot for folks in trouble because they've been there, too. Those have an advantage over the others."

Jake stared out the window at a passing wagon.

"The wise ones have Jesus. He promised that He'd never leave us, Jake. Once you tie in with Him, He'll stay with you and help you through the worst that life can hand you."

Jake finally looked him in the eye. "That your sermon for today?" he asked, his voice low and weary.

Banjo leaned back. "I guess it is. I'm trying to help you, son. Please think about it."

Their meal arrived, and Banjo let the subject drop. Even if Sally ended up leaving the ranch, her boy needed the Lord, or he'd likely come to a bad end. If only there were some way to get through to him.

They were finishing the last of the coffee and enjoying the warmth of the dining room when Virgil Ganss came in with his wife. Mrs. Ganss wore a peach-colored dress of draped silk and had a long white feather in her hat. Ganss seated her at a table near the door and stepped toward Banjo and Jake.

"Hello, gentlemen," he said, sticking out his hand. "How did you folks pass the winter?"

"We got by," Banjo said, briefly gripping the man's soft palm.

"Please pass my compliments to Mrs. Newcomb," he told Jake. "Remind her that my offer still stands. If she accepts it before the end of the month, I'll add a hundred dollars to it."

Watching him through narrowed eyes, Jake nodded.

His smile still intact, Ganss made a half bow and returned to his wife.

"How do you like that?" Jake whispered to Banjo. "I wouldn't trust him as far as I could pitch a buckboard."

Banjo drained his cup. "Let's take care of our business and head home," he said. He dropped four bits to the table, added a dime for the waitress, and stood up. "We can still be home before suppertime if we keep moving."

An hour later they had loaded the pack horses with two fifty-pound sacks of oats and two burlap bags of other supplies. Feeling relieved and eager to be home, they set off down the trail. Sally had packed them a meal of fried ham and corn bread. Banjo had brought along a small bag of ground coffee and his coffeepot for a stop along the way. They'd need it come early afternoon.

"I want to thank you for caring about us," Jake said after a long pause. "Things just get worse and worse. I'm getting scared."

"Have you thought about what I said?" Banjo asked. "Have you thought about taking Jesus?"

The boy looked down then nodded. "I know I need to," he said. "I've known it for a long time. I guess I'm just that stubborn or proud. I've had a time admitting it."

"I fought it myself," Banjo said. "Most folks do. The important thing is that you're willing to admit that you need Him now."

"I do," Jake said, his voice so low that he could hardly be heard.

"Let's pray." Banjo stopped Kelsey, and Jake drew up beside him.

Banjo led out in prayer then said to Jake, "Go ahead, son. Tell Him all about it."

"Dear Jesus," Jake prayed. "I'm an awful sinner. Please forgive me and make me clean. Make my life worth something. Amen." He looked up and drew in a deep breath. His shoulders relaxed, and his mouth curved into a natural smile. "He's real," he told Banjo. "I can tell. He's real."

Banjo nodded. "You're on target there, Jake. He sure is!"

They rode for another hour, deep in discussion about what it meant to be a Christian, when Jake said, "What do you reckon's going to become of us? It was bad enough when it was just me and Ma. Now we got Carey to tend to."

Banjo let a few yards pass under the hooves of their mounts before he replied. He shifted his hat to an easier position and squinted into the distance. "At some point your Ma's going to have to make a decision about the ranch. I've been praying for her to do the right thing." He hesitated. "If I can help her along, I'll surely do it."

They passed the crest of a hill and made their way toward a winding stream in the valley below. A tiny wisp of smoke caught Banjo's attention. He pointed it out to Jake. "Let's mosey on down there and see what's cooking," he said.

The animals picked their way across tree roots and around rocks until they were within sight of the camp.

"It's Preacher Monaghan!" Jake said. "Where's his black suit?"

Dressed in jeans and a sheepskin coat, the preacher was hunkered down beside a tiny fire. He had a stick in his hand and was roasting a strip of bacon. He looked up when they drew near.

For an instant he looked startled, then he stood and smiled. "Well, howdy!" he called. "Come and sit a spell." When Banjo and Jake drew near, Monaghan said, "You got any coffee? I've got bacon and some beans I'm warming up, but I'd give my eyeteeth for a cup of hot coffee."

Banjo turned to his saddlebag. "I have that and some biscuits."

The preacher looked pleased. "I'm glad you happened along. I've been on the road for three days, and a body gets mighty cold and damp outdoors this time of year. Yesterday I dropped my frying pan and cracked it in two. I've been trying to get along without it until I can get to town. Fact is, I was planning to stop in on the Bar N as I was passing through."

"Where you headed after that?" Banjo asked, bringing the food bundle to the fire.

"Durango," Monaghan said. "I've got a brother there, and I'm anxious to see him. A brother in the Lord, I mean."

Jake found a chunk of wood and hauled it near the fire to use as a seat. He cast sidelong glances at the preacher. Banjo filled the coffeepot from the cold, rushing stream and returned to the fire. He found the packet of coffee in his food bundle and shook some grounds into the pot.

"We just came from Juniper," Banjo said, making conversation. He never felt at ease with this preacher. Every time he looked at the man, Banjo remembered him making calf eyes at Sally. It didn't set well. He took a piece of corn bread and a slab of meat from the packet and passed it to Jake. "Tell me, Parson," Banjo said, "what's your opinion on the redemptive work of Christ? Was it for everyone or just a select few?"

Still roasting the bacon, Pastor Monaghan eased his legs and shifted his body away from Banjo. "That's a good question," he replied, watching the fire. "I reckon I've got to study on that one some more. I've heard both sides of the issue."

Banjo pushed ahead. "But what's your best guess? I've wondered about that for years. Didn't your teachers at the Bible school talk about that any?"

When the preacher didn't answer right away, Banjo asked, "Where did you go to Bible school? I've been thinking of sitting in on some book learning myself one of these days."

"I went to the Pueblo Bible Institute in Colorado Springs." He glanced at Banjo. "Have you heard of it?"

Banjo nodded. "I knew a fellow that went there back in '68. Name of Ivan Guthrey. You know him?"

Monaghan shook his head. "I was there from '64 to '66. Sorry."

"So what did Pueblo teach about that question? Did they believe Jesus died for all or just a few?"

The preacher pulled the end of the stick from the fire to check the bacon's progress. It hung limp, white on the top and black on the bottom. "I guess I'm not as good at this as I thought," he said, eyeing the meat with distaste.

Banjo said, "Get a smaller stick and thread it through the bacon a couple of times so the bacon stays along the stick. Then just turn the stick a few times while it's cooking."

"Now why didn't I think of that?" Monaghan propped his stick against a rock and strode away, saying over his shoulder. "I'll be back in a minute."

Banjo watched him go.

"What was that question about?" Jake asked.

Banjo's cheeks widened as he grinned. "It's an old question that preachers have been jawing on for years. I learnt about it from a pastor that came out to visit the troops during the War of Northern Aggression. He held a little Bible class, and one of the men asked him about it. Since then I've asked the same question to many a preacher, and I've never met one yet that didn't have a strong opinion on it."

"But what does it mean?"

"It'll take too long to go into that now," Banjo told him. "We'll talk about it on the trail home."

Monaghan returned with a slender branch in his hand. It was limber and swayed as he walked.

When the preacher reached them, Banjo said, "That piece of wood puts me in mind of a hickory my Ma used to fetch whenever I sassed her."

Jake stared at him. "You sassed your Ma?"

Banjo laughed. "I wasn't always a saint, son. Every person is a sinner from birth." He turned to Monaghan. "That's in Romans. . ." He stared into the distance. "For the life of me, I can't remember the chapter. Do you know it, Parson?"

Monaghan finished skewering the strip of bacon and didn't answer.

"I don't think he heard you," Jake murmured to Banjo.

Banjo didn't reply. At that instant Monaghan leaned forward to resume his crouched position, and the back of his coat came up. At the small of his back, lodged under his belt was the pearl handle of a Peacemaker. Monaghan leaned back, and the coat covered the gun.

With a warning glance at Jake to stifle any comment the boy might make, Banjo checked the coffeepot and returned to his saddlebags for two tin cups. He handed one to Monaghan and said, "I just remembered something that I've got to do. I'll have to turn back. Since you're going on to the ranch anyway, maybe you could side Jake and give him some help unloading the pack animals."

Monaghan showed his teeth in an easy smile. "It'll give us a chance to get acquainted." He looked at the boy.

Jake's expression darkened. He stared at his outstretched boots. When the coffeepot was empty, Banjo carefully drained the last drops of moisture from the coffee grounds at the bottom of the pot, careful not to lose any of the grounds, and returned the pot to his pack. Jake strode up from behind him. They were on the offside of the horse and out of Monaghan's sight.

"What're you doing?" he whispered. "Where are you going?"

Banjo lowered his chin and spoke near the boy's coat collar. "I just got an idea he may be up to something. He's packing a hideout gun. I've seen preachers carry Colts and Winchesters, but they all did it in plain sight. If he's hiding a gun, he's hiding other things, too. I'm going to backtrack him and make sure he is who he claims to be. Go home with Monaghan and keep an eye on him. Try to keep him from speaking to your ma alone. I'm hoping he'll just take a meal and ride on."

"What if he don't?"

"Just watch him. Trail him when he leaves the ranch if you can."

Jake's eyes narrowed. "You think he's the one we're looking for?"

"That's what I'm about to find out." He busied himself with tying down the pack, and Jake turned to Haney.

With a brief wave to the preacher and a nod for Jake, Banjo turned Kelsey around and headed down the trail. At the foot of the last hill he saw Juniper Junction to the northeast. Its buildings formed a small brown mound on the edge of the horizon.

He took the right fork in the trail and headed south for Colorado Springs. His old friend Sykes Maddock had lived in Colorado Springs for all of his sixty years. He'd know where Pueblo Bible Institute was located. A conversation with the head of that school could prove mighty interesting.

Banjo's instinctive dislike for Garrett Monaghan might have been something more than just irritation over the preacher's attitude toward Sally. The tone of the preacher's messages was always harsh and condemning, and that had grated on Banjo. Monaghan didn't seem to know anything about the love of God or the forgiveness that's available through Jesus Christ. Banjo knew other preachers who had the same tendency, but Monaghan was different even from those.

Banjo pulled up on the reins as Kelsey started down the final hill at the edge of the plains. He removed his hat, swiped the bandanna across his brow, and urged the donkey ahead. If Kelsey kept up a good pace, he could be in Colorado Springs by tomorrow evening.

At the Bar N that evening, Sally heard a call from the yard and stepped out to the porch to greet Banjo and Jake. She shaded her eyes when she saw the preacher's black stallion. It was the first time she'd seen Garrett Monaghan in cowboy dress.

"Do you mind taking in some weary wanderers?" the preacher called when they came near. "We're tired and half-starved."

"Where's Banjo?" she demanded, worry in her tone.

Jake avoided her eyes. "He had to take care of some business. He said he'd be back in a few days."

"A few days?" A dozen questions came to mind, but she didn't speak any of them. Instead, she smiled at Pastor Monaghan. "Come in and sit by the fire. You've got to be frozen. After the sun goes behind the rim, it gets cold real fast."

"I'll tend to the horses," Jake said, reaching for Haney's bridle.

"Let me help Jake unload these pack horses," Monaghan told her. "We'll come inside directly."

"I'll fill the coffeepot," Sally said and stepped back into the house.

"Where's Banjo?" Carey asked her. "I saw the preacher but not Banjo."

Sally filled the coffeepot from a bucket beside the stove. "Jake said he had to take care of some business."

"What business?" she persisted. "He didn't say anything about that, did he?"

"No, he didn't." When Carey opened her mouth again, Sally said, "Let's not talk about it in front of the preacher, Carey. It's Banjo's affair, not ours. Come and stir the stew. We need to get things on the table. Jake and Brother Monaghan are probably half-starved."

"But Banjo is ours," Carey declared. She laid aside her book and hurried to help. "I miss him."

Sally reached for the stack of enamel plates on the shelf. She missed him, too. But that was just because she depended on him so much. Maybe it was good if he did stay away for a few days. She ought to get some of her independence back. The Newcomb family wouldn't be living here too much longer, and she should start standing on her own two feet again.

The door opened and Pastor Monaghan stepped in. He set down his saddlebag and rubbed his hands together. "Whew! It sure feels good to be inside." He glanced down at his jeans and flannel shirt. "I hope you'll excuse my appearance, Sally," he said. "It got cold, and I changed out of my suit into some warmer things."

Sally lifted a bowl piled with yeast rolls and set them on the table. "Don't think of it," she said, looking up at him. His warm expression caught her off guard, and she felt her cheeks growing hot. Confused, she turned away and made a show of being busy with the meal.

Monaghan slipped off his boots and set them inside the door. He pulled off his coat then stepped closer to the fireplace. "M—m—m. There's nothing better than a warm fire and hot food on the table," he said. "Thank you for your hospitality. This place has been a haven for a worn-out preacher." He gazed at her, a light in his eyes. "I want you to know that."

Sally glanced at him and felt her cheeks burn again. Irritated, she turned away and tucked a strand of loose hair back under her bun. What had gotten into her? She wasn't some starry-eyed teenager. She couldn't keep acting this way in front of Jake and Carey.

Abruptly she said, "You can wash up at the basin by the back door." With a hard swallow and a pause to collect herself, she placed the last of the silverware on the table and took her seat. Carey sat beside her as Jake came inside. Pastor Monaghan returned from the back of the kitchen with his dark hair slicked back.

"Wash up, son," Sally told Jake. "We'll wait grace until you're ready."

Jake sent her a hard, wide-eyed look.

What did he mean by that? Baffled, her gaze followed him as he walked past her to go to the washbasin.

"This looks mighty good," Monaghan said, taking a seat at the corner beside Sally. "Yeast rolls line up right along with apple pie in my book. I can't get enough of either one of them." He kept his mouth busy with the food, so there was little conversation. After the meal, he picked up his thick Bible and opened it. Jake fidgeted and fumed. If only he could have thirty seconds alone with his mother.

After the dishes were finished, Carey went to bed. Jake sat beside the fire with Carey's copy of *Little Women* in his hands, reading by lamplight.

Monaghan stood and opened the cabin's front door to look outside. "It's a clear night out there," he told Sally. "Would you like to go for a walk by moonlight?"

Jake glanced up. "It's cold enough to freeze your breath in five seconds," he said. "I'd not go awalking out in that, Ma."

She was about to agree to a walk, but something in Jake's voice drew Sally up. She glanced at him again and got that strange wide-eyed look. What was the boy up to? He was starting to get her riled.

"I guess we'd best not," she told Monaghan. "Let's stay here where it's warm."

The preacher fetched his Bible from his saddlebag and pulled out a chair at the table. He spent the next fifteen minutes reading silently from its thin pages. Sally pulled a chair closer to the fire. She picked up Carey's sock from her mending basket and slipped the darning ball inside it. Threading a needle with wool, she began to sew.

Why had Banjo left Jake? She couldn't think of a single reason, and she couldn't get Jake alone to ask him without making an obvious move. She didn't like to think of Banjo lying somewhere out on the cold ground with nothing to warm him besides a saddle blanket. Maybe he found a place in someone's hay mow or maybe in a bunkhouse along the way. She hoped so. If only she'd packed more food for the men to take along. Being cold was bad enough, but being cold and hungry was torture.

Monaghan closed the Bible. "I'm worn-out," he said, standing. "I believe I'll turn in."

Sally smiled. "There's an extra cot in the loft. It's the first one on the left."

He beamed at her. "Thanks again for your hospitality," he said. "I know the good Lord will bless you for it." He lifted the saddlebag and deftly climbed to the loft.

Sally slid the needle through the sock and prayed for a weathered cowhand who had a twinkle in his blue eyes.

⁀

Still on the trail at nightfall, Banjo camped among three fir trees to gain shelter from the wind. There was just enough room to bring Kelsey in with him and tie him with a short line. The heat from the donkey would bring up the temperature a few degrees anyway. Rolled up in his blanket, he adjusted his Stetson over his face to keep his nose from freezing and tried to sleep.

About all he did was try. He was back in the saddle before the first gray beam came over the horizon. It was still half a day's ride to Colorado Springs, and he wanted to return to the Bar N by the next day. He had to get back to Sally right away. No telling what that smooth-talking scoundrel might do while he was away.

Colorado Springs was a thriving city of the wealthy. The giant flat-topped mound called Pike's Peak formed a backdrop to the town. This was a place where the rich and the noble of the world came to build mansions, to play croquet, and to drink from the mineral waters so famous for their benefits.

He took the trail that swung wide to the west and turned toward town. Sykes Maddock owned a hardware store on the west of town, and Banjo hoped to catch him there.

Maddock's General Mercantile bore little resemblance to Harper's Emporium. Where Harper's was cluttered and pleasantly crowded, Maddock's place had the precision of a surgical suite. To the left stood a shoulder-high coffee grinder with a giant wheel on one side. A glass-topped counter made a giant U-shape around the front room. Inside, tools and watches, cooking pots and carpenter's gear lay in neat rows, organized by size and type. A husky young man wearing a tight smile and a white bib apron stood behind the closest counter. He approached Banjo the moment the old cowhand stepped through the door.

"Is Sykes Maddock in?" Banjo asked.

"Yes, sir," he replied, adjusting his sleeve garters. He pointed toward the back. "He's just through that door. I'll fetch him for you."

Banjo sauntered to the base of the U and waited. A moment later a flat-faced man with almost no upper lip came out. He saw Banjo and gave a loud laugh. "Banjo! You old coot! Where've you been hiding?" He reached out to shake hands.

"I've been down the river, and now I'm going down the pike," Banjo replied, grasping his friend's meaty paw.

Sykes chuckled. "This is the pike, all right," he said. "But business is not at its peak."

Banjo shook his head. "Keep trying, Sykes. One day you'll master the art of the joke."

Sykes laughed. "What brings you to our neck of the woods? Can you stay for a checker game?"

"I'm sorry to have to turn you down. I'd enjoy a game, sure enough. Actually, I'm here to get a little information, and then I'll have to move on." He cocked his head and leaned closer. "Have you ever heard of the Pueblo Bible Institute? I'm looking for directions to the place."

"Wait a minute. . ." Sykes worked his bottom lip up and over his sinking upper lip. "It seems to me there's one over at the Colorado Springs Tabernacle on the edge of town. It's just west of here—a white clapboard church."

Banjo nodded. "I think I passed it coming in." He shook the storekeeper's hand again, thanked him, and hurried away. This was better than he'd hoped for.

An old preacher was sweeping the front steps of the church when Banjo rode up. A small man, he wore the standard black broadcloth and had a neatly trimmed gray beard. He looked up and smiled when he heard Banjo's "howdy!"

He folded both hands on the top of the broom handle and waited for Banjo to get out of the saddle. "What can I do for you?" he asked. His eyes had deep crinkles at the corners.

Banjo strode to him and put out his hand. "I'm Joe Calahan, and I'm looking for the Pueblo Bible Institute."

"You found it." As he shook Banjo's hand, the man took in Banjo's appearance. "Come on in by the fire. You look like you've been on the trail for a while. I've got coffee on the potbelly stove in my study. I'm finished here, so let's go in and sit where it's comfortable." He opened the door to the church and led Banjo to the back of the auditorium. It was a spare room with two dozen handmade benches and a small pulpit at the front. The white plaster walls were bare. The six windows contained clear glass.

"Here we are," he said. He opened the study door and stood aside for Banjo to enter first. As soon as Banjo stepped inside, he felt warmth sweep over him.

The room had the same stark appearance as the rest of the building. A thick oak desk filled the center of the room. In the corner behind the desk stood a small stove with a coffeepot and a tiny cooking pot. Two straight-backed wooden chairs faced the front of the desk.

"Have a seat," the old pastor said, moving to the stove. He picked up a cup from a small shelf nearby and poured coffee. The odor wafted through the room.

Banjo dropped his hat to the seat of one chair and sat in the other. "That coffee smells great," he said.

The pastor smiled as he handed Banjo the cup. "I'm Amos Hostetter," he said. He moved to his chair behind the desk. "I started the Bible Institute, so I know as much as anyone. Were you thinking of enrolling?"

Banjo sipped the hot brew and felt the warmth travel down to his stomach. "Actually, I'm here to ask about a former student. His name is Garrett Monaghan. He claims he was at the Institute from '64 to '66. I was wondering if you know him."

Hostetter didn't speak for a moment. Finally, he steepled his fingers low across his middle and said, "I don't recall the name."

"He's tall and skinny with a nose that puts you in mind of an eagle's beak."

The preacher picked up a ledger and leafed through it. He ran his finger down a couple of pages. A few moments later, he shook his head. "He's not listed here, so he wasn't a student. I'm sorry. I wish I could help you more." He closed the ledger.

Banjo drained his cup. "You have helped me." He set the cup on the desk. "Thanks very much, Pastor. I'll be on my way. If I leave now, I may get home before dark." The longer he was away, the more anxious he was to get back.

Sally tipped up the edge of her washtub and dumped the dirty water out on the ground. Carey was hanging up the last of the washing. It was time to set the table and call the men in for lunch. Garrett was standing outside the corral fence watching Jake train a yearling to the rope, the first step to saddle-breaking a horse.

As she crossed the yard, Sally analyzed her son's technique and wished that she could be inside the corral with him instead of washing clothes and cooking beans. She glanced toward the mouth of the canyon, hoping to catch sight of Kelsey. It seemed ages since Banjo had left. How much longer until he came home?

"Can we have butter on our bread today?" Carey asked, skipping up behind her.

Sally turned toward her, still far off in her thoughts. "I suppose," she said. "Go ahead and dip some out of the crock."

The girl dashed ahead of her into the house, leaving the door ajar. With another glance across the meadow, Sally followed her.

After the lunch dishes were finished, Garrett stretched his arms out. "What do you say to a walk, Sally?" he asked. "It's a fine day."

"How about a ride?" Sally asked. "I haven't been in the saddle for a coon's age."

He grinned. "You've got a deal there. I'll saddle the horses." He stood, retrieved his hat from a peg, and headed out the door.

Jake stared at Sally. "Ma! Don't go out with him!"

"Why on earth not?"

"Well, take Carey with you," he persisted.

"I'd like to ride, too," the girl said.

"Why don't we all go?" Sally asked. She turned to Carey. "We can finish our work tomorrow." Heading toward the bedroom, she cried, "Let's get some fresh air!"

"*Eh bien!*" Carey cried and ran after her.

An hour later the four of them formed a ragged square as their mounts headed toward the pasture.

Carey shouted to Jake, "I'll race you to the gap!" She put heels to her horse, and the mustang bounded ahead.

With a whoop, Jake set out after her. The next moment his hat went flying. Intent on the girl ahead of him, he ignored it.

Sally laughed. "You should have seen Jake before Carey came," she told Garrett. "He's like a new person."

"I imagine losing his father was hard on him. It would be hard on anyone."

She nodded. "I was afraid he'd never recover himself. He was always a pleasant child. It's nice to have my old Jake back."

"Sally. . ."

Something in his tone made her heart skip. She looked over at him to see his eyes intent on hers. The next moment he reached out and grasped her horse's bridle to pull their animals closer together.

Sally's breath stopped in her throat. Whatever he was about to say, she was terrified to hear it.

"Sally, will you marry me and let me take care of you?" he asked. His voice grew mellow with a pleading undertone. "I grew up on a ranch. I could take care of things here and relieve you of all the worry you're under." He let go of the bridle and reached back for the pommel of her saddle. "I've come to love you, Sally. I tried to fight it, but it's no use. Please make me a happy man and say yes."

She swallowed a hard knot in her throat. With a second man to help them, the ranch might thrive again. Besides, how long would Banjo stay with her at the ridiculous salary she was paying him? She glanced at Jake and Carey, who were riding shoulder to shoulder across the field. What would they say about Garrett's proposal? She pushed the thought aside. Children didn't have the wisdom to know what was best. She'd have to make this decision on her own.

She turned toward the preacher. His gaze was so intense, so full of passion. At that moment something melted inside her.

"Yes, Garrett," she breathed. "I will marry you."

Chapter 12

Darkness was less than thirty minutes away when Banjo found a campsite that night. He had put off finding a place in the hopes that he might get close enough to ride on in. However, Kelsey was stumbling with weariness, and Banjo couldn't justify his pushing the faithful donkey for even another hour.

Pulling the saddle off the donkey to let him roll, he gathered a few sticks for a small fire to chase away some of the chill. There was nothing to eat in his saddlebags except a little jerky. No matter. It wouldn't be the first time he'd spent a slim day on the trail. A small sack in his kit held enough coffee grounds for another pot, and that would have to do. If he was back on the trail before first light, he could get home in time to eat some of Sally's biscuits.

At the thought of her, the cold inside him warmed a little. She was the toughest, sweetest gal he'd ever known. She could work shoulder to shoulder with a man, but she was every inch a woman. He unrolled his bedding and sat on it with his feet stretched toward the flames to warm his icy toes. Sipping coffee, he stared into the night.

He'd always figured that he'd spend the rest of his life alone. It was funny, the way the Lord worked. He rubbed his two-day stubble and pursed his lips. Well, he hadn't exactly staked claim to her, had he? She probably wouldn't look twice at the likes of him.

Flinging the grounds from the bottom of his cup, he lay back with his arm under his head and prayed, *Lord, You take hold of this problem for me, will You? Sally's a fine woman, but she's so young for the likes of me. She deserves better than I can give her. If she's not for me, take these ideas out of my head.*

With that, he rolled up in his bedroll and tried to sleep. This time exhaustion took over, and he slept soundly until an hour before dawn. When he awoke, the fire had died. He didn't have enough coffee grounds left for a decent pot of coffee, so he left the campfire alone. Cold, hungry, and irritable, he set off for home.

The gap to the Bar N canyon opened up before him just after the sky lit up, and it cast a long shadow over the meadow. Reaching the interior of the canyon, Kelsey picked up the pace of his own accord. He was as anxious to get home as his rider was.

They hadn't covered a third of the way to the house when Haney galloped out of the barn with Jake in the saddle. When they met, Jake was breathing hard.

"Ma's gone crazy!" he panted. "She's made up her mind to marry the preacher!"

"What!"

The boy nodded. "I don't know what's come over her. She won't talk to me about it." Panic filled his voice. "That man's running a ringer, ain't he, Banjo? Is that what you found out?"

His jaw set, his face grim, Banjo nodded. "You said it right, son."

"It's my fault," Jake cried. "I shouldn't have been so mean to her after Pa passed away. She got enough meanness while he was living without me carrying on after he died. Ma's always been good to me. I just made things worse."

Banjo reached out to put his hand on the boy's shoulder. "Let's pray."

Jake bowed his head while Banjo called on God for wisdom and strength. He prayed for divine protection for Sally and Jake and for little Carey. Then they rode to the house together.

Taking the animals to the barn, Banjo and the boy headed for the house. Banjo felt his throat tighten as he stepped up on the porch. He braced himself and reached for the door latch.

When they stepped inside, Monaghan sat at the table drinking coffee. Sally stood across from him, making biscuits. When the door thudded shut, Carey peeked out from the bedroom.

"Banjo!" the girl cried. She ran to him for a hug. "You came back!"

He leaned down to put his arms around her. "Yes, honey. I'm back." Releasing her, he took off his hat and dropped it over a peg.

"I've got some news for you, Banjo," Sally said. She had a stiff expression as though she were confessing some misdemeanor to a stern parent.

Banjo didn't answer her. His eyes were on the preacher. Monaghan sent him a look of triumph that was a gleam in his black eyes. Forcing his gaze away, Banjo looked at Sally.

"Garrett asked me to marry him, and I accepted," she said, her voice level. "I think it's for the best."

Jake moved away from Banjo and circled wide around the preacher's back on his way to the fireplace. Banjo still didn't speak. He moved along as though following Jake. When he came behind the preacher, he lunged at him and grabbed the gun from under his coat.

"Say! What's this?" Monaghan whirled around and grabbed at the revolver.

Banjo backed off, aiming at the man's midsection. He said, "You thought you had things wrapped up here, didn't you, Monaghan? If that's your name."

"Banjo, have you lost your mind?" Sally demanded. "What are you doing?"

"This hombre's no preacher, Sally. I just got back from the Pueblo Bible Institute where your friend says he went to Bible school. Well, he was lying. He's never been anywhere near the place."

She stared at Monaghan. "Garrett? What's this all about?"

"You'd better answer her straight," Banjo told him, "or I'll ventilate your gizzard." He glanced at Jake. "Fetch his saddlebags. I think we'll find some interesting things inside."

Monaghan stood with his hands up. "You're making a mistake!" he growled.

"Sit down!" Banjo cried.

The tall man dropped back into his seat.

"Scoot yourself backwards until your chair hits the wall."

Banjo circled around to put the table between them as the preacher moved back. A few seconds later, Jake arrived with the saddlebags and dumped them out on the table.

The first thing to catch Banjo's eye was a pair of red wire cutters. They were almost new with a dozen scrapes across the blades. Banjo reached into his pocket and pulled out a small paper twist. He handed it to Jake. "Open that real slow so the paint chips don't get lost," he told him. "See if you can match any of the chips to the scratched-off places."

Jake laid the paper on the table, his big fingers fumbling with the tiny bits inside. "Fetch me a book," he told Carey who stood beside him, her eyes big as dinner plates.

She dashed into the bedroom and brought back a copy of *Ivanhoe*. Jake opened to the center of the book. He placed the small paper of paint chips on one side of the book and the wire cutter on the other side. Drawing up a chair, he bent over them for several minutes.

Sally stood with her hands still in the bowl of flour. Her face was as white as her biscuit dough.

"He's not going to find anything there," Monaghan snarled. "This is insane, man! Let me go!"

Banjo held the gun steady and didn't answer.

"Looky here!" Jake cried. "And it's the same color."

"What?" Carey asked, bending closer.

Banjo glanced down at the book. "Tell me what you've got, son," he said, not wanting to take his eyes off his prisoner.

"This big paint chip fits into this scratched-off spot on the wire cutter." He glared at the preacher. "What's a preacher doing with a pair of wire cutters anyways?"

Sally shook her hands in the air. Bits of flour and dough flew everywhere. "What are you talking about?" she cried.

Banjo said, "You're looking at the mischief-maker we've been hunting." He bore in on Monaghan. "Ain't that right, Parson?"

Monaghan grew red around the ears. He glared at Banjo. "Don't believe him, Sally," he said. "He's got a wild imagination."

"You were here just before the stampede," Jake said. "I remember it."

"That's right!" Sally said, looking from Jake to Banjo and then to Monaghan. Signs of doubt showed on her face. "You left; then those steers almost killed us all."

"That's no proof," Monaghan insisted. "It could have been anyone."

"Have you got some rope in the house?" Banjo asked Sally. When she nodded, he said, "Go and fetch it for me, please."

Monaghan's Adam's apple moved. He licked his lips. "What are you going to do?"

Banjo said nothing.

When Sally returned with a thick hank of rope on her arm, Banjo said, "Jake, tie him to the chair. Make sure he's sewed up good and tight. I'm gettin' tired of holding this gun on him. Besides, I want to look through his things myself."

Jake took the rope and used all of it. When he finished, Monaghan was tied to the chair by his hands, feet, chest, and waist.

Banjo nodded. "That'll hold him. But keep an eye on him anyways." He laid the gun on the table and slid onto the bench. Something caught his eye and made him pick up the revolver again. There was a corner missing from the mother-of-pearl inlay on the pistol's handle. He looked closely at the missing space.

He shot a look at Jake. "Fetch me your cigar box, son," he said.

Jake scuttled up the ladder and was back in a flash. He handed the wooden cigar box to Banjo.

Sitting at the table, Banjo lifted the lid and dug through the items inside. Sally stepped closer to lean over his shoulder and see what he was doing. He lifted out the mother-of-pearl fragment that Jake had found on the canyon rim where his father had died. Turning the piece in his hands, Banjo slid it into the missing place on Monaghan's gun. A perfect fit.

"Looks like we caught more than just a vandal," Banjo said, looking up at Sally.

"What was that?" she asked.

"I found it at the place where Pa went over the edge," Jake said. "It was pretty, so I kept it."

Banjo shook his head. "I never thought this would be the end of things," he said, letting out a deep sigh. His shoulders slumped for a second. He looked up at the woman beside him. "Sally, I've been afraid of this for some time." He pulled out a chair for her. "Sit down and get a grip on yourself. I've got some bad news."

Fear tightening her mouth, Sally blindly reached for the chair beside her and sat down hard.

He put his hand on her arm. "Mickey was murdered."

"What!" Her face twisted. Sudden tears streamed down her cheeks.

Carey ran to Sally and threw her thin arms around Sally's neck. The ladies held each other for a long moment, sniffling and whispering to each other. Carey had bits of dough on her back from Sally's pats.

"What are we going to do with him?" Jake asked, nodding toward Monaghan. "We could use that rope for another purpose, you know."

Banjo shook his head. "I'll escort him into Juniper Junction and turn him over to Buckeye Mullins, the magistrate. He'll lock him in the stage station storeroom until the circuit judge comes to town in June."

Sally turned Carey loose and looked at her hands. "I've got to wash this off," she told the girl and hurried to the washbasin beside the back door. A moment later she returned. She had a handkerchief pressed to her cheek. With a muffled sob, she sank into the chair beside the fireplace and turned sideways so she couldn't see the bogus preacher.

Kneeling beside her, Banjo spoke softly and slowly, each word distinct. "I'm here, Sally. You're not alone anymore. Do you understand that?"

Gently clasping her fingers, he lowered her hands so he could see her eyes. "I'll be here as long as you want me."

She nodded and dabbed at her streaming eyes. She whispered so only he could hear, "I was actually relieved when Mickey was taken, but now that I know what happened. . ." She shivered. "That's a horrible way for anyone to die!" She closed her eyes and drew in a quavering breath. "I feel so guilty!" Tears streamed down her face. "I'm a miserable person, Banjo. A sorry, ungrateful. . ."

He covered her trembling lips with his fingers. "That's enough of that," he murmured. "You've been hurt in a hundred different ways. You're not to blame for any of this."

She nodded. Still weeping, she wiped her face.

Banjo stood and faced Monaghan. "What were you up to?" he demanded, advancing on the man. "What were you after?"

"You think you're so smart, cowpoke," Monaghan ground out. "Figure it out yourself."

Banjo considered him for a moment then turned to the items on the table, the things from Monaghan's saddlebag. He ran his hand over the ball of twine, the dented compass, the tiny tin of matches, picking up various things for closer examination, looking for something but not knowing what.

"The book!" Jake said. "I bet it's in there."

Banjo picked up the small black volume and sat down to look through it.

"It's a common tally book," he said, turning pages. Near the center he found a page folded small enough to fit into the book without showing. He unfolded it and read:

Dear Johnny,

Yesterday I chanced upon an opportunity that could benefit both of us. A silver strike as rich as the Comstock Lode. I won a map from a no-account gambler named Mickey Newcomb. Believe it or not, he's the owner of the property, but he's too lazy to mine the ore. I've made him two offers to buy the place, but he won't sell. If intelligence was figured in dollars and cents, he'd be living on credit.

If we can come up with a plan to get hold of that land, we'll never have to work again. Come to Juniper, and we'll talk about it.

Your cousin,
Virgil Ganss

P.S. I've drawn the map out for you here.

Below the writing was a map, crudely drawn in thick pencil. It was smudged at the creases but still readable.

"Silver!" Sally cried. "Is that what this is all about? I can't believe it."

"Look at this," Banjo said. "What do you make of it?" He handed the page to her.

She stared at the drawing, turning it sideways and then back again. "It's a map of the back pasture," she said. "See the stream and that small pond?"

Jake moved closer to see the drawing.

"There's a triangle on the stream," she said pointing. "See it?"

"That's it, all right," Jake said nodding. He looked at Banjo. "What's this mean? Are we rich?"

"It's hard to say at this point," Banjo replied, folding the map and sliding it into his pocket. "I've worked in several mines, and I can tell you that a silver strike doesn't always mean millions of dollars." He turned to Sally and asked, "You want to ride out there? We ought to look the place over."

She nodded. "I'll get my buckskins on," she said. Ignoring Monaghan, she hurried to the bedroom.

Before she shut the door, Banjo called after her, "Throw me a blanket before you close the door, will you? Nothing that's any good—we're going to take it to the barn."

She handed him a folded piece of stained wool, and the door banged against its frame.

"What about him?" Jake asked, eyeing the man tied to the chair. He sat like a statue, staring straight ahead. His Adam's apple was the only thing that moved.

"We'll lock him in the feed room until we can move him into town," Banjo said. He took stock of the prisoner. "Untie his legs, Jake. Just his legs. We'll get him bedded down with the corn sacks. Then I'll saddle the horses."

Jake reached for the knots and had the counterfeit preacher loose around the ankles before Sally returned from her room.

Banjo held the gun on him. "Stand up," he said. "You're going to wear that chair like a backpack whilst we get you to the barn."

Monaghan said, "I can't walk like this. Nobody could."

Banjo pursed his lips and squinted. "You know, Jake," he drawled. "Now that I think about it, I'm inclined to believe it will be more trouble than it's worth getting this hombre into town. He may try to escape, and we can't allow that chance, can we? Nobody would fault us if we just strung him up here and delivered his carcass to Buckeye Mullins. That way we're sure to get him in."

With a loud *umph*, Monaghan leaned over and heaved himself forward. The chair came off the floor behind him. Hunched over, the outlaw took tiny steps toward the door. "Where's the feed room?" he grunted.

Banjo reached around the man to open the latch. "Step right this way," he said. "Your quarters are in the barn."

Banjo and Jake followed Monaghan to the feed room. Inside, Jake untied him and stepped back until he was in the doorway. Monaghan stood up and sent Banjo an evil look. "You'll be sorry about this," he said. "My cousin will have me free in no time. Then I'll come after you!"

Banjo cocked his head and stared at the man. "Be that as it may," he said. "Me and the good Lord know how to take care of varmints like you. Take off your pants."

"What?" Monaghan's face grew beet red. He stood staring at Banjo, not moving.

Banjo cocked the pistol. "You've got to a count of three."

The bogus preacher reached for his belt buckle. Ten seconds later, he handed his jeans over. "I'll freeze in here!"

"Count yourself lucky. When I found out you was running a ringer, I wanted to sharpen your heels and pound you in like a fence post." Banjo threw the blanket to him and backed out of the room.

Jake slammed the door shut and shoved the padlock into place. "You think he'll get out?" he asked Banjo as they headed for the horse stalls.

"Naw. He won't be running afield in his long drawers. Not in this weather. It would be suicide." Banjo gave the jeans and the pearl-handled gun to Jake. "You'd best keep hold of these in case he gives you trouble while we're gone."

At that moment, the door creaked open, and Sally stepped into the barn, wearing her riding gear. Banjo always had to smile when he saw her suited up like a cowhand. She was the liveliest, most lovable gal in the country.

He led her favorite mustang, Joey, from the stall. "Here you are, m'lady," he said. "Want a leg up?"

She slanted an indignant look at him. "Since when do I need a leg up?" she demanded. She slid her small boot into the stirrup, then grabbed the pommel and cantle. One smooth leap had her in the saddle. Joey pranced a little, and she pulled on the reins. "Steady there, boy," she said, patting his neck. She turned toward Banjo. "I'll take him outside. He's always frisky when we first start out."

Banjo chuckled. "Just don't leave me behind." He saddled Sassy. Kelsey was too tired to go out again so soon. Tying a small shovel to the cantle, he lifted his boot to the stirrup. To Jake he said, "Give us a couple of hours or so to find what we're after." With that he set off out the doors. Sassy was stepping high. She must have caught Joey's mood.

Neck and neck, the horses cantered across the meadow, heading for the canyon mouth. The wind still had a little bite, and the ride sent a thrill through Sally like she hadn't felt for a long time. She felt free as the breeze that chilled her cheeks and pulled at the fringes on her jacket.

For at least five minutes she immersed herself in the euphoria of relief. But before they were outside the canyon, she realized her troubles were far from over. They still had precious few cattle for starting the new year. She had to make a decision about the ranch. The silver strike put a whole new slant on their situation. What should she do?

Banjo beckoned to her, and they slowed their mounts so they could talk.

"What do you think about this silver strike?" he asked.

She shook her head. "I'm tired with thinking, Banjo. Things have been happening so fast this morning, I don't know up from down."

They reached the stream and stepped to the ground. It was a quiet place with a sandy beach. The water made a gentle curve. The far bank rose high above the surface of the stream, but the near bank came flat away from the water.

"This is a perfect spot," Banjo told her. "The curve makes the silt slow down, and heavy metals like silver and gold will drop to the bottom of the stream." He untied the shovel. Walking near the water's edge, he dug into the gray sand right at the water's edge. Sally walked up to watch him.

Pausing, he said, "I've panned more dirt than I care to remember. More than I ever care to pan again, to be honest." He turned away from her and stared across the water for a long moment.

"What is it?" she asked, coming close to him. "Can we tell if there's really silver here?"

"That'll be easy enough," he said. "If we dig awhile, we'll find it. The question is, What if there is silver here? What then?" He turned to face her. "Do you know what this means for your spread, Sally? Do you recall what happened to Sutter's Mill in '49? People ran over Sutter's property like ants. They dug up every square inch of the place until it looked like a quarry pit."

"Is that what will happen here?" she asked. Frown marks appeared on her brow. Suddenly she sighed. "I might as well admit it. I don't want to stay here anyway. There are so many bad memories, so much hardship."

"You could sell the ranch to a mining company. There are plenty of those around these days. You'd have them bidding against each other for the place." He paused, his lips working in and out, considering. "What do you want to do, Sally? With this strike, you can have just about anything you want. What do you want the very most?"

She gazed at him, a light in her eyes. "A horse farm," she said. "I'd like to breed them and train them. But most of all, I want to ride them." She started to turn away, considering it. "Yes! That's exactly what I want to do."

He dropped the shovel, reached for her elbow, and drew her back. "There's something I've got to ask you," he said.

At his sober expression, an icy finger of panic slid down her spine. She had an impulse to run, but she stayed put. Her mouth went dry.

"I know I've probably no right to say this," he began. "But I've got to at least try." He paused and drew in a breath. "Now that you're an independent woman, you can make up your mind without any worry about needing help or anything like that. And I don't want you to be scared about hurting my feelings. All I ask is that you be honest with me."

He hesitated a moment longer as though gathering a last bit of courage. Then he burst out, "Sally, I love you, and I'd be proud if you'd be my wife."

She stared at him, her mouth slack. A dozen thoughts collided in her mind. "You want to marry me?" she demanded.

He backed away and rubbed his jaw. "You don't have to give me an answer now," he said doubtfully. "I just thought I'd put it up to you."

Suddenly she tore the Stetson off her head and threw it to the ground. "You asked me to marry you while I'm wearing buckskins and this old hat?" She laughed aloud. "You asked me while we're out here digging around in the dirt?"

His face grew sober. "I didn't mean it for a joke."

With another loud laugh, she skipped toward him and caught him by both arms. "I'm not laughing because it's funny. I'm laughing because I'm such an idiot that I never thought of anything like this before. You are the sweetest man on the face of the earth! You mean you want to marry me even though Jake has been so rude to you? You want to marry me even though I can't cook worth anything?"

He looked into her eyes, and her laughter immediately ceased. "I want to marry you because I love you," he said. "I want to spend the rest of my life with you, Sally. If you want to ranch, I'll ranch. If you want to run horses, I'll run horses. The main thing is, I want to be with you. I want to make you happy."

She couldn't say anything. This was too wonderful to absorb in one heartbeat. Finally, she found her voice. "I love you, too, Banjo. I didn't realize it until now, but you've been special to me since the day we sat on that flat rock beside the Chamberlins' stream. I've been so confused and wrought up, I didn't understand what I really felt. All I knew was that I enjoyed your company more than I could say. Every minute you were away seemed like a thousand years. I never thought of love."

His lips formed a soft smile. "I've been thinking of almost nothing else." He brushed his fingertips across the hair next to her temple. "Will you do it, Sally? Will you marry me?"

Her smile deepened until a dimple appeared at the corner of her mouth. She looked straight at him and said, "Yes. I will marry you. As soon as we can do it proper, I'll marry you." She lifted her hand to touch his cheek. "This is forever," she murmured.

He drew her into his arms.

Sally clung to him, and time stood still. Her doubts and fears for the future melted away in that one sweet moment. This was a godly man, so faithful and kind, so gentle and wise. And he was hers. All hers.

Epilogue

On a Saturday morning late in June, Steve Chamberlin and Chance Calahan set up a dozen benches in the front yard of the Circle C. It was a wedding day, and the whole county was invited. Jeremy dashed in and out of the house with Carey following his every step and Katie right behind her. Jake declared himself too old for such foolishness and perched on the front steps with baby Stevie on his lap. The smell of roasting beef, corn cakes, and apple pies mingled with the heady aroma of freshly baked bread.

"Is Pastor Tyler here yet?" Sally asked, peering out the front windows. "He should be here by now." She wore a taffeta dress of pale pink with a white satin sash at the waist. A giant bouquet of fresh daisies tied with pink ribbon lay on the table.

Megan came to put her arms around the nervous bride. "Don't worry, Sally," she said. "He's at Em's house with Banjo. They'll all come together."

Sally hugged Megan and laughed. "I'm so bedazzled that I forgot where the preacher was! You'd best keep an eye on me."

"I'm so happy for both of you," Megan said, beaming at her. "God's given Banjo a new start and a new song. In the process, he did the same thing for you. Isn't that just like the Lord?" She sighed. "Your new house is so beautiful. I can't believe the men finished it so fast. Six weeks from start to finish has to be a new building record."

"Everyone's been so wonderful!" Sally said. She let go of Megan and turned toward the side bedroom. "I'd best see to my hair. I want to do a high chignon, and I'm not sure if I can manage it or not."

"I'll help you," Megan offered, following her. "It took me half a dozen tries before I learned the trick, but I finally got it right."

Sally sat in a chair, and Megan stood behind her. She picked up the wide brush from the dresser. "I'm glad we're neighbors," she said. "I always worried that one day Banjo would ride away, and we'd never see him again. He's so much a part of the family that it would break our hearts to see him go."

The glow on Sally's face lit up the room. "He's not going anywhere now," she declared. "Once we got that piece of the Hohner place, I knew we'd always stay here. It's so perfect for a horse ranch." She sighed. "I feel guilty being this happy, Megan. It's almost like I don't deserve everything—twenty thoroughbreds, a registered stallion, a clapboard house with real painted siding, new furniture. . ." She sighed "It's too much!"

Brushing Sally's dark tresses, Megan clucked her tongue. "Don't even think that way. You deserve every bit of it and more." She laughed. "The way Banjo tells it, he's getting the best part of the deal."

"I guess we'll have to argue about that later." She giggled.

The last hairpin was in place when the first of the guests arrived. Soon the trail around the cornfield was filled with one wagon after another—the Sanders family, Wyatt and Susan Hammond with their ranch hands, the Feiklin family, Kip and Ruth Morgan of the Running M, Joe and Peggy Harper from the emporium, a dozen families at least. The yard became a moving mass of humanity. Kitchen chairs were brought outside. Men perched on the porch steps, the porch railing and the edge of the porch floor.

Jeremy rode to Em's house with a message that she should bring more chairs in the buckboard when she came with her food.

Half an hour before starting time, Megan left the house to rescue Jake from Stevie's fussing. She put the baby on her hip and stepped into the yard to greet the guests.

Wearing a red dress and a wide-brimmed white hat, Mrs. Feiklin hurried toward Megan, her chubby face eager to tell her news. "Hello, Megan. Did you hear about our Lisa?" she asked.

"No," Megan replied with an encouraging smile. "How is she?"

"She had a baby boy last month! He's got blond hair like his daddy, he has." She clapped her hands. "I'm going up there come September and stay for two months. I can't wait!"

Megan beamed. "That's wonderful news! Please tell her that I've been praying for them, will you?" She touched the stout woman's arm and moved to Susan Hammond, who sat on the other side of the group with an eighteen-month-old girl on her lap. The child had red hair, freckles, and the cutest little nose.

Megan sat beside them. "I'm so glad you were able to come," she said.

"This is one event I wouldn't miss for anything," Susan declared. "I can't wait to see Banjo suited up like a preacher with a string tie and everything." She laughed.

"Sally's too nervous to sit down," Megan told her. She looked across the yard. "Here comes the preacher and the groom with Em."

They watched the buckboard stop near the front steps. Several men carried pots of food into the house for Em. Chance helped her down, and she went inside the house, her navy dress swishing along the floor.

For the next ten minutes, Banjo stood apart from the group with the pastor beside him. He held himself stiff, his arms at his sides except for when he made frequent adjustments to his tie and tugged at his coat.

At last everything was in place. Children scrambled to find seats with their parents. Banjo and the preacher took their positions at the front. Sally came out of the house on Steve's arm and joined her beloved at the front of the crowd. She pressed the daisies to her waist with her left arm. Smiling at the world, she had eyes for only Banjo.

As always, Pastor Tyler's words were simple and direct. Ten minutes later he said, "I now pronounce you man and wife." Banjo claimed his bride with a lingering kiss and a long hug.

"Ladies and gentlemen," the preacher said, "I present to you Mr. and Mrs. Joseph Calahan. Please come forward to congratulate them."

Light applause followed. Everyone stood to form a line that moved toward the front. With his left arm tightly around Sally's waist, Banjo shook hands with his friends, endured endless backslapping and kidding, and shared many smiles with his beloved.

Carey was near the end of the line. When she reached the front, she shook Banjo's hand, put on her sober expression, and asked, "Does this mean that you and Sally are my daddy and mama for keeps?"

"I guess that's right," he replied with a warm smile. He touched her shoulder. "Is that okay, honey?"

Suddenly, she giggled and reached up for a hug. *"Eh bien!"*

A Letter to Our Readers

Dear Readers:

In order that we might better contribute to your reading enjoyment, we would appreciate your taking a few minutes to respond to the following questions. When completed, please return to the following: Fiction Editor, Barbour Publishing, Inc., P.O. Box 719, Uhrichsville, OH 44683.

1. Did you enjoy reading *Colorado*?
    ❑ Very much—I would like to see more books like this.
    ❑ Moderately—I would have enjoyed it more if _____
    _____
    _____

2. What influenced your decision to purchase this book?
    (Check those that apply.)
    ❑ Cover   ❑ Back cover copy   ❑ Title   ❑ Price
    ❑ Friends   ❑ Publicity   ❑ Other

3. Which story was your favorite?
    ❑ *Megan's Choice*   ❑ *Lisa's Broken Arrow*
    ❑ *Em's Only Chance*   ❑ *Banjo's New Song*

4. Please check your age range:
    ❑ Under 18   ❑ 18–24   ❑ 25–34
    ❑ 35–45   ❑ 46–55   ❑ Over 55

5. How many hours per week do you read? _____

Name _____

Occupation _____

Address _____

City _____ State _____ Zip _____

E-mail _____